WHAT CAN I DO WHEN

EVERYTHING'S ON FIRE?

WHAT CAN I DO WHEN

Translated
from the
Portuguese
by
GREGORY RABASSA

ANTÓNIO
LOBO
ANTUNES

EVERYTHING'S ON FIRE?

W. W. NORTON & COMPANY

New York · London

For information about permission to reproduce selections from this book,
write to Permissions, W. W. Norton & Company, Inc., 500 Fifth Avenue, New
York, NY 10110

For information about special discounts for bulk purchases, please contact
W. W. Norton Special Sales at specialsales@wwnorton.com or 800-233-4830

Manufacturing by Courier Westford
Book design by Charlotte Staub
Production manager: Devon Zahn

Library of Congress Cataloging-in-Publication Data
Antunes, António Lobo, 1942–
    [Que farei quando tudo arde? English]
    What can I do when everything's on fire? / António Lobo Antunes ;
translated from the Portugese by Gregory Rabassa
        p. cm.
ISBN 978-0-393-32948-3 (pbk.)
I. Rabassa, Gregory. II. Title.
PQ9263.N77Q8413 2008
869.3'42—dc22   2008013189

W. W. Norton & Company, Inc.
500 Fifth Avenue, New York, NY 10110
www.wwnorton.com

W. W. Norton & Company, Ltd.
Castle House, 75/76 Wells Street, London
WIT 3QT

1 2 3 4 5 6 7 8 9 0

DEDICATED

to Marisa Blanco for her pitiless friendship

*to my cousin José Maria Lobo Antunes Nolasco, who's gotten
me out of some tight spots*

*and to the poet Francisco Sá de Miranda, so much at home
here, coming from the sixteenth century to
supply the title of this book.*

I am you and you are me; where you are, I am, and in all things I find myself dispersed. Whatever you find, it is me you are finding; and when you find me, you find yourself.

(Epiphanius, Haer. 26.3)

DRAMATIS PERSONAE

PRINCIPAL CHARACTERS

PAULO ANTUNES LIMA son of Judite and Carlos
CARLOS/SORAIA drag queen, father of Paulo, lover of Rui
JUDITE (maiden name is Claudino Baptista)—teacher, wife of
    Carlos, mother of Paulo
RUI Soraia's lover, Paulo's friend
MR. COUCEIRO (Jaime Couceiro Marques)—Paulo's guardian,
    retired World War II veteran
DONA HELENA Mr. Couceiro's wife, Paulo's guardian, housewife
NOÉMIA COUCEIRO MARQUES the Couceiros' dead daughter
DONA AURORINHA Carlos's neighbor on Príncipe Real
ALCIDES later lover of Soraia
DONA AMÉLIA candy seller at the club, friend of Carlos
GABRIELA MATOS HENRIQUES maid in hospital dining room, lover
    of Paulo

SECONDARY CHARACTERS

ABEL LOPES MARTINS Mr. Couceiro's grandfather, Isabel's father
ALBERTO Dona Amélia's uncle
AQUILES father of Gabriela
CAMÉLIA Judite's blind mother, Paulo's grandmother
CARMINDO new lover of Gabriela

CRISTINA (and Elizabete and Márcia)   fellow teachers of Judite in Lisbon

CORA   grandmother of Judite

DÁLIA   girl on tricycle in Bico da Areia, later seen by Paulo in Chelas

ELISA   lover of Luciano

FIRMINO   uncle of Gabriela

FLORIANO   store clerk, lover of Judite

MR. FREITAS   Marlene's stepfather

ISABEL LOPES MARTINS   Mr. Couceiro's mother

JOÃO   Rui's father

JÚLIA   Paulo's girlfriend in Personnel

LUCIANO   Paulo's doctor at the hospital

PROFESSOR MAIA ONOFRE   newspaper columnist

MARIA DA SOLEDADE   Mr. Couceiro's grandmother, Isabel's mother

MERCÊS   Julia's mother

OFÉLIA   Rui's mother

ORLANDO BORGES CARDOSO   Rui's grandfather

OTÍLIA   sister of Gabriela

PEDRO   Rui's uncle

PILAR   friend of Rui's aunt

SERGEANT QUARESMA   Dona Aurorinha's uncle

ROSENDO   former fiancé of Dona Aurorinha

VIVALDO   orderly at hospital

DRAG QUEENS (in order of mention)

ANDREIA

BÁRBARA

ALEXANDRA

NINI

SAMANTA

CAROLE/ANTÓNIO (has a daughter in France, niece of Aura; childhood neighbors are Dona Eunice, Álvaro, and Fernanda)

VÂNIA/MARCELINO Gonçalves Freitas

MILÁ

MICAELA

MARLENE/JOAQUIM (son of Lurdes)

RICARDA (Brazilian)

DINA

SISSI

LUCI

CRISTIANA

VANDA

CARLOS/SORAIA'S LOVERS AND CUSTOMERS
(in order of mention)

RUI	BEATO
FAUSTO	ELISEU
LUCIANO	AGOSTINHO
TADEU	ERNESTO
MÁRIO	FLORIANO
DINO	EURICO
JÁCOME	FERNANDO
LICÍNIO	ROMEU
HERNANDO	

MAP OF LISBON AND ITS ENVIRONS

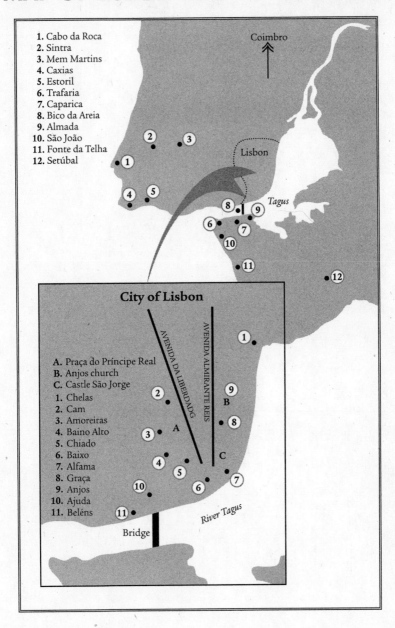

1. Cabo da Roca
2. Sintra
3. Mem Martins
4. Caxias
5. Estoril
6. Trafaria
7. Caparica
8. Bico da Areia
9. Almada
10. São João
11. Fonte da Telha
12. Setúbal

Coimbro

Lisbon

Tagus

City of Lisbon

AVENIDA DA LIBERDADG

AVENIDA ALMIRANTE REIS

A. Praça do Príncipe Real
B. Anjos church
C. Castle São Jorge
1. Chelas
2. Cam
3. Amoreiras
4. Baino Alto
5. Chiado
6. Baixo
7. Alfama
8. Graça
9. Anjos
10. Ajuda
11. Beléns

River Tagus

Bridge

WHAT CAN I DO WHEN

EVERYTHING'S ON FIRE?

CHAPTER

I WAS SURE I had that dream last night or the night before
   last night
   and that's why, without waking up, I kept thinking
   —Why worry I know damned well that I'm
   not interested in any episodes I knew weren't real
   —I'm asleep
   that might have scared me yesterday, I'm not scared of them now
   —Why should I get all worked up if it's nothing but a lie
   aware of the position of my body in the bed, a twist in the sheet
under my leg that's hurting me, the pillow
   as usual
   sliding between the mattress and the wall, my fingers
   by themselves, on their own
   looking for it, grabbing it, pulling it up, tucking it under my
cheek, which was tucking itself into the pillow in turn, which part
of me is pillow and which part is cheek, my arms were holding onto
the pillowcase and I was helping my arms
   —They're mine
   amazed that they belonged to me, aware of one of the plane trees
outside there, a blur on the windowpane at night and day now, getting into my sleep, making me lift up my head
   just my head because the twist in the sheet was still hurting me
   looking through the window to the office where the doctor was
writing out a diagnosis or a report
   the desk, the chair, and the cabinet all old, the door always open

where the patients would lie in wait to beg for cigarettes, unshaven, with dead eyes

I could never eat fish eyes in a restaurant, my uncle would stab with his fork and I would be blinded, screaming

they don't pay any attention to me, nobody ever pays any attention to me, all the orderlies do is shove me along

—Let's go let's go

and the fishes sitting on benches, their hands out, begging for cigarettes, my uncle lowering his fork

—Don't you like eyes, Paulo?

the desk, the chair, the cabinet, the doctor signing something or other, looking at me, quickly picking up his fork, moving it toward the sea bream or the gilthead, I do like eyes, uncle

—You can go home tomorrow

and while I was waking up and a dove was bobbing up and down on a branch of the plane tree, the twist in the sheet stopped hurting, the fish that I am separated itself from the pillow which isn't me after all, my uncle was amused and retreating into last night's dream, in which pills had changed into conger eels into puppets, and were asking me for cigarettes

—Don't you like eyes, Paulo?

the man gasping on my right for example rising up on his mattress like a drowning man on a slow swell, his wife would visit him on Sundays with a small bag of peaches and he would dismiss the peaches which he never finished with a wave of his hand

—Did you bring me any butts, Ivone?

my mother Judite, my father Carlos, the doctor, not this one, a fatter one,

I remembered the doctor's red necktie when they brought me in, a Gypsy woman who was hollering

or was I the one hollering?

the doctor

—*What's your mother's name?*

along with that I remembered the attendants, who were holding me by the wrists, from the ambulance Dona Helena had called

—*Take it easy, fellow*

*all those plates smashed in the kitchen, the pitcher still intact, the hands on
the clock keeping watch over the stew*

—Destroy us

*maybe it was the attendants who had helped me instead of the fat doctor
with the red tie, not in this office but in a room with no windows or a closet
where the Gypsy woman or I was hollering or maybe neither one of us, the
noise of the dishes*

—What's your mother's name?

my mother Judite, my father Carlos

—Did you bring me any butts, Ivone?

five cigarettes on Saturdays but you run out of cigarettes, a chit
for a glass of milk at the bar but the milk can't stand up straight
and it spills all over the counter the minute you touch it, the orderly
cleans the counter, cleans our jackets and chins with a rag that's the
fossil remains of a towel, the television ranting up on a high shelf

—Damned pigs

cake that crumbles as soon as you bite into it, sandwiches with
resistant meat, the cigarette lighted with the tenth match on the fil-
ter end as a tiny little flame devours the cotton

—They don't even notice it, the poor devils

the match goes out too soon or refuses to go out and burns your
skin, the certainty that I'd dreamed those days last night or the
night before and so why worry since back beyond the day before
yesterday, all I can remember is a Gypsy woman hollering and my
being strapped down to the bed, by the ambulance attendant
maybe

—Take it easy take it easy

the cup I stole from the dish rack smashed on the floor, Dona
Helena in tears, I've got to break these plates, the pitcher intact,
offended

what I liked about the pitcher

asking

—How about me?

the doctor with two or three psychologists or students or customers from the disco where my father worked and the branch of

the plane tree finally quiet as always at noontime, its elbows on the wall pushing back the row of sparrows over its brow, cats in a thicket of thorns or beside the garbage from the dining room where a girl wearing a cap was emptying buckets, the doctor to the students

—They live inside themselves, they have practically no feeling, it's so hard to help them get to feel again

giving me a basket of peaches no, giving me a cigarette, the match lighting when it should light, going out when it should go out, the ashtray full of ashes and with it like that where can I put my ash, I think Dona Helena's husband went along with the attendants pointing to the carpet, the floor

—He gets ashes on everything

I think the doctor

They live inside themselves, they don't even know their own families

and the psychologists or students or customers from the disco who made fun of my father repeating in obedient notebooks they live inside themselves, they don't even know their own families, the doctor's wedding ring advancing across the desk,

—See now

the pen tapping on the desk top, waking me up, aware of the position of my body in the bed, of a twist in the sheet under my leg

—Paulo

smashing the pen and the plates in the kitchen, Dona Helena took the pitcher with the line of a break where they'd glued it back together, away from me, the pen still moving along on the desk stopping me from smoking

—Paulo

the second coffin and my pretending not to notice it

—What's your mother's name?

and at that point, almost without realizing it, I began to laugh, when my father died I began to laugh just like that, people on long benches, a little old man with a painted mouth and a lap dog in his arms, the second coffin that I pretended not to notice, the priest came out from behind a curtain and I was lying over the casket laughing

—What's my mother's name you say, what's my mother's name you say?

preventing the psychologists or the students or the customers from the disco from getting a look at the corpse and ridiculing it, my father's a clown with feathers and spangles and a wig, padding on his behind, his breast, the painted mouth of the old man with the dog bristling at me barking, once I took my father's mastiff with a bow to Príncipe Real park where they used to play with me on the swing, there were fish in the pond, I never threw cracker crumbs to the fish

—Eat your cracker, Paulo

I unhooked the leash

—Get lost

and the animal was hesitant, hiding under the furniture dribbling piss on the rug, if we'd bought him a glass of milk at the hospital bar he would have spilled it on the counter, my father cleaned the dog's snout with the rag that was the fossil of a towel, I threw stones at him until I made him disappear around a corner, terrified, confused, the bow was becoming undone and wrapping around his legs, if only I could have thrown stones at my father

—Get lost

until I made him disappear around a corner, the feathers, the spangles, the wig, if only I could have stopped laughing

—They live inside themselves they don't even know their own families

without a single tear to hide the coffin, the music, the cone of light that was rising up onto the stage and my father singing

not my father, a clown with feathers and spangles and a wig

not the clown, a woman, all those plates to smash in the kitchen, the bottles of perfume in his room, the nail polish, the lipsticks, the razor to hide his beard, skirts and more skirts on a clothes rack, if only I could have thrown stones at the . . .

—What's your mother's name?

I say, my mother lives in Bico da Areia on the other side of the Tagus, a bus, a second bus, Lisbon upside down in the water, if I knock on the door the leash gets unhooked from my collar and a man on the first step at the entrance, my mother

—Get lost

catching a glimpse of the light on, houses with only tin or wooden roofs, shacks for black people, small gardens with wilted flowers, chestnut trees, in my father's time the flowers never ended up that way

—Go see if the faggot's kid is still out there

always fresh flowers in the living room, what's the reason for your purple fingernails, Father, the painted line that makes your eyebrows, the man came out onto the step chewing, a napkin around his neck and the wilted flowers

—Go see if the faggot's kid is still out there

the Tagus was going back and forth uncovering the float, that is it seemed to be going back and forth but it was staying right there, the Gypsies' horses were grazing on dune weeds, I heard a cricket or a night bird by the road, the man with the napkin around his neck wiped his slippers on the step and went back to the table chewing

—Nobody is out there

ruffled curtains, cardboard magnolias, my mother washed pots in the tub in the backyard, not dressed like a bride, barefoot, no pearl tiara on her forehead, my father and she cutting the cake and on top of the cake a pair of wax figurines, I woke up on the mattress in the kitchen as their arguments pulled me out from the bedcovers and I brought the rubber crocodile with me, my mother no longer a bride but not barefoot, not washing pots in the tub in the backyard and emptying the tub into the flower bed, was holding up a bra for my father to see

she kept the pearls in a button box and the figurines from the cake were displayed on the radio

—Do you wear this, Carlos?

my mother's name was Judite because that time I promised not to tell

when my mother's eyes looked strange and my uncle pointed at them with his fork

—Don't you like eyes, Paulo?

the crocodile got away from me and curled around her legs

—Mother

and I was thinking I hope the psychologists or students or customers from the disco didn't notice, I wonder where the figurines from the cake are, where the string of pearls can be, one of the Gypsies appeared with a switch and drove the horses toward the pine grove, as I curled up under the furniture along with the dog shedding hair and dribbling piss, do you wear this Carlos, and my father not saying anything, throwing stones until I made it disappear around a corner while the crocodile

—Mother

don't let them leave me all alone when they close the blinds and the man with the napkin

—Judite

not a man, the slices of a man seen through the slats in the blind, they drive me along toward the pine grove with the horses, the crocodile staying stubbornly by the entrance

—Let me stay with you people

explaining to them that I'm not me, I'm not to blame maybe if I grab them around the legs, the slices of my mother getting bigger, half of her glasses looking at the floorboards

—Did you hear the door creak

I thought I could make out the slices of a bottle that went back to being the slices of it placed on the slices of a sideboard, you could hear the pine trees rustling and the river by the float cleaning its teeth with its tongue, the slices of bottle rose up and the man with the napkin appeared on the step with it annoyed and scratching himself

the refrigerator with the dwarf from Snow White on top, the one with the pick on his shoulder who bossed his companions around, the dwarf to my mother

—You can't hear anything Judite, it must have been the horses

who were trotting along on a flat stretch where there were tents, wagons, the bottle was sliced up again on the sideboard into little strips of only glass now, another bra, jars of cream, a woman's boot, on the top shelf in the pantry, thrown at my father in a burst of scorn, the slow way algae and pebbles underwater, I can't tell whether they're moving or are just shadows

—Do you wear this, Carlos?

running your hand over the surface of things in the way that it's the crash step that's moving backward, not the train, you're standing and then a sigh of steam and metal, the platform that's moving away, the same with time, with death, the faces of the dead within our reach and yet so very far away, more serious, more dignified, maybe if my mother

—Do you wear this, Carlos?

my father not answering in his coffin with me defending him laughing, they'd dressed him in a necktie, a shirt without lace, a vest he would have hated, they combed his hair where before there were feathers, spangles, and the wig, the figurine in the picture was cutting the wedding cake, his cheek up against my mother's cheek while my cheek is up against the pillow with the plane tree pulling me out of sleep, aware of the position of my body in the bed, of the smell of the creolin they washed the floor with

—You can go home tomorrow

and at home the tub in the backyard waiting for morning

—Go see if the faggot's kid is still out there

and in the house

—Did you hear a creak from the front door?

the other home, the one on the deserted square of Príncipe Real, Rui's coffin to the left of my father's, a necktie, a shirt with no lace, and a vest all quite identical he didn't die like the clown

both their shoes, coming out their pants legs, pointing to the ceiling

they'd found him on the beach with the dog with a bow sniffing him or barking at the waves

not sniffing not barking at the waves, running in circles, all excited by a stick or the neck of a bottle, in my father's apartment it was the designs on the rug that interested him, hours on end contemplating diamond shapes

—Get lost

the police asked

—Do you know who he is do you know him?

four stakes and a rope surrounding Rui's body, the headlights of the cars lighting things up the way they do in a theater, any minute now first drums, then music, then silence because the music broke up, then some invisible running about, then

—You'll never learn, you idiot

then

—It's not my fault they unplugged it

then loud music, an oval of light on the curtain marked by burns, my father with his legs relaxed and a tiara tilted to one side singing with his arms crossed in forgiveness of sins, my mother turning over and over the tiara that was short on diamonds

—Do you wear this, Carlos?

if I lived in Bico da Areia I'd run through the pine grove or along the beach where there were tents, wagons, a trailer with no tires, the Gypsies would blindfold me the way they do horses before they shoot them with me on my knees, me laid out, me in a coffin in a church, when we went to the village my blind grandmother would run her fingers over my features with the motions of a potter, making adjustments to my nose, my cheekbones, my jaw, I'm changed, I don't recognize myself in the mirror

—Your grandson, Mama

my grandmother in the darkness of the small sitting room surrounded by images and candles lengthening my ears and giving me more teeth, she's going to eat me up and spread me over the land the way pigs do, her fingers suddenly stop short, caught around my neck, a dark question was making its way out through her kerchief dressed in mourning right down to her soul

—What do you mean grandson, daughter?

speaking not to my mother but to a chicken that was preening itself under its wings on a jumbled pile of trash, her hands pushing the shadows aside and she stopped

—What do you mean grandson, daughter?

while she put my features back in place with quick movements, if I lived in Bico da Areia I'd run faster than the orderlies, than the horses, my grandmother was searching out my mother, she was taking stock of her face with her thumbs

—You've gotten thinner Judite

one time or another I went to visit her in the village under the elm trees, avoiding the nettles, the mice, her eyes sensing my steps without her hearing them, her fingers kneading the emptiness intrigued, they said my dead grandfather would come in during the night with his hoe in his hand

—Camélia

uncovering pots and pans with that hunger the dead have, their musty breathing too, we wanted to live, we didn't get to run away and everything was quiet all around, the schoolteacher was strolling along the road to the cemetery with school over, bees and more bees on the trunks of the poplars, my grandmother to the hoe

—You're not coming to rob me are you?

I'm not coming to rob you, grandmother, I'm coming to ask you to touch me, to watch while you work in the garden, draw buckets from the well, change the afternoon with your hands, if you'd been at the church you'd have been quick to shape a decent face for my father and I wouldn't be ashamed anymore, a man, not a clown with feathers and spangles and a wig, on the afternoon when he visited me in masquerade at the hospital

one of the orderlies whistling or coughing, the maids making faces from the laundry, I wanted so much to be a horse and trot along the beach far away, for them to cover my eyes, take a shot at me, the animal kneeled down and stopped thinking, the Gypsy kicked me up on the flank, when the tail stopped quivering the music got louder, the oval of light on the curtain with burn marks disappeared, I knew no performer had gone up to any microphone wearing a stole and a diamond tiara, the policeman

no, the doctor to me

I've already dreamed this dream, I've already dreamed this dre . . .

—Do you know who he is do you know him?

no, I didn't dream this dream, four stakes and a cord surrounding the body, the dog barked at the waves, was hit with a stick, leaped to one side, came back, my father and Rui had another dog but it was run over by a truck, its back legs crushed the mouth still talking

—*You can go home tomorrow*

we took him home, we wrapped his back legs in a blanket to stop the blood, Rui was waving his arm to keep the flies away

—Wave your arm keep the flies away

starting in March on Príncipe Real, father, the flies, flies in the living room, in the bedroom, in the closet with the wash basin, the vet getting his syringe ready, my father cried and his eye makeup was dark wet streaks, he ran his handkerchief over them and more streaks and smudges

—Be quiet father

four stakes and a cord surrounding the body at the place where they always came in the summer, my father didn't go into the water because of his wig, first drums, then music, then silence, then

—It's not my fault they unplugged it

then music again

—Sing father

even though it was the music that was singing, not him, the voice from the loudspeakers and my father picking it up, toss a ball in the living room and the dog would go right and left, fooled by the echoes of the sound, the clowns

the women

the clowns who went on with my father, younger than he, with not so many feathers, moved their hips in the rear, adjusting the hooks on their dresses, one of them, without a wig, was shaving himself in a small pocket mirror, going after recalcitrant hairs with a tweezer, the policeman to me

—Do you know who they are do you know them?

no, the doctor

—What's your mother's name?

my mother Judite and my father Carlos they have practically no feeling it's so hard to help them get to feel again

I haven't got a mother, I've got two mothers and Rui in the second coffin in the church, people on long benches, the little old man with the dog in his arms and me leaning on the brass handles laughing, an old suit of Dona Helena's husband with cough drops in the pocket and an empty toothpick case

no, a single toothpick tock-tocking

which was small on me, they brushed my hair put on a drop of hair lotion, turned me around to see how I looked, satisfied, funeral aside, they'd really put me together

—It's not too big in the belly dress him

they stood me in front of a dressing table, Dona Helena's husband moved about studying me, avoiding him I asked silently

—Wouldn't you like being my father?

they have practically no feeling it's so hard to help them get to feel again

and he was busy adjusting the shoulders, he knew the names of the trees in Latin, he'd stroke their trunks and the trees were thankful, I think

—Mr. Couceiro

he'd served in Timor where a bullet in the rump

—The Japanese, lad, up to my neck in a rice paddy with buffaloes

I don't believe it

when he came to get me at the station house because of the drugs and with my guts floating all by themselves I could hear his cane before he came in, I knew exactly the moment when he was going to dry the back of his neck with the handkerchief which, all twisted into knots, kept coming out of his pocket, the cane searching for me among the roots of hedges, horns, native corpses

—The Japanese, lad

he put the handkerchief away to help me keep my stomach intact, a lung, the arm I thought I was going to thank him with and it floated up to the ceiling, hiding under the furniture, dribbling piss on the rug, if they gave me a glass of milk I would have spilled it on the counter, Mr. Couceiro wasn't throwing stones at me, wasn't ordering me to

—Get lost

he'd say hello to the trees, recall the Japanese, he showed me his corporal's uniform which the rice paddies had stained, three days and three nights up to his neck in the water and they gave up because they were tired lad, he looked at me the way my mother looked at my father

—Do you wear this, Carlos?

not even disillusioned, humble when the light of the lamp

caught him, he had no eyes, wrinkles above and below and instead of eyes small spheres of light, Dona Helena

the doctor's wedding ring was tapping the pen on the desk top
—What's your mother's name?
and there was no dove bobbing on the plane tree
with me in her arms
—Look at what I've got here Couceiro
a hidden floor, plants in paint cans, the curled-up doormat that I always tripped on, bedrooms boxed inside one another
the dining-room table ended at the bed
where the doorknobs turned uselessly, you would grab any one of them and it would stay in your hand, a porcelain ball and a rusty shaft, tiled panels in need of repair, Mr. Couceiro coming from the antipodes where a radio was playing, not the one I broke, an older one next to the patched-up couch, Mr. Couceiro with a cane, in line with a current of air that was puffing out his shirt
—Just like the monsoons in Timor, lad, all those fallen palm trees
Dona Helena with indignant clicks of her tongue whirled as if someone had been attacking me and went off with me in her arms into the trenches of the pantry, gave me some pears in syrup, gave me some cookies, showed me the music box and the little waltz started up
—You scared him and he started crying who's going to quiet him down now?
all I have to do today is think about them
they have practically no feeling it's so hard to make them get to feel again with a little luck medicine sometimes
and I remember all the notes, I find myself repeating them if I go soft, I don't have two mothers, my mother's name is Dona Helena, she showed me the music box again, sat down on the couch beside the sewing machine, exiled Mr. Couceiro far away to the radio
the needle moved along the dial and foreign languages whistling, scratching, it stopped where the priest was saying the six o'clock rosary, icy echoes in the chapel, half from his prayers and half from the women, they paused and the women would begin and

the priest would stop, after the heroin the voices would mingle, the sewing machine

back and forth sewing me up, I tried to cry out and my throat closed up on me, the lamp to heat the spoon slid along the mat, I couldn't get the needle out, a tiny drop of blood appeared and trickled down, Mr. Couceiro concerned

—What's wrong with him?

my mother Dona Helena and my father Mr. Couceiro he started crying it's all your fault who's going to quiet him down now try entertaining him with your Japanese your buffaloes the months you spent up to your neck in a rice paddy tomorrow when he comes back from the hospital don't bother him leave him alone talk to him about trees turn on the radio rosary for him

in the back of the apartment a balcony facing the Anjos church, a stretch of river and almost never any ships, I was sitting on the flowerpot with the lemon and the syringe, I tightened my fist the way Rui had taught me to find the vein, he would come with a ring or a bracelet or the money from last night's show toward payment for the washing machine or repairs on the stove

—Don't worry about it, it's your father who's paying

my father's name is Mr. Couceiro, my mother's Dona Helena, the clown who Rui thought was my father isn't my father I swear, I don't know anything about him, I don't know him, my father went away or maybe I didn't have one or maybe he vanished into thin air and materialized years later so I could lean over his coffin laughing, the old man with the little dog fluttering with indignation

—Good heavens

the clown who wasn't my father fussing with containers, bottles of silicone, cotton balls

—What about the envelope with the money, Rui?

searching through the blouse rack, pushing waistbands, head-dresses, capes aside, my father's a man, he knows everything about the Japanese, he knows the names of trees in Latin, he killed buf-faloes in Timor, his name is Mr. Couceiro

—You scared him and he started crying who's going to quiet him down now?

we came to a broken-down wall as we left the Cape Verdeans not along the road, on a path through the weeds, pieces of a garden fence, what had once been a statue

Neptune or Apollo?

but without any arms, a battered mess kit begging

—Hit me

I understood her quite well

—Please hit me

the same with the oranges falling off the fruit cart and I said

—We haven't got time now

we unfolded the newspaper and there was some white powder, stop it from slipping all the way down the crease, separate part of it, put the other part away, on the broken-down wall a whole lot of lighters, rubber bands, footprints, writing carved with a jackknife impossible to read, we handed over the money through a small door without seeing anybody, we waited a little, received the newspaper, a Mulatto stood guard at the corner opening and closing a jackknife, the palms of his hand were softer than mine, pink with black wrinkles. I thought I was afraid but I wasn't or maybe just less afraid than I thought I was, studying the powder, maybe it was chalk dust, maybe limestone, how do you do it Rui, show me how you do it, my father's husband

not my father's husband, the clown's husband, they slept in the same bed and therefore they were married, there'd been others before this one, Alcides, Fausto

the clown

—Let me introduce you to Alcides let me introduce you to Fausto up against the Chinese chest where my father was doubled over moaning

look, my father said, I made a mistake

—You shitty fag

he snatched the chain from him, put the chain in his pants and the clown

—I'm sorry

Rui's wife came to Príncipe Real once, railing at them while the tenant on the third floor

Dona Aurorinha said

—Miss

she walked slowly, she never got excited, a half hour for each floor with her bag of groceries, she was breathing hard as her chest tightened

—It's all right I'm fine

she insisted that I taste her guava jam, the rooms were dark because the light bill hadn't been paid, she lighted a candle

—Electricity upsets me

you opened the faucets but not a drop came out

—I don't need water I keep myself clean

the furniture white with mold, a desperate flight of cockroaches, in April an aneurysm carried her off, Rui's wife at the empty door

—Come out of there you slimy worms

she tried to force the lock with a piece of tile and Dona Aurorinha

—Don't hurt yourself, Miss

she kicked the garbage can which rolled down the alley, and went away

—Slimy worms

my father

Mr. Couceiro

my father?

my father holding the artificial lashes from one eye in the tweezer, the other one quivering with annoyance

—Such a bother

and something else quivering on his face, a tendon or a muscle, his eyes cloudy with cataracts like my grandmother's, almost falling against the chest without Fausto even hitting him, Dona Aurorinha offering him some guava jam

—Mr. Carlos

coming down step by step with heroic difficulty, the clown, arching his pinky, was consoling his annoyance with camomile tea, holding out a cup

—Would you like some, Dona Aurorinha?

he was sticking on the artificial lashes before the mirror where years before he used to comb his mustache, Alcides or Fausto then, yes, with

mustaches and my father frying cutlets, wearing an apron, while he gave them his wristwatch, gave them necklaces, hopeful, submissive

—A remembrance from a friend

Alcides or Fausto suspicious of the gift examining the treasures

—Is this worth anything at all?

shawls, sashes, poppies, plastic vicuñas, my mother trampling those splendors I thought belonged to her

—Do you wear this, Carlos?

we came to a broken-down wall as we left the Cape Verdeans not along the road, on a path through the weeds, pieces of a garden fence, what had once been a statue

Neptune, Apollo?

but no arms, no arms at all, we unfolded the newspaper and a bit of white powder, on the ground by the broken-down wall a lot of lighters, rubber bands, footprints, Rui squeezes the lemon like that way, mixes it in with the water that way, does it that way with the spoon, heats it that way and as soon as it's boiling a little he ties a rubber band around above his elbow that way, it seemed to me there was a jackdaw in a stone niche

its head bobbing, spasms in its tail, in just a few minutes I'm a bird, I reach the top of the fig tree all excited but then I'm calm, contented, the needle by the widest vein, don't be in a hurry with the shot, that way, a kind of heat, a kind of cold, the broken-down wall, the jackdaw, heat in my belly again, inside my chest where my heart wasn't beating, I was spreading out, losing weight, breaking away from myself, I caught a glimpse of it almost purple in the bird's nest, what's your name, what's my name, tell me what my name is and Rui tightening his rubber band, that way

—Shut up

wind where there's no wind, thirst where there's no thirst, I can understand everything with the powder Rui, I can understand everything, the words from the jackknife possible to read now, do you want me to read them to you Rui, you're cold too, you're hot, you're a jackdaw too, don't lie down in the mud, head bobbing, tail in spasms, the little bitty fruit on the fig tree, look how my leaves cross over each other, look how I'm growing, don't lie down by the weeping willows, get up, what's the reason for your scolding me Rui, don't scold me, don't tell me to shut up, the jackknife words say

—They don't mean anything

they say

—It's hard to get them to feel

They say

—Go see if the faggot's kid is still out there

not one fig tree, two out of the same trunk, Rui covered up the hole the needle had made and the crimson drop

darker than crimson, crimson is what people think blood is, garnet

—Shut up

the Mulatto was going over to a pickup without any tires opening and closing his jackknife, a small click when the blade came out, a small click when it went back in, Dona Helena with me in her arms going off toward the pantry

—You scared him and he started crying who's going to quiet him down now?

the Mulatto rested his sandal on the landing where there was a speck of rain, those remnants of October and the remnants of October while I was counting the gratings in the garden fence, sixteen

—Not here

counting again, I wasn't sure whether it was fifteen or sixteen, I was right, four near us plus seven and plus five, the Mulatto pointing to the city down below

—Not here

sure that I'd dreamed this dream yesterday or the day before yesterday

and for that reason, not waking up, I thought

—Stop worrying I know all that already

not interested in any episodes I knew weren't real, the jackknife at my throat, the sandal stepping on me

—I'm asleep

and since I'm asleep I don't worry, everything's a lie, aware of the pillow sliding between the mattress and the trunk they were slamming me against

—I don't have any necklace you can take from me

Dona Aurorinha with her bag of groceries

—Paulo

half an hour for each floor, her huge, exhausted feet

—Don't worry you're doing fine

walking ahead of me lighting a candle and me following the candle in the dark until Dona Aurorinha tells me

—Sit down

in an invisible chair and the two of us stay there, not talking, listening to the sounds of the building and something distant that was mocking me

A jackdaw?

that was mocking me.

CHAPTER

WHEN I WAS LITTLE I would settle down outside there near the horses and the sea so the waves would muffle the voices inside the house and thank God that for an hour or two I could forget about them, my father next to the refrigerator with the dwarf from Snow White on top, turning it round and round without looking at it, my mother asking him in a hiss that carried to the pine trees and made me call to them, pounding on the clothes rack or smashing the car with wooden wheels the minute my mother said

—Why Carlos?

and her

—Why Carlos?

wasn't in the living room, it was going from tree to tree and mingling with splotches of light in the haze, the dwarf from Snow White going from one side to the other on the refrigerator and my mother's question without my mother

—Why Carlos?

that same question even today

even yesterday

even today in the hospital by the row of plane trees, looking at their trunks and at every branch those same sounds, pounding on the clothes rack, not hearing the pigeons, the maids in the dining room, the man in the next unit lying belly-up in a whisper, his navel

yesterday

today, he said today

—*They're not attuned to time*

—Why Carlos?

I am so attuned to time, I know how to tell time on clocks, five minutes to six, seven-twenty, eight-twelve, where did the doctors get the idea that I'm not attuned to time, show me your wrist and I'll tell you instead of having me draw a family and the person in skirts, dressed as a bride, with pearls in her hair, bigger than the husband, and the son, the husband next to the refrigerator, the son smashing the car on the straw mat and the mat torn

—Why Carlos?

the bride grabbed the dwarf from Snow White and stopped it from dancing, my explaining to the psychologist who gave me paper and pencil that it's not a question of a watermelon or anything like that

—It's not a question of a watermelon or anything like that

it's a question of the dwarf from Snow White that the bride is moving away

—Stop messing with that, it makes me nervous

she was stopping her husband from touching it, this is the husband, this is the son, this is the son's car with wooden wheels, I had a big one, if you don't ask the plane trees to be quiet I'm leaving, the man's navel on the wall, I didn't hit him, I hit the clothes rack and the orderly as though I'd hit someone and I hadn't hurt him, I was the one hurt out there by the horses and the sea

—Let go of it

where the voices didn't reach, the shower out here too and the dripping on concrete all night long, a puddle where there were yellow jackets in August, you'd turn the faucet on and the soap was on the windowsill, or rather it was with my parents that the soap was on the windowsill, with me I'd hold it for a second and then because I was a child and couldn't control anything, it would slip down to the ground and I'd grab it quick before the yellow jackets, on Sundays they'd come in through a hole in the window screen which would put the waves into squares, beyond the soap my father

deodorant, perfume, my mother's cold cream on the sly, I peeked and my father stopped rubbing it on and looked at me, there's something strange about the person in the sketch, not him, timid-

ity, bashfulness, a kind of qualm, the psychologist making an oval
mark and an arrow, cream on the buttocks, on the shoulder blades,
on the chest

—Is he your father?

one of the neighbors, the one who owned the terrace café,
perched on the wall to prevent him from seeing him and telling the
customers I elbowed the clown out of the way and there I was all
alone by the corner of the house spying, the horses were trotting
along under the whip, one of my feet was unfinished in the sketch
and it stopped me from running, I picked up the pencil and made
a shoe, as I got out of the sketch and into the yard, the hospital
fence, the river

—Take care of yourself

the river tomorrow as I say goodbye to the doctor, today the yard
and the fence, a friendly cigarette, a coin for a friendly cup of coffee,
I'm not a patient, friend, they've imprisoned me here, the basket of
peaches abandoned by the plane tree, Mr. Couceiro helped me with
my suitcase, clothes, slippers, a poster of my father in an evening
gown that I hadn't even remembered bringing with me

—Why Carlos?

—No

—Why father?

and Mr. Couceiro quickly folded it up and it disappeared in
among the shirts, if I asked

—Why father?

my father would be mute, it looked as though he was going to
speak and he was mute

speak to me tell me

I'd wake up in Bico da Areia with the bedsprings moving on the
other side of the partition, with the springs my mother's leg

ever so slowly

on top of a sleeping leg, an endless pause during which the
horses

the sea

a silence, the sleeping leg escaped with a creaking of boards, my
father's voice

—No

—Why father?

and the horses or the sea or neither sea nor horses, my mother's slippers on the floor and the grumbling bedsprings moved back into shape, I could tell that she'd hurt herself bumping into the clothes closet, we always hurt ourselves bumping into the clothes closet, our house tripped us up, startled at first and then angry, we'd grab our knee with both hands, the furious reflex before our mouth came out with

—God damn it

I could sense her going down the steps, her hands on the outer door from the creaking of the hinges, no moon no pine trees, only the scaly surface of the water, I sensed her strange breathing, her night-gown pulled up, something white that was leaping about and I said

—Don't cry

no sea no horses, blowing her nose on her sleeve, her hands half embracing me and half pushing me away

—Go inside you'll catch cold, dummy

finally embracing me, gathering in her nightgown more, her body so warm, tears that didn't belong to me that became mine now, don't cry Paulo don't cry, and Dona Helena would pick me up and take me away, maybe Mr. Couceiro would talk to me about Timor, maybe they'd fill my mouth with spoonfuls of guava jam, when I lifted my head I saw my father at the window

oh to trot with the horses

when he saw that I'd seen him he disappeared from the window frame and the frosted glass, when I went in I saw him crucified up against the wall far behind me there, not in a nightgown, in pajamas

—Do you want to borrow my hose father?

the nightgowns only at Príncipe Real, red, silvery, not cotton, silk, if I happened to catch him without his wig a small irritated cry, little fingers that shooed me away

—Oh! Paulo

and without the wig the bald head, the freckles, he'd put on a kerchief when he went to bed, the cedar at Príncipe Real said to me

—Don't stare at cripples it's not nice

Dona Aurorinha in the vestibule with her shopping bag, her cheap ring, two potatoes, wilted vegetables, feeling her way upstairs

—Let me give you a hand

pondering her worries as she put her foot on each step

—How's Paulo's father, Dona Aurorinha?

her uncle a sergeant

—My uncle was a sergeant

and consequently an important matter for Dona Aurorinha, poor thing, if people didn't show her respect she'd threaten them with the Army

—I'm going to report you to headquarters

she'd introduce herself to the sentry with her ring, the potatoes, her rundown blouse, she'd raise her umbrella in a solemn salute, take the photo of an old man in uniform from her purse, clean it with the hem of her jacket with dignified pomp, examine the flag with the familiarity of a relative

—I'm the niece of Sergeant Quaresma of the Second Infantry

sure that the colonels, fearful

—She's the niece of Sergeant Quaresma and that makes everything all right

Sergeant Quaresma's niece coughing all night long, at the funeral no colonel, no sentry, no military honors, some sparrows in the cypresses but inattentive and few, my father and I accompanied the casket, he was wearing pants fortunately and didn't have any polish on his nails, almost a man except for some vestiges of a clown on his eyebrows, from last night's show, my mother pointing it out to him with her finger

we had a crystal lamp with a painted shade

—Who is she, don't lie

words in the mirror in front of his mouth, the light of the lamp on the most expensive, prettiest wardrobe, like a trim or a caprice, broken garlands of flowers in a lilac fringe, fell onto his reflection soundlessly and as it fell, an eternity followed

—Who is she, don't lie

a storm of flashes, congealed time waiting, the horses in suspense despite the whip, a wave reaching out its arms along the beach and gathering debris

I was a piece of debris, take me with you, not these baskets, not these algae, me

my mother

—Get away Paulo

throwing the pieces into the pail, reliefs, that ruffled part hand-painted they told me

—It was hand-painted keep away don't touch it

not throwing me away, my father was washing his face in the basin, Dona Helena stopping her cooking

—Throw you away, Son?

she called me son, see? she called me son

she smelled of fried food, starch, goodness, I could go to sleep on her lap, Mr. Couceiro after hesitating put a finger to my forehead, his cane idly tapping

—Have you got a fever?

their wardrobe never bothered me, a large, benign mirror, with the whole room inside it, the mirror on the dressing table in front and three Dona Helenas, three of me, three Mr. Couceiros, corporals in the Timor rice paddies, leave your finger on my forehead, it doesn't bother me, I like it, Dona Helena

—Don't frighten him be careful

I let him take off his earrings, change the position of his hairpins, when they brought me in, the doctor spoke to Mr. Couceiro, while the paramedic released my wrists, cramps from a lack of heroin, my father dead and even so laughter

laughter

explaining to me that if I didn't laugh, if I didn't keep on laughing

—I need to laugh so much, do you understand? I need to laugh doctor

the doctor to Mr. Couceiro

—Is he your grandson?

Paulo leaning on the coffin of his own father how awful on the coffin of his own father between embracing him and rejec...

25

the light on the roof of the ambulance was swinging from wall
to wall

—Paulo

I stole money from Dona Helena and Dona Helena didn't report
me, I broke open the strongbox with the Minho chains and not a
single earring, clasps and powder on it so she could tell if someone
had been stealing, asking for a loan in her name at the grocery store,
at the butcher's, the grocer gripping his broom

he didn't hit me

—Get out of my sight you little sneak thief

making more holes in my belt because the pants are too big and
Dona Helena soup, quinine extract, syrups

—Take your tonic, Paulo

put your finger on my forehead, Mr. Couceiro, while you keep it
on my forehead the cramps grow less, all those needle marks on my
arms, the hard, black veins, they're not arms, they're tree branches,
I'm a bush, Dona Helena, my gums are dissolving, I hide my missing teeth with my lips, the ashtray on the doctor's desk, desperate,
anxious

—Break me now

while the light on the ambulance obliged him to exist, I sold the
wall clock and from Dona Helena not a word, from Mr. Couceiro

—*Is he your grandson?*

not a word, the naked hook accusing me, a second hook on the
left, the cane looking as though it was going to move but not angry
at all

for God's sake get mad, shout, get mad at me

Dona Helena held him back with her eyes

—Jaime

Jaime Couceiro Marques

she pulled out the hook so it wouldn't accuse me, facing me at
dinner time, Mr. Couceiro in his easy chair, Dona Helena in the cotton velvet upright chair, sometimes I'd find her in the kitchen putting the touch of a smile over a mask of pain

—It'll go away

the smile was smaller than the mask as could be seen from the corners of her mouth, when she thought I'd left the smile would disappear, she'd come along leaning herself on the backs of the chairs

the toaster was taken too, the meat grinder, I stood in front of where they'd been pointing at the hook

—It wasn't me

no

carnations in the unbroken vase, starflowers

—It was me, kick me out, it was me

two tulips

no, pretended indignation, the open hands of innocence

—I wasn't home today, how could it have been me?

two tulips and some geraniums, don't answer, please don't argue with me, Mr. Couceiro knew the names of trees in Latin, he would stroke their trunks and they'd answer him, the huge hook, maybe I could ask the Cape Verdean for the clock back

—Lend me the clock for a week, I'll bring it back

the jackknife opening and closing, the sandal nudging me

—Are you still there?

a labyrinth of alleyways and no way out, old walls, small cracked windows, where is the city, there was a statue but what statue what square, at night my father in his wig looking for Rui, the clown in a ball gown and high heels that lifted him up over the cobblestones, I didn't even exist

—Rui

Rui on the muddy ground

—You shitty fag

and the clown, my father, cleaning his wound, getting his scarf dirty, he

did I say kissing him, mother?

kissing, the pair of them

sorry

in the same bed, my father with a kerchief on his head, I don't even exist, he laid Rui down in the car, fixed the blanket around him, the headlights quivering over the bumps, me in Chelas all by myself can't you see that you've scared him, who's going to calm him down now, the jackknife changing tone, interested

—That shitty fag is your father?

in Príncipe Real the pond in darkness, the trees that Mr. Couceiro knows the names of and I don't, the key in the lock stopping me from getting in, the garbage trucks were collecting boxes under a spotlight

two

on the roof too

yellow, not blue

pointing me out and then hiding me, going away and coming back

and I was going away and coming back

Dona Aurorinha's shopping bag with the potatoes, which she, dead in the cemetery, certainly wouldn't be cooking, suffocating from her bronchitis, the Anjos balcony so clear before I got to the doormat, Dona Helena stumbling about in her insomnia, relieved, content

—Son

with me thinking, hating her, I could steal her vacuum cleaner, the bronze inkstand, her in-laws' wedding rings on a cotton cushion, take the toolbox

—Can't you see that I despise you, that you make me sick, that I detest you?

and the thumbing of the radio rosary program as she accompanied the priest without interrupting her crocheting, praying for me, Mr. Couceiro from the clothes bin where there was a smell of lime

—Is it the boy, Helena?

don't let me hear the cane, God help him if it's the cane, luckily it's just his slippers on the floor and the throat-clearing of old people, emptying out the teapot

burn everything, destroy everything, Dona Helena said

—Paulo

not son

—Paulo

I'm not her son, never was her son, the key in the lock of my father's door stopping me from getting in, fake chinchillas on a wire hanger, muslins, fans, Rui and the clown who pay no attention to my presence playing checkers, if Dona Helena dares say

—Son

I'll break the soup tureen right then and there

—You're not my mother

heat at first, followed by cold, followed by an urge to crush myself, I don't know what dying is like but they're disentangling me from my body, conversations that get away from me, scarecrows in smocks holding a basin up against my chest

—Vomit

while I was a jackdaw incapable of flight, a sick bird, a bundle tied together with a cord of nerves asking for a needle, a lemon, a rubber tube to help the needle, when I was a wet bundle that toppled and fell, Mr. Couceiro's Japanese or orderlies or doctors pushed me under, shouting into the rice paddy of Timor, the drifting buffaloes prevented me from breathing, the heads with dead empty eyes watch, asking for the borrowed clock to sell again, if I can recite the table of sevens or the tributaries of the Guadiana I'll get better, the hospital orderly

—You're back in school dummy

once I offered to accompany Dona Aurorinha upstairs and carry her shopping bag, the potatoes, the wilted vegetables, a small bottle of olive oil dripping green tears, we went one behind the other quietly up the steps, she was nothing but some disconnected rattles of bronchitis, me with the Cape Verdeans on my mind

—Don't die on me now

the rattles came together with a struggle, a shudder, a falling apart and more bronchitis, it seemed to me that some loose screws were releasing her from her flesh, her neck was so thin, the cartilages of an insect, every so often the question in the form of a wheeze

—Aren't you tired, boy?

not a question, a hope

—If you're tired you can lean up against the wall I'll wait for you

and accompanying the invitation with the sound of a dozen

screws in a tin tube, and the skylight farther and farther away, the endless banister, the coin purse gleaming with age and its small chrome clasp

—How many coins have you got, old woman?

no wristwatch, no ring, a parasol that wasn't worth shit, if you were only a rich old lady, silver flatware, watercolors, crystal, instead of watercolors and crystal flower boxes on the landing, just boxes, no flowers, with dirty sand that stank of cat, a pigeon on the sky-light or a jackdaw walking across the glass

I could swear it was a jackdaw walking across the glass

the key coming out after some difficult maneuvers

another screw falling out

from the depths of her skirt, with a muddy little laugh that drenched her with joy, the left corner of her mouth sliding down toward her jaw

if you fell apart, who'd care?

the key was searching for the hole and scratching the paint

—Thieves can't find it, boy

the hinges sounding like the click of a switchblade and the latch leaping out, the same cat smell that was intriguing because there wasn't any cat, Dona Aurorinha fluttering around I don't know where, the location of furniture guessed at in the dark, me with my hands out before me in fear that a dresser or a side table might attack me, maybe if she said something to me, if she took me in her arms

she used to take me in her arms

if she said

—Boy

I'm not robbing you, help me, the orderly at the hospital with a pitying push

—The boob got a notion to call for help

jackdaws not just on the skylight, but on the cedar in Príncipe Real, on the trees that Mr. Couceiro knew, jackdaws, don't you cry, jackdaws, get inside you'll catch cold dummy, jackdaw waves, jack-daw horses, jackdaw orderlies, the boob got a notion to call for help, jackdaw doctors ordering them to tie me to the bed

—Is he your grandson?

Mr. Couceiro's cane rising up with some strange arabesques and going off to confront the Japanese

—He's not my grandson he's my

if he calls me son I'll smash the tureen right here and now

jackdaw four times seven, five times seven, six times seven, you've gone back to school, dummy, colic, vomiting, this coldness in the belly, a spoon, the match, don't give me any medicine and I won't smash the car with wooden wheels, he's not my grandfather he's my father, who's going to keep him quiet now, my father, the clown

—*Why Carlos?*

in his wig with no lipstick on his lips, the straps of the dress not on his shoulders, on his arms, through a chink in the window

the drapes, the chandelier, a metal frame and the light bulbs in a circle, three of them lighted

how much is seven times three?

the rest of them dark

—Go back to Dona Helena's you'll wake up the neighbors

a voice so different from the songs in the show, jewels that don't get to shine without light bulbs, there was no bathtub, a stucco washbasin and Spanish perfume instead of cat smell, the water was heated in pans, wobbling in the midst of the fumes, a handle on both sides, the steam spreading, the clown

—I scalded myself

Rui lying down reaching for the newspaper

—Did you scald yourself, sweetie?

a scarlet splotch with blisters, my father looking for the tube of sunburn lotion and lavender, acetone, pictures of him as a redhead, as a blonde, as a Sevillana with a great show of castanets and mantillas, Rui between two pages, checking his cigarette

—Can't you find the lotion, sweetie?

on the stone lid a cluster of woolen forget-me-nots, Dona Aurorinha nowhere to be found, a tenuous presence in the distant past, days like nostalgia for the dead, the bronchitis rattles breaking apart elsewhere, a palsied claw have a hard time gathering them together

31

—Come here

the Venetian blinds rose with a creak of bones that showed an empty cage holding a rubber stamp, would someone clear up for me whether or not rubber stamps can sing

how much is a rubber stamp worth?

a small trunk open just for me

thank you, trunk

with a couple of postcards where grease stains have dissolved some letters

M ss Aurorinha, please believe that if I live a housand years I'll not for et that Saturday, yours orever Rosendo

the boyfriend dead any number of years from some undefined illness, July sunsets in which he kept getting thinner

gently

at the baths drinking cups of bicarbonated water while the musicians quavered out waltzes on a bamboo bandstand

M ss Aurorinha, tonight the fever went down and I'm no longer spitting blood

lilac messages, dried herbs in books, declarations of love, a complete sentence that the Cape Verdeans wouldn't swap with me for anything

—Why do I want this?

crowned with a star-shaped smear

As soon as I'm cured and if you'll have me, let's get married

and in the end he wasn't cured, the waltz was inaudible, doctors in top hats prescribed cupping glasses, baked chicken, naps

With the rest I feel almost strong and I took a wa k this afternoon, I kiss yo r hands Rosendo

Dona Aurorinha in a hurry with her trousseau, linking initials, convincing her sergeant uncle to accompany her to Luso, trains slower than oxcarts, linden trees, mists, cottages, characters who were nothing but eyes and mouths wrapped in shawls in wicker lounge chairs and the creaking of the wicker prevented us from understanding who was complaining, not just one Rosendo, ten or fifteen Rosendos in their unknown beards, in their empty boots, in the softness of their asthma, the spring of bicarbonated water was weeping in the woods, kites were hanging down from the sky in a line swaying wires, ten or fifteen Rosendos

If Miss Aurorinha could only dream how much I love her, my odfather has promised me a partnership in his firm and a share in a house in Arroios

those who recognized her couldn't remember her, then recognized her, elated

—Miss

the return train broke down in Coimbra, the sergeant uncle on the platform consulted timetables with the kites hanging down from the sky in his mind and no more delicate passion, no more postcards, and the man with the jackknife jeering at me

—What am I going to do with this?

what am I going to do with If I live a housand years I'll never foret that Saturday please accept y sincere best ishes Rosendo, what am I going to do with legitimat ly happy I can tell you that I am almost back in shape I only ost one pound during the past eek and I go to the dining room with the help of the attendant, what am I going to do with a beautiful day oday in the hot baths remembering a certain unforgettable Su day in Alges during which

I swear it

I valued her as I never had, arguing with the Cape Verdeans while the cold, the heat, an itching that made me keep scratching myself all the time, pulling off my skin with my nails, pulling me out of myself, freeing myself from the impossibility of not moving, from this apartment in the dark, from this cat smell with no cat, from these invisible pieces of furniture that watch me, threaten me, attack me, take a good look they're expensive postcards, a lot of collectors would give a fortune for them, they'll sell like hotcakes in those stores where rich people go and Dona Aurorinha coughing on the stairs with her shopping bag, her two potatoes, her skeletal vegetables and the screws and their thread

—Aren't you tired, boy?

so nice to me, always so attentive

—If you're tired, rest on the landing I'll wait for you

Rosendo accompanying her up the steps with his polite ways,

discreet about his illness, and his painstaking handwriting, my father had a nib like that, he'd put it in the penholder and write with it, making no mistakes

if you will allow me a bold expression of my daring I adore you

the teacher asked for the names of the kings of the first dynasty and the penholder

if you will allow me a bold expression of my daring I adore you

the notebook exhibited to the circle of schoolmates

—Get a look at this

Ricardo spelling it out, following the syllables with the tip of his finger

if you will allow me a bold expression of my daring I adore you, the Mulatto torturing his ears and fighting off the thorny consonants of I adore you, coming down off the postcard toward me

all those fixes in his pocket, all that peace, the broken-down wall, the needle, the rubber hose that woke up the veins, a stone where I could fold up my topcoat and rest my head

—What am I going to do with this?

I put them back in the trunk, I don't put them in the trunk, drawers and in the drawers no clothes, one last postcard

Now that I'm saying good-bye to you I'm tire

just what I'm saying

Now that I'm saying good-bye to you I'm tire

on the other side a lady and a gentleman with painted lips like the clown's, girlish smiles, cheeks that are too rosy, if you put a wig on him

—Good morning father

the lady and the gentleman in chaste modesty, framed in a heart of flowers, now that I'm saying good-bye to you I'm tire

another clay whistle, another trolley ticket, holiday jaunts to Belém and Graça, the gentleman with cheeks that are too rosy

—Miss

and all this even though the apartment was just like ours, the same tiny rooms, that is, the same narrow hallway with missing floorboards, Dona Aurorinha in distant areas where spices were boiling no, tasteless little herbs, leftover vinegar, remains of coriander, maybe the Cape Verdeans would accept some coriander, a heroin fix for a bit of coriander, would accept a trolley ticket, a holiday, a heart of flowers, would accept this bronchitis, these screws, this solicitous little squeak

—Would you like some soup, boy?

searching in the bedroom and in the bedroom a rundown bed with no sheets, a rag doll with only its left leg and inside the doll what looked to me like an inlaid cigarette case, a silver medallion, gold that

Miss Aurorinha I ask of you the favor of keeping in your posses-sion as a token of affection and legitimate respe t this simple keeps ke of my late mother's

my classmates gathered around clustered in astonishment, the teacher exhibiting the notebook and the pen

Miss Aurorinha I ask of you the favor of keeping in your posses-sion as a token of affection and legitimate respe t this simple keeps ke of my late mother's

—Read

the walnut tree in the playground that I never saw give any nuts, berries the size of peas that just as soon as they appeared would fall off the branches and swarms of horseflies in a hole in its trunk, would you like some soup, boy, and I bet the shopping bag, brought back to life, was sailing about in the pot, the eye that my uncle's fork was offering me

—Don't you like eyes, Paulo?

so

—Have you got a fork you can lend me Dona Aurorinha?

tugging it out of the dishrack

from the fluted drain beneath the faucet where a teacup, a bowl, the cluster of peas that passed for a glass, a saucepan, a teapot, Yours forever Rosendo, cheeks that were too rosy, long hair that was too black, the ring finger arched

—You shitty fag

elegantly kissing the forehead of the lady inside his heart of flow-ers or my mother's forehead in Bico da Areia excusing the lipstick remnants or the traces of eyebrow pencil and she followed him over to the refrigerator

the dwarf from Snow White wobbled and was silent

—Don't you even dream that I'm going to forgive you Carlos hurry up and pack your bag

the horses were trotting in the pine grove and with the pounding of their hooves you couldn't hear the sea, you heard the person who wasn't me

was me

blowing his nose on his sleeve by the doorway and in order to stop being me blowing his nose I tore Dona Aurorinha's doll just the way I'd smashed the car with wooden wheels flinging it onto the floor, the doll's stuffing was straw and sawdust, let me have the inlaid cigarette case, the silver medallion, the gold, last night my temperature went down and I didn't have any sweats, as soon as I'm cured, two three weeks at most, they assured me we'll get engaged, please accept my greetings with indul ence Rosendo, Dona Aurorinha at the bedroom door with the can smelling of soup

of cat

of soup

of her mouth

—Paulo

without saying

—Paulo

her blouse more frayed than my mother's apron in Bico da Areia

—I'm not forgiving you Carlos

I was hanging from my perch on her shoulders as we watched him leave on the Lisbon bus, the trace of eyebrow pencil, the pink cheeks, what looked like a woman's jacket over his arm

—Why Carlos?

smashing the car with wooden wheels, tearing the doll with the fork and finally straw and sawdust that crumbled in my hands, where do you keep your money old woman, confess to me where you keep your money, don't invent things like it's only trash, a clay whistle, don't stay silent, don't forgive me, don't touch me do stay silent I mean, do forgive, do touch your puppet, your clown, your dead faggot, feel this cold in me, this heat, these cramps

Miss Auro inha if I'm lucky and with God's intervention my lungs

I mean Dona Aurorinha I can't handle it, help me

I mean Dona Aurorinha even old the way you are, even sick the way you are, even incapable of moving the way you are, let me sit down on this broken-down wall for a while, sit down on the ground for a while, light the lamp, find the needle, help me tighten the rubber hose on my arm, push the plunger, and then if it's all right with you, stay with me for a while until I

I'm sorry

fall asleep.

CHAPTER

I LIKED GOING to Príncipe Real on Sundays because of the hats and the headgear, top hats with satin ribbons hanging down the back, headpieces that looked like metal but were made of felt and had blue feathers on them, at Bico da Areia the mirror on the wardrobe where the image became deformed right before our eyes, feeling no pain we'd examine our knees because the image was examining one and we'd put some tincture on it because it was putting some on it, the wardrobe was almost empty, a few rags, a few belts, a few woolen jackets while at my father's place women's clothes filled up the kitchen, the pantry, were spread out on the couch with their sleeves sprawling, Dona Helena would push away the perfume the way you push away cobwebs and put me down appalled, Rui

not yet Rui at that time, Luciano, Tadeu

would retreat to the rear

naked I think

without a good morning or a hello, in my memory I can see a man with graying hair slipping a banknote under the lamp, glancing at the telephone, my father, saying

—Are you sure your wife doesn't know?

the billfold coming out of the jacket, two bills, three bills, my father calming him down covering the telephone with his hand

—She doesn't know

Mr. Couceiro bothered about something or other picked me up on the way back to Anjos, lifted me up an inch or two and Dona Helena

Jaime

the man with graying hair, pretending he was a visitor, was putting on a toothy, complicated smile calling my father madame, checking his chest for the mascara the clown wasn't wearing, begging our pardon as the drops from his eyes stained the knot of his necktie, the mastiff with a bow nuzzled intimately against his legs and the man with graying hair was sort of begging, believe me, if it's not too much to ask please believe me

—I've never crossed paths with this beast in my life

at Bico da Areia, in December, the rain mournful like that against the windowpanes, I'd watch the clouds arrive one by one, storming out of the east over the crest of the mountains, clouds afraid of their comrades, their friends, their wives

—If it's not too much to ask please believe us

I went over to the window where the sea was close to the house, when the waves withdrew, a drowned horse on the beach and an albatross keeping watch over us from up above, the Gypsies tied the horse's legs together with a rope, attached the rope to a van and dragged it off with the wind to the pine grove, my mother was leaning against the door after she'd covered the windows, fussing with some towels and with fear covering her face too, legs and arms tied together by the rope, the slippers and stockings left behind, the horse buried, my mother buried, and winter chasing me into the house, maybe it was the dwarf from Snow White or one of the bedsprings

—He's there

they never discovered me, the springs on my father's side where he'd be rumpling and smoothing out the quilt, checking the folds of his shirt, thinking there was a stain, protesting, bustling, checking his hair with cupped hands, everything in place father, don't be so concerned about yourself, studying himself in profile with the posture of a bullfighter or an Egyptian frieze and no trace of a belly, father was satisfied

did he quiet down?

stop rumpling and smoothing out the quilt, returning to the stain that stood out on the cloth

—I could have sworn that a scab

once my mother's buried who's going to take care of me, feed me, put me to bed, not my father, always smoothing out the quilt, pushing away an invisible hair or feather, holding them up against the light, the suitcase on the step outside, the wardrobe open, the mirror toward the wall and yet we

what a mess

nowhere unless it's here, when I'm in the mirror I'm far away and left-handed, I'm living among things in reverse, which don't tell me anything, my name isn't Paulo, the clown at the bus stop beyond the pine grove carrying the coat like a living thing, still checking to see that there was no stain, at Príncipe Real headdresses, top hats with satin ribbons, gold berets, plumes, not Rui during those days, Luciano, Tadeu, the skinny Indian clerk in a jewelry shop, motionless on the threshold watching Dona Helena, giving back the money to the man with graying hair

—Keep this

a voice I didn't know, her lip quivering, what could there have been in her gestures

—Be quiet

I touched the headdress, pulling it down so as not to see it, only the floor and on the floor the ankles of the barefoot Indian, my mother at Bico da Areia rumpling the quilt without ever smoothing it, going to get some scissors in the dresser to cut it up, every twenty minutes the Lisbon bus would pass by on the highway and the rubble in the livingroom got more scattered, a dim bulb gave us the shadows that the scissors were cutting up, the shadow of the chandelier, the shadow of the dwarf

—Cut up the dwarf, scissors

the bulb grew brighter and the dwarf was whole

even today, twenty years later, I'd smash him if I could

on days when he had a cold Mr. Couceiro would fold up the newspaper like an accordion as little pieces dropped onto the floor, then he would open up the page and there was a string of people holding hands, the church clock fluttered through the curtain the curtain was all right, it was the clock that fluttered, its hands, the Roman numerals

and right after eight o'clock a rush of birds, Dona Helena saying

—It's five o'clock

she and Mr. Couceiro came to pick me up at Bico da Areia I don't remember the sea or the horses on that day, I remember the car with wooden wheels, pounding and pounding on the wardrobe, not out of hunger because I wasn't hungry, because

my mother offering them chairs, the two we had, that is, and the canvas couch held up by the stepladder because it was missing a leg, the house was looking more and more modest with their visit, the social worker, a strong woman, and a man with a cane waiting by the outside door and if they'd let him would have pounded on the sideboard like me, the terrace café, a wooden shack with tiles and bags of cement and a deserted bar, with spirals of scallops the waves had rejected, pounding on the wardrobe while my mother shaking a teacup with a fly inside and the fly

enormous

on the rug announcing

—I'm a fly

I don't remember the sea or the horses

none of them were gray, all of them chestnut, growing old

on that day, I remember my mother with no quilt to rumple and smooth

—Sit down, sit down

covering the fly with her heel, pushing it under the stove and the fly

—I'm not leaving

if only December and its rain at least, if only we could die so we wouldn't die of sickness at least, the social worker was signing papers on the oilcloth table cover, the strong woman was signing papers, my mother's name came out of the bent-over head, the lips tightened as when threading a needle

Judite Claudino Baptista

my mother Judite my father Carlos me Paulo

my mother is the strong woman, my father the man with the cane scratching marks on the flower bed and then erasing the marks, if I could have imagined the newspaper dolls, the Japanese, the trees

the month of July and butterflies in the woods, I remember the butterflies, they'd alight on the wall with a single eyelid waving back and forth, the top of the wooden car a few strips of wood and some nails

smash what's left, step on the fly that's accusing us under the stove

—Weeks go by without their cleaning the place

maybe a horse, the lame one that didn't go along with the others but no, it was Mr. Couceiro on the step, the eyelid, the transparent mustache going back and forth, an instant later the mustache flying over the wall

good-bye

pounding on the wardrobe

—*What's your mother's name?*

—*I don't know*

—*The poor devils lose every notion of things, some aren't even capable of remembering their birthdate or where they are*

that's not true I'm under the plane tree by the hospital, have you got some change for a cup of coffee, a butt, have you maybe got a butt you can spare, friend

and keeping on pounding so that the hospital no, the social worker to my mother

—What about the child's vaccination booklet?

Mr. Couceiro's mustache as he stood on the step kept going off and coming back, give me a butt friend just when they were looking for the vaccination booklet in the sewing case, in the bread box, in the envelope with photographs, give me a butt friend where the social worker has just found the picture of my father with a coat on his knees rumpling the quilt

—Don't send me away

and smoothing it out immediately after, my father at the bus stop for Lisbon, abandoned, orphaned, give me a butt, the doctor to the orderlies in the hospital

—Tie him down

stop the Gypsies from tying his arms and legs, tying the rope to the van and dragging him off with the wind to the pine grove, folding him like an accordion, dropping little pieces onto the floor, and a garland of people holding hands, some change for a cup of coffee friend, a butt, the man with the cane waiting for me on the step

my father's name isn't Carlos because the clown's name isn't Carlos, it's Soraia, my father up to his neck in the rice paddies of Timor, Dona Helena

—Don't scare him with your tales

they're not tales

your Japanese, your buffaloes, who's going to quiet him down now?

he knew the names of trees in Latin, he seemed to feel sorry for my mother, looking at the waves, coming to the door, closing the door on us and when she closed the door on us she never knew us, never knew me

did she know me?

what will become of the bride's pearls, I can describe her smell when she held me in her arms, my mother looking at the green morning waves, almost brown in the afternoon and it was the first time I noticed the bottle, a second bottle behind the stove, a third empty in the sink

no, decorating the grass that was replacing the flowers, dirty water and sand in the sink

no, dirty water and trash and a bottle in the sink

two bottles

Mr. Couceiro put the vaccination booklet in his jacket and that was the end of home, I didn't have one, it might be one roof in the midst of a lot of roofs, but which roof, oh God, I'll bet my mother didn't see me because the bottle, the glass, the dark kitchen or maybe the scissors cutting something or other, the quilt, newspaper dolls, the clown, send the faggot's kid away before he stays there hanging around the outside door and knocking for us, the Lisbon bus stop came up to meet us and dissolved into the pine trees, the doctor or the Mulatto with the jackknife, Dona Helena to the social worker

—He's fallen asleep poor thing

the orderly telephoned my mother at the same time that six pigeons alighted on a single branch of crutches and she said

—It must be some mistake, I don't know who he is

she drinks a lot, mother doesn't drink, how long ago did she start drinking?

and the scissors cutting me, there are pictures of my father, there are pictures of her, as far as I know there aren't any pictures of me except on Dona Helena's dresser hugging the car with wooden wheels that Mr. Couceiro repaired, my mother locking herself in the bathroom with the wine

—He's gone away

a sour smell through a crack in the boards and a motion of her arm, a different smile as she looked at me again, not my mother's smile, a different one that had the look of swallowing me and spitting me out right after, the floor had an unexpected tilt, the furniture hindered her walking

—Beat it

the owner of the café snarled the way dogs snarl if a bitch . . . stuck his hand in the openings of the knit jacket

five or six pups sniffing her, obstinate, ferocious, always a small dog

me?

five or six pups also means the owner of the café, the electrician who lives three shacks down, boys not much older than I was at that time, throwing pine cones, chasing each other, pulling each other to the ground

—I won, ma'am did you see how I won?

I watched them go down to the sea after my mother, the gulls not moving from their heads up and dancing from their heads down on the sheet of the water, the owner of the café was barking and the electrician and the pups were taking shelter in the skeleton of the trawler, a compartment with engines where they step along a stretch of lead, the small dog

—Mother

not in the trawler, in the backyard near the Bakelite tub or the umbrella that was in shreds, small ripples not even waves almost, like fish scales, picking up a stick, my mother naked and the whistling of the pups, she straightened up, chatted with the owner of the café and dressed again and the pups silent, they followed her up to the house threatening and biting each other in an urgent little trot, the electrician with a sore on his loins was examining weeds, it seemed to me there was a howl and the shudder of a pack of hounds in the Gypsy encampment, skinny, dark, barking in the pine grove, my mother was buying undershirts from them and taking a lot of time in the store, everything silent except the thicket of broomweeds, the old powder storehouse, the Alto do Galo, the thicket of broomweeds

—Your mother's a

I'm covering my ears

It doesn't interest me

my mother is Dona Helena, my father is Mr. Couceiro, not Judite and Carlos, not a clown and a

covering my ears

It doesn't interest me

the pups weren't throwing pine cones at me or tossing me to the ground, the electrician with his tail up searching for a track that was slipping away from him

—What became of that character, the fat guy too?

if I could die in the sea my bones would rise to the surface floating weightlessly, bits of chalk, Mr. Couceiro might worry about me, my mother

—It must be a mistake, I don't know who he is

my blind grandmother reading the bones with her fingers

—I don't have any grandchildren, gentlemen

she didn't turn on the light, she was breathing in the dark with the whistle of a teakettle, when we got to the wall the dogs up on the edge with the small one running around them, so comical

Rui to me, when I stopped him from pawning a necklace that wasn't worth anything

—*You're really ridiculous you know you're ridiculous you and your old man really ridiculous if I ask him he'll give it to me we went into pawnshops and the pawnbrokers acted like they didn't see it on the counter*

—*Are you pulling my leg?*

If they only could have seen it on stage with the lights and the music, they would have taken it, called over the clerks with the pride of someone getting a relic

—*Do you see what we've got here?*

not just one fix from the Cape Verdeans, five or six fixes, what do you mean five or six fixes, ten fixes, twenty fixes, fifty fixes at least

the one with the jackknife

—*Gentlemen*

he didn't hit us, he didn't send us away, he respected us

—*Gentlemen*

he cleaned off the broken-down wall for us with a deferential whisk broom
the small dog stopping Rui from taking the necklace, not the necklace, it's not worth anything, and Rui to me

—You're really ridiculous you know you're ridiculous you and your old man really ridiculous if I ask him he'll give it to me

the owner of the café on the steps handing my mother a bottle, a flock of herons crossed the Cova do Vapor woods on their way to Caparica, one of them fell like a napkin and the electrician galloped over to pick it up in his mouth, the clown would hide his rings at Príncipe Real, he would lift up a corner of the rug, unfasten a floorboard and a small bag of jewels that the ambassador

—My tribute Soraia

the strands brought out one by one, starting at the ear

—*Draw your family, a street, a tree*

—*They've forgotten their families they don't feel anything it's no use talking to them*

they disguised the lack of hair and made it even more evident, he squeezed my father's hands with slow intensity

—He isn't Soraia, he's Carlos, he's a clown can't you see?

my father introducing Rui

—A friend

introducing me

—My nephew

a carnival masker you understand, a comical merrymaker, he was adjusting his wig, but he'd been in the army, he made me, the owner of the café chased the pups away, in the space between his undershirt and pants a portion of his belly was strangled by his belt
  —Riffraff

the electrician dragged the heron up to the gate of the yard, they built their nests among the bridge beams, anyone who tried their eggs would get sick in the lungs, a couple of my mother's cousins
  she swore to me

they died that way, she went to wake them up in the morning because it was time for school and they were dead, you can't imagine what dead people go through Paulo, try looking at them and me leaning on my father's coffin laughing, the electrician vanished on the beach with half the heron, the half that was left over there dirty with earth, the pups stopped throwing pine cones at the roof and threw them at me, one of them hit me on the shoulder, another on the behind, maybe if I could run away through the hole in the pieces of tile and a pine cone on the thigh
  —*They don't feel anything we don't exist for them they can't draw your family tree in case you've got a family*

I haven't got a family
  —*They never have a family draw a street a tree*

the bench where nobody was sitting, your father hasn't died yet and even so your sorrow, crawling on the wet cement of the shower stall, you're not even a heron
  —*Don't scare him, Jaime, you've scared him*

half a heron, its beak, a shred of a wing
  —*He drew a bird, look how instead of his family he drew a bird*

and the pups attracted by some kind of call

a dying horse of the Gypsies, a mouse that the flood

trying all along the waves and the heroin needle feeling around and getting off course, I tightened the tube on my arm and cold, heat, cold, an upper tooth moaning, insignificant and moaning, they would moan and right away they would stop bothering me, they were all jumbled up, Rui
  —Not that vein that vein there's dried up

Rui a friend of my father's, after all, since my father said to the ambassador

—A friend

a friend mother, a friend creeping along the desk or maybe the pen, the wedding ring

—I'm going to discharge you tomorrow

I was confused, the doctor or the plane tree, the plane tree

—I'm going to discharge you tomorrow

but how can I be discharged tomorrow if I'm standing in Bico da Areia, by the back of the house, marigolds in the flower bed

me to the psychologist, correcting a petal, rounding it out better, showing him the notebook

—*The marigolds*

marigolds and a gentian propped up by wires and nails, the stems just like my veins

—*That vein's dried up*

today nothing but wires and nails, a small branch at best

me standing in Bico da Areia behind the house trampling the marigolds that I'd drawn, the door with no padlock swung open and hello how goes it, before going to work at the disco at night my father

—Hello

my father

—How goes it?

having fun with the pups with the pine cones, running away with them along the sea, I closed the door

the psychologist isn't believing the notebook

—*I asked you to draw your family and you're drawing dogs for me are your family dogs?*

my family are dogs, I'm an adult dog today with the Cape Verdeans in Chelas, farms, workshops, the cookie factory with the broken windows, the one who gave orders to the one with the jack-knife, with straightened kinky hair

—Are you still there, dog?

his jacket had a bulge from the butt of his pistol, besides the chimneys there were only little lemon trees, a group of Chinese hunched over instead of talking and cooking owls on a spit, the day your father breaks up with me

my father's not breaking up with you, he's not breaking up with anyone, you're the ones who are breaking up

—Bye-bye faggy

and the clown having forgotten to cover his bald head with the kerchief

I'm picking up my bundle and heading for the cookie factory, Paulo

the clown tripping over a shoe and caressing the shoe, then catching sight of me

behave yourself father

his eyes changed

—*What doll is that now?*

—*A clown with a shoe*

—*A clown with a shoe did you hear that listen to that, his inner world is falling apart, you never know what they're thinking*

until I find a new friend with him in the small parlor, the lipstick is redder, the blouses tighter, the eyebrows thinner, nothing but lashes and arched pinkies giggling merrily, thank God I'm happy Paulo now, you can't feel how happy I am, he'd enlarged his hips and breasts with a thick liquid, he'd rounded out his cheeks, the ambassador

—Soraia

just one syllable, Soraia just one syllable, my father gave thanks in church for his luck, wearing coral earrings, until the sexton put him out with whispered indignation, you couldn't catch the words, you caught the cassock billowing in a buzz of scandal and the forefinger pointing to the exit, I arrived at Bico da Areia, and the lower hinge of the door, a small voice inside the hinge

—Paulo

I always felt that the hinge was in pain, I tried again and the hinge was silent

—It's a joke I was wrong you're not in pain

the cistern had been soldered twice and there were still drops or maybe the same drop I don't know falling eternally and going all the way back to the beginning, slow, dark, fatigued from the trip, in the hospital we bathed on Saturdays, no towel to dry with, the sheet, matchboxes used as ashtrays, they fixed up a patient in a wheelchair on a tripod under the shower and the orderlies

—Hurry up

going in so fast at Bico da Areia that there was no time for the hinge to say

—Paulo

and the owner of the café buttoning up his shirt, looking at the dwarf

—Your mother's asleep don't wake her up

a bottle on the pillow, not hers

—Is it morning yet Carlos?

the hand coming out from under the pillow looking for nobody, I think maybe the smell of the mimosas in my grandmother's yard

—If only you could have lived with that smell of mimosas Paulo

when we went north I'd pause at the edge of the village, just after the station, where all I could see was coal and dust, she'd squeeze my fingers asking

—Can't you catch it Paulo?

all I caught was locomotive smoke, sleepiness, fatigue, eucalyptus berries on the ground and I didn't see any eucalyptus trees, only a single solitary plane tree and the silence of things, I think that maybe even today it's the mimosas that matter to her, not the men, not the sea, not the wine, not me

I don't matter to her

the mimosas

—Can't you catch it Paulo?

she'd go searching in the pine grove, where the Gypsies were, the horses coming from who knows where, I watched her come back indifferent to the pups, to the electrician, to the thorns on the century plants that would catch her skirt, the owner of the café lingered a moment looking, straightened the dwarf, left, his wife was setting the tables without getting mad at us, I stayed in the bedroom by the bed and then the idea of the mimosas came to me, I tapped her on the shoulders

—Get up mother, the mimosas

I'm sure it was the mimosas or maybe my fear of being all alone at home, in the hospital, up above the Anjos church and its changed hours, the clock proclaiming eight o'clock when it's five, proclaiming seven o'clock and it's three, Dona Helena

—Where are you going son?

—*I'm not your son*

Rui with the Cape Verdeans in Chelas

—I've got some dough from your father here

we were climbing up the hill through broomweeds, no mimosas, oaks, what might once have been a chalet or a convent

a house?

the first pains, the first cabins, the bottle on the pillow

—Is it morning yet Carlos?

I'm not your husband, mother, I'm not your faggot, it's not morning it's night, around this time, if he were alive, the clown would be making up, putting on perfume

not from mimosas, from a French vial

changing the blonde wig for a redheaded one, sewing the dress that was torn in the armpit, but keep in mind that my father didn't die, Rui didn't commit suicide, no cop pointing at the body

—Do you know him?

and Rui lying on the beach

—I died can't you see that I died what are you going to tell them?

keep in mind that I'm carrying a lemon in my pocket to cut the drug, cold and heat and cold at the peephole where the bills are passed through, I'm not a fag, I'm not afraid of needles, I dilute the powder while the music starts up, do you want to see father dance mother, do you want to see him along with me sheltered by the broken-down wall, don't be upset by his cheap dress, you're the performer's wife, mother, the customers will understand, don't be afraid to bring the bottle, everybody watches father dance with a bottle next to him, applauding him, people jeer at him and applaud him, they jeer at him on the street, at the movies, in stores, my father's voice begging under the muteness of his lipstick

—Don't let them humiliate me Paulo

of course I don't let them humiliate him, he's much more than what they are, a dancer, a singer, and a performer and in payment this rubber tube squeezes me until the veins stand out, hold the

needle, help me not to have diarrhea, colic, see the calm, this afternoon light, everything peaceful, with us in Bico da Areia without needing anybody, next year we'll enlarge the house, another floor on top of this one, a bigger living room, a porch, plaster swans on the pillars by the entryway, and mimosas, instead of the marigolds mimosas, the social worker

what a lot of hooey

swearing to Mr. Couceiro that they'd abandoned me, a lie, they didn't care about me, a lie, that my mother an alcoholic, that my father a

lie, just notice this calm, this afternoon light, everything peaceful, with us in Bico da Areia without needing anybody, it's not worth turning me over to Dona Helena because you two will take care of me, just tighten the rubber tube until the veins stand out, lay my jacket on that stone so I can rest my head and yes, mimosas, tap my mother on the shoulder

—Wake up mother, the mimosas

the locks of hair changing position on the pillow, the bridge with moss on the beams where the herons hide their eggs, if I approached, they'd fly up shrieking, they ate garbage, trash from the Tagus, refuse, the splotches that the clouds go about drawing on the waves, I remember a water snake, chopped in two, twisting, tomorrow, as soon as I come out of the hospital, I'm going to visit them, once a little bit before Dona Helena and Mr. Couceiro and the social worker said

—Come here

and me, as though I hadn't heard, smashing the car with wooden wheels on the floor, I found my father hiding behind a dune spying on them with a beauty mark on his cheek and the huge lashes, the pups all around him and the pine cones and my father to me

—Go away

I thought they're going to bite him, tear him apart, running off toward the woods with him, giving out with victorious barks, eight pups, nine pups, ten pups, the electrician too with the wound on his rump, I'm not sure whether my father spotted the herons or spotted us coming off the bridge to Bico da Areia avoiding the neighborhood, the café, my mother

avoiding my mother, the figurines on the wedding cake, the pearls that they might have bought in Chelas, show me the pearls I'm going to bring you tomorrow mother, the wedding dress put away in the chest, trying it on by the wardrobe

—Look at this Paulo

a whisper of silk and a whisper released from the kidneys probably only in the mirror, not on her

not on me, not on me, give me the bottle Paulo, I was elegant wasn't I, I was so well groomed wasn't I, the faint candle of a voice

—Why?

and the questions made me uncomfortable, me and the mirror, don't bother me question, most likely it's nothing but a defect in the glass, a speck of dust in the eye

tears without thinking, what's the reason for tears?

it might be a round tear that's not about to fall, that doesn't fall, filling her face, if my grandmother would only stroke her face

if my blind mother would only run her slow, questioning fingers over my face

—What's wrong daughter?

nothing's wrong, it's you who don't understand, do you remember throwing rice at us when we came down the church steps, the beret with a bent feather that a neighbor woman lent you, nothing's wrong, I'm me, I'm not me, what am I, who am I, who am I not being me, don't talk, be quiet, rose petals, rice, the photographer, they were smiling, people I didn't know who they were, that cousin, that uncle, my husband coming off the bridge to Bico da Areia in spite of the electrician, the pups, the pine cones

—Do you catch the smell of the mimosas Carlos?

even if you don't believe it and I don't think you do believe it, you never believed it

—You're so handsome

and my father wanted to see you Judite, he wanted to know

about us, looking at you, your pearl accessories, your maroon blouse, I left the disco without taking off the wig, cleaning off the makeup, changing, I waited on the ferry platform for the connecting bus to here, the same one that you sent me away on two years ago, the same one that you didn't want me to go away on two years ago, the same one that two years ago as soon as you

—Carlos

I come back to visit you, I go around the house, I don't dare knock, I watch you through a corner of the curtain and you're all alone at the table, I'm a crack in the ceiling, a broken tile, the bottle of oil waiting for you in the cupboard, that thing in your belly that no pup can smother, lend me your handkerchief because of the lipstick, fill up the basin so I can get rid of the makeup, tell me about a place where I can throw away the wig, don't get worried that it's already dawn, it's not going to dawn as long as I'm with you, after the photographer coming out of the church, everybody move in close so the best man and maid of honor can get in, after the lunch, the wedding cake, your mother's carrying on, the Beato boarding house where during lovemaking, the clerk with the key to thirteen because thirteen is lucky, the horseshoe on a hook to bring good luck too

—Is it for two hours or all night?

noticing the wedding rings, giving a ten percent discount, shaking our hands, telling the lady in charge to let us in

—It's for all night isn't it?

and me incapable of hugging you out of love for you, so hard to hug you out of love for you, not repugnance, not what your family whispered, love, me on the edge of the sheets wanting you, asking for you, forcing myself to want to not want to ask, there are times when I wonder if Paulo

I'm sorry

it's obvious that Paulo, it's clear that Paulo, there are surprises aren't there, there are mysteries aren't there, it's obvious that Paulo, my hands, it's clear that Paulo, my way of walking, this mark on the wrist, my mother Judite my father Carlos and that's that, Paulo to the doctor in the hospital my father Carlos see, so hard to embrace you and my father Carlos see, children don't lie, they discover, they know, they find out, she would pick him up if he cried because he was hungry, put her thumb in the sugar bowl and take my thumb, these steps are me, this shuffling in the hall is me, this

—Judite

it's me, not the owner of the café, not the electrician, not the pups with pine cones bulging in their pockets

—Dona Judite

it's me, their greediness, their bashfulness

—Shall I take off my clothes ma'am?

the legs stuck in the pants, you guiding them in their trouble, amused, pitying

—Wait

and I couldn't see any more because my son

my son

pounding on the wardrobe, smashing the car with wooden wheels, starting to shout and the doctor

—Quick

the orderlies held his ankles, they stuck his head into the pillow and as they stuck his head into the pillow they moved me away from you, the herons calling on the bridge prevented me from hearing, I think waves, horses, the east wind in the pine trees, I think the tide is coming up to my knees, my waist, my neck, I think it had dawned that the bed of marigolds was rising up along the wall, that the gentian was budding again, that on that Sunday in Lisbon

—You're so handsome

and then it was over, me at the bus stop with the jacket and my suitcase and a last pine cone I didn't notice, one last jibe lasting until today and before Paulo wakes up and spots me in the bedroom, lend me your handkerchief because the lipstick.

CHAPTER

IT'S ONLY BECAUSE I just can't do things any other way: I laugh when there's nothing to laugh about; I make fun of someone who looks at me disapprovingly
—Paulo
I put people down because I worry about them, I get mad at myself because I put them down and I punish myself by putting them down again. I want to stop it but I can't get to stop, I want to say
—Maybe I'm rough on you people but this isn't the person I am, but
I don't say it like that, not with words, I show them I'm worried by making them suffer the way I'm suffering
I'm not suffering
it's fine that you're not suffering but take it easy Paulo
pushing Dona Helena away so
—Son
she'll take an interest in me,
pushing her away means
—Take an interest in me
it means a lot more
—Take an interest in me
so much more if she doesn't complain
complain do you hear me, make me stop this, complain, why don't you stop me from living with you like my mother, my father, my father's brother, all the rest of them, made excuses

I haven't got time
avoided me
Don't bother me now
said good-bye
—I don't want you here do you hear can't you understand I don't
want you here
and me going down the stairs
—I'm sorry
while Dona Helena didn't make excuses, didn't avoid me, didn't
say good-bye, let me go to sleep with the light on, tried to pick me
up and put me to bed in her bedroom, I
—Let me
Mr. Couceiro
—Your arthritis Helena
she'd give me money on the sly, would lie for me at the bank
—This order for payment came in, ma'am
and she
—The writing may look different but I was the one who signed
the check
so upset over me that the teller took pity on her, asked for a loan
to cover the amount, the manager in a low voice in my direction
—Swine
take the manager home instead of me Dona Helena, give him my
chicken soup, my steaks, my quinine extract, the manager in a low
voice leading me away by the arm
—If it wasn't for the old lady you'd have been in jail a long time
ago
their daughter dead before I was born, bangs and skinny little
legs, Mr. Couceiro steadying the bicycle and the bicycle with flat
tires now, rusting away in the laundry room, push on the bell and
there'd be a feeble little ring, the easy chair would be pushed back,
Mr. Couceiro's cane would come along in a happy rush
—Noémia
and nobody on the seat, his smile turning into something that
made me sorry if there was anything that could make me sorry,
Sunday outings, Easter at the circus, a hamster

the hamster's cage on top of the wardrobe

Mr. Couceiro taking his handkerchief out of his jacket, examining the handkerchief, putting it away, trying to put it away, that is, without finding the pocket, the voice that was slow in picking up strength

what good are the names of trees in Latin?

—Don't ring that again

the defeated cane on its way back to the easy chair, pencil marks measuring height on the door frame, three feet seven inches, three feet eight, three feet nine and that was all, after three feet nine nothing remained but meningitis

—It can't be

the promises, pounding on the coffin pillow, I rang the bell again and the easy chair was quiet, tell me about the Japanese if you're up to it

he went over to Noémia's picture on the wall, an expensive frame, poor thing, Aurea Photo Shop, if I could only feel sorry

I can't

when I'd hear them on the stairs on Saturdays back from their visit to the cemetery I'd get up on the seat and keep ringing the bell, Dona Helena changing from mourning clothes into her kitchen apron as though she hadn't heard, Mr. Couceiro would go straight to the photograph on the crocheted mat with a handkerchief hanging out of his pocket and a hamster pedaling on its wheel inside his head, a gouache that showed a sun with long lashes

This landscape is for the best father in the world your always loving daughter Noémia Couceiro Marques

looking for the gouaches in a drawer, tubes squeezed by fingers, the brush with missing bristles, I tried it out on the gas bill, I began with the dedication

This landscape is for the best foster father in the world your loving foster son Paulo Antunes Lima

but the Lima was covering the Antunes, a cloud blotted out the best foster father in the world and the twisted oval sun, whose rays reached beyond the gas bill and continued onto the towel, erasing the clouds and the sun and a horse that looked like a mouse appeared

a hamster

where Mr. Couceiro was galloping in armor and with a sword through the rice paddies of Timor, I scratched out those idiotic scribblings and tossed them onto the easy chair

—I don't want this crap take it

I locked myself in the laundry room and traveled on the rusty bicycle until it was night; I went around the world, and I got to Paris with the Noémia Couceiro Marques in the picture rubbing up against me with her bangs, outings on Sundays, the circus at Easter time, the Phantom Train, I wasn't afraid of falling asleep in the dark, holding her by the hand, you'll get to be four feet on the door frame, I'm four feet two, I'm huge, what if I asked

—Will you be my girl?

what would your answer be, her bedroom that we never went into unless it was Dona Helena changing the flowers in the vase, the quilt that was pale with dust, the metal owl with glass eyes on the triangular corner table, out the window the buildings on Avenida Almirante Reis that never smiled would chat from time to time with the disconnected tolling of the church, the fat, wise, mistaken, salivating clock hands full of sparrows from the square, the tolling would stop and not a single sparrow left, only the jaws of the roofs chewing their cud of treetops, Mr. Couceiro looking at the picture

—Don't you think her color is better this afternoon?

the birds waiting somewhere or other for the whim of what time it was

—Do you know anything about the sparrows Noémia what have they done to the sparrows?

shadows and more shadows shrouding things, shrouding you, painting everything blue and pink and green

the gouaches that were left

I could steal rings from my father and give them to you, not to buy drugs with, to give to you, how did they dress you on the day you died, what did they put on you, who dressed you, tell me about

the coffin, the wreaths, about the place where you are today, Dona
Helena chopping cabbage in the other end of the apartment

—What?

Mr. Couceiro pulling up his sleeve with his fingertips to wipe a
speck of dust from the frame

—I asked you if you didn't think her color is better this
afternoon?

the blue and pink and green tubes of paint in a small wooden
box filled with tarnished coins and a dried beetle, in another drawer
colored pictures of actresses, a bracelet made from wire twisted into
artistic shapes, the school notebook, Dictation: The Beatitudes,
blessed are the poor in spirit for theirs is the kingdom of heaven,
blessed are the pure in heart for they shall see God, didn't get indignant if Rui said

—Are you going with a dead girl Paulo?

blessed are the humble for they shall be exalted, the charm
bracelet with hearts, little hoops, we die and the things that
belonged to us take on a solemn mystery, the bracelet confessing to
me

—All my life

and repenting it, delving into the notebook, Copy: My Country,
my country is located at the westernmost point of europe bathed by
the atlantic ocean it is thirty-five thousand square miles in area and
is called, not bothered by the doctor's bewilderment

—You've got a girl named Noémia and you never go out with
her?

Dona Helena drying her hands on a dishcloth, with pieces of
cabbage in her hair, on her arms, going up to the picture, two
sleeves delicately wiping off the speck, straightening the frame in
its crocheted oval, the picture wobbling

—Don't drop it

a fingerprint on the glass and cleaning it again, Dona Helena
looking over her glasses

—Her color does look better to me, yes

the roses in the vase withered and rusty, the water muddy, one of
her stockings the right one, the second stocking gone, time was dis-

solving her nose, her eyebrows, her left hand down along the length of her skirt, in a short time there won't even be a trace, the right stocking gone too and then

how many weeks, how many months?

no stockings, a blur where a solitary sandal resists the centuries, it is thirty-five thousand square miles in area and is called Portugal, sandals, a shoe, those boots with a pad to correct her walk or just a reflection from the bulb if we change its position it disappears or maybe it's nothing, you don't exist and not having been anything, you're nothing, the doctor to Mr. Couceiro

—He says he has a girlfriend named Noémia do you know her?

Mr. Couceiro's fingers looking for his handkerchief as if the handkerchief were more of a cane than his cane itself, going into his pockets, his own fingers a second handkerchief, also made of cloth, lost on his forehead too, Mr. Couceiro not a corporal in Timor, a neck without a body looking at a picture

—I asked you if you didn't think her color is better this afternoon?

settled in the easy chair with a happy little smile, Composition: To My Daughter, contrary to what I expected my daughter arrived, Rui hold it, I'm all mixed up in the head you're going with a dead girl who died before you were born Paulo, I was changing the needle in the syringe if I could only stop being a damned jackass, if I could only get to feel sorry for Mr. Couceiro and I can't just like I can't get to suffer, I can get to break saucers and repeat the table of sevens, I can't get to suffer, the cane, diabetes and Rui, forgetting to tighten the rubber hose, three feet nine you say, eleven years old you say, the jackdaw there all the while without our seeing it, maybe its tail or its beak in the fig tree, Rui throw a stone at it Paulo

we thought it had gone away and its little chirps were making fun of us, Rui loosening the hose and no vein, a constellation of small scars, throw a stone at it Paulo, a piece of brick, a clod, a piece of shit, anything because the damned thing is getting on my nerves, my room at Anjos next to the dead girl's room, almost every night I'd wake up thinking I'd heard her, I'd sit up in bed listening until I realized it was Dona Helena and the next day fresh roses in the vase, bought at the market along with the meat, the tomatoes, the oregano, not scarlet closer to pink, looking for the gouaches and painting them blue, painting the sun on the wall and waves, not the waves at Bico da Areia, serious waves, large, how many times coming back from Chelas did I find Dona Helena on the couch with Mr. Couceiro holding her hand and since I'm incapable of doing things any differently I hurt them because I worry about them, getting mad at myself for hurting them and punishing myself by hurting them some more

—I'm all you've got since your daughter's dead
or
—I'm all you have and I detest you
or
—I'll bet you'd like to have me die the way the other one died
two old boobs
I hate you
I don't hate you
I hate you
hugging each other in a corner of the living room, they were drinking tea, they weren't eating dinner, they were consoling each other with the picture of their daughter, two frightened boobs examining the bangs that were disappearing under the glass, don't you think she's got better color this afternoon, they don't console each other, don't have any illusions, don't make up things there aren't any colors, there aren't any features, be quiet, tomorrow they're taking me out of the hospital and it'll be an end to the plane trees, the doctor

—I've got no time for chitchat today let me go
and me with so many things to tell him if he'd only ask me
—What is it?
I remained mute, overflowing with words the same as when they operated on my father, they removed his breasts and in place of his breasts two

if I can put it that way

dark scars, a face where the features could barely be made out, eyes where maybe eyes and the maybe eyes

—Rui?

no

—Paulo?

I never stole anything from you, I never made fun of you and what was left of him

—Rui?

the joints of the bones in his bald head, do you want your wig, father, your lipstick, your creams, do you want me to put the music on, applaud you, bring you the gold dress and the feather stole for the final glory, I say

—Dance, father, dance

until they throw me out

—Have you gone crazy, boy?

I imagined my father's arm rising up before they turned off the music and the lights, thanking them with a bow, accepting orchids, champagne, chocolates, smiling from the pinnacle of his glory

—Aren't you proud of me?

and the doctor

—I've got no time for chitchat let me go

but it was all right because an end to a butt friend, an end to a coin for a cup of coffee friend and the cup steaming as it wobbled on the counter, Dona Helena in the Anjos apartment with currants and a cake and the chicken she imagined I like and which I don't like

—Son

in spite of my having warned her a thousand times that I won't have her calling me that

—Just because the idiot girl in the photograph is rotting away in the cemetery do I have to repeat year in year out that I won't have you calling me that?

detesting the Avenida Almirante Reis, detesting Mr. Couceiro who would change from his street jacket into the scarecrow rags he wore at home if you could call those half dozen cramped little rooms a home, with the glassware shaking every time the church bells rang, a bus outside, the dead girl's roses quivered their petals, Dona Helena

—Wouldn't you like some chicken Paulo?

and I'm certain my father's eyes with no rest

—Paulo?

Paulo was interested, don't tell me otherwise, don't lie, the maybe eyes

—Rui?

Rui in Chelas at that time pawning the fake jewelry or committing suicide at Fonte da Telha and the mastiff with a bow licking his knees, the two coffins in the chapel and me laughing, me laughing, I was remembering Bico da Areia, my mother, the man with the napkin in his hand trotting in the Anjos hallway, trotting in the hospital, where's my car with wooden wheels so I can smash it on the floor, what my father had injected in his face, in his cheeks, that is, by his cheekbones, he was breaking out in purple scabs on his forehead and he

—Rui?

the windows at Príncipe Real were open, the carpet taken up, the floorboard had been pried up by a knife on one corner, the empty jewel bag and the clown was blind to it

—Rui?

so what else could I do but laugh, Dona Helena was alarmed

maybe because the simpleton in the picture is rotting away in the cemetery I'm going to repeat time and again that I forbid her from calling me son, and she as though she understood, but she didn't understand, if she really understood she'd have had the good sense to leave me alone, do some crocheting in the evening if she wants, go to the dead girl's grave if she feels like it, wait five or six hours at the clinic so they can warp her backbone even more, she could enjoy cooking her chicken but if you've got the least bit of sense left, leave me alone, in spite of my suggestions she tried to grab me by the shoulder

—Paulo

Mr. Couceiro, the hero of Timor, cane in the air, was climbing up out of the easy chair or out of the rice paddies with buffalo corpses where the Japanese were searching for him shouting

—Helena

still to a regiment that was his cane
—Helena
and just when the Anjos clock was flinging down the first clump
of sparrows
—Dance father dance
the glass on the photograph
my fault?
my fault
broken on the floor, Dona Helena
—Jaime
an almost blind old couple on their hands and knees on the floor
putting together what was left of the frame and their daughter, Dictation: My Death, I died on the seventeenth of February nineteen
sixty-eight and every Saturday for thirty-two years my parents visit
me, when they first started living at Anjos they would bring me
along with them to the cemetery and to an iron square laid out
among other iron squares making a kind of wall with grass on the
stones, I scraped the grass off with a dirt-covered piece of glass and
Mr. Couceiro
—Don't
I imagined he was convinced that the clover, or whatever it was,
was part of their daughter, a ring for the chrysanthemums that
were sold at the entrance and Noémia Couceiro Marques's words
thickened by fungi, the jackdaw that would chase us much later in
Chelas invisible now whistling its two notes in the willows, Rui
deciding
—It can't be the same jackdaw, stupid
even so he looked for it frightened, as a child they'd made him
kiss his grandmother in her coffin and he swore that her hands
those vines that grab you and pull you
they tried to carry him off, he asked me for half of my fix so he
could forget her, both of us in a cold sweat like my mother when the
wine ran out and she'd wave her arms around bumping into things
—Go ask for some on account at the café, Paulo
the pups with pine cones at the corner of the neighborhood
keeping watch on the gate, the herons lined up along the bridge

beams predicting rain, clouds on the Cova do Vapor, clouds of sul-
phur at the Alto do Galo, a lost mare trotting aimlessly along the
street, her eyes just like my father's

—Rui?

the same despair as though there was someone who could take
him away from there and save him, no one can save your father, it's
over, the mare was scratching her haunch on the trunks of the fir
trees, a vein on the neck which if I had ones like that I wouldn't
need any rubber hose, the ring on my father's throat appeared and
disappeared as he breathed, his empty gums sort of spongy, pale

—Where are your teeth father?

the mare turned around among flowerpots and my mother
unaware of the rain, of the waves of the northeaster that was coming into the backyards, of the wailing of the herons unable to protect their eggs

—Go ask for some on account at the café, Paulo

and there I was along with the mare unable to find my way, a
watering can and pieces of newspaper in the bottom of the gutter,
the awning drawn up, the owner's wife, barefoot on the terrace, disappearing off with the tables, an apron spread out in a shadow
where glasses gleamed

—Your mother's asleep don't wake her now

me motionless in the doorway not daring to go in

the café owner leaned over the bar looking at me just as a Gypsy
struggled with the mare covered with a hood my father disappeared, Rui disappeared from the beach but the policeman was asking me

—Do you know who he is do you know him?

and they didn't have to tie me to the bed, I wandered about the
yard chatting with the box trees, a coin for a cup of coffee friend, a
cigarette friend, he was picking up the butts the orderlies left burning attracting the pigeons, the wife of the owner of the café came
back struggling with the ribs of the umbrella

—What does this one want here?

and her husband to me

—Your mother's asleep don't wake her up now

my mother wasn't asleep, a lie, she was in front of the wardrobe and calling him while she trembled, chasing spiders that weren't there in the corners of the room, shaking imaginary mice out of the folds in her blouse, Mr. Couceiro watching her cleaning a speck from the glass

—Don't you think her color's better this afternoon?

soon the dwarf from Snow White split in two, soon the drawer with the flatware in the flower patch, soon she was speaking to no one

—Why Carlos?

and I was rumpling the quilt and smoothing it as though there was makeup left on my cheeks, in a little while she told me

—Get out of my house Carlos

and I was all alone on the stoop, all alone by the main entrance trying to explain to her I'm not father mother, I was five years old

they cover me with a hood and don't even inject me

trying to explain to her

—I'm your son mother

don't throw pine cones at me, don't squash me against the pillow stopping me from breathing, seven times eight fifty-six, seven times nine sixty-three, don't tie my wrists, don't bring an old couple for me to live with in the name of some bangs, some skinny little legs, a bicycle with a flat tire rusting in the laundry room, give me a bottle of wine, half a bottle of wine, a pint of wine, we'll pay at the end of the month and saying that Dona Aurorinha with her bag of groceries hanging from her hand gathering her strength on the step, my mother

—Wait there Paulo

to the tallest pup

two small figures on a wedding cake, what can have become of the pearls, the perfume, the wedding?

—How much money have you got pup?

and me with my mind made up not to listen, hearing from beyond her the waves down there, not the sea yet, the dampness left by the ebb tide covered with straw and mud, smudges of motor oil, boards, on one occasion an almost intact cradle with a rattle hang-

ing on it, a plaque carved with a saint, my mother was counting out
one small bill and three or four damp coins in her palm, translating
them into wine, she rose up in the mirror and disappeared from it,
excuse me for keeping on ringing the bell on the bicycle Dona
Helena but I don't want to come upon her

—Come in

I don't want to sit on the step waiting, noticing how Lisbon only
exists upside down in the river, the bottom half of playing cards,
buildings, monuments, lights and no sound in the house, during
that time when my father was working as a photographer he'd put a
red bulb in the washroom, cover the door with a piece of oilcloth,
sink white tapes into a tub and at the bottom of the tub traces that
came together into the faces of clowns, the bodies of clowns, too
much hair, never Noémia Couceiro Marques, well-built clowns, smiling triumphantly, my mother brought the bottle and didn't wave her
arms at the mirror, she wasn't shaking and the dwarf was safe

—Who are these girls Carlos?

let me ring the bell on the bicycle and stop the question

—Who are these girls Carlos?

stop Mr. Couceiro from cleaning that speck off my eyelid with
his sleeve

—Don't you think his color's better this afternoon?

my mother Judite my father Carlos

as though I belonged to them and I didn't belong to them, I
don't belong to anything unless it's the Cape Verdeans in Chelas, as
though I was their son and I'm not, as though I was only a gravestone in the cemetery and I haven't died yet, I'm not dying, tomorrow I'm going back to Anjos, help me with my suitcase in the
hospital Mr. Couceiro, no more coins for a cup of coffee friend, no
more a butt friend, the plane trees calm, all the pigeons where
there's a basket of peaches, the tallest pup left our house and went
down the steps without seeing me, my mother searching in the living room, under the pillow, in her apron

—Did you see the money Paulo?

hearing the waves, not hearing her, the gulls on the bridge
beams, the imbecilic jackdaw from chimney to chimney

—It wasn't me it wasn't me

my mother rummaging in the coffeepot where on happier days buttons, keys, pennies and where my father stored herbs in a bag and heated tisane, she was staring at me in the mirror

—Did you steal my money Paulo?

no pup outside, the café deserted, the two of us all alone at Bico da Areia, peeking into a boot because sometimes there are things there, my mother went over to the mirror taking the jackdaw away from me

—It wasn't me it wasn't me

—My money Paulo

my father never got mad at Rui, he'd see him with his wallet open on his lap, wouldn't ask any questions, wouldn't shout, wouldn't threaten, tell me you don't understand Paulo, I'm not asking you to understand, tell me to get rid of him, he was working in a different place in order to pay the Mulattoes, not a disco with a foreign name, a place in Caxias, you turned left at the prison and there was a dirt road, you went past an arch and some unfinished buildings, a shed under an elm tree, my father in a dressing gown, with more frills and makeup than in the places with music

—I'm a clown Paulo

two or three men drinking in a small room with him, black leather couches that had silver legs with the paint peeling, someone working with my father had a small whip under his arm and was helping one of the gentlemen to take off his necktie and the gentleman with his eyes closed

—Are you going to punish me Andreia?

my father whispering, not touching me, luckily, if he touched me I'd kill him

—I'm a clown Paulo

as though he loved me, as though I loved him, the proof that I didn't like it is the fact that I wasn't the one suggested

—Let's leave, papa

it was my mouth and I was furious with my mouth, the gentleman who's taken off his tie was unbuttoning his shirt and crouching on the sofa, such a white belly, his round little shoulders

—Are you going to punish me Andreia?

I wanted to correct the mistake he's not Andreia he's Abel, he works during the day at a restaurant in Almada, if you pull off his wig you'll find a man didn't you know, he didn't inject the vials that my father injected to puff up his breasts and he was complaining of pain, I thought I heard a train but what train and where, only ferries, furze, maybe a tanker looking for the river mouth, maybe my heart in my ears imitating railway cars, it used to happen to me from time to time, it would make me weak or I'd cry

I'm not crying

or give me an appetite

I'm not saying

the gentleman pointed at me to my father while his chauffeur, in the hut, was opening up his newspaper

—Tell your lover to come over here Soraia

and the train again, the one I took when I was a kid when we went to Beira, a bunch of jackdaws always, out of sight, not just one jackdaw, a dozen of them, twenty jackdaws, fifty jackdaws laughing in the treetops like me in the church, lend me the bicycle Dona Helena I'll bring it back, let me stay in the kitchen while you chop turnips, don't let Mr. Couceiro come into the pantry where there's no light

—Tell your lover to come over here Soraia

you frightened him, you scared him, who's going to quiet him down now, cover my ears, stop me from catching on

—I'm a clown Paulo

not my father, Dona Helena swears to me that he's not mine, he lives in Bico da Areia with my mother and me, we have fun during vacation in Arrábida, in Tróia, I resemble him in the way I walk even though my mother

—Your father the pervert

shut up mother

my father's like that, he likes circuses, applause, entertaining people, when I was little he'd deck himself out in netting

—Don't you think I'm funny Paulo

plus a cap with a tail like the jackdaws' and their two mocking notes

—No more jackdaws

without my ever spotting them, patent leather pumps, a high little voice like a woman's

but not a woman, obviously not a woman, a clown, the gestures
of a clown, the twirling of a clown with me pounding on the
wardrobe, smashing the car with wooden wheels, not upset you can
see not upset, satisfied

I was satisfied

Dona Helena

I'm lying, Dona Helena one or two years later, my mother so elegant, so sound, with me in the yard where the marigolds and the
gentian were and the door hinges didn't creak

—You scared him Carlos can't you see that you scared him, who's
going to quiet him down now?

Bico da Areia new at that time, ten or eleven houses if there were
that many, the girl my age who wouldn't lend me her tricycle, she
went off to study to be a secretary and I've got the feeling I met her

it can't be, she was blonde, her name was Dália and they washed
her head with camomile and lemon

dragging one of her legs where the Cape Verdeans in Chelas
hung out, maybe if I

—Dália

the look that didn't see me, her good leg up, her hair in a beret
I'm not sure whether blonde or brunette, she didn't need any rubber hose to find her veins, going down stone by stone and getting
all dirty with mud, her aunt fixing her curls with the iron, slow,
haughty

—With hair like that and your porcelain face you ought to be
able to land yourself a doctor

Dália concentrating on her pedaling of the tricycle, maybe if I
asked

—Did you ever land the doctor Dália?

a nose that snorted, a twisted step as she went away from me, the
tricycle faster and me looking at her with a wonder that's lasted
even till today, if I'd gotten to be a doctor, an accountant, a quarter-
master, owned a motorbike, not had a clown for a father

—Tell me where you live Dália

the beret, the swollen leg, a topcoat in August and so much cold isn't that right Dália, if she hadn't brought any money she'd huddle on a rock waiting and between the open buttons were a pair of torn pants and an army shirt, her aunt chasing me away afraid of contagion

—Beat it, you scamp

when no one was watching I'd pull up my father's marigolds, roots and all, and spread them out on her doorstep, on tiptoes I managed to catch sight of her after dinner seriously examining a picture book, busy educating herself for the secretarial course and the chore of landing a doctor while her aunt perfected her curls

—Don't move, precious

why should I have any interest in her

—Tell me where you live Dália

because she wasn't living in a rose garden with a doctor, she was living alone among the fruit stands in Beato with her plate for donations at her feet, her little face all wrinkled and stucco cracks were visible in the porcelain, her aunt dead centuries ago, the curling iron used by the Gypsies to wave their horses along, I pledged, stepping on squashed orange rinds, over boxes for packing plums

—I'm here Dália

—It's me Dália

—I've never forgotten you Dália

I took her by the arm and she drew back huddling in a doorway in the midst of sacks and rags, the money from her donations rolled onto the pavement and Dália

—My money

my tricycle, my picture book, my blonde hair, my money which Rui

—It's empty

which Rui

—Take it

and Dália limping toward him on her lame thigh, her wide nostrils helping her lungs, the eucalyptus trees of the Ateneu in endless remorse, Rui farther and farther away between two trucks

—Go get your money

I convinced myself that the water from a fountain was falling over them, my father in a dressing gown, with more décolletage and makeup than he wore in music halls

—I'm a clown Paulo

the money in an open ditch where there were pieces of pipes, if only I could have given you the marigolds from the yard, the dwarf from Snow White for you to sell in Chelas, Rui finally came out from behind the trucks fixing his fly with your beret in his hand and everything was calm in Beato, everything so calm in Beato that if we'd stopped walking and paid attention and paused for a moment we could have heard in any point in the darkness

in Madre de Deus, in Marvila, in Bico da Areia

a tricycle pedaling along by the waves in the river and a street urchin following it, hiding behind a wall nearby, anointed with camomile and lemon.

CHAPTER

IN THE AFTERNOON I used to sit in the backyard not thinking
about anything, not feeling anything, not looking at anything, time
was motionless thank God, me alone free forever from what limited
me and was holding me back, free from myself, the yellow clouds on
the water side and blue ones on the pine tree side, neutral, not moving, the night that wasn't coming and the morning that wouldn't
be coming, if they called me

—Judite

if they called me

—Dona Judite

I hated them for making me exist like them, realizing that my
solitude had ended starting with the moment when they were able
to offend me with their hands, their voices, the words that something in me understood without my understanding them and to
which something in me replied while I stayed silent, I became aware
of the absence of my husband and my son and no desire to see them
again, I saw the herons and that was all I needed, the waves coming
and going, devoid of meaning and importance, I was little when my
father would come up out of the temple and carry on about Jehovah and the blood of the Lamb, convinced that he knew the blood
of the Lamb and that the blood of the Lamb was in my blood which
was flowing, me an adolescent here in Bico da Areia, listening in the
darkness to the plants that only speak to us in the dark and they
weren't talking about religion or the Bible, they were talking about
themselves just like the ones calling me

—Dona Judite

it's about themselves they're talking, about their selfishness, their fears, me a teacher in Almada, almost the same age as they, concerned more with springtime in the yard and the way April was finding its way up along the roots of my thighs and it made me sin against my father's religion, leading my fingers, even during class, through tiny flaming places that promised hell and which I didn't know I had, me back in Bico da Areia, arriving on the bus at dinner-time when my father would put on his tie and standing at the head of the table would recite the psalms, drinking in the pine grove hidden from us, the way they might be calling me

—Judite

I hated them the way I hated my father and the blood of the Lamb inside a bottle for him and what was coming down for me, between two moons, from my thighs onto the sheet, my father and his discourses about the Lord, His gospels and His apostles, Purgatory which in his words was nothing but engravings which he wouldn't let me see and where I lived burning in secret, hurt by the branches of the almond trees and the eyes of men making me vibrate without a stop all up and down my nerves, eyes, expressions, the sticky hidden smells under their clothing with which they approached me as I was sitting in the yard not thinking about anything, not feeling anything, not looking at anything, not loathing myself when

—Dona Judite

—I've got the money here Dona Judite

—I'm not like the others Dona Judite, I don't run away after I pay

the beach was just as much out of it all as I was and the city was off in the distance, yellow clouds on the water side turning white as my name is transformed into what they expect and it pretends to be expecting them too, where it lingers along with them leaving me here, darker stains where during ebb tide there's a promontory, bushes where the wild geese and sea swallows, a kind of silence in which I

the other woman

motionless afterward, remembering the time when my father

tormented with visions would warn me, hand on my shoulder filling out the sentences, about the severity and the punishments of the Angel, not me, the other one, Dona Judite, rising up from the pillow, grabbing her blouse, catching me in the mirror, ordering me pointing to the bread bag

—Take care of the money we've earned Judite

his fingers with nothing and the three banknotes in mine, buttoning up, putting on my skirt, putting on my shoes before opening the door to my son

no, my son was twenty years ago no, I haven't got anyone to open the door to

the bread bag on the kitchen doorknob and nighttime at last, an end to the roofs, the light, the pine trees, I thought that they might be spying on me from the wall and they're not spying on me from the wall, because sometimes my husband

and my husband never

wanting to come, packing his suitcase for him again

—Leave, Carlos

not packing the suitcase

—Stay with me Carlos

take it easy because I'm not asking you for anything at all unless it's to stay with me Carlos, the promontory and its bushes had disappeared in the tide, the blood of the Lamb in the bottle was all gone, my hands fail me so much, I'm forty-four years old, I can't believe it, it's so funny, lie down here, I'm not asking you to caress me, we didn't caress each other remember, if I tried to embrace you in the boardinghouse, the almond trees in the schoolyard ran up and down my nerves, my knee was surprised by your absence, it didn't understand where you could have gone since you're still with me here, I mean maybe not you, maybe a sob imitating you, breathing like a hare

—What was it Carlos?

the terror of the chickens when my mother would grab them by the legs and hold them in the air facing the knife, I wanted so much to save them the way I want to save you even though their throats grow smaller in my hand

—What was it Carlos?

defenseless, small, me huge, my hair standing on end, the small
bones a child's running away which affected me all the more,
explaining I haven't got my knife see and the throat so quick, the
breast so quick, my name

—Judite

a refusal or a request

a refusal

a request

your solitary heel and your clothes on the floor affected me,
cooking for you, taking care of you, your shirts, your dinner, your
colds, you'd come by to me pick me up at school, you'd wait on the
sidewalk, awkward, cigarettes and you didn't know how to smoke,
you'd run from tree trunk to tree trunk so they wouldn't see you,
the other teachers

—It was funny

I'm going to write him a letter Cristina, I was furious and at that
time yes, the knife, you're not leaving

—It was funny

without the courage to write you, what I mean is I'd start writing
to you but that's not the way it was, there was more than that, and
I blushed, and I stopped, Cristina

—What's this?

snatching the paper, showing it to the other women and the
other women

my darling Carlos

and the other women laughing

my love

I was furious, the dull knife missed and wounded, my mother
feeling sorry for the chickens

—Go get the big knife Judite

dumping your guts into the pail, throwing your heads away,
pulling out your feathers

—Let go of my letter

not blushing, pale, make them feel small, hit them, complain to
the supervisor who hung around at recess and stole chalk, you were

going to pick me up at school with a flurry of matches, burned-out matches scratched for hours on end on the box, you'd go with me on the bus to Bico da Areia not looking at me, not talking to me, maybe Cristina wrote to him because she knows how to write and I don't, because it wasn't the way that I, there was more than that, I wanted to talk to you about the almond trees and the blood of the Lamb and I never said anything, talk to you about us in the board-inghouse and about my name gasped out

—Judite

making things clear isn't important, I'm not worried, we'll get married won't we, we'll be happy won't we, I copied a poem from a book written by a man so I changed everything to make it female and it didn't come out that way either, maybe Cristina wrote to you and I ask

—Do you love Cristina, Carlos?

—What's wrong with me Carlos?

—Why not with me Carlos?

hating her, hating you, hating both of you, grabbing them by the legs and holding them up in the air as my mother helped, no cataracts yet, no hand on my face yet

—What happened child?

as we got farther away from Almada the campground, the Jeho-vah's Witnesses temple and my father wearing a necktie

—You sinned you sinned

I sneaked off with the blood of the Lamb I got from my father, the pine trees

not pine trees yet, fir trees, pines later

the river, only the smell of the river that is, just like the smell of an animal lying down and sand quarries and dunes, Santo António da Caparica, São João da Caparica, two-story buildings, houses with outside lights, the bakery where the clerk wouldn't let me pay

the words weren't coming out of his mouth but from around his mouth slugs that I shook off

—We've got plenty of time to settle our accounts, girl

the Gypsies' horses snorting in the dark

if we turn off the lamp in the room at the boardinghouse will you let me kiss you Carlos?

and you changing places with me and protecting yourself from the mares, the backyards at Bico da Areia, marigolds, pups, if you'd let me take care of you, if you'd marry me, my father appearing from behind the trunk of the walnut tree hanging from his necktie with the twisted face of a hanged man

—What kind of devil are you bringing me Judite?

lighted up by the flaming oil of the wine, the shadow of his hand gobbled up by the shadow of the glass, Cristina's father would have received Carlos in a proper way, come in, come in, her mother would have bustled about him, have a seat, his fluttering eyes taking us both in, don't whisper to me again that you write to him Cristina, don't invite me to your birthday party, don't talk to me anymore, they would have him to dinner, serve him first, if I could have spied from the street I'd have noticed the starched curtains and their stretching out their necks to avoid spilling the soup, the flowers you brought all wrapped in cellophane in the center of the table while what I give you are my father, the café, the whole neighborhood, I was on the verge of tears

—For heaven's sake will you leave my fiancé alone

you in the boardinghouse moaning on the pillow

—You've got to give me time to get used to you

if I was Cristina you wouldn't need time to get used to me, something about her that I don't have

let me have the bottle, father, don't pretend to be scandalized, be quiet, let me have the bottle

a Gypsy woman coming from the river with two buckets, walking like a crow, they cut the feathers off their clothes and they walk on the ground, incapable of flying, at night the whinnying would make me restless, and make the waves restless, running fingernails over the body with a shudder of pine trees until the wind or the blood of the Lamb make openings I don't dare peep through and never peeped through, your apologetic smile which would go out if I blew on it, poor Carlos and you

—I'm not capable Judite

the wind and the blood of the Lamb shouting inside me, I'm forty-four years old and everything's dead, finished, my son at the door, bigger than I am, and since I don't recognize him I don't let him in, your son Carlos because I was thinking about you when the clerk in São João da Caparica was refusing my money

—Don't worry about paying we've got plenty of time to settle our accounts, girl

you went with me by the post office and the houses with outside lights and it was you I was going with, Carlos, not him, with you, there was a warehouse or a garage and behind the garage a chicken coop, rubble and chicken droppings, the clerk closed the screen door and that dull peace, those feathers in my mouth, an old man hoeing weeds and the blade was slicing me, cutting me, emptying me out of what I have

I don't even have a core, don't push me I'll lie down, don't break me I'm ready, don't cover my mouth I won't say anything, don't worry I won't report you and he said

—Your husband never gave you anything, right?

I was remembering the pearl tiara, that dull peace, those feathers in my mouth

—Of course he did don't be silly

he didn't believe me, scraping the ground with his shoes

he looked like just one more hen but he wasn't, the pail of corn, the trough of water

—In that case it's time to settle accounts, girl

the day my father died the Jehovah's Witnesses were singing and I was in the pew listening to them, vengeance is mine proclaimed the Lord because my God is a jealous God, dozens of candles on the stove, on the bureau, a drop of wax running down his face and right afterward the shadow of his hand in the shadow of the walnut tree

—What kind of devil are you bringing me Judite?

on Sundays without wine he'd spy on me from the washstand while I dried myself, eyes on my breasts and my thighs, pulling on my towel, at the moment when some part of him was meeting some part of me a hesitation, a pause, my mother as her eyes grew weak

—Floriano

and he on his knees on the damp cement hugging my waist

—I'm a wretch forgive me

his pockets stuffed with nails that he was using to make his coffin behind the house, I remember the holes in the lid so that he wouldn't suffocate underground, his mouth open

—Judite

the gulls were leaving the bridge beams heading for Alto do Galo in hopes that flotsam in the river, they tell me my son is in the hospital and I say

—I don't know who he is

they say that my husband

—Your husband never gave you anything, right?

Cristina during recess at school

—Are you really going to marry Carlos, Judite?

and the other teachers laughing, not listening to them, cleaning the blackboard vigorously, they tell me my son is in the hospital and I don't remember my son, I remember the old man hoeing weeds, the blade didn't cut me because I wasn't there, I remember the chicken coop with the remains of a roost and a rake in the corner, it's possible, I can't swear to it, but maybe there'd been a cradle there, it was a long time ago

twenty years, twenty-five years?

a car with wooden wheels, someone I told to wait at the gate and then the social worker and the man with the cane on the front steps, and then all by myself, I locked myself in so I wouldn't hear them going away, the dwarf from Snow White

—Now, Judite?

it was my husband who'd bought it at Christmas, the owner of the café visited me that afternoon

his wife was setting the tables watching us, I refused the pint

—Not today

the gulls had come back to the bridge beams from Alto do Galo, Carlos was waving good-bye from the edge of the neighborhood and his lips were getting away, never the lips, the cheek, on one occasion the ear and drawing back in panic

—Seriously are you keeping company with Carlos?

he was thinking about my father, Jehovah, sin

—I'm sorry Judite

I got the idea that the man at the boardinghouse was making fun of me when he gave us the key, if only I could have stained the sheet with the blood of the Lamb the same as in the chicken coop when my mouth got covered, I'm not going to holler take it easy, nobody's going to catch us and he

—Your husband never gave you anything, right?

I was me and I was him, I was both of us and Cristina, Elizabete and Márcia threw roses and rice at us as we came out of the church, the school supervisor puzzled

—You're going to marry that fellow?

because he combed his hair better, dressed better, we could sketch his movements in pencil, his cautious little feet didn't hurt, get mad at me Carlos, don't let me leave, don't pretend you don't know they're waiting in the bushes for me, stay with me today, the owner of the café in the doorway not caring about you

—Let's go to Trafaria, Judite

he looked back and nobody, you weren't even at the window

—Don't you want to ask me anything aren't you interested in me?

you were twisting your fingers, knotting them, turning them around, your throat was too full of words to be able to speak, your son

my son

—I don't know who my son is

pounding on the wardrobe

I'm not lying if I swear that I don't know who he is, I fed my son in sin with the flesh and blood of the Lamb, father, my body changed because of him and I don't know him, I brought him with me and a stranger, I let them take him away from me because I never had him, when the social worker, acting as though she didn't see the bottle or the clothes strewn about or the unwashed dishes or my hair without pearls impossible to comb and graying now, or one of the pups after throwing a pine cone against the window, I'm not like the others Dona Judite I can pay, not saying anything, imagining the police, going away, the social worker warning me, don't think for a second that I didn't hear, that I'm not going to put it in the report that I'm not onto your life, but we can't call in the judge, we can't

possumus

arrest you, the social worker wasn't getting involved in anything who can say why about the sicknesses these people give us

—Please fill out the form ma'am

the form about the son I don't know who he is, they telephoned me from the hospital

—Your son

and his voice

—It's my mother it's my mother

under the voice that was telling me

—Your son

I said very quickly to the stranger

—I want to talk to my mother, mister orderly, let me talk to my mother

—You have the wrong number I've already explained more than a thousand times that you have the wrong number I'm sorry

leaving the receiver off so they wouldn't call me, I said to the social worker and the man with the cane on the front step

—Take the child he doesn't belong to me with his pounding on the wardrobe and smashing a car with wooden wheels

and luckily the horses were trotting toward the woods and preventing me from hearing what was said, the wind or maybe the Gypsy's whip filled the house, at the age of sixteen I'd broken my calf bone, it healed poorly and the stretcher-bearer from the Temple had to break it again, my father held me by the arms, a Jehovah's Witness squeezed me around the waist

—Quiet down, Jesus suffered more from Satan

and because I expected so much pain I didn't find any pain, I found a white space hanging above all of you in which I was floating serenely, I saw my father singing a hymn while the hammer was searching for the bone, a whack on the shinbone and no pain, an enormous distance, Judite getting agitated, falling silent, the sound of the joints in the pieces coming together and missing again, I saw her expression, a smile

not a smile

her expression

—No

and now her features asleep, the hammer

—I think I was wrong

and it was all right, I'm not me, it isn't Judite because Judite is forty-four and has graying hair, not chestnut, uncombed, without a ribbon

Judite

—Dona Judite

—It's time to settle our accounts, girl

—I've got the money here Dona Judite

—I brought a bottle from the store don't drink it all at one time don't fall down on me now

Judite, without a job, without a husband, without a son, sits down in the backyard not thinking about anything, not feeling anything, not looking at anything, just herself and the city in the distance, the yellow clouds on the water side and blue on the pine-grove side, night that doesn't arrive and morning that won't come, I was wrong about the bone, it happened, just one more tap, be patient, even today if I'm tired

and I'm tired, a tired mare of the Gypsies that the one with the pistol kills in the pine grove

—Kill me

me begging

—Kill me

the pistol next to the left eye

—Please kill me I don't want my husband to find me in this state I don't want his hurt I don't want his pain I don't want

—Do you need anything?

kill me, even today the leg catches me when I walk, when I was young wearing an insole and with a little care people didn't notice, didn't know, Carlos, for example, never caught on to it, never knew, maybe on an incline or going down stairs I would lean to the right and I'd distract him by talking, noticing changes in the weather, even when the sky was clear, by a change in my leg, not really discomfort, a gurgling in the tendons

—It's going to rain

and right away movement in the marigolds, the gentian drooping, the alarm of the herons as they sobbed in the woods

I don't like herons if I had the courage

my father died here, my mother went back to the village, my husband was in Lisbon working as an entertainer

he's not an entertainer he's

Bico da Areia was too humble for a singer, discomfort in the leg and no cloud at the moment, my mother's eyes snuffed out on a living face, hands that searched for me in the small parlor

—Daughter

perfecting the air, the body that she remembers and had lost

—I'm not like that anymore it's been ages mother

none of us is like that it's been ages and I wonder what we are now, for example, I had a son and I don't have a son, for example, I'm so slim, so healthy and so deformed, for example, there was a boardinghouse and there isn't a boardinghouse, for example, I was a teacher and I'm not a teacher, for example, hug me Carlos, don't be shy, hug me, for example, I'm incapable, at night the vine would sigh on the window frame, it doesn't sigh today, the social worker checking the form, underlining, erasing

—I need your husband's profession ma'am

the bone was broken a third time and I said that's all right even though they were pushing me down against the floor

—No

I don't want my husband to find me like this, he'd make fun of me, he'd laugh, the supervisor disguising his surprise, I can't believe you're going to marry that fellow Judite and I said you don't understand do you, you don't know what suffering and shame are do you, you don't understand that Carlos needs me, the women's clothes in a locked suitcase under the bed, photographs, letters, I was smashing the car with wooden wheels, pounding on the wardrobe, crying with hunger, refusing to eat

—What have you got hidden away there, Carlos?

smoothing the quilt rumpling the quilt, smoothing the quilt rumpling the quilt, the first pine cone on the roof, don't hold me down, don't break my bone, don't hurt me, my husband

—Nothing of any importance

rumpling the quilt

—Really nothing

smoothing the quilt

—Nothing

looking at me with the eyes of the cemetery guard who was watching me among the flowers with a piece of apple in my pocket

after we buried my father I stayed by the grave listening to the laurels, I remember a hoopoe swaying on an angel, medallions with tarnished profiles, I was sure that the nails of the dead grew under the ground and my doubts

—Who takes care of them?

you could catch sight of Trafaria and the sea or maybe the mouth of the river through a break in the poplars, the sandbars at ebb tide, the city where my husband

—I need your husband's profession ma'am

was famous and sang, who are you sleeping with, where are you sleeping, how are you sleeping Carlos, the laurels weren't talking to anyone anymore except me

—I have the money Dona Judite

I thought about leaving him a pint on the tombstone

—The blood of the Lamb, father

the hanged man's necktie came to mind, waking up with his pulling the sheet off me

an albatross with his gullet wide open

me covering myself with the blanket

—Father

the albatrosses of Bugio, Praia da Rainha, and Fonte da Telha continuing on up to the huts beyond the man with the cane and the social worker an old woman in mourning, the callus on the bone telling me it's going to rain and the lamp lighted at three in the afternoon, a melancholy eternity turning the curtain pale, what will forty-four years be like, Carlos, writing forty-two on the form and the social worker dusting off the chair and settling her behind, feeling the seat

—Forty-two?

your suitcase is still under the bed and as long as the suitcase stays there I promise I won't make a fuss stay with me Carlos, the one who wasn't my son in the car with them, I could swear my husband was at the bus stop, his little hand waving but no, a branch, at night on that path there were always nighthawks, owls, the echo of the waves, not from the water side, from the pine-grove side

arriving at Fonte da Telha they told me to go down a ramp tripping over tiles in the dark

—*Watch out, fellow*

every step squashed some living thing as it twisted, one of the cops with a lantern even though the lantern wasn't lighting to show the way, to light up the walls of shacks, a woman behind a peephole, alleys where last week Rui and I, a plastic arm on a stake pointing to the beach and after that a house with no chimney, the dune, the mastiff with a bow barking at the corpse on the bath towel, the headlights of the Jeep focused on the towel, the unlighted cigarette in his hand and Rui jolly as he always was when he came to get me at Anjos

—*What did you steal from my father today Rui?*

not seeing me but merry, the lemon, the syringe like the ones we used, but no heroin, empty, the pants and the shoes nobody had stolen, nothing but the smell of water, not the smell of death and the whisper

—*Paulo*

every so often Dona Helena was in the kitchen and he would be peeking at the pictures, the trays, at Noémia Couceiro Marques fading away in the molding

already faded away in the molding

the old lady never had anything worth anything, they're poor, we've already taken the clock, the veneer ashtray, the case that wasn't ivory at all, was fake, they would examine the place where things had been without say-

ing a peep to me, not afraid of me, afraid that I'd leave, last week I caught the old woman kissing my jacket before hanging it up, at first they tried to drag me into their daughter's room to try on the Panama hats and the bibs with the smell of the closet and I

—*No*

everything ancient, threadbare, if I'd had the car with wooden wheels at least, a wardrobe I could pound on with my fists, Mr. Couceiro to me, no, to the picture, to the iron box where there was a bouquet of chrysanthemums

—*Noémia*

even today sometimes when I enter the apartment, before I get to the living room

—*Noémia*

Noémia Couceiro Marques with no eyes, with no mouth, with no face, reduced to a bicycle with flat tires, the petals in the vase that evaporate when you touch them, a little bell on the handlebars that would arouse the whole building, Rui with the bath towel under the headlights of the Jeep

—*Noémia*

son of a bitch

while the mastiff with a bow leaped to avoid a policeman and came back whining, my father begging them to hide the scars on his chest, to stop the serum, to sit him up on the bed, and his husband mother

—*Rui?*

since she doesn't see either of us, Rui, why is she throwing me out, not letting me come in, telling the man with the napkin

—*Send the faggot's kid away*

and the breathing of the horses mingled with the echo of the waves not from the water side, in the pine grove, me at the bus stop the way he was before and nighthawks and owls and mother and father and Dona Helena and Mr. Couceiro and don't abandon me here

the one who wasn't my son at the bus stop like my husband at some other time but without a suitcase or a topcoat and finally nobody, just a stick, so I could open the blinds, take away the broom I'd jammed against the doorknob, turn the key in the door, go out, settle down on the doormat with a pint

no, not with a pint, take a bath, fix myself up, find the vial of perfume that Carlos gave me and that I haven't used in twenty years twenty-two years

behind the rice tin, I mean not really perfume, what's left of some perfume, half a dozen drops, turn it upside down, touch the stopper to my ears, the back of my neck, try on a dress from my younger days, the old pink and brown one, not really brown, maroon

maybe brighter than maroon, purple with a green sash

lilac with a green sash

purple with a green sash, the purple dress with a green sash that I only wore once after I was married, before I got pregnant, a year after school, holding it up to my breast and my breasts were too big, stopping with the dress, throwing it onto the bed, why was I insisting on the dress, getting rid of it and going back to cooking, what's the use if you're not going to caress me, hug me, look at me crossing my fingers, knotting them, twisting them, your shoulder getting away from my hand and me the dummy the blind woman

—What was it Carlos?

—What's wrong with me Carlos?

—Why not with me Carlos?

detesting me

I'm ugly

not Cristina, not Elisabete, not Márcia, I'm ugly, what don't I have, Carlos, for heaven's sake tell me what you don't like and I'll change it, it's my fault, I'm to blame, I don't know how to get it right, teach me, don't hide in the pillow, don't sink into the mattress, a creaking of springs

—It's not your fault Judite

when it's obvious that it is my fault, don't ask me to forgive you, put your head on my breast because I'm not asking for anything, see, I'm not laughing at you, the desk clerk making fun of you, don't worry about it, noticing something I don't know what

—He noticed Judite

he didn't notice, he's already forgotten about us, the school supervisor noticed, the other teachers noticed, nobody noticed, everything's normal Carlos, anxiety, shyness, don't be frightened I'm waiting

—Waiting for what, Judite?

don't talk, don't worry, I'm waiting

—What's that racket Judite?

it's the Gypsy wagons, the horses, the sea, it's my father

—What kind of devil are you bringing me Judite?

it's the gulls on the bridge, don't look at me as though you were saying good-bye to me, don't take all the pills again and me in the hallway of the clinic, the mulberry trees deconstructing the sun on the avenue, sweeping the sidewalk with the gleam of their leaves

—Hasn't he died yet gentlemen?

Elisabete calling me aside where there was a smell of iodine and a sign No Smoking, a cigarette with an X across it

—Forget about him Judite let's go they told me that

an X across it and me

—Beat it I don't want to see you anymore

they let me go where you were while they muffled their laughs, showing me a lace handkerchief more expensive than my own

—The guy's handkerchief, imagine

asking me with charming surprise

—You're his girlfriend aren't you?

and behind my back the signals, the expressions, you putting on your shoes, fixing your collar, the pups' teeth

—I've got money Dona Judite

the clerk's teeth growing out of his gums

—There's plenty of time to settle our accounts, girl

the comb missing your hair and slipping through your fingers

—Your husband never gave you anything, right?

a little old man hoeing weeds and the blade slicing me, cutting me, emptying me of what I have

I don't even have a single intestine left

my giving you the comb

don't push me I'll lie down, don't hit me, I'm willing, don't cover my mouth I won't report you

—Of course he did, sir

a pine cone on the roof, the pups or the electrician or the owner of the café

—Judite

and telling them no, not today, putting on his shoes today, fixing his collar, parting his hair, putting the handkerchief in his pocket

—Your handkerchief

taking a scab off his lip

—It's a scab, wait

I can't today

I'm sorry

I have to help my husband we're coming out of the clinic, the mulberry trees deconstruct the sun on the avenue, the bus

only the driver and us

to Bico da Areia, yellow clouds on the water side and blue ones on the pine-tree side, the horses chasing gulls on the beach, my brown dress

lilac

maroon

purple

my purple dress with the green sash, the door open, the dwarf from Snow White greeting you

—Mr. Carlos

the plates in the sink, the floor mopped, not a single bottle peeping out of the oven, the bed made and waiting, a bouquet on the windowsill

—Good morning

bushes where the wild geese and the sea swallows were, sit down on the beach with me not thinking about anything, not feeling anything, not looking at anything, don't answer if they call me, I'm staying here, I'm not going, I'm not packing my bag, I promise you I'm not packing my bag

—Stay with me Carlos

stay with me Carlos, I'm forty-four years old, I don't believe you, that's strange, you don't have to hug me, caress me, we didn't do any hugging remember, standing up, two figurines on a cake and the photographer motioning us in with his hand, so elegant, so healthy, do you want to see what we were like Carlos

—Nice and quiet

one beside the other until night and morning and the sea swallows getting away from high tide, just let me take off the cold cream and the wig

an entertainer, a singer

let me look at you before you leave, before

—I'm not capable Judite

before the owner of the café with a pint of wine and me imagining it's you, me imagining it's you, me certain it's you and saying

—Yes

agreeing

—Yes

closing my eyes under your weight and feeling happy.

CHAPTER

NOW THAT MY FATHER'S dead I think I've begun looking for him but I'm not sure. I'm not sure. I keep turning it over and over and the answer I get is I'm not sure. It all seems so hard to me, so complicated, so strange, a clown who was a man and a woman at the same time or a man sometimes and a woman other times or a kind of man sometimes and a kind of woman other times with me thinking

—What am I supposed to call him?

During the times he was a woman or a kind of woman and I'm not sure

I'm not sure

I'd turn my head away and I'm not sure, people my father lived with didn't know either, sometimes they treated him like a man who wasn't a man and sometimes like a woman who wasn't a woman even though he paid for their clothes, their upkeep, cooked for them with all the humility of somebody asking to be forgiven

forgiven for what?

he'd get mad over the remorse I represented for him

—Get out of my sight

let me have something, anything, a train ticket, Dona Helena's hand, a horse from Bico da Areia so I can get out of here

the fingers that seemed to be trying to touch me and didn't touch me, the voice that was suddenly masculine

—Didn't I tell you to get out of my sight?

sorry, folding up into pleats of tears where there weren't any tears, the perfume that he would give off and when my father'd gone away would still linger in the living room, stagnant, thick, accusing him

a horse from Bico da Areia will do, not a train ticket because the horses at Bico da Areia never leave the woods unless the Gypsies sell them or finish them off with a shot and trains disappear into the night for good, even as you hear them go off beyond the houses

I didn't dare ask

—What's father blaming himself for?

while he was getting dressed for shows with his eyes enlarged with makeup and liner, maybe the sound of a faucet or a glass in the kitchen, his eyes growing smaller investigating, the antennae on the back of his neck deciphering the sounds

—Did you hear that Rui?

under the metal lamp where two bulbs were missing

maybe Dona Helena could help me leave, Noémia had left, Mr. Couceiro will reach the vestibule any day now, lift his cane

—*Good-bye*

and which when I went into Príncipe Real today was missing all its bulbs, a van at the door, guys carrying out the wardrobe, the chairs, the cane rack with enameled mouse ears, everything scattered about on the street, cheap, poor, with decorations and bindings that made things look even poorer although they looked almost new and rich behind the curtains

be patient Dona Helena put me to sleep now, the bed too, the dressing table with a mirror swaying on the stairs where I thought it was looking at me and ignoring me, me in the glass for one instant and then nobody, Mr. Couceiro lowering his cane

—Diabetes, lad

wrinkles and bones pretending to be happy, Dona Helena in the doorway

—Jaime

the cane rising up again

—I feel fine Helena

The dignity of sick people aspiring for a sudden recovery with death living underneath it, at Príncipe Real, the workers with the

washing machine that hadn't worked for years push a button and
it sobs out some water along with dust, the landlord

—What do you want, boy?

putting little cases with tubes and brushes in a cardboard box,
sometimes I'd go to Fonte da Telha with my father and Rui

and before Rui, Mário, and before Mário, Dino

to the spot where three months ago the policeman and the body
were, my father in a bra and earrings, his lips so thick, soft gestures,
curves, the hair on his thighs tingling from the hair wax, me
ashamed of them swearing to everybody, to the fishermen tarring
their boats that is

—I don't know them I never saw them before

the landlord pointing to the van where the Spanish doll and the
shells on the bracelets were

—Seven months' back rent, boy, I've come to collect what's owed
me

he'd appear every month with the bill and my father, after peeking out the window, would signal Rui

or Mário or Dino

changing shoes, replacing the blonde wig with a black one

*give me anything, a train ticket or a full syringe in order to get away from
here, the maid from the hospital dining room who went to Chelas with me*

—*I loved you, did you know that?*

—*I don't want to, it hurts and I don't want to hurt, people think it hurts
and it doesn't, just try a little bit you'll see, the jackdaw on the broken-down
wall agreeing with me*

—You'll see

*you don't feel heat she said, you don't feel that you're not moving and
you're flying, better than Dona Helena, than the horses at Bico da Areia,
than a train ticket to Spain or Paris*

my father in a black wig

—Come in come on in hey

a song on the radio, a liqueur, Rui

or Mário or Dino

shut up in the closet where the ironing board was

—Come in come on in hey

and sit down here beside me, what's that piece of paper, let me guess, don't tell me, I bet it's a love letter, a proposal, a poem, didn't anyone ever tell you you have a romantic look, if you could only guess how many things a woman can spot, the rent bill, what a surprise, but written like it was a poem, a businessman poet, good heavens, all those qualities, I wonder if your wife has even thanked the angels for all the luck she's had, my father's voice now flat now a thread that didn't settle into any tone, his knees uncovered, his forefinger and thumb removing a speck from the landlord's lapel, studying it tenderly and dropping it into the ashtray as carefully as he would a diamond, his ear on the closet, don't screw things up Rui

or Mário or Dino

don't breathe, don't move, at Fonte da Telha, when we got back to the car, insults on the glass

faggot

one of the headlights shattered

Isn't it true that you're flying, isn't it true that you're flying?

the mudguard dragging against the stones, my mother

my father making a show of folding up the rent bill and tucking it into his pocket, with so many important matters to be resolved between us why waste time talking about money, take this note Paulo, buy me some cigarettes at the stand and stay out for a bit playing in the park I'll call you in a little while

and the sunset and trees, and the darkness and trees, and fear and trees, rain beginning in the trees, the pinky touch of a drop on the back of my neck

—Paulo

and how do I answer the drop, the bench by the cedar tree and me curled up on the bench, the bulb in the ceiling replaced by the lampshade on the small table, a silky halo, a violet light, the branches of the cedar stretching out toward me with a challenge of leaves, a second pinky on the neck and a third on the forehead blinding me, the bench wet, a branch on my shoulder

—Get away fast Paulo

our stopping the car, looking at the mudguard, my father on his knees

not a kind of woman, a man ordering Rui

Let go

fixing the mudguard and cleaning the windshield, getting to the house the landlord beside the van next to the radio, the lampshade, the shoes from times gone by

—Seven months in arrears, boy

my father not a man, a kind of woman adjusting her neckpiece and the landlord confused, pleasant

me to the maid from the dining room

—*Isn't it true that you're flying, isn't it true that you're flying?*

the voice that finally found its range, slow glycerine that was dressing and undressing him

—I never could have imagined that a poet

releasing Rui

or Mário or Dino

from the closet with the ironing board where I'll bet there were rats, sometimes I imagine feet, scurrying, the maid from the dining room flying on the broken-down wall and cold and heat and cold

not right now, heat right now, everything so clear, so simple, that's life after all, I understand everything, I know, I can't explain it but I know, amusing myself with the jackdaw's whistling, my job, the hospital, the German shepherd before I got to my place, when I was a little girl I'd always change my route and keep looking back when I heard it barking, my sister who got married five months ago on the twenty-fifth, don't run, when you run they bite you, the seat at Príncipe Real empty except for half a dozen fashion magazines, a poster of my father making his thread of glycerine stand out with touches of mockery in it

—I never could have imagined that a poet

Dona Helena without stopping her crocheting to repair a stitch that had become broken from rubbing her back, as she got older her twisted spine, a growing hump

—You never could have imagined what, Paulo?

why can't she leave me alone and not make me holler at her, Mr. Couceiro noticing my annoyance and I

Don't get involved in what's none of your business be quiet

maybe he still gets up in the middle of the night to take a look at me sleeping, he'd realize I'd noticed him and would go back to the door stumbling on the sill, we'd place the fork in his left hand and the knife in his right, we'd tell him this is the knife, this is the fork, we'd lay out his food, the napkin wrapped around his neck

—There's your chicken Jaime

the fork picking at the tablecloth, the knife hitting the pitcher, someday going into the Anjos building, other dressers on the stairs, a different landlord in the building

—Seven months in arrears, boy

and looking for my father I'm not sure

I'm not sure

I go round and round and I'm not sure, staying on the bench by the cedar tree or with the maid from the dining room on the wall in Chelas, all the horses at Bico da Areia motionless on the beach, all the trains halted in the station

—There aren't any tickets, boy

the cellar club where the clown worked right off the Praça das Flores, a woman in a gray smock who during the shows sold the customers candy, cigarettes, perfume, gifts for the performers which nobody bought, waxing the floor among the tables, a small window almost at ceiling level where a difficult day poured in where sometimes there were legs, a three-wheeled cart with vegetables, the instantaneous

hint

of a cat, the doorman lining up imitation champagne bottles along shelves behind the bar, the reflecting ball that spun from the ceiling announcing whatever it was that no one was listening to, the woman picked up a crushed camellia and threw it into a bucket, my father crossed the room with little tango steps

—Hello Paulo

a current of air coming from somewhere puffing out some

draperies that shook and he was silent, never hello son, always hello Paulo, he would introduce me to his colleagues

—My nephew

or

—My cousin

and now that the woman in a gray smock was beginning to wax the floor around him, with a pirouette of unimaginably worn velvet

—Hello Paulo

—Hello nephew

—Hello cousin

during the fall when I had the flu he visited me grudgingly at Anjos accompanied by a fellow with a mustache whom he introduced to Dona Helena with a baroque flourish

—An engineer friend

and whom I recognized as the worker who handled the lights at the club, he looked disdainfully at the furniture that had no gilt or spangles or ribbons, a beat-up door disguised by the cupboard and behind the cupboard the neighbor

—Cecília

Mr. Couceiro offered him a spoonful of my syrup, realized his mistake with a nervous leap

—What could have got into my head how stupid of me I'm sorry

my father on a corner of the mattress after checking the firmness of the bed mistrustfully and a whiff of cologne embalmed my nose, his ruffles

so cruel

they made the age of things stand out along with the defects of the plaster, the neighbor

—Cecília

sharper, closer, the clock in the church dislodged the silence tossing its sparrows at the window frames, my father smoothed and rumpled the quilt as at Bico da Areia but I was in Lisbon, there were no horses, there was no beach, there were no Gypsies, somebody where there couldn't be a gate because an old fourth-floor flat

—Dona Judite

and my mother asleep beside me, somebody

—I've brought some money Dona Judite I can pay

I seemed to see Dona Helena with her hand cupped behind her ear to hear better and not getting to hear, Mr. Couceiro with the spoonful of syrup, intrigued

—I'm not like the others Dona Judite I won't run off afterward

my fever or maybe what was waves or the tide coming in, what could be called pine trees and yet what pine trees in Lisbon and what east wind in September, nothing but an automobile horn, the loudspeaker for the lottery for the blind, my father with blonde hair holding out to me the candy that the woman went about selling in the club

—Hello nephew

the clown's colleagues, with a rustle of feathers, were moving legs with lipstick guffaws over the hysteria of their mouths, a pause with no gulls or pine cones on the roof and during the pause

—Cecília

candies with the names of the performers in bleeding hearts Bárbara Alexandra Nini, dressing-room bustle over the customers and watch your tongues the little one might hear, changes of clothing and be careful Samanta a child

me?

pounding on the wardrobe, my mother in the yard

—Carlos

the fluttering of the herons on the bridge beams or in the next apartment and my father kissing me with repugnance

—Hello Paulo

—Hello nephew

—Hello cousin

trying to but I'm not sure

I'm not sure

candy, cigarettes, vials of perfume, Dona Helena sniffing the vial because of good manners, Mr. Couceiro declining the tobacco

—I don't smoke

the man with the mustache startled by the little porcelain Dutch shoes that a cousin of Dona Helena's had sent from Rotterdam and that were used to cover up a pipe in the wall

—just take a look at this horror Soraia

the haze of the flu, since I couldn't speak, correcting him to myself

—He's not Soraia he's Carlos

the doorman was washing glasses at the bar, his braided jacket on the coatrack, at the small window by the ceiling a greasy afternoon, clotted, like Alto do Galo during the time when the swallows startle the woods and only afterward the breeze that would wake up my mother and make her drink, my father with apprehension of the thunderclaps

—Judite

putting the perfume and the cigarettes in his bag, moving his fingers toward me, thinking better of it, putting them into the pocket of his blouse, calling to the engineer who'd moved from the wooden shoes to the fringed cover of a candy box with a little donkey turning a well-wheel

—Good-bye Paulo

Mr. Couceiro's cane in the hallway behind them now heavy now light, in the middle of the horses that lame mare, the mist of the flu

everything so difficult, so strange, the maid from the dining room after all that's life, don't ask me to explain it to you, I can't explain it to you but I know

—Your father?

the woman in the gray smock in weary fatigue

and dusk through the small window, a change in the afternoon

—Have you come to fix the coffee machine?

the lights with cellophane leaves held by clothespins were abandoned in a corner in a tangle of wires, an overcoat on the cane stand was moving its lapels demanding that it be put on

—*isn't it true that you're flying isn't it true that you're flying?*

—You're Soraia's nephew aren't you, I've kept your aunt's things in the office

give me whatever there is, a train ticket or a full syringe so I can get out of here, a door that said Restrooms and to the right of the door a boy peeing into a pot and on the left of the door a girl in braids on a second pot, the woman wiping her hands to get rid of little pieces of wax climbed up some steep steps and there at the top, waiting for me, God

no, and there at the top another door without any pots or children that said Manager, the last sky of the day

with clouds in pink makeup

its distant blue persisted on the balcony, I sensed trees nearby from the tint of the air, the picture of the manager's children

one of them wearing glasses

the bag with my father's toiletries soft at the bottom, the son in glasses, with the look of a manager already, getting interested in me, photographs of clowns that poured out of an album, the doorman pulling on his suspenders in the doorway

—That's everything, check it if you want

and heat and cold and heat, this uncomfortable feeling, this thing in the chest so a little lemon friend, a needle friend, a match to heat the powder with, maybe Mr. Couceiro carrying my bag and resting at corners because of diabetes, urea

—All your aunt's belongings are there, check it

me not there, me and the maid from the dining room in Chelas, me getting mad at the jackdaw's teasing or the Mulatto with the jackknife opening and closing the blade looking for us in the neighborhood, the pictures of the clowns

Bárbara Alexandra Nini, another one more on in years who didn't drink with the customers, didn't talk would tie the little dog to the doorknob of the dressing room, go off in a car without makeup

Carole

a kinship with my mother as she looked at herself in the mirror on the wardrobe in Bico da Areia with the same incomprehension and the same rancor, one night she didn't come to work and the people waiting for her, the boss, the doorman, me with the candy tray already, cigarettes, perfume, it was with me that she'd chat sometimes, not really chatting, my name

—Amélia

two or three words along with my name

—I'll tell you someday Amélia

while she adjusted her clothes making faces and twitching,

replaced a fingernail, lingered at the entrance indifferent to the music, the manager pushing her on stage

—Have you fallen asleep Carole?

The little dog barking anxiously the whole time tied to the doorknob, the manager

—Will somebody do me the favor of killing that mutt?

and she to me as she came back from her number which no one applauded except for one or two old men who'd known her for years

—I'll tell you someday Amélia

she would drop her plumes and I'd gather them up from the floor, leaving by the rear entrance dragging the animal along without paying any attention to it the way children do with a squashed doll they've become tired of, on the end of a leash, a voice without falsettos or trills, the voice of an exhausted man

—I'll tell you someday Amélia

or not exhausted, in some place I wasn't allowed to enter

—I'll tell you someday Amélia

she had a daughter in France, had worked on ships, was a cousin of the manager who took her on out of charity, the boys would chase him on the street with the persistence of crows

Poor Carole

they'd imitate his walk, his gestures, he went from rooming house to rooming house unable to pay for them, they'd ask him for the money and his hands were empty

Take it

so that deeper and deeper into the outskirts and farther and farther from the river, four suitcases at first, one suitcase afterward, then a knapsack, the chain sold, the ring sold, afternoons at the window waiting for I don't know what, a memory of packet boats, Amsterdam or Hamburg, but the ships were old and rotting away in Seixal, in Montijo, in Amora, sharing some leftover fish with the little dog and the manager

—You've lost weight Carole

how to disguise those wrinkles, cover that throat, hide those hips, she didn't disguise, she didn't cover, didn't hide, looking like my mother looking at herself after some wine in the wardrobe at Bico da Areia with the same incomprehension and the same rancor, one night

—I'll tell you someday Amélia

she didn't show up at the club, didn't answer the phone, didn't answer a letter breaking her contract, we discovered her after a week of searching and asking, creditors who showed us receipts, bills, a postcard from France

Puteaux

where there was too little ink and too much contempt, after what she'd done to my mother she doesn't dare write me, after a week in the slums to the north of the city, people afraid of the police, chickens on garbage heaps, information in broken Portuguese leading to nonexistent alleys and vacant lots with trash, another postcard from France

Creil

that increased the anger, and she still has the guts and a wave without a hand

—I'll tell you someday Amélia

asking me for money and finally after an address in pencil on a page from a notebook

27, Jardins Boieldieu

covered by two marks of eye shadow, some construction on a slope in Pontinha, Bosnian immigrants roasting a rabbit

or a mole

the entrance to a building where there were stork nests and the bills of irritated storks could be seen through the planks, a rebuilt ground floor

Puteaux, Creil, Jardins Boieldieu maybe the same thing. maybe like here, Ukrainians, blacks, Romanians, a rabbit or a mole, after what she did to my mother and me she didn't dare write me and then the smell, you understand sir, that I associated it with poverty

pick me up Dona Helena, I don't weigh much, pick me up now

the knapsack open, a French stamp in the handbag reminding her of her daughter as if it were a picture, a draft of a letter signed António, Carole in the only chair mocking us my mother in front of the wardrobe in angry incomprehension

the little dog not barking for the first time, lying at her knees, both with wounds at the neck and not really much blood not really much blood, almost no blood at all, two little scratches, that was all, there must be pine trees around here, there must be pine cones around here in Alverca

or Massama or Loures

around here in Pontinha, horses and waves and gulls and pine cones, throwing them off toward the roof

—Dona Carole

or

—Dona Judite

—I have the money here Dona Carole

—I won't run away like the others Dona Carole I'll pay

Dona Carole getting up out of the chair and opening the door for me

Dona Carole without even looking at me, the letter for her daughter signed António

When you get this

which never reached Puteaux or Creil, 27 Jardins Boieldieu, after what she did to my mother and me, that father of mine rumpling the quilt and smoothing the quilt, didn't justify himself, didn't ask for forgiveness, took the bus, went away, preferred the horrible creature who sold candy at the club to us

—I'll tell you someday Amélia

the candy on this side, the cigarettes in the middle, the perfume on the other side, candy filled with liqueur, American cigarettes, Spanish perfume more alcohol than perfume, one of the Bosnians at the door, hat in hand, the little dog on a spit or in a dark pot, a fallen brazier, a fan

When you get this, father

Carole in men's pants, the feet of a man, no bottle of wine, no dwarf from Snow White, no refrigerator, the image of the wardrobe wounded before us and the people

—Why?

the hand that rubbed at the same time that the image

or before the image?

two identical hands in identical movements, the manager wiping them on his sleeve with surprise, no

—I'll tell you someday Amélia

a nervous whisper

—Call the police Amélia

and the bills of the storks hitting the boards up above, a camellia on the bedstead and Carole caressing the camellia, only her mouth forming the words, not her voice

—Thank you

or not even her mouth, the closed curtain, a moment of darkness at the club, the disk jockey making a mistake with the next piece, the Bosnian asked for the little dog, sir, before the police

a coin for a cup of coffee friend

the police and hours of waiting and the doctor and hours of waiting and the ambulance and Carole calm, hours of waiting and the stretcher, no light on the streets, the little flames of wood fires at some point in the darkness, a train that was leaving for Spain without me, the ambulance orderly's flashlight on the manager's face, on mine, on the woman in the gray smock

not on Carole's

the wound on the neck, the man's pants, the man's feet with one of the toenails painted, this isn't carnival what's going on here, the manager's hands in the sweep of a bow a colleague gentlemen, a performer that is, the sheet over the stretcher enwrapping the performer

if I only could have told you Amélia, in Amsterdam, in La Coruña, in Hamburg, I never had a chance to go to France before dying, Puteaux, Creil, the Jardins Boieldieu, number twenty-seven and my daughter

—You

forgiving me, if there was a camellia she'd throw me a camellia, I'd go back on stage surprised, content, the disk jockey spinning the turntable backward and my number one more time, pretending that I'm singing, that I'm dancing while the stretcher off in the direction of Lisbon, a stone table where they undress me, weigh me, test my liver and after undressing me, weighing me, and testing my liver put me away down there in the freezer among frozen people, an item in the paper or not even an item, who cares about me even in Puteaux or in Creil, I didn't drink with the customers, I left all by myself, no Mário, no Dino, no Rui, the car with faded paint going down the Praça das Flores on the way to São Bento and past São Bento if I could have told you Amélia, you who saw us arrive, helped us with the ashes, my daughter

after what she did to me and my mother she still had the guts
the gall
the bitch
I looked for her one Tuesday
you didn't look for her Dona Carole don't lie it's a sin
I looked for her one Tuesday, not so long ago, in July not dressed this way of course, I hadn't shaved for a week, I'd left my eyebrows alone, I walked among the people with an umbrella on my arm
realizing that an umbrella in July
in spite of the umbrella without which they would notice or pay attention to me, a woman looking at me and not just looking, she was looking with interest, words
or am I imagining words
I didn't imagine words, I wasn't mistaken, words and the six o'clock light gilding the window frames, me a child in summertime I would nest in the kitchen to watch the light pass by, after my aunt got widowed, my father
—What's the matter Aura?
and my aunt
—It's the light
in front of the kiosk I turned and my aunt and the woman watching the light pass, they didn't recognize me by the kiosk in spite of my not having changed all that much
eight years, nine years?
a touch fatter, half a dozen freckles
fewer

a touch fatter, three or four freckles but my hair just the same, I combed it the way I did before, the part, the sideburns, Tomás's hair tonic, he wasn't home and he would have been mad at me

—Do you want to be a man Carole?

I squeezed the lump of it onto the sidewalk in front of our house I spotted them immediately and a strange joy

the neighbors from before, Dona Eunice, Álvaro, Fernanda, Fernanda's sister whose name I can't remember, Álvaro looking at me hard for a second and shaking his head

—It can't be I must be mistaken

shacks made of aluminum instead of wood, an attic at twenty-three where there was no attic, a girl dressed as a lady with rings in her ears that I must have found as a child

how many years exactly?

I didn't find

I found

that I found as a child, the steps that separate this walk from the next one where I lived with you and to a third set of stairs with streetlights on, I always liked it when the streetlights went on, my aunt

I can't understand why

she thought it was sad and I didn't, she insisted that lighting the lamps reminded her of the dead, bats around them and they told me they screamed but I didn't hear any screams, a sound of something felt or canvas as they grazed the roofs, at the end of the steps the restaurant also unchanged, bullfight posters for Alcochete and Évora, the plaster matador on the walnut base, the proprietor

he was all shriveled up, poor thing

closing up the menus with the care shown a missal, my wife at the window

how many years Ivete?

plucking off the dried leaves in the flowerpots, going over and searching for something to say, putting a hug together, you're going to hate me for not bringing a present, a veneered box, a silk neckpiece, maybe from the notions store that closes at eight on Fridays, counting the money in my pocket and going there, I've got to get there so I can go back, I go quickly back and my wife still watching me, seeing me I imagine like the woman in the telephone booth even if it might be hard with the streetlights on, to see that I smiled

I smiled, I certainly smiled

I smiled even if it might be hard to see if I smiled just as it's hard to see if the window that slammed shut was my wife or the July wind that almost always comes on with the arrival of night.

CHAPTER

SOMETIMES I THINK I'm the one who's dead, that I died instead of my father and I, my father, live on Príncipe Real I mean the park and all that, the cedar tree and all that, the café up ahead there and all that, the old lady in a fur cape in August giving corn to the pigeons and the pigeons running away from her and all that, one day I could have sworn my mother was spying on us, I ran into the kitchen like a shot

—Mother

my father was on the verge of a faint it was obvious as his hands pulled at the shade all nervous and getting the cord caught in the roller, and he squatted down to peek, the room got dark from top to bottom, the walls disappeared, the crack in the plaster with the shape of a wry face mocking us, fix the crack father, my father checking to see if his heart could take it with his open hand, peeking again, the blind flew up and day came back with a jolt, from bottom to top and the face on the wall with a corner of it behind the molding ha ha

—It isn't your mother it's the old lady

the old lady with her bag of corn surrounded by kernels, maybe when my father gets to be her age he'll be waiting too for whatever the old lady was waiting for, you couldn't figure out what she was waiting for but she was waiting, she was waiting for what she knew wouldn't ever be coming and she amused herself with the pigeons while whatever it was took its time in calling her, two or three hours later she would pick up the corn that she'd left on the bench and go off with the strut of a duchess, what would happen if I said

—Hello

I said

—Here I am

I said

—I got here

the small myopic look running up and down the boxwood trees, some little-girl thing in the timid question

—Cesário?

just like my father

—Rui?

forgetting the ironing whenever the key was in the door, the small myopic look a few years from now father, not too many, his glasses falling to the ground and his two sad fingers brushing leaves away to pick them up

not finding them, looking farther off, asking him if I could help and your face father, if you could have seen your face with a smile just like the smirk on the wall except not one of mockery but of entreaty

—My glasses Paulo

maybe even, but it's not true

—My glasses son

son finally, not nephew, not godson, son, his feeling around like a blindman, discouraged

—My glasses son

on hands and knees around the bench

—My glasses son

and

—Rui

and since there wasn't any Rui, there isn't any Rui, there never was a Rui, father, it was unclear what he could have been waiting for but it was obvious that he was waiting

—My glasses son

Rui who didn't even sleep with him, would come in the morning smothered in scarves and excuses, my father accusing me about the Cape Verdeans, I who didn't know a thing about Chelas, it was Rui who introduced me to the Mulattoes, an air of mystery, promises,

I'm going to show you something come here, just about the time
when the face on the wall began to mock us, bring along a bag for
the pigeons father, put the leftover corn in your pocket, leave with
your little duchess strut, Dona Aurorinha telling my father about
the other woman, a doctor, a piano it seems, maids, a chauffeur,
Dona Aurorinha's mother her seamstress on Thursdays, baskets
and baskets of clothes, expensive shirts, neckties, and now this idée
fixe, giving corn to the pigeons, explain to me why, they'd bring my
mother a tray with lunch to eat at the machine and my mother
afraid that a pitcher, a piece of crystal, a knickknack on the floor,
tapping me on the hands

—Don't get into anything Aurorinha

paintings on the ceiling of gods and nymphs and now corn for
the pigeons, an aunt who gave my mother an egg candy

—For your little girl, Lucinda

my mother in a rush timidly shaking me by the arm

—Thank the lady where are your manners

and while

—Thank the lady where are your manners

a second mouth on the gods, on the nymphs muttering at me
with my mother's voice

—Wait till you get outside to eat the candy, ninny

her thumb and forefinger or those of a nymph on the archway,
that chubby one, naked, with a twisted pinch

—That's the way you little rapscallion I'm sorry ma'am

not completely naked, covered with a sheet, half-naked and
angelic, me clutching the candy curious, the nymph with her eye on
a goat that was playing a flute leaning against a rock, its hair in
braids like those of the aunt with the egg candies and the insistent
pinch

—Wait till you get outside to eat the candy, ninny

*Rui doesn't sleep at home father, don't make excuses, don't lie, getting up
whenever there are steps outside*

*how many months is it that Rui hasn't slept at home, his wave of an arm
showing boredom, annoyance*

Leave me alone Soraia

if his expression could only be seen, if he could only show it to you in a mirror

the niece in a fur cape a little worn don't you think, where are the gods, the nymphs, my mother's friend leaning against a board that was changing into a rock and eating a pomegranate

—Aurorinha

my father always got up when there were footsteps outside, he would go over to the doormat not daring to open, the slippers back to bed because it was the slippers that were holding up his body, his body wanted to stay there until the next cough or the next key, the slippers at rest sleeping one beside the other and you in bed smoking, a sigh that came from the pillow, not of disappointment, of weariness

a wish to die father?

take it easy, you're not dying

—Did you ever see me Paulo?

the cedar tree and the café outlined by the halo of the night, the circles of a flower bed in the shadows, a barrel by the cedar where he told me to wait, the pond where the water was resting without any stuff of dreams, Dona Aurorinha maybe awakened too while people with wings, naked women, gods

—Thank the gentleman Aurorinha

not really naked, their chubby feet stepping and stepping on her, the insistent pinches

—Wait until he leaves Aurorinha

my father on his back

I died in your place father, I left you alive, if I could be capable of forgiving you, accept it, if you want I'll go with you to the park and maybe at four in the morning the pigeons, my father on his back listening to the rain

don't you hear the rain father?

me listening to the rain at Anjos and the church clock shuffling the night and forgetting about its hands full of sparrows, insomnia's gigantic strolling, noises that were scolding me

—Thank Mr. Couceiro be polite

—Have you lost your manners Paulo?

—Cat got your tongue Paulo?

and me with my tongue out

—I do so have manners

the distance to the infinite window, the light switch I don't know where, would you like a syringe father

would you like a heroin fix?

would you like to fly?

Dona Aurorinha's mother's gentleman friend offering her the pomegranate

—Soraia

I met Rui and I fell in love period, almost at my son's age period, fifteen years younger than me period, it never happened to me with the others, I would think it was love and it wasn't, I would debase myself, let myself be robbed

everything so dark

Rui never debased me poor devil, if he robbed me he suffered more than I did, I would take him to my dressing room to stop him from taking drugs

my father on his back in bed, the bedstead with marble decorations that were obviously pine, the image on the glass of the dresser, listen somebody on the stairs, listen a cough, listen his name

—Soraia

listen the key in the door, the money box for the saint where from time to time a coin for the Easter candle, lighting the wick, pouring wax onto a saucer, sticking the base into the liquid and the candle leaning a bit, too much smoke

a black oval on the ceiling, dark soot swirling on the curtain but the saint grateful which can be seen immediately, if she wasn't thankful punishment, gallstones, problems with the plumbing, my father on his back forgetting about the annoyance of finding a beauty spot coming unstuck, they swore to me at the boutique that this mark

—We can fix an amputated arm if necessary sweetie

and a lie, the mark in place and annoyance again, give me another handkerchief Paulo this one is a rag, pouring a drop of cologne onto it to soften the sadness because cologne you may not believe it but it helps, Rui opening the saint's money box with a knife, I took him with me to work to prevent him from turning on, I would go up to the dressing room before the last applause and he would be carefully inspecting the cards in the frame of the mirror, not admirers, a bill for the car, the gas bill, a note from an angry creditor

always angry, creditors

or maybe chatting with Vânia, Vânia playing the flute up on a rock

no, Vânia his age, not mine, on the makeup table swinging her legs, stroking his knee

higher up than the knee

oh to kick Vânia with the tip of my shoe, starting the motion and having to go back and thank the audience, so many nights with empty seats, the workers chatting at the bar with no respect for art, the doorman with his jacket unbuttoned tugging on his suspenders, Dona Amélia who worked on commission walking her candy through the empty seats, only a businessman from the north who threw us kisses or kissed the camellia and threw it onto the stage, the nuisance of picking up the camellia whose petals were dry already

what am I going to do with this?

and kissing it too, putting it in my décolletage and pretending enthusiastic movements with the flower scratching me on the breast, a wave with two fingers as the curtain closed, crossing paths with Vânia and shouting at her I'm going to demand that they fire you, did you hear, Vânia

Marcelino Gonçalves Freitas, I went so far as to protect her, just imagine

shrugging her shoulders why don't you retire Soraia, Bico da Areia for a moment, my wife finishing dinner, no Vânia to torture me, if we were careful the wages from the jewelry store were enough, the payments on the vacuum cleaner up to date even if I'd suffer sometimes when a boy on the street, not exactly suffering, something else, a guilty desire, wanting to run away, the thing that made me grow smaller on the mattress and my wife

—Why Carlos?

the shape of the legs changing on the sheet, the voice that repeated hurting me more

—Why Carlos?

and the echo trembling inside me just the way I was trembling, Judite, drinking water out here in pajamas I think

in pajamas, I never took off the pajamas

while the pine trees

not the pine trees, something else, an echo that was fading, coming back, repeating why Carlos

—Why Carlos?

pulling the leaves off the gentian one by one until the echo was silent, the house calm, the dwarf from Snow White not daring to accuse me, the glow from the river imprecise in the silence or maybe recalling those animals in a corner of the field afraid of people

a hare or a rabbit but an enormous rabbit

breathing in the darkness, a fever of owls in the strip of woods, the same ones who during the day peck at the sun with a stubborn rage, my first boss at the jewelry store was like that, I was repairing a pendulum and he with his wings folded

—Mr. Carlos

places I was learning about little by little, subway stations, urinals, the beach where there were only men and I don't dare, I don't go, I walk by the beach and I dare, going over the dune with my shoes in my hand and I go, sitting down in a corner with my chin on my knees, next to me

—Hi there

and I don't dare, Bico da Areia, my wife

—Carlos

maybe I can make it with her, I'm going to make it, I'm sorry Judite, I don't know what's in me, I don't want to go, I'm not going, even not wanting to go and an impulse to run away Alcides

—I'm Alcides

with a silver ring in the shape of a snake, an initial gesture of coiling himself, a chuckle that hurt

—Why all the rush?

feeling that I was getting rid of an uncomfortable lie when I got rid of the wedding ring, it took my wife a week to notice, she couldn't believe it, she looked for my finger again, poured herself more water and more water

—What happened to your wedding ring Carlos?

my fork poking about on the patty was answering for me

—I lost it

a silver ring in the shape of a snake taking the place of the wedding ring, Alcides who seemed to have dyed hair

—It's too big for you isn't it?

the owl with folded wings, reproving, peevish, while I was fixing the pendulum

—*What are you doing Mr. Carlos?*

my co-workers Pedro, Felipe, Francisco, me Mr. Carlos and the pendulum I could swear not inside the wood, the owl one afternoon a sob, a

—*Mr. Carlos*

detesting me but only slightly, it seemed to be sighing, whacked against the cash register, a vein of coins bled from the drawer, Francisco lifting up his chin

—*He's done for*

one of the Gypsies' horses was gasping in the alley just when the glass of water came back to the tablecloth and the fork tormented the patty, I buried the wedding ring at the beach

I remember the forefinger that was digging, digging, after the forefinger the hand, after the hand the forearm, after the forearm the arm, after the arm the shoulder, withdrawing the shoulder, the arm, the forearm, the hand, the finger and the ring on the other side of the world, the memory of the wedding cake appeared and went away, the photographer moving us closer together on the steps of the church, me happy and unhappy, me not knowing whether happy or unhappy, me thinking

—What now?

and with the wine and the food the embraces the best wishes and congratulations Carlos, me cutting the cake

which we were to return the next morning without a tear, without a lump, intact, to the photographer who'd rented the marriage ornaments, me almost happy, I think almost happy, me happy, the toasts, the winks

—Watch out how you behave don't screw us up tonight

the certainty of screwing them up tonight, I'm sure

—Of course I won't screw you up tonight

and I didn't look for the ring, maybe with the wind always shifting dunes, changes because of tides, or some tramp looking for debris with a bag, a stick, it was lost

I miss the marigolds father, I miss the gentian and the way we used to be

the glass returning to the tablecloth, the fork on the patty

—Why Carlos?

not angry, every day why Carlos in a soft voice, colleagues at the school had warned me that you, and it's not true, swear that it's not true Carlos, they wanted you to marry them, they were jealous, they were lying, and me putting out the light from lethargy, from sleepiness

—They were lying

missing the marigolds father, the mirror on the wardrobe that laid out the world, the great big world, remember, woods, sea parrots, the never-ending Sundays

—*What time is it?*

—*Two o'clock*

always two o'clock, the hands not moving, do you miss us?

Alcides and through Alcides Jácome, Licínio, Hernando, the Praça das Flores, clubs with clowns where the clowns would hold back a laugh that wasn't a laugh for a minute, there was a casting of fishhooks that scratched the skin and they'd stare at him without any envy or interest

or with envy and interest

—Who's that?

yellow kerchiefs, yellow braids, yellow bracelets, a spring almost snapping inside the breast, a spring snapping and a disappointment, a diminishing

—Oh! Carlinhos

the marigolds father, now that I've died in your place I remember the marigolds, maybe if I spoke to Dona Helena I don't know maybe if Dona Helena

that I can make out the gulls and the horses in spite of its being night, the mare that ran off from the tents and was wandering about the terrace café, a huge shape knocking things over, turning around and more tables tipped over, don't knock over the tables on the terrace father, go away with little duchess steps like the old lady with the fur cape, don't pay any attention to

—I have money Judite I'll pay

go away with little duchess steps with your remnant of makeup and your slow walk, Alcides getting him to use makeup, Licínio all you have to do is grab the microphone, dance a little and remember that you're singing, the wig was squeezing his head, the long hair swept across his nose, one of the false lashes hurt him to the point of tears, he tried a casual step, stumbled on a step, a woman in a gray smock not Dona Amélia yet, not a friend yet, asking the manager while she was polishing the floor

how sad the club was in the afternoon, those scratches on the floor, the curtain not holding any mystery, the window up above driving the sun away

—Did you hire a new performer Mr. Sales?

stuffing that changed my body and no pine cone now, no step that was mine, no thinking about you, no feeling myself, no getting annoyed that

—Dona Judite

—I've brought money Dona Judite

—I'm not like the others Dona Judite I pay

not getting annoyed with the owner of the café who made fun of me, the electrician, the pups all around you sniffing you, biting each other, going into our house with a pint of wine or some money in their hands

—Good afternoon

not getting annoyed that you got pregnant with my child, that the teachers

—I could have told you Judite

pointing me out with my belted jacket, my neckties

what's wrong with the ties?

my ways, it doesn't bother me that you don't notice me Judite,

I'm dancing take a look, the manager applauding me, Licínio and
Alcides applauding me, I don't belong in Bico da Areia, my wife
—Just a minute
waiting for me to leave so you can receive them and I'm leaving,
you have my word, the gauze glove cutting the cake under my hand
and the forefinger that wraps around mine, noticing that it was
wrapping around and getting away from the photographer, the
guests, the wig that stopped feeling tight and that I'm beginning to
like, the teachers showing you a breast without any stuffing since
the woman in the gray smock injected me with a liquid, since I
injected the liquid
—Did you notice Judite?
my face, thin once, full now, the round behind that holds up my
pants, pills that the orderly sold me with mystery and looking all
around
—If they ask you don't you even dream about my name
to get rid of hair and lighten the voice, maybe in that way the
owner of the café, the electrician, the pups with pine cones
—Dona Soraia
but the pups with pine cones with you, not with me and an
absurd haze
—Such stupidity Soraia
a kind of dampness inside the eyes as though I were jealous
—Such stupidity Soraia
or remembering the step, not you, as if all that was making me
suffer, you must believe that it doesn't make me suffer, what makes
me suffer is sitting down one day with a bag of corn on Príncipe
Real waiting for I don't know what since I'm waiting, what would
happen if I said
—Hello
if I said
—Here I am
if I said
—I've come
the little myopic look running over the boxwood trees, the hesitation of a little girl in the timid question

—Cesário?

no, the hesitation of a little girl in the question

—Rui?

putting down the flatiron whenever the doormat or the key, getting up from the bed and trotting out into the hall adjusting the wig, the quilt I keep smoothing and rumpling

—Where were you Judite?

which because of you I keep smoothing and rumpling, a face wrapped in scarves, where were you Judite what nonsense, almost smiling at the idea that a pine cone

—Where were you Rui?

Rui passing him, running away, something that doesn't belong to him breathing in his mouth, on summer afternoons, for example, you get the notion that the heat is breathing us, Rui

—Let go of me

puffs of dead leaves come out of our throats, Judite I don't know who I fixed a step for in days gone by

—Just a minute

and almost smiling about the pine cone

do you think there are pine cones in Chelas?

Rui as though his stomach was upset

—Let go of me

I followed him into the bedroom where he doesn't go to lie down, stays looking at the saint

and the street cleaners' truck with its hose on the street, workers in orange coats washing down the dawn

stays looking at the saint, taking in things, looking me over the way you look over an intruder

Dona Soraia

squatting down on the rug

—I'm cold

and I was blankets, my dressing gown, the new mantilla that they brought me from Spain, convincing him he should lie down, a cup of coffee, a brandy, Dona Aurorinha's mother respectfully studying the crack in the wall as though gods and nymphs

—Don't touch anything Aurorinha

only my father and I visited her when she had her attack, Dona Aurorinha tiny on the pillow saying good-bye with her eyebrows, Dona Aurorinha's mother

confused, grateful, shaking her by the arm

—At least say thank you, where are your manners?

with a pillowcase to be ironed in her hand

which one of us is telling this, father, I think it's you, I think it's me, I think both of us together even if we were never together, I died in your place and you're alive on Príncipe Real, the park and all that

what's the good of descriptions, what's the good of details, we know everything so well

the cedar tree and all that, the café and all that, a statue where I read the name and I can never remember, there I go getting close to it to make it out and I forget it, there's a metal letter missing on the base, the ground-floor flat empty today and no landlord to receive me, you annoyed with me, disheveled, without earrings, with an old faded vest

—Is that you?

remnants of remnants, a piece of curtain on the railing, a broken-down brush, your junk pointing in the direction of Estrela, you defeated, you all alone, Rui not wanting the blanket, the shawl, the Spanish mantilla, living somewhere else, in some other time, in a dimension that rejects you father and to which you'll never have access

—I'm cold

while at Bico da Areia

I could bet on it

a man with my mother, not the owner of the café, not the electrician, not the pups, that fellow with the napkin who interrupted his dinner to look for me at the entrance or on the wall, his clothes in the closet and you kissing a camellia at the club pretending that you were dancing, his razor on the shower shelf and you accepting the invitation of a customer, receiving the glass of bubbly that the manager

—A bit of champagne for the lady

placed on the table, the customer whimpering his feelings on your neck following a sigh that summed up his life, venturing to lay an arm that weighed a ton on your shoulder, my mother on the other side of the river brought more wine from out of the cistern, the customer choosing a perfume from Dona Amélia's tray and putting it in my purse

—A small token from a friend, girly

the lights going on and off announcing closing time, the signal from the manager to the worker and from the worker to me to ask the fur cape giving corn to the pigeons

an egg candy all wrapped in paper Dona Aurorinha with the paper in her mouth

—How do I eat it mother?

—For your little girl, Lucinda

where can the gods and the nymphs be, the friend of Dona Aurorinha's mother, hairy and with horns, playing the flute on a rock, the manager handing me the fur cape

—Remember my ten percent Soraia

leaving the club with my little duchess steps, collar up to protect me from the vulgarity of the street, the customer

—Where are we going, girly?

and somebody I don't know where, I think over an oilcloth table cover in São João da Caparica or in Alto do Galo, in Trafaria or in Cova do Vapor

don't lie father, the lying's all over, what's the good of lying, no matter how much it's hard on you

and it is hard on you isn't it, and you're surprised that it's hard on you

the oilcloth table cover at Bico da Areia, green and white checkered squares, I can still see the green and white squares, the burn marks that always bothered you

such a nice tablecloth

and no matter how many attempts or cleaners we couldn't get it really clean, somebody in my house in Bico da Areia, somebody besides the owner of the café and the electrician and the pups

—Dona Judite Dona Judite

capable of giving you what I never gave you, treating you the way

I never treated you, not humiliating you in front of your colleagues at the same time that the customer with me in the little room in Beato, the bellboy

—Sixteen is taken Soraia you can have twelve but it's a dump

tiled walls because it used to be a kitchen, the marble square where the stove used to be, the stove itself pushed up against the bed and the stove legs four rusty things, pothooks serving as a clothes rack and in the middle of all this a lamp shade with fly specks and the floor made of bricks, the window blocking out whatever was beyond the window casement, somebody in my house in Bico da Areia and Judite was hugging him, somebody in my chair using my knife and fork but that wasn't it, what do I care about the knife and fork, what mattered to me was your way of looking, my nonexistence in you, my not mattering, the customer struggling with his shirt

—Give me a little help here, girly

without noticing that one of the buttons had popped off

I noticed it

and I'm so clumsy, and I'm sorry, to myself

—Shut up

what could there be beyond the window panes, the marks of the stove that seemed to be calling me talking about you, about your plans for a bigger house with a proper living room, if my wife would give up the owner of the café, the electrician, the pups, the bottles of wine and me there, I don't see how but there, can't you see, my wife

—Carlos

and I swear to you I won't stay silent like that smoothing and rumpling the protection

the quilt

I don't stay silent like that smoothing and rumpling the quilt, I lie down beside you, for the first time in my life I lie down by you without any fear and the design of your legs doesn't change on the sheet, I'm not sleepy, I don't invent excuses, I'm not frightened, beyond the windowpanes of the boardinghouse the woods, the Gypsies' tents, the gentian that I'm going to take care of tomorrow in spite of the customer's clothes on the hooks all orderly, topcoat, pants, in spite of the

 —Girly

 the

 —Don't squeeze so tight, girly

 it surprised me that it wasn't him I was squeezing, how could I squeeze him if I'm not with him, I never was with him, I'm with your abandonment, your contentment, your thankful peace and the marigolds

 so close by

 glowing for us.

CHAPTER

I THINK IT WAS Rui one night at the club, when my father was trying the plumes on his head for the finale, older in spite of the
makeup

or was I just thinking older

thinner judging from the way the fabric hung loose around his
waist and over his shoulders, taking longer than usual to get ready,
every so often a wince I didn't give much importance to, a pause as
he gathered his strength while he pretended absentmindedness, he
wasn't absentminded, isn't that right father, he'd move his hands
about among sprays, brushes, dropping pieces of lacework that
slipped

how come I didn't notice that?

from his fingers, not wanting us to turn on the radio or talk to
him, telling us to be quiet with a gesture that wasn't a gesture or an
order or a request, which maybe wasn't whatever it was supposed to
be except

—I feel so tired

(but you've felt tired so many times, daddy)

and he would accompany it all with a yawn that made his teeth
larger and that frightened me, finally standing up as though he
didn't see us and I think in fact he wasn't seeing us, his eyes weren't
blinking outwardly but inwardly, my father realizing that the music
was waiting for him, his colleagues were on stage, the manager's
nephew

—You're the only one missing Soraia

one of the plumes falling off beside the door and his shoulders hunching over annoyed

his shoulders not hunching over annoyed, a lie, that's not the way it was, he was concerned, he turned back, tied it on, studied himself in the mirror asking

—How's that?

as the sound of his heels went off Rui went to the table to filch a cigarette, sneaking open my father's bag as though he were still there with us, they say your old man's sick, they say he's going to die Paulo, like that or with other words

it's doesn't matter

it's hard for me to remember but it was something like that I think

—They say your old man's sick, they say he's going to die Paulo

and objects became different all at once, my father's comb, my father's watch, his key case, things worth nothing suddenly frightening, Rui with the cigarette hidden in his hand even though he's not there, dancing down below

—Your bronchitis Rui

waving the smoke away with his hand, they say your old man's sick and a song the loudspeakers were distorting, they say he's going to die Paulo and ashes on the floor I study my face in the mirror to see if I'm surprised, if I'm sad, Rui scattering the ashes with his shoe, unscrewing the top of a cold-cream jar and putting out the cigarette, the grand finale with the whole cast dancing off the stage, cardboard hats, laughter like shattering glass, my father back here in a rush, not sick, obviously not sick, taking off his shoes, sighing, undoing the fasteners on his back that were scratching his spine

—Hurry up and get these plumes off me

Rui and I pulling on his hairdo, the wig coming off with the plumes in a tug and my father furious, hating his baldness

—Can't you people be more careful?

and me I don't know whether I'm relieved or sorry for him, for that very old face coming out from under the painted one as he cleaned off his jaw, his cheeks, his mouth, under the jaw, the cheeks, and the mouth were another jaw, other cheeks, a different mouth, underneath the others still others maybe and which of them was you, the father I knew or a man I don't know emerging from the woman who was hiding him

I don't know how to explain this

a woman

in the end a woman, explain that to me

replacing purple lipstick with red lipstick, a pearl vest with a black dress, tin bracelets with a gold bracelet

no, Rui had pawned the gold bracelet, or they'd pawned it together

tin bracelets with a silver bracelet, not genuine silver, the kind where street jewelers carve their mark with a jackknife, wanting to ask him

—Aren't you glad to be dying and putting an end to all this aren't you glad to be free of all this?

when really I was the one who was glad to be free of all this, of the people who turned to look on the street

—Father

and my father adjusting his skirt offended

—Don't call me father

running his hand through the air petting an invisible lap dog or Persian cat, we didn't have any lap dogs or Persian cats, we had a mastiff dragging his leash between his legs, the one from Fonte da Telha on that night when Rui and the headlights of the Jeep and the policeman

—Do you know him?

the doctor removing his white fingernails, the sound of the waves coming from somewhere and the smell of the sea in front of me or next to me

next to me I think even if the water wasn't next to me, farther off, and its glow by which I mean a lot of little scattered glows, the policeman

—Do you know him?

and me

—I don't know him

while my father was arranging the bangs of his wig over his forehead

—Can't you people be more careful?

while a muscle in his poor arm was trembling, the wish for a place somewhere I could escape to and walk among the trees down to the river

to Chelas because in Chelas we

or maybe it wasn't Rui one night at the club, it was Mr. Couceiro in Anjos as though he were still carrying my suitcase from the hospital, we were in Campo de Santana where the question-mark swans slipped along with idle questions, weightless but making painful wounds

—What about you Paulo?

—What about tomorrow Paulo?

—What are you going to do with your life Paulo?

me, obviously, crushing a leaf from a bush

—You people stop tormenting me, shut up

and while at Anjos

—Paulo

while fearfully

—Paulo

and Dona Helena setting the table in silence, no flower in Noémia's vase, the picture in need of cleaning, the neglected bed

—Have you forgotten your daughter Dona Helena have you grown tired of her already?

the clouds not just in the window but here inside too brown, I mean in the window I can't remember, here inside brown, opaque, Dona Helena and Mr. Couceiro slower, more resigned, more useless, a Japanese was spying on us from the trunk aiming his rifle and on taking a better look it was an umbrella sticking out of the cane rack with a cap on top, as always when the clouds were like that I thought about the bicycle in the laundry room, the bell that for weeks now

or months?

I hadn't touched it, I looked at it and didn't feel like touching it what in hell made me not feel like touching it?

the bicycle and I we don't need any heroín, me to the Mulatto with the jackknife, to the maid from the dining room, to Dália, to all of them

—I don't need any heroin

pedaling through the Baixa not to Príncipe Real, not to Bico da Areia, just pedaling through the Baixa, I didn't touch her, I looked at her and I didn't feel like touching her

why in hell didn't I feel like touching her?

the bicycle and I didn't need any heroin, I said to the Mulatto with a jackknife, to the maid from the dining room, to Dália, to everybody

I don't need any heroin

pedaling through the Baixa, not to Bico da Areia, just pedaling through the Baixa, the cane feeling along the carpet and all those corpses in the rice paddies of Timor, all those names in Latin, all those strange bushes when Mr. Couceiro

—They say your father's sick they say he's going to die Paulo

Dona Helena putting dinner onto the plates

there were times when I liked seeing her putting dinner onto the plates, peaceful almost, a conviction that I belonged to a home, the questions from the disenchanted swans

—I have a home do you hear?

or maybe it wasn't Mr. Couceiro, Mr. Couceiro not daring to tell me, what's the use just another buffalo corpse, those nostrils, those open eyes, it was my father one Sunday when I found him lying there with no makeup, bald, talking to the ceiling, still talking to the ceiling even when he knew I was there, that tasteless ceiling

the idea of talking to the ceiling would never have occurred to me

the lumps and the stucco rosettes of an aged ceiling, I remember sheets on the balcony clothesline, clothespins on the floor, the garden and etc., the cedar and etc., the café and etc., the mastiff with a bow that I pushed away with my knee, a lozenge of sunlight dragging its snot across the mattress and then my father

—They say I'm sick they say I'm going to die Paulo

not to me because he was reaching up to every spiral in the

stucco in that void of past times, on the other side of the river when he was running away motionless and my mother was suspicious of I don't know what

—Carlos

my mother a minute earlier

—Carlos

and I was imagining my mother a minute earlier

—Carlos

when Carlos, because Carlos interests you, ma'am, in Lisbon, on this side of the Tagus, uninterested in everything with a cup of soup warmed for him by someone I don't know who and that he'll never drink, making me come closer in order to hear his voice as though he were talking about someone else in some other place, in some other time

—They say I'm sick Paulo

and when you come to think about it, he was talking about someone else in some other place, in some other time, a piece of news that had nothing to do with him, a piece of news of no interest, what's so important about

—They say I'm going to die Paulo

compared to the bathtub that had been out of order for a long time and that he was using as a storage bin, the washbasin propped up by a broom handle with only the left faucet giving out a stingy trickle and all the while chandeliers, damask bedspreads, the hole into the cellar by the baseboard where mice were all moving about when you put your ear to it and scurrying and squeaking, the mastiff with a bow making the hole bigger with his claws, it rained on him in the bedroom and the living room, because there wasn't enough money to keep up the apartment, because they paid him so little, why that notice from the court about the rent

because as a matter of fact you are sick, because as a matter of fact you are going to die father

have the saint on the dresser and the candle in the saucer been of any use to you?

and as the trees in the park evaporated and the park evaporated into a filthy dome where streetlights and shadows fluttered about, helping him get ready for the night's show, painting his mouth and eyes which the Easter candle filled with tremors as they reached me in a tidal fluctuation while my mother in the garden thought she'd spotted the clown on a corner along with the wine and the pups, taking her inside, looking for a blouse in the wardrobe and fixing up both of them, the collar button that was slipping out of my fingers and their annoyed faces in the mirror, existing only in the mirror because for me they were only hands grabbing mine, the heads of both in one single head, their voices in one single resignation

—I never saw anyone so clumsy damn it

putting on their stockings and long gloves, knocking over the picture of an actress or the dwarf from Snow White while choosing a vial with some perfume among dozens of empty vials, empty jars, empty tubes, getting confused over the earrings in the jewelry box where there were also shells, rubber bands, a stamp from the Congo

a zebra I think

with a piece of envelope, my father rejecting the earrings dropping a brush

—It's the white ones, ninny

and for an instant we're in Bico da Areia and Príncipe Real at the same time because you could hear the waves and the cedar and I seemed to be hearing horses

—Do you hear the horses Rui?

Rui putting out his cigarette in the cold-cream jar and covering it with the lid, I think my mother is looking at us and finally the curtain or maybe my mother making excuses to her colleagues

someday I'm going to get Rui and take him to see the horses

—I'm not going with him anymore

my father's not sick, they were wrong, a lie that he was sick, tired, and the cup of soup

—They say I'm going to die Paulo

horses and more horses coming back from the sea, sometimes along with the herons on the bridge beams at other times running on the Alto do Galo with the cadence of dreams, my father doesn't reach for me, doesn't lose his balance on his high heels, from the Rua da Palmeira, practicing a curtsy or a polka step horses and more horses Rui, dozens of horses

he bows to a performer from a neighboring club, and the two of them linger fluttering and twittering discussing lovers, sandals, and nylons, the performer takes the picture of her stepdaughter from her purse

what do you mean dozens, hundreds of horses, thousands of horses, billions of horses

whom she hasn't seen for twenty years

—She's an engineer Soraia

and she whispers

—I can still get into my clothes, I haven't gotten fat at all

in the coffee shop by the factory door, the performer is a middle-aged gentleman among middle-aged gentlemen blocking the window having forgotten his coffee cup, taken by a freckle-faced creature lacking in any beauty and my father who miraculously still had some pity left

—Quite beautiful

the creature waiting for a bus unable to see him, not an engineer why all the fibbing?

a factory girl more likely, the performer cleaning the window muttering proud remarks, I imagine like

—She's an engineer Soraia

his glasses fogging up making it hard to define things, rain or something like that, I'd say rain, it might be raining on us, attempting a signal that no one answered, the bus hid the freckle-faced girl and as it disappeared around the corner no bus no freckle-face, the wave of a magician's hand and an empty stage, cleaning them better in hopes that habit would scrub the lenses and nothing but buildings, a cat, other working girls

other engineers waiting, the coffee machine spouting steam, my father hiding his pity

—Let's go Milá

and the performer

and the middle-aged gentleman blending into the window, blowing his nose or his forehead, a line of mascara on his cheek, imploring

—Soraia

a kiss on the tip of his fingers that nobody received or a few hours later a customer in the first row would put into his pocket and the middle-aged gentleman

—It's not yours

knocking over the champagne, looking for the kiss among datebooks and change, the chicken-like fluttering of the dancers, the manager

—Missy

the tatter of a kiss that didn't get beyond the coffee shop dripping down the glass, gathering on the cigarette butts and the rinds on the floor that my father and the middle-aged gentleman stepped on as they went to the door while the customer in the first row was adjusting his lapel, accepting the apologies of the management, a bottle of champagne with the compliments of the manager, two clowns for free to finish out the night and even so indignation, datebooks and change on the table, the lining of his pockets exhibited all around

—But what kiss what kiss?

the kiss swept away with cigarette butts and rinds, the factory invisible at two in the morning, only its gullet of an entrance and a garage on the left, the horses were licking the salt on the bridge beams, the flamingos in a farewell circle off to the rivers of Tunisia, Milá resting in the dressing room with the help of the works inspector with whom she would wake up at the start of each month until the money ran out

the honking of the geese that I think I'm hearing

and a pill for the nerves that my father gave me, the honking of the geese that I hear as I sleep, Rui sneaking open the bag and stealing a cigarette as though my father were there

—They say your old man's sick they say he's going to die Paulo

and the flamingos and the geese swirling over the poplars, Dona Helena tottering with rheumatism incapable of helping me, my father isn't sick, he's going along the Rua da Palmeira with me, practicing a curtsy or a polka step, he may be leaning on my shoulder but it's because of a loose paving stone you understand, he needs a cup of soup or to spend the afternoon talking to the ceiling and looking out the window at the park and all that, the cedar and all that, the café and all that, Mr. Couceiro would visit the cemetery with the angry expression of an asthmatic bothered by the air, needles pricking his lungs

—Oh! doctor when I breathe

—Shall we be going, lad?

diabetes, urea, not a body, pieces that were wasting away each by itself, the liquid my father injected into his breast exploding onto his skin, Dona Amélia without cigarettes or candy or perfume laying a camellia on the grave and that was what Rui didn't want to see, refused to see, that must have been why he went to the beach in the afternoon with the syringe and the spoon, whistling to the mastiff with a bow who was off sniffing at trash, at the cemetery no flamingos or geese, sparrows, butterflies, one big one, emerald green, hopping about through the laurels, my mother playing hopscotch along the village graves

shelves with doilies, paper flowers, curtains

she would mark the gravestones with pieces of chalk, numbering them, toss a pebble, and leap onto them with one leg, the wind brought the smell of mimosas down from the mountains and now my mother not playing on the gravestones, not playing with anything, so far away and grown up

—Do you have a picture of when you were little, mother?

Mr. Couceiro waiting for me at the cemetery, impatient with me

—Shall we be going, lad?

his cane hanging from his wrist and a bouquet of gillyflowers forgotten in his hand, incapable of placing it on my father's coffin, taking the bouquet to the maid from the dining room without knowing how to give it to her

—Take it

and her thanking me at the movies as soon as the lights went slowly down and I was fascinated by the world that ceases to exist, by my mother who disappears, maybe the smell of the mimosas fainter and more distant, the maid from the dining room happy with the gillyflowers squeezing my fingers, the breathing of a drowsy boat that rocks and calms me, Rui must have gone to the beach in the afternoon

there's a bus at three o'clock

and after taking the train from Costa da Caparica to Fonte da Telha holding back the mastiff who was barking at the waves, touching the needles and the piece of newspaper afraid of losing them, finding the place near the rocks where Soraia and I, the mastiff as though he understood

he doesn't understand

licking me on the ears, the wound on its haunch that the vet can't cure, Paulo at the movies stroking a neck that doesn't move away, accepts him, the gillyflowers sliding down from the lap of the maid from the dining room, muscles that stiffen, permit, relax, the look of recognition and all the gillyflowers on the floor, the hand over mine almost inert, wet, it seems to me that

—Paulo

in spite of the sound of the film, her mouth

—Paulo

sketching out the letters of my name one by one

—Paulo

asking her to repeat

—Paulo

and

—Paulo

and

—Paulo

and

—Paulo

my name changing when spoken by her, deeper, fuller

—Paulo

Mr. Couceiro with an asthmatic whistle

—Shall we be going, lad?

without, thank God, the maid from the dining room, wearing a blouse with fish and anchors which I'm not sure I like

I like it

wearing the necklace with a cross, it looks to me like the solemn communion picture back home in the living room, a childish appetite for lollipops and cake, they tell me I'm sick, they tell me I'm going to die

—Paulo

after the movies over the broken-down wall in Chelas, the impression of a wig, false fingernails, eyes suddenly open that run away from me, protest

—You're pulling out my hair Paulo

sure of padding on the breasts and hips, a clown with me pretending to be you, pushing her up against the bricks, grabbing her head, breaking the chain

—You're a man

tearing her skirt and underneath the skirt, where I'd expected something, no toy, emptiness, the jackdaw who won't leave us alone, a damp heat that contracts and gets away from me, letting go of her blouse, her hair, a foolish smile instead of a bouquet of gillyflowers

—I'm sorry

and you not saying anything why, scared why, looking around for help why, kneeling and looking for the chain with the crucifix why, the glint of the little cross in the grass, your hand closed over the cross that you wore for me over the anchors and the fish, the desire to make love to me, for me to marry you, to live with you in Bico da Areia and then wine, right? and then your body swelling, right? and then why Paulo?

and then why Carlos?

the owner of the café with a bottle

—Judite

the smell of mimosas and the mountain wind, the crucifix that you wore for me and hide from me now, Paulo's mother in the cemetery leaping on the gravestones and winning a game from the electrician, the pups, an insistent owl on the bedroom blind, there isn't any Bico da Areia, only the mountains and the mimosas, shelves with doilies, paper flowers, curtains, the blacksmith's forge dribbling sparks, everything so slow, everything so eternal, they're eight years old and therefore they don't call

—Dona Judite

they don't appear on the step

—I've brought money I can pay

the schoolbooks that they leave on a gravestone, their pebbles for playing hopscotch

—Can I jump, Juditinha?

my grandmother's brother

Grandmother Cora, she made pumpkin sweets in cardboard cups

he was a harbor pilot in the Azores, Corvo, Pico, Faial, I remember the names of the islands, even today I do a good job brushing my teeth, my brain goes along repeating Corvo Pico Faial, Corvo Pico Faial and the taste of pumpkin sweets on my tongue, heating the spoon more than once so the fix will melt and the syringe is full, the first vein showing up under the rubber band too dark, the second vein larger, the needle finding it swelling, tendons and this warmth in the chest, this acceptance of what, the mastiff nipping at my shirt with a strange whining and no pain, no discomfort in the kidneys, Paulo, Soraia's nephew, Soraia's cousin, Soraia's son

Soraia's son

repairing the gold chain in Chelas

—I'm sorry

Mr. Couceiro accompanied him from the cemetery to Anjos the way he'd accompanied his father at night to the show at the club, they say your old man's sick, they say he's going to die Paulo, Dona Helena going out to the doorway on a nutty impulse, the memory of Noémia where silence was growing in the dust of the corners, where bangs and skinny little legs, a stack of school notebooks, a broken pencil sharpener, when the sound of dishes stopped in the kitchen and the clock on the church forgot about the sparrows, the three of you

the three of us quiet in the living room waiting for what, thinking about what, wanting what, the Avenida Almirante Reis which never changed, furniture stores, lunchrooms, dentists, on Mr. Couceiro's birthday a comrade from Timor with a decoration in his lapel and whose hand hung from ours like a dead hare, we grasped the hare

—Where shall I put this?

we stayed looking at the hand when the corpse disappeared into the sleeve reappearing in a kind of slipping, the little paws of his fingers wobbling trying to grasp the spoon, Dona Helena afraid that the hare would cling to her arm and stay there slowly decomposing, the rest of the comrade also a hare, maybe only moribund, gobbling potatoes, his grandson came to get him after dinner and led all of that, the decoration, the animals, far away from us and I got the feeling that pieces of gray fur were floating in the living room

my mother used to get the feeling that owl feathers were floating in the bedroom when she opened the window, the village cemetery, the graves of the soldiers gassed in France, flowerpots taller than the treetops glistening in the sun, autumn leaves spinning around the chapel the way voices spun around in Bico da Areia

—Dona Judite, I can pay

not from the pups, from the soldiers from the war without uniforms without skulls

—Dona Judite, I can pay

even today for example the owner of the café with me, and I repeating to myself Corvo Pico Faial, Corvo Pico Faial, a hint of mimosas, a taste of pumpkin pudding, the sideboard they'd painted red with a trim of roses, my grandmother

—Juditinha

the first rains of October scattering gulls, the month when they say my father's going to die, mother, the month when Rui at Fonte da Telha not lying down yet, waiting, the distance that was growing between what for him was him and for the mastiff and for us

the cop

—*Do you know him?*

and I don't know, I don't know this man

a stranger with a stolen cigarette in the dressing room putting it out with his fingers so that I to the cop

—I don't know this man

similar to Rui with his loafers, his clothes, but not Rui, not Rui, Rui arriving at Príncipe Real, wrapped in mufflers, not like this, not undressed, one of his socks on, the other that the mastiff had pulled off and that high tide would carry off, Rui

make note of this

at Príncipe Real, bronchitis at the door, the clown who got up out of bed to insist on some tisane, soothing syrup, and a hateful arm, not listless, hateful

—Let go of me faggot

while what wasn't an arm was folding up on the living-room couch among nickel-plated deer and mice on candlesticks, clowns' treasures that didn't make me sad, made me laugh, in Vânia's room a velvet hippopotamus, in Micaela's garret a theatrical pause

—Take a look

the light was dimmed and the signs of the zodiac were fluorescent on the ceiling, down below we were blue, skin, hair, envy, pointing to Sagittarius, Libra, soda crates with small knitted cushions serving as chairs, Micaela a tiny character floating head down from Capricorn to Gemini, not a person, a planet with no orbit in a blue immensity, indifferent to the pawn tickets piling up on a spindle

—Isn't it beautiful?

just the way Rui was floating at Fonte da Telha, indifferent to the train that was going off on its toy rails through bushes, willows, the mastiff who was nipping his pant legs, the ever-so-distant voice of someone beside him and he didn't care whose it was

a fisherman, the cook from the seafood stand on the beach, a tramp with a battered bucket hunting for mussels at low tide

—What's this?

Juditinha leaning over to check the stone and advance along the chalk marks, sounds that came and went without belonging to the cemetery or the waves, it might be people calling, footsteps, Rui's aunt on the telephone with a friend

—Listen to this, Pilar

an attention full of raised eyebrows, her hand completely covering the surprise on her mouth

—I can't believe it

my aunt putting down the phone, crossing the room and Fonte da Telha, leaning over me as I hid the syringe in my pants

—Really Rui what a dumb thing to do, killing yourself

going back to the phone shaking her head and then telling Pilar

—Listen, Rui committed suicide

eyes on the wall as though she were listening with them, her hand sliding down her face

—Are you serious?

covering the water, the beach, the sun wasn't a cloud, it was she, Pilar's buzzing as she knitted comments together, the disapproval from the Chinese masks in the niches on the shelves

—I swear I never would have thought it Rui we gave you everything didn't we?

the Indian rugs, the English easy chairs, the first floor where the study and the bedrooms are, the plastic giraffe floating motionless in the swimming pool, the chauffeur in an apron with a rake

—We gave you everything didn't we?

tidying up the garden, we gave him everything, schools, vacations in Switzerland, a place in the business

the cop

—*Do you know him?*

and Paulo

—*I don't know this man*

and look what happened, you put us through such shameful situations with your awful friends

—*I know Rui, I don't know this man here*

he sold the apartment we'd bought for him he stole from us

playing hopscotch on the gravestones, shelves with doilies, paper flowers, curtains

they told us about drugs, strange goings-on, a wretched woman twice his age

a man aunt, a man

be quiet, a wretched woman twice his age in a beggar's hovel on Príncipe Real

explain to Pilar it's a man aunt, I'm living with a man

a beggar's hovel on Príncipe Real, naturally we forbade him from coming into our home

the gravel path, the lignum-vitae warrior just inside the door

Corvo Pico Faial, Corvo Pico Faial

his uncle had them tell the gardener not to let him come looking for us, it seems that the wretched woman

—I can't believe it

I swear to you that the wretched woman

and her hand completely hiding the surprise on her mouth

—Are you serious?

hiding the water, the beach, the sun, it wasn't a cloud or the albatrosses who at this time of year, the albatrosses, it was she, the chauffeur who knew me as a child not on Príncipe Real, in Ajuda, at that time a first floor in Ajuda with Tapada left behind

—Boy

surprised at the beat-up stove

I'm just brushing my teeth or getting lunch or ironing and the taste of pumpkin sweet on my tongue

a wig on the cane stand, Soraia in a bathrobe straightening the padding on her breast

—Your uncle sends word that you shouldn't try to look for the boy

I don't know him, I don't know this man here, it's not Rui it's a sneak thief with a stolen cigarette in my father's dressing room putting it out between his fingers, the cigarette that Dona Amélia

—*A little gift for the one you've chosen, sir?*

or candy, or perfume, my father with a flourish of refusal pushing away the tray

—Chocolate is fattening

and not just the beat-up stove, the lunch plates that didn't match, the cheap wine, my aunt coming back from the telephone

really Rui what a dumb thing killing yourself, we've given you everything, schools, vacations in Switzerland, an apartment that you sold for drugs, a job without any responsibilities or

the mastiff barking at the waves, won't stop barking at the waves, pulls at my socks with his teeth

—*Rui*

easy work in the firm, we brought you to us after your father's accident, you never lacked for anything, right, we've never treated you badly and now

well done

the train that was going away toward the beach on little toy tracks through reeds, weeping willows, and now you see, everything far away from you, an unawareness of what, the difficulty of seeing only shapeless silhouettes

—What's this?

or maybe tramps with a battered bucket in search of mussels at low tide while Paulo at the movies with the maid from the dining room, the blouse with fish and anchors, the cologne that reminds me of Bico da Areia and my mother waiting for my father opening her décolletage a little, noticing me, closing it, it seemed to me that one of the Gypsies' horses is beside the wall or maybe it's the marigolds in the flower bed, my mother noticing me again and opening it again

how old is my mother?

—Carlos

the mouth of the maid from the dining room

in spite of the noise from the film

sketching out one by one the letters of my name

plane trees, plane trees and doves, a coin for a cup of coffee friend

—Paulo

the broken-down wall in Chelas and the two notes of the jackdaw, the little handbag that must have belonged to you mother, your older sister's earrings, Rui going up to the dressing table

—They say your old man's sick they say he's going to die Paulo

her body getting smaller on a corner of cement and bricks, sure that just like my father a wig

—You lied to me you lied to me

artificial eyelashes, the enormous eyelids lamenting, protesting

—You scared me Paulo

sure of a clown with me, the beat-up stove, pages from a magazine on the walls at Ajuda, grabbing her head, breaking the chain

—You're a man aren't you, you're a man aren't you?

and you not saying anything because, scared because, crying but why, wanting to please me, for me to marry you, to live with you in Bico da Areia or at Príncipe Real or in Ajuda

—You're living with me in Bico da Areia or on Príncipe Real or in Ajuda don't be disappointed don't get mad I'm going to be a woman I promise stay with me Rui

Paulo, my name is Paulo

stay with me Paulo, sell the chain and the cross to the Cape Verdeans but stay with me Paulo, wait for me in the dressing room, go home with me, help me along the Rua da Palmeira because I'm tired Paulo, I haven't grown thin, my clothes don't bag on me around the waist or across the shoulders, it doesn't take me longer than usual to fix myself up, the lace doesn't slip out of my fingers, I still have a lot of years left Paulo

I still have a lot of years left Rui

I still have a lot of years left Rui before I get old, stop dancing, a lot of years for us to go to Fonte da Telha, take the little train along the beach through reeds, weeping willows, turning the dog loose and watching him run alongside the waves, stop, call us, chase a gull that lingered there, bring us a piece of seaweed as a present, a piece of willow, a twisted branch, really Rui what a dumb thing killing yourself, hear the manager's nephew calling me

—They're all waiting for you Soraia

so if you'll excuse me I'm going down on stage and if you peek through the curtain you'll see me, in the middle of a tango, saying good-bye to you.

CHAPTER

WE USED TO LIVE near Sintra and when my father would take us to Cabo da Roca on Sundays he'd always announce here's where the world begins, this is the beginning of the world, I'd look around and nothing was there but the desolation of the wind, crags, bushes blown over and the sea down below, the wind was stronger than the sea so there was only the sound of the wind, no sound of waves, all of Europe behind us, Uruguay and Canada waiting to be invented like my father used to say leaning out into the distance mixing in with the clouds, nothing existed except us and the schoolteacher's tiptoe caravels poking around in the emptiness looking for the latitude of an island waiting to be discovered in that extent of shadows, there was Sintra and beyond Sintra, Madrid or France a long time from here, not now, taking a bath because the heater jet was a full corolla and not just one small petal, my mother serving the soup, telling us to be quiet

—Stop playing with your fork Otília

every day of the week

(and us with plenty of days of the week to spend, Fridays, Thursdays, Sundays, I can't remember a greater number of Fridays, for example, except during those times

—Stop playing with your fork Otília)

Wednesdays and Tuesdays and Saturdays, what we had plenty of were days, ask me about just any one of them and I'll fill you up a whole stack of them right away, take Thursdays, Wednesdays, take Sundays with Otília playing with her fork at dinner, as soon as she stopped playing with her fork she got married, my father got run over, and the petal in the shower never turned into a full corolla again, America must have begun because movies and all that, as soon as my father was gone my stepfather arriving with his suitcase

—Good evening

my mother to him

—It hasn't been a week since I got rid of Otília and now I've got the other one with the same manias, leave that fork alone Gabriela

I started working in the dining room at the hospital and the number of days began to get smaller right away, if you ask for any Mondays I'll have to steal them off the calendar because I have almost none left, on payday morning my stepfather would go to the office with me and collect the money

—I'm going to hold it for you don't worry

and he would hold it so efficiently that I never got to see it, from my sister now and then a pair of shoes, a blouse with anchors and fish that her husband doesn't like, I imagine Cabo da Roca and the crags and the wind still there far away sometimes on the Malveira road, my father on the bus with nostalgia for the sea

—When are we going to go look at the waves Gabriela?

I don't know whether I was intrigued or happy looking for him and nobody there, the conductor

—Did you lose something miss?

my father back from his grave number two hundred forty-eight in the Sintra cemetery, no gravestone, just earth and a number marked on a stake among lots of numbers marked on stakes, continuing on to the old station where we pretend they still sell tickets at a window with no grating, going into the vacant lot where the circus was in December, if you were quiet you could hear the tigers at night, a Chinese man with a pencil behind his ear was feeding them chickens, with me opening my mouth and wanting some chicken too and my father insistent, forgetting he was dead, and my mania of going there and not getting to touch him I caught his smell, I saw the full corolla of gas

—When are we going to go look at the waves Gabriela?

a chair at the table that squeaked all by itself, the tureen moving and nobody else noticing it, the bushes where the world begins bent over in the living room, the schoolteacher's tiptoe caravels at anchor on the high seas and no mother no stepfather

—What's all this?

no mother no stepfather

—A whole lot of Wednesdays for what?

long, terribly slow, full of multiplication tables and rivers, father unscrewing a light bulb and the soup growing dark, his place isn't here, be patient, go away, this guy is here haven't you noticed, you've got grave number two hundred forty-eight waiting on the strip of land next to the circus, stay with the trapeze artists, have some fun, rest easy, my stepfather checking my pay

—Who are you talking to, Gabriela?

my father mocking him

—Who are you talking to, Gabriela?

my mother who hadn't let out a sound to me

—Are you looking for a slap in the face, you fresh kid?

an invisible dog in the yard just before ours, nothing but a black snout between two boards, teeth showing, throwing his body toward me unable to get to me, above the yard a window with no light and hiding behind the windowpane my father maybe fighting against the wind

—Where the world begins Gabriela

laid out so nicely in the coffin, so distinguished, so serious, a proper dead man that my mother was proud of

—He looks like a doctor don't you think?

the flame of the candles was pouring light over his face and changing the shape of his features as though he was speaking, maybe he was speaking, making his silent speech about Cabo da Roca, the bushes, the cliffs, the poor little tiptoe caravels looking for a latitude, if I think about it today I can picture my stepfather in the chapel among the neighbor women and the smell of the vinegar they clean dead people with, my sister

—That's him

pointing to my stepfather, to the cap he was twisting in his fingers, the suitcase in the center of the living room, that is

—Good evening

taking charge of everything, regulating my time, stopping me from going out

—I won't stand for much foolishness Gabriela

a desolation of wind and bushes with no Uruguay or Canada, the plane trees around the dining room at the hospital, my fellow worker laughing with me at a patient in the yard, not Paulo yet, a little old man with an untouched basket of peaches and a wife whining

—Have you lost your appetite Dionísio?

imagining my mother in her Sunday clothes begging for explanations from the orderlies, the doctors

—He's lost his taste for peaches

buying cigarettes because my father had rejected the basket, a butt friend, and at that point Paulo with a woman I took to be his mother and the woman

—I'm not his mother I'm his aunt

a princess or an actress my fellow worker was envious of her necklaces, her hair

—She must be an actress Gabriela

a young fellow Paulo's age with her and the woman

—My boyfriend

one of the waiters whistling in derision and she not hearing it with the disdain of a queen, perfume so thick you could grab it in your hand, it carried into the building and covered the frying smell from the kitchen, my fellow worker, actresses are like that, boyfriends too young or too old trailing after them with trained love, the plane trees that never noticed whatever it might be, agreeing, of course, they said that nothing mattered and with their lack of personality

—Obviously

the young man Paulo's age spent a long time in the visitors' bathroom taking a spoon out of his pocket and he came out after what seemed like years stumbling through the pigeons, glowing as though his cheeks had been polished with an oily cloth, his smile going along all by itself ahead of his lips, Paulo made me think of the cabins at Cabo da Roca that protected you from the wind and maybe that was when I took an interest in him, all those cliffs, those bent-over bushes, a swirl of rain toward Sintra and him standing in the yard, not asking for cigarettes, not asking for money, accepting a peach from the wife with the basket and lingering as he rolled it in his hand, the actress

—Paulo

the caravels moored to a promontory or an island when they finally found that latitude they could trust, the actress's boyfriend not looking at anyone, rubbing his arm and leaning against the trunk of a tree while his smile billowed out and traveled over nameless oceans with him, the actress waving her fans and gold jewelry about, me, poor me, the solemn communion chain and the ring my godmother had given me as a child and my stepfather

—Let me see, it's fake isn't it?

he sold it, I know because my father from grave number two hundred forty-eight

—He sold your ring Gabriela

Madrid and France didn't exist for now, a Europe with roads that didn't lead anywhere except to eucalyptus trees and villages of emigrant workers on the slopes of mountains, the dog ready to bark at me, bite me, the eye between the boards turning into my mother's eye serving my father and me our meal

—Are you looking for a slap in the face, you fresh kid?

not to my father because there wasn't even a picture of my father on display, dead, my mother was thinking, and me without her hearing that's a lie, he's not, we go to Cabo da Roca, we have long talks, she must have thrown away the pictures, the stamp collection, the Spanish razor, but forgot and kept the jacket he wasn't wearing in his coffin

not the Sunday one, the one I like best, with diamond shapes in the weave

and my stepfather was wearing it, my father was leaning against the doorframe with my mother mistakenly thinking it was me

—Doesn't he look just like a scarecrow Gabriela?

my father who when he was alive, during the time when we had

plenty of days, lots of days, more days than you could shake a stick
at, Fridays, Thursdays, Mondays and with us not knowing what to
do with so many idle hours, the silent memory of the tweezers and
the album trading stamps from Singapore for some from Denmark, maybe my mother

—Aquiles

he would raise his head and the magnifying glass at the same
time and look at her with an enormous eye, lids larger than window
shades in the glass disk, a very normal body that is but on top of the
neck the eyeball that made my mother draw back with a sudden
fright

—Aquiles

the magnifying glass would be lowered a little and the mouth
with no end was rolling pebbles around, giving off a normal, ordinary voice instead of thunderclaps

—What's the matter?

hairs on his chin as thick as fingers, gulleys in his cheeks and
after his mouth his shirt collar suddenly growing large, the stamp
album bigger than everything else around, a hero from Denmark,
modest up till then, taking over the whole planet, the lens poised
over the album and the universe in peace, my mother walking pru-
dently and avoiding the glass

—Will you please put that thing away in the drawer, Aquiles?

the magnifying glass that she'd wrapped in a handkerchief with
outstretched hands, turning her head away, and had buried in the
drawer, for weeks

every week with hundreds of days, Fridays, Sundays, do you like
Sundays please help yourselves

I caught her watching my father, eyes, mouth, collar, with nervous apprehension, just like the actress with her boyfriend who
would have floated about the yard if she hadn't taken him by the
wrist

—Rui

he gave a little leap or something like it and flew away, Paulo on
the other hand, holding a peach, was earthbound and calm, a kind
of plane tree except he was spilling milk on the bar, I helped him

with the sugar, I wiped his chin with a cloth, I stopped the cake crumbs from dribbling down over his pajamas

I remember the too-sweet milk and their ordering me

—*Drink it*

a cat in a bramble patch, their wiping my chin, I don't remember you or maybe I only remember you coming into the dining room or in my father's funeral chapel with a bowl in your hand, the two coffins side by side and you in an apron and headscarf not knowing what to do, upset by the clowns

—*Excuse me*

or me upset by the clowns and yet laughing, calling you, your clogs on the stone floor of the chapel, plane trees or candles alongside the coffins while you were wiping my chin with a rag and the doctor shaking off a pigeon that was hanging from his throat

—*They lose their sense of reality get all confused get everything all mixed up it's so hard to get them back into life again*

life Mr. Couceiro waiting for me that is, Dona Helena at the door and meat tarts and cheesecake and luckily you're here and

—*My son*

so I don't know if I feel like getting back into life again

my sister when I asked if I could borrow a pair of stockings

—So are you going to the movies with a patient at the hospital Gabriela?

the stockings a size smaller than mine making me walk slower and Paulo waiting for me at the entrance to the theater with a bouquet of gillyflowers like the ones for dead people, eyes that bug out with the drive of animals trying to kill us

he handed me the gillyflowers with a dozen blossoms waving and taking on manias, how can I get hold of the spreading flowers, how can I get this thing calmed down, a mess of stems and fingers hard to separate, thirty fingers and fifteen stems and fingers hard to separate, thirty fingers and fifteen stems coming out to meet me, petals, fingernails, leaves, knuckles all mixed up, intertwined, falling to the ground, arms chasing after all those petals, messed up, awkward

—Take it

two left arms, no right arm, my sister

—Is he the one?

luckily I don't know where my father is maybe in grave number two hundred forty-eight, maybe looking for the magnifying glass in the sewers in Sintra, my mother sold the stamp collection for a song

—Not even his stamps are worth anything

and I found my father rummaging under the bed, digging in the cupboard, maybe if I told him

—All we have left of yours is the jacket with the diamond-shaped weave don't you know that you're dead?

he didn't believe me, he went off offended, I called him

—Father

and he went down the steps with a little good-bye wave, taking the bus to Cabo da Roca with the idea of being present at the beginning of the world, and I forget about my coat and close the street door

—Wait for me father

my stepfather with a piece of meat between the plate and his mouth, my mother

—Where do you think you're going Gabriela?

if only there was a light on the landing and he waiting for me, going into the movies I noticed the gillyflowers and Paulo's eyes not angry, defeated, seeing me, I'll put the sugar in your milk relax, I'll help you with the cake, I'll watch the movie with you, I'll protect you from the plane trees, from the orderlies, from the pigeons, whenever the actress went away my sister was puzzled

—You call that thing an actress?

I think some sound, I don't know what, like horses or Gypsies or pine trees by the hospital fence, bottles in a cistern, a woman

who?

counting wrinkles in a bureau mirror, Paulo smashing a car with wooden wheels

I'm not going with my father, I'm staying here, I'll help you

Paulo following her as though he hated the actress

—You call that thing an actress?

or as though he hated himself for hating the actress, my fellow worker not noticing the pine trees and yet the needles, the treetops, for her there was nothing but the fence and the patients and a butt friend

a butt friend, be patient friend, a coin friend

—Horses?

and as a matter of fact there were horses, the horses were perfectly perceptible and only afterward the hospital again, the woman by the bureau and my fellow worker

—The woman by the bureau?

fading into the air, don't put on that face, wait, didn't you get to see her fade into the air, why don't you like the actress Paulo, who's the woman by the bureau Paulo, who owns the plot with the marigolds that are drying up and Paulo's eyes not angry, defeated, I'll get the gillyflowers out of your fingers don't get upset, you can hide your fingers in your pockets, keep them there all through the movie in spite of my blouse with anchors and fish, the stockings my sister lent me, we're in the dark and no horses, right, the lights going out and I thought music and the actress on stage dancing

—Do you like being the nephew of an actress Paulo?

in my family the closest thing we had to performers was my father, he played the accordion when he was young before I was born, then he got arthritis and the accordion was left in a corner, whenever a shoe touched it the bellows would deflate and a long drawn-out moan brought chills to the whole building, my mother traded it in at the store for a flatiron that never gave anyone any chills, on rainy Sundays

you like rainy Sundays, ten rainy Sundays, you can keep your rainy Sundays and deliver me from winter, from this shawl on my shoulders

my father would glance at the empty corner and move his hands as though he was running them over the keys, the building would shake with all the afflictions of days gone by, my mother would put her fingers in her ears

—You're out of tune Aquiles

I'm fooling, I would put my fingers in my ears

—You're out of tune father

my father with his head tilted to the left agreeing, correcting the note with his little finger and my mother and my sister surprised, sometimes I feel like

I've bumped into some metal object and a sigh comes from the bellows, a pause, that moan again, my father's knuckles all deformed, red, he doesn't complain about the pain, he moves them back and forth asking

—How about a little tune Gabriela?

we would take the knife from him and cut up the apple, we would bring a bowl with sodium borate, my father would settle into the chair with his head down

—How about a little tune Gabriela?

even during the funeral, belly up with a handkerchief over his face

what happened to your face father?

a rosary wound around his fists and the priest blessing this side and that, putting the straps over his shoulders and an anxious wait a deep sigh, in grave number two hundred forty-eight a little tune Gabriela, my mother

—This wind

and no wind mother, admit there's no wind, the laurels not moving, beyond the wall Europe, Madrid, butterflies in the boxwood trees, the gillyflowers falling, Paulo's knee in the movies avoiding my knee, or my elbow and his slipping away, my sister let me sprinkle her perfume on my blouse and after the perfume I was worried that I wasn't me, I was her, swearing to Paulo I'm me, check me out, I'm me, I went to the hairdresser this afternoon, I put on lipstick, if it bothers you I'll wipe if off with my arm and get rid of it, but I'm me, give me your hand because my father in a soft voice

—Don't be bashful give him your hand Gabriela

Paulo's hand growing smaller in mine and a big hand but without any bones, a piece of soft meat resting on my leg, eyes popping out in anger, silently barking inside the film, my stepfather staring at me and my mother in the kitchen or at mass, my father

—What's all this?

but what could my father do starting with the moment they covered him with a handkerchief and handcuffed him with prayer beads, I'm eighteen years old, I'm grown up didn't you notice, play the accordion father, don't be nervous, footsteps on the floor above pounding down on me, with every one my stepfather closer, there aren't any trees on our block, there are blocks under construction, cement mixers

where the world begins

my stepfather clearing his throat a bit, grabbed me around the waist and the cross on the chain quick, hiding in my blouse embarrassed

—Did you say eighteen years old Gabriela?

I borrowed some money from a fellow worker and went to the hairdresser this afternoon, he gave me a beauty mark with a kind of pencil

—Be careful now and don't go ruining it

and I grew older, twenty-three, twenty-six years old, luckily the hand came to life you might say, muscles, tendons, a vibration of gills, a kind of crab at low tide going along diagonally with tickling claws, my stepfather far away, my mother coming from the kitchen or from mass, I remember you with brown hair, how do you explain this, at a baptism with my father, what happened mother, I can't believe that one of these days I'm just the same, bladder, gallbladder, blood pressure Dona Gabriela, rhinoceros ankles, pick up your accordion father and give us a tune quick, his body lonesome crags, bent-over bushes and grave number three hundred fifty-seven or three hundred ninety-one or four hundred eighty-nine waiting for me, not the sea like at Cabo da Roca, a grave and me surrounded by gillyflowers that drown out my sister's perfume like here at the movies, the seats rising up, the screen dark, my stepfather eighteen years old Gabriela and that little mocking clearing of his throat, Paulo's hands taking refuge in his pajamas, the actress all bracelets and pigeons and him going around a plane tree, his eyes up against the grating threatening her

—No

—*Why do you hate your aunt Paulo?*

—*I don't hate my aunt I don't have an aunt there's a brother of my father's but I haven't heard anything about him for years he doesn't look us up he has no interest in us* his eyes against the grating, us outside and Paulo

—I'd like to show you a place

I found out where he was working, I looked him up at his job, they told me to wait in the office, coils of wire, stickers, a Coke can serving as an ashtray, mechanics who were setting off torches in an echo chamber, no satin cushions, no dress, no jar of cold cream, a man completely different from my father, a cut from shaving growing dark on his cheek, tugging off his glasses

—I'd like to show you a place

with one of the braces bent, fogged over at first and then something growing on them, a film of tobacco from his tongue

—I'd like to show you a place

on the wall a torn ad for a brand of mufflers, with half of it falling off

—*If you're Carlos's son you can get the hell out of here*

he didn't go to the funeral, he must have read about it in the papers and

—*All right*

his little finger was missing, I wonder where he could have lost his little finger, go back and ask him where he lost his little finger

—*Why do you hate your aunt, Paulo?*

—*I don't hate my aunt I never had an aunt*

—*If you're Carlos's son you can get the hell out of here*

he wasn't going to say Carlos he was going to say

—I'd like to

another name, right? he was going to say another name, his glasses quivering in his hand, his lungs stormier than the sea at Cabo da Roca where the world begins, the words galloping along with the clouds, I forgot the workshop uncle

I didn't forget, Avenida Afonso III, you go by the police station, the Jewish cemetery where the trolley turns, more and more buildings

visit the model apartment

and still poor people, old people, little shops, the barber without customers with mustaches to be trimmed, I won't punish myself by saying the other name, all these years my mother who confused him with me or with the tops of the bushes, she'd repeated it a thousand times worked up by wine, the owner of the café who took pity on me

—*Judite*

Avenida Afonso III between the insurance company and the medical

clinic, people with X-rays, tests, three weeks now a small pain when I press
here

    cough

    when I press here

    a deep breath

    just a little higher up, doctor, a jab when I press here, Mr. Couceiro dia-
betes, urea and Dona Helena doesn't it hurt when I press there, the day they
die just me and Noémia at home staring at each other, the vase without any
flowers, the bicycle in the laundry room, the crocheting left on the easy chair

    nothing

    less than nothing

his eyes against the grating with us outside Paulo

—I'd like to show you a place

only he and Noémia at home staring at each other, the bicycle in
the laundry room, the crocheting left on the easy chair, nothing

    less than nothing

to show you a place on Príncipe Real and the cedar and all that,
not the church in Anjos, farther on, the smell of gillyflowers and my
sister's perfume

—Are you going to the movies with a patient Gabriela?

sure that the hairdresser's hairdo has come undone, I still had
the blouse with anchors and fish and the chain with the little cross,
they promised me a new blouse for my birthday

—Did you say eighteen years old Gabriela?

and in the end an insignificant package, and in the package an
imitation-leather change purse and a pair of woolen gloves, I
counted the candles on the cake and two were missing

—It's missing two

my mother opened the fuse box, searched among the fuses,
brought out the candles we used when the lights went out, stuck
them in the frosting which didn't have my name written in
chocolate

—There

two long candles and sixteen tiny ones, in my father's time they
were all the same, his wiggling his fingers as though it was a real
accordion

and a real accordion, I'm sure keys, buttons, the silver decorations, grave number two hundred forty-eight deserted

—How about a little tune Gabriela?

the wind where the world began, all of Europe behind us, no train with laborers returning from France, passengers waving their arms out of windows looking like castaways, bundles, baskets tied with cords, the islands and promontories to be discovered, only a desolation of escarpments and the sound of the waves, Sintra yes, the Moorish castle yes, bus twenty-nine with no empty seats, me hanging from the pole with dozens of other passengers

let's imagine café owners, Gypsies, pups stepping on me, pushing up against me, London and Russia not for now, my stepfather at the cemetery, he watched the lid being screwed on, the coffin going down, the spadefuls of dirt, he grew calm, my mother with the knife over the birthday cake looking uncertain, the deserted chair

—Do you hear an accordion Otília?

she put down the knife to listen better but the waltz had stopped, a drunken argument in the beer parlor, or a dog against the planks of the fence in the yard, my sister picking up the fruit again

don't play with your fork Otília

—It was the dog

if I told you it wasn't the dog you'd disappear down the steps, never visit us again, exorcisms for a week, prayers, pins in a wax doll to kill ghosts, Paulo's eyes through the grating, he was walking slowly because his leg hurt or he was imitating the gentleman with the cane who was looking for him at the hospital without the courage to come forward, to speak

—*Is he also your uncle Paulo?*

—*I haven't got any uncles shut up*

so dreary, so old, he would secretly give cookies, jam, and juices to the orderly, go away through the mud of the swamp dragging along buffaloes, roots

—Is he also your uncle, Paulo?

and his eyes strangling me, shouting

—Shut up

a syringe, a rubber band, a box of matches, Paulo showing half a lemon and hiding it again

—I'd like to show you a place

not really a place, a spot in Chelas with blacks, small gardens with lettuce and archways of palaces from where the world begins, if only my father and I could live alone with a lettuce garden or in a palace where the world begins, I suggested to him

—Father

but he pretending not to hear me or on the other side then grave number two hundred forty-eight

letting myself hang back so Paulo wouldn't notice

—Don't pretend you can't hear me daddy

gardens, palaces, pilgrims counting coins and receiving pieces of newspaper in exchange, huddling on a slope with brambles that scratched their penitent state, asking my sister to stick pins in wax dolls, pray for them, bless them, pour water from Fátima over their heads and they're cured, the Mulattoes who took coins for newspapers unemployed, one of them opening and closing a jackknife leaning on a corner greeting Paulo, my sister trying to hold me back

—Gabriela

and I imitating my father pretending not to hear

—I can't hear you mother

how did she find out about me, how did she find me in this neighborhood so far away from Sintra, my stepfather

—Did you say eighteen years old Gabriela?

Otília in a blouse with no anchors or fish and her six-month-old son in her arms

you promised me you'd be his godmother and I wasn't

—How did they find out about me how did they find me?

not on the path that went along the slope, in a small alley closed in by little windows, doorways, a corpse on one step, maybe not a corpse because he blew his nose and died again or maybe a corpse awake for a moment

my father?

showing me missing teeth and a silent accordion

—Father

no accordion, a beggar who's snoring, Paulo the actress's nephew

where does your aunt perform Paulo, what theater, what stage?

he came back with a piece of newspaper too, I can imagine your aunt in a scarlet dress singing, showing me missing teeth and a silent accordion

—Father

no accordion, a beggar who's snoring, Paulo the actress's nephew

where does your aunt perform, Paulo, what theater, what stage?

he came back with a piece of newspaper too, I can imagine your aunt in a scarlet dress singing, I can imagine the presents, the invitations, the flowers, why a boyfriend your age and well-off like you, every so often I see her taking a small lace square out of her purse, drying the corners of her eyes that were never wet, making an effort to obey the invisible stage director

disguised as a pigeon from the hospital who demanded a look of scorn

—A look of scorn madame

it was because of your aunt that you dragged me to Chelas, wasn't it Paulo and that piece of newspaper and the lemon and the syringe and the broken-down wall where we're squatting now and a jackdaw

what must be a jackdaw

with two notes on the branch of a tree, the matches you can't get to light and me

—Wait

lighting them for you, pouring the powder from the newspaper into the lid from a bottle, holding the match underneath and the match turning to ash, burning myself, wrapping the rubber band around your arm and hold it father, just a minute don't interrupt us, it's not my fault that I can't pay attention to you, you should have answered when I called you, don't come to me now with the story of not wanting to alarm me, tripping over your body on the step, don't argue you blew your nose on your shirt, you looked at me with your toothless mouth and you didn't pay any attention to me daughter

let me wrap the rubber band around Paulo's arm, around my arm, let me pick out a vein

this bigger one, the other one?

deciding on a third one almost on top of the bone which put a little red spiral into the syringe

I who had a horror of blood you remember, with a little scratch I'd make them cover me with bandages, dressings, coverings, warm water, the accordion playing

one or two millimeters more and a second spiral wrapping around the first with the slowness of algae and the dancing about of a fish tank, don't hold my shoulder mother, don't hold my shoulder Otília, loosen the elastic, push the piston down slowly, remembering pushing the piston, Barreiro or Almada on the other side of the Tagus, ships dead for centuries with tufts of reeds coming out of the openings in their stacks, pressing the actress's little lace square against my skin

pressing a corner of my blouse against my skin, a stitch at the ankle on my sister's stocking that stretches out with a tearing sound with every movement of my leg so not leaving here father, settling down on this stone like you in grave number two hundred forty-eight and remaining quiet, with no thoughts of music or accordions that don't exist, looking at the ships all decorated and more present, more clear that night

night beside me in Chelas and day on the Tagus, that kind of vague little chill even in September, gentlemen, the clearness at the end of the afternoon, however

how amusing

daytime on the river, Sunday, Thursday, Tuesday, which do you prefer, choose, help yourselves since I don't notice Paulo getting close to me, examining me, getting uneasy

—Gabriela

taking me by the chin, giving me a little shake, careful that I don't hear him and worrying, deciding that I don't hear him and terrified, throwing me against the broken-down wall

he or my mother or my sister
he and my mother and my sister
—Gabriela
as if
isn't that so?

why should it bother me if they hurt me, handle me like some inert object, smash my temple or the back of my neck

the temple the doctors wrote that the temple

against the corner of a tile, as if I cared about their concern, their fright, my toothless mouth staring at them from the step since I'm on a ship decorated for centuries with tufts of reeds in the openings of its stacks, since my father

—How about a little tune Gabriela?

bringing his arms together and then apart with his head leaning down, running over the keys of a real accordion.

CHAPTER

WHEN ONE SUNDAY leaving Chelas I told the maid from the dining room that my father was my father, that the actress

what she took to be an actress even though her fellow worker or the waiter or the orderly

—You call that an actress?

and me with a peach in my hand listening to them as though I wasn't listening to them or listening to them without realizing I was listening to them recalling the funeral when they'd dressed him as a man, an old man

forty-four years old, not quite an old man

with the remains of eyeliner that nobody else seemed to notice except me, a man

the jacket, trousers, and shoes of a man

that my mother wouldn't have recognized, my uncle wouldn't have recognized, I wouldn't have recognized if it hadn't been for Rui next to him, my father who'd asked that they dress him that way in the hope that he'd be taken to Bico da Areia and a bed of marigolds that rustled all night long in January where in spite of everything

who knows

living might not be so hard for him

no, where living would be harder for him without any applause, without an audience, without music, nothing but the sea or the river and my mother waiting for what he couldn't give her, her women friends

—I can't see how you stand for it Judite

the nakedness of a lamb on the butcher's hook coming out from under the sheets

—Carlos

inviting

—Lie down with me Carlos

but not dressed as a man in the hope that he'd be taken to Bico da Areia but because of the saint in his dressing room or the fear of God, Dona Amélia without any candy or cigarettes or perfume hugging me as I laughed

—He asked us to dress him as a man Paulinho

among the camellias that they'd brought from the club to the church where at any moment you expected a curtain lighted by a spotlight, performers shaking their plumes on stage, my father rising up with a swirl of spangles from the coffin and instead of applause and music Marlene, Micaela, Vânia, the Brazilian whose name escapes me

Ricarda

sitting in the chapel in their clown masks, I got a picture of my uncle and his sliced-off little finger, Dona Helena and Mr. Couceiro at one of the tables by the bar while a light swept over the audience between numbers, with camomile tea instead of champagne

diabetes, urea

and the stage manager directing the funeral, telling the priest when to enter, the sexton, the funeral-parlor attendants adjusting a crease concealing a wrinkle, ordering them to change a lamp because of a smudge

—We can't wait all night for you people to come on stage, hurry up

giving orders from the wings to speed up a prayer or make a change in the blessing, getting annoyed with Dona Helena

—Did you forget your daughter's bicycle, lady?

calling the pine trees together, suggesting to the gulls that they hang from the ceiling and to the Gypsies' horses that they gallop on the platform, lowering a set with painted waves, handing my mother an empty bottle and fluffing out her skirt

—Make believe you're drinking Judite

the closet between my father's coffin and Rui's, me smashing the car with wooden wheels on the church floor and spotting Mr. Couceiro in the mirror with his useless gillyflowers

—Come on come on, do you think we've got all the time in the world to finish the show, well we haven't, lad

Noémia's picture without a frame now, a hazy mist, had found a spot on the dresser, come on come on and my grandmother strolling among the people there, bumping into the clowns, the priest, the workers from the club, touching faces at random

—Who's this Judite?

for the first time in so many years far from the village, in Lisbon, her sister emerged from her grave in Bragança shaking the soil off her blouse to guide her with a muddy hand

—This way, sis

in the direction of the dead, she went back to her grave begging forgiveness, the electrician and the café owner fixed the gravestone, straightened out the name and the enameled photograph, Noémia fortunately locked up in an iron box impossible to open with the words rest in peace engraved as if bacteria allowed any rest, my father's eyeliner, asking the manager for some cold cream

—Look at the eyeliner on my father

and the manager furious

—There's no time, you ninny

busy packing the Bico da Areia bridge into a box on stage and the gull eggs that the sea was carrying off

where to?

undoing the nests, telling the pups to come closer, a confusion of pine cones and Dona Judite I have the money here, what will they write above the dates on my father's grave, what are we going to call him

Soraia?

Mr. Couceiro or my mother visiting him every month with gillyflowers, the maid from the dining room thinking she hears the tinkle of bracelets, earrings, fans, my uncle beside the tombstone

—Don't you dare appear to me Carlos never appear to me

maybe I should lend him the car with wooden wheels to smash on the marble, the maid from the dining room listening to the bracelets underground and the manager who was handing my mother a mourning dress

—It's your entrance let's see how you handle it don't forget the wine

the hairdo from a cheap hairdresser, the touch of perfume that was even cheaper

—Are you really sure it's your father Paulo are you sure it's him?

maybe time, the roots, the rain

not the rain in Trafaria or Príncipe Real or Anjos, the rain of laurel leaves that were falling onto the crosses

Carlos or Soraia on the tombstone or neither Carlos nor Soraia, only the dates with a dash connecting them

separating them

were the dashes separating or connecting them?

it must be connecting, let's say they connect, connecting them, a dash without any names connecting them, you didn't exist father someone else existed for you going to pick up my mother at school and fixing the gentian so it hung on the wire, someone else who spied on us from a distance waiting for the café owner to visit us with a pint of wine going off through the bushes, up to the bus that crossed the Tagus to Lisbon, the maid from the dining room was coming down to Olaias twisting the little cross on her chain

—The actress is your father Paulo you're not lying to me?

without noticing the condolence cards and the unpaid gas bills stuck in the mirror frame where the bulbs were blinking, Vânia getting undressed in front of us and Rui putting out cigarettes in coldcream jars, maybe all still alive, maybe Rui with us tomorrow in Chelas with an envelope with banknotes and the topcoat that had served him as a shirt for so long, he had an apartment, a car, a job, he was rich

—Your old man gave them to me

or maybe

—I stole them

I caught him sleeping and I stole them, tomorrow when he looks for them underneath the mattress he'll get all upset because the payment for the washing machine was two months overdue

—Where's my money Rui?

and the bank taking it away, he had a swimming pool

—Do you remember the giraffe floating in the dark water at night Rui?

a place with a garden, Rui's aunt on the phone with a friend he signed my name to a check and disappeared somewhere Pilar, the manager of the club changing the position of her body after calling for a slanted blue light on her

—Don't talk to the mike, lady, talk to the audience again

and she at the same time that the maid from the dining room and I were on our way to Príncipe Real

—He signed my name to a check and disappeared somewhere Pilar

the Rua da Palmeira drawn in charcoal on the set, sketches of four or five balconies, four or five roofs, a spot for both of us too, the manager's nephew shouting up to the light man on a scaffold

—Be careful it's the son

the son coming from Chelas accompanied by a cheesy blouse with anchors and fish and the needle, the syringe, the lemon in his pocket, the newspaper too with hopes of some little leftover drug, thinking it's all gone and shaking it into the spoon or the jar lid found in the weeds almost a fix of heroin stomach tight remembering Mr. Couceiro always at attention

a corporal

in the album he in dress uniform, straight and stiff, holding his daughter on his shoulder like a rifle, don't forget Mr. Couceiro now, and the manager to my mother with her empty pint, standing in center stage feeling ashamed at being fat in the dressing room, braiding and unbraiding her hair

—Your son's name is Paulo isn't it?

that skinny little man whose eyes leap out at us now and then curled up humbly in a corner of the house, arm in arm with a girl who smells of cooking

they light her up

the cheap blouse of a hospital attendant condemned to borrow or to palm a few pennies when they sent her shopping

who'll tell me her name, what's her name dammit

biting the little cross, winding up the chain, letting go of the cross while her fellow worker

where can her fellow worker be, let Marlene come here and play the part of her fellow worker

while her fellow worker on the dining-room stairs

—You call that an actress?

the girl

let's say it's Gabriela for lack of anything better, Gabriela will do and it goes with the blouse, the earrings faking a necklace, a little tune on an accordion, a hard-to-place wind from where the world begins, crags, bushes that bend over, little clouds running away, fingers crippled from arthritis

and which nobody else noticed

—Not now father

grave number two hundred forty-eight in Sintra, when I can I go into the mortuary and buy a plaster angel to weep for him, the clerk warns me about the limestone

—After a couple of rainy Januaries the angel will fall apart

the angel weeping for himself, not for my father, carried off by the tears are his nose, his ears, the curls on his forehead arranged by the same hairdresser who did the girl's hair, if it rains on you Gabriela, you'll dissolve onto the ground like the broken-down wall after the heroin when we'd lean against the bricks hearing the jackdaw rising up over Chelas and the muddy clothes, over Dália who didn't get to marry a doctor somewhere on the hillside with her beggar's plate

let me repeat your name Dália for the tricycle on the sidewalk, for the notebook with pictures, I loved you so much

I mean if it rains and one of these days it will rain, it always ends up raining doesn't it and you dissolve onto the ground like the plaster angel, you, your blouse, Otília's accessories, the manager calling for a tolling of bells and a curtain of laurels and small coffins of dead people that rolls down from the ceiling covering the random brushstrokes of Príncipe Real, your mother, your stepfather, your sister holding your nephew along with the small pearl necklace that you thought so elegant and that she never lent to you, Vânia, with a rag doll, twisting her neck to show off the necklace imitating your sister for the audience at the club at the same time that Marlene, with sprigs in her hair, was pretending to be a poplar tree and Micaela, unable to button up her blouse with anchors and fish, was asking me near Conde Redondo where the streetcars used to turn

—How could the actress be your father Paulo if the actress isn't a man?

the Campo de Santana swans are missing, sir, don't forget the swans, put in some swans there, the swans and an old man hunting for cigarette butts with a stick that has a nail at the tip and then yes Micaela tugging at my sleeve, lingering on my shoulder and taking me by the wrist

a few swans please, even if they're clay like the ones in cribs and the mirror in the dressing room acting as a pond, a few swans, friend, just as many as are needed to forget him

—It isn't your father Paulo how could it be your father?

so that I can forget him once and for all, the maid from the dining room or the horror of the other one, of my mother in Bico da Areia

a dozen albatrosses croaking at the equinox and I forget her too

sitting on the bed looking for a jacket since October was here and the blinds can't keep it out, because at Alto do Galo the dampness, the mist, the first flock of crows, since she needed the spark of wine and the floor

the floorboards that had managed to hold up

her shipwrecked upper deck tilted forward, the other one coming together on the sheet, throat, knee, which changes into a foot, lighting the gas jet but the gas has run out, looking for a chair and the chair running away from me

running away from her

pounding on the dresser, hit the dresser lady, don't let go of the bottle and hit the dresser with the chair, the chair smashing a cup or a chalice and falling to one side, hips independent, autonomous, let them live by themselves fighting with the walls also independent, autonomous and right then horses' hooves or Gypsies' voices on the way back from the pine grove, the fever of the pups

—Dona Judite Dona Judite

around the wall, the orange-colored clarity of autumn coming down from Trafaria where they were setting fire to the brush, the gentian that was losing its vigor, the curtain at the club suddenly opened

a hat was visible on a hook and a broom in the rear

and my father walking on stage and waving to us, the woman with the candy back from the cemetery trying to kiss him

—Soraia

in a joy of weeping, Dona Helena who was scaling fish in the kitchen, Mr. Couceiro, the maid from the dining room

—It's not your father Paulo how could it be your father

the little cross and the chain, her concern over the stockings, kissing me as I held the rubber band in my teeth, the policeman reduced to a flashlight

—Do you know this man?

pointing to Rui at Fonte da Telha laid bare by the headlights of the Jeeps, Rui stiff with pain messing about among knicknacks, bills, dried flowers, lilies, gardenias, roses in hiding places in the apartment, drawers he was pulling open without closing them, the towel rack, the pots and pans in the kitchen where there were ants and cold food

—Shit where's the aquamarine ring?

coming upon the flattened medallion in the linen closet, the one with copper decorations that my mother used to wear and I thought was pretty, a horrible imitation Pilar, one of those things cleaning women wear, seamstresses, poor people, you don't understand the pleasure they get out of bad taste, my mother would put the medallion on the side of her neck and her body would become more harmonious, taller, one of those things cleaning women wear God knows why they think they're more important that way, one of the maids we had for example got herself a rabbit stole and stopped talking to us, the swans at Campo de Santana, sir, it's all right by me and you can put the swans there, I don't care if they

172

—What are you going to do Paulo?

I don't care if they

—What about tomorrow Paulo?

just limit yourself to putting them there so I won't run into my mother, let's not keep coming back

and coming back and coming back

from a lunch years ago in Cova do Vapor, even though it was several lunches it's always the same, the only one, my grandparents, my uncle

I mean I would have liked it to have been my grandparents and my uncle instead of strangers in the restaurant, if I remember right on one occasion a teacher from the school where my mother taught, on another the brother-in-law or a cousin who as soon as he caught sight of my father pretended not to see us, I understood that he was talking about us because he was hiding secrets behind his hand and I don't know how many squints of his eyes as they lighted on us, a swan who'll defend us from them and stop me from hearing them talk about it from then on, about the effeminate man, he dresses up as a woman, he left his wife and child for a young drug addict and don't bring along the swans no, don't help me with the swans, the medallion that I'd thought was lost, my mother covering her shame with the napkin, more harmonious, taller, my father disappearing in the glass, give me what's left in the syringe Rui, that little bit left over in the syringe that might help me and is no use at all to you, looking at the swans' question marks or those from Dona Helena one afternoon, her nose rising from the crocheting needle, a glimmer on her glasses as if from sorrow

what nonsense

or fear

fear and nonsense both, I've grown up, convince yourself of that, don't upset me when I'm reading the newspaper, me who never read the newspaper

—What's going to become of you Paulo?

and her nose

sorry?

blending into the doily, the crochet needle working intensely, actually I don't need the swans, leave them in Campo de Santana, all I need is to pick up the newspaper, Mr. Couceiro scolding her without a word, the cane flourishing a touch and me extremely interested in an article that's hard to read

why in hell do they write articles that are hard to read?

please don't try to protect me, don't imagine that I love you not even for a second, you can be sure that I don't love you, when Rui with the medallion my father

—Rui

not angry, pleading, already so thin in the bed, a more comical clown than when he'd had his health, a true clown at least, now that he's going to die I recognize his talent, I appreciate his art, I applaud you father, plead again

—Rui

please, not angry, a perfect sigh, the

—Rui

almost not spoken, an entreaty that gives up and I was admiring you father, tossing candy on stage for you, perfume, a pack of cigarettes, congratulations to the head on the pillow, the tiny bones of your fingers, the lock of hair on your bald head sticking to your skin, the hand that shakes a little and doesn't grab Rui, congratulations for having thought about Bico da Areia and my mother and me

—Paulo

or maybe if you take a close look you can decipher that it's

—Paulo

and nothing but a tunic against the draft from the window whispering good-bye to him, or the concave mirror where he fixed his lashes, or hearing the pups throwing pine cones at the house, or

for one last time

the herons coming from the bridge attracted by what the ebb tide has left on the beach your lipstick that is, your rouge, a piece of a poster where my father was throwing us a kiss

an actress, an actress, I swear to you an actress

the herons wiping off his kiss with their feet, their bills, I don't know who I don't know where, maybe the dwarf on the refrigerator or the few lamps that didn't have broken bulbs

—Why Carlos?

and when they go along great ruts of shadow on the rooftops, gentian stalks, you at Príncipe Real

—Do you think you're going to die or don't you?

far removed from me, from my mother as she comes out of the closet to go to Cova do Vapor and her hesitant vanity, all that childishness in her gestures

—Do you love me Carlos?

answer that you love me even though you might be lying and you are lying, you never stopped lying, I love you, a lie, I missed you, a lie, and I want to get married, a lie, you don't love her, you didn't miss her, you don't want to get married, you crossed your fingers on us while you lied mister, what the hell difference does it make to you

—I do love you

look at the electrician, the pups, the café owner, not

—Rui

Judite, try Judite, you never speak her name, never chat with her, you remember the swans don't you, questions that have no answer moving along the pond, do you want me to stop Rui from making off with the medallion, do you want me to put it back in the linen closet, how much more time on the pillow until the leaves in the cemetery swirl up into a whirlwind and devour your face, what are they going to write on your tombstone, what are they going to call you

—What are they going to write on your tombstone father what are they going to call you?

the maid from the dining room with me at Príncipe Real, the park and so forth, the cedar and so forth, what's the use of details, tree trunks with names in Latin that Mr. Couceiro knows, the mastiff with a bow discovering the lemon in my pocket and licking the lemon, how do you say lemon, how do you say Noémia in Latin Mr. Couceiro, how do you say Soraia, how do you say clown, dresses on the carpet, on the telephone stand, a fork in a bowl and inside the bowl seeds, gloves with missing mates, hair, a workman in the cellar pounding day and night, you go down and the workman looking at us from among beams and buckets, as soon as we close the door the hammer starts again, the landlord to my father

—What hammering is that friend I have no workmen here

he kept on denying it on the dark stairs, what hammering is that friend, where's the hammer, on every step a match that flickers and goes out and before it goes out caverns of tile, the door

how strange

closed, but matches until he finds the key in a bunch on his ring and as we lighted more matches a washroom, a china doll, the atmosphere of a tunnel, the workman among beams and buckets and the landlord

—What workman?

the manager to the sound man

—A hammer dammit

a hammer dammit, open a peephole in the curtain dammit so the worker does and through the curtain the park and so forth, boxwood trees that bow to us

—Good morning

what are they going to write on your tombstone father what are they going to call you, the leaves in the cemetery swirl up into a whirlwind and devour the stone where Soraia, where only the dates and Dona Helena

—Poor fellow

my mother with the bent medallion and the manager to my mother

—Hang onto the bottle

on the cemetery paths trying to find him, they met at a dance, in a coffee shop, at a bus stop, an umbrella and so much water miss, don't think badly of me miss, you'd better get under cover miss and the warnings at home about strangers you know him quite well, a clerk in a jewelry store, me a schoolteacher, the wind was puffing out the umbrella and twisting its ribs, gray building fronts that were taking away our color, noticing an ink stain and blushing because of the ink, the smock over my arm, the briefcase with the books, repeating like a little girl, I'm a schoolteacher and he was nodding not listening to me, telling him I lived in Seixal because

Bico da Areia was so rundown, so ugly and beggars too, Gypsies, and the garbage from the river, the pups and the pine cones were there already then, the café owner already there

—Judite

the side glance and me naked in the store, the owner's wife washing glasses and cups

who's going to write on my tombstone, the electrician, my son, my mother running her fingers over the letters

—Judite

my daughter Judite, my girl, she would repeat to me, smell the mimosas mother, she doesn't notice the mimosas, she was holding her son in her arms you don't smell the mimosas, her husband all alone in Lisbon and then

it was to be expected

the wine, when he left she'd rattle the bottles and the empties, I woke up because of the mimosas and even though I won't swear to it men

—Judite

in her room sometimes but maybe it was the chicken coop, the bustle in the dovecote, who's going to write on her tombstone, the electrician, my grandson, the pups, on my husband's they wrote for me when the ulcerous memory of we miss you husband, we miss you father and he was bubbling up underground so that when we got close we could hear him evaporating, in his last years nothing but cigarettes and insomnia, his mouth muttering

—Oh if you only knew how heavy life weighs on you

he asked us to leave him in the rose garden with a blanket over his kidneys, the beloved husband with his cigarette out giving his despondency to us, the beloved father spitting up blood into his handkerchief before he bubbled up in peace and became a quiet liquid mingling in with the water of the irrigation wheel, I left the bench in the bower and the blanket on the bench and I looked at my daughter playing hopscotch on the tombstone, dividing her loving father into chalk squares without noticing the boiling until the doctor in Bragança

—You have a cloud in your eye, auntie

the doctor hazy, my daughter hazy

—Can you smell the mimosas mother?

the beloved husband hazy, the insomnia hazy, a mist in each eye auntie until they stole the bench and the blanket on me, his beret must be there on a hook in the kitchen or on the scythe handle, there must be a vest, a box of cigarette papers, we never argued, what was the good of arguing, almost at the start of our marriage he came back from a fair to me with a medallion trimmed in copper, he didn't give it to me, he laid it on the table, soldered a pin onto it

beloved husband, beloved father

so I could pin it to my dress and he went off into the garden, I put on the medallion and he was coughing by the fireplace, so many roosters crowing at the same time hurting me outside there, I found him among the mimosas where a patient, monotonous hammer, in a square I don't know where a cedar, a park, where my grandson to the maid from the dining room take it easy I'm going to introduce you to the actress, she's waiting for us in her room, what she thought was an actress in spite of her fellow workers, the waiter, the orderly

—You call that an actress?

when she visited her nephew in the hospital and those pigeons my God so skittish, so angry the actress calling

—Rui

not angry, requesting, make a note that she was requesting, she wasn't mad at him, she was angry with her companions because of a mantilla or a customer, actresses are such special people, so picky about unimportant things, just like us, so sensitive right? and poor people's ground floor, the bathtub used as a trunk, the dining room where we never dined, they say my father's very sick, they say he's going to die but don't pay any attention to them, my father stayed on in Bico da Areia rumpling and smoothing the mattress

no, my father's having lunch in Cova do Vapor with my mother who's come out of the wardrobe mirror with the mother-of-pearl medallion, better groomed, taller

—Do you love me Carlos?

and my father a man, I swear a man

—I love you

and

—I love you

and

—I missed you

no café owner, no electrician, no pine cones on the windows, my aunt really my aunt and your fellow worker doesn't understand, the boob

—You call that an actress?

just like the waiter and the orderly they don't understand either, the actress my aunt, besides being an actress a dancer, a singer, there she is Gabriela

I called you Gabriela did you notice, I can call you Gabriela now

waiting for you in the bedroom, before watching you linger, first the satin sheets, the tunic in the breeze from the window whispering good-bye to you, the throat may be too thick but still feminine Gabriela, the hands too broad but there are women like that, don't believe your fellow worker, the waiter, the orderly

—You call that an actress?

I painted his mouth, cheeks, forehead, put the soup cup out on the balcony, changed his men's pajamas, those of a sick man, an old man

an almost old man

for a red nightgown, I announced her entrance into the room

—Gabriela my aunt

and it's too bad the rain in Príncipe Real had carried off the cedar sprigs

or the laurel leaves, the poplar leaves and no name on the tombstone

a lie, a phrase on the stone that I paid for, I'm going to pay for when I get the money and I'm bound to get some money, Dona Helena will lend me some, write beloved husband, beloved father, my mother drawing the hopscotch square on the stone

—Why Carlos?

and forgetting about him while throwing the pebble onto number six, onto number eight

—I win

while I'm with you in the bedroom where the velvet garlands that I soaked with perfume and where the actress, a little pale from last night's show looks to you as though she's sleeping but she's not sleeping, she's awake, interested, she asks thinking you're

—Rui

and it isn't Rui, you made a mistake, it's

—Paulo

it's

—Gabriela

those are our two names, she recognized you, be happy, she's thanking you for the visit and we can leave before the rain starts up again, loaded down with cedar sprigs

or laurel leaves or poplar leaves

she prevents us from looking at her as she says good-bye to us because she likes

it's not right to go against the superstitions of actresses

getting to the theater early.

CHAPTER

YOU START TO THINK about it and life becomes so strange, and yet there are still days

or maybe just a handful

I was in the hospital, the psychologist if you don't draw a house and a family and a tree I'll tell the doctor and you'll never get out of here and all of a sudden

with no transition at all

there I was in the laundry room in Anjos pushing the plunger of the syringe into my skin, as the plunger gets closer to the needle I change into a gas balloon up against the ceiling with its cord hanging down

the same one I used to find the vein as I tightened it around my arm

except that two hours from now the gas starts escaping and I come down to find Dona Helena ironing, Mr. Couceiro in the easy chair and the psychologist studying the house, the family, and the tree, I tried to draw the one at Bico da Areia and what I got was waves and a girl on a tricycle, I made the swans bigger, the psychologist what's that and me swans asking nobody knows what, the psychologist handing me another sheet of paper we're not in some art museum fellow, when I said a house I meant a house, period, just like when I say a family it's a family and that's the way it is and when I say a tree it's a tree so okay, there's no room in the test for marigolds or swans so pick up the pencil and make me a nice little house quick, with me remembering Avenida Almirante Reis and giving him a five-story building without an elevator, the puff of sparrows that the church belfry flings at us along with the time and I was flying on the ceiling of the laundry room with the help of the syringe, the psychologist what's that there, me explaining that it's me flying on the ceiling of the laundry room with the little strap for enlarging veins hanging from my sleeve, the psychologist what strap, me if you'd come to Chelas with me and lend me some money we could both fly over the plane trees and mix in with the pigeons, the psychologist complaining to the doctor this guy's sure he's flying today and the doctor if he's flying I'll trim his wings pretty quick don't you worry, he called the orderly get over here Vivaldo, and as soon as Mr. Vivaldo you calling me doctor, the doctor our friend here's got the idea he's flying can you beat that, and while I was watching the faucet in the washbasin as it gave off rusty drops that were turning the porcelain brown Mr. Vivaldo, who was in the habit of setting himself up in the bandage room with the other maid from the dining room, the redheaded one, sounds of falling metal objects coming through the door and she oh keep that little hand to yourself Mr. Vivaldo, that sneaky little hand, more than likely the same one he placed on my shoulder asking the doctor if he wanted him to bring him down to earth or not, the drops from the faucet growing round again, going back to stretching out when they decided to fall and they became completely spherical and with the ceiling light inside in miniature, the orderly took his sneaky little hand off my shoulder, disappeared into the cavern of the corridor where a maid was washing the floor and imploring wait till it dries wait till it dries, the doctor with a pensive little hmm not looking at me, tapping his pen against his thumbnail, so we're birds then fine fine, when one drop slower than the rest stretched out and drew back, the psychologist showed him my drawing of the house, the doctor do you think I've got time for games Teixeira, he kept on repeating fine fine and perfecting whatever it was on his thumbnail until the orderly came back with a pill on a saucer

introibo ad altare Dei

white, large, with a slit in the middle, he winked at the doctor, invited me to stick out your tongue canary, precisely the trill that followed the sound of metal objects and the redhead's protests about the sneaky little hand, the doctor interrupted him fine fine looking at the pill with benevolent approval, the sneaky little hand popped it into my mouth, the rascally hand gave me a cup of water and closed it, the world

you start thinking about it and life gets so strange

began to grow smaller take a look, the universe a drop from a faucet that contained everything, house, marigolds, the girl with the tricycle who wasn't Dália after all, she was her cousins pedaling along at the same time whispering to each other, calling to each other, pretending not to see me

—We don't see you we don't know who you are

from time to time a look of indifference and under the indifference the joy of having an audience, circling close to me chin held high and on one occasion, I'm sure

I'm sure

—Be well

the house, the family that is me alone, the tree I wanted to be a cedar but was just a tangle of lines although it hadn't been done all that bad since we're not in an art museum boy, the orderly the walks outdoors are over you're a slug now, the woman in the hallway was starting to clean the floor again while they dragged me out of the office to my bed couldn't you have waited until the tiles dried, the doctor satisfied that the canary was still there, I was still waving my arms it seems, I wasn't even shaking on the mattress, the redhead to the orderly you killed him didn't you Mr. Vivaldo, a plane tree came to spy on me from the window and ran off

life is so strange

before falling asleep it seemed to me that my father

—Dance Paulo

so I executed a step to the right, the floor gave way on me and I crashed into the wall, the redhead with a squeal of surprise he didn't die Mr. Vivaldo, I remember asking on the other side of the Tagus

—Was that what it was like with wine mother was that what it was like with wine?

my mother answering yes hugging the empty bottle against her knitted jacket, the doctor with a wrinkled brow studying his fingernail comparing it to the other fingers he was holding out, the pen was far, far away fine fine, Dona Helena

—Hi there Dona Helena did you see how I'm flying?

leaving her flatiron and coming up to me on the ceiling among the stains of time, they're only aging photographs, the frames too, when I arrived here as a child the windowsill was up there and the balcony is worn away today, the tiles are as dingy as the clothes and the faces

yellow, yellow, my father yellow

—Hand me my wig before Rui gets here

not a clown, a scarecrow, a skeleton of beanpoles and a head of cloth with eyes and mouth of red lead, what happened to his teeth so real, so well defined, I put them in my pocket with that sneaky little hand, oh that little hand Mr. Paulo

—He doesn't need them anymore

and since the Mulattoes still chew, sell them in Chelas, just like the dark glasses in the shadows by the peephole fumbling in the pocket, showing his gums and his lewd little hand, didn't they teach you how to be quiet Mr. Vivaldo eh and right after that the metallic objects in the bandage room, the window latch closing and you in the dark, right? if my boss finds out, furniture knocked about, a weakening protest don't squeeze me like that you're crushing my ribs, whatever I imagined

fine fine

an uproar of pigeons scraping with their wings, the orderly breathing along with the staggering breath of someone carrying a piano and asking the piano what kind of a mania have you got stop laughing wait, a pause in the middle of the carrying and after the pause an intriguing slowness, what's the matter Mr. Vivaldo do you want me to open the window, the psychologist showing the page what the hell kind of a tree is this and I said a cedar

the cedar from the nights when it was raining at Príncipe Real with me on the bench waiting for my father to call me

—Step outside for a moment because I have to take care of some business with my friend here

the orderly or the piano or irritated footsteps can't you keep your mouth shut dammit, resentment, disappointment

fine fine

feet back and forth on the linoleum if you talk about what happened I'll kill you, with every drop from the faucet a puff of sparrows in the doctor's office, a Mulatto in dark glasses examined the teeth that in Chelas, I don't know why, weren't smiling, no bolero, no greeting to the audience

—Are they yours?

a Mulatto girl came out of the shadows with an enamel teapot, put them in her mouth and disappeared into a deeper shadow where glasses, you call this scrawling a cedar, you stick a marigold on top and you call this triangle a house, we're not going to release you, you're not going to leave here Jorge

Paulo

Paulo or Jorge I don't care you're not going to leave here, the window of the bandage room open, the orderly in the hallway buttoning up the buttoned buttons, the redhead coming down the steps as though she didn't know him, I to the Mulatto in the dark glasses your mother took my teeth and the Mulatto you gave them to her don't you remember

fine fine

get out of my shop, the jackdaw behind me and a second Mulatto do you want to rob a lady you crook so I was coming down from the ceiling of the laundry room and Dona Helena

—Where've you been Paulo?

Paulo or Jorge whichever you want, where've you been Paulo, the redhead far off now you didn't make it Mr. Vivaldo and the orderly whore, pushing the plunger of the syringe and no discomfort, no pain, so long Dona Helena I'll be right back, when I was drawing the family I put my mother and my father together and their son flapping his wings flying, the redhead pointing out the orderly to the waiter, and the waiter to the orderly

—Is that true?

and the orderly

I'm so high up now, you can't see Anjos

—Are you going to believe a slut like that?

maybe that church there, that little square of turf, that neighborhood and in the neighborhood Mr. Couceiro staring at the wall I'm not sleepy Helena, he asked her to turn out the light and he turned into a thing, a cupboard, a wardrobe interrupted by the creaking of wood, Noémia had been freed from the photograph and was flitting about the rooms, the orderly stopped questioning me you gobbled it up in a trill, canary, as soon as the redhead arrived with the food trays he would stumble toward the pigeons and lean against a tree trunk and unable to work his lighter with his flirty little hand, I bet the same one with which he tied the rope to the plane tree during the night shift, the one with which he set up the crate, the one with which he tested the knot, we didn't hear the crate topple or maybe we heard a cat, it's a well-known fact that cats, in the morning his socks were fallen showing his shins, the cigarette lighter in the grass that one of us picked up for the butt they might give me friend, Mr. Couceiro as a counterweight not even a coin, staring at the wall while a buffalo crossed the room in the May fog, the waiter climbed up on the crate with a pair of shears, he told us to hold him there

I got the notion that the redhead was hiding up his sleeve

and the smock and the sock in the grass where the lighter had been, I don't know which patient

me?

bringing a sheet, when my father goes and Mr. Couceiro I'll bring a sheet too, I'll ask Rui and Dona Helena hold them there, draw me a tree, a house, the orderly who took Mr. Vivaldo's place take it easy, the plunger was getting close to my skin and me so calm, so content, they brought

we brought

the sneaky little hand and the lewd little hand to the bandage room, a comb slipped out of his pants and one of us used it

I was straightening my part and combing my hair with it

we left him in the laundry room rolling his eyes and with his neck twisted, I locked the window, I scattered some metal objects here and there, I told the redhead who was being served a glass of red wine and what's all this and take it easy

—Mr. Vivaldo's waiting for you miss

with that a flurry of pigeons, the breathing of someone carrying a piano

—Don't laugh now

and the day was back on track again, nothing had happened, this isn't his comb, this isn't his cigarette lighter, the fellow on crutches gave them to us when his son-in-law took him home, we were together in his room and this pen is for you, this shaving brush is for you, this brush is for you, don't lose it, we watched him going off with his withered leg wobbling in a swirl of pigeons, he would toss it ahead of himself and meet up with it through a push of his body, he shook his arm in what I took to be a good-bye wave, got into a taxi bit by bit

his chest, his shoes, his crutches finally inside with the effort of an oarsman, the son-in-law with the haste of someone loading baggage

—Settle yourself in

and with the windows up he no longer existed, he held the chess board close to the mirror, he was challenging himself

—Do you think you've got me stumped?

and he was beating his reflection, if his daughter visited him he wouldn't even answer her, then father and he mute, how do you feel and not a peep out of him, then the son-in-law

—Mr. Pompílio

a surprised sideways glance

—Do you know me from somewhere?

the daughter in tears with her back turned talking to the waiter and the waiter

—He doesn't connect

Mr. Pompílio called us aside and explained, pointing at his own image

—That fool's the father I can't stand his relatives

he would chat with Mr. Couceiro about Timor because during his time in the navy his ship sometimes, he would suddenly interrupt himself, make a sign to Mr. Couceiro to wait and pinch his face
—When will you stop lying, you scoundrel
they would serve him two portions at mealtime
—For you and for your friend Mr. Pompílio
Mr. Pompílio furious, refusing one of the plates
—That blockhead my friend?
snorting with disdain at the empty chair, he would refuse to lie down on the bed to avoid sleeping with someone else
—Am I some kind of fairy or what?
and a battle under the blanket, a shout for the orderly
—Get me out of here this son-of-a-bitch hit me
stable sounds in the nearby rooms, the dribbling faucet that was turning the porcelain brown, the son-in-law to the doctor
—Why in hell do I have to take who in hell knows who home?
draw me a house
and leave my father-in-law in his mirror and really, after the taxi went off, I had the impression when I was shaving of someone on crutches on the other side of the glass, a silhouette getting ready to check and the movement of the pieces, the other one's plate and chair, in the dining room, waiting, the redhead leaping away from the solitary place settings shaking something or other
—Oh your sneaky little hand Mr. Pompílio your flirty little hand
one afternoon I followed up on a move and he beat me
pushing the plunger of the syringe into my skin with all my strength
the daughter in the hospital bathroom
—Get out of the mirror right now
as soon as I began to fly dozens of horses galloping on the beach
no, dozens of clowns dancing on stage
no, a girl on a tricycle
no, Gabriela with me on the broken-down wall I'm afraid, don't tie my arm
no, where I am now
until finally

I took so long

on the carousel with my parents, riding the hippopotamus, the zebra, the antelope, happy and afraid until my father's hand on my shoulder and then only happy

carnival lights on the trees

draw me a tree

and all along the river, the lights on the river too dancing on the mud, sometimes a wave and the lights were shattered, then no wave and the lights whole again, a section of shadows on the vacant lot to the right

but don't look, don't look

where a man in a bed and an empty wardrobe

what section of shadows, no damned section of shadows, the colored lights, the Indian who was walking on broken glass, he drank some gasoline, pointed his nose at the moon and gave off flames, the old woman telling fortunes by shaking seashells in a bag

—You're going to be a lieutenant, little one

and above it all the carousel with a creaking of boards, the owner moved a lever and the hippopotamuses, the antelopes, the zebras gave a jerk, every time it passed by the side of the vacant lot that man in bed asking for something or other or not asking for anything, just stretched out on the bed in wordless terror but don't look, don't look, fortunately right afterward the Indian, the old woman, the maps that exploded in the Tagus all perfectly settled in the trees

—*What the hell kind of tree is that?*

—*A cedar, doctor sir, and me on the bench in the rain until the signal on the curtain*

I told you not to look didn't I, don't upset me, don't look

the Indian dressed like us eating a pork sausage sandwich without any flames in his esophagus, was wiping the grease off his face and turning white, my mother protecting her hairdo and me noticing how smooth her neck was, how green her dress was, she wore it at a cousin's wedding and the following year it was transformed into a portiere and the next year into drapes to cover the window and the year after that the drapes disappeared, the owner of the carousel pulled the lever, the animals and the planks stopped with a screech, the animals scared you but when they weren't moving like that they didn't startle anybody, you went off down some iron stairs stumbling on every step, my mother testing the stairs cautiously the way back home she would use her finger

—*Draw me a real house what the hell kind of house is that?*

—*Marigolds a clay dwarf who's missing his pickax bottles in the laundry tub in the backyard*

maybe if I mentioned the pine cones maybe if I told him I have money Dona Judite I can pay

cautiously to test the soup, right after we'd left the river, the small wall that separated us from the water, leaning forward and finding my father and my mother in the shattered light, my father in a blonde wig and my mother fixing her hairdo, dozing off on the bus to Bico da Areia and the certainty of their never growing old, or not exactly sleeping, crouching against the broken-down wall in Chelas and on the broken-down wall the Indian, the old woman impressed by soldiers, if you behave yourself you'll get to be a lieutenant, boy, I'm going to be a lieutenant and in command of a whole lot of people Gabriela, coming through the spinning of the carousel was the motor of the bus and the bumps in the road, garages, workshops, the campground with fireplaces by the tents, the halo around a drugstore cross

beloved father beloved husband

finding our way in the dark by the trawlers and their coughing, when I had trouble getting air near dawn they'd wrap me in a blanket, my father

—It weighs a ton

and the cross was always running away from us, not this corner, the corner up ahead, not the corner up ahead, the arch at the factory entrance, counting your steps helps, three hundred ninety-eight, three hundred ninety-nine, four hundred, a goat lost like us grazing on a slope,

my wife

—Is Paulo going to die Carlos?

before the drugstore a scattering of pipes, a darkness of pipes and roots that can't drink me in and over which my mother is flying, my father hanging on the bell bringing out sounds all around, protests, shades, the crying of a child and maybe the accordion player who wasn't there

—How about a little tune Gabriela?

deformed fingers modulating the air, Noémia on her bicycle on an Easter Sunday

no, Noémia sick and pale in bed before turning pale in the picture

don't look, you're happy don't look

until the nut-cracking of a lock and along with the nut-cracking the druggist in his undershirt, the goat hazy, dirty hair, it can't reach you and you're flying over it Paulo, the jackdaw doesn't even bother you, my wife perched him on a corner of the bar, not my son, the son of the café owner or one of the pups or

not my son because I'm not a man, I'm not interested in being a man, I never felt myself a man, every time Judite kissed me I

my son four or five years old, four years old, the week before turning five his mother

I loved his mother

Judite

I wanted so much to be capable

my son

I said my son

who didn't whine, didn't cry, didn't ask for help, I remember

—Is Paulo going to live, mister druggist?

his feet in a single wool sock of mine, his neck getting thin and getting fat

just like you at Príncipe Real, just like you now

the goat spying on us from the show window as they put the oxygen mask on him

—He might not die

on his mouth, the drugstore cross on the Tagus along with the carnival lights and the hippopotamuses, zebras, antelopes, the Indian who was drinking gasoline with nails through his ears, the hairpins on the head of the druggist's wife let's get you better little fellow, the fish bowl

with a fish opening and closing its lips and reciting the multiplication table silently and me along with it eight times five, eight times six, eight times seven, eight times eight, each eye a little sleepwalking pearl with a red seed inside, my wife

—Paulo

wait father don't get tired, the words are so hard aren't they, don't stay in bed chatting with the cedar tree

draw me a tree, what the hell kind of tree is that

and I warm up his soup, fix him a cup of tea, cut an apple into little pieces or break it up with the fork, my mother

—Are you going to die Paulo?

with the brooch at her neck, one afternoon after my father had left I tried to pin it to my shirt, the pin tore the fabric and pricked my shoulder, my mother appeared out of the kitchen with something in her hand that at the time didn't look like a bottle

—Take that off, stupid

I remember a man I never saw again on the front steps, maybe the Cape Verdean opening and closing his jackknife, maybe the policeman at Fonte da Telha under the headlights of the Jeeps

—Do you know him?

maybe a Gypsy or the café owner

—If you don't have any money, it's not worth the trouble coming in

a man I never saw again

who?

waiting for the bottle to drop to the floor, for my mother to snatch the brooch off my shirt tearing it some more

—Take that off, stupid

the mirror on the wardrobe empty and I in the yard where the gentian was disappearing branch by branch into its wire supports and with it my father and the hand on my shoulder, just the hooks and the bridge with the gulls with their cries and eggs were left, just the stones of the broken-down wall were left crumbling in the sunlight, an old man on crutches limping in a yard, me drawing houses, families, and trees, a person

who?

calling

—Paulo

like my parents

—Paulo

in the drugstore

and even though the faces were close to mine it wasn't me they were talking to, it wasn't me they were speaking with, they laid me on a couch separated from them by a bedspread hung on a wire, in the windowpane beyond the bedspread the woods that mingled with the sounds from the bed, my mother was an arm looking for a body and finding only sheets because my father was at the kitchen table

—I can't I can't

two parallel lines descending down his face, hands that covered his eyes, a curiosity to know about the electrician, a teacher at the school, and in a panic for my mother to answer him

—Which one of them is Paulo's father, Judite?

hippopotamuses, zebras, and antelopes on the carousel with gaudy lights at the same time that a clown with a blonde wig dances for customers who toss him candy, cigarettes, and camellias

and me, Judite, at Bico da Areia while my son was flying and no man with me, a pebble on a flagstone and it could be the scent of the mimosas

with luck it could be the scent of the mimosas

answering

—I don't know

the days that were so much the same and the men so much the same that I didn't know, there was another child afterward

how many years after?

for only eleven days, I hid it on my mattress almost under my body, so they wouldn't hear it cry, with my breast, my milk, the sound of my steps on the floor, a girl only eleven days old, without any name, almost without any life, that I separated from me, fed, hid, when they visited me I'd cover her with my bathrobe and

—What's that Judite?

or

—What's that Dona Judite?

or simply

—What's that?

and I

—Nothing

they were a little intrigued looking at the bathrobe because there was movement, a tiny little breathing, I was protecting my daughter by not letting them find out about her, older than I used to be when during the day I sometimes would take dolls to the cemetery and set up homes inside the tombs, older than I am now

—Nothing

allowing them to make use of me without finding her, hugging her in the mirror after they'd left and calming her with my warmth, my stomach, calming myself with a pint, two pints, three pints until my lips stopped trembling, until my fingers grew steady

—They've gone away now you can rest easy

the pups at the windowpane, the electrician

pushing the syringe plunger down, only water and no spiral of blood on the glass pushing the syringe plunger into the skin

lighting a small fire in the woods and shadows on the red tree trunks because it was winter and rain and the shack had lost half its roof, the café owner pretending he was annoyed with me, he who was never annoyed with anyone, you never know with women and the customers agreeing

—You never know with women

especially with sluts Mr. Figueira, you never know with women, his wife as though she hadn't heard, on one occasion the two of us at the greengrocer's and she said leaving

—I feel sorry for you

you start thinking about it and life is so strange

the café owner unsure when he came in

—You've lost some weight you've got thinner are you sick Judite?

the impression of a different kind of weeping, a different kind of sob, a different kind of calm because my daughter was sleeping so you must be wrong, I haven't lost a single pound, I'm not sick sir and the door closed, my back to the door listening to the calm, one of the pups calling me from the wall, the chair propped against the doorknob so that

don't look Paulo don't look

—I have money Dona Judite

they couldn't come in, lifting up the blanket from the bed, not understanding my daughter's silence, understanding her silence, thinking that when they bury children bells ring in the village all morning long, the little coffin open all the way down the street, so many spikenards, my mother and the neighbor women in the midst of the brass band, the sexton carrying the coffin lid carefully like a tray

don't look Judite don't look, the little pink dress, the fingers holding a spikenard that's too big, you're going to dream all night about corpses Judite, you're going to wake up without daring to ask yourself

—Am I alive?

don't look my back up against the door and the little coffin to the right and to the left on the square, the blind man from Cardal putting his nose forward without anyone answering him that there aren't any clouds of course not, the acacias coming together up above, the café owner

—Judite

outside

—You'll be sorry if I get sick because of you Judite

not understanding my daughter's silence, understanding her silence, not lifting the sheet from the bed, lifting the sheet from the bed, the bells, one after the other, chasing away the finches, the brass band deafening me, my mother lifting her head and noticing me, signaling me to stay home, the post-office clerk

without any cuff-holders on his pants

stopping his motor scooter, taking off his cap, turning older and I'd never imagined he was bald, playing hopscotch and leaping on all the chalk squares without stepping on the lines, looking for a clean tablecloth for my daughter, the one they gave us when we got married, with lace trim and my name in blue thread on one corner, wrapping her in the cloth, sitting down to wait on the bed, getting the bottles from the cistern, draw me the cistern, draw me your daughter, hungry and not hungry, sleepy and not sleepy, not eating, not lying down, waiting for tricky little hands to darken the balconies, for lewd little hands at the windows, the electrician who nobody cared about looking at the waves

there

and as soon as the Gypsies were quiet in the woods walking diagonally with little fox steps to the place on the beach where there are weeping willows and reeds

for a few days or maybe for a few minutes I was still a patient in the hospital and now I'm here with her, go over there mother I'll dig the grave in the sand, go back to the house

you never drew a house for me, why didn't you ever draw me a house?

don't look

the breast that's on fire because the milk hasn't dried up, the shoes that were wide once which made it hard for her to walk, the swollen ankles, covering the blanket that lies waiting with the remains of high tide, a little murmur right here but don't be frightened it's the river, take a bottle out of the stove, sit down by the wardrobe mirror so as not to drink all alone, get happy with the scent of the mimosas mother, act as though you were still wearing the brooch at your neck and in a little while go to sleep, your arm on your forehead like the necks of swans that ask questions

ask questions?

and mother doesn't hear the questions, she's descending inside herself, she's forgetting and not forgetting, it seems to her that there's a character masquerading as a clown singing and not singing, her blood at rest, the swaying of the cedar

me on the bench

the little coffin open, Noémia in the niche in the cemetery with her wilted flowers, a knock and nobody inside, Mr. Couceiro tapping with his cane and hollow and empty, Noémia on her bicycle without paying any attention to you all, look at her bangs, her thin little legs, her refusal to live in all that

junk, the cane insisting or the doctor's pen on his fingernail fine fine
—*Noémia isn't here Helena*

just as I'm not mother, I'm not spying on you from the outside entrance, I don't trot around the wall in the middle of the pups, I push the plunger down and I fly, leave the cloth ma'am, don't stay down on your knees scratching in the sand and getting caught up in the reeds, get yourself a little spoon, warm it up with Mr. Vivaldo's lighter, I'll help you tighten the rubber band and then, word of honor, mother

as soon as the Gypsies were quiet in the woods I walked diagonally toward the beach the way my uncle said foxes did, we would only get wind of them when the chicken-yard wire had been lifted and there were half a dozen feathers on the ground, the tablecloth that my colleagues at school gave us when we got married and no weight at all and silence, so expensive a tablecloth that we didn't dare open it up on the table, guiding myself by the gleam of the Tagus and past the settlement, where an invisible hollow had been cleared out, the weeping willows, the reeds, what you could guess at was the bridge from the sighs of the herons, sometimes on Saturdays I'd be sitting on the beam and the trawlers, today I'm sitting on the beam with my daughter in my arms, a daughter who wasn't a daughter, the cloth with lace trim and my name in neat letters

Judite

opening a grave in the sand and burying her, why, because there was nothing to bury except a soft little sob, a moan, why, get rid of the cloth because I could trade it for some wine in case the café owner wasn't interested in me, his wife checking the quality of the cloth, the embroidery, a way of undoing my name from the back of the linen

—I'll give you two pints for it

or one pint or half a pint or the cloth handed back with the lack of interest of someone turning down a rag

—What do I want with this?

the mouth not toward me, toward far away

I don't know who I am, I don't exist

checking for stains and putting it away in the drawer, closing the drawer, today the weeping willows, the reeds, the bridge beam where my daughter and I

where the cloth and I, where they didn't spot us, little by little in the darkness the gull nests, the little piggy-bank slosh of the water, pennies that some hand

what hand?

was spreading out and bringing back together again, gave the idea of three o'clock, four o'clock, five o'clock, that soon

soon?

tomorrow, I was sure that soon tomorrow one last owl, the lights of Lisbon out, buildings that were hard to make out in their wrapping of haze, what looked to me like a hill, what looked to me like trees

—*What the hell kind of a tree is that?*

—*A cedar and me on the bench waiting*

soon the tents of the Gypsies, a girl turning the horses loose, the faucet on the tap open, soon the gulls scolding me, the electrician or the pups in circles on the beach spying on me, wrapping up the empty cloth, pointing at me barking, teasing one another, asking

—Dona Judite

and me receiving them satisfied, adjusting the copper brooch and smiling the way I always smile when people show an interest in me.

CHAPTER

AND A MAN who was going about there by the church entrance asking questions and writing down the answers on a pad said just as they were bringing up the hearse with the two coffins and the flowers that's Soraia's son, so five or six photographers bunched up in front of me with their cameras and flashbulbs covering their faces, one of them kneeling down commanded don't move so you'll come out nice in the paper, they were removing rolls of film from their cameras and putting them into a bag, they were taking rolls from the bag and sticking them into the cameras announcing just one more young fellow waving their hands like a flag in the wind pretend we're not here just look at those buildings over there, buildings with nothing special about them that didn't deserve being looked at, clothes hung out to dry of course, cages whose birds had flown away or died

of course

an old woman watching the funeral as she was putting knitted socks on a cat, one of the clowns, Marlene I think, straightened my tie, the one on his knees be patient straighten out his tie again so they can snap the both of you miss, Marlene showing her teeth to him while she tugged at my neck and the photographer all twisted, with a strip of belly showing between his shirt and his pants, great great now put your arm around him miss, Vânia left the cortège to lay her black lace glove on my shoulder, the photographer as his belly got wider perfect, Marlene in a low voice to Vânia still showing her teeth beat it you tramp, her arm wrapped around my arm pulling me toward her and face powder, perfume, a trace of lipstick on my ear, Vânia's glove gripping the back of my neck, her forehead up against mine, swaying her hips to accentuate her waist, beat it you bitch, the funeral attendants working hard to place my father's and Rui's coffins side by side crushing purple ribbons and wreaths of flowers with me obediently looking at the buildings in the background, the ones beyond the churchyard that is and the roofs on the next street where it seemed to me my mother

obviously not, only the mastiff with a bow wandering about aimlessly, the photographers

each one with his own face now

were putting their cameras away having forgotten about me, five or six mastiffs with a bow barking in one last outburst at the coffins or at Rui's aunt who years before had chased him away from up on the steps with her huge forefinger, Rui said good-bye to the giraffe float in the swimming pool and the giraffe with a sorry expression visible on its face

—Aren't we ever going to see each other again old friend?

he thought of taking it with him, went over to the tiled edge of the pool, changed his mind, limited himself to taking out his syringe and puncturing its belly in order to shut it up and the giraffe grew thin with a little whistle, the sentence broken off

—Aren't we ever

silent, turning into a rag the gardener would throw into the garbage along with the leaves, maybe if I'd stuck an adhesive plaster over the hole, blown into the animal I could have put it on the hearse on top of the flowers, with the float pointing toward the cemetery

—This way this way

Marlene and Vânia went with me in the taxi in hopes of more newspapers and photographers, I was the dead woman's best friend gentlemen, don't pay any attention to my colleague here, don't waste your time with her she's only lying, I tell you, so absentminded, so blind they were

—A giraffe where?

incapable of seeing the swimming pool on the morning when

Rui went away, without any luggage, any bag, any suitcase, his aunt you've got your gall haven't you close the gate on your way out you ingrate and when I got to the street I looked behind maybe

   maybe?

   and how strange there wasn't any light in my room, the light was on in my uncle's study, my aunt on the telephone I'll bet with thank God we've got that burden off our back Pilar, when her friend would visit her

—It's something you couldn't ever imagine my dear

shock, indignation

—Are you sure?

they'd brought me from my grandmother's at the time my father had died, just look at my bad luck Pilar, my sister-in-law pregnant and right after that her husband, the child getting up at all hours and coming into our bedroom not crying, no tears, all of that at the time my mother-in-law was getting everything all mixed up, me

—Hello mother

and she to Pedro

—Who's this João?

João dead of course, Pedro ever so patient he was always very patient with his mother

—I'm not João I'm the older one Pedro

she puzzled echoing

—Pedro

there were moments when she would stumble into some distant episode and a sweetness with which she would recall vacations, bees in the cherry grove, the swing in the garden and my mother-in-law in a white hat pushing the swing

—Pedro

and right away her fingers on the hat that wasn't there, her glasses surprised that there were no roots coming out of the floor, an adult without a pacifier near her

—What Pedro?

Pedro in despair shaking her bones remember the bees all around us mother, remember Alenquer, don't rob me of that time, father used to come on Saturdays

—Leave me be I'm sleepy

and lying down all afternoon, remember how we found a sparrow in the fireplace and we fixed its leg with toothpicks and thread, uncle an important man, very successful, with no children, shouting remember how we fixed its leg with toothpicks and thread, a sparrow from forty years ago that wasn't worth a penny, more important than his business, the rise in value of his stock, his deals, his whole existence, depending on a sparrow, his raised fist turning into a childish sob

—Don't rob me of that time

instead of the country place buildings and yet, in his reasoning, the cherry trees Pilar, sometimes even with visitors and in the middle of dinner he'd go over to the fireplace almost scurrying like a salamander, stir the ashes with a poker gleefully at first, then with disappointment, I said

—What's wrong Pedro?

he was always so careful but he dropped the poker onto the rug that cost a fortune to get cleaned not to mention the live coals, that hole there, for example, look at the fringe on the sofa, he would glare at the guests as though he hated them, hated me

—It wasn't anything

on one occasion when I was going through his clothes looking for signs of lovers, telephone numbers, notes, a comment in his datebook, I came across half a dozen toothpicks and a roll of thread, if he could have imagined what I found he would have killed me, we paid a nurse to take care of his mother who doesn't recognize us at all, mute in her easy chair and Pedro dragging a stool over next to her

—Who am I mother tell me who am I?

so if you paid attention you'd hear the bees, see the flowers on the cherry trees dropping to the ground, catch the squeak of the swing that needs oiling, my husband's mouth by the sick woman's ear waking up all of Campo de Ourique

—Tell me who am I mother?

my mother-in-law's eyes staring at him, stopping their stare, hopefully

—Who are you?

hopefully

—Mother?

having a hard time getting back from a useless trip, lost, exhausted

—I don't know

while right then and there sharing some candy with the poor lady, the prolongation of Alenquer, of his brother, and of the white hat in the garden, my idiot nephew, Pilar, who wasn't interested in who he was in spite of what my mother-in-law said to us, accepting the piece of candy that Pedro was unwrapping for her and pointing to him with her chin, puzzled

—Who's this?

this one that we had with us and who had no connection with the sparrows, accustomed to my mother-in-law's apartment where it was February all the time with the dust, a decorated little garden extended out from the kitchen, a linden tree, herbs, giving me the picture of a pedal car and somebody going around a flower bed

the notions we get, isn't it so, the fantasies we get

and just as I was about to call him

—Pedro

Pedro watching the car too, I took a better look and nothing but a bucket dark with rust, no girl in a white hat in the frames, brigadiers, an adolescent in a sailor suit

my father-in-law?

some prince or other with what was left of a date and a dedication

With my best wishes Afonso

rubbed out, Pedro waving a picture book

Pharmacies of Portugal

with the useless illusion of finding what had been stolen from him, my mother-in-law in the easy chair squeezing the same pair of glasses hours on end saddened by some meaningless annoyance, when we would say to Rui

—Give your grandmother a kiss

the flurry of a little parrot flapping its muddy wings

—Who's this?

after the wings a lack of interest that mingled with the cushions and the shadows, with no garden, no cherry trees, no bees, Rui not even looking like Pedro's brother getting up at all hours and coming into the bedroom with eyes like my mother-in-law's glasses, like a pair of abandoned lenses, two circles that

—I don't know

with a throat clearing and a sigh, angry because never any beehives or any revelation of who he was, only a child

not João, not him, an intruder

going into the bedroom, she wouldn't let me help him get dressed, take him to school

—He's not João don't bother with him

I'd find the kid in the pantry with the maids or by the edge of the pool talking to the giraffe until seven or eight years ago my mother-in-law got up from her easy chair, I could see a white hat on her and it started up the motions of catching a sparrow and right away my husband pulled out some toothpicks and thread from his pocket, right away the swing began to dance

now yes, dozens of cherry trees in the orchard and the breeze from the hives, my brother catching a toad

—A present for you Pedro

me with my hands behind my back

—They're poisonous I don't want it

the blacksmith so far off and the hammering so close by, you could see the man pounding, our waiting for the sound and after a bit the sound right beside us as though we were at

will you please explain the reason to me

the entrance to the smithy, Alenquer a mile and a half away, the well covered with planks where we were forbidden to play,

you lifted up a board and echoes, you dropped a brick and the gleam of the water at the center of the earth gobbling it up, the caretaker's stepson swore that his cousin had drowned and when they fished her out with a pole, all covered with slime, her blue lips were saying

—I committed suicide

my mother was ready to push me on the swing that time, I was steadying myself on the small seat and holding the ropes tight

—So?

I was sure I'd knocked over the glasses with my sandals, I caught the smell of the medicines, the nurse's nervousness

—Madame

and she, selfish, with no love at all for me to sustain her, she paid his rent, bought his medicine, slipping out of the easy chair, the blacksmith

far away

hammering away at my blood and after a little

will you please explain the reason to me

the white hat rolled into the orchard and I lost sight of it, the bees were possessed, I was possessed, kneeling at her feet

—You've got no right to go away without telling me who I am

at the funeral when Pedro's employees shook hands with him they were surprised to find a small child's fingers and a piece of thread, cherry trees instead of poplars, beehives instead of crosses, my father-in-law dressed in old-fashioned style

a topcoat with a velvet collar, spats

—Leave me be I'm sleepy

bursting into the chapel looking for his siesta couch, Alenquer two miles away, my brother-in-law with a toad in his hand

not dead, with a toad in his hand

—Buddy

as night fell the garden full of ghosts and the howling of dogs, Pedro poor thing running away from the cemetery shielding himself with the arms of his employees, from his father, from his brother who was coming back to torment him with animals

—Get me into the farmhouse quick

you have no right to bother me just because you died before me, just because mother deboned your snook for you while for me

—You're old enough to take care of your own fish

just because you weren't rich, didn't study, worked in a bank

did you work in a bank?

you worked in a bank for one week of rest between trips to Spain, chorus girls, gambling houses, you came looking for me at work without waiting for the secretary to announce you, you listened to her excuses you can't go in you can't go in and you looked as if you were about to pat her on the behind I'm not going in, sugar, nobody went in, showing me some sheet of paper aware that I understood you were showing me some sheet of paper you requested from the receptionist, the switchboard operator, a third employee who was wrapping packages surrounded by rubber stamps or maybe a crumpled label, a page from a pad with idle scribblings knowing I wouldn't read them, that I would pretend not to see it, you picking a hair off my jacket, praising the secretary to me

—Nice girl don't you think?

changing the position of my ivory letter opener, my carved inkwell

—Countersign this note for me and get me out of a bind, old brud

as you examined the watercolor on the office wall

—Nice oil painting Pedro

hefting the bronze horse that my wife at Christmas

—You've really got a pile of dough haven't you?

counting the money and smoothing my lapel and tossing the bill away without tearing it up

why tear it up

into the wastebasket

—You're my savior you've stopped me from getting arrested

and you can still perceive, even if my wife doesn't believe it I could even swear that you liked me

it's so important for me to be sure that you liked me

unlike you, your son didn't lie to me with pages from a notebook, didn't look for invented hairs on my jacket, he'd slip into the kitchen

disagreeable, withdrawn

chatting with the maids by the edge of the pool drawing secrets out of the giraffe, so different from you, I showed him Alenquer and he didn't know the town, I showed him the labyrinth of buildings that the farm had become and he was bored with the farm

—We've scarcely missed a single Easter here

he wasn't impressed by a part of the main entrance, the limestone column that stood at a corner of the square, that is

—We'd gotten through the gate and were all beaming

just like the mother you'd dug up I don't know where

not in Spain, not a chorus girl, not anything, an ordinary working girl, stupid, sluggish, so that instead of a Spanish girl, a chorus girl, a prostitute from the word go, João, you brought her to me at the company, guiding along her sheeplike obedience with an invisible crook

—Meet my millionaire brother, Ofélia

while you could have been saying

—I brought you this toad, Pedro

and I with my hands behind my back

—They're poisonous I don't want it

someone who curled up on the sofa fiddling with the catch on her handbag, give her the giraffe from the pool or conversation with the maids so she can enjoy herself with people of her own kind

—You're not my nephew you're the son of a common maidservant get lost

and Rui immediately under the table unwrapping candy, why don't you get up, are you afraid to show some little piece of paper, a crumpled bill, a page from a notebook with doodling

—Cosign this note and get me out of a bind uncle

why don't you get a job in a bank sometime and during breaks at work poking me in the belly with your finger, making fun of me but still my pal, I'm still thankful

—You're my savior you stopped me from getting arrested old pal

why do I always remember you as so serious you were never serious, lying on the bedspread with a crucifix on your shirt assuring me

—It's all over, palsy

with a solemnity I don't recognize in you, get up, come out from under the table, leave the candy alone, do you remember the widow who received us in Alenquer in the little house right next to Mr. Machado's property, a pinch on the cheek and

—Take off your clothes

she would wind up the phonograph, get out of her clothes smelling of violets, tiny, chubby, jolly and what am I doing now, don't mess up her eiderdown quilt

we only had shoes and socks on

above all don't mess up her eiderdown quilt

—I'm sorry Dona Clarisse we've messed up your eiderdown quilt and her breast

my mother probably had a breast like that

—You messed it up you messed it up you're a naughty boy come here so I can punish you

no, my mother doesn't get undressed, my father always sleeping and my mother dressed, the music from the phonograph an opera with a woman annoyed at us repeating in the midst of violins, eiderdowns, and Mr. Horácio's elms, naughty boy naughty boy

—Disobedient boys bad boys

asking each other in our heads what now, little porcelain angels fluttering on the dresser, one of us, who knows why

—I'm sorry father

or maybe I think I know but I don't know, a clock with Roman numerals in a glass case

we have one in the living room

who am I, tell me who I am

a hairpin sticking into my back

you on the right and me on the widow's left, my darlings, my well-mannered little boys who won't kiss me on the arms, kiss me on the arms, I was bothered by the vaccination mark

me on the side with the vaccination mark, just my luck, the widow went deaf years later, I was back from the army and the little house needed plastering, the clock with Roman numerals stopped at some lost hour, my mother to her

—My son Pedro

not full voiced, not jolly, bent over, taking her time remembering

—You had two children didn't you ma'am?

how to tell that to Rui

to João

how could I blame him for my always being on the vaccination side, having to close my eyes because of the scar, how could I ask him

—Change places with me today

I bought some little porcelain angels so they could fly over the dresser Pilar

Pilar incredulous

somebody was incredulous

—That's awful

an eiderdown quilt of fake satin, an attic phonograph, she had the chauffeur build a chicken coop next to the garage, studied it for a moment, got mad at the chauffeur

Alberto, I think that back then

she called on Rui as a witness

—It wasn't like that in Alenquer was it?

she ordered Alberto

Alberto or Amadeu?

Amadeu

she ordered Amadeu to cut the roost in half, raise the netting, remove a shingle from the roof and calmed down

—That's fine you can go now

the chauffeur was baffled, he shut himself up in the shop muttering about us

—They'll never understand

he left the door ajar so Rui could go in but he didn't, Pedro was complaining that his nephew was just like his mother, a good-for-nothing

—Better some Spanish woman a chorus girl a prostitute but somebody with life

and Rui in the kitchen with the maids asking for lemons, the first time I found a syringe in his room and told my husband, my husband pointed out his thinness to him, upset and stammering

—Have you decided to imitate your father and die on me too?

João, we never spoke about him, if I just happened to mention him I'd be pierced with a look and he'd waddle off away from me, insisting that he had no family, he wouldn't let me mention him

—Do you think there was any brother?

my brother-in-law would make fun of me all the time, would lift up my skirt and in a tiny little voice, completely rude, naughty boys, wicked boys punish us punish us, he would put an opera on the turntable and say he was going to tear off my blouse smiling at Pedro

and Pedro, I swear, took his side

the widow didn't pay any heed brother, tiny, chubby, if our mother only knew, my mother-in-law who didn't have an inkling of anything was getting the names mixed up

—I don't know

like I'd gotten pregnant Pilar and my brother-in-law was feeling my belly

—Nobody would have looked at her twice and still

maybe I've been capable and left barren for my sins, reduced to telephone calls and teas, and João doing a mocking pirouette

—I spotted it right off little brother

whenever he wasn't shut up in his room Rui would have fun with his lemons and his giraffe, I'd go over to the pool and I could hit him and tell him get out of this house nobody wants you here, my husband didn't say anything, the giraffe didn't say anything, I was even afraid that the giraffe

—Don't be mad at him ma'am

but all it did was get thinner while a little whistle turned into a rag that the gardener pulled out of the water along with the leaves, if only my brother-in-law would stop appearing to me from time to time, even today when we're alone and I can see him quite clearly with his leg stretched out on the chaise longue as though the house belonged to him and I was the guest, as though the money hadn't come from my parents, get it into your little head that everything's in my name, understand, your brother works for me, understand, if I felt like it I could kick out the two of you, understand, and in his impudence asking Pedro

—Haven't you had it up to here with her little brother?

inviting him to some house

a shack in Alenquer next door to Mr. Machado's property where

there was a widow and a phonograph howling operas and a pinch
on the cheek and

—Get undressed

he was naked with the widow, with me wearing a bathrobe, Pilar
rubbing his knees with her hands

—Rui?

and me noticing that his mouth was saying

—João?

his mouth the whole time

—João?

João, the one my mother liked best, she would debone his snook
while with me you're quite old enough to take care of your fish by
yourself, she'd push him in the swing longer, when my time came
I'm tired, when he got close to the well and all those bees good lord,
wasps driven crazy by the smell of the water, the bloom in the
cherry trees that I never saw so beautiful

thousands of such beautiful blossoms

those threads left by the little seeds as they sailed through the
grass, the bad things

soup, aspirin, brushing teeth

not existing, when he got close to the well she barely spanked
him and if it had been me how'd you like a good whack on the
behind, I tried to give her my arm at the funeral and she pushed it
away or stop it don't you feel guilty at being the one who's left, my
secretary can't get in can't get in and João pretending he was
stroking her behind, amused, merry, going down into his grave, signaling them to cover him with dirt, getting undressed

—So long little brother

João to the secretary I'm not going in sweetheart, where'd you
get that crazy idea, nobody went in, until the gravestone shut him
up or maybe not even a gravestone since in the middle of meetings
you'd appear before me in the office

—Peekaboo

interrupting the Englishmen with the farm equipment, with you
drinking my coffee, suggesting

—Shall we go now?

shuffling the order of the files

—Don't let yourself be tricked little brother you're such an innocent

the Ping-Pong table set up on a paved spot at the farm, the case that I imagined contained the bones of our grandfather the notary, the respect shown by the family in front of the frame with a skinny fellow made dignified with praise

—Your grandfather notarized more than a thousand deeds in Coimbra

and the skinny fellow writing his name with a pen that was missing its tip and was displayed with all the pomp due a relic

—Grandfather's pen

the Ping-Pong table, the Englishmen waiting, grandfather the notary from inside the chest, impatient

—Well?

more than a thousand deeds in Coimbra and now his bones, clean of flesh, gleaming in the chest, when they opened it up with a crowbar no grandfather, moldy curtains and empty cookie tins, I don't remember if it was raining, I remember my mother folding her fan, complaining about the heat

—Such heat

I remember the widow, my darlings my little boys, the Englishmen waiting while I picked up the Ping-Pong paddle and the ball

while I picked up the pen that was missing its tip

while I was taking the pen from my jacket and in place of the pen given to me by the Industrial Association the pen for signing deeds, my brother helping himself to the cigarettes from the head of the English delegation and blowing smoke in my face

—Surprise

I'd better pick up the paddle, concentrate on getting the ball over the net, my father dozing in a rocking chair and in spite of his being so very chic, hair tonic, suit, ring

I wanted that ring so very much

what you could spot was the pair of patent-leather shoes laid out at the head of the bed at night, the label on the lining

Mimosinha Shoes

which carried him through the rooms with a sleepwalking
slowness
—Leave me
the cherries that the wagtails were pecking at, Mr. Machado's
property, apple trees, vines, Dr. Elói who played the big mandolin
or the banjo, or the guitar
on holidays, inaugurations, weddings, he would wear a medal,
he would visit the widow with a flask of liqueur, he would leave,
combing his hair, smoothing his jacket, the widow would give me
the yellow liqueur to taste where shiny little pieces of straw glowed
in the light
—Try some of the lawyer's liqueur, boy
she pronounced it liquior
Dr. Elói's shaving lotion everywhere
and after tasting it I took pleasure in relaxing without any interest in the little angels, the phonograph, the world, I was sinking
into some sweet jelly with the vaccination scar rubbing my cheek,
the Englishmen with the farm equipment looking at each other,
our accountant pointing to the line where the contract was to be
signed
your grandfather, the moldy curtains, and the cookie tins, he'd
signed more than a thousand deeds in Coimbra, his name strong,
decisive, precise
Orlando Borges Cardoso
my secretary with cologne that was unfamiliar to me, tell me
who bought it for you, don't make any excuses
—Pedro
we can't get married but we can do everything else if you behave
yourself, me, who'd always kept telling her to be careful because
there were lots of vultures and gossips on the loose
—In your apartment I'm Pedro or whatever you feel like calling
me but in the office mister architect don't you forget that
our accountant quivering with her
—Pedro
dozens of little pinball-machine lights were lighting up in her
head, trying to put them out before I caught on

Mimosinha Shoes

—Anything else you want to add mister architect?

and as a result I pick up the pen without a tip and write Orlando Borges Cardoso, I started to write Orlando Borges Cardoso in an antique hand, a skinny fellow in Coimbra with more than a thousand deeds signed, admire him, the Ping-Pong ball luckily on the other side of the table, I made it, the Englishmen, relieved, my oil paintings

watercolors

relaxing on their hooks, my mother leaping out of the rocking chair to explain things to them

—He can't compare with his brother, I never expected much of him

the watercolors that belonged to my father-in-law and that I never thought much of

—I can see why

we can't get married but we can do everything else if you behave yourself, Friday afternoons, business trips to London, the purse you spoke about to me the day before yesterday, our accountant calling my father-in-law's associate instead of me, copies of letters, a report on internal services

—Mr. Simas did you know that the architect?

Mr. Simas changing his long-distance glasses for his close-up ones, making a mistake putting them away with his handkerchief and a third pair that I figured belonged to the girl from accounting

—Is that true João?

—I'm not João, I'm the older one, Pedro

Mr. Simas puzzled echoing

—Pedro

Mr. Simas becoming aware of the third pair of glasses, hiding them in his pants pocket, turning to me with a note I didn't remember having sent, Tomorrow at our nest after the dentist

—Is that true Pedro?

the Ping-Pong ball too fast onto my side of the table where a warp in the wood sent it off, my brother, don't miss, don't lose the game, explain to Mr. Simas that it's not your writing, your writing

doesn't go from thick to thin, baroque consonants, it's not full of
commas and the family used to admire it back then, yes, it's right
out of notary Orlando Borges Cardoso who was praised so much in
Coimbra, look at the faded paper, the near-lilac ink, my mother's
enthusiasm, my father's, my uncle's, the one who retired from his
Angola cotton business and understood about books, holding the
note up to the light with the unction of lifting up the host and
exhorting me to venerate the example

—Your grandfather, João

—My name is Pedro

—Your grandfather, Pedro

an insignificant skinny little man with the beak of a blackbird,
he won over your grandmother

and the good Lord knows how demanding your grandmother
was

with capital letters that softened her heart

—They don't learn any of that in school these days

my parents to Mr. Simas and I don't think he saw them, exhorting him to venerate the perfection of the tilde

—The perfection of the tilde Mr. Simas

of course that's not João's writing

Pedro's

Pedro's, yes, of course it's not, it's Pedro's writing, Pedro obviously, always so awkward, incapable of that harmony, Mr. Simas
convinced that I'd been the one who'd spoken

—What's that you were saying about the perfection of the tilde?

bringing the note closer to his long-distance glasses, trying on
those of the girl from accounting, tracing the wave of the accent
mark with a fingernail, his hand got away from him all by itself, independent, riding through the air drawing camel humps as it went

—The perfection of the tilde?

getting his hand back the way I got the ball back, quickly tucking it up his sleeve, clenching it and straightening out the knuckles
making sure that it was, in fact, his, my parents helping him, my
mother in her white hat, wearing her beltless dress for strolling in
the garden, the patent leather shoes

Mimosinha Shoes

squeaking on the carpet in the study

—Don't worry it's your hand, Mr. Simas, relax

Mr. Simas having trouble freeing himself from the perfection of the tilde, distributing the glasses among his pockets in a perplexed daze, coming to with some difficulty

the Ping-Pong ball on his side, what luck, we got the ball onto his side, mother, an opinion falling from on high underlined by a pat on the back, the complicity of men that mother will never accept, brotherhood in sin

—These things are done cautiously boy

the last piece of advice with the right hand

clenching and opening up his fingers again, there's no mistake, it's mine

on the doorknob

—And please hurry up and change your shoes because the patent leather squeaks more than I can take

without noticing that I'm not with him, I'm in the church with my nephew right at the moment when they were putting the coffins into the hearse and the flowers and a man who was asking questions and writing answers on a pad

—He's a relative of Soraia's husband

so that five or six photographers right in front of me with their cameras covering their faces don't move so you'll come out nice in the paper, they were removing rolls of film from the cameras and putting them in a bag, they were removing rolls of film from a bag and putting them into the cameras just another minute sir, they were waving their hands like a flag in the wind lift up your chin as though we weren't here and look at those buildings there behind us, not Alenquer, not the widow's little house up against Mr. Machado's property, buildings with nothing special about them that didn't deserve being looked at, clothes hung out to dry of course, cages whose birds had died for lack of someone to take care of them with toothpicks and thread and at that moment a woman

my secretary?

she straightened my tie you're not going to appear in the maga-

zines with a crooked tie mister architect, the photographer farthest
to the left lighting up and turning off his bulb quickly be patient
miss straighten his tie again so we can get the two of you in, my secretary showing him her teeth and the photographer with a strip of
belly showing between his shirt and pants great great now take his
arm miss, my wife left the cortège to place her black lace glove on
my shoulder, beat it you tramp, and my brother all aglow

—Your wife little brother who would have thought

powder, perfume, a trace of lipstick on my ear, the photographer
sticking out his perfect navel, the glove gripped me by the nape of
the neck with her forehead up against mine swinging her hips and
lifting her waist, my secretary beat it you bitch, with me obediently
looking at the buildings off to the rear, the church steps, the roofs
on the next block where it seemed to me my mother

—Who's Pedro?

obviously not my mother, my mother sick, somebody smaller,
maybe me on a swing

no, even smaller, I think a giraffe float in the swimming pool and
me calming it down

—Rui will be here any minute now, calm down

while it emptied out in my hands with a little whistle of wind.

CHAPTER

SITTING ON THE FLOOR. Sitting on the floor like a child. Sitting on the floor like a child twiddling his fingers. I asked him

—What's the matter Rui?

and he was sitting on the floor twiddling his fingers like a child facing the picture where three nymphs, almost naked or wearing transparent veils, which made them all the more undressed, their arms in a motionless dance, barefoot in the grass with petals of different colors

blue yellow brown

here and there, the nymph on the right wore a necklace made of a string of tiny grapes and was brushing against the knee of the nymph in the middle, it seemed to me that my father was singing in the kitchen but it might have been the recordplayer that he was using to rehearse in the mirror as he shook his plumes in the short little flight of a turkey

—Do you miss your aunt and uncle, Rui?

and all he did was stop twiddling his fingers

in my mother's village they'd fatten them up on farina

when my father and the recordplayer stopped or somebody went into the chicken coop with a knife

it was usually my grandmother who went into the chicken coop with a knife putting all the hens into a flutter, the turkey would puff up in a corner with his loud managerial laugh, the blade would reach his back, his breast, his belly, Rui sitting on the floor

or inside the picture of the nymphs

petals of different colors here and there, my father from the kitchen to the bedroom along the unlighted hall

instead of running away the turkey was stock still, resigned, the cold was coming down from the mountains into the houses, my grandmother grabbed his head and covered it with a burlap bag, his throat exposed

sing now father

and the bag on the ground, the roost, which was held up by a stepladder with paint drippings, fell one step smashing eggs and straw together, Rui coming out of the picture and back to the floor

—Do you miss your aunt and uncle, Rui?

at the moment when there was rain on the square and my grandmother was quartering the turkey, blood on her skirt, her apron, her blouse, drops of red on the roost on the stepladder, my mother forgetting the mimosas

—I don't want you out in the rain Paulo

blood on her skirt too, her apron, her blouse, they fastened the bird's ankles with wire to stop it from running around with its throat cut, I remember a duck bumping into the fig tree, a few months back I came across my father like that on the stairs, a rope around his wrists, a rope around his legs, at first I didn't understand because the bulb in the entryway had burned out a long time ago, I thought it was a bundle waiting to be picked up in the morning but the bundle was moving, my grandmother dragged the turkey along in the rain, brushing against pumpkins, the cookhouse, they tore off what was left of its neck with a piece of burlap, as always, the door at Príncipe Real wouldn't accept my key, while my grandmother asked my mother for

—The pail for the innards Judite

I turned on the Chinese lamp by the door with its carnival dragons and its fuchsia fringes and my father was sliding down the wall with no rings on, no bracelets, no wig, the rain was making the tomato plants hazy and the hopscotch squares in the nearby cemetery

you're going to have to draw everything all over again mother

my grandmother was plucking the turkey on the bread-kneading table, pulling out my father's feathers at the same time, the padding, the lace

it was grandmother who went to get him in the chicken coop with her knife and you sobbing in your throat, they gave him grain to fatten him, father, and father with his split lip where there wasn't any lipstick, something else it was hard for me to recognize, the same as on my mother's skirt, her blouse, the wrapper she was covering herself with now

—What's grandmother doing to father, mother?

why are his guts in a pail what was their reason for killing him?

dragging him upstairs and saving him from grandmother and from himself, one of his shoes lost, the one he had left stained with lipstick

it wasn't lipstick it was

the one he had left stained with lipstick in the street with paper and trash, dragging him over to the blanket that served as a rug in the living room, emptying out entrails, taking off the elastic belt, and the skin all bristled, white, which my grandmother, my mother, and I rubbed with alcohol, my grandmother to us, me to myself that is with a towel and a basin of water

—Take care of that cut on his back

Rui sitting on the floor like a child, twiddling his fingers

—What's the matter Rui?

not

—Who was it father?

that how it should go

—Who was it father?

and Rui sitting on the floor like a child, twiddling his fingers, isn't it true that you didn't pay the Mulattoes Rui, that you owe money in Chelas

that wound in the back

the same as my mother's owing money at the café and the café owner I'll come to your place whenever you want Judite, the way my father owes money to the butcher and the butcher's man facing Dona Aurorinha who said

—Leave her alone leave her alone

you liar, you fibber, with your aunt and uncle the butcher's man coming from behind the counter wiping himself with a cloth, mister architect, ma'am, do you miss your aunt and uncle Rui, in the window the café and so forth, the cedar mingling with the night, not just the lipstick of a wound on the back, on the nose, on the mouth, on the tongue that was trying to free itself smiling at me

and it wasn't a smile because the only open eye was blind for me, my mother in suspense on the third square of the hopscotch because a kite was above over the chicks' panic, if I can get back to the farm fast, if I can only protect them, the caretaker at the cemetery coming over with his hoe

—Where are you off to, Juditinha?

putting a match to the turkey covered with alcohol in order to make the meat firmer, more tender, and my father wrapped in a blue flame or maybe little waves of flame along his chest, don't sit on the floor like a child, don't twiddle your fingers, all you people coming from the disco and the Mulattoes

—Good evening

it's not true Rui, it's not true that you ran away, you were off in the trees with names in Latin, Mr. Couceiro explaining them leaning on a trunk and my father

—What's wrong Rui?

it isn't true that one of the Mulattoes with a broken bottle I think, a switchblade, the chain from Noémia's bicycle in the laundry room at Anjos, don't let them take the bicycle chain Dona Helena, my grandfather putting firewood and pine cones in the stove, grabbing the bottle of oil, taking the fan from the hook on the wall, it's not true that a car waiting on the Rua da Palmeira, a broken bottle or the knife cutting through the shawl, cutting through the shawl again, one of the Mulattoes pointing to the vestibule

—Stick him in there

you watching from the cedar and my father

—Rui

it isn't true that the kite was heading up into the mountains with a rabbit in its claws, the caretaker at the cemetery if you don't leave Juditinha I'll give you a doll, my grandmother to my mother hand me the spit Judite, it's not true that you were thinking my stomach hurts and the intestines that those peasant women poured into a pail, my father all alone Rui, except for the mastiff with a bow growling in the doorway, maybe if it was raining on the shanty too, it was also raining at Príncipe Real and me, ten or eleven or twelve years old, waiting on the bench for a man to come out of the building and my father by the curtain counting the money, the Mulatto with dark glasses was emptying out the purse, datebooks, aspirin, two or three coins

no, the little Fátima medal

—I have to go to Fátima, Paulo

when he was in trouble he would go to Fátima, go to Fátima while the Cape Verdeans are beating you, father

—Aren't you going to pay up what your boyfriend spent on you?

your aunt on the telephone holding the mouthpiece toward us did you hear Pilar, what the gardener pulled out of the pool wasn't branches or leaves or the plastic giraffe, it was a drowned clown, two weeks without dancing at the club until the bruises and the swellings and what are you going to eat, father?

—Can he eat?

asking for credit at the grocery store, pawning the Chinese lamp, Marlene

—I haven't got a penny if I did I'd be happy to give something, I'm sorry

Dona Amélia feeling sorry, secretly giving him the change from her tray

—Just look at the way they've left you Soraia

your aunt showing the mouthpiece to my father, talk into this little lady

—Did you hear, Pilar?

João's son's sweetheart, he's lived off us and made a fool of me

—The wife you picked up at a raffle, little brother

he gave me a smile and when I took it into my hand it wasn't there and the idiot was amused

—Surprise

while Rui, afraid of the blacks from Chelas or sitting on the floor twiddling his fingers, someone else

they say Paulo

shaking him by the arm

—What's the matter Rui?

the Mulatto in dark glasses searching in the lining of the purse, inside the dress, under the wig where

you won't believe that Rui and the little lady and my husband

—Shut up

not wanting to see the blood that his boobish son was calling lipstick, just imagine

—All that lipstick, father

the Praça do Príncipe Real where retirees play cards with the pigeons, a part of Lisbon where people pass by without looking, the Cape Verdean with his boot on the little lady's finger squashing her ring

—Aren't you going to pay up what your boyfriend spent on you?

the dwarf on the refrigerator or the manager to my father, blocking his way from the dressing room

—Are you going on like that Soraia?

covering the bruises with ruffles and sleeves or maybe a comedy number that the audience likes, sir, a penguin for example, pretending to be a penguin and Vânia who's learned everything from me

—A penguin, ridiculous

I brought her here, I made her what she is today, I helped her when they fired her as a notary and her name was Raul, after the rain in the village the mimosas so evident, I mean the smells of my childhood with me, the voices of my childhood with me

—Juditinha

the years of my childhood and my life as a woman with me, my body different from me or maybe too big a body I was living in without knowing it, the train trip to Lisbon, the school where I taught and no man, my God, most of all, no man, I was free at night although sometimes, getting undressed, not knowing who I was, these legs for example incapable of playing on gravestones where I couldn't discover the legs I had before, the school principal checking my papers, looking up from the papers, up and down at what I wasn't sure was me and the caretaker at the cemetery

both the same age, both old

—Juditinha

at the same time as the principal

—Are you the one called Judite?

and me thinking about Judite, when my son began to take shape I didn't believe it

—I don't believe it

I was afraid

—I'm afraid

I tried to go to the mountains but there weren't any mountains, only houses, streets, my husband's shirt on the board to be ironed, a fleck of shaving cream on the drain, the letters that my mother dictated at the post office about kale and rheumatism, the woman behind the counter licking the envelope with her tongue

—Any more message for your daughter Aunty Vivelinda?

my mother wanted to say something to me about Paulo, hesitating, embarrassed

—No

I was afraid when my son was on the way because I'm too small, my mother would take off her shoes and put on my father's for work in the orchard and the garden

Judite, when you come in August the lemon tree

the shoes not waiting under the bed, leaning against the stove to dry from the rain, when you come in August we'll prune the lemon tree, the principal gave me back the papers looking up and down at the body that I wasn't sure was mine and on which I'd pinned the medallion so I could be recognized if someone saw me

and through the window Almada, my mother pounding on the lemon tree

—Are you the one called Judite?

no, the principal

—Are you the one called Judite?

Judite to the caretaker at the cemetery settling onto a gravestone where she arranged the candles from the coffins chatting with them

—I live here

Judite folding the papers and putting them into her briefcase surprised by the too-large body, which was living without me, becoming obedient, taking the body back to the boardinghouse noticing the sound of my father's shoes

my shoes

on the linoleum and the landlady out of the distant shadows, made larger by her emphysema

—This is a proper residence I lock the door at eleven o'clock, miss

through the window Almada, the statue in profile, maybe if my mother hung out the wash in profile she'd stop being my mother, me an orphan

—Mother

until the profile turned and my mother again, if she fell asleep she wasn't her either, something like my mother who was taking her place that is, a defect in the eyebrow that wasn't there when she was awake, her shoulder poured out onto the sheet

the only part of her that stayed alive

getting smaller and larger, where did you go mother, where are you, in the yard, in the shack, I asked the thing

—Is the shoulder you?

the shoulder linked to an elbow, the elbow holding back the light, the defect in the eyebrow disappearing, eyelids that rose up, saw me, everything in motion between forehead and chin, lips that were chewing on the remnants of phrases from the remnant of a dream, not really phrases, echoes of people and me happy

—It's you

my mother and I, my son and I since my father and my husband were intruders, only shirts to be ironed and shoes under the bed or propped up against the stove just like the principal and the cemetery caretaker were intruders too, the electrician, the pups, the man in the coffee shop after class got up from the table with his cup almost falling off the saucer

—May I, miss?

how could it have been like that

—Don't leave Juditinha

or

—Are you the one called Judite?

what does it matter because no man, my God, most of all no man, me free, the other body with them having nothing to do with me, me and the mimosas in the cemetery, in Almada, in Bico da Areia, my son thinks that with my husband I

—Carlos

me

—Why Carlos?

and with my husband I was all alone too, watching him smoothing and rumpling the quilt, cleaning off the makeup, hiding the women's things, defending himself from what I wasn't accusing him of, sorry for what I was grateful for while not listening to him

why should I listen to him?

I'd throw the pebble onto the first square and the laurels bowing, you did it, onto the second square

—We're so proud of you, Juditinha

on the fifth square the piece on a line, I looked around and nobody, I fixed it with the tip of my shoe and the laurels pretended not to see

—We didn't see

the same way that my colleagues pretended not to see in the coffee shop swallowing their giggles as soon as the cup began to shake, the spoon, the lump of sugar, and the knot in his tie, what I remember about him isn't his voice

all the smells, all the voices of my childhood with me

isn't his age, isn't his wristwatch

no, I remember the wristwatch

it's the knot in his tie

—May I, miss?

the wristwatch and the knot in his tie, if my husband

—Who's the father of your child?

I answer him no man, thank God, no man, I'm free, the father of my child is a second hand quivering all it wants from tick to tick and a knot in a tie that's blue and green I think, blue or green I think, the laurels scolding

—Juditinha

they've been scolding me for twenty years

—Juditinha

I was sorry for the second hand, rearranging the location of the pebble, drawing my hand away from the necktie, that is from

—There's nobody with me, shut up all of you

the man from the coffee shop in Bico da Areia while I helped him with the coffee cup he didn't have, nothing was trembling except him and the pups who were growling on the beach, a pine cone on the window frame and the second hand afraid

—May I, miss?

smelling the marigolds that my husband planted reaching out toward the night, the wristwatch that hesitated as it met the care-taker at the cemetery or the principal at the school or my husband with me and me alone all the same, the body that wasn't mine sleep-ing in the mirror, a defect in the eyebrow that hadn't awakened, the shoulder spreading out on the sheet

the only part of me that was still alive

getting smaller, larger, where did you go Judite, where are you, in the yard, in the shack, I was searching in the yard, I was searching in the shack, I was asking the shoulder

—Is the shoulder me?

becoming aware that the necktie had left me, that the shoulder linked up with an elbow, the elbow holding back the light, the defect in the eyebrow disappearing, eyelids that were opening up, seeing me, everything in motion between forehead and chin, not really phrases, echoes of people and me happy

—I'm me

Rui's aunt on the phone, they get pregnant like animals, you know, they don't know each other's name, they don't suffer at all, they live in hovels and think they're houses, they sit on the floor twiddling their fingers or play on tombstones where a girl drew some lines in chalk and the caretaker telling her in the light of the laurels

—Don't leave, wait a bit

she to the caretaker

me to the necktie when he approached again in the coffee shop
and sat down at my table

—I don't need you anymore

me to the caretaker

—Do you want to play with me mister?

and one Saturday afternoon at the time when the horses were
coming back from the beach, my husband bracing the gentian with
a piece of wire

—A child?

distributing the bunches along the wall so that the sun, disappearing into the kitchen to fill the watering can and the sound of
the faucet inside there, coming out of the kitchen, looking at the
branches, helping the smallest one get some light, my husband
shaking off the dirt

—A child?

with no rage, no insults, his hair gave me the feeling that it was
lighter, dyed

—Did you dye your hair Carlos?

his fingernails shining

—Did you paint your nails Carlos?

but that was in the mirror and in the mirror the other woman,
the grownup, the one who has nothing to do with me or doesn't
worry about the mimosas, that smell that takes me back to a time
of pictures that, after my mother's death, stopped recognizing me
out of their frames the way I stopped recognizing them in spite of
their names in pencil

Octávio Juliana, cousin Sequeira, if they could only imagine
where I'm living now

—What kind of a life do you call that Juditinha?

and on whose graves I laid palms and poured holy water in
hopes of winning and I won, I got the idea that the dead were complaining about the game

—It's not them it's the wind

not just in the laurels, in the weeds covering the graves, my
mother at dinner

—Have you noticed the weeds by your uncles and aunts?

and they were annoyed

—Your daughter, niece

although at that moment I was there when the Mulattoes got to Príncipe Real, coming out of one of the establishments with posters of naked girls, which made me stop pretending I was fixing something or other on my collar

a button that had come off, something like that

thinking that I'll never be that pretty, I got the idea that there were three Mulattoes but no, four, no, five, five Mulattoes in dark glasses at a café table until they turned off the lights and after the lights were turned off for a few minutes there and afterward in the trees in Mr. Couceiro's Latin who were examining the texture and calling to my son

—Do you know him?

after Mr. Couceiro's trees the Mulattoes on the bench by the cedar, in the place where

in the place where Soraia's nephew, she never admitted to being a father and sometimes said my nephew sometimes said

and got to tell me when I interviewed her a year before her death from the illness that kills fags and street women

—My younger brother

waiting for the signal at the window, two tugs on the curtain and the wig in a myopic search, how many times have I told her to get contact lenses

—You can even change the color, girl

and I offered to lend her the money that I knew she didn't have and she insulted me bumping into the furniture

—I can see perfectly well

Soraia squinting and hazy outlines, two cedar trees instead of one, before the interview she put on her glasses

a pair that did her no good

to get rid of a stain on her belt she asked me in a way that would have moved me if I'd been capable

thank God I'm not

still of being moved, you go along drying up over time and in my case, besides time, there was the cyst in my pancreas and the hospital that had withered my soul

—Don't say in the paper that I wear glasses, promise

followed by

where was I going?

the Mulattoes conferring under the cedar where in July there was still something left over from the rain, one solitary drop, two solitary drops, several drops that you couldn't say were solitary because a lot of them were falling from one branch here and one branch there although inevitably and, from pure perfidy, onto the space between collar and neck, they moved over next to the bench keeping a simultaneous watch on Soraia's building and the annoyance of the drops, ready to move toward the first in order to escape the second which made him do a kind of dance step as soon as a green tear began to take shape on a limb, the second Mulatto

who worked the neighborhood and knew the police

anchored himself some six feet from the door and lighted the cigarette he lights when he wants to give the impression that all he's doing is lighting a cigarette, the third and the fourth on the corner by the car where the fifth Mulatto with a small white woman next to him was and I was sorry for not having brought the photographer, calculating whether there was time to call the paper and before they got mad at me for being late, tell them right off I need a photog quick, the problem is that the photog would get there complaining and scaring off the Cape Verdeans who would be back God knows when and the story would be lost along with the pat on the back by the editor, and I was in need of some peace and quiet and at the age of sixty-two

what's the use

I stayed ready for battle, mingling with the taxi drivers waiting for fares by the statue that paid homage to some famous anonymous person and the kiosk that was all shuttered up, a couple holding a small child passed by arguing about payments on the refrigerator, the usual beggar with his usual bag, lifting the lids of garbage cans one by one with the delicacy of a chef inspecting his courses and my boss, with another pat on the back in front of my colleagues gathered there, you can relax I'm not going to fire you, that bit about the chef I can only call first rate, people will read it and wow, like they're seeing it before their eyes, where do you get all those ideas, old man, to top it off the beggar was wearing gloves and the boss what did I tell you, what did I tell you, that's what we call the gift of observation, by next week, without fail, put together a story for me about panhandlers, okay, he pulled out a greasy piece of paper and an empty package, sniffed into a tin can, which he threw over his shoulder, missing the container, the boss stick with it, dammit, pride in penury, the nobility of the unfortunate, all summed up in just one observation, learn something you dummies, one single phrase, he held out his glove waving the greasy paper at the drivers and me, one of the drivers looked at the glove without saying anything until the beggar, covered with more rags than he needed, looked at it too, front and back, with a new curiosity and went off with his hand in the air still studying it, now with one finger now with another, with the joy shown a trophy, he checked it under the streetlight, showed it to the Mulattoes from a distance and vanished forever, the boss was enthusiastic, I don't know about next week, I'm not going to wait a week, tomorrow without fail I want the panhandlers in the second supplement, the couple with the child passed again in the opposite direction, they interrupted their argument, interested in an old easy chair waiting for the municipal garbage truck, which suggested to me for a moment

or was I the one who suggested to myself, sixty-two years old and with the beginnings of glaucoma

the doctor scratching his nose in a stern tone

—You have the beginnings of glaucoma

as if glaucoma was some childish thing I'd done or that I'd picked it up in passing during the intimacies of a guilty relationship

sixty-two and the prospect of a seeing-eye dog, no matter how competent the dog might be, feeling no weight of the years

the easy chair

I said

which for moments suggested that I get in among the trash containers where the beggar had drawn out the miracle of his hand, the
woman left her husband and child to check out the fabric, one of
the taxi drivers warned her that just minutes before I'd found a rat
making its nest in the cushion and the woman moved away from
the chair, let's go Júlio

the boss red-lined this part

—You were doing so well with your description but you're
spreading out too much here

and right there we got back onto retirement

—You've ruined this piece of writing for me with your mania for
details, old man

while, in order to avoid details, old man, I suggest

no, I'd try to avoid any unnecessary tendency toward factual
exaggeration that could cost me my job

be concise

that the Mulattoes around the ground floor of Soraia's place, the
funeral of someone you'd describe a year later and the boss wiping
out a whole afternoon's worth of my work with the simple stroke of
a pencil

—If you keep on with this stuffy mishmash we won't get anywhere, old man

with a parallel series of red lines, do you think anyone is interested in the funeral of a drag queen, nobody is interested in the
funeral of a drag queen and, therefore, in hopes of hanging onto my
job and avoiding their laying me out on a chaise longue on a balcony to enjoy the skimpy March sun

—Make good use of the skimpy March sun on the balcony

I changed the thrust of the paragraphs, I proclaimed with two
ballpoint scribbles and the boss

—Not too far in this direction and not too far in that, old man

the Mulattoes around Soraia's ground-floor apartment while
the small white woman fixed her eyelashes, paying no attention to
them, with the help of what looked to me like a small brush

and finally a pair of tweezers

in a small mirror framed in tortoise shell, a small one like the one I had when I was a kid

maybe the same one

and after four and a half months he exchanged me for an actor in radio soap operas, I went over to the car because upsets are hard to smooth over even after thirty-five years

I'm lying, thirty-seven

and the boss with his finger over what I'd written do you think anyone's interested in your life, old man, will you please take that out?

I felt like answering that even if you take it out of the piece you won't be taking it out of me but I kept quiet and the boss to my colleagues, he's getting senile poor fellow, the only reason I don't fire him is because I feel sorry for him, handing me back the piece, indifferent to the best part which, in spite of its being short, cost me hours of work and deals with the moment Soraia gets home, I wrote it with the memory of the feelings I had as a way of seeing that I wouldn't lose it

time has taught me that there's nothing as volatile as sorrow

and as proof that there's nothing as volatile as loss is the fact that the doctor, during my first consultation, when he announced glaucoma, declared with fraternal solemnity let's both fight it with courage and these drops in the morning and at night and during the eighth or ninth visit I heard him at the door of his office sighing to the nurse to send in weak-eyes, the nurse before smothering her giggles in the bathroom, come in mister weak-eyes, while I went off with the articles in my hand, back to my desk farthest from the window where there wasn't even a hint of sky, a horizon of desks, staplers, erasers, and newspaper clippings on the wall, the boss to my colleagues, the poor devil is trying hard but sixty-two years is a long time, just look at his typewriter, falling apart and with keys missing, practically the whole alphabet, he gives us flounders all covered with the flotsam and jetsam of half a dozen vowels floating about at random and I don't understand his thread of eloquence, the corpses of consonants all adrift, the detritus of emotions and sentiments with which he's overstocked in his old age, great, people read it and it's like they were at the scene, where are you going to get so many ideas, old man, only a few more days, don't carry it any further

and in your case you can go way back because the depths of age are infinite

don't clutter up my desk with that tale of some Mulattoes and a drag queen all mixed in with a turkey in the oven, a slum of a house in Bico da Areia with a defunct gentian, a damsel four or five years old playing hopscotch on the gravestones of a provincial cemetery

don't you catch the confusion?

saturated with the smell of mimosas, going back and forth across the newsroom and he almost landed in my lap, with that drive senile people have in their wheelchair-cradles, repeating over and over to the reporters it's nothing but a stack of pages with the vowels missing, the person's name is Soraia sir, she was buried the day before yesterday, we could narrate her life in episodes and then circulation, do you want to bet, will take off, he was showing me pages with the transvestite, the turkey, and the girl and her game of hopscotch, a shipwreck, I could go back and forth there in a lifeboat without finding the slightest trace of people and yet there was the old geezer with the hopes that parents have waiting right up to their last day, the child devoured by squids, look at this episode on page fifty-seven sir, the Mulattoes waiting in Príncipe Real, a square where in my story it's quite clear that it's raining because the drops are fluttering down, I wrote it just like that, not bad I think, look at this line, the tenth one from the bottom and there was no line as was to be expected, a question mark a third of the way down on the left, a comma an inch or so farther on and he was proud there it is, drops fluttering down off the cedar, see, the light of the café turned off and the cigarette machine up against the counter and on a hook the jacket with yellow buttons that belonged to the owner, see the trees in Latin, see the cedar and the cedar bench where the transvestite's son was sitting waiting for his father

see Soraia on that corner

an accent mark and a capital letter missing because the ribbon didn't print them

coming home from the discos on the Rua da Imprensa Nacional, basement clubs with steps down into the darkness and at the bottom of the stairs music, dancers, lots of beer, the candy woman

Dona Amélia

with a tray of candy, perfume, and American tobacco, the paradise of the pure of heart, homosexuals, addicts, depressives, transvestites, lesbians, and lonely people like me who'd lost their ideal thirty-five years ago

who'd lost their ideal thirty-seven years ago and think it's only a matter of eyelashes, not noticing me, finding again in a small mirror a small girl fixing them with a touch of powder and a tortoiseshell frame

page one hundred sixteen

an accent mark or capital letter, completely lacking except for a grease stain from an index finger maybe the boss's or mine even though the boss said

scandalous

—It's yours

and even so it was completely lacking from the very beginning

and it's not true

missing, any unprejudiced reader, any reader

because we're so used to fawning on them

being strictly objective, any reader

because we're so used to sugar-coating their intelligence

minimally missing as will be seen in my complete, detailed story, without any breaks, Soraia's son

—What's the matter Rui?

and Rui on the cedar bench, not Soraia's son, Rui on the cedar bench while a piece of lead pipe or a switchblade or the neck of a bottle, since you won't pay what your boyfriend owes, faggot, and the faggot

the character I'd toss a camellia to on Fridays that is, and the faggot my father, that is, without any protest, without any complaint, without calling for help

one of the pure of heart, understand?

covered with what at first I thought was lipstick on the doormat, let them take off his wig, tear his dress, crush his ring with their heels, to my grandmother approaching with a knife and terrifying the hens

page two hundred

with a sprinkle of lime, she stuck its head in a burlap bag, the roost fell a notch squashing eggs and straw, with blood on her skirt, her apron, her blouse, a rope

or a roll of wire

on the turkey's ankles to stop it from running with its head chopped off, so they could cut out its liver, its stomach, its intestines and my mother

the mother of his son

—I don't want you out in the rain Paulo

at the same time as I put my pages away in the drawer, took my jacket off the rack, went out, crossed over by the taxi drivers waiting for fares by the easy chair next to the garbage containers in hopes of meeting Eveline again fixing her makeup in the parked car, asking her to

—Come with me Eveline

confessing that

—I set your plate on the table every night Eveline

and I don't have to look at your picture because we're together again, you're silent as always, impatient, nervous with me wanting to say

—I love you

(isn't it true that I'm not all that old, isn't it true that I'm not so bad off for someone sixty-two?)

and I was silent too, not saying anything, so happy, squeezing your hand.

CHAPTER

DONA HELENA SAID

—Paulo

I'm sure she called me, she said

—Paulo

in the bedroom at Príncipe Real or in the laundry room in Anjos in the laundry room in Anjos

and yet I'm sure I didn't hear her just the same as I'm sure she didn't have her hand on my shoulder worried that I'd be annoyed

—Don't touch me

my elbow moving away

—Leave me alone

my eyes lingering on her fingers, not fingers, slugs, the thimble on the middle finger, the forefinger with a cracked nail

—Get that off me please

I heard her and I didn't hear her since the fact is I'm not at Príncipe Real, I'm not in the Anjos laundry room. I'm watching the audience at the club, following the spotlight that was moving up to the curtain while the drums were announcing the music, the tape

and one of my father's legs

came to a halt and my father's leg was waiting, I'm going back, I'm not going back, starting to go back

I'm going back

when the tape started started up again, the music was too loud and the leg that was already dancing stopped, the sound man low-

ered the volume and the leg was dancing again, Dona Helena in the
laundry room in Anjos

no, at Príncipe Real grabbing my arm

—Don't worry about him Paulo

the second leg, a fan making his hair wave, it seemed to me that
his knee had lost its strength, was putting his body off balance and
my father leaning over onto the other hip, the thimble

—Why do you stay here watching him die, let's go Paulo

his mouth or not his mouth, the lipstick on his mouth, the
authentic mouth at Príncipe Real to Mr. Couceiro, to me, to Dona
Amélia who kept repeating don't wear yourself out, nobody's stopping you from taking it easy dammit, the authentic mouth

—Rui

always

—Rui

I don't exist isn't that right father and at the club mimicking the
words while he rehearsed in the mirror, one same song one afternoon after another which even when he was finished would chase
after us hollering at us like certain children, certain bits of remorse,
certain pups, the memory of the blind woman inspecting my face

—Are you my grandson?

and I was on the verge of tears

—Don't hurt me please

how many times, with the maid from the dining room, do I
think about my grandmother, sense her moving in the darkness
beside me, the sigh from the mattress or the stool in the kitchen

from the stool in the kitchen, you've turned into my grandmother Gabriela, her bones creaking like a beam, asking you don't
hurt me please and you

—Why Carlos?

don't get upset, I thought that you

—Why Carlos?

and you in a shawl with white hair and a jar of plum jam in your
lap

—Why Paulo?

not in Bico da Areia, in the rented room where we're living now, a boarded-up window, it makes me think of pigeons, Mr. Couceiro and Dona Helena whom I haven't seen again

—Why Paulo?

dead maybe, so many months have gone by, so many years, two weeks ago I passed by the place in Anjos and the building had a board fence around that was saying dead, just as long as they don't put their hand on my arm

—Leave me alone

I'll go look for them I promise, playing hopscotch on the stones but during the time I'm talking about, Marlene is saying to my father as he adjusts his clothes with some pins

—You've gotten so thin sweetie

only half-clowns or one eyelid green and the other normal that's because it's inflamed you see, I got a speck in my eye, half in dresses, skirts that is, the other half men, the shape of their feet, unshaven chins, their voices

—Can't you hear their voices Gabriela?

and the maid from the dining room

—Take it easy I'm not going to hurt you it's a dream

my father to Marlene during a precarious bow, thanking the audience

—Hold me up

tiptoeing to the curtain, taking off a garter and offering it all around, the medicine bottles and his frightened question, drumming up courage from word to word

—I'm still fine don't you think?

drumming up courage from word to word and losing interest in the answer, what do I care what the answer is, they replaced my poster with Vânia's but I'm getting the show ready here, lying in bed, spinning around the living room, Marlene's helping me, the doctor's helping me because I'm still fine don't you think and candy, cigarettes, perfume, on stage the camellias from the gentleman in the first row and Dona Amélia with a calling card, happy for me, did you spot his big expensive ring

—Table nine Soraia

help me up Rui, fix my wig, close the fastener on my tourmaline

necklace, table nine is waiting, the herons were leaving the bridge
for the backyards of the houses, I found them pecking at the
marigolds with their breasts puffed out, croaking at people or chasing weasels in the Gypsies' pine grove, the wind from Alto do Galo
was rattling the windowpanes calling me
—Carlos
pointing to it, happy for me
—Table nine Soraia
corpses of abandoned herons to the disgust of the pups behind
the house and which the electrician buried in a ditch in the woods,
Dona Helena was alive at the time
the building wasn't boarded up, my bed, the couch where Mr.
Couceiro would curl up in the afternoon with his malaria reciting
the Latin names of the trees in the rice paddies of Timor
Dona Helena was alive at the time grabbing my arm for some
reason or other you can stay here and watch him die if you want
we're going Paulo, but he wasn't going to die because the manager
was announcing his song, they turned on the lights and got the
spots wrong, not that one, the yellow one and the yellow one
searching for him offstage, finding a thigh that was rising up out of
the sheet, the tip of a fan, a sigh, the gentleman with the calling
card changing his place
—Sit on my right side because I can't hear out of this ear
Marlene
—Soraia
taking her home while she kept on asking me to come up
the doctor
or the transvestite disguised as a doctor with huge glasses and a
fake belly, covering my father with the blanket don't worry friend
the manager's waiting for you and then him among the dead
herons waving to nobody
—Judite
sit down by my right side because at the age of sixty-two and
with the typewriters at the newspaper all afternoon I can't hear out
of this ear, they told me they call you Soraia and the boss gave me
an article about a drag queen you're out of your mind

he was waving to nobody as night came up over the lake in Príncipe Real and invaded the park

—Judite

not in the trees like I'd thought, on the lake, if I light the lamp our submerged bodies, weightless, Marlene and more pins, more catches, my father worried

—I'm still fine don't you think?

you've gotten so thin, sweetie, when I took Marlene home she would always ask me up, a building in Alcântara with the trains down below

how long ago was it

an oak tree on the corner

don't you feel like relaxing a little Paulo, Gabriela and me in Algés and the old woman who rented rooms demanding money in advance, I hope you're married, Marlene who liked me or felt sorry for me

—Don't you feel like relaxing a little Paulo?

the picture of a man she'd turned around

—He tricked me

clearing a chair of articles of clothing, socks, blowing away a dried-up beetle along with its dusty remnants, leaning over to cough, straightening up flushed and fanning herself with a newspaper

—Sit down

pay me in advance too Miss Marlene like you do with the rent, Dona Helena who understood everything

I'll get it I promise

excusing herself be patient ma'am he's just a child don't ask any questions Paulo, all those fringed pillows, all those Japanese knick-nacks, all those glass forget-me-nots, I looked at her building, Dona Helena and nobody, a piece of shelving, bricks, the bicycle in the laundry room that wasn't the bicycle, it was the sewing machine in a mess of debris, so when you tell me in Príncipe Real

—Let's go Paulo

where to since you haven't got a home anymore, while Marlene is passing me a fringed pillow

—I'm your friend don't you know?

and my father

—Marlene

a second floor in Alcântara, if you went onto the balcony you could touch the oak tree, a man with his chin in his plate having soup in the next room swallowing hurriedly and hiding the bread as though we were going to steal it from him, Marlene

—My stepfather

wearing workboots and the satin shawl from an old show, when he finished the soup he sat staring at the empty plate leaning forward, his eyes hidden by a dirty straggle of hair

—He was a dockworker and the crane hit him on the head years ago

the stepfather circling about aimlessly pulling off pieces of crust that he put into his mouth along with his fingers chewing on his knuckles with a kind of shiver, Marlene following him with the drops from the drugstore all right it's not bitter, saying over her shoulder to me

—He hasn't got a tooth left, poor devil

he didn't have a tooth left and over the years he must have swallowed the muscles that were missing, he squatted down tightening the shawl around his neck, brooding over the drops, his hanging hair muffling a complaint

—Tough luck tough luck

until I figured he'd fallen asleep because the shawl was all entangled, Marlene not a penny of pension did he get and only

—Not a penny of pension did he get

one of the glass forget-me-nots agreeing as it fluttered in the light, a worker was roasting some finches on the scaffolding at Anjos, no place for Mr. Couceiro to go up unfortunately, no landing where he could rest his emphysema unfortunately, bricks, plaster debris, the old buildings in the next alley, what can Mr. Couceiro do now to get up there, what cane will give him some help, what jacket not too worn can he put on for Sundays, Marlene wiping her stepfather's chin with the shawl, the stepfather tough luck and Dona Helena

—Who are you talking to?

the scaffolding replaced by Japanese knicknacks and fringed pillows, Mr. Couceiro from the grave

—Nobody

how many times in Lisbon, when at dawn the municipal van
heads toward Beirolas, I watch the shifts in the tide at Bico da Areia,
the maid from the dining room who only understands what's going
on in the bedroom and doesn't notice the wind and the agitation of
the mares, doesn't hear the albatrosses at Cova do Vapor barking at
the rain and therefore shakes me by the shoulders, brings the lemon
and the syringe worried about me

—What's wrong Paulo?

and in spite of the syringe I'm pecking at the forget-me-nots
incapable of flying, the pups that grab me by a wing and drag me
into the woods, what's wrong Paulo, tightening the rubber band,
picking the vein and while the plunger it was nothing what an idea

—It was nothing what an idea

except for the treetops all puffed up with leaves every time a
lightning flash, in the village the fever of the pots as they shook on
their hooks and my grandmother to my mother looking for her
where she wasn't

—Was that lightning, daughter?

her nose probing in the air from one side to the other, the eyes
that think we're up on the ceiling, the faraway look of her expressions that told her nothing while she was cooking, Marlene
intrigued

—Don't you see me Paulo?

I don't know if I told you that when Soraia was sick her nephew,
or maybe her cousin, or maybe her younger brother, or maybe her
son, that's it put down son because it can't bother her anymore

I sit down by your right side, wait

he wasn't paying attention to anyone, the dame who raised him

—Let's go Paulo

and he was shaking his elbow away

—Leave me alone

every so often inviting him here to my place to get his mind off
it

don't pay any attention to the mess I just haven't had time

he sat in the chair where you're sitting now except he was sitting up straighter and not trying to kiss me, my stepfather worked his whole life unloading ships and one afternoon the crane dropped a crate, he couldn't be seen under the crate, only his boots

—Tough luck

just like right now in my shawl

not him he doesn't say anything, he goes from room to room with his pockets stuffed with bread, the shawl from an old show

—Tough luck

when Soraia and I, Paulo poking through the makeup and the wigs

—You clowns

the nephew or cousin who never was a nephew or cousin or younger brother, the first time Soraia brought me he was looking at me without seeing me, the way people who are lying always try to convince us of what they're convincing themselves

—My younger brother, Marlene

and then pretending not to understand I understood his son, who lived with a woman I don't know where but not far from the sea because on certain nights she'd forget to zip up her dress and talk to me about marigolds and gulls, every so often the look that wasn't seeing, her voice had forgotten how to talk scaring the words away, her useless gestures

—I can't go on with you today Marlene

and she'd take the bus to the other side of the Tagus, I heard about a Gypsy settlement at Costa da Caparica or Fonte da Telha, the dim pine grove that made the beaches bigger, the past that the ebb tide always leaves on the sand

in my case my father who'd laid his forehead on his shotgun

a terrace, a bridge, huts that held off winter with a stubbornness of shrubbery, those skinny little branches with no roots or stalks coming out of the rocks with a drive for eternity, we discovered my father in the olive grove through a flight of hoopoes, my mother was still holding the grapes she was eating touching him with her foot, rejecting a grape, calling to me

—Marlene

not Marlene, a different name, you noticed how I looked at you without seeing you when I said

—Marlene

a different name obviously, a boy's name and five years old at the time, it happened in February and my birthday is in May, a name that's of no interest for you and that doesn't exist for me, she picked a grape for herself and a grape for me drawing back her shoe

—Would you like a grape Marlene?

or make it

there's that look again

—Would you like a grape Soandso?

we finished the bunch by twos, the hoopoes in the cork tree there, my father prone and no smell of gunpowder, the shotgun that we left by the door frame when we went out, the hoopoes had come back to the olive grove and we were happy because everything was the way it should have been and we enjoyed the peace

—They came back

I'm sure my father was satisfied too because he hated disorder in the world, a rug out of place and he'd straighten it, if the pitcher wasn't where it should be he'd place it right, at dinnertime he'd arrange his plate so that the picture on it, a waterwheel and a girl with a flower in her hand, faced him, my mother would open the ironing board and while the iron was heating up

—Don't let it burn

she telephoned the police, I didn't think it was worth the trouble because everything was the way it should have been, the rug straight, the pitcher, the picture on the plate facing my father's place, the coat and pants he would wear on the hanger by the window bar and there was no reason for any complaints about us, no reason for any complaints about anything next to an olive root two hundred feet from the house, hard to make out because of the night and impossible to make out when the Jeep got there, my mother

—Take care of the iron

and the policeman

—Good evening

at a time when it wasn't necessary to wash the grapes because we didn't spray them and the wine that year was grade twelve and cleaner, I tested the iron with spit on my finger and waited for my mother to send away the police and put it down again to iron a towel

—You can let me have it Marlene

did she notice my look?

—You can let me have it Soandso

I never could understand my name, it didn't look like me, no name looks like me, if we repeat them over and over they don't mean anything no matter what they might be just like the language foreigners talk that doesn't mean anything, for a glass a collection of sounds that doesn't look at all like a glass, if a glass isn't called glass how can we use it, my mother Lurdes and if I say Lurdes Lurdes Lurdes for a minute she doesn't exist anymore the way Soraia doesn't exist, Vânia exists but she isn't Vânia she's Raul, and yet if I say

—Raul

nobody, Vânia taking care of her throat, Sissi amused, she arrived last week and only works in the chorus, she helps Dona Amélia with the candy and cigarettes, the manager sized her up maybe you can be Bárbara, she got mixed up with her eyelashes

—What's that?

the manager thinking it over better Bárbara doesn't go with brunettes, Samanta, Vânia said we had a Samanta in October and the manager you're right let's call her Dina, the one who'd arrived the week before

—Dina?

don't argue you're Dina, one of my wisdom teeth is aching, I can't think, what I remember about my father is the coat hanger and the cartridge I found days later not where his body had been, more toward the front and crushed and burned, I covered it over with dirt and no more cartridge and since the coat hanger was put in a closet and we kept it for a bodice of mine I stopped remembering him, a few months later the plate with the picture full, a chicken leg hiding the waterwheel one of the girl's braids showing

the rug was crooked, my mother pointing out the braid to me

—He works unloading ships

and in the silence of the light bulb his boots still the same

did you notice the boots?

the house filled up with flags, spars, and that collection of things from inside a ship's engines, a Greek oil tanker with its hull with letters around it that I wrote down on my breath on the window-pane before I knew how to write, ships you can see from here and that don't remind me of the docks but of olive groves and hoopoes, a flight of hoopoes, the tip of my mother's shoe examining I can't remember what I'd wake up and the taste of grapes, the nephew or cousin or younger brother or son of Soraia there in her chair sitting up straight on the seat

—Grapes?

thinking of some way to leave without offending me as though I could be offended by him, Soraia and her son taking different buses, not knowing each other, to the other side of the river and I was noticing the gulls, noticing the pine groves, the terrace café with a fat man behind the bar

—If you won't give me something I can't sell you a bottle Judite

and a pack of pups waiting, I said again

—Paulo?

I asked him again

—Don't you want to come up with me Paulo?

not for me to do anything with him you understand, just so I wouldn't be all alone because we were all alone for ten years in Alcântara my stepfather and me, deaf from the noise of the trains

—Sit down by my right side because I can't hear out of this ear

I was on my way home to rehearse and he was missing the Greek tankers, shivering in a black shawl like a crow in a barroom, grumbling about the crane

—Tough luck

Soraia and her son each one on a different corner of the wall watching from the gate as the woman was leaving the café, older than I'd imagined with wrinkles on her throat and face, poking in among bottlenecks in a stone tub, and yet in spite of her ugliness, her frumpiness, her wrinkles, something about her hair or her lips brought back to me the idea of the picture on the plate and the girl in braids

I can see her now

playing next to the waterwheel and it was like mother and me, back in some impossible time, walking in the olive grove again, me five or six years old and she

—How about a grape Soandso?

examining my father with the tip of her shoe in the midst of a flight of hoopoes, as though we'd opened the ironing board and she was bringing in a basket of towels and pillowcases while the iron was heating up, something I can't explain about the woman, nothing to do with her hair or her lips, where mimosas were calling and I have trouble saying what I want to say, my body stock still, what I took to be longing or being disconsolate or none of that, a kind of mood

not really a mood, you tell me you've studied these things

I who was never sad, not sadness, maybe a feeling to want to get away, for people not to talk to me and to leave me alone for an hour or so which later went away, it always goes away, it got to be late so slowly, without my realizing it, I go to the window, I don't answer the phone, I don't pay any attention to my stepfather and at night I go down to the club, I feel great, a rustle of olive trees, a pitcher out of place, one or two hoopoes at most but it doesn't upset me, my father with me straddling rocks and fishing in the brook, see how I see him without seeing him and they're not lies now, don't touch me, wait, not a fishing pole, a broomstick with a string and a pin on the end, whole Saturdays like that listening to the trees, with him paying no attention to the broomstick and me pestering the ants with clods of dirt and stones, once I thought I heard partridges or maybe not partridges, a rustle of cloth, people hiding, someone who said

—Hurry up

maybe

—Don't be afraid hurry up

certainly

—Watch out for Joaquim

not Joaquim

Quim

all right, that's it, I'm Joaquim, I mean I was Joaquim through some mistake, Joaquim, how silly, that business of names, Joaquim Joaquim Joaquim and Joaquim doesn't exist, Joaquim never existed, I made up Joaquim and I tricked myself, don't think for a moment I'm Joaquim, I'm Marlene, but I did think I heard partridges and my mother, a man and my father's shotgun aimed at us against the man's shoulder, my father tying the pin onto the line, my mother seeing me, grabbing the barrel and saying

—No

the shotgun aimed away from me, the man

—Tough luck

the day by the olive tree, the bunch of grapes, and the hoopoes settling down into the cork tree there, it wasn't the shotgun my father was carrying, it was the hoe, the shotgun was by the door frame with my mother grabbing it, letting go of it, asking me to

—Heat up the iron Marlene

not Joaquim

Quim

not Soandso, Marlene, forget about my look

—Heat up the iron Marlene

and while the iron was heating up my mother taking out a cartridge from the dresser drawer as though she wasn't taking any cartridge out of the dresser drawer, taking the shotgun into the yard and sitting on a board waiting, I heard the rustle of cloth from the day before, the partridges that walked with the sound of boots

—Tough luck

my father's hoe into the ground once or twice

more than once or twice, several times into the ground and then nothing, then my mother mad at me

—Shut up

in spite of me shutting up

in spite of a girl shutting up

of me shutting up

Joaquim Joaquim Joaquim and that was the end of Joaquim, it doesn't mean anything at all, I'm Marlene, my mother getting up because of the iron just when the birds

—Shut up Marlene

did you hear, not Soandso, not Joaquim, Marlene

—Shut up Marlene

just with the flight of birds into the priest's cork tree, my mother checking to see if there were any peaches but the peaches were green, straightening the rug wary of my father, realizing that she was straightening the rug, getting mad, making it all the more crooked, watching me with the suspicion I was guessing what I wasn't supposed to know I tugged at her skirt

—What's wrong mother?

and she didn't hear me or didn't want to hear me picking up a bunch of grapes from the fruit bowl, waiting for the rustle of cloth or the partridges nearby, what I figured to be a cough or maybe a rat in the woodpile, my mother holding me back from the window when I wanted to take a look

—It was a rat in the woodpile

in spite of its being Tuesday and not Sunday, the coat hanger by the window with his coat and pants, his shined shoes, his tie for processions on the ironing board along with his shirt, the wind was silent because the cork tree wasn't moving, my mother was pointing toward the olive grove

—Go outside there Marlene

the picture on the bottom of the plate the next Thursday, an identical waterwheel, the same three clouds, the woman older than I'd supposed on the other side of the river, with the wrinkles of time on her neck and face, I was quite certain that a blind woman was pointing at the ceiling with her nose and was going over my features with her fingers

—Who's she, Judite?

Paulo in the dressing room going through makeup and wigs

—A clown

every so often I get the idea I don't know why, maybe because of

the girl on the plate, of asking them to stop the music, getting rid
of the jewelry, the makeup, the plumes, not caring about the audience, the manager

—Marlene

—You're fired Marlene

—You can go beg on the street Marlene

and I was leaping about on the floor of the stage with my feet
together following chalk marks that nobody but me uses, indifferent to my colleagues, the stagehands, the doorman who tries to
grab me and me so light you understand, just like the mimosas
impossible to grab, with only vegetable restlessness a sigh in the
corner of my memory, some outlines by a brush on clay

a waterwheel, a girl

who's holding a sigh in her hand, Dona Amélia arranging the
perfume bottles on her tray let me talk to her, it's loneliness, it's
nerves, who can put up with this life

—Marlene

I was standing up, fluttering about, not in Lisbon, in an olive
grove where there's a highway now, buses and palm trees around a
restaurant where the house used to be, a team of oxen looked at me
through the bars

—Why did father take both the shotgun and the hoe when all he
needed was the hoe, mother?

my mother putting it away in the chicken coop

pet me if you like but forget my eyes for a moment

—What hoe Marlene?

bringing in more charcoal for the iron, pulling a splinter out of
her hand, the splinter was out and she didn't pay any attention to
the cut in her hand which surprised me

you promised to forget my eyes didn't you?

—What hoe Marlene?

the hoe near the dead man's arm, the shotgun farther off, my
mother moving it closer to my father the way he would move the
pitcher when he got home

the hoopoes sat on their eggs on the Frenchman's wall with
feathers all around their bodies like the skirts of the Gypsy women

or Dona Amélia in the dressing room rolling up and unrolling a tube of lotion

—Don't you feel well Marlene?

my mother in the kitchen to the crickets in the night

—The police have gone, so beat it

a smooth cloak of crickets on the ground all across the fields, broken by a rooster or a dog, Dina was pounding on a slipper with the spatula she used for waxing her legs preventing me from hearing a rustle of cloth and my mother making the crickets quiet down by closing the window and with the crickets some heavy breathing

—Tough luck

people hiding and she pointed to the hollow by the stove where the kindling was piled up

—What people, it was a rat in the woodpile didn't you hear it?

but I feel fine Dona Amélia, why shouldn't I feel fine because it was a rat in the woodpile just like it was a crane for unloading ships, not at home, what a silly idea, at home, on the docks, a slip-up on my stepfather's part just his luck and a cable went slack, a mistake with the levers, the maneuvers of a beginner

why do they take on green people?

my mother came into the room and I let go of the hoe

—It was the crane didn't you see?

and my stepfather prone in the picture on the plate, what plate mother, a Greek ship with its name in the letters that you write on your breath on windows before you know how to write, it's here in the window frame, I read it before what was left of it faded away, I'm not completely sure but I'll bet it was a Greek ship don't you think, sailors talking in some foreign language that means whatever it wants to mean, glass for example a strange collection of sounds that has nothing to do with a glass, if they don't call a glass a glass how are we going to use it, stepfather for example they say rat, crane they say hoe and as a result he didn't see the crane, Dina finished pounding on her slipper and in spite of Lisbon the crickets again, Dona Amélia imitating the hoopoes incubating the tray on the small bench in the dressing room

—Don't you feel well Marlene?

a smooth cloak of crickets on the ground all across the fields, no rooster to puncture it, no dog, the shotgun harmless by the door frame, no rustle in the olive grove, the ironing board closed up, cold water and handkerchiefs on the spot on his head where the crane broke the picture on the plate crippling my stepfather, the rats behind and in front of the woodpile, his brain dried up too bad but let him have the shawl because your husband's cold, not my shawl from working at the club yet and Dona Amélia

—Don't you feel well Marlene?

a piece of wool that covered her in January, the music man came to call Dina who'd lost one of her necklaces for the finale, the crickets were expanding and contracting, sewing up the darkness, fix him some soup, give him a crust of bread, unbutton his collar so we can lay him down ma'am, a moment before I said no rooster and yet Dr. Magalhães's rooster scratching inside our bones with the abrasiveness of a crow, Dina looking under the clothes have you seen my necklace maybe Dona Soraia, I to the police taking my stepfather as a witness tell the sergeant maybe it wasn't the Greek's crane that fell on his head sir, my mother not a peep and he was hiding the bread in his pockets

—Tough luck

leaving the kitchen hauling the inert half of his body that the crane had shriveled up and I who felt sorry for sick people, take the broomstick my father fished with to help you walk please, the broomstick, the string, the hook and both of us not moving

I remember

a whole afternoon by the brook, or better a tongue of murky water lingering along the stones going from stone to stone with the slowness of the earth itself, olive trees that took their time for years on end to reach their death agony, the cork tree I'm not sure whether alive or not turning to granite, my father weakened by drowsiness and no fish of course, what fish, threads of slime, the proof that I feel sorry for sick people is that after my mother's death

a mixup with rat poison

a crane on a Greek ship

a mixup with rat poison

I brought him with me to this second floor in Alcântara where the trains shake the furniture and hour after hour repeat it's time to leave, Dina desperate for the necklace I'd stuck it in my bag

—The necklace the necklace?

since I'm not young anymore, one of these days the manager's going to give her my dresses and my songs

—You're all through Marlene

and me without a job gnawing on the plaster of the wall and the embroidered pillows, maybe Paulo in that chair with me or not even Paulo since I can't pay for his visits to the Cape Verdeans in Chelas, me on a corner in a daze from the trains, using more perfume, using more padding in my breasts, keeping out of the light and hiding my age, lighting a cigarette instead of a smile and the cigarette going out, the women or the ones in charge of the women

—Beat it

in the neighborhoods of Lisbon where first thing in the morning, before the lights go out, the delivery trucks and the drivers with a wave of the hand

—Come here

suckling pigs, fruit, vegetables, dolls swinging on rearview mirrors, getting out of the trucks with lipstick on their cheeks

—What do you mean pay, faggot?

—Did I do you a favor or didn't I, faggot?

—How much have you got there tell us, faggot

my purse on the seat, glasses, bus pass

—Haven't you got a fucking cent, faggot?

—Has business been bad, faggot?

—Who's this a picture of, faggot?

—Doesn't anybody love you, faggot?

the glasses tossed into a bush and me crawling, unable to see, the way my father couldn't see my stepfather thirty or forty

forty-four years and two months ago, busy with the root of the olive tree in spite of the warning from the hoopoes

—Mr. Freitas

just the way I didn't see the drivers getting rid of me

—Can't find your glasses, faggot?

my stepfather in a ditch cocking the shotgun, checking the trigger, turning the gun toward my father, looking around to make sure I wasn't there, the waterwheel and the girl in braids at the bottom of the plate weren't there, waiting for my father to stand up and the hoopoes all upset, jumping from limb to limb, fluttering around him

—Mr. Freitas

the trucks heading north, only those red lights, sometimes not two, one, getting smaller as they went away, me finding the glasses just when my father stood up and finding my mother's eyes as she held the iron over the board and seeing in them the trees, the birds, the brook that was drying up over the stones, the spread of the fields

if I could only live there, if only the house was still there

my father staring at my stepfather with the hoe hanging from his hand, my mother handing me the grapes

—Would you like a bunch Marlene?

Joaquim Joaquim Joaquim Joaquim

—Would you like a bunch Marlene?

my name is Marlene, it's always been Marlene

—Would you like to come up with me Paulo?

I'm sorry, it's not that, after the age of thirty-five you get everything mixed up

—Would you like a bunch Marlene?

would you like to come up Paulo and relax in what's left of the afternoon, Dona Helena didn't put her hand on his arm, afraid of annoying him

—Don't touch me

if I could only live there again I'd straighten the rug, put the pitcher in place, chase the rats out of the woodpile

Paulo's elbow moving away

—Leave me alone

I'd open the window to hear the crickets

fingers that weren't fingers for him but slugs, the thimble for repairing a mantilla on the middle finger, the forefinger with a cracked nail

—Get that off me please

a veil of roosters lighting up the night and Paião in the distance, the new housing project, the firefly of the radio antenna throbbing on a hillside, bringing the fruit basket

—Would you like a grape Paulo?

at the same time a spotlight on stage and me pushing Dina away

—It's for me

the drums announcing the music, the tape starting up

moving a leg toward the stage

it got stuck

the leg hesitating, waiting, I'm leaving, I'm not leaving, Dina the dummy

—What's wrong Miss Marlene?

starting to draw back

I'm leaving

the tape starting, what a relief, I'm not leaving, the music too loud and the leg that was dancing stopped now, the sound man lowering the volume and the leg dancing again

—Paulo

the second leg, a glove

we all wore gloves

spangles, twirls, Dona Amélia very good Marlene, the manager finally with

—Would you be offended if I said I liked you Paulo?

you can still make it Marlene, you don't have to look for some corner between streetlights, you don't have to disguise your age, we're not firing you, we're raising your billing, we're putting you on a poster by the entrance, don't take off your makeup, take all the time you need, we're firing Dina, you're fired Dina, you don't have to drink with the customers or accept the invitation from table nine, forget about table nine, which we're giving to Vânia, don't be in any hurry, let the people wait, you're not a drag queen you're an artiste, Marlene, our own artiste, now that you've found your glasses clean those leaves off your breast and your knees and smile,

don't grab the shotgun, don't turn it on yourself, smile the way the
girl in the picture on the plate was smiling
do you remember?
a little hazy now and still so beautiful, shaking her braids and
saying hello to you.

CHAPTER

WHAT'S THE REASON for your eyes being so far away when you hear the rain falling Paulo, why don't you talk, connect with me, say

—Gabriela

why do you sit on the bed all by yourself and explain to me without speaking

—You're the maid from the hospital dining room, you're nobody

hearing voices and steps I'm not aware of and I stop existing for you, what does exist, is it those voices and those steps I don't know who they belong to and you're there listening to them without saying anything, every once in a while you'll speak to them but in such a low voice that I can't catch it

—Who are you talking to Paulo?

and the leaves of an elm tree answer through the boarded-up window where in September there are echoes from a backyard we can't see, the flapping of neighbors' clothes on the line, my sister worried about me and looking at the bed, the washbasin, the wardrobe, she'd press money into my hand

—So are you living with him Gabriela?

if only my father could pick up his accordion, start a little tune, take me with him, I'd say

—I'm going with my father Paulo

and Paulo deaf, worried about the rain and what the rain brings out, a man with a cane explaining the maple trees to him in Latin, for example, an old woman in a laundry room where he used to fly before he flew with me, for example, the actress's lady friends who would visit us sometimes and leave a happiness of laughter in the room, for example

the singers were so happy

perfume, traces of makeup as they pinched my chin and kissed my cheeks

—Your wife's very nice Paulo

they would twirl around the bed in a kind of merry dance, Miss Micaela, Miss Marlene, Miss Sissi, missing was Miss Soraia who'd died six months earlier and when I forgot she was dead and asked

—Where's Miss Soraia?

Miss Micaela, more respectable, older, coming over to me with a tango step

—One of these days when you least expect it you'll have Soraia here my pretty one

while I wondered why my father hadn't taken me out of here, it's been so long since we've seen you father, you don't look me up, you never put in an appearance, my sister

—Still working up that mania about father what a silly notion

and Paulo listening to the rain fall, I even thought about going with him to the doctor at the hospital but when I was thinking about going with him to the doctor at the hospital who when he passed me

—Susana

me

—My name isn't Susana, doctor

and he, in spite of being important and serious without ceasing to be important and serious, had a flirty little hand like the kind Mr. Vivaldo had except that he hadn't committed suicide yet

—I'm sorry but you have a Susana face, Susana

when I was thinking about going with him to the doctor we went up to the Cape Verdeans in Chelas, we looked for the broken-down wall or a shack with half the roof missing that had been a garage because of what used to be a cement floor and today was cracks, seeds, dried oil stains and a tire where we'd unroll the newspaper, cut the lemon, heat up the spoon, and the trip would start, my father opening and closing his fingers, I would say

—Thanks for the tune, father

and I'd forget about the doctor, that I had a Susana face, and about Paulo listening to the rain in the bedroom, while I fluttered with open arms over the beams of the garage without my sister's angry judgment as she hugged my nephew to her breast

—Gabriela

made me come down and when I came down I found myself with no wish to find myself, that is, a girl in a hairnet carrying patients' lunch and dinner from kitchen to dining room followed by plane trees and pigeons, the actress in the center of the yard blinking indecisively, animated, merry

the singers are so happy

—Have you seen my nephew, sugar?

sometimes the actress at other times someone who must have been the actress's twin brother excusing himself with fancy words

—Have you seen my nephew, sugar?

the same faces, the same rings, a graying bald spot instead of blonde hair, a suit instead of a dress and yet a scarf that was exactly the same, it seemed to me that there was the same mole on the chin and that a penciled mole on a man was impossible, it must be a real mole

—Is he your uncle, Paulo?

one of the two of them was sick at Príncipe Real while I hesitated

—Which one of the two?

so that whenever Paulo's eye went far off as he listened to the rain falling I would cease to exist for him, he didn't talk, didn't connect, would excuse himself to the man with the cane who was explaining the maple trees to him in Latin

—I'll come visit you one of these days, I promise

because Lisbon isn't all that big that I won't run into you, the coffee shops where you meet your comrades from Timor, the bench where you sit to rest your lungs, the maid from the dining room interrupted me, the boob

—Do you miss your aunt and uncle, Paulo?

I don't miss anybody, I can't stand anybody, the owner of the café brought a pint of wine while I played with empty matchboxes on the floor

—Send that spook away Judite

or pulling out the cork with his teeth because his other arm was where I don't care to remember

—Open your mouth, spook

pulling my head back, giving me a drink and everything warm, tickling my stomach, my mother getting free from him

—Alfredo

she wiped me with her sleeve and the sleeve turned purple, the floor wouldn't let me walk

my mother on the hippopotamus on the carousel, I on the elephant, do you remember the lights on the Tagus?

if I tried to take a step it went soft on me, I came up for an instant, swimming in the mirror on the wardrobe and right after that I wasn't there, I searched for myself with my hands and what I found was me without being me because my hands were slipping around without reaching me and I began to cry, the café owner, the floor hadn't changed for him

—What's all this Judite don't get mad at me, come here

I appeared in the mirror again along with the corner where my mother had run over and then only the café owner and then one of us, the refrigerator that rose up all of a sudden and something hurting me on the back of my neck, I tried to get a grip on the mattress that was getting away from me, the café owner grabbed me around the waist

—I'll help you up, boy, it wasn't anything

stronger than my mother, your son looks skinny and he weighs a ton the little devil, the floor settled down, the bulb in the ceiling got smaller as the rug got bigger, through the open kitchen door a gull was preening its wings, my mother helped me down the steps by the entrance, the café owner don't worry everything's okay give the big chief a big kiss pussycat, my mother's body shaking, wait

—You go play on the beach for a while

not on the beach because herons were on the beach, in the garden where a lizard scurried off through the opening in the wall, I thought maybe I could grab its tail with my thumb and forefinger but the opening beat me, came up and swallowed it, the sound of shoes, the neck of a bottle on a glass, the café owner invisible, imitating a child whose big kiss hasn't come, the café owner's wife was cleaning the tables and watching me silently, that is, she kept on cleaning the same table while I hid in the gentian where the branches were scratching my nose

—Are you my grandson?

a small dark parlor, my grandmother never turned on the lamp at night, she'd walk without making a sound and then the heartbeat of the clock would change, a gray splotch would get larger among the shadows

—Judite

and changed as the lampshade turned into mourning sleeves and brazier ash, in winter, when the cat died, she put it in a drawer with some pill bottles, letters, and those throat ribbons from when she was young, faded now

—Don't bury him on me Judite

my grandmother behind us stumbling in the corn patch in spite of the rain that was erasing her features

—What happened to your head, grandmother, your chin?

fingering her rosary beads one after another and grinding her gums

—Don't bury

the pump on the neighbor's well confused her and we went to get her at the barrier fence where she was tearing at the boards in hopes that the animal

—Don't bury him on me Judite

the cat who didn't need any light to settle down on her lap, its eyes round, turned into nothing but hair and coming out of the hair a lump with claws, my father patted down the grave with the shovel, also erased

—What about your forehead, father, your chin?

my mother erased, me erased, the well and the lemon tree erased, the drawer with the letters empty, my mother gave her the drawer, grabbing vials, buttons, I think a picture with a book in her lap, a bouquet of violets that smelled of scented memories

—Here's your drawer, mother

the next day my mother was out in the corn patch looking for the cat talking to it

—When you hear the rain falling and you don't talk to me are you thinking about the cat Paulo?

when I hear the rain falling and people without any foreheads or chins I'm thinking about my grandmother in the photographer's studio, the photographer handing her the book

—Put your index finger on the page and pretend you're reading

my grandmother who didn't know how to read, rolling her eyes at the writing in front of a curtain with a tropical background

bays, coconut palms

where the shadow of the camera extended and he was calling for attention with an authoritarian arm

—Smile

a girl that none of us knew with a hat that must have belonged to her mother and her feet together, who's blind today

tell me about it

keeps looking at the bays and the coconut palms, my father patting down the cat's grave with his spade

—Look, it's raining

because of the rain you couldn't see the vegetable garden, you could see the bread oven and the chicken coop, too, but hazy, dim, those lenses on the glasses grownups wear that distort everything

—When you put them on, doesn't everything look terribly strange father?

faces at a slant, objects falling apart, my grandmother searched through the drawer and for a second the girl with her shoes together was surprised at us, an arm ordering her

—Smile

I took a better look and there was no arm no girl at all

—She was never young, didn't you know?

only my mother getting sentimental over the picture and my grandmother warming her feet on the brazier, I was waiting for the lizard to come back along the wall, the café owner passed by scratching himself

—You can go back to your mother, spook

while his wife was cleaning the table and wasn't looking at the café owner until he said

—Bernardete

even today I wonder if it was me she was looking at, we brought the picture with the bays and the coconut palms to Bico da Areia and one day we lost it

I lost it

I didn't lose it, I tore it up, I thought it was unfair, my grandmother dead and the girl with her finger on the book was alive, they lowered the casket using ropes and I said

—Aren't you going to pat down the grave father?

my mother gathered the pieces together looking at me with an expression like the one gulls and the cleaning woman have, a Gypsy came out of the waves whipping a horse with the remains of a belt, what happened to the box with pill bottles and letters, on top of the wardrobe, in the tub among the bottles, a part of the café owner in a part of my mother that I preferred not to know

that I don't know

that I know

that I preferred not to know, the Gypsy erased in a tone that intrigued me

—Give the big chief a big kiss, pussycat

pulling the cork out with his teeth because his other arm was where I'm not going to remember

where I didn't want to remember and still I do remember

—Open your mouth, spook

so that a few months ago I bought a can

before spring because Alto do Galo was fogged over and the flowers on the gentian closed up, my father at Príncipe Real

—The gentian flowers, Paulo

so that before spring I brought a can of gasoline to Bico da Areia with the flowers on the gentian closed up, I leaned against a bridge beam until a bit of moon was over the water, rags and bottles, that is, and a piece of shopping bag with no electrician, no pups or Dália's aunt noticing me it's been ages since anyone's been pedaling the tricycle two houses away

Lisbon across the way and the lights of ships, several Lisbons and several ships set on top of one another by the movement of the Tagus, one Lisbon folding into another and another into another and at that point the first one again, my mother chatting with a man, the man dumped a pail out into the yard and pushed the door open, wearing Rui's topcoat I brought a can of gasoline, the syringe, the newspaper, and the cigarette lighter to heat the spoon, it's been ages since anyone's been pedaling the tricycle two houses away because the niece there didn't become engaged to a doctor, she begs on the street, they told her that her niece is begging on the street

—Don't bother me, shut up

Dália spinning around and spinning around in a little blue dress, she looks like an angel, she looks like a fairy queen, she looks like a princess, don't you think

—Shut up

I said to Dália on the hill in Chelas

—Do you want your tricycle Dália?

and Dália, open-mouthed, shaking in her rags, what happened to your teeth Dália, what happened to your doctor's wife's teeth, did you know that the tricycle's waiting for you with new wheels, Dália, did you know that your aunt

—Shut up, I didn't hear you, be quiet

closing the curtain, the lock, the blinds

—Don't bother me, shut up

Dália in Bico da Areia trying to remember

—Where did you know me from?

crouched at the entrance to the settlement, hoping for some coins, those cuts on her fingers, those faded nails, the wind from Trafaria could be felt along with some shreds of music hanging from your shoulders like your jacket, Dália, when the gentian flowers open up in May we'll get engaged, would you like that, Dália and the spook

—Get rid of that spook for me, Judite

the spook waiting along with the silence, Gypsies, the mirror on the wardrobe empty, no light in the settlement, pulling the cork from the can of gasoline with his teeth, at the café ordering

—Open your mouth, baby

Dália with the help of the spook pushing the plunger into a vein in her tongue, both her arms and legs bloodless, she was searching under her clothes and the lines of her bones gnawed at her skin, Vânia got thin like that and the manager was studying the looseness of her blouse

—Could you be sick by any chance, Vânia?

if my grandmother ran her fingers over her face she'd understand, my grandmother in a grave that my father didn't pat down, it was patted down by two characters in caps while the priest held his missal against his chest complaining about the cold

—Hurry up

no bell to toll for her, the girl with her finger on the book with us

no, a neighbor girl

no boxwood tree no tree of any kind, a rectangle at the start of the slope with a crucifix at the entrance

the Marrano cemetery, they said

cypresses in burlap to be planted later, willows, Judas trees, Vânia

—I never felt better

on one occasion we brought my grandmother to Bico da Areia, everything getting left behind through the window

that is, the memories I had were running through the train window as though they'd grown old in an instant, separating us from things that were ancient in the end, the house, the cat, the mimosas, my mother's smile halted on her mouth

—Open your mouth, spook

we brought my grandmother to the steps by the gate, the pigeons' whispered lullabies and she was worried trying to hold onto us

—I don't understand the sea Judite

in the small room to the rear where the basket with the sheets to

be washed was, the almost empty box with the metal table settings
that we were selling or turning in at the café where the gasoline now

the spook would turn them in at the café where the gasoline
now, the owner would scratch a fork or spoon with the knife, heft
them in his hand, look them up and down and half a pint of wine,
my mother to my grandmother

—Come eat, mother

and she was all huddling with fear

—I don't understand the sea Judite

—*Is the café owner my father, mother?*

my mother silent or maybe

—*What do you want here, go away*

and before I went away the spook, helping Dália with the vein in
her tongue

or before the spook was all alone thinking if I could only help
Dália with the vein in her tongue, the rest of the can of gasoline on
the canopy, one of the pups trotted by right next to the last house
and sank into the dune, if I'd only known Mr. Couceiro at that
time, I would have asked him to speak to my grandmother and
explain the sea in Latin, the city across the way, the ships' lights, the
spook bringing the lighter up to the newspaper and the newspaper
to the gasoline, the café owner in the house just to the left of the
settlement with a saint in a niche and bricks and cactuses, his wife
in her apron knew for sure

—*Is he my father, mother?*

*and my mother on the bed with her eyes closed unable to stand looking at
me*

—*Get away from here*

the customers knew for sure, the electrician, the neighbors, my
other father, Soraia

—*A nephew Dona Amélia*

Dona Amélia picking out a piece of candy

—*Do you like candy, spook?*

such nonsense

—*Do you like candy, child?*

my other father, Soraia, knew, my nephew, my cousin, my

younger brother, call me Soraia, Paulo, don't mess up my life, Dália with the spook

it isn't the maid from the dining room that I love, it's Dália, with me when I hear the rain fall in the room, if only Dália were with me, a butt friend, a coin for a cup of coffee friend, draw a family, the chess player telling himself to shut up

—Bastard

the doctor to Gabriela

—I'm sorry but you've got a Susana face, Susana

excuse me, the doctor tapping his pen on the desk, calmly, terribly

—You set fire to what, Vivaldo?

me spying on the hospital kitchen, a patient in pajamas pissing on a post, my father brought Micaela to visit me, the perfume of both of them wiped out the mimosa and my mother in the village

—Can't you smell the mimosas, Paulo?

Mr. Vivaldo with mocking bows

that flirty little hand, that rascally little hand

—Madames

Micaela enchanted, with a spiral of jewels

—How nice

that fool set fire to a settlement of poor people in Caparica or Fonte da Telha but the whole awning didn't burn up, some Gypsies found him in the morning leaning on a bridge beam chatting with the gulls, calling them

—Dália

and trying to stick an empty syringe into his tongue, Mr. Couceiro's cane was writing on the ground, Dona Helena holding back tears with her nose and trying to hug me

—Paulo

not in Caparica not in Fonte da Telha, near Trafaria, in Bico da Areia, one of those settlements with shacks along the Tagus, small plots with marigolds, pine groves that need thinning, among some gentians a woman whose age is hard to tell, not the one in the apron wiping a tabletop, the one fishing for something in a tub under the clothesline and the orderly, it's his mother, doctor, the wife of the clown who visits him by the fence straightening her wigs with her fingertips, see her using the broom to threaten the pups barking at her from the beach, throwing pine cones against the window panes, I'm your friend Dona Judite I'll pay, she'd open the door to them and they with an urge to run away, digging into their pockets

—I guess I was wrong, this is all I have, ma'am

not men, puppies, thirteen, fourteen years old at most, the wife taking the quilt off the bed

—Hurry up

and a desperate glance at the herons outside, noses holding back tears like Dona Helena, childish voices that withdraw, fade away

—Come to think of it, we don't feel like it Dona Judite, let us go

—*I'll take you in my arms if you want, do you want me to take you in my arms?*

Mr. Couceiro never took me in his arms, the old lady was barely holding me around the waist

—*Take your daughter in your arms I'm not a girl, go take a shit for yourself, Dona Helena*

if only I could have said something when I saw her crying, if only I could have managed

—*I'm sorry*

pull the handkerchief out of her hands

—*I was only fooling don't pay any attention to it*

resting my head on her shoulder, helping her, helping myself

the café owner who really wasn't burning to give half a bottle of wine to his mother and the spook in the office at the hospital, proud of I don't know what, showing us his hair held in an elastic band, his eyes red

—Cute, don't you think?

the spook going up the steps by the gate with a can of gasoline repeating Dona Judite Dona Judite, a pup like the others, I'll pay Dona Judite, don't worry I'll pay

the maid from the dining room rising up from the pillow

—*Paulo*

and Paulo with his back to her listening to the rain

looking for bills and coins in his pocket and neither coins nor bills, the plunger of a syringe, a needle, a piece of newspaper, the spook not recognizing the wardrobe, what was once a car with wooden wheels smashed on the quilt, the woman at the kitchen table tipping the neck of a bottle

—What happened to my mother's medallion?

the smell he caught of mimosas and, checking it better, of sludge in the Tagus, what mimosas for God's sake, the things people invent, mimosas and graves and laurels and the conviction of having been happy when

it's obvious

so unhappy, like today, poor devils, the clowns, Marlene, Micaela, Vânia, Sissi

—Speak to your mother don't be bashful

the spook leaning against the refrigerator

no, the spook leaning against the plane tree at the hospital, a butt friend and Mr. Couceiro's cookies on Sunday, he didn't have the courage to speak to his mother, he balanced on the bridge beam, the café owner shouting from down below you set fire to my awning, didn't you set fire to my awning, didn't you, and he escaped to a higher crossbeam, slipping

—Dona Helena

as though the dead woman who'd brought him up could save him, the dead woman to whom the spook, to whom I said

—Don't bother me leave me alone

I didn't mean to say

—Don't bother me leave me alone

I meant to say

—Dona Helena

I was sure of saying

—Dona Helena

saying

—You shouldn't have died, understand?

and I said

—Don't bother me leave me alone

horrified at having said

—Don't bother me leave me alone

maybe you don't believe me, but every so often it happened that I felt protected with you, watching you turn on the radio, crochet, cook, the café owner said you set fire to my awning didn't you, on one occasion I changed the flowers in Noémia's room, I made a cardboard mat in school, took away the dried petals, put fresh water in the vase, when I turned around Dona Helena was by the door, her jaw quivering

—Paulo

I didn't mean to break the vase I swear, why would I break the vase, it was a surprise for you, my mother decided to break it, I was angry with my hand, I stood looking at the pieces of glass, the spilled water on the floor, the roses

I asked the woman at the store to sell them to me on credit, I told her

—Those white roses, the big ones

I'm sure she heard me

—It wasn't me, Dona Helena

in spite of my silent mouth, just like Rui after selling my father's rings

—It wasn't me Soraia

in spite of his silent mouth, you could see

—It wasn't me Soraia, quite healthy

I was silent while the café owner said you set fire to my awning, didn't you, the gulls were so close, one of them, filthy with slime, set apart from the others but the same ferocious cruelty, the same hate, a pup

two pups climbed up onto the bridge, the café owner

—Let me get rid of that son-of-a-bitch, let me settle with him

they got up over the beam, hit me and I wasn't hurt, what hurt was the

—Send this spook away for me, Judite

the vase hurt me, if the building in Anjos still existed, I'd run up three floors, ring the bell, and take my place in the living room, the doctor's pen

—*You have my daughter's name, how funny, how'd you like to have lunch with me, Susana?*

insisting in the office

—It looks to me like he's taken a beating, Vivaldo

without my noticing the horsewhip marks on my chest, on my kidneys, my mother opened the gate and stayed by the gate, at intervals during the whipping of the gentian by the wall, one of the branches bent over onto the chimney, wavered, surrounded by wasps, my father at Príncipe Real

—The gentian Paulo

me at Príncipe Real

—The gentian father

and from the way my son looked at me I understood that he didn't remember either the gentian or his mother, I was sure that in all those years he hadn't found her again, on Saturdays I'd go to pick him up in the laundry room where the old lady was ironing and he was there with a basket, I'd take him along with me out of pity, if I happened to be busy

because my life isn't all that simple

I'd ask him to wait a bit by the cedar tree while I handled a problem with a friend and I'd look at him through the curtains, quiet in the park, the café had its lights on, the buildings were changing color at that moment while the streetlights went on, I told my friends with an agitation I couldn't understand

—I've got my son there

no, I told my friends, pointing to the curtain

—I've got my nephew outside

the ambassador, the economist, the partner from ready-to-wear that the manager and Dona Amélia sent me

—Kid gloves because they're respectable people, Soraia

mistrustful, tense, they asked me immediately if there were any photographic devices, of course not, they insisted that it was the first time, they were sweating, livening up with a bit of cognac

—Doll

they would settle down on the sofa, my nephew saw us I was sure, and it was then

my stopping listening the same way that Paulo stops listening to the rain that the gentian appeared, I was not with them, I was with the watering can in the afternoon with no horses now or herons on the beach, the customers were ambling out of the living room, looking at the posters, promising tips and I couldn't hear them, even if I was interested I couldn't, given the fact that I was so far back in time with my wife

I was just fooling, I never had a wife, a woman, what for, since I'm a woman aren't I

I was working at the jeweler's, I'd just met you Judite, I was in the schoolyard with a bouquet of hydrangeas, putting on a smile, if I can get rid of the smile I'll be serious and you tug at the bouquet and I hold it tight, the important people on the sofa beside me

—Nobody will find out I came here, will they?

the shoulder strap falling all by itself, my knee

—I'm a discreet girl, don't worry

I didn't recognize the knee

—I don't know you, knee

getting my face in order so I could build a smile and handing you the hydrangeas, the amount of rubbish I had to take care of, eyebrows, jaws, ears, the teeth I don't know if I should show you because one of the front ones is brownish, how could I do all that, how could I get all that together, I managed to get the right eye looking friendly, but maybe not so friendly, because Judite looking through the bouquet, alarmed

—Don't you feel well Carlos?

my nephew in Príncipe Real, I'd swear he saw us, incredulous with the lifting of the dress strap, the knee, the cognac

—It's the first time, doll, I swear to you, I never

jackets on the body that resisted, collars impossible to open, thinking about the gentian on that summer afternoon, asking my wife for the clothes sprinkler for the sick branches, when the vine gets all the way around the house I'll be able to be with you Judite and be the father of my son, isn't it true that I'm the father of my son, the one five or six years old

no, older, nine

by the cedar tree outside, the lampshade was knocked over in an anxious movement

if I managed to feel sorry, maybe feeling sorry didn't matter to me

and they were on their hands and knees picking up the pieces

—Don't get mad, I'll pay for it don't get mad, I'll

kid gloves because they're important people, holding out the pieces in the palm of their hands Soraia, take this bottle of plum brandy, this one of Jamaica rum

—Where's Jamaica?

not interested, who cares where Jamaica is, this bottle of French sparkling wine as long as you don't notice the scratch on the label, which even if you add water to it, makes for an expensive drink

pulling out the cork with his teeth because his other arm is where I don't want to remember

—*Open your mouth, spook*

you must have some drinking glasses in the place, everybody has drinking glasses in his house

—Did your lover pawn the glasses, Soraia?

Dona Amélia asks the bartender to wrap up half a dozen glasses for her, the green ones that went out of style and luckily are cheap in case the boyfriend pawns them again

the gentian I planted was tiny, two stalks that were like nothing

what a crummy bunch you all make, I need your wristwatch, where's the wristwatch, an urgent debt, next week I'm getting a late payment, I'll get it out of hock and everything'll be fine, the important people were lingering over my glass-bead stars, my image of the saint, the silence of someone who can't believe, the hesitation

—I'm leaving

stopping

—I'm not leaving

so while my mouth fawned on them, the barefoot saint in a plaster cloud, the conch-shell caravel, their curiosity appalled

at what?

—Did you buy this stuff, doll?

the collar easier now that we're friends isn't that so, the topcoat

over the shoulders while a little finger picking up courage poking
me in the belly, a whisper letting me know

—I don't want it to get wrinkled, catch?

the green glass on the nickel tray

—Fine fine

the vine growing toward the sun in August, the Tagus was washing the wave towels back and forth on the beach and they were talking to nobody, not to me, I don't know their names, I never knew
their names, even if I wanted to, I couldn't get to see them from this
bank of the river, don't leave any makeup on my throat, doll, don't
get upset, your nephew can take it, he must be used to it, isn't he,
the gentian spreading out from the wall rounding out its clusters

—It's good you've come back, Carlinhos

if I open the window at Príncipe Real I'm sure I'm going to see
the terrace, the horses, my son in our bed laughing, my wife to him
birdy birdy what a beak let me have a little peek, the first front
tooth at four and a half months, the second at six, the manager they
phoned me to complain that they're not paying you to lie on the
bed talking about front teeth, making fun of them with kiddy
songs birdy birdy what a beak and I said don't you like the vine
Judite, I had the watering can in my hand

—What customers, sir?

since one root was having a hard time in the bricks of the flower
bed, give it some phosphate, fix my eyeliner to make my eyes wider

—What customers, sir?

what customers, sir, because I've been here the whole time with
the plant that was muted by the tide of the Tagus and the folds of
tar on the beach that I forgot to cover with powder to disguise their
age, the one who knocked over the lampshade, intrigued

—Tell me the truth, don't lie, haven't you seen the last of thirty,
doll?

the gulls fleeing, the horses retreating shaking their manes, last
October

or December, close to Christmas, at the time when my son
started walking, we set up a barrier of boards and stones and a few
hours later, in the middle of the night, the marigolds drowned, I

peeked out from the kitchen and an albatross croaking at us imitating the bats, me, with my eyelid all fixed now, spinning on the stool abandoning my reflection which was still fixing itself up

—Birdy birdy what a beak, sir?

are you saying customers, a nickel tray with a couple of empty glasses and some bills on it, sir, a cigarette lighter that they left behind on the table, a voice or footsteps

not Rui's, not Paulo's, not mine

afraid they'd be noticed, asking

—Don't come out I know the way

hoping that the landing is deserted, the stairs empty and thank God their landing deserted, the stairs empty, the kiosk closed, nobody except for the boy coming over from the cedar tree

his nephew, his younger brother, maybe his son what do I care, Soraia not seeing me maybe she did get to see me, I asked her something and she said

—I beg your pardon?

—I'm sorry?

—What?

or maybe words that seemed to me to be coming from a jingle back when I was little, the girl cousin who took care of me birdy birdy, as soon as she stopped me

—More

there are times with my wife when I come out with birdy birdy what a beak let me have a little peek, my wife

—What's that, Henrique?

and me of course

—Nothing

with the birdy birdy tormenting my mind, but it must have been some confusion on my part, how could the wretch have known my cousin, I was in the street now with the birdy birdy and the old lady pounding on me, angry at her for having died on me, raising my hand and Soraia on the ground floor plucking at the curtain as if she was pulling the leaves off one of those vines that peasants and riffraff in the outskirts adore, arranging bunches, supporting branches with a twist of wire, asking what I took to be a woman on a step

—Do you like the gentian, Judite?

not a bougainvillea, not a young vine, a gentian she said

—Do you like the gentian, Judite?

in a flower bed made with bricks painted blue, I tried to touch the vine and my cousin

—Hands off

changing me from my parents' bed to mine, tucking me in, leaving the hall light on, ordering me

—Go to sleep

coming back to give me a kiss, disappearing upstairs into the piano room and from there nothing, a polka or maybe there wasn't any music and only the rain outside, the rain outside certainly, my wife what's the reason for your eyes looking like that when you hear rain outside, Henrique, not understanding birdy birdy on the windowpanes, and complaining that she doesn't exist for me, never existed for me and you smell of cognac, Henrique, you smell of cheap perfume, your cousin's or from that strange singer at Príncipe Real the one that I've been given hints you're seeing, you smell of gentian, such poor taste, don't pretend, don't call me doll

I just can't believe it, Henrique

above all don't call me doll while you hug my knees asking me to forgive you, offering me money, picking up the pieces of a lampshade from the carpet and holding yourself as though you were a stem with a wire brace around you.

CHAPTER

I THOUGHT MY office hours at the hospital were over and I was putting my papers in order with hopes of having a peaceful lunch with
Elisa when the nurse came in without knocking

—You have one more patient, doctor

one of those young nurses who seem to have been mass-
produced in some high-class ceramics shop, it's hard to get mad at
them or say no, not a wrinkle on her glass-smooth skin, a small
defect on one tooth that maybe makes me feel sorry for her, something about her waist that makes me feel old and superfluous, like
a piece of antique furniture, a sideboard or dresser, looked at without interest, capable maybe of seducing her aunt, not her, the girl
didn't understand that the crooked tooth that almost bit into her
lip caught me and made me feel happy, I smoothed my hair with my
hand and she didn't notice my hair, which made me look through
the folders slowly and grumble

—I can't see any name here

underneath it all I was glad to find myself close to a body that
was getting the better of me even before it started conquering me,
the back of her neck where there was some fuzz that curled out and
if it was touched there was no fear, no rejection, only sincere
surprise

—Are you crazy?

Elisa, three or four years younger, even though she'd been
ground down by unemployment and the problem with her foot and
even so she was uneasy at the movies and on the street, pulling her

elbow away and pretending not to be pulling her elbow away, looking embarrassed at someone who wasn't looking at us, asking me in
a low voice

—Don't take my arm Luciano

walking a step in front or a step behind, exaggerating her limp
with an unworried expression so as not to offend me, hoping that
strangers would think she was walking alone, I was supporting her
and her parents, I would go into the laundry room and her mother
had her back to me

—Don't you even dream of losing that gold mine of a doctor, and
you a cripple on top of it all

not catching the signals from her daughter's eyebrows, her flip-
pant father laying a piece of paper on the table

—I pawned my wedding ring, friend

in the beginning it was doctor sir, then doctor, now friend, any
day now it'll be Luciano, pawning my paintings, borrowing my car,
occupying my armchair

—I pawned my wedding ring, Lucianinho

Elisa on the phone with her cousin or prancing about among us,
bored, irritated, settling down in a corner of the sofa within reach
of my hand, opening a magazine without reading it, staring at me
out of the corner of her eye

thinking I didn't notice

wishing me dead, Elisa shrugging her shoulders and her mother
taking the remote from me to raise the volume on the TV where
some idiot was singing

—What do you mean dead, doctor, she's looking at something
else

when the only thing she was really seeing was the idiot blowing
kisses to her from the screen and Elisa not pulling her elbow away,
fluffing up her dress, sometimes I wonder why I don't come to my
senses and go back home, stop dyeing my hair, let out my belt a
couple of notches, breathe freely without stiffening my muscles like
when the nurse at the hospital straightens her cap and as she
straightens her cap I melt away with feeling

you could pour me into a chalice

shuffling through X-rays

—It's not here, your colleague in the lab asked for it on the phone

you could pour me into a chalice or dump my ashes into a pail, when I shave in the morning it's not me I'm shaving, I'm invisible and with no white hairs lathering a gray chin that doesn't belong to me, in front of our window in Reguengos in the summer Mr. Dimas was taking the chair out of his shop, setting it up on the square, tying the towel around his customers' necks

the wild doves were rising out of the fields

and he'd give them a close shave in the sunlight, I remember the smell of the aftershave as they got out of the chair and the proud Mr. Dimas wipping his razor and patting them on the cheek

—Like a baby's behind like a baby's behind

Reguengos, a row of warblers along the balcony of the co-op, the traveling bullring they would set up at the edge of town with the bulls shut up in a truck that reeked of lye, the owner would take care of their wounds from the last fight's banderillas with clover salve, we'd peep inside and there was unhappy lowing, if I were to go to Reguengos the barber's been in the cemetery for ages and not a warbler to be seen, if the nurse or Elisa could only guess that when I was their age, if they could only believe me, just when I was going to tell them where the warblers slept, one of them the nurse, I think, because Elisa and her cousin

—Also, I don't really know if it's a female or a male patient, he looks like a man to me, but he has a husband with him

the bulls in the truck scratching themselves on the nails and the sole matador drinking beer with the divorcee from the boarding-house. Elisa, who was getting fat in the hips, waiting for me, holding up her funny ankle, one of my colleagues calling in the corridor

—Bernardino

and a faucet turning on and off, quick footsteps

sometimes the warblers would circle around the square like drunken sailors, in every consultation room were prints of French paintings stained with grease and funguses

—Wait a minute Bernardino

taking the chairs from the medical office out onto the square and shaving his colleagues in the sun while the bulls, which looked to me like a single one with different heads, were rubbing up against the planks, Bernardino must have been waiting because

—I thought you'd gone deaf

the cleaning woman's stepladder on the floor outside and at that moment the fireworks from Évora with a handful of salutes and my saying let me set one off Mr. Borges, it's hard to be fifty-eight years old since September, lumbago, high blood pressure and still having a liking for firecrackers, the nurse was in a hurry to leave me

everything's leaving me these days

—Shall I send them in, doctor?

another one who'd started with doctor sir, now she's on doctor and any day now

that's the way the wheels go round

slipping a piece of paper onto my desk, taking a quick look around, like an accomplice, amused, let old Methuselah pay

—I pawned my wedding ring, friend

and I went for my glasses and wrote the check because that tooth, Mr. Borges handed me a bunch

—How time passes, lad, fifty-eight really?

he was just the same because I never saw him again, me with this damned spine and the masseur guaranteeing me, with pity, that I'm in very good shape for my age, when he asked me about it I lied, I'm sorry I lied, I explained that I always get my figures mixed up, his pen changed the two to a seven, the humiliation of cops and cabinet ministers younger than I was, when my father reached seventy he showed me a news item, unfortunate seventy-year-old run over by a train and in the last sentence they removed the old man's corpse to the morgue, the nurse, the nurse studying my remains on the railroad tracks, no problem with her foot, her flesh firm, glowing, kissing Bernardino, her arms, my God, a smile if she would only give me one

—Shall I send them in, doctor?

lumbago nonexistent and my cholesterol that of a child, only in homage to that smile while firecrackers were exploding with little clouds and the pigeons of Cardal Florido huddled in fear

—Show them in, Risoleta

the name on a badge at chest level, in Cardal Florido my grandfather's farmhouse a stone's throw away and my grandfather speaking to me from inside his mustache

—Scratch this shoulder for me Luciano I can't reach it with my
nails

the yellow mustache between his nose and his lip

—Tobacco, lad

underneath the yellow some exceedingly yellow gums from
which he'd extract a damp cigarette, his skull showing and his face
two hollows as he dragged on the tobacco, a hot coal rose up out of
the ashes and glowed for an instant, the farm here in the hospital,
the tractor gobbling up rocks, Bernardino running into Elisa in the
coffee shop and straightening his jacket

—Hello there

the cleaning woman passed me at the door on her hands and
knees with a brush and a cake of soap, there were metallic sounds
coming from the bandage closet, I went to medical school because
the doctor in Reguengos served the water crackers at mass and men
took their hats off to him without his saying hello to anyone, if you
were interested in fireworks all that was needed was one little word
and Mr. Borges haughtily

—They're yours

while as for what concerned me

—Use good judgment, boy

the little cloud and the explosion not in the sky, here below,
echoing off the walls of the church and the orange trees on the
square dropping their fruit onto the ground, Risoleta led that
woman and her husband in

—This way this way

fifty-eight years old and possibly the prostate

certainly the prostate

realizing that one of the temples on my glasses was wobbling on
its screw, catching sight of a dress and a pair of pants floating
about, pointing out the barber chairs in the sun as its rays bounced
off the walls of the church onto them, if my grandfather had his

beard trimmed he would fall asleep under the towel, the barber would extract the cigarette from the grip of his canines and his skull all startled sucking on nothing

—What's going on?

my skull begins to appear, I swear, see where the bones are joined together, if you see me fall asleep cover me with a handkerchief

—He's dead

just like my grandfather's corpse sleeping stretched out in the parlor under a linen napkin, Risoleta's bracelets from India growing quiet in the hallway

—Good-bye

the dress and the pair of pants took shape on the bench and changed into faces, a blonde wig, earrings on a skull similar to mine and the skull of a young fellow next to it, both silent, no tongues, no skin, inanimate skeletons handing me the lab report, the frayed blouse where the arm was, through the window an attendant in coveralls came out of the administration building, opened the lock on the storage room, five or six tanks shaded by an elm tree, a sign

no fires or flames

began shaking on the grillwork of the gate, the doctor gave out the water crackers at mass and didn't say hello to anyone, he took the stethoscope out of his bag, ordered me to cough, and would go off in silence, during the mating season the doves cooed all day in the oat field, Dona Isaura in her bathrobe on the Dutchman's terrace and my mother, I don't know why

—Idiot

the two skulls were watching, looking at me, arriving at the hospital on consultation mornings dozens of dead people like these, umbrellas, do you want me to scratch your shoulder grandfather where your nails can't reach, I to the blonde wig

—What's your name ma'am?

a pause in the cooing of the doves, the attendant in coveralls closing the gate and the sound of the lock coming after him, just one firecracker Mr. Borges, the other skull, the young fellow's

—Soraia

a small bag of gunpowder tied to the stick, a lighted match, the match touching the wick, you don't have to show me Mr. Borges, the blonde wig pulling off an earring massaging the ear

the piece of ear that skulls sometimes

contradicting the young man

—My name is Carlos

when I put my glasses on a piece of ear, really, pieces of jaundice that lipstick and creams no longer hid, the kind of glow that enshrouds the dying, my mother for example, they'd bring her some chicken soup and she was searching for the spoon without finding it

—Do you find me different?

so I wrote Carlos

the barber lathering up my grandfather before they hid him in his shirt, his suit, lathering up my father

not thinking about Elisa, about my wife by herself in the living room, about my empty armchair

I made a mistake and wrote Luciano, I erased it and wrote Carlos, and the young man doubling over as if he had colic

—Her name is Soraia I'm her husband

looking for something or other in his pocket, leaving the pocket alone, no doctor sir or doctor or friend, I should have said to the nurse

—I can't

have said, forgetting about the defect in her tooth and that business about her waist making me feel old

—Tomorrow

tomorrow because fifty-eight years old, cholesterol, prostate and a row of warblers waiting for me in Reguengos, one or two before, now dozens, hundreds, I look at the balcony and there they are, I look again and the railing is deserted, Elisa pulling up the quilt

—What's the matter now?

and even without turning on the light I knew that the warblers again, inside her face, pecking me, the skulls huddling and as they huddled a creak of ribs, vertebrae, I'm sick aren't I

or maybe the clouds from the fireworks and me spelling out the clouds before the blonde wig

—I'm sick aren't I?

one afternoon in the Alentejo the skeleton of a calf that the foxes had stripped, pieces of cartilage on the ground, a shred of hide, the birds that eat dead meat slipping about, not afraid of us, my sister and me

—Run, Luciano

us running home and at home no bones, curtains, rugs, my mother polishing the candlesticks on the piano that never held any candles

why don't they put candles in them mother?

the blonde wig taking off her cranium, her name is Soraia, my name is Carlos, her name is Soraia I'm her husband, a fear just like my sister's when she came upon the calf's skeleton

—I'm sick aren't I?

except no house to run to, in the office a tableau of a man in riding breeches asking a lady with a necklace I'm sick aren't I, run, you were never here, they never found your bones in the hospital although home, an ancient ground-floor apartment, a fringe of handkerchief on the artificial lashes, and underneath the artificial lashes the cedar in Príncipe Real noiseless rain, if only the Cape Verdeans from Chelas could help them

—Help us

the husband wearing a vest with spangles, lying like Elisa if I ask her

—Do you love me?

(can I love her?)

a sigh to the ceiling, her waist disappearing out of my hand, sorry because don't you even dream of losing that gold mine of a doctor, and you a cripple on top of it all

—I've told you twenty times

lying like Elisa, arguing that maybe I'm not sick, let's do the test again and the cedar missing, the blonde wig smiling, the caretaker who buried the calf, guaranteeing to the skulls, guaranteeing to my sister

—You had a bad dream you were mistaken I didn't see any bones, girl

I can continue working because I'm fine Dona Amélia, a passing fever, these autumn upsets, my old weight back in three weeks at most, tell the manager I'll make tonight's show, tomorrow's, every day in the week, a lab mistake, a mistake in numbers, hanging up the phone, calling Marlene

—Can you guess what they told me at the hospital, silly?

looking about serenely, reconciled, happy, and in that instant, in a chance reflection, the skull looking at her, not me, not me I swear, a dead man Micaela, the mummies in the House of Horrors that rise up slowly waving their arms between the hanged Judas and the witch who's petting a lizard, not a rubber one, even if your lover swears it's all fake, it's a real animal, the two of us

—Good heavens

see how my pulse is quivering, see what's happened to my pulse, if you put your finger there, you'll see that my heart's giving out, Micaela covering me with the quilt

—Don't get yourself all upset, it's nerves

so many shows we did together, we toured the provinces with a circus, do you remember the Jehovah's Witness who handed us the Bible

—Convert

showing us how God's breath had destroyed cities, we closed the first half dancing with the extras, the one who smelled of wine grabbing us

—And then?

Micaela to my son

—Bring some water

my son just like his mother, how should I know what place years ago, pouring water on the ground, probably in Bico da Areia or married again to someone, she doesn't torment me with accusations, suspicions, nosing into my pockets, checking out my clothes, finding a picture and showing me the picture, Alcides and me embracing on the beach

—Why Carlos?

tearing up the photograph, throwing it out into the marigolds, me not moving, give me some reason why I should move a finger and in spite of my not moving my wife

—Please don't touch me

Micaela held me, tipping the glass, just a sip go ahead, explaining to Dona Amélia who's peeking at me from the door not daring to come in, just like the woman who was talking to the man in riding breeches in the tableau at the hospital, timid, beseeching, calming her the same way Micaela

we toured the provinces with a circus and at ten o'clock the band was playing to an empty house, a piano, that is, and two trombones

the same way Micaela calmed me, don't worry Dona Amélia because after all I'm fine, tell the manager I'll be working quite soon, tomorrow at the latest, a passing fever the doctor said and Dona Amélia snuffling into her handkerchief

—Of course

if you don't believe me ask the doctor at the clinic, what do you think doctor, his eyebrows a flock of doves in flight

the fireworks in Reguengos

next week, my dear lady

me a lady, me a lady, did you hear Dona Amélia that's right

the doctor stirring calf bones, not bones that belonged to me, calf bones, next week a conference in Vienna, back from Vienna have them do a second test for me maybe it's not sickness, her husband do you hear that, Soraia, maybe it's not sickness, my mother not finding the spoon, she didn't know the purpose of a glass, a plate

—Do you find me changed?

she stopped, asked us what time it was, not

—What time is it?

an incomplete flourish pointing at the clock, we told her the time and she

—So early

next week Vienna, the conference, the Hotel Mailberger, there'd be no skulls, no dead people, no Elisa, my wife knitting before an empty armchair, the cleaning woman peeking into the office leaning on her brush or maybe peeking at the blonde wig

—Good heavens

and the blonde wig

—I'm an artiste, doctor

I'm a singer, I'm a dancer, I'm an actress, my parents would take me to the theater in Beja where people were all excited, were hollering in a foreign language, a curtain closed, all twisted, I tugged at it, and one last howl, a dog was barking backstage or in some nearby alley, near and far away like the sounds in the country starting at dusk, the rustle of the walnut tree among us at the table, the goats huffing in the closets, you'd open a drawer and only lavender, the eleven o'clock mail train, and a lantern swinging between rails, my mother

—Did you hear?

as the lights went on in the theater, the performers

the false lashes, the rings, the earrings

—I'm a performer, doctor

come out from a curtain that an old man was opening

I could have sworn also fifty-eight, cholesterol, lumbago

just like me by the car door so Elisa could get in, her father in a suit that belonged to me

belonged to me

winking at his friends

—The doctor's a gentleman

they told me to hand a bouquet of I-don't-know-what to the ones hollering, I went up a side stairway where scenery was piled up and a man

—Go ahead

one performer waiting for me with exaggerated niceties, seen from close by, her mouth was in acid folds, my mother to my father

—You should have brought the camera Raul

also a wig, also false fingernails that picked me up, they made me acknowledge the applause, instructing me, furious inside her nice manners, nod your head idiot, and following aloud, without any fury, stroking my ear although it seemed to me to be a slap of disdain

—What's your name, boy?

throwing pieces of the bouquet of I-don't-know-what to the audience, a second performer tripped over me in my timidity

—Get out of my way

maybe this one here picking up the test without noticing the cleaning woman

—Good heavens

when my parents hollered at each other

no one there to applaud them

—Do they want a bouquet too?

the blonde wig and her husband in front of me and on stage Elisa moving her elbow away, pretending not to be moving her elbow away

—Don't give me your arm, Luciano

the cleaning woman

—Good heavens

my wife on the sofa agreeing, I'll come back home, give me another month two more months and Elisa's scorn

—Who's that old woman, Luciano?

every so often, without my realizing it, I'm fine in the car and I come to the avenue almost in front of the building without daring to go in, when I think about going in a neighbor, the dentist with the Jeep, opening the mailbox, thumbing through his letters, looking up and before he spots me, I step on the gas and good-bye, the old grocery store, a fashionable shop, one of the mannequins

—Doctor sir

the art gallery deserted, the pastry shop whose name had been changed, looking back to see if the lights in the windows are on, and they seem to be

on

the electric kitchen gadgets, the kettle, the round clock which I didn't know how to set when they changed the time, locked into a time sometimes right sometimes wrong, but when was it right and when was it wrong, if I took a drink of water from the bottle in the refrigerator I'd look at the hands with hate

—What are they trying to tell me?

and the hands paying no attention, my wife

—Who are you talking to?

and how can I explain to her

tell me

that my mother back there, the Dutchman's hill bordered by lemon trees, rocks with weeds around them which the teacher made us respect

—The graves of Lusitanian warriors, show some respect

and only snipes among those enormous rocks, how could I explain

—Who are you talking to?

that my mother there in the clock, the smell of medicines, female cousins with rosaries, careful little steps, my father to us

—Go play in the dispensary while the orderly

they were changing her sack or something like that for her lungs, with us, swabs, tinctures, how to explain movements that are looking for something in a place where she didn't see them

—So early

finding her very voice strange, her eyes

—I didn't say anything

how to ask you to give me another month, two more months, if at least you took down the kitchen clock, lying, silent, your taking it off the nail without understanding, how could you have understood, it's impossible for you to understand

—The clock?

it's not impossible for you to understand because you didn't know the dispensary

—Go play in the dispensary while the orderly

the basins, the flasks, my mother's Pierrot from when she was small that frightened me, my mother to my father

—I can't throw the doll away I'm sorry

and since she wasn't capable of throwing us away either

—I can't throw you away I'm sorry

we were in the dispensary so the orderly could change the sack for her lungs, the dentist with the Jeep in the elevator with me opening a letter with a key, saying hello to me and while saying hello to me the floors slower than when I'm by myself, first, second, third while the 3 lighted up and the 2 went out, going from 3 to 5 with a pause at 4 burned out, you could see it was 4 from the grayish number, right there he interrupts his letter, takes a nail file from of his pocket, moves close to me

—Let's see about this

a doll that in May with pumpkin sweets relegated to the bottom and only the tip of its hat, invisible

—Raquel

my mother Teresa, my grandmother Manuela, my sister Manuela too, she inherited the farm, which her husband sold to foreigners

they sold me they were Scottish

and still he

—Raquel

—*What's your name ma'am?*

words are so hard dammit, you forget that words are hard, placing the card on the mat and the other skull, the young fellow's

—*Soraia*

too quick to be sincere

—*Soraia*

too tense, not even like a challenge, from fear, I'm not a faggot, don't think for a minute that I'm a faggot, doctor, her name is Soraia, I'm her husband, doubling over as if with colic and the blonde wig taking off an earring, rubbing her ear, contradicting the young fellow

—The Pierrot says my mother's name is Raquel

and my mother

—*My name is Carlos*

and my mother in the middle of the living room

—How strange, Raquel

an aunt of my grandmother's I think, they said that at night

the overseer said that at night there was a soul in torment looking for her wedding ring in the well but overseers poor devils believe in tormented souls and werewolves and ghosts, on that night or on the following night my mother by the well, we went to get her with the lantern and she was poking in the mud with her umbrella

—Wait

she was trembling so much

my father with his pistol in his pocket to defend himself from the ghosts

although only overseers poor devils

he had them burn the Pierrot in a basin, falling apart, inert, as soon as it stopped burning they threw the cinders into the edge of the field and the pistol went back to the desk, on holidays when he came out where the linnets were with us, my sister said

—Look

I saw the gleam of a piece of mica and instead of the piece of mica a wedding ring that said Rolando and my father didn't pick it up with his hand, he hooked it with a stick and ordered us not to tell anyone and repeating Rolando, he asked my grandmother at dinner

—What was the name of your aunt's bridegroom, Raquel?

—*Don't lie to the doctor Rui why lie to the doctor my name is Carlos my name isn't Soraia*

and taking closer notice I found that she didn't smell of perfume or deodorant or any of those creams they put on, she smelled of gentian and cheap bouquets, something like the gulls on the river, the false thumbnail lost without her having noticed, the blonde wig that fell over her forehead while the vine grew, hiding the traces of a beard and the purse with the broken clasp and the young fellow

—*I'm her husband*

insisting with pride

—*Her name is Soraia, doctor, don't listen to her*

and suddenly, I don't know why, I was in the car spying on my building waiting for a lighted window, waiting for you

a bronze pheasant in the center of the table, Saint George fighting the dragon in a carved frame

selling the farm

—What was the name of your aunt's bridegroom, Raquel?

they sold the picture too, the impression of my coming across it in an antiques shop in Sintra but I put it aside because I wasn't sure, Saint George on horseback in armor and helmet, the dragon rising up to the sword with a snort of light, covering her ears, not listening to the answer, and before covering her ears my grandmother said

—Jerónimo

spying on my building waiting for your window, two months more and I'll come back asking

—Forgive me

the dentist with the Jeep making room for the baggage and the dentist interrupting his letter, studying the suitcase, studying me, getting out on the sixth floor and his doormat new, going down to the ground floor in spite of your being alone in the living room, going off, running away, asking for forgiveness without your hearing me, putting the baggage into the car swearing to you

don't think badly of me

because I don't belong here, Elisa brushing her teeth annoyed at seeing me, leaving the baggage by the door, maybe if I tried to kiss her

—With this heat, Luciano?

so taking a magazine out of the basket, not thinking, not reading, waiting for her to go to sleep in order to lie down next to her, hesitating about hugging her, hugging her, sorry at having hugged her because her shoulder

—What a bore

and me uncomfortable with the idea that the dentist with the Jeep had heard her, I don't belong here, my father put the pheasant back by the window where the shadow of the wall

—I think it was Rolando

I asked about the painting of Saint George in the antiques shop in Sintra and a fat man with a child's pacifier

—To quit smoking, old man

came out weaving his way among dressing tables, sideboards, large mirrors

—It's not for sale, old man

there it was no doctor sir, no doctor

old man, in a moment now Luciano and a familiar *tu*

—It's not for sale, old man

trying to put me off

or console me

with some Louis XV chairs, dozens of cowbells along the wall, the pacifier with the tedious tone of someone testifying

—It's what they use in vacation homes, you push the button and instead of a doorbell a cowbell to recall the country, understand

in the end not the familiar *tu*, the formal *você*, on a second wall tile fragments hanging from wires, the remains of landscapes, wild boars, martyrs, I thought I caught sight of the bronze crest of the pheasant but at that moment the sun from the window and with the sunlight worthless pieces of junk, not the Saint George, a canvas with a conquistador leaping over a ditch, the dragon a wounded Indian with ridiculous feathers, my father to my grandmother, not really to my grandmother, to himself

—I thought it was Rolando

my mother

—Rolando?

the doctor assured me Micaela, he says there are a lot of viruses going around in the fall, I'll repeat the test and when he returns from Vienna on Tuesday or Wednesday

Hotel Mailberger Hof on the Annagasse, Hotel Mailberger Hof

He'll see us in his office, we'll give him the test results

—Completely normal ma'am no need for concern

and right then, he reminds me to send him an invitation to the show, after the visit, on leaving

—I promise

—You smell of gentian did you know that?

just like that, I looked at him, Rui was flabbergasted

—You smell of gentian did you know that?

and immediately Bico da Areia, Judite, the Gypsies' mares coming from the sea, I was

how else can I put it

content, not nostalgic, content, the albatrosses, the bridge, my son

my nephew was small, it was gratifying

you're going to laugh at me, don't laugh at me

dancing, luckily Rui pulled me out of it

—Soraia

*and the cleaning woman looking at us with that face they put on when
they look at us, crossing herself*

—Good Lord

but I shook his hand and he shook mine, we shook hands and I understood

Hotel Mailberger Hof, me in the Hotel Mailberger Hof with
prints of Flemish masters

Spanish, Italian?

imitation Empire furniture, two small bottles of Sankt Leopold
on a square tray

*understanding that he was calming me, finding me fit, wishing me luck,
his lips without any sound to be heard, he was standing very straight and closing his mouth, Rui*

—What's the little man got?

and me getting clo . . .

two small bottles of Sankt Leopold on a square tray

me getting closer

—Doctor

and the doctor

—Rolando

the room was large, with prints of Flemish masters

Spanish, Italian?

imitation Empire furniture, two small bottles of Sankt Leopold
on a square tray. The bed seemed too big, with the look of having
served for the wake of an important corpse the previous night. It
also gave the impression of a glimpse of a gentleman in patent
leather shoes lying on the quilt, a crucifix between his fingers and
his face covered with a handkerchief. From the window the Annagasse was visible

a street with no cars

and a Neapolitan restaurant a hundred feet down. Peeking at the
bed again after closing the window on the Annagasse, the gentleman in patent leather shoes had disappeared. The mark of his body
on the quilt was still there, however. He picked up the ballpoint pen
that came with the wine and began filling out his breakfast order, a
hole on top for the doorknob. He hesitated about putting down
two persons or one because of the corpse. He decided on an inter-

mediate solution and ordered *2 Eier im Glas*: thirty schillings isn't a lot of money. Besides, Austrians are pleasant people; a placard proclaimed WIR SIND IMMER ZU IHREN DIENSTEN

WE'RE ALWAYS AT YOUR SERVICE

and the lady at the reception desk, with painted eyelids behind her glasses, gave him a kind smile over the map of Vienna. Wien. An odorless and weightless city

maybe the aroma of sugar

which vaguely reminded him of Paris although lighter, softer, more intimate. The biscuit-like texture of the girls' skin enraptured him, especially when their laughter broke like a crystal glass. He filled out his breakfast order, put it outside, and thought about lying down: the memory of the dead man in patent leather shoes held him back. There was an armchair in front of the TV and thirty-six channels. He didn't turn on the sound out of respect for the dead. The first little bottle of Sankt Leopold, with a palace printed on the label, tasted like a gum remedy and therefore he didn't open the second one with the metal implement. The telephone maintained the look of loud objects when they're not making any noise. The electric clock with red numbers was announcing 2234. A Virgin with lowered eyes was protecting the Infant Jesus and a chubby little friend against spectral branches and a stormy sky. He counted the toes on the Infant Jesus and the chubby little friend and it annoyed him that they were correct. In spite of being no more than three or four years old the friend suffered from bunions. It must have been something esteemed during the painter's time. On turning his head to the left he caught sight of himself in the mirror on the wardrobe. He took the opportunity to turn sideways and measure his belly. He tightened his belt and measured again. Besides his belly he didn't like the fact that his shirt didn't match his necktie and neither the necktie nor the shirt matched his pants. He found himself too old. The clock had gone from 2234 to 2243 without his having noticed the time. No: 2244. He looked for the menu with a photograph of various vegetables

und so gesund

a pepper mill and a bowl of sauce, he ran through the pages, he came to *Rahmgulasch*, he stopped, *Rahmgulasch mit Servietten Knödel*. He leaned the menu back against the lamp and the clock, implacable, 2249. He wanted, without understanding the reason, a Bible on the night table. There wasn't any. He made the best of it and read the instructions in case of fire, with explanatory drawings. The last one showed a woman smoking in bed, with the cigarette covered by a red X: RAUCHEN SIE BITTE NICHT IM BETT. He cast a glance at the quilt: the worthy gentleman, one who respected instructions, wasn't smoking. Maybe if he lifted the handkerchief from his face. He lifted it. That is, he had the intention of lifting it but on touching the quilt no one on it. 2255. Rural scenes in black and white on a double print next to the bathroom. On the left panel a pair of hunters with shotguns on their shoulders and some quite tall trees. In the background a building with an abandoned look about it. In the print on the right the same building from a different angle, the same trees, scattered people. The label was identical on both of them: PROMENADE PUBLIQUE DE VIENNE, in nicely shaped lettering. Maybe Vienna had been a kind of farm in 1779, since under the label it stated it was drawn

d'après nature

by Laurent Janscha, a student of the famous Professor Brand, whose fame must have evaporated by 1780. Or 81. He decided to make a note not to forget to ask at the desk about Professor Brand, for whom the public promenade of Vienna took on the proportions of a provincial panorama. The lady with painted eyelids behind her glasses would clear up everything in the didactic manner of a librarian before he went out to take a streetcar ride through the center of the city. With a little luck he might run into the hunters with shotguns. Nor did he understand the reason for the soap in the bathroom being called Ginkgo Classic. He tried the Ginkgo Classic and his hands were left smelling of cedar. Besides that, there was the picture of a cedar tree on the Ginkgo Classic and at that moment he came upon eight fauns on the wall balancing on blue crags. If the hall is full of smoke, close the door and remain in the room. Attract attention from the window. Wait for the arrival of the firemen (*Sollte der Fluchtweg voller Rauch sein schliessen Sie die Tür und bleiben Sie im Zimmer. Machen Sie vom Fenster aus auf sich aufmerksam. Warten Sie auf die Feuerwehr*). Who was going to notice 329? Speaking of 329, the electric clock 2327. The Infant Jesus and his chubby friend five toes on each foot. Counting the fauns, 100 digits, speaking only of those below the knees. He took the metal implement and opened the second bottle. It also tasted like the gum remedy but it diminished his fear of dying.

CHAPTER

IT DIDN'T TAKE THEM long to forget my father because nobody remembers a dead clown, the same goes for Marlene, Micaela, Sissi, Vânia, too far on in years to dance at the club, too shapeless for the privilege of a street corner, coming out under a streetlight

—Hi there

and then nobody, I thought I caught a car looking me over, wondering

—How much a trick

and nothing but a fireplug or the reflection of the name of a hotel fluttering over the sidewalk

QUARTOS CHAMBRES ROOMS ZIMMER

fluttering over the sidewalk, *se habla español*, English spoken and neither Spanish nor English, flags behind the desk, a guy rising up out of a newspaper I don't know how many weeks old and pointing twice at the price on the sign in pencil, folding down his pinky and ring finger as accomplices in a discount and even so eight fingers, nine with the cigarette, nine bills *caballero*, nine bills *monsieur señor* sir, there's no bathroom but there's a small washbasin although unfortunately and for no apparent reason they've turned off our water, a stairway to the top floor where we're closer to God, sometimes we can hear His footsteps in the attic back and forth bringing order into the world, I could never understand people who don't believe in Him because God is changing the station on the radio and knocking over chairs with his unsteady knees, His cataracts, eyes worn out from searching for lost sheep among so many sinners destined for hell, loan sharks, cops, bill collectors for the gas, God is a little clumsy it's true but He's forgiving, kind, determined to forgive

—Come unto Me come unto Me

the hotel guy would bring up alms in the form of a little soup now and then because God is a widower and hasn't any stove there, wearing pajamas and a rubber cap ever since that tile

—That devilish tile

broke off because of the hail or the angels

—You've read about it in the Bible haven't you?

who because they revolted against Me I exiled them to the utter darkness, put the soup down on the floor, straighten out the stool, stay with me for a bit because I'm bored in Heaven, tell your boarders to do penance because the hour is near, prepare the Ark, Monteiro, because it's only waiting for the company to turn the water on in order to set up the Flood, the flags behind the desk are loose, Australia's has fallen off its staff, the ashtray in the shape of a metal turtle, if you lifted the lid you got the smell of stale tobacco in its shell, nine bills then

make it eight

eight bills *caballero* and with God as your neighbor what more do you want, He'd been sitting on the edge of the bed governing the universe ever since His wife's aneurysm, when she was alive He'd disguise himself as a desk clerk and watch over us in a bow tie, meticulous, judicious, studying our virtues, good morning, good afternoon, unsure we wouldn't suspect His divine nature but as soon as she'd been lowered into her grave, it must be five years now, He decided to reveal Himself

—I am what I am

Marlene, Micaela, Sissi, Vânia grow larger in the rain

—Hi there

Dona Amélia too, they told me Dona Amélia was without her candy tray ever since her husband's surgery but not with the others, all by herself, the expensive medicines, the dressings, the tiny roast chicken, I thought that another customer

—How could it be Soraia, as if my father who never grew old, because underneath the photograph

not written with a pen, printed and therefore true

Soraia the Star, I thought a customer

what foolishness

—Paulo

and I realized the maid from the dining room was stopping getting dressed

the blouse with the anchors

how many months has it been, how many years Gabriela?

I'd forgotten about her as she filled up the room, worried about me

—Paulo

as though all of a sudden Dona Helena and Mr. Couceiro were in her, the same expression, the same quivering mouth, the fear that I

—Don't bother me

me to her or to the customer in the car

—Don't bother me

drawing back toward the entrance offended, a faggot, a transvestite, a dead clown while God, in His pajamas, was spying on me in the seraphic heaven of the little attic window without being able to see me, maybe if I called Him a freak, a fright, the feeling that He'd been in a hurry creating everything in six days and a small guilty blessing, my father always paused even though the music had already started and the spotlight man said

—Let's go

he'd do a dip with his right leg and cross himself before the curtain went up on stage, Rui wearing for the first time the vest that Vânia had given him and my father in the middle of his prayer

—We'll see about that

Rui leaning against a column smoking, money in the pocket of the new vest

—Promise me you won't say anything to your old man

and the two of us in Chelas, *caballero monsieur signore* sir English

spoken, on Mr. Couceiro's landing in Anjos, or the Esperanto
teacher trailing after us maybe, a small man with a white beard and
a Siamese cat that was getting out of his arms just the way doves get
out of a magician's pockets vanishing into the air, the nameplate by
the door next to the bell *Esperanto parolata*, he would pause on the
steps assured, fraternal, never a wrinkle, a crease, all his pleats perfect, with the Siamese leaping from his arms and immediately
disappearing

—In a matter of months, not too many two three we'll all be
speaking the same language, brothers

the nephews who didn't speak the language had sold his dictionaries and grammars by weight, the bust of the distinguished Polish
gentleman who invented those verbal orthopedics, Vânia was
studying my features with pity, how long have you been on drugs
Vânia, your knees are so skinny

—If only you were cute like Rui, Paulinho

if God could only come down from the attic and correct my
imperfections, straighten my nose, the maid from the dining room
watching me as I tried to make the nose bone thin

—What's wrong with your nose Paulo?

not just the knees Vânia, your body is so skinny and I never saw
you in Chelas, Dália yes, you no, they'd stopped sending you notes
from the tables, you've got number nine waiting for you, girl

a fire hydrant, my father coming out of the entryway

—Hi there

with the bashful smile of not having slept at home making my
mother despair

—Where've you been Carlos?

before Bico da Areia we lived in Lumiar for a month, my father
repeating

—Do you remember Lumiar?

me

—I don't remember anything

and he was disappointed in me, some brownish buildings just
beyond the military post, I used to take you to Ameixoeira on Sundays, there was an abandoned factory there, if we coughed there

were echoes and echoes like people walking, Lumiar while he repaired a redheaded wig and I didn't think much of it

—You're not going to wear that piece of shit are you?

a redheaded wig to go out into the rain on a step by the entryway

—Hi there

I asked the hotel guy to take me up to the attic where God lived, a small stairway disguised by a wardrobe on the third floor, you moved the wardrobe to one side and the stairway was there in darkness, difficult but necessary

smelling of dried urine and mildew

the eye of the needle that comes before the Kingdom of Heaven, the desk with the keys are so earthly, so unimportant, the guy climbing up with me, pots all boiling up in his lungs

—You wouldn't think this could tire you out

the dried urine and mildew grew stronger, a hint of light where surely Paradise was and people exalting the Power and the Glory with psalms, a movement of martyrs and seraphs closer and closer, the guy, who was familiar with the corners of eternity, rapping on some invisible thing in the shape of a door, not with his knuckles, with the strength given for spinning out millenniums and for the destruction of cities without just people, God's eardrums had hardened a bit, pounding therefore, getting impatient because man's nature, unfortunately, is to be anguished and avid

—Mr. Lemos

someone shaped from too much clay was on the floor here below, still prisoner of a worldly state

—The law again?

the maid from the dining room grabbing me by the lapels

—Don't leave, Paulo

she'd set up a lamp from the hospital which went on if you shook it and you'd blink your eyes not used to the light, she'd put together a kind of sideboard with shelves from the storeroom, if we uncovered the window maybe we'd see the Tagus, a park, people just like us shaking out rugs across the street, my lapels were being gripped the same way my mother would in times past

—Don't leave, Carlos

—Don't leave, Paulo

a silence that was demanding, begging, give me the car with wooden wheels

I can't hear the waves though

so I can smash it on the floor

where the stairs ended rarefied solemn air, much higher than the clouds, the hotel guy, sacrilegiously, working on the lock with a piece of wire, twisting doorknobs

—*The old bastard's deaf*

the Esperanto teacher would drive away his Siamese cats with sweeping gestures, it was his hands, designing the cats, in the beginning there was nothing and then a nose, a paw, a curled-up life that stretched out with a leap and an animal running off

the doorknob came off with a bang, he lifted the latch to the dull glow of good fortune where the windowpanes hadn't been cleaned and a rubble of comets, lunar detritus, the bowl of soup from the night before or the night before that, cold on the windowsill

—*Haven't you eaten, Mr. Lemos?*

and no one in the little room, just as it was

se habla español, on parle français, English spoken, from time to time a wandering foreigner, a Japanese an arm raised protesting

—No no

a barefoot girl asking for a handout, angry, *si parla italiano* and the Japanese right out into the street

—No no

the first time I slept with a woman

not really a woman, Micaela

the first time I went to bed with a woman I stayed motionless waiting, a tureen with the picture of an aqueduct saying Cidade de Elvas and before taking off my shirt, before taking off my pants

—Elvas Elvas Elvas

shrinking away if she got close to me, pushing her hand away, the lamp on the night table had the nose of a seal balancing the ball that was the lampshade, next to the seal a shaving brush with the dried remains of lather and I kept my eye on the tureen Elvas Elvas

Elvas, no matter how much I tried to say something else and I really wanted to say

—I don't want to

a fever inside of me Elvas Elvas Elvas, if only I could have been able to run away over the aqueduct, if only I could have run away over the aqueduct, Micaela tugging as she put on her bra

—I'm doing you a favor and you push me away

the seal turned off and we all disappeared, no viaduct over which

so the Esperanto teacher with a long caress showed me a nose, a paw, a life all in a ball, I straightened out with a leap and

what a relief

good-bye

—I'm sorry Miss Micaela

no viaduct over which I can escape, Micaela a man after all, fingers without rings pointing to the doormat

—Get out of my sight

and instead of

—I'm sorry if I upset you Miss Micaela

—I didn't mean to offend you Miss Micaela

—I'm so ashamed Miss Micaela

my throat disobeying me Elvas Elvas, I ran through the tureen toward Spain, a sulkiness that was disappearing

—You ingrate, I was doing you a favor

beyond the mailboxes by the entrance no Seville, no Elvas, Lisbon was emerging, I took shelter next to a cement mixer near some construction work

Elvas Elvas

with the certainty that as long as there were tureens

and thank God there was no lack of tureens

I could keep on running

a folded mattress, old furniture in the shadows, the bowl of soup from the night before or the night before that

I could keep on running

the hotel guy looking at the bowl

Elvas Elvas with an indignation not worthy of God even if God was rheu-

*matic and deaf, surrounded by angels who no longer flew, nestling casually
in pitiful dejection*

—Aren't you eating, Mr. Lemos?

*nobody in Paradise, martyrs, seraphs, that is, my grandmother, for exam-
ple, who was in torment because of her blindness*

—And this one, Judite?

*His wife's nightgown on the armchair with just one arm from where He
annihilated Gomorrah and governed the navigation of the nebulae, the skylight in the ceiling open, vapors from the constellations made on the Second
Day beyond the span of the bridge and the statue of the Son blessing us, most
lovingly, from the heights of Almada, the hotel guy leaning out the window,
one shoe on the floor, the other hanging*

—I can't believe that the filthy bastard

Micaela who was changing earrings at the club in a quiet little
voice

—You don't like me, do you?

the hotel guy called me over, waving his hand in the air

—Come over here

*and God was hugging the chimney pulling off pigeon crud, I asked Him
about my father and He*

—What?

*I explained that he lived in Bico da Areia, he likes marigolds, one after-
noon he left the house on the highway bus, he took pride in masquerading you
know he worked as a clown in a club I don't know if you understand*

Elvas Elvas, no farther, even last night when I woke up in the
middle of a dream, Micaela or the maid from the dining room kissing me

or me thinking they were kissing me and right away the tureen
on three wire hooks

*he worked as a clown in a club lip-synching songs, he went with the man
from table nine right after the show, they're asking for you from table nine
Soraia and table nine*

—On my right, girl

*you must remember him when he'd come back to Príncipe Real hooted at
by the city workers washing down the square, taking off his rings, loosening
the elastic of his wig, kicking off his heels, it was impossible not to notice him,*

I waited for God to peel off the pigeon crud, leave the chimney, see fit to look at me while the hotel guy I'm going to call the firemen, Mr. Lemos, and God was listening to me thoughtfully

—There's such a lot of you, boy

I got up onto the roof catching a whiff of the birds' dead feathers, the birds' crap, the weeds growing in the gutter crud, the Lord to me in His infinite goodness, in the mercy of His heart and in His celestial stench of dried urine and mildew

—on my left, boy

let them come unto Me

and I was prodding his memory maybe you know Bico da Areia right after Caparica, near Trafaria and Alto do Galo, not a rich neighborhood don't worry, a place for people like Your Majesty and I said, whenever the Tagus came up it would pull our yards back toward the woods, I should say something about the Gypsies to you, the pine grove, the wife of the café owner looking at my mother without paying attention to her wiping of the tables, it's possible that you don't know my mother or that you can't distinguish her from her colleagues as they come out of school but you certainly must remember the park with retired people like you, with a trump card in the air waiting for the first slam, of the cedar in winter and a little one

me

waiting for the signal, the curtain being drawn back and a clown, not a woman, a clown

my father

—Paulo

and God in His infinite condescension finally paid attention to me, examining a shoe that's slipping off His foot, leaning on the chimney

—Wait

Micaela changing earrings again, huge pearls now

—Do you still not like me, Paulinho?

a man, make it a man, getting into the tureen and escaping over the viaduct until whatever was left of me is glazed ceramic

Elvas

while God, more relaxed in His measureless condescension thanks to the shoe He managed to get on

—Wait

noticing my father

blessed be thee

appearing on His face, the sleeves of the pajamas reaching out and pointing from the ceiling to some spot among dozens of spots, a street corner, a doorway

—Hi there

the hotel guy behind me thinking that he existed and didn't really exist, we existed on the roof taking off the pigeon crud, the Lord in His prudence advising me

—Wait

a horizon of antennas, courtyards, and extinguished neon tubes, for a moment my grandmother running her fingers over me, pausing to think

—Is it your son, Judite?

a gravestone where a girl was busy drawing squares in chalk, the hotel guy chasing the girl away by raising and lowering his stiff forefinger

—I swear to you I've phoned for the firemen, Mr. Lemos

and God indifferent, the creator of Abraham, Isaac, and Jacob, Exterminator of first-born, Headman of Nineveh, Hangman of the Sodomites, extending to me curved little fingers stained with the blood of the impious or liver spots trying to button up his collar and missing the button

—Would you happen to have a newspaper or something like it to wrap me up in, because it's cold?

God in His pajamas, tied with a cord, putting on the glasses that were missing a lens

—I think someone is out there

Micaela leaving her earrings alone and taking a drink from a small bottle and coughing at me while Dona Amélia are you still here children

—*If you wanted to, Paulo*

all I feel like doing is talking I swear, feel that somebody's with me, that there's somebody in the room, they tell me that this cough and doctors and I don't know what and I say don't even think about any treatments, I've always taken care of myself by myself, a customer years ago, almost a friend, after a time you start feeling affection for them, worried about my lungs

—Take care of yourself
you may think he was an idiot but he was always
—Take care of yourself
I look at the aqueduct, the landscape, I answer him
—Elvas
and I keep thinking why Elvas, why did I answer Elvas, I never lived in Elvas, a city almost in Castile they tell me, a fort with prisoners they tell me, the tureen was already there when I rented the place, maybe the previous tenant too
—Elvas
like me, left it on the hooks to free himself from some fate or maybe from us and our mouths
—Elvas
the customer
just an eyebrow
stopping to tie his necktie
—What's that?
and me holding back my cough trying to stop my mouth Elvas, trying to replace
—Elvas
with
—Nothing
I tried to adjust my wrapper just so I'd be adjusting something

God adjusting the glasses that were slipping off His face because of a bend in the temple, moaning without paying any attention to the hotel guy about this damnable cold that pours water into My bones, waving His arm can you hear the water plop plop, don't you have a newspaper there or something like it, when My wife would go to get Us some papers at the newsstand, the man at the newsstand pointed out to her that the day was over

—Auntie

handing over the leftover newspapers after gathering up his things

—A soft quilt if Dona Berta will accept it

Almighty God and the fountain of salvation that comforts souls in the joy of His presence in spite of the castanets of gums chattering with cold

—Enough to freeze your balls, boy

huddling by the chimney in order to avoid the treachery of the north wind and the dampness in His joints making it almost impossible for Me to walk, I've got a crutch somewhere but it's got no padding and it hurts My armpit

—Isn't someone there who might be your father

among the mortals

praise unto Thee, praise

only buildings, a fountain with the king's coat of arms

MDCCCXXXIV and a spigot where once upon a time the coach nags, the ferns in the Botanical Garden rustling their mysteries, even in the daytime mysteries, even in the afternoon mysteries, mostly before it gets dark while birds are still warbling, the ferns revealing to me what was to become of me

—Pzgtslm

Mr. Couceiro asking them

—Repeat that

searching for pzgtslm in his Latin, complaining in confusion pzgtslm pzgtslm

—I don't understand

the ferns waving their evidence and I annoyed with the ferns annoyed with him

—Maybe they're talking about Noémia, Mr. Couceiro, saying that she's complaining about not having any visitors and she asked them to tell you that she's suffering

a trembling of the cane because Noémia was dying again, the meningitis, the coma, the orderly inventing cures, you never know, when least expected, we think one thing and you'll see something else turns up, Dona Helena consulting a knowledgeable neighbor woman who read the cards, this red queen is smiling she noticed, this jack of clubs, and this miraculous five in the middle, don't worry, a little baked fish, a hot-water bottle on her feet and she'll be cured, the ferns in a hurry pzgtslm pzgtslm and Mr. Couceiro at the door of the room searching in his dictionary

—I don't understand

God, however, Who understood leaning over the date on the fountain with the divine cloak of His rubber cape flopping about

—Let me take a better look because it might be your father

a faggot, Lord, a transvestite, a clown whom the Son pardoned in Your Holy Name, let he who is without sin cast the first stone remember, and God far removed from me, a mere grain of dust in the vastness of the galaxy, blowing on His fingers and going back to the newspapers with gums weary from dictating Commandments

—Not even a single page from the supplement, boy?

His mind on the newsstand and His wife, you take a step and the newspapers right away

—Pzgtslm

like the ferns, boy, He lifted a skeletal shin, showed me the step, slipped along four tiles, a sleeping pigeon went off moaning, the hotel guy despairing

—Mamma

I never imagined there could be so many veins in a face

pzgtslm

—I already warned Mr. Lemos that within five minutes we'll have the firemen on the stairs

and not just the guy, an alarmed woman tenant, a second woman tenant looking for a deal that if I don't pay the room rent for a week it'll be all right

—The other day you asked me for twenty minutes didn't you, Mr. Lemos, if you come down quick I'll give you a whole hour

the customer to me

—*You said Elvas didn't you?*

not a customer, a friend, he put a schoolgirl uniform in the closet for me, bought me rulers, multiplication tables, asked me to sit on his knees feeling around under my skirt

—*Naughty girl naughty girl*

he thumbed through my notebooks where I copied dictations, subtractions, the names of mountains and rivers, he begged me to draw big smiling suns in colored pencil, that I erase them and draw them again, he would stop to look

*for the watercolors putting more money on the night table, one or two bills,
three bills sometimes*

  *—You don't have a beauty spot on your face do you want a blue beauty
spot on your face Micaela, you're a naughty girl*

  *he gave me dolls, wind-up animals, puzzles and he was running around
me, let's play Micaela, he'd fondle the doll would be disappointed with me*

  —You're thinking about something else

  *and I really was thinking about something else, about the aqueduct, about
Elvas, about my daughter sometimes*

  although my daughter

  the customer stopped looking at the tureen

  —What is it about the tureen?

  *without noticing that I wasn't there, coughing, I was past the aqueduct on
the way to Spain, this pain in the ribs, this trouble with the air, it gets in and
refuses to get out, it gets out and refuses to come in, I sit down and the air
doesn't move, my throat's tight, the aqueduct where I'm not walking, it's a
different one I'm walking on, I stay there watching it go away, so I don't even
hear the customer holding me by the shoulders*

  —Micaela

  *thinking about opening the door but who can I call, waking up a neighbor
but what do I tell the neighbor, what I am, and what if the neighbor says
you're all cut from the same cloth who cares if your clown is dying, getting her
out of her school uniform, the low-heeled shoes, the schoolgirl socks, hiding the
notebooks in the closet but in the closet there are scarves, mantillas, frippery
with feathers, pocketing the money on the night table so they won't think that
I, instead of the stairs use the aqueduct even if it's poorly painted and crooked*

  Elvas, a city with a fort and prisoners coming up the hill carrying barrels

  *and getting to Badajoz or Cadiz or somewhere farther off, in the end Lis-
bon, at the end of an alley off a square, luckily dozens and dozens of alleys
and while there are alleys I keep on running, my wife who refuses to dress up
as a schoolgirl*

  —What a silly idea Eduardo

  putting another pillow under my neck

  —Did the company meeting tire you out?

  *the air that goes in and won't go out, goes out and won't to go in, doesn't
move not going in or out and my throat tight, my wife*

—Eduardo

unable to hear her because of my steps on a distant narrow path, low houses, warehouses, barking all along a poster, visit the model flat, every so often a ground floor lighted up, beggars on a tarpaulin, a big ship, the Tagus, Micaela

—Elvas

me

—Elvas

and yet settling down on the sofa and calming my wife, the meeting didn't tire me out, I don't need any pillows, I'm fine, leave me just like this for a minute to think about work, a couple with a child happily suggesting visit the model flat, the father dark-haired, the mother blonde, the child blonde too, the child and the mother smiling at the father who

—The other day you asked me for twenty minutes didn't you, Mr. Lemos, I'll give you a whole hour

was embracing both and beyond the family a development with a halo of sanctity in a grassy plot, deluxe accessories, central heating, kitchen trimmed in oak fully equipped, come see us

COME SEE US

don't buy without seeing us, come see us and all along the poster barking come see us

a whole hour and God letting me go, settling down on the bricks, fixing his gaze on the hotel guy

—Did you people say an hour?

Taking off His glasses and the date on the fountain

the MDCCXXXIV

invisible, the ferns in the Botanic Garden pzgtslm

—After all, look, I made a mistake it's not your father, boy, it's a mailbox

and me forgetting that the ground I was treading was holy and that no one, not even Moses, permitted himself to cast his eyes on the eyes of God, it can't be a mailbox, Mr. Lemos, with just a little careful attention you'll discover a faggot, a transvestite, a clown at Príncipe Real at five in the morning, orient yourself by the cedar, the café, the lake and He was coming forward across the bricks

—What we have plenty of in this country is cafés, boy

his pants rolled up, sleeves hiding his fingers, the boarder at the skylight with the hotel guy, with a flashlight, lighting up His hair

—This way, Mr. Lemos

and You who spoke to men pure in heart do not abandon my father, the doctor guaranteed him that he's not sick

—Rest easy you're not sick Dona Soraia

and my father

—My name is Carlos

lying out of pity, he's got a fever, he's sick

—I'm sick Marlene

thinking about Bico da Areia, my mother, the gentian, filling the watering can from the spigot at the washtub, I won't let it die Judite, notice how he got pale, it's hard for him to move, the watering can dropped from his hand and he can't bend over, a dizzy spell, a faint

—Be patient, nephew

or cousin or younger brother, or a little one without a family that I take care of poor thing, my father to the little one without a family that I take care of

—Be patient, nephew

it can't be a mailbox Mr. Lemos, it can only be my father, he's wearing a blonde wig isn't he, a circle of lipstick between his nose and his chin, artificial lashes that darken his face, ask him his name Mr. Lemos, try asking him his name and in spite of Rui

—I'm her husband her name is Soraia

he'll answer you

—Carlos

how much do you want to bet

don't leave, we're almost finished, how much do you want to bet he'll answer

—Carlos

and answering him

—Carlos

I'll stop bothering him I swear, I'll talk to Dona Helena and a mass in Your honor, I'll ask the maid in the dining room and the offering in the same alms box

Souls in Purgatory

pzgtslm

which Rui and I cracked one afternoon with a nail and a hammer, a cracking of wood and half a dozen coins that the people

you know quite well

the people, not me, became greedy and selfish Lord, give me back my father resting at a corner on his way back home carrying his cross smaller than Your Son's and which only You and I know

a faggot, a transvestite, a dying clown rumpling and smoothing a silken quilt, getting up, leaving

don't let him leave, command him

—The gentian, Carlos

and he obeyed You, put down the suitcase, limped over to the wall

Kyrie Eleison

where in winter the gulls were wary of the waves and the bridge and the horses, the same way that I limp over to the edge of the roof scattering the pigeons and the hotel guy who hears and doesn't hear

—Be careful, you boob

so far behind me, so distant Lord, my father removing the dried leaves and taking care of the branches, fixing up a small shoot that was leaning over with a piece of string, straightening out a branch that the rain

or the pups or the wind

had pushed down to the ground

—Tie it here, nephew

and while I slide off the roof

thank you, Lord

I tie it here, I keep on tying and I help him and I fall into the noise and the hate, keeping in mind the peace there can be in silence, certain that fear is born of solitude, of fatigue, and the absence of discipline and looking after myself, a son of the Universe no less than the trees and the stars and even though bright or dark for me at peace with God no matter in what form I conceive Him and whatever shape my efforts and aspirations take, maintaining my soul serene in the vain disorder of existence because in spite of all the error and madness and unfulfilled desires this world of Yours, my Lord, is a perfect world. And I will be careful. And I will try to be happy. And nature will strengthen my spirit protecting me from the mishaps of life. I will not be blind to virtue. I will try to be humble before the changing fortune of the years: facing disappointment and darkness the soul becomes perennial like the grass and, like it, it will survive forever at the same time that I fall and by falling I begin to live again and I fear nothing, my Lord and my God because my father

a faggot, a transvestite, a sick clown

—Tie it here, nephew

and the scent of the gentian that folds and enshrouds me defending me from death rising up to You from among the pigeon droppings, the satisfaction and the hope of the love I bear You.

CHAPTER

I CAN'T SAY it was every day but at least once a week she did come to visit us, my husband and me, in the little flat that belonged to my mother-in-law where we lived, almost smack up against the castle, hearing the peacocks that kept us awake with their screeches in the ivy on the battlements, from where as eight centuries ago it was down with the Saracens, up Portugal, the doctor recommended rest and a kind of diet for my husband

no fried food and this bottle of drops for the swelling in his legs, ten after lunch and ten after dinner in half a glass of water with a little sugar because it's acid, see?

my husband would lay out tins of corn with roach killer, complaining I can't stand the damned things but it was the gulls that were dying, not the peacocks, the next day there were gulls hanging from the peach trees or drowned in the water troughs in the poultry pen scaring the geese, the peacocks untouched in the towers down with the Saracens up Portugal and my husband said to my mother-in-law, digging into the trunk and coming across pictures of the boy who had died inside and had kept on dying with every new white hair, every new wrinkle, every new hernia spasm, where's my father's shotgun, a single-barreled one with a loose butt that so many years ago he'd scare the neighbors with, going bang-bang with his mouth, going down three flights with the shotgun, saying bang-bang to the peacocks, it's likely that the peacocks, the same as the neighbors, would lift their hands to their breasts, roll their eyes, declare you've killed me, until he left, happy, the castle in silence, and handed my mother that gibberish about being proud that he didn't have to pull the trigger in order to get rid of the peacocks, as you can see, the boy with his face peeping out and settling down, wearing a lace collar, onto the lap of his grandmother who I never got to know and who swore at me from the picture frame, dropping her smile when she caught sight of me, you're no wife for Álvaro, and maybe I really wasn't a wife for Álvaro because we hadn't met at the club where I'm working now, because clubs didn't exist in those days, it was a place on the outskirts where you forgot the miseries of a life that instead of going forward only walks backward what can you do, with paper streamers, cheap beer, an accordion and a piano on a platform, I was seventeen

make it sixteen and in spite of my being afraid of the dark and going to bed with a little Bakelite hen that if you wound it up would flap its wings and lay a glass egg, a body of thirty and features thirty-five that scared me because they gave me the idea that I was my own stepmother, ordering me to throw away the hen Amélia because it doesn't even have a beak, sixteen and the profession of sitting down under the paper streamers and the moths around the bulbs waiting for men whose lives were only going backward, what can you do, dancing with them, listening to their complaints of have you ever seen worse luck dammit, going to bed consoling them in one of the rooms in the annex thinking I hope they don't turn out the light, the Bakelite hen, all ready to protect me, within arm's reach until my husband one night or other, not daring to approach, all lost in embarrassment at the bar with that forlorn look in the photograph in the trunk, maybe I could wind it up and he'd be taken with the egg while he admired the accordion and the piano, spending hours nursing a beer following me with his eyes and forgetting about his glass, when during a waltz or a tango I'd go off in the company of a man whose life, what can you do, to one of the rooms in the annex, where sometimes a glass egg would fall all by itself without a sound and I'll bet that the boy in the photograph was listening, lots of times I'd wind it up for him without my husband's suspecting that every egg was my way of telling him a name I didn't know, I'd wind it up and the one whose life was what can you do I'm not here to watch your hen, while I waited for the wings to stop flapping and let me know that you can leave Amélia, looking for what was left of himself on the sheet and it looked to me like he was afraid of the dark just like me, the men would pick themselves up after lying down and pick up their clothes, look at this leg, this elbow, this little finger I didn't lose after all, funny, putting themselves together until they took the shape of a creature fighting with its shoelaces mixed up and a voice out of the darkest of the dark where there were threats of witches that were just trees, thickets

—Let me get dressed in peace

not an adult voice, from something in the trunk, maybe a baptism dress, maybe the whistling of rabbits

a long time ago

on a corner of the farm after the grape harvest, the oxen that were carrying the grapes sniffing the ground, the shoelaces and the fingers

it was the shoelaces that were knotting the fingers

my husband followed me with relief, having forgotten about his glass, when I came back from the annex during another waltz, another tango and settled down onto the chair pulling down my skirt to cover

he thought

my shameless knees, not understanding that it was the smell of the vines and the hares running away that my hand was hiding, those quick little noses eternal for a second, my life which in those days wasn't going backward what can you do, was going forward especially after the rain, the door would open and the wintering tomato plants would say hello to me

—Amélia

I'm not exaggerating

—Amélia

my husband was propped up at the bar warming his beer with his hand until the dancing was over which means the piano was a useless piece of furniture up against the streamers on the wall, the accordion player was tugging at the straps of his instrument with the movements of someone getting undressed and instead of undressing he was putting it away in its case, turning up the collar of his jacket and disappearing into the street without anyone's knowing where on the outskirts he was heading, maybe not the outskirts at all, maybe nobody was waiting for him, a little wave that wasn't unhappy, indifferent, until tomorrow ladies and gentlemen, with the ladies and gentlemen he was referring to the cleaning people who were pushing back the furniture and giving the floor a quick scrub, except for the man who was paying my aunt counting the bills with saliva from his thumb, three bills tonight madame because your niece left a customer unable to leave the room all caught up with the hen, they went to get him and he had his fingers all knotted chasing runaway hares

—Do they catch the smell of the vines?

not to mention the boy in the photograph at that hour of the morning growing old with fatigue, white hair, wrinkles, hernia spasms, mumbling into his beer or to my aunt while a small flicker of sun coming from Góis knotted the paper streamers that night had stitched up and put together, I'll give you six bills for her, convinced that I had the thirty years in my body and knew how to wash and iron and take care of a little flat almost stuck up against the castle where the peacocks for eight centuries in the ivy of the battlements called down with the Saracens up Portugal, and sew his clothes and cook his meals when all I knew was how to wind up the hen, pick up the egg in my hand, and watch my husband who'd run out of roach killer take out the shotgun with a loose butt and a single barrel that had belonged to his father, raising that useless combination to his shoulder with the falsely competent look of unnecessary objects it had, lifting it slowly with one eye closed in the direction of the patriotic cheers now at this stone now at that one, he waited for one of the cocks to fill up his throat pointing it toward the clouds, as soon as down with the Saracens my husband with his mouth

—Bang-bang

and a gull was hanging from the peach trees in backyards or drowned in the troughs in poultry pens scaring the geese, my aunt to my husband eleven bills, my husband who couldn't look at her, in the same way that he couldn't look at anyone, he'd talk to people with his head down studying his thumbs and now studying his thumbs yellow with foam from the glass of beer six bills and a half and let's not have any more talk about this, I remember my new shawl

blue

and the flicker of sun that brought an acacia with it

a fern

pzgtslm

the shadow of an acacia dragging along over joints on the boards and climbing up to the platform hidden from us, my husband rubbing one thumb against the other and the thumbs in agreement

—Eight bills

I always call acacias ferns don't mind me, if the fern or the acacia could guess I was noticing it, it would say hello right off

—Amélia

my mother interrupting the deal

—Are you sharing secrets with the trees?

and even though I wasn't saying anything sitting on the chair with the shadow on one of my ankles and the other ankle free, as soon as both feet got caught who'll help me walk

answer me

my shadow was behind me and I was afraid of it

—Let me go

I stopped and the shadow stopped too making it hard for me to move, little bitty head, great big hips, we held out arms at the same time and who's obeying whom, which of the two of us is in charge, I leaned frontward on my hips, I'm not afraid of you, my hands five fingers then none at all, blending into my waist, I moved my fingers away and the shadow, imitating me, had five too, longer than mine, the middle one was on a stone the others on the grass, I scratched my head and they disappeared again, my chin was normal, its chin was strange but there weren't any eyebrows, any nose, just one ear if that and still it could hear me, if my husband aimed the shotgun and went

—Bang-bang

with his mouth the shadow fell dead on the floor, covered with ants like the corpses of toads, it would come back the next day and almost not a shadow anymore, half of the head, half of the lumpy hips, the rest the crows had carried off, my aunt to my husband ten bills and the hen as a present, the fern

or the acacia

fastening me to the chair and how am I going to get out of here, covering my face I stop breathing and then, my husband examining the hen

—It isn't worth a red cent it has a broken beak

he grabbed it, found the windup key

—Is this how?

and the wings went up and down in a slanting effort, out of my hand I thought it was ugly and lifeless and it wasn't just the beak, the left leg was cracked, when it didn't move its wings it was a creature that wasn't capable of defending me from the dark, my husband put it in his pocket and for the first time his eyes moved away from the beer to me

—Your name's Amélia isn't it?

while the acacia

or the fern

went off toward the piano and I was free, from inside the little flat almost stuck up against the castle there were only clouds crossing the balcony toward the sea and time that had no need for clocks because it was always three o'clock, no rabbit whistle, no vine smell, a cricket in a cage of twigs and I'd been inventing tomatoes varnished by the rain, starting with the cricket, anxious little legs, that is, antennas searching, crickets in the roots, on the ledges, inside the wind, along with the crickets there are oxen sniffing the ground and I was

ah the ground

sniffing along with them, lying down in the eucalyptus grove while the dowser moved around in circles, paying no attention to the stones, with a forked apple branch and everybody was waiting, he'd go back and forth, walking like a blind man, the branch would

dip, trembling, insisting on a slope that the plow had left intact and
he had the look of someone waking up on the other side

—There

they dug a well and our reflected faces making and unmaking
themselves down below, I was on the ground in the eucalyptus
grove for once without any shadow because the ants and the crows

my husband to my aunt trying out the hen

—*What about her clothes ma'am?*

they'd carried off half my head and half my hips, I was only a
leftover part of myself all lumpy and twisted, I don't exist, I'm not,
and the sound of the eucalyptus trees crossing through what I'm
not while the shadow of the dowser, that yes, whole, the dowser
exists, thank God one of us exists, thank God the shadow of one of
us in the branches and the branches are bending over in spite of his
not weighing anything, I saw the shadow of his hat, the forked
branch, his pants tucked into his boots, I never saw him, his real
shadow, not him, in circles, paying no attention to the stones and
the shadow with him, my family was working the field and waiting
for the forked branch to bend suddenly

—There

on a slope the plow had left intact and reflected in the bottom of
the well unmaking and re-making itself in a shadow on the water
was the shadow of the dowser taking me by the elbow, I thought

—If I push back my hair will I still have an ear?

I thought

—If I separate my fingers will there be some finger in the leaves?

and of course no ear no fingers because the ants and the crows,
a fox, the dogs, three dogs fighting over my shoulder, running off
into the brambles and no shoulder though, what do you think
you're doing it's only your shadow, not mine, among the tree
trunks, look how the wind doesn't stop on my body, goes right
through me, look how bent I try to make some kind of movement
there's no movement at all, it only touches berries and pebbles, it
only unbuttons an absence, the hat gets bigger, the forked branch
is on the ground but then the forked branch doesn't exist either,
that is, it exists but it's not a shadow and therefore there isn't any,

or there it is suddenly turning down, if I lift myself up a little and take a look I can see the plow, one of the oxen, the weathervane on the barn, broken for years, always pointing south, the forked branch not pointing where I am but pointing at my aunt and uncle

my husband looking through the drawers

—*Are these the only clothes your niece has, ma'am?*

a mystery of mud, the water black at first and then brown and then invisible, or, rather, you could hear the sound, you felt it in your flesh, pouring into bowls and the varnished tomatoes, red, the eucalyptus trees

—Pzgtslm

while the shadow of a knee was splitting the knee I didn't have, while a breath of wind the weathervane couldn't hold with its beak of a rusty rooster, open, on what had been my neck, probably talking to me but I couldn't hear because I have no ears, I pushed my hair back and

just as I'd imagined

no ear really, I probably could have talked to him if the ants and the crows or the fox we kill in the trap

he was caught by the thigh and then the hoe, the pruning shears, a knife

—Son of a bitch

going in and out, hitting a bone, missing the bones, the lungs pffff, I remember my aunt

—Don't ruin the pelt

and they ruined the pelt that stank of woods and blood and entrails, if they'd left me

and they hadn't left me

a tongue, I would have asked

—What about me what do I stink of?

the shadow where my neck must have been you stink of mud, the water black at first and then brown and then invisible, of eucalyptus leaves and berries, of woods, of blood, of entrails

my husband

—*Are these the only clothes your niece has, ma'am?*

my aunt to my uncle, to the others, to an arm of shadow that was
straightening its hat, grew smaller on me, picked
—Don't ruin the pelt
up the forked branch and the forked branch was a shadow too
you stink of water
my husband never told me I stank of water, my husband ne . . .
saying that I stank of water and went off with her, in the place
on the outskirts where I worked, my shadow gone, I was all alone,
men whose knuckles were like ramrods and whose lives instead of
going forward went backward, really, something due to the fact
that there was no shadow for them, not even a shadow for them,
nothing for them, at the very most, voices
—Let me get dressed in peace go away
face down on the mattress picking himself up thinking he was
picking up his clothes
—*Are these the only clothes your niece has, ma'am?*
until taking shape as an adult with the picture of a dead child
inside, I would help them the same way that I helped my husband
—Wait a minute, you have the buttons wrong
I would help them
—Wait a minute, you have the buttons wrong, sir
the same way that I helped the girls, Marlene, Micaela, Vânia,
Sissi, Soraia, poor thing, before she got sick and who I can't say
came every day but at least once a week she'd visit us in the little flat
that belonged to my mother-in-law, almost stuck up against the
castle, with a different lover on each visit
—I want you to meet my boyfriend, Dona Amélia
until a certain time only her younger brother and Rui, Soraia on
the balcony trying to make out the other bank of the river
—You can't see the other bank, what a pity
and when I asked her why the other bank, she answered me
marigolds, I showed her one of the backyards where there didn't
happen to be any dead gulls, you have marigolds there, Soraia,
those aren't the marigolds, Dona Amélia, without my understanding what marigolds she was talking about, flowers that she must

have lost years ago just the way that I'd lost my shadow and the
hares running away, there are times when I think I've found them
in the club when the lights are turned on and a shape flutters on the
wall, I think it's the dowser but it's Sissi singing, my husband asked
my aunt who was packing my bags, one almost empty little bag,
that is, nothing but glass eggs and the smell of hares

—Her shadow, ma'am?

my husband was trying to find the marigolds because he, too,
when he was small

—I can still remember, Amélia

and his eyes turned inward where I could make out a cradle in an
empty room and right away my husband

—You couldn't understand

only the frame of the cradle, a string of seashells crumbling in a
rusty curlicue and a little lullaby music box with its music gone, I
felt sorry for his orphan look

—Did you see my cradle, Amélia?

showing me an empty room much smaller than when I'd left it,
a tiny window opening onto some stalks that weren't even
marigolds and in what was left of the iron skeleton the little music
box covered in a spiral of rust that my husband hadn't been able to
clean off

—I haven't been able to clean it off, Amélia

in spite of having taken it apart to study the mechanism in
hopes of a slow jingle spelling out hey Mr. Bogeyman get off our
roof and in spite of all my efforts not a note, Amélia, all I ask for is
one little note that will give me back my mother when she was
eighteen, wrapped in perfume on a March day with swallows and
the six o'clock light that I thought came out of a basin of lye, not
this old woman I barely know and who shows no sign of knowing
me and passes me by the way she would a stranger, ordering

—You're blocking the hallway

hanging out my dead father's shirts and annoying the peacocks,
my husband in a voice that he was taking out of the trunk along
with the pictures and I was holding fear in my hand the way I'd
hold those old ribbons that tear if you touch them

—Help me find the person I was, Amélia

a room I don't know, in what neighborhood, on what street, in what building, and he would swear to me sometimes it was big sometimes small according to the whims of his memory and he would repeat you don't lose the six o'clock light the way you lose a key Amélia, Soraia, the six o'clock light Mr. Osório, do you think the six o'clock light, Rui wondering if he could sell it to the Cape Verdeans in Chelas, heat it up in a spoon, cut it with lemon, inject it into his veins, you're the six o'clock light Rui, lifting the lid of the trunk and nothing but papers, mildew, the six o'clock light, what happened to the six o'clock light, my husband smiling at a cradle with its new music box that was asking Mr. Bogeyman to get off that roof, my husband, while my mother-in-law stopped blocking the hallway

—Where was home, mother?

a liar who called himself my son as though I didn't know my own son, as though my son wasn't with me peacefully playing with a string of shells, a worn-out man accompanied by a woman without a shadow almost as worn out as he is, a creature with a lot of earrings and rings and two skinny young fellows who open my drawers and rummage in my pots and pans

—Where was home, mother?

if he really was my son he'd know where home was, he'd pick it out without any hesitation, the Travessa de São Bernardino and the second door on the left, he wouldn't have to ask, threaten the peacocks with a shotgun saying bang-bang with his mouth and killing the gulls, the Travessa de São Bernardino just before the convent, every so often a novice would pick up tangerines from the ground, at four in the morning prayers in the chapel and the door knocker echoing prayers all over the place, the creature with the rings intrigued, all you have to do is look at her and you can understand that a cradle just like but more modest than ours and not made of painted iron, cheap wood where I'd be ashamed to put my son to bed

—What's the matter Mr. Osório?

the perfume ahead of her, you caught the perfume before there was anyone on the stairs, the perfume in the living room asking permission

—May I come in?

and the worn-out woman to the one who wasn't my son

—Hurry and get yourself fixed up, here comes Soraia

with me feeling like a tangerine too, and, catching sight of the cradle, because with children you never know if they're hungry or have angina, the worn-out woman as though my duties as a mother

—She's been in her own world for a long time now, don't pay any heed

I say to Soraia she's been in her own world for a long time now, don't pay any attention to her, she doesn't talk, she doesn't care about us, now and then she gets the notion, not fussing around anybody's body because nobody's that small but that can't be the reason, it must be rheumatism, some spring in her brain that vibrates for no reason, little threads of memory that will float up and disappear and go away, in my case

it's an example

it was the dowser with his broken forked branch and the pruning shears stuck in his back, missing half a head because of the ants and the crows and a shadow of blood covering the shadow, what seems to me a kind of peace in my uncle as he looks down at him, my aunt looking for neighbors, left and right, washing the shears, praying into the palm of her hand for the wind not to carry her words toward the vineyard after ours

—Don't you want the shovel, Alberto?

a single boot, fingers hoping that they can still hold me, you smell of the woods Amélia, you smell of water first black, then brown, then invisible, I pour it into bowls for you, the varnished tomatoes, red, you smell of mud and roots, the smell of woods, of entrails, the dowser breathing pffff in the fox trap and then the hoe

of course

the poker from the kitchen, as we got closer he looked at us, covering the metal teeth, his hat on his head, concerned about a hole in his stocking

—I didn't know there were any foxes around here

the iron teeth where the bait, a piece of lard, and the weathervane on the barn were spying on us, my aunt worried about the
weathervane

—Alberto

why worry about a rooster who can't crow, an aluminum comb,
a yellow tail

you smell of berries Amélia, don't worry, wait, let me smell the berries,
you smell the way oxen smell when they smell of earth, the way hares smell
in the barley, those quick noses eternal for an instant

the dowser asking

—Lend a hand over here, Alberto

the dowser asking for a leg massage

—Lend a hand over here, Alberto

noticing the shears with which we cut branches, falling silent,
the shadow denser now, the two arms just one arm only drawing
back, retreating, the forked branch pointing at my uncle before
falling into the leaves and ceasing to be a shadow of the forked
branch to be only the forked branch, a piece of apple bough shiny
from use that my uncle stepped on, the hatless head two ears, that
is, which were growing larger, the shadow of the free boot stamping
on the ground, reaching my uncle and moving away from him
because of the pruning shears, what must have been a mouth

the shadow of a mouth

what was a mouth, what I found out later was a mouth

—We're friends aren't we Alberto?

the hat close to me, not the shadow of a hat, a hat, green with a
hatband and in the hatband a cigarette

a match was lighted while they were digging the well, the flame
made no shadow, when the dovecote burned down I can remember
the shadow on the wall of the chicken coop, the shadow of the
flames and the shadow of the smoke, of the buckets that the neighbors came running with, the mixed shadows of the pigs, one single
pig with a lot of snouts, a lot of tails, the fallen washtub, the shadows of the neighbors mixed in too

you smell of eucalyptus trees Amélia, you smell of berries, you smell of
woods, entrails, of what animals smell like and me face down on the ground

Mount Caramulo was visible

remembering the mulberries on the road in the pine grove, my aunt if you eat mulberries you'll get sick in the liver, my uncle against the doctor's orders, serving himself from the bottle in the cupboard, I was waking up and his bare feet, drinking, not all my uncle, his bare feet, I could hear the sound of the bottle as he put it back, the doctor

—*You're not going to last even six months Alberto*

and he didn't

my uncle buttoning up his jacket after the examination, his belly bloated, his nose so white

—*Just as long as I have time to get rid of a fox I know about*

the shadow of the dowser fox crouching in the trap, the shadow of his hat that my aunt squashed with her shoe, Soraia in the little flat almost stuck up against the castle

—I don't want to see, Dona Amélia, I can't see

in each of the fox's hands five fingers and every finger separate from the rest

—If it's because of your niece she's still a virgin, Alberto

before the first time with the shears, and when it was the second time with the shears

—Don't bring any trouble down on me and tell your uncle you're still a virgin, Amélia

Looking at me I imagine and yet who can tell where shadows look, the third time with the shears the fox silent and its tongue dark in its mouth

the shadow of its dark tongue in the shadow of its mouth

or a clump of earth then, or a stone then, or my aunt then because her shadow was on top of him covering his throat with a piece of cloth to stop him from speaking, black water on the cloth and then brown and then transparent, the empty lips in the leaves, the empty clothes

you smell the way oxen smell when they smell the ground

I wasn't the one who smelled of berries and woods, of mud, of roots, of water, he was the one, I had the impression that

—Alberto

and it wasn't my aunt

—Alberto

it was the rooster on the weathervane, it was he, I can't be sure, I think it was he

—If it's because of your niece she's still a virgin, Alberto

cleaning the shears on his shirt

or on his pant leg, Soraia running out onto the balcony where a peahen

which one?

was sobbing

—I don't want to see, Dona Amélia, I can't see

the lemon trees in the yards breathing outside and my mother-in-law in her own world for a long time with her deafness and her trunks of rubbish winding up what she imagined was a music box

and now throwing the body into the well and covering the well

—There wasn't any water, it was a mistake

in spite of the reflection down below, my aunt, my uncle, me, three heads with one cloud above

no cloud, a ripple of water

no ripple of water, a bag of quicklime on top of the hat and the forked branch

you smell of eucalyptus leaves, you smell of branches, if it's because of your niece she's still a virgin, Alberto

we erased the marks with branches, we hoped that the underbrush would grow over the spot where he

where his shadow or a flock of herons from the dam at the lake, how many nights, I wonder, am I sure of finding Soraia on the landing waiting for me

—I have to talk to you, Dona Amélia

and reaching the doormat

God knows how hard it is for me to reach the doormat at seventy-three

seventy-three, not sixteen not thirty, seventy-three years old

putting the key in the lock, inviting her to

—Come in

I see that I'm all alone thinking about the peacocks, I wouldn't say that she came every day but at least once a week she would visit us my husband and me in the little flat where we live almost stuck up against the castle and even though she had no money and pawned her hairpiece always a nice gift, a little package of tea, a ceramic piece that might not have been expensive but that caught your attention, Micaela told me that before leaving with the customer from table nine for the hotel or the boardinghouse

se habla español english spoken

where she reserved rooms

a counter with small flags

even from the Ivory Coast, Dona Amélia

a little old man on the roof chatting with the pigeons

she would go into the kitchen and ask for leftover sandwiches that my gentleman, the dog

a mastiff with a bow

adores and it wasn't my gentleman it was the dog that ate them on getting home, it was she, the manager bawled her out for going with an important man carrying a bundle under her arm, there are customers who don't like that Soraia, you look like some poor woman scavenging leftovers, her gentleman, the dog that appeared later at Fonte da Telha muttering its displeasure around Rui's corpse and was carried off by some wave, the policeman noticing he was missing

—Where's the mastiff?

as if the mastiff could tell them that on Tuesday the twenty-first of September nineteen ninety-eight we got to Fonte da Telha by bus, the deceased and I, we walked along the dunes where there were necks of bottles and filth and cans, we spread out the blanket on the sand, we lay down where we always lie down, past the shacks, where the larks laid eggs on an outcropping with weeping willows, looking at the sea, as it so happened that time more green than blue, caused

I think

by a bunch of algae from last night's tide, which brought about a movement of gulls toward Costa da Caparica, to be exact, or even farther down on Santo António da Caparica, that is, São João da Caparica, Bico da Areia, Alto do Galo, or even Trafaria, those death-trap shacks where except I was wrong about Bico da Areia, I needed additional information to back me up better, what I'm declaring is

where, however, and with reservations, a woman between forty-seven and fifty-three years of age was using her apron to wipe the tables of a café not far away

seventy feet?

from a house

from a shack

from a rundown house with a gentian

of this I'm sure

fading all around, and picking up again, after this brief and perhaps unnecessary digression the declarations that I shall read, find accurate, and sign, we spread out the blanket and got undressed looking at the sea, making sure that the syringe was in our pocket along with the spoon, the lighter, and the equivalent of eleven heroin fixes picked up in Chelas during the week immediately preceding the day I mentioned above from people whose name, domicile, and profession

in addition to marital status, nationality, and any specific information

we swear on our honor we don't know, after which we raised our elbows over our eyes to obviate the excessive solar light that the empyrean

devoid of clouds

was making uncomfortable for us, with sight already made fragile by the regular administration, according to all probabilities, every other day of stupefacients with an elevated degree of impurities, some of which are hepatotoxic and at least one nephrotoxic

for further elucidation of what we state, consult appendix 2

(two)

of the autopsy report

with our sight already made fragile by the regular administration of stupefacients in addition to the unquestionable existence of congenital glaucoma

appendix 4

(four)

of the same report

with a probable reduction of fields of vision especially the left, lying in dorsal decumbency on the blanket listening to the

(marginal note without the initials of the deponent although accepted by the presiding judge after a telephone consultation with the Port Captain of Lisbon where they kept me waiting for an eternity in spite of their having been informed of my status of magistrate, motivating on my part a strong protest, still without a reply which, judging from the delay on the telephone, I do not believe will be forthcoming, marginal note, low tide at twelve thirty-three, adding, if it was not twelve thirty-three, it was sixteen four because on the captain's desk there is such a jumble of papers that your honor can't imagine)

we, as I was saying, were on the blanket, listening to the monotonous succession of the waves, basically the same as on winter Sundays, I was writing on the typewriter while my helpmate feeds our son suggesting, couldn't you put that aside for a bit and help me with this messy mush the child keeps getting me dirty with, which brought on two mistakes that I corrected by hand at the bottom of the page, hoping that the section chief

—The day you make a proper report I'll send up a rocket

doesn't make me pound it out all over again, we, consequently, were in dorsal decumbency on the blanket, until

approximately

at eighteen thirty according to testimony of doubtful fidelity in light of the notorious intoxication of the person questioned and, however, the only person it was for us to detain, in accordance with Chapter 4

(four)

Discussion and Conclusions

of this report, and the only one possible for us to detain in view of the hostility

and mistrust

shown by the inhabitants of Fonte da Telha

with the exception of the friendly alcoholic

with regard to the efforts, goodwill, and legitimate desire for accuracy on the part of the police and the ingrates, avoiding the truth and involvement in legal procedures

in which they had been, on several occasions, involved

repeating I don't know anything, I didn't see anything, I'm not talking to you, release my brother-in-law first and then we can have a chat, and thus it is only correct for us to imagine that Rui

that I

indifferent to the mastiff because I never liked him and the Cape Verdeans didn't want to buy him, with a bow on his neck

so stupid, gentlemen

trotting on the tar and barking at the reeds, every time he came over to me I'd push him away with my knee

—Don't bother me

and the boob, instead of understanding, filled with even more loving, convinced that I was Soraia calling him lovey and sharing the leftovers from the club with him, at six o'clock, when the sun stopped bothering me, I was heating up one of the packets maybe too dark but what did that matter if you didn't want to fly, if at nine o'clock in the morning

(nine-eleven, the words of the deponent Maria Alice Nunes Garcia, nurse 2nd class

second class who'd come on duty a bit late to the annoyance of the head nurse, about fifty minutes before)

they'd called me from the hospital to inform me that Soraia, I was staring at the phone as if the phone

putting it back in the cradle, pulling the cord out of the socket as though the telephone

banging it on the corner of the kitchen table until the Bakelite broke, I smashed the ball, destroyed the insulation, undid the coils, threw away all that stuff that had lied to me

not Soraia

on the rug drying at the rear of Príncipe Real where no one saw me from the business with offices on the other side of the street where a stenographer would smile at me sometimes

or I would pretend that she smiled at me sometimes, a skinny little blonde, who knows why so sad, and blondes bring on more

pity than brunettes because they don't cry, don't fall apart, nurse
2nd

(second)

class Maria Alice Nunes Garcia having heard that uniform and
monotonous sound

not monotonous like the waves that break off and start again

the monotonous and continuous sound of broken connections,
in view of which, my obligation of reporting the demise of the
patient and keeping in mind the bed that urgently needed changing and the forthcoming bureaucracy of death that fell to me to fulfill, calling the doctor, the stretcher-bearers, informing the business
office, marking the corpse with the obligatory tag and the unit
stamp on the head, I hung up, having on the following morning
received news of the fatal end of the patient's living companion,
who had appeared, abusively declaring himself to be the husband,
referring to said patient as a person of the female sex, of which, as
has been proven, he was not, having received knowledge of the fatal
outcome in the newspaper, and now that we are here and in order
for it to be clear in this thick head here

pardon me if I offend you

I don't have the time or the wish to have lunch with you, mister
detective, especially since you're wearing a wedding ring, tell me
where to sign because I have to get on with my life

I threw away all that stuff that had lied to me

not Soraia

on the rug drying, I can barely remember lifting up the brick
where I hid the heroin, I don't remember whistling to the mastiff
although I just might have done it because Soraia, loving as she was
and wanting us to get along with each other

—You'll take care of the beasty won't you promise me that you'll
take care of the beasty

she would have liked, I know her that well, for the animal to be
with me, I have a hazy image of the bus to Fonte da Telha, especially
of an elderly lady sitting next to me who asked

—May I pet him?

at the same time as she got bogged down in a tale all full of ramifications and details about a basset hound that had disappeared on her in São Domingo church, stolen by some martyr or other I presume, perched on the altar with an innocent little look among candles and flowers and the lady, running her fingers through the mastiff's hair, let me hug him around the neck and bring back memories even if just for five minutes, with my finding a certain happiness in the fact that there are people even more alone than I am, a happiness that no doubt gave me the courage to lay out the blanket on the sand, heat up the heroin fixes in the spoon

not eleven, correct the eleven, ten gathering them up one by one into the syringe without its mattering to me that people were watching me and I can't guarantee that the fishermen and the people living in the shacks weren't watching me because maybe I had some money, maybe my shirt or my loafers or some ring that the druggie maybe wore and that they could certainly sell in Barreiro or in Almada, I could feel their hope and their hope helped me almost not to notice the rubber band on my arm, the needle, nothing understand, almost noticing nothing that wasn't the sea.

CHAPTER

MY FATHER WAS SEWING a hem while I sat on the sofa, legs out, tapping one shoe against the other, looking at the ceiling and waiting for something interesting to happen because down below here nothing of interest was happening and right then and there I got the idea that the chandelier was finally beginning to come unglued and at least there would be a feast of broken glass on the floor, my father's face was looking for mine and I was pretending I wasn't noticing, and I said to the chandelier

—Will it be today or when?

with hopes that the quivering of the prisms would turn into a cascade, I stopped knocking my ankles against each other to pound on the floor and bring about the collapse at the same time that my father was puckering his features around his nose, all in my direction

—Paulo

while the prisms came to rest because it had only been a bus on the street and the bus was long gone now, if we'd opened the window I would have got the notion that the chandelier was a tree too, except planted upside down with its fruit of hollow bulbs waving along with the other treetops, a transparent tree

except for the brass trunk and the branches of bolts whose name Mr. Couceiro knew in Latin, he would write bolts in the air with his cane and explain to me, explain to me now the reason for my not being able to shake your hand and say good morning, I mumble, I disappear, I shut myself up in the laundry room angry at shutting myself up in the laundry room, if only I could, if only I could manage it, if only I weren't ashamed

and I can't, I can't manage it, I'm ashamed to go into the living room and keep him company, I don't want to

can it be that I don't want to?

I don't want Dona Helena, lifting her happy gratitude from her knitting, I don't want them to grow old, to die, to scare me with your medicines at table with your small fingers meditating

the capsule or the pill?

deciding on the capsule but picking up the pill, helping it down with water, the urge to get involved, afraid of the answer

—What did the doctor say?

because I could swear more hunched over, slower, when they brought me with them Dona Helena didn't have liver spots

she never slopped her food

no need to lean on her chair, I was annoyed with that little bit of theater

—Don't pretend, you have trouble walking

along with a desire to hit them and along with an urge to hug them

no urge to hug them, only the desire to hit them, a couple of fakers thinking they could move me with their stumbling as if in matters of clowning my father wasn't enough, in the middle of the night they would walk to the kitchen, bumping into corners and waking up the building with pretexts of being thirsty, not slippers scratching on the floor, chalk that scraped a blackboard and made my hair stand on end in the depths of sleep, pulling off the adhesive from my skin which was also me, the dishwasher in a frenzy of uncountable objects we'd never had, hundreds of pots, silverware, cups, strainers knocking against each other, falling, rolling, walking up to me with metallic rumbles and then, in the silence, the thread of water in the glass

a glass with no bottom that never stopped filling up

a deafening thread, a cascade of lead entering their throats which I never imagined could be so wide with an immense gurgling, the slippers back to the bedroom in spite of the pillow over my head and my being adhesive tape, and my being skin, or then a hope that lasted for infinite seconds, taking the pillow off my head, adjusting my ears in growing apprehension, a body lying across the bread bag, features in a mask of horror, the sleeve drooping onto a cluster of dead fingernails

don't die

the suspicion, the probability, the certainty that maybe they'd fainted, getting up out of bed, getting tangled up in the sheet

seeing that they might just have have died

getting myself untangled from the sheet

don't die

pulling up my pajama bottom loose at the waist, which falls down to my knees because in spite of mentioning it three months ago Dona Helena with a pat on the head

—You're right, son

don't call me son

she didn't replace the elastic

they might die again

stumbling, holding up my pants toward the kitchen, bumping into the same corners as they did except I was barefoot, a nail and infection, tetanus, delirium, fever, pains

—There's nothing to be done ma'am, the vaccine didn't take

I went on to the bathroom with its smell of perpetual tide where even in the dark the mirror gleamed, calling me, worried as I was

—Hurry up

the bedroom where Dona Helena or Mr. Couceiro

I didn't know which one would survive the other

was coughing in time to the alarm clock along with the enigma of a fly inside the glass which the minute hand would try to harpoon every half hour and in the kitchen that was enlarged by the streetlights

don't forget the way the streetlights would enlarge the apartment when you got home up the lightless stairs, when you would have one step to go and your leg would sink into an unexpected landing, don't forget that before the key was in the lock you'd light a match, the flame from the match would fall onto the doormat don't forget the flame from the match falling onto the doormat

and the building just like you would cease to exist but, still, the key was turning all by itself, the lights enlarging the living room into other living rooms, revealing to you shadows of sofas that weren't there and you were questioning strangers

don't forget

who didn't exist and still were talking to you in the emptiness of the silence, the lights on rainy Fridays crossed the street with crooked lines, even though there was no wind, your reflection in every drop on the glass, dozens of you in the window frame looking at you with no interest because it's this, only this, you don't know who you are and who you'll be, only this that frightens and intrigues you, you go up to the curtain and nobody there

not even you

in the reflection it's useless to question yourself, assume anything, feel afraid, the evidence of your life is before you, don't forget thinking

—Who am I?

even though you won't get an answer and you don't get an answer, there's nobody with you. nobody can simulate you, you simulate yourself and your heart has stopped, you drop the curtain because you found the future, not your future, that of others, your future is finished

don't forget

if you tried to speak where would you find the words, don't think that by turning on the light you'll get back what you've been, what you imagined that they're waiting for you

don't say that they're waiting for you

they're not waiting for you

don't be upset, put away your handkerchief, stop, maybe if you put away your handkerchief you'll discover some apple seeds, in your pocket a pencil stub, a lost jackknife that will help you reconstruct an archaeology of voices, your father, your mother, your blind grandmother making a mistake

—Is it my grandson, Judite?

and the smell of the mimosas that you never got to catch so get on with your story, don't forget that you went to the bathroom, the hallway, the bedroom, and in the kitchen enlarged by the streetlights

and in the kitchen enlarged by the streetlights

don't forget

in the kitchen enlarged by the streetlights neither one of them slipping away from the refrigerator with a tear of margarine hanging from the package, waiting for me to get really sad, the Anjos church worshipping misfortunes

—Too late, Paulinho

and

it's obvious

a lie, what do you mean too late, Mr. Couceiro on the stool from which he'd feed me when I was small, that is Dona Helena would feed me and Mr. Couceiro would count the spoonfuls, eight to go, seven to go, six to go, five and a half to go and after five and a half, since you couldn't see the bottom of the plate, Dona Helena would give a signal and Mr. Couceiro, while Dona Helena was scraping the edges, five and a quarter to go, five to go, four and three quarters to go, four and a half to go, going from four and a half to zero so that Dona Helena

—All done

or maybe he would happen to speed up his count, dividing the unit into smaller and smaller snippets, three quarters to go, half to go, a quarter to go, half a quarter to go, half of half a quarter to go, almost nothing to go, half of almost nothing to go, Dona Helena with the spoon in suspense and me with a bib around my neck fascinated by the elasticity of that endless arithmetic, even today it occurs to me to count the forkfuls when they serve me lunch

—Seventeen to go, Paulinho

increasing or decreasing the asparagus in order to hit zero, the cane pounding against the tiles inside my head, popping my eyes out in the restaurant because I'm sure Dona Helena's with me, I got to zero Dona Helena

—I got to zero Dona Helena

because I'm sure that Mr. Couceiro's with me

—Did you hear me get to zero Mr. Couceiro?

Mr. Couceiro standing by the stove

don't forget that either

seeing me come in as if I hadn't come in, following me without following me, pointing at the box for me a basket of clothes on top of it

not pointing at the box for me because none of us used it because of the basket, the church telling me a lie that was immediately noted

the Anjos church, if you think about it, not too late, I was wrong, the margarine clown hiding his eye in the eyelid of the package, we planted parsley in tin cans on the windowsill, they let me water the parsley with the port-wine glass with gilt decorations, they would lift me up by the waist and I would empty the glass into the cans

—The parsley belongs to me doesn't it, Dona Helena?

parsley or rosemary?

in the afternoon the sun on the pots and pans, on the cloths, Dona Helena didn't dare season the rice if I was nearby, on one occasion I caught her chopping a leaf

—Don't hurt my parsley

rosemary?

and Dona Helena letting go of the knife as she would a living thing, the bicycle even with flat tires you could have said had just come back from the park, if it had had cheeks they would have been flushed from the wind, at dinner the little pearl of the porgy's eye was wheezing with a goiter, Mr. Couceiro and I in the center of the world and when we got back, along the way Ghana, Alaska, China the poster with palm trees

VISIT THE BAHAMAS

in the travel agency, at the end of the month the Bahamas were wrinkled, the clerk substituted a black woman in earrings offering pineapples, papayas

VISIT CURAÇAO

I was madly in love with that black woman for a whole year and also with the Bahamas and Curaçao on our return, I was going to say there was a bird scratching on the window of the laundry room and yet from its electrocardiogram flight it was a bat, I think, just so long as you don't call me son don't squeeze my shoulder

don't squeeze my shoulder

I feel fine this way, we could spend hours without looking at anything, if only the hand of the alarm clock, in its fury to harpoon the fly, didn't bring us day, the first buses came down the Avenida Almirante Reis making it stretch from intersection to intersection all along the traffic lights and all of a sudden faucets, people, sparrows, the world off center

don't forget the night when a girl danced without paying attention to you you were nobody, you were nobody

on a lighted balcony, Noémia disappearing from the picture frame and in Noémia's place the girl who grabbed a pitcher and danced with it, Mr. Couceiro changed the order of things on the wardrobe and Noémia again, don't forget that you were doing the same thing with the comic book and the schoolbook, as soon as you heard their steps the schoolbook on top of it

Mr. Couceiro left the stove on his way back to the bedroom, his knees wobbly, his mouth twisted, the church radiant through the elbow with which he was resting on the table

—Can it be this one, Paulo?

but it was only many years later when I wasn't living with them, they never got to know that

they never got to know that I loved them

I loved them, I won't say a lot

I'd rather not say a lot, why say a lot, I loved them, half past four, a quarter past four, four, a quarter to four, half past three

I loved them

what's happened to my parsley, my napkin ring with the Big Bad Wolf printed on it, which I would scratch with my fingernail, whenever the Big Bad Wolf would look at me a little drop of gluttony dripping from his jaw, who could swear to me that he hadn't eaten Noémia, one bite and that was that, that he's not going to eat us, pulling up the covers, the silence hurting me or maybe my father at Príncipe Real sewing a hem while I was on the sofa with my legs stuck out in front knocking one foot against the other waiting for something to happen, the chandelier to start getting detached and a festival of glass on the floor, my father waving to me with a clown's good-bye

—Paulo

saying without saying

—Paulo

saying

—Paulo

not in the voice I remember from Bico da Areia and in October the gulls, a sharper voice, Micaela's voice

—I'm your friend didn't you know?

Marlene's, Vânia's, Sissi's arguing in the dressing room over lipstick, powder, glue for the wig that should have been here and isn't, who stole my gold lashes you sneak thieves, who ruined my heel, look at this heel, the bottle of perfume without a stopper that smells only of alcohol, wax flowers reduced to the wire of their stems, the prayer card of a saint who protects against illness on which they'd drawn a mustache and glasses with eye pencil, Marlene indignant

—Was it you Rui?

and Rui to whom Vânia gave what looked to me like money taking the lemon out of his pocket and studying the lemon, my father in the small living room at Príncipe Real where the prisms on the chandelier were quivering, with every bus that went up the cross street

—Why can't they let me be a woman like other women Paulo?

my grandmother running her hand over his face puzzled, winter was coming down from the mountains whistling in the roof tiles

—*Did you bring along a lady friend Judite?*

look at my man's hands Paulo, my man's neck, the falsies that slip down on me ever since I lost weight, the first time that he visited me at Anjos masquerading as a clown I didn't recognize him, feet together beside the chair that Dona Helena was offering him without daring to sit down, from one foot to the other fighting the cold even though it wasn't cold

—I won't stay long madame I just wanted to see my son

taking candy out of his purse and giving me the candy, that is not daring to give me the candy that was melting in his fingers, putting it down on the tray on the sideboard with a little smile of apology that seemed to slip off his lips and fall withered to the floor

—If you put it in the refrigerator it will get hard again

something in Mr. Couceiro's belly jumping, Dona Helena

straightening a mat, my father leaned over for a kiss, a breath of cologne came close to me

Dona Helena clutched the mat

and he didn't get to kiss me

Dona Helena let go of the mat

the whiff of cologne grew fainter and the belly was quiet, my father in the vestibule

—Don't bother, I know the way

threatening a vase, putting it in a place that wasn't where it should be

—I'm terribly clumsy aren't I?

and as he put it in a place where it shouldn't be, the cane was in a frenzy, Dona Helena turned the dragon around frontward and the cane was quiet, in spite of being out in the street already, my father remained there in the candy on the sideboard, picking it up with thumb and forefinger, as far away as possible, and dropping it into the garbage, by the door of the closet with its plastic bag meant for leavings and the lid that opened when the door of the closet opened, the candy in the midst of milk containers and bones and rinds, closing the closet and now yes, the house without any clown, we were in peace, everything in order, Mr. Couceiro moved the vase two millimeters and Dona Helena, the critic, judging perspectives

—Not quite

Mr. Couceiro with his head back examined things with her, rolling the vase, cleaning the dragon with his sleeve, trying one millimeter, Dona Helena

—I think it's right now

and still the dragon wasn't exactly right, I don't know, maybe the tongue, maybe the scales, maybe the wings, Dona Helena with her nose over the animal

—Don't do anything more to it

during dinner when one of them got a whiff of cologne a panicked glance at the vase, Dona Helena serving me my soup and Mr. Couceiro not counting the spoonfuls

fifteen, fourteen, thirteen

fearful that my father would take me away in spite of my father's straightening his hair, checking his earrings, lowering his décolleté, making an effort not to seem he was asking and yet asking, playing horseback with me on the beach

you were ordering him

—Gallop

don't forget

hooked around his shoulders grabbing him around the head, his cap, his ears, your thinking

—I'm going to fall

while your father was stumbling over the uneven sand, you could tell he was tired from the way his hands slipped down along your sandals, from his panting mouth and yet

—Gallop

the bridge getting closer, a wave that wet his pants and went off, one of the pups summoning its comrades that were looking for mussels on the beams

—The faggot's playing he's the kid's mare

and at a gallop, a trot, and not a trot, an exhausted stumbling, if you'd had a stick, a whip, some barbed wire wrapped around a pole, if you could have whipped him, ordering him

—I order you not to stop galloping

and your father reached the bridge, leaned against the railing, stared at you the way

my father stared at Dona Helena looking for a hook that wasn't there to hide the stuffing in his breast

—I won't be long madame I only wanted to see my son

the lack of courage, the shame, like the coldness underlying I won't be long madame I only wanted to see my son

—Why won't they let me be a woman like the others, Paulo?

the comic book under the schoolbook, in order to avoid the dragon vase shattering they'd take me to Príncipe Real on Saturdays, wait for me on the bench by the cedar tree where I would wait later on, the bell on the ground floor was pushed with a dull plea that gave the impression of an echo in an endless chain of caverns

dust, cobwebs

a man who wasn't my father with his watch on his wrist and his ring on his finger looking at me on the doormat

—A miniature person to see you Soraia

the man would vary from Saturday to Saturday but the watch and the ring always belonged to my father, through the window I saw Dona Helena and Mr. Couceiro on the bench with the cane leaping between them impatient, annoyed, my father dressed as a clown the rustle of lace and the fateful cologne, broad gestures with rings on his fingers, the impatience that he was trying hard to turn into merriment

—Have you met my godson Eliseu?

or Eurico or Agostinho or Ernesto or Floriano

—Have you met my godson Floriano?

the ground floor of an ancient building among ancient buildings without any Gypsies or sea, a broom stuck up against the wall supported the washbasin, there's no gentian, father

I mean godfather

there aren't any marigolds here, the usual candy going soft in his hand, afraid that Eliseu

or Eurico or Agostinho or Ernesto or Floriano

would suspect, guess, look down on him because of me, a whisper that looked like we were having some fun

—Call me godfather, Paulo

the mastiff with a bow relieving itself against corners, wouldn't you rather be in Bico da Areia, wouldn't you rather be with my mother, do you remember the pine trees, the albatrosses in June, having sardines for lunch at Cova do Vapor and mother cleaning you off with her napkin, laughing at you

—You're a bigger baby than your son, Carlos

the old man with the mouth organ stopping his playing and saying nice things about us

—What a lovely family what a lovely family

the customers clapping for the music and with the clapping you didn't notice the sound of the water that was rising, rising, the reed roof made the sun print lines on the ground, if I held out my arm over the necks of bottles and smoke from the fish

sea breams, conger eels

my arm caught the black and yellow stripes and my mother

wasn't saying anything, my father stuck out his arm, his arm
caught the black and yellow stripes and my mother laughed
—You're a bigger baby than your son, Carlos
don't you remember that, father?
—Call me godfather, Paulo
—Are you sure you don't remember that, father?
his eyes showing annoyance, the rest of his face motionless, my
father's friend was combing his mustache with a toothbrush and
my father gave me a hard pinch, a few hours later the mark was still
on my back, a pair of brown spots that were turning blue, the next
day the blue became skin again
—For the love of God call me godfather, Paulo
it's all right by me if you want to be a woman like the others,
godfather, I'll forget about Cova do Vapor, the sardines, my mother
picking bones out of your plate to put in hers, picking out the best
fish for you, giving you the roe, taking the onions out of your salad
because you don't like onions, if a little piece was left in the tomatoes and the lettuce she'd beg your pardon
—You're so picky Carlos
if
—You're so picky Carlos
annoyed with me, if
—You're so picky Carlos
tender, happy, she'd serve him the oil, the vinegar
—Don't dirty yourself, wait
if his napkin fell off she'd take mine
—Use the tablecloth Paulo
not noticing that the water in the river was rising, rising and the
fishing boats were at eye level, the old man with the mouth organ
was dozing, a toothpick in his gums, the man who was combing his
mustache with a toothbrush was moving his mouth from right to
left arranging the hairs
—How old are you, my little man?
picking up a small enameled box that I didn't remember from
Bico da Areia, lifting the lid, lowering the lid, putting it in his
pocket, whispering to my father

—I haven't got any bus money Soraia

a woman's bag, a woman's change purse, a bill, two bills, three bills, the man

—That's still not enough Soraia

four bills, a knife of wrought copper added to the small box

—I'll give you back the change later

if only my mother had been with us to forgive him, to call as a witness the old man with his music but the old man was deep in discussion with a glass of berry brandy to which he was telling secrets, misfortunes, calling me as a witness but I was wiping myself with the tablecloth, proud of my black and yellow arms, trying to guess the number of toothpicks in the toothpick holder and emptying out the holder to see if I'd gotten it right, my mother with no witnesses, with a resigned murmur

—You're a bigger baby than your son, Carlos

the man disappeared into the café, Dona Helena was nudging Mr. Couceiro

—Did you see?

the cane pecking at the ground, the cedar

what do you expect from cedars?

agreeing with her

—Yes indeed

its upper branches so broad they had to support it with iron braces, even in August it was always October on the bench, I couldn't play piggyback with my father because there wasn't any sand or any bridge so we shared the candy on a settee that has imitation gold arabesques whose paint, as it peeled, showed dark zinc, both of us idle, bored, if only a gentian on the wall at least, some marigolds maybe, a car with wooden wheels to smash on the floor, we finished the candy and I went about counting the breaks in the baseboard

odd or even?

while my father, his ankles together the way my mother used to sit, was examining his fingernails, the trim on his blouse, an imperfection in his skirt, he examined me

—Do they feed you at least?

but I was still me and you weren't you anymore, you'd unlearned how to make paper airplanes that almost flew even though they'd fall down down right away, how to talk to me, you looked on your wrist for the watch that Eliseu had carried off and even without the watch it was two o'clock at last, how do you take care of a child for two hours

teach me

because there aren't any games or toys or hard candy in the place and he gets the settee all dirty on me with his filthy fingers, I wash his hands and three minutes later if even that long and there's an hour and fifty-seven minutes left, I'd let him have the doll from the head of the bed, the peasant girls on the oil and vinegar carafes, the little bird in a bamboo cage that you wind up by the tail and it whistles the national anthem, he'd let me have a little bird in a bamboo cage that didn't whistle at all with whistling music that was full of drumbeats that weren't coming from the bird but out of the bottom of the cage while the creature went back and forth and didn't give off any sound at all and I'd pretend I was interested in it just in order to please my father while my father was convinced he was pleasing me

—A real little bird, Paulo

when the drumming was over, the bottom of the cage would stop shaking and the bird was left with an idiotic expression, my father pointed to the creature that was masquerading as a canary the same way he was masquerading as a woman

—Don't you think it's cute, Paulo?

the bird and my father begging, ridiculous, asking for something or other with their little painted beaks, while I listened to them without hearing either one of them as through the window I noticed Dona Helena taking out her crocheting and Mr. Couceiro, helpful, explaining to the tree trunks in Latin who in fact they were, my father set the cage down on the dressing table and the bird was looking at me, defeated, as if I were asking

—Why Carlos?

you were rumpling and smoothing the quilt and it was the one at home, not at Príncipe Real not at Anjos, our own house, the electrician, the café *don't forget the sound of the water that was rising, rising*

our home in spite of the fact that they never took me to Bico da Areia, the social worker arranging some papers I can't make it today you see, next week, next month, there's no hurry, not getting to

—Your mother doesn't want to see you

to

—Your mother doesn't want to see a faggot's son

and there was the shaking of the cane, the words just as if she was shouting, not see a faggot's son, not see a faggot's son and the sound of the water

calm down I haven't forgotten

which was rising, rising, the faggot's son refusing his soup, Mr. Couceiro

—Just ten more spoonfuls Paulo

and me with my mouth closed

—I won't eat

the turnips were running out of my mouth down onto the cloth tied around my neck, if you eat something we'll go to the movies, to the Ghost Castle, to the circus where the other clowns play saxophones in the ring, one of them very proper, elegant, with white cream on his face and eyebrows like your father's when he got annoyed with his colleagues' remarks

—Vânia doesn't know how to dance at all I can't understand why they took her on

as soon as one of them started crying the water would pour from her eyes, my father never cried like that, maybe if he talked to me about the dwarf from Snow White

and anyone who mentioned Snow White would be talking about the time we lived on the other side of the river

he'd turn his head to where he wasn't, he'd take that imbecilic bird out of the drawer of the dressing table and with the drums from the anthem you couldn't catch anything, not any horses not any gulls, maybe the cedar saying all the while

I never met anyone so selfish

—I'm me and I'm here

if it figured out that we weren't paying any attention to it, it

would call to us with its needles, peeved at us, holding out its
branches until we connected
—What a pretty tree all that shade
I told my father that I believed in plants and my father
—Don't be silly Paulo
he didn't believe in plants but he believed he was a woman
—I'm a woman
he stood straight up before me, his arms out, chin held high
–I'm a woman
I was searching with my tongue for the remains of a piece of
candy lost in my molars
—You're a woman
in order to avoid any flood from his eyes, I think he was squeezing a rubber ball in his pocket so if the clowns were crying I could
cry too, the man who was combing his mustache with the
toothbrush
—Cut that out, you dummy
at lunchtime Dona Helena would start rolling up her knitting,
would say something to Mr. Couceiro and my father would bring
me my coat a little too fast
—I'm sorry but they've come for you Paulo
I got the idea that a seam was coming undone and he'd spotted
the break and was getting rid of me
—It doesn't show, it's all right
if you stood on tiptoe you could make out the river and beyond
it Bico da Areia where I never returned for years on end, the mares
must still have been trotting by the waves, when a Gypsy died the
others would gather together like a flock of crows, playing the guitar, singing all night long, the soles of their feet would explode on
the ground and I wondered if it was hollow and so I asked
—Is the ground like a tambourine, mother?
the dead man's wife was leaning on friends who were scratching
themselves and shouting, everybody drunk on the terrace of the
café in spite of the owner saying
—Closing time closing time
always some shot, some switchblade, more shots in the pine

grove, the dead man I came across one afternoon smiling on the pine needles, an insignificant little hole in the back of his neck, almost no blood and he looked so happy, my God, my mother put her hands up to her mouth, the café owner walked around the body wondering what to do, suggesting while he looked over at the tents it would be best if we forgot about this, but he ended up coming back with the police and not a trace, an oriole amused by us, the corporal to the café owner are you having fun with us, have I come up with a joker in the lottery

if it hadn't been for the police I might have got the oriole even without a spear

the café owner said it was right here sir, I even told Judite that we should forget about it in order to avoid any complications, the one who would come into our house without knocking and order me

—Beat it outside, you

respectful now, submissive, the oriole flew off just when I found a stone that was perfect, the tide was coming in or going out

coming in

and the Tagus was different, one of the soldiers in leggings

I remember that the leggings needed polish and had buckles missing

he got out of the Jeep struggling with a lighter that refused to light, his thumb was turning on a little wheel and there was a spark but, the cigarette went out right away

—We should invite our joker here to come to the station house so our comrades could have a laugh, the corporal too

the tide wasn't coming in, it was going out as could be seen from the slower, more peaceful sound, in just a little while now lots of algae on the beach

the café owner kept walking back and forth whispering to my mother

—You just wait and see what I'm going to do to you Judite

he took some matches out of his pocket with the idea of helping the soldier

the oriole came back for an instant swaying in the high treetop but the matches got away from him because he couldn't get a grip on them, the soldier put the cigarette into a crease in his cap

—You just wait and see what I'm going to do to you Judite

and he put out the matches with his boot, I grabbed my mother's hand and her palm was wet

there couldn't possibly be any mistake, even a child could tell that the tide was going out

the soldier invited the café owner

—That play with the matches is funny too, let's go have a laugh at the station house

as they left I thought I saw the happy dead man a few pine trees up ahead but I was wrong, a piece of blanket hanging on a branch, the owner came back to the café the following Tuesday holding his sleeve up against an eyebrow, one of his legs slower, his wife who was cleaning the tables came over to him along with the pups and their pine cones, she was carrying a basin and some soap, Dália's aunt and Dália on her tricycle were watching the healing operations frightened, that night they cut off our lights, pulled up our marigolds, broke three windows, we could hear them in the yard stealing the sheets that had been put out to dry and pouring lye into our cistern

wandering reflections in the mirror on the wardrobe were growing larger, my mother on the bed hugging me, her breast heaving, tears, I could have sworn, I looked with my finger and I found hair, my face was on her neck, do you miss the smell of the mimosas, do you miss the vineyards, do you miss the car with wooden wheels, mother, and my mother didn't answer, do you miss father, mother, do you want me to call father and her hair covering my mouth

my father Carlos, my mother Judite

Carlos Carlos

the mirror on the wardrobe calming down or maybe it was then that I fell asleep, the maid from the dining room who fell asleep, we who fell asleep mother, they can't hurt us while we're asleep, that's not knocking on the door, it's the wind, there's nobody outside, it's the gentian branches sprouting, tell the maid from the dining room that we're all alone, we're all alone Gabriela, not you and me, I'm sorry to tell you this but you and I don't matter, my mother and I are all alone and now it's only the sea coming in or going out

coming in

don't forget the water that's rising, rising

just a few minutes from now there won't be a single bit of algae on the beach, or any bridge, or any house, or any Bico da Areia, or us

Sardines

if someone stood on tiptoes he could make out the river, he couldn't make out Cacilhas or where we'd lived years ago, only waves mother, not the bridge, not Alto do Galo, not them in the yard, the maid from the dining room

—Paulo

looking for the lamp, getting out of the sheets, turning on the lamp with the window covered, Lisbon mother, Lisbon, when we were in Bico da Areia

piggyback on my father

—Gallop

holding him around his forehead, his cap, his ears, thinking

—I'm going to fall

while he stumbled along over clumps of grass, garbage, rubble on the way to the bridge and not at a gallop, at a trot, if only I had a whip, a branch, a stick wrapped in barbed wire, if only I could have ordered him

—Don't stop do you hear I forbid you to stop galloping

don't pretend you're tired as your fingers slide down my sandals, don't think the maid from the dining room is defending you when she calls me

—Paulo

swearing to me poor thing thinking I believed her

—It's nothing Paulo

because logically it is nothing, how could it be anything new, I know quite well it's nothing, it's some guy

at most

some guy or other climbing over the beams where there are gull eggs and mussels and slime, leaning against a rail

do you still want me to call him, mother, seriously do you still want me to call him?

taking off a shoe to get rid of some pebbles, shaking it, putting it on again and I right away with my heels into his kidneys

—Gallop

look at how the faggot

the pups say

is playing mare for the kid and still at a gallop, don't try to amuse me, don't give me candy, don't show me the cage and the music of the anthem, don't think that Dona Helena and Mr. Couceiro will be of any help to you

they're of no help to you and Eliseu isn't any help for you didn't you know, not even my mother

—Let him go

I let you go didn't you know, don't get dressed as a woman, don't put on mascara, don't put on makeup, don't disguise yourself with a wig, don't ask me

—Do you think I'm a woman like them?

plucking an eyebrow in a way so that one doesn't match the other at all

and it won't match the other one sir, you're a clown and clowns use different eyebrows, the left one normal and the right one higher

don't ask me why they're stopping me from being a woman since I'm more of a woman than they are, take a look at my waist Paulo

—Did you take a good look at my waist Paulo?

when he turned me over to Mr. Couceiro he held out his hand to him and Mr. Couceiro didn't hold out his and ignored the selfish cedar

—Look at me all of you, here I am

held up by iron crutches and putting out branches annoyed with us, we go through the park on our way to Anjos and I notice the curtain being drawn, becoming a kind of blur and as soon as the blur disappears I'm an orphan, all I can expect tonight are the slippers scraping on the floor bumping into corners on the way to the kitchen, the dishwasher frantic

hundreds of pots, pans, strainers, all I can expect is the faucet open and a bottomless glass that doesn't stop filling, all I can expect is one of you by the stove waiting for me, don't forget the way the streetlights lengthen the living room and reveal to you shadows of sofas that weren't there and you asking strangers

your mother, your father, your grandmother

—My grandson, Judite?

who didn't exist, who never existed and yet they were talking to you in the emptiness of the silence, nobody's there with you, nobody can touch you, you're touching yourself, the maid from the dining room

—Paulo

—What's wrong Paulo?

—It's no good this way Paulo

—Don't scare me Paulo

there seems to be someone next to you but if you take a better look there are boards on the window and beyond the boards is Lisbon, Lisbon mother, Lisbon, I thought it was Lisbon and yet the rain, you're crossed by slanting lines even though there's no wind outside, your reflection is on every drop on the windowpane, dozens of yous in the window frame telling your father

—Gallop

while you manage it you tell your father

—Gallop

so you're not sure that you have any flesh left, only teeth, only eye sockets and teeth gleaming with the astonishment skulls have, cover yourself with marigolds, pull the sheet up over your head, if the maid from the dining room says

—Paulo

don't answer, sink down into the mattress so you won't bump into the future, not your future, the other one's future, your future is all over.

CHAPTER

WHAT I WOULD HAVE LIKED was having a business of my own, a small neighborhood establishment that wouldn't make me get up dead tired from lack of sleep at half past six in the morning with this cold all winter long and no light outside, starting to get dressed in the dark under the bedcovers without getting out of bed, buttoning myself up lying down there, pulling on my skirt while raising myself on my heels and my shoulders, thinking I'm going to go back to sleep, thinking they'll mark me absent, thinking I'll lose my job, feeling the floor with my chilled right foot, finding my left shoe and surprised that I'd changed shape during the night, if I close my eyes a little I can get my body back but I haven't got time to get my body back because of the fact that Paulo's not working, finding the second shoe next to the wall where I don't remember having left it and it fits me after all or maybe I changed when I woke up, putting my hair in the elastic band I always leave around my wrist before it gets the urge to run away on me too, pulling my coat off the hook with such force that

the hands begin to change into my hands and they're still not my hands

that the loop inside the collar tears, proof that there's something in my hands is the fact that I drop the umbrella, I don't know where Paulo is because I've lost track of the bed

—Can't a person get a little rest Gabriela?

in my ear right then because it scared me and far away because I don't care in spite of my being more me now, there are bits and pieces of not me still there, this shoulder, for example, the heart that doesn't beat, for example, starts working, misses, stops, in the chest now in the belly now, unable to find its place until it gets settled in my ribs, calms down and right then, me finally me, arms, fatigue, legs, an urge to lie down on the floor, to die, I could see the room, I could see the wardrobe, I could see the frozen doorknob impossible to turn a short while ago and now so easy, a gray light with the tatters of March floating over the landing because the skylight on the ceiling has been fogged over by the pigeons

not just the stains of their droppings, feathers too, a cloud that's chasing after the night and can't catch up with it

certain as I go down the stairs that I'd stayed behind up there, so heavy, absent, half of my teeth squashed against the pillowcase, one eye blind, the remaining eye searching in the shadows, looking back and becoming just as blind when on the wall, in charcoal, Marina & Diogo with the Diogo x-ed out and replaced by Jaime, the Jaime bigger than the Diogo but it still can't get rid of him, Jaime lived with Marina in the basement, I never ran into Diogo in the building so that farther down Marina & Jaime and us, not connecting with Jaime, looking for Diogo, concerned about his absence

—I wonder where Diogo is?

with an urge to x out Jaime and give Diogo to Marina, who worked for the city, Marina & Jaime on the ground floor where someone had started to rub out the Jaime, every week the Jaime got more and more faded and Diogo, in spite of not being there, was filling up the space, one afternoon I ran into Marina leaning over the trash rubbing her sleeve against the Jaime, the landlady told me that Diogo

—He abused the poor thing, she always was a ninny

had run off to Australia with their savings, she showed me a tiny little Diogo inside a heart drawn in pencil stuck to the mailboxes in hopes of a letter and in spite of the hopes never any letter, every day the anxious little key, looking for Diogo in a flood of supermarket flyers, advertisements for electric gadgets for the home, announcements from African spiritualist clairvoyants in caps and dark glasses

Professor Isaias, Professor Claudecir

who brought people together and separated people, in the case of Diogo a medium-like neutrality that got Marina stirred up, when she went out onto the street the cloud that had followed her at night was a little pink mist at the end of the block, not Marina, Jaime unshaven adjusting his cap at the bus stop, I

—I don't know why you should have an effect on me

was making up my mind to underline his name on the ground floor first thing in the morning

maybe I don't know why, his fingers are like my father's up and down the keys

—*How about a little tune, daughter?*

and I was annoyed you shouldn't have died do you hear

the buildings

just like me with my blouse and skirt ten minutes earlier

were getting dressed in windows and on balconies without turning on the light, moving around under the window drapes, this print here, that fruit bowl there, Jaime kept his hands in his pockets and I hated him for making me miss my father at the lunch table with the accordion on his knees, the little smile that annoyed my mother and made me happy, the instrument more whistles than notes a sick cough but it was all right, I liked it, even today when I feel depressed I can hear him playing the accordion and I feel better, if he could have dreamed of what became of me, where I work, how I live, that the orderly

that naughty little hand Mr. Vivaldo, that sneaky little hand

would call me into the bandage room when the redhead wasn't there, couldn't you find a man with a decent job, Gabriela, instead of a patient, some proper young guy who could take care of you, my father forgetting about the buttons and the keys, worried, sad

—You were always so thin

a timid little ray of sunshine touching the patches

—So frail

from the rain, the bus stopped with a sigh, agreeing with him, Jaime waiting for me to get on maybe with Diogo written in charcoal somewhere on my coat

I tried to clean it off without his seeing it, the landlord despised him, that dimwit, that cuckold, I don't remember Marina talking to him, the day was getting itself organized, Lisbon was getting things ready all along the way, small squares, trees, the hoists along the Tagus in places where there was a deep shadowy emptiness and Paulo's knee against my belly, two or three hours before, at the time when neither of us was neither of us, I thought

I was just imagining

I was seeing treetops through the boarded-up window and yet I wonder if they were treetops in the boarded-up window or by the sea at Peniche years ago when we visited my grandfather at the fort

I was very young

hallway after hallway and the unseen waves could be heard, crashing against the stone wall, my grandfather

—They haven't hurt me

I don't remember him, that is I remember his voice

—They haven't hurt me

my mother pulled something out of her skirt and gave it to him, one of the guards to my mother

the sea at Peniche with such force now

—You there

such force that you can't hear the little package hitting the floor, they gave my grandfather a shove, the guard lifted up his arm, looked at me and his arm wasn't moving, waiting, I remember the fishermen's huts

they told me afterward that they were fishermen's huts

they'd caught my grandfather with pamphlets against I-don't-know-who in his pockets and they took him away, something to do with politics, they opened the little package, cigarettes, almonds, butter, a card with a diagram and some writing on it inside the butter, the guard called another guard and the other guard asked my mother

—What's this?

just as I was going into the hospital and the plane trees were

greeting me right away, shaking their branches and leaves and leaping around me like happy chickens

—I don't have any corn, get away

the eyes of the doorman in the glass booth detached from his
face so they could run up and down over my body, dripping wetness
that stuck to my clothes, what I would have liked was having a business of my own, a small neighborhood establishment, a laundry,
Paulo's father's lady friends

Paulo's aunt's

would bring me the dresses they wore when they danced at the
theater and the customers would show me respect

—We never would have guessed that you knew actresses Dona
Gabriela

not just my grandfather, they gave my mother a shove

—What's this?

they went through her bag, went through her blouse, communist, communist, if my father and his accordion would only leave us
in peace

—Play a little tune father

and my father

it was the only time he didn't do what I wanted

ordering me

—Shut up

not with his mouth, with a wrinkle in his forehead, ordering my
sister

—Don't cry

and my sister stuck out her neck and swallowed herself, all that
was left was her open mouth with all her upset inside, weeks later
we got a postcard from the fort along with my grandfather in a
closed coffin that they wouldn't let us open, the guards attended
the funeral with us, they stopped us from carving his name on the
tombstone

there wasn't even any tombstone

they wouldn't let my grandfather's friends go into the cemetery,
three or four old men wearing neckties that weren't the color for
mourning, bright red

—Only the family, gentlemen

a few months ago I went through Peniche and there were the waves pounding against the stones, after the funeral the police were by our door, the friends in red ties were on the sidewalk and the four of us were in the room wearing our Sunday shoes and the lace tablecloth was laid out, the friends finally went away one by one, the guards rang the doorbell to warn us

a business of my own

—We want you to keep your mouths shut

no crucifix, no priest, no sexton praying, my mother gave my sister and me a thimbleful of wine, a drop flowed down onto the label, kept going down, they catch it with a napkin, they won't let it fall, my sister to herself inside her stomach and facing my father as he twisted the cloths in his hand one into the other

—Don't cry

going to get the stepladder from the kitchen, going through the apartment with the stepladder catching on the furniture, placing it in front of the bedroom wardrobe, climbing up the steps I was thinking I'm a drop of wine, they hold me with the napkin, they won't let me fall, I got the feeling that my father was saying

—Like a dog just like a dog

but in such a low voice that I could have been wrong, he was bringing the accordion that moaned with life, breathing on my lap

—Play a little tune father

my mother ran to the window where her shoulder was going up and down, my father was imitating my sister swallowing himself too, the accordion lying on the floor became quiet, its silver decorations shining, its lungs collapsed, dead, my mother was nothing but a back, she was crumpling up the curtains without looking at us, when Paulo's father

aunt, godmother, cousin died, there was no pounding on the stones at the fort, no accordion on the floor, his colleagues at Príncipe Real were arguing over the ostrich feathers that might not have come from an ostrich, Paulo was leaning on the radio laugh-

ing while the mastiff with a bow licked the tip of his shoes, Dona
Amélia was looking for money

that's not how it was

because there had to be money, he must have left some money
in the drawers, in the trunk, in the bread bag, Rui

it couldn't have been Rui, Rui was in Fonte da Telha at that time
poor fellow and the mastiff too then, everything's all mixed up in
my head

Rui to Dona Amélia

that's not how it was

—It's no use poking around in his belongings he was just a clown
didn't you know?

Paulo laughing and taking it all in, laughing and onto everything, he got away from Marlene

a not very young chanteuse but better dressed than the others
and beautiful

he went down the steps without hearing me

—Paulo

he went out into the park without paying any attention to anything, unbuttoning the jacket Dona Helena had lent him, his feet
like in beach sand, his elbows pushing away someone I think was
Mr. Couceiro and then gentian branches that I imagined, I couldn't
see, if I could only set up a business, a neighborhood establishment,
Paulo was still laughing until we got to Chelas

a while later the dead body of a rooster appeared, the remains of
some cartilage, some bones

cartilage or bones?

laughing at the Cape Verdeans who didn't understand why he
was happy, sitting down on the grass

I thought that a dead accordion couldn't get to play and yet my father

for one second his eyes were different like sad or something, thank
God because right away happy again, the Cape Verdeans told us

and a switchblade I think

we're not selling you anything, go on back down, as if Paulo had
scared them, so insignificant, so calm, I thought that a dead accor-

dion couldn't ever get to play and yet one Sunday morning, I was already getting ready for school, I was scared when I heard it until my mother said

—Ruben

when we were going down to Príncipe Real to the aunt's apartment, the godmother's, the cousin's

why pretend, Paulo's father's

vacant

he wasn't even an artiste, he pretended to be singing, in spite of rehearsing in front of the mirror, the repetition, the efforts, his lips didn't keep time with the violins, he'd stand in front of the mirror again, hold out his hand to catch the sounds sometimes slow, sometimes fast, they were determined to humiliate him, he'd drop onto the sofa, ask for his fan

—The fan, be patient

my grandfather my mother's father in Peniche, if you asked my mother about him she always watched out for the neighbors, footsteps, chinaware, her breathless panic

—Shut up

he'd grip the fan to stop it from flying away from him and instead of the fan it was his face that was fluttering its eyebrows behind the ribs

—I'm not capable

I don't know anything about my grandmother, I don't think I had one

—What about grandfather's wife, mother?

and my mother like a secret because of footsteps, because of chinaware, because of ears on the other side of the wall

—She died

no photograph, no letter, *my grandfather's friends would cross over when they saw us, every now and then an explosion, a ship sunk and their photographs, those, yes, in the newspaper opened up at the table and as soon as the photographs appeared my mother, pointing to the page*

—Burn that, Ruben

a tiny flame and the picture curling up in the washbasin, rising up out of the letters around it and trying to stay alive, and then yellow and then black and then ashes and then the faucet sending them down the drain, the water kept on running with nothing to carry along with it now, on one occasion, before Peniche, there was a knock on the door, my mother hid the crack in the door with her body along with furious whispering aimed at the empty landing

—Don't mess up my life father, go away

as far as I could think there was nobody at the door at all but we were never sure because she'd lean against the doorknob looking at us, terrified for us, she would lean over the windowsill, go back to the doorknob, one of her knees was moving all by itself

just her knee, her hip and her ankle were motionless

—He wouldn't rest until he killed my mother with his politicking and now he won't rest until he kills me

and yet, in spite of my grandfather's wanting to ruin her life, there was a loose plank in the pantry floor where there were notebooks, packages, tubes wrapped in a piece of oilcloth and tied with string, my mother would send us into the bedroom before she lifted up the board

—Stay in there for a while

a creaking of wood, a muffled sound, my father on the stairs leaving his soup half eaten, his knee toward us, with an affliction that prevented us from saying anything

—He went out to buy some cigarettes

my father, who didn't smoke, who detested tobacco, he'd come back and settle down at the table with his pockets empty, he'd pick up his spoon and the spoon would slip away from him, his knee was scared too, the napkin not touching his mouth

—There it is

one of my grandfather's friends

—Isn't he the one in the newspaper mother?

and my mother

—What newspaper?

I pulled whatever it was out of the garbage can, the accordion without any little tune, the apartment seemed to be all knees too, the calendar, the faucets, my mother that is to the apartment

—No noise, dammit

until a few nights later a bomb in a munitions factory, this burned, that burned, some the fan closing as though its life had ended, Paulo's father rising up from behind the ribs with a sparrow chirp

—I'm not capable Rui

airplanes destroyed, burned, the waves at Peniche pounding on the wall, my mother to the doormat in a whisper that everybody heard

—*This finishes it, what do I care about the dictatorship, I'm not*

the ground floor at Príncipe Real vacant, even the chandelier, just imagine

helping you anymore

the apartment that had quieted down a bit was getting all agitated again, I had no idea that the glasses in the cupboard could jump about like that, my father didn't try not to say anything and he was trying hard not to say anything, my mother going to the door

—*I'm the one who's talking to that fool of an old man of mine, understand?*

on the ground floor at Príncipe Real a tube, all rolled up on the dressing table, squeezed by fingers

my grandfather

that fool old man

was rowing out on the Tagus straight up to the frigate, his friends knew where they were supposed to be going, the sandbars, the currents

women's makeup and clothes I wouldn't dare wear, maybe he wasn't a man, Paulo was playing with me, lying to me, it couldn't be a man, if it wasn't your aunt or your godmother, it's your father, who's your mother, you were fooling me weren't you, you were lying, weren't you, how could it be your father

don't fool around with me

if she lives with her husband, her name is Soraia, do you know any man named Soraia and then her friends, Dona Micaela, young Sissi, those men who visit them, the engineer, the doctor

the friends knew the sandbars, the currents, the places where smugglers or Navy launches

Paulo showing me the syringe, the spoon, tying my wrists to the bed without any force tying my wrists to the bed

—Where'd you connect for the heroin Gabriela?

—What are you talking about Gabriela?

—What kind of a story is that about my father your grandfather how long have you been this way Gabriela?

incapable of understanding that his aunt

—I'm not capable

that my grandfather and I rowing in a boat, stopping me from rowing

—Don't tear the sheets

I won't let you stop me, nobody can stop me, if your aunt is your father, show me your mother I dare you and he said

—Gabriela

unable to bear the fact that I had no nausea, no pain, maybe a touch of chill but everybody knows how the Tagus is in February, don't lie on top of me, don't cover my mouth, don't cry

—I'm not crying

there's no reason to cry because the friends know the sandbars, the currents, and my picture in the paper tomorrow, in February I'd go walking with my father along the wall by the river and my father would tighten the scarf around my neck, he wouldn't squeeze me the way you squeeze me

—I'm not squeezing you I only want you to rest a little, who squeezed you Gabriela?

he tightened the scarf around my neck, no need to talk, we never had any need to talk, not even by the closed box that the police prohibited me from opening, it wasn't a coffin, a box with no crucifix or any handles, with hinges nailed down at random, with a number in chalk on the wood and my mother with her knees together, stiff

—What proof do I have that my father's inside there?

calm, not upset, not angry

—What proof do I have that my father's inside there?

not at home, in the chapel at the cemetery, at the entrance some flower beds and a character taking care of them with the calm of someone tidying up a yard, there was no priest, there were two guards and the box on the brick floor

more than two guards my sister swears

what does it matter

there were two guards

or three or four or five

with a document for us to sign, my father with a black band on his arm, my mother in mourning, my sister and me, I can't remember, we didn't have any black dresses so most likely black bands on our sleeves too, fastened to our arms with a safety pin and me proud of the black band

—I'm grown up

the guards laid the documents on the box

coarse men, not in uniform, if you ran into them on the street you wouldn't notice them, my mother not picking up the pen

—Who says they have my father in there, I want to see him first

and the guards we haven't got time for that, don't make any work for us, look at the seal, the warden's initials so my father signed, not quickly, letter by letter learning the words, I have received from the Director General of Security, he paused looking at the box and the guards who were getting to be more, seven now, ten now, twelve now

my grandfather not dead, rowing in a boat on the Tagus toward the anchored frigate

a chapel with a platform and on the platform a table that served as an altar, the stained-glass window that they'd repaired with a piece of tape, the black band slipped down to my wrist, I showed it to my mother who fixed the pin and it must have been one of those few times when I felt her hands, you couldn't hear the waves pounding on the rocks, the guards took the document away, to my father

—That'll do for a signature

I said you couldn't hear the waves beating on the rocks or the oarlocks or the hinges or the boat getting close to the frigate or Paulo's father

or aunt, godmother, cousin

—I've got to take care of him, there's nothing else to do, so small trying to get rid of his worries with the fan

—I'm not capable

you could hear the cart on the cemetery path, my mother was going to kiss the coffin but my father stopped her from leaning over don't hold me onto the bed, don't cover my mouth

one of the guards helped her, mocking

—Go ahead and kiss the little box, lady

thinking my mother didn't like her father, the way you don't like your father, why should she like her father since he screwed up her life

didn't your father screw up your life Paulo?

a path alongside the wall, not just the February cold on the Tagus, the February rain, the detonator's all set, it's in the oilcloth wrapping

—Your father screwed up your life Paulo don't come to me with the story of your father not screwing up your life your mother the marigolds Bico da Areia Dália paid no attention to you

you're rocking in the boat, you hold out the package and a magnet holds it up against the hull, I think they helped me to walk in the cemetery because my legs ached, I think they lifted me up, I think my father lifted me up Paulo

you were hitting him on the forehead, on the shoulders, on the ears

—Don't stop galloping don't lean up against the railing of the bridge I forbid you to lean against the railing

and the gulls, isn't it true, you hated them and yet you haven't forgotten the gulls, the way they devour fish, their babies squalling in the afternoon

and then no tombs or angels, a hole all ready beyond the other graves, not among them, a rake that asked me

—Please, Gabriela

asking me I don't know what, wanting I don't know what, my mother turning away from the coffin for a moment

—Don't listen to him, Gabriela

and maybe, because she was distracted, the cemetery workers dumped it into the hole with something rattling inside

those cookie tins we keep empty and when we pick them up it sounds as though there's still a cookie inside

this time it wasn't her knee, it was my mother's lip and her teeth showing, growing in size as they start shoveling the earth, her lips teeth, her features teeth, her body teeth, my father repeating

—Like a dog just like a dog

but in such a low voice that I might have been wrong, but I wasn't wrong because one of the guards, the one with the document

—Is there any doubt that your father-in-law was a dog?

and my mother's teeth disappearing one after the other

he was a dog, he was a dog, you're right mister guard, he was a dog, the dog was rowing on the Tagus straight up to the frigate and Paulo's arms were gripping mine, the palm of his hand was covering my mouth

—You're going to wake up the whole building, Gabriela

beyond the wall uninhabited houses, trees from China, gates, the air seeming to be boiling with bees, a little woman prodding a turkey with a stick, the man with the document saying to my mother so you put on your mourning clothes for a dog friend, you just tell me whether it's worth putting on mourning clothes for dogs, they bite you, they betray us, we've got the kennel at Peniche full to overflowing, when they can't find people to bite they bark at the government, bite themselves, I swear, the shadow of a cloud

not a cloud, the shadow of a cloud, Paulo, it passed over us, its blur made the plaster cherubs dark for a minute, the Our Ladies, the too-white statue of a girl my size

a little bigger

Eternal Longing

and the girl's prayer card in a copper oval

praying on a tombstone, the statue, not the prayer card, the girl puzzled that they'd put her there

—Did something happen to me?

you couldn't see her forefinger on her breast in the picture arguing that it can't be me, it's a mistake, puzzled by their sticking her onto the marble above Beloved Daughter, her name and two dates in gold, looking all around, worried

—Come clean with me whether something has happened to me or not

and what can I tell her Paulo, you tell me, I showed her the little vase with small wilted flowers, the iron fence missing a spike, I confessed to her

—I don't know

because I felt incapable of disillusioning her, you understand, but the thought still came to me of finding out where your mother is, your father, swearing to her that her mother and father were coming back to get her it won't be long

and the shadow of a second cloud almost next to us, you looked at the sky and it wasn't round, it was stretched out, with golden edges, if I could have managed to read, I would have called her by name or maybe called her father, her mother

—She's here waiting for you don't forget her

they've gone to take a walk, don't be frightened because they're not lost to you, they have money, they sleep with the lights out, they're older, and the girl in the copper oval calmed, content, settling into the decorations, taking on the responsible and serious look that dead people have, they never lie, you can trust them with a secret, they won't tell anybody, what they promise they do, once I stole a coin from my parents, looking at the picture of my uncle, my mother asked

—Was it you Gabriela?

my uncle was silent, he probably wasn't on my side but he was mute, my sister, even if she was on my side

the third or fourth time that my mother said

—Was it you Gabriela?

she couldn't hold back and she snorted, my uncle, on the contrary, was beside me, not dressed like my father and the other adults, in a fireman's uniform and a medal

Uncle Firmino

if he took off his helmet I'll bet his bald head would show so he never took it off, the cemetery workers finished smoothing over the grave without bothering about the rake

—Please

not to my sister, to me and I let it be understood that it could still work

—You can still work I'm sure

although for every five leaves, two got picked up if they were lucky, as soon as the cemetery workers put their shovels into the wheelbarrow, the guards said to my mother not two, several of them Paulo, my sister had been right

jeering at the workers, look how the boobs are scared of us, we don't hurt anyone who doesn't get involved with the State, they don't thank us for solving the problem of your dog, lady, he doesn't bark at your heels anymore, he doesn't bother you, he doesn't annoy you at night scratching at the door and you scared about the neighbors who might phone us, write a letter, turn him in, the dog barking in your ear hide this for me Isabel and you in a women's prison, you doing a good stretch of years making handicrafts in jail, potholders, baskets, crocheting while the matron teaches you to love your country

—Love your country Isabel!

a lot of guards Paulo, you can let go of my arms because I won't run away, this heroin was cut with so much talcum powder, a lot of guards went along with us and my grandfather near the too-white statue whose parents, getting on in age, were capable of sleeping with the lights out and probably haven't lost her, have taken her home, given her some supper, put her to bed, and that's enough of cemeteries, iron fences, vases

—Nothing's happened to you, can't you see that nothing's happened to you?

the way nothing's happened to me, don't give me any camomile tea, don't warm my feet, nothing's happened no matter how much Mr. Vivaldo might have hinted otherwise, nothing's happened Paulo, my grandfather's friends at the cemetery entrance and the guards

eight guards, definitely eight guards

spotted those dogs, look at those dogs who won't have to wait long for a box for each one of them and that'll be the end of their fleas, communism, disrespect for the church, your husband throwing packages into garbage cans lady, what a rotten life, what a stinking smell, you were scared that they're screwing up your life, the floorboard at rest finally, the rowboat alongside the frigate, those lights on the water that aren't even blue, reflections, but of what if it isn't the moon, let me sit for a while Paulo, let me breathe, I don't feel anything see, I'm not hollering, I'm not trying to hit you, I'm fine, it's been a long, long time since I felt so fine, notice the way I carry the trays into the dining room without a single spoon shaking, the dogs at the cemetery entrance all in a pack, sneaky, look at what cowards they are, if we throw a stone they'll run away, your father wasn't any different, lady, if you threw a stone at him he'd run away, how do you want us to bury them except in boxes that aren't worth a penny, the mine's not sticking, help me, the glue on the mine isn't catching, and now try a little farther on where there's no paint, there on the bedroom wall between the bed and the window, take advantage of the rising and falling of the river, it's got to stick, damn it, when in just a little while the wall of the room and we can forget all this, Príncipe Real, Anjos, Chelas and go to sleep in peace, the guards along with us from the cemetery home to protect us from any bad meetings, friends, and my mother nodding yes, my sister clutching her legs and my father's fingers playing the accordion on his vest, I told the girl in the copper oval

—I'll be back

and the silly girl believed me, I fooled her, I'm not coming back, the way you look at me sometimes like that, I don't think you're coming back Paulo, the guards took their leave by the entrance landing don't make us get mad at you, friends, holding out their hands to my father, shaking hands, holding out their hands to my mother and my mother not moving, looking at them, don't you think that's enough, won't you leave us in peace, the ceiling light mixing us all in and, even so, the girl recognizing me, pulling on my dress

—Will you really come Gabriela?

And I didn't know where the cemetery was, relax, I'm really coming, what a silly question, have I ever lied to you, my mother closing the door, they've tormented me enough, they won't bother me anymore, we heard them talking to each other on the landing, going down the stairs, disappearing into the street, from the pantry we brought out the mourning wine, water crackers, and the mourning figs and no neighbor with us to pay our respects to the dead, afraid that we'd invite them to the supper for the deceased, I took advantage of the ups and downs of the river and I stuck the mine to the hull, I set the clock, I connected it to the mechanism with a couple of wires, half an hour, Paulo, twenty-nine minutes, twenty-eight, twenty-seven, inside of twenty-seven minutes if the alarm clock works as it should, if my grandfather's friends were right, and they are, we'll finally know after so many months what there is behind the covered window, whether it's the sea at Peniche, whether it's Dona Micaela dancing, whether it's Mr. Vivaldo in the bandage room with his naughty little hand moving away from the dinner-time pills

—Every day that passes you grow more appetizing, my little one

when we didn't have any money Paulo looking at the Cape Verdeans in Chelas, sizing up them and me, deciding

twenty-six minutes

—If you spend a little time with my girlfriend will you give me a fix in exchange?

he stayed sitting on a log drawing on the ground with a small stick, when I gave him the heroin, he kept on drawing, if I kissed him

—Let go of me

if I said to him

—Paulo

he erased what he'd drawn, turning his face to where I wasn't

—Don't talk to me, whore whore

if I stood in front of him and I didn't feel them Paulo, I don't know them, I don't remember them

—Get out of my life, beat it

twenty-five minutes

with the tone of someone begging don't get out of my life, don't go away and the invisible jackdaw making fun of us, maybe the girl in the copper oval, used to

twenty minutes

their fooling her

—Will you promise you'll keep your word, Gabriela?

I had to adjust one of the connections on the clock better, I mean there was a screw that was out of line and right away, the hand wasn't jumping in leaps, it was slipping along over the numbers, you thought twenty minutes, there they were, twenty minutes and then, all of a sudden nineteen, eighteen

Paulo, in spite of his cramps, his pain, that jab in his liver

—Shit on your drug, you inject it and everything's fucked up

if I only had a business of my own, a neighborhood establishment, a laundry, a newsstand would be nice, I remember the girl and I really feel sorry but how can I make room for her in this place where there isn't even room for a couch, we have the night table, the trunk, we eat sitting on the bed, the next day I leave the paper plates in the garbage can and when I leave the plates in the garbage will I run into my father hiding the communists' package, I thought he'd died and he hadn't

—Good morning father

nervous until he recognized me and when he recognized me he moved his arms back and forth, moving his fingers on an accordion that wasn't there

—I'm going to play a little tune for you daughter

we'd never had a little tune that belonged to the two of us, he never told me

—This one's for you daughter

he never wrote in charcoal on the landing Gabriela & Father, I would be coming out of the dining room or from school

out of the dining room

looking at the plaster maybe, spotting in the midst of so many scratches, so many cracks, so many tiles showing us on the mailbox or where the stairs curve up Gabriela & Father, not at all, always Marina & Diogo, never

twelve minutes

us, I tested the screw and the wire and they must have been right because the clock was working, a vibration going on inside the mine, whatever it was, it was expanding slowly in the same way that I'm expanding slowly in myself, if I could only tell you but the little stick was drawing on the ground

—Which one of the blacks got you pregnant Gabriela?

a whore like the Gypsies' mares who don't pick their males, my mother, for example, because my father, looking at me and asking which one of them, the café owner, the electrician, the pups

—If you tell me I won't get mad, Judite

or maybe going down into the yard worrying about the gentian

eight minutes

he was worried, so little time to get the boat away, eight minutes, my parents, my sister and I, the four of us in the living room wearing our Sunday shoes and the lace tablecloth, a drop that went across the label and continued on down, hold it with the napkin, mother, before the accordion lies down on the floor, stop the silver decorations from shining, its lungs are deflated, defunct, Paulo's mother without answering his father or answering

—He's just mine

two minutes and I'm not going to have enough time, I can't make it, if I stop in the middle of the sentence you won't get to know, Paulo, I only wanted one for you and me, I only wanted

I only really wanted

don't get mad at me, I only really wanted

the four of us in the living room wearing our Sunday shoes, Sunday clothes, the water crackers, the figs, for the first time no sound of my neighbors, scared of the police, communists

—They're communists, those people

and the waves lowering

one minute eleven

beating and beating on the rocks at the fort

no pipes, no faucets, no voices, the building deserted and it was just as well the building was deserted because when at one minute eleven from now

when at one minute from now, when at fifty-three seconds only the four of us in the neighborhood, only the two of us in this room waiting finally for the covered window and at the moment when the covered window loosens up, the orchestra begins, a yellow spot and a silver spot swirl over the audience showing necklaces, glasses of spumante, Dona Amélia with her tray of cigarettes, candy, and French perfume, the spotlights showing a velvet curtain as the sound grows louder, the manager signaling to Micaela, Marlene, Soraia

Soraia

Vânia, Sissi, an ankle peeking out of the curtain, a leg, a long glove, I was squeezing the lemon into the spoon, heating the spoon, coming to a stop because the girl in the copper oval

—Gabriela

—I've been waiting for you for more than fifteen years Gabriela

—You don't even remember, of course not, do you Gabriela?

the statue, the vase, the fence around the stone, if I didn't remember then I'd remember today

sixteen seconds, seen from the side they seem like sixteen seconds and yet they're fewer, Paulo his head down, drawing on the sheet

—Don't talk to me

convinced that I was talking to him and I wasn't talking to him, how could I be talking to him when I was talking to the gravestone, swearing to the girl

—Nothing's happened to you

calming the girl down

—Your parents went for a walk don't be afraid they haven't forgotten you

and the shadow of a cloud almost coming down on top of us, you took a look at the sky and it wasn't round, lengthened, with gold edges, now that I know how to read the name above the dates, the date of my birth, and today's date, and on top Gabriela

Gabriela Matos Henriques

the vase with withered flowers was just like my parents' jar, my name

Gabriela

smiling at the girl

—It's me

still smiling when the hand is on zero seeing my grandfather rocking on the Tagus, a hazy glow, the covered window open, thank God, and in the window a man stops playing his accordion, lays it on the sofa and takes me with him

I'm so weightless

over the trees in the cemetery which no matter how hard they tried, so ugly, so dark, couldn't hold me back.

CHAPTER

ALL I NEED AT NIGHT are some headlights lashing out across the ceiling of this room for just one second over the wardrobe with my suitcase on top to let me know that sooner or later

later

I'll have to leave

there's nothing left for me to do except leave

the tulip design on the chandelier that I hated at first and which I've got to like because of the clumsy symmetry of its petals that a worker in some unnamed factory put together with patience and bad taste, all I need before I go to sleep, kept awake by the street sounds that are deformed by darkness

the hose that's washing down the sidewalk, a certain change in the rustle of the trees, the leaves that make the lake frown with the concentration that a forehead shows when it's searching for memories that it knows are there but is still trying to get away from, all I need is your arm brushing against mine after a sleep where gestures are heavy, like the algae of dead women lying on the shore, asking

—Is that you?

all I need, in short, is to sense that you're present in your absence, outside of time and your body, of which I can only see two or three fingers, is still on the pillow and not over the shape of my features but over a face that's not mine

some other man's, someone who'd earned the right to take my place and seems to be giving you the tenderness and peace I never brought you, the hollow silence where you lay your fears to rest, the right direction I couldn't follow because I'd lost my way, no screwdriver to tighten life's hinges one by one until they were secure,

solid, livable, putting weeks, months, years together in a tranquil harmony I couldn't live in, so used to the change of a wave that lifts me up and carries me off and doesn't set me down right away all covered by flotsam that's just as useless

aluminum bowls, straw hats, those mutilated dolls on which an unchanging happy smile beams out and which instead of making me happy makes me sad and I envy it, it gives me an urge to destroy, with all the sick remorse of evil, that's all I need

I said

for me to feel all alone when I'm next to you surrounded by the numbered pieces of the puzzle of an existence that are scattered across the table and that, in spite of its being easy, I refuse to put together, just so I can understand that I have to stand up again, pass through who you know I am to who I also am and whose existence you're unaware of, the thing I hide from you, don't confess anything, don't talk about it, my parents, the maid from the dining room, Chelas, the old couple who thought they were raising me in an apartment in Anjos where the church seemed to be made of sparrows because every time the bells tolled it would grow thinner with a swirl of wings, me, who told you my name was António and my name is Paulo, I'm not in this building with officers and engineers and women with golden braids and German cars but in a laundry room on the Avenida Almirante Reis, just imagine, where Dona Helena ironed in winter and in summer would bring in a wicker chair, take off her shoes and rest her heels on a sack or a stool to get some rest from her arthritis, her husband would keep her company with a matchstick in his mouth

I remember the floor tiles so clearly

and strange as I may seem to you

there are times when I seem strange to myself

I loved them even though I wasn't capable of telling them that, just as I'm not capable of telling you that I love you in spite of the fact that if you were to ask me I'd tell you yes, maybe asking myself

—Do I love you?

maybe replacing the words with a caress that would get lost on the back of your neck or your throat before going back to my cigarette, conscious of my age and an age like that carries with it bashfulness and fear, afraid of a heart rotting under a stone

or miraculously intact, who the hell knows, me, who doesn't believe in miracles, I'm the bottle I was talking about a while back and if it reached shore a rock would break it, but me up on a girl's bicycle whose light was drooped over the wheel when the mudguard was missing, its tiny eye turned off, the old couple looked after me with a zeal that bothered me at the time and now, if I could only get back my heart from under the stone along with the tears my mother stole from me so she could use them to weep for herself, maybe it would give me a few tender feelings, but the sounds keep alternating and taking on an October tone while afternoon is coming to its end, the sparrows cluster together to build the church, I can hear you tossing the keys onto the entrance table and in just a moment now your smile

always the first smile, your puppy-dog smile as you stand in the center of the living room waiting

in just a moment now the quick click of your heels, in just a moment now my smile too, wrapped around my tongue, half hidden in my mouth with an urge to meet yours and to curl up, run away, I'm not in this easy chair

imagine

I'm up on the bicycle between my two old people from the laundry room who are so formal with me, submissive, humble, Dona Helena holding the iron up over the board and her husband, Mr. Couceiro, reaching for the jacket he'd left on the coatrack, all cloaked in embarrassment

—Forgive me ma'am

worried about the floor that should have been mopped and the sideboard that should have been dusted, the tea that should have been ready on the lacquer tray hanging on the wall with the pride of a hunting trophy along with its little mother-of-pearl roses and its worn wicker baskets a pincebeck can't you see?

the mat on the tray, the copper sugar bowl missing its top

the sugar served with an unmatching spoon because the spoon for the sugar bowl

—Two spoonfuls ma'am?

the uncertain little hand

—Two spoonfuls ma'am?

had also disappeared, the poor old-timers going inside to change clothes and you didn't understand, stealing a little peek at the door, you were counting on dining with some friends, shaking your head at the teacup with the Statue of Liberty printed on it

—Are we in some kind of play António?

Dona Helena combing her hair and gathering in the wisps that were getting away from the brush and anxiously forcing on her shoes with a shoehorn, Mr. Couceiro borrowing one of Noémia's flowers to decorate his lapel, a puppet show, you're right, look at the stage setting of the wallpaper, the detail on the carpet that doesn't stick to the floor, the tray with ceramic ducklings in a descending row, two of them without any tails, puffing up a muted protest, the sugar in unbroken lumps, the tea that tastes rusty like the bottom of a tin, the leaves that stick to your gums with a sour insistence, pulling them off with a finger but what can you do with them good Lord, your friends waiting and you impatient, looking at the teacup and the old people standing there, waiting for a phrase that you're looking for and that doesn't come and since it wouldn't mean anything it's all right, but the wallpaper, the carpet, the ducklings, one half of your face is giving kind looks to Dona Helena and the other half holding back desperate frowns held in a vise of growing irritation says

—António

so I reluctantly leave the bicycle in the laundry room with no time to pump up the tires or raise the light, I run a little finger of thanks over the ceramic family, taking a moment to straighten up the smallest member, I notice that Dona Helena has her skirt tightened with a safety pin on the waistband because the doctor's pills are consuming her or maybe it's the anemia, her paleness and the bags under her eyes come from some creature inside her breast that has a horrible name I don't dare think about, the sad hopes, the deceptive improvements

—I haven't felt this well in ages

the fatigue, the hospital, the little tidbits she doesn't eat

fruit, cakes, almonds

can't eat, magazines she doesn't read, held for a moment, falling without her noticing it from bedcover to floor, her look which even as it follows us to the door as we leave and stops, grows dark and stays that way

an object with no place

until the nurse adjusts the pillow for it and gives it a tranquilizer or some soothing syrup, Mr. Couceiro who mistrusts nobody, no matter what, believes the surgeon and confuses pity with hope, pointing to the teapot

—Wouldn't you like some tea ma'am?

going along with us

do you hear his asthma?

up to the old furniture by the door, the umbrellas in a stand, the bolt on the door that he doesn't have the strength to lift

—Did you like our place ma'am?

worried that you're not interested in me because of him, that you decide I'm just like him, crippled and old that is, that you don't want to see me anymore, that you're rejecting me and you are rejecting me, a thoughtful slowness, a nose sniffling out lies

—Did the little man call you Paulo, António?

the headlights that sprayed the ceiling of this room with light revealing to me for a second the corner of the wardrobe with my suitcase on top, the tulip chandelier with its awkwardly symmetrical petals that some worker

Mr. Couceiro?

and thinking about Mr. Couceiro your face

—This one?

in some anonymous factory put together over the fire with patience and poor taste and which I don't know why

why?

you like, I'm kept awake by the sounds from the street deformed
by the darkness, thinking about the conditional freedom of my life
with you, in this daily postponement of a separation

without any scenes or drama

that we both know is inevitable and about which neither of us
says anything

different interests as we explain to others when there's nothing
to explain, why justify ourselves when there's nothing to explain
and since there's nothing to explain we talk about different interests, different interests João

or Eduardo or Daniel or Gonçalo

different worlds, characters so different and accentuated by rou-
tine, I'm not thinking about you, about the two or three fingers
sticking out of the sheet and tracing along the pillow the contours
of a face that doesn't belong to me, João's, Eduardo's, Daniel's,
Gonçalo's, imprecise memories of imprecise creatures, imprecise
squeezing of hands at imprecise parties that suddenly become concrete when I run into you people in a restaurant or at the movies,
the short hair that makes you younger, a dress I don't know, pearls
I don't remember, your artificial pleasant way

no, your natural way

the lightheartedness of your casual introduction your

—You know Daniel, don't you?

an arm that leaves your shoulder to greet me and after greeting
me and after a half-dozen condescending niceties

or that my jealousy imagines are condescending

which I don't get to hear, have no curiosity in hearing, refuse to
hear, leads you away, on my shoulder again, far away from me, for a
moment I can make you out between two heads, I can't make you
out anymore, I stand on tiptoes and you've disappeared with him

where to?

I'd rather not think about where to, I keep still, a road sign that
announces anonymous villages or chapels in ruins, the ruins I am
for you, a pleat in the past that's not disguised because it's not
noticed, that one, the one I almost didn't recognize, how awful, the
one I still don't understand today how I was capable, the one who

sees you go by in a car and lowers the mirror on the sunshade to examine your makeup, the one with a wave or a request with the slow lifting of his sleeve, the fellow on the sidewalk who doesn't notice that it's raining until the first drop lands between his forehead and his glasses and extinguishes an eye, and then he takes off his glasses, and off fights the drop, but the drop persists

everybody knows how stubborn rain is

the fellow without glasses, looking at the small square and the confused buildings, sure they're flower beds

—Aren't they flower beds, drop?

a complicated fluorescent sign that's hard to read in spite of his being able to read disconsolation and remorse, seeing me in the living room where you'd moved the furniture, the glass ashtray we never got to buy the size of the drop or of my pity for myself on the end table, the print that in my time I'd exiled to the pantry

apples, pears, brown and blue cherries on the corner of a tablecloth, a red background and at the bottom in pencil, 35/200 and a hasty signature

presiding over dinner, checkered sheets I swear, a different wristwatch on the night table beside me, a book in English, I can barely read English, the miniature of an idol from Thailand making faces at me and pitying me

—Oh Paulo

I mean

—Oh António

Dona Helena in the cemetery squeezing her rosary between her thumbs, not daring to go against the terracotta god who, she knew, never went against anyone

—António

putting my glasses back on with the remnants of a drop

you know what rain is like

wavering, insisting, the buildings on the little square are clear, the fluorescent sign, Club Something-or-Other, maybe a cellar club like the ones where my father worked and for an instant my father called by a colleague

Marlene, Sissi?

appearing at the entrance in a blonde wig, making excuses, pulling up her décolleté

—I'm really sorry but I can't help you

so without noticing it

noticing it

almost not noticing it, I leave the small square, I leave the small square quickly before another drop lands between my forehead and the glasses because the rain won't stop

won't stop

even if the rain does stop

and it must have stopped, I swear it's stopped and it isn't stopping, I can hear it on the windows of the living room where the glass ashtray, the print with apples and Daniel, taller than I, grabbing your hips, turning you toward him

I leave the small square furious that you don't protest, that you let yourself go

why do you let yourself go?

you grab him too, the rage at not being able to close my eyes and get you out of me, to have you disappear with the drop, have you dissolve along with it, have your short hair and the dress I don't know evaporate out of my imagination, driving the car to the Tagus bridge with the windshield wiper pushing away this rain that multiplies headlights and your image in endless reflections, you in profile, you seated, you laying down your bag beside the couch, you kissing me on the ear

kissing me on the ear

without taking off your coat, deciphering the message from the maid on the pad in the kitchen, amused by the mistakes, your squeezing an elbow that wasn't mine

—You know Daniel, don't you?

and it hurts, hurts, hurts, it makes me put on the brakes, skid, straighten out the wheels, calm the fluttering in my heart that took a long time to calm down

—Did I kill you?

until you understand that I didn't kill you, not you, not a man with you, a cardboard box that the wind was blowing along the bridge with no rain finally, burying you in my pocket all mixed in with the drop or burying the handkerchief, Micaela beside me fixing the snap on her purse with her teeth

—You love me don't you, Paulo?

using her eyebrow tweezers to make it close better, answering her

—I love you a little

looking to the side with the pretext of a motor-scooter, her seat empty, on the Caparica road, next to a cone of stones, a girl smoking who looked like Dália, the cigarette glowing, now resting, now between her mouth and her slacks, when it was glowing a peasant beret covered her eyebrows, when it wasn't, a child in Bico da Areia different from me, stopping beside her, saying

—Dália

drawing back in fright and the beret again, turning to the right in order to get away from the beret, two-story houses and then vacant lots, the Judas tree where a cousin had hanged himself somewhere back before my time, swinging like a pendulum, the earth didn't want him and he didn't want the earth, the Council president had to cut the rope to interrupt his dance and the cousin stared at him from the stretcher with wild-eyed wonder just as when he'd lose his temper during the time he was alive, he would only change expression when calculating shots in the poolroom, roaming around the table shooting an azimuth, cue on his shoulder, stalking like a hunter, lifting his right foot up in a ballet position while the rest of him flowed down, his forefinger in a ring, right over the cloth, the cousin was a piece of fruit in a coat hanging stiff from a branch, passing the cousin whose existence was limited to the attic of other people's memories, so that without thinking about that

thinking about that, it's not worth repeating that you didn't think about that

Santo António da Caparica and the two-story houses replaced by modest homes, workshops, a baker's oven that was beginning its work and coloring my jealousy red, São João da Caparica where we come to the drugstore, the butcher and no drugstore, no butcher, a traffic circle that went somewhere, the campground with its oil-burning grills not tulips with symmetrical petals that some old worker etc.

a boy my age was coming up out of the tents and aiming a toy machine gun that fired Ping-Pong balls at me, he'd squeeze the trigger and a dried-up ball would fall at his feet

—I killed you

even today I can remember that I died that time, I stopped existing at the age of six, from then on who am I, the frightened boy

—Why don't you fall down?

my mother who was coming out of the butcher shop saw me dying on the wire fence, she pulled me up by the armpits because I was getting my socks dirty

—What kind of monkey business is this?

while the murderer was firing a second dried-up ball at her and I was unable to save her, my mother, invulnerable

—What kind of monkey business is this?

I died at the age of six from a Ping-Pong ball that, because it didn't touch me, went through my aorta and consequently what do I care about whim or insolence

insolence

—You know Daniel, don't you?

because Daniel and you, the print with the pears, the glass ashtray, the wristwatch, because the checkered sheets that I didn't see again but that I know by heart the same as I know the lace nightgown you bought after I'd left, the care you took of yourself, depilation, massages, small surgical implements

tweezers, scissors, chrome sticks with a brush or a swab at the tip

because you'd perfected the surrender, going through São João da Caparica, before the detour that you changed too, I remembered that I've been dead for a long, long time and being dead calmed me down, a path through the pine trees from before, almost an avenue now, entering Bico da Areia without seeing Bico da Areia because there are lots of backyards, the café with different chairs, five or six side streets and which one did we live on, the bridge beams rising up with the tide

could any gulls have existed there?

the sewing-machine waves speeding along to sew up the rocks

folding up the foam into a line of algae, I thought I saw the pups but no, the pups from my time were incapable of running, of throwing pine cones, of

—I've got money Dona Judite

think of new smaller pups that were barking at me afraid, running away from me, your cabin Dália with no backyard or windows, sinking into the ground like a dove asleep against a chairback, your aunt, the same type as Dona Helena, and her ferocity, didn't come over to order me

—Beat it

on the contrary

—Come in come in

in hopes I'd bring you back from Chelas and marry you

—She was a princess, sir, the poor thing a bad break

the Dália that the Cape Verdeans had come across long ago coming down from Chelas, jacket slipping down off her shoulders covering her red guts that a switchblade was holding together while ten steps away from her, fifteen steps away from her, a bearded skeleton with a needle was looking for the vein in his throat

—They cut out her guts Dona Alice

a porch with a lantern, a gentian maybe and speaking of gentians that plant there, no, the other one after that one, the violet bunches, looking like bottles in the cistern, marigolds, the dwarf from Snow White on the refrigerator, supporting the woman who was moving about in the kitchen

—You know my mother don't you?

not my mother, not a woman, an old man

the man from other days in my father's place?

picking through leftovers in a pail, a drop of rain that was slow in falling and that I didn't wipe away with my sleeve

—I can't introduce you to my mother, I'm sorry

and you to Daniel who was taking you far away from me

I could make you out for a moment, I stopped seeing you, I stood on tiptoes and you disappeared with him

—How António has changed

I'd rather not think about where, so I'm in the café at Bico da

Areia waited on by the owner who wasn't the one from other days, outside, I could have sworn, a lost mare going in circles on the beach and a Gypsy with a switch whistling at her from behind, asking the owner of the café

—Whatever happened to the gentian?

the way you're sleeping under the glass tulip now, who is it you're sleeping with now, Eduardo, Gonçalo, João, who is it you're playing hand games with, the ones I always lost

—Shall we play some hand games?

and my hands on yours, the one with the ring hitting me all the time

—I've never seen anyone so slow

the faded little hairs on your arms, once a week you'd shut yourself up in the bathroom in mysterious maneuvers, the drawer in the washstand stuck in its frame, a clatter of bottles and boxes

—Don't come in

I peeked through the keyhole and muffled my cough, a small sound in my throat, you were irritated

—It's no use Antonio

and a wax mustache, when you tugged at the mustache a little cry of pain, my bathrobe that reached down to your ankles

—Don't look at me

episodes that I hated at the time and that I miss today, you with your chin on your knees putting polish on your toenails, putting your feet up around my neck to dry and while they were drying with the toes sticking up, the bathrobe would open, a nipple of your breast challenging me and I would pretend not to see, you'd tighten the robe, disappointed in me for not noticing that your breast was showing

another game without any hands on hands and you, my God António, you don't understand anything, when you kiss me you hurt me, look at the mark on my neck, it shows even with a turtleneck and I hate turtlenecks, what can I tell my friends, the boy with the machine gun came out of the campground, aimed the Ping-Pong ball, killed me, I checked my smock looking for blood before my mother made me get up because I was getting my socks dirty

—What kind of monkey business is this?

I can't introduce you to her, she doesn't live here anymore, she was a teacher in Almada, she'd draw squares, they were almost always crooked, when they were too crooked she'd erase them with her hand, she'd draw them again and play hopscotch in the cemetery in the town

in the village

in the town, it's been a town for a few years now, they're going to have a court, she wore a cameo

having a court makes me proud

a mother-of-pearl cameo, during the last days pine cones on the windows, on the roof, I've got money Dona Judite, let me in Dona Judite, I'm not like the others Dona Judite, I can pay, the café owner, not this one, the old one

Bico da Areia will never have a court

with a pint of wine, ordering me, outside, pest, and chasing a lizard into the gap between two bricks

—I can't hear you I can't hear you

the woman who cleaned the tables at the café staring at me, the pups were approaching the wall, I died years ago in the campground at São João da Caparica, I'm dead, on the way back to Lisbon I spotted my corpse on the fence, a kid with a Ping-Pong ball in his heart, I turned away so I wouldn't feel the pain, what you might call cramps as though the heroin still, the hospital, the plane trees, my father visiting me in pink satin with a huge hat over his wig

—Your aunt, Paulo

settling down by the hospital walk, grabbing my fingers, a hip almost sliding off and I said

—Father

or maybe

—Don't embarrass me, father

or maybe

—They're making fun of us, father, go away

and he waved his arms around, avoiding the pigeons, they might ruin my dress I don't even want to think about it, taking me by the chin, bracelets jingling

—You've gotten thinner, Paulo

his face under the clown face biting his lip as when my mother

—Who's the woman you're going with, Carlos?

showing him a lipstick, a vial, a tube of cream, his hair dyed now
I think

why reddish tones, if my mother

—Who's the woman?

he would look at himself right away in the wardrobe mirror,
pushing back a strand of hair half black and half blonde

—Can't you see it's from the sun?

a butt friend, a coin for a cup of coffee friend, the ridicule of the
orderlies, the waiters, dozens of elbows in dozens of ribs, the ambulance driver forgetting about the stretcher

Mr. Peres

open-mouthed at the wheel and I to myself don't worry, you're
dead, do you think the dead have any worries, getting up

—Good-bye father

lying on the bed where through the window there was a bit of
roof and the four o'clock sky where sometimes storks were making
their nest in the chimney of the garage at Bico da Areia a flamingo
would blink with fatigue on a bridge beam and the pups would
throw stones at it, one made it fall onto the beach and there was a
swirl of paws and bites and pinches, pink blood carried away by the
first wave so that instead of your looking for the little room with
the boarded-up window, Gabriela waking up at six-thirty because
the dining room at eight o'clock, the certainty that she'd pause by
Marina & Diogo in charcoal on the wall, the neighbors she'd greet
and I wouldn't, the landlady all wrapped up in mourning, which
increased her outrage as she complained about the back rent due,
my father taking out the small chest at Príncipe Real from its hiding place in the pantry, and seeing that the chain on the padlock
was broken and the chest was empty, muttering it can't be, calling

—Rui

and no one there, eyes hazy, a pinky that stopped a trace of lipstick from reaching his cheek, squeezing his shoulder hard, kicking
the chest where there was a piece of paper, I'm sorry

—Don't make a scene father

don't kneel down, dammit, and clear up those eyes for me

noticing he's sick, the back of his neck thin, something on his skin, they'll do the tests again and it won't be anything you'll see, labs make mistakes, give me the note you were folding into your bra

—For you

the landlady was suspicious, smelling the perfume, it spread over her, she crinkled her nose

—Is he a fake, young man?

getting to your building at ten to five in the morning

I was dead in the campground and dead in your life and by being dead and since the dead don't feel suffering anymore, what nonsense, what I needed was a little suffering, it doesn't bother me that it's raining, it's not raining, there's not the tiniest drop hanging from my eyelid or fogging up my glasses, ten to five in the morning when the first small trucks were going through Lisbon

fish, poultry, vegetables

my father was coming back from the club, staggering on his high heels, you were with Daniel

or Eduardo or Gonçalo

still on the pillow with two or three fingers not going over the shape of their features but a face that might be mine

I was another man who seems to give you

gives you

the tenderness and peace

people change, why won't you believe that I've changed?

that they never gave you, today at ten to five in the morning I'm in the building where I've lived for sixteen months with the maid from the dining room and the Marina & Diogo by the mailboxes with the numbers of the floors in the middle, I'm the one who could have written our two names

I thought about writing our two names

I decided to write our two names

I would have written our two names if I'd had in my pocket

and I should have brought it but childhood was so far away you understand, the pleasure of putting letters together had been lost such a long time ago

a pencil, a piece of charcoal, a stub of chalk instead of the ballpoint they'd guaranteed me was dirt-resistant and whose tip, after no time at all, began to get clogged and later got bent on the plaster, preventing me from making us eternal with a heart and an arrow, why not a heart and an arrow, there are thousands of hearts and arrows on the walls of Lisbon but never us, never us, I stuffed the useless ballpoint angrily into my pocket, I tested the light switch in the vestibule, sure that it wouldn't work, and it didn't, it's never worked, I lingered, getting used to the stairs again sometimes too high, sometimes too low, answering my unsure steps with too much noise and vibrating with warnings I never got to understand, starting with the third floor the skylight showed me the outline of doormats, a demijohn, bags of garbage with a rancid smell, on the fourth floor the skylight wasn't black, it was lilac, the Marina and the Diogo were larger, enclosed in a rectangle of little blue flowers, the first pigeon or the last bat was soiling the windowsill, a light that reminded me of the sea on Sundays when we'd have lunch at Cova do Vapor, my parents and me, and the whistle of a freighter would fall over us with the slow drift of its ashes, the memory of my parents, almost happy, almost interested in me, gave me the drive to climb the remaining steps more quickly

two steps, the insignificance of two steps and right away disorder and poverty

I'm not afraid to say it, you can make fun of me if you want

which I scorned at the time and, right now, strange as it seems

and it seems strange to you

I like it, I want it, the brass lamp stolen from the hospital that wouldn't turn on with the switch but with a whack on the table, the blanket made from the screen the doctors opened up

—Get away from here

around a bed where someone was dying, Gabriela's father playing the accordion and Gabriela nodding her head to the rhythm of the tunes that, no matter how hard I tried, I couldn't manage to hear

—My father

two steps, two little steps covered with a leap, two stinking steps and I was there, and all set, it's over, I've freed myself from you and I'm home again, the skylight was almost within reach, the pigeon up there

not a bat

preening its wings over my head and helping me to read a second rectangle of little blue flowers

roses, jonquils, lilies

inside the rectangle not Marina & Diogo, Gabriela & Paquito, what a horrible name, Paquito, so hair-tonic and tie-pin, so suburban-slum, so cheap

not Daniel, not Eduardo, not Gonçalo, Gabriela & Paquito, the file clerk who'd linger in the dining room sometimes to chat with you, knowing about me, with respect and distance, Gabriela & Paquito, how impossible, what a foolish idea, repeating Gabriela & Paquito to the closed door behind which, who knows, a huffing little tune, repeating Gabriela & Paquito going down landing by landing while the vestibule and the mailboxes came up to me, repeating Gabriela & Paquito endlessly, monotonously, mechanically on the sidewalk in front of the building, fighting off a raindrop between my eyelash and my glasses while, because of the cold, I stamp my feet on the pavement, raise my collar, blow on my hands or dance to the rhythm of the accordion, those little tricks that help.

CHAPTER

IT CAN'T BE

I don't believe it

it makes no sense for my father to be only this, a clown changing things around at Príncipe Real asking me to help him drag the sideboard over to the other corner of the living room with all that glassware shaking inside, to hang the print in a place where the afternoon light as it passed through the curtains transformed the trees into movements of water that flowed endlessly across the wall, the lines of the branches where a fish that was a pigeon or the old men on the benches also went back and forth, it makes no sense for my father to be in the manager's office, a cubbyhole on the first floor

PRIVATE

newspaper clippings, posters from shows, the manager not inviting him to

—Sit down

concentrating on his pinky, he removed a piece of skin, went back to his observation, took the scissors out of the drawer

—We'll have our talk in just a minute

and trimmed the edges, he shuffled the file folders protesting to the cleaning woman that she kept getting them out of order, barking

—Not now

when there was a knock on the door, with a movement that consisted of fingers disappearing into the drawer, he picked up an invisible speck of dust from the desk and shook it off, no substance to it but enormous when it went into the wastebasket, he concentrated on a spot over my father's shoulder with such fierce intensity that the blonde wig took a quick peek and caught sight of a picture of Marlene, the blank square of a missing photograph with the rectangle of a poster announcing Soraia, the eyes of the manager fastened on the ledger with figures he wasn't looking at, his hands had more knuckles than they'd had before, were arguing for him, at the same time as he looked at the woman waxing the floor of the club

—We have to accept old age, Soraia, I'm getting old too but I'm not a dancer

as I thought why should I listen to him, all I had to do was look at his knuckles and understand right there, they would pick up an eraser and drop it, they would move a glass from right to left quickly and from left to right slowly, they would get in between his collar and his neck, they would disappear into his pocket, they would reappear out of his pocket with a ring of keys, they would rise up with a friendly wave, pulling out a chunk of air and offering it to me, you could go on the road Soraia

as though I was all through, as though I could go on the road and Paulo, seeing me sitting up in bed, it can't be

I don't believe it

it makes no sense for my father to be just a clown, just that, imagining who the hell knows what, telling him there's no way for you to understand that I'm no good for you, telling him go look for your mother and leave me alone, telling him go back to those people in Anjos, don't bother me anymore, and he moved around me wanting to help without being able to help, I don't need any help, the knuckles cut out a second chunk in the air and held it out to me, going on the road means emigrant workers' festivals, means campgrounds, Paulo got all worked up about the campgrounds

—Campgrounds father?

as though I was above that and I'm not, never was, at least they're not putting me into any hospitals, I'm not going after any people and giving them hopes, how many times when I came out of the show did I find him leaning against a tree or a shop window or something like that, thinking that just because I'm nearsighted I didn't see him, following me from a distance if I was alone, from farther back if there were people with me, I'd go to the window and he'd be outside, I'd tell him to go away, he'd pretend to obey me, he'd drop back thirty feet and stay there because I could sense his presence quite well even without my glasses, I couldn't be sure whether by the lake or by the statue or by the newsstand, he was looking after me he thought, worrying about me as if there was some reason for him to worry about me and there isn't, look at all this air, all for me, that the manager's holding out to me, bouncing it in the palm of his hand because on the road, festivals, campgrounds

—You've grown old, Soraia

the month when I started at the club, filling in during breaks and waiting on tables

my name was Luci at the time

I came across Dona Soraia packing her accessories in her suitcase without folding her clothes, piling them up any old way, forgetting a shoe, a sash, a veil, I asked what's wrong Dona Soraia, Marlene said nothing, Micaela said nothing, the makeup mirror with its rim of light bulbs sending back the silence, nobody in the frame, I leaned over to find myself and it was empty, the club workers were putting the chairs onto the tables, Dona Amélia was turning over her candy and perfume money at the bar, they'd put out the lights, a kind of dirty morning outside, there were no trees or workmen

a dirty morning outside

Dona Soraia pushed her knee onto the suitcase to close the snaps, cleaned off her makeup with the beard starting to show

—I've been let go

the doorman was arranging the bottles on the bar, the music played for two or three seconds on stage and stopped, Marlene tried to help with the baggage but the mirror or Dona Soraia answered her

—No

so the three of us were left in the middle of clothes racks, open

wardrobes, the irises from a customer from Beja, every so often
Judite would telephone from the café and I had trouble hearing her
because of the gulls that were screeching at her
—You're a fool you're a fool
—Aren't you coming home Carlos?
as though I had a home, as though there was a home, as though
it was possible for the two of us and it wasn't possible, so with the
receiver at my ear I went along counting the waves
—I know you can hear me Carlos
or the in-and-out of her breathing, the dice game the pebbles
were playing back and forth with the coming and going of the foam
—Don't hang up
and I hung up, I drowned the cats in a tank, they say, it's so simple, you knot a cord, you watch the frenzy subsiding, the animals in
the bag trickle off into inert arms and legs, my wife was silent, facing the doorman
—Some crazy woman
had killed it and along with it the sea and the gulls that kept
pounding in my ear, we saw Dona Soraia dragging her suitcase at
the club without saying good-bye to Dona Amélia, we saw ourselves
in the mirror that had decided to notice us sizing up defects, freckles that we disguised with creams and sashes, the mirror said to us
—You're no good anymore, you've grown old too and they don't
invite you to table nine after the show
pointing out imperfections, scars, this problem of my back that
kept me from taking a bow, thinking better of it, I do have a home,
maybe there is a home, with a little luck they'll take me back at the
jewelry store, Paulo won't have any need to spy on me from a shop
window, from a tree trunk, Dona Soraia on her way to the train or
the river, at first we thought it was the train but the mirror showed
us the direction of the river, Marlene grabbing at the dressing table
and trying to turn her away, Micaela fogging up the glass and asking her not to, in the windows there were buses, trolleys, street ven-
dors spreading out their goods on the station steps, the telephone
ringing and I'm not going to answer, I don't answer, I'm not interested in the waves, it's some crazy woman complaining, marigolds,

horses, the sea stirring up pebbles and I won't talk to the sea, Dona
Soraia laid the suitcase down next to the little wall by the Tagus,
Dona Amélia

—Soraia

taking her by the arm and the arm got away, the manager arrived
at the door just as the suitcase was falling without any sound, one
circle, two circles, a small change in the water, maybe it wasn't a
suitcase, we were wrong, Dona Soraia was thinking about absences,
my wife

—I know you can hear me Carlos

I, who'd stopped listening, because I'm deaf now, one of the ped-
dlers at the station standing there, a tugboat with its smokestack
cigarette in its mouth and a package to deliver over its shoulder by
the river mouth and coming back with a whistle of contentment,
Micaela, even though in the dressing room, was trotting along the
dock and holding her hip

—Dona Soraia, wait

I was sure she'd caught her, we all saw that she'd caught her,
thank God, but Dona Soraia's jacket slipped away from her, Marlene was staring at the jacket that was heaped up on the stone, leaning over into the mirror in the direction of the oil stains that were
quivering there below, what looked to me for an instant like a floating body, mouth, nose, ears, the vending woman who was calling to
her fellow worker, someone with a pole I think, the tugboat with its
hands in its pockets filling up the mirror

—Good morning

everything in the mirror getting larger except Dona Soraia, a
screw, two linked circles and the river indifferent, Dona Amélia

—Micaela

Micaela who was coming back to the dressing room and dropping scarves, her legs piled up on the floor like scarves, my wife was
seasoning my salad at Cova do Vapor and her laugh

—Carlos

a telephone that was wailing in the club, when the Gypsies'
mares got sick they would complain like that, and Paulo it can't be

I don't believe it

it makes no sense for my father

the way it makes no sense for the three of us in the mirror that was ringed with colored light bulbs and notes from lovers who were never lovers

—They were robbing us Paulinho

between the wood and the glass, we were there at the club with Dona Soraia, who was being taken off the wall, a torn dress, a piece of dirt, a wound on the forehead that I couldn't look at, the oil stain had disappeared from the water and was clinging to her neck as Marlene cleaned it off, Micaela was twisting open her lipstick and trying to paint her lips, asking Dona Amélia for the silk blouse, give me the silk blouse and the stockings please, the spangled tiara she liked so much, Dona Soraia all naked in the funeral parlor at that time and being dressed as we helped without eye shadow, powder, hair curlers, the doctor adjusted the light over the body on a marble table and she said to Dona Amélia without noticing the little knife that was opening up her ribs

—Paint my nails blue, Dona Amélia, I feel good in blue

I think

it can't be, I don't believe it

other slabs, other dead people laid out, in just a little while it would be eleven o'clock at night and the doorman would be putting on his uniform, the curtain, the music, Dona Soraia putting on her rings while a song and the dancers were on stage, looking at herself in profile in spite of a little knife that was tearing at her lungs, adding folded newspapers to her waist

—It's your turn, girls, I'm old I'm not good for anything

and don't call me because I won't answer the phone, why should I worry about that sound of pebbles, those pines, the woods, my wife at the café

—I know you can hear me Carlos

one time she caught me coming out of work, she must have put our son to bed in Bico da Areia, taken the same bus that I'd taken ages ago, crossed Lisbon, got the streets mixed up, found the place by chance and found me with a Sevillian comb in the middle of the poster, and waited hours on end with the cameo on her throat, clutching a small bundle with a sandwich maybe, a slice of apple, a bunch of grapes that she didn't know where to put, I was kissing the doorman, leaving with Alcides and that scarecrow was staring at me, just as gawky as in the village mooning over the mimosas, her mother was going through the backyard with the slowness of blind people alert for a misplaced scythe or a branch that was too low

—Judite

in the village cemetery the viscount's grave with a basalt angel weeping for us all, the tree where the sun dragged itself through the leaves and rose quickly to meet noon, my wife as a bride speaking to me and me behind a smile, while the priest was turning the pages of his missal

—And now?

a worker at the funeral parlor washed Dona Soraia and Marlene was stopping him, getting all excited in the mirror

—You're going to take off the lipstick

after the burial, Dona Amélia's hydrangeas, the manager calling me aside at the moment when they were lowering the coffin, smothering her again except that instead of oil stains and a circle, two circles, the earth swearing I haven't got anybody here, good-byes from handkerchiefs with a life of their own, wanting to leave, and if we didn't grab them they would have kept on going into the neighborhood nearby and mixed in with the birds

—You're going to take her name, Luci, you'll call yourself Soraia and we'll build it up in the ads

her name, her fripperies, her table drawers, her way of going down the steps with plumes and fur pieces, Dona Amélia insisted on leaving one last hydrangea and she didn't know where, since there was no gravestone, no cross, a small mound with a shovel on top, Dona Amélia waiting for some voice to help her

—Soraia

if you needed help my grandmother would find you, I was in the green bean patch and right then and there boots marching around me

Judite uncomfortable with the package

—Carlos

her fingers on my face

—You'll never stop growing, boy

I'm thirty years old, I haven't stopped growing, grandmother, you wouldn't recognize me

and Dona Soraia under the shovel, she was living on a small square with a bronze general ordering around pots of geraniums along with stubborn balconies that were driving the French invaders into Spain, in the dressing-room mirror we saw that we weren't ready to go down on stage when the music man called us

Micaela was putting on more lipstick to reduce her annoyance.

but cats were cushioned all about except for the little lights in their eyes, the wounded war veteran who roasted chestnuts on a broken-down tricycle, a staircase that didn't go up onto any stage, it went up to a small room where Dona Soraia in a paratrooper's uniform stood out in profile alongside medicine bottles and a votive candle, her mother was pointing at her with a spoonful of syrup meant for her as Silvestre while out of the trunk he dug a uniform and a medal in a case, saying to Dona Soraia

—Mother

begging our pardon with a wave of pity, she's half crazy, don't pay any attention, get rid of these things, mother, my son works at night, he comes home to me smelling of perfume, sleeps on the little couch there where the girls sit

we were facing the mirror

the manager

—How long does it take you to go into the Burmese dance, Marlene?

watching us sitting on a sofa plucked clean by the tips of slippers that peeked out of the fringes, a rubber kangaroo on a tray, the shirtwaists on the line covering our faces

—Don't look don't look

and yet

obviously

we're not looking

—Be quiet, father

in the kangaroo was a tiny kangaroo you could pull out

—You can pull it out

and Micaela holds up the kangaroo, in a different frame the paratrooper in civilian clothes with a girl in a straw hat dead from typhus two months before they were to be married, just imagine the evil omen, girls, I remembered Judite, her silhouette, her bearing when I would meet her coming out of school

the fir trees at Almada, they were beginning to build the court-house and a machine was laying down quivering cement, I almost didn't notice that we were walking toward the river where her mouth was on my face and

evidently I said

—No

—*I already told you to be quiet, father*

not out of fear but from revulsion, because it's strange, I don't know how to explain it any other way except that you were kissing me and it was strange, Judite's smile turning off, turning off, two steps that maybe were

me with revulsion, fear

preventing the smile from turning off

—No

Dona Soraia's mother forgetting about us

—What, son?

—*It can't be, I don't believe it, it makes no sense for my father to be this*

with the spoon for the syrup not moving, getting the solution ready he adds some water right up to the edge of the label and shakes it, makes sure there are no dregs, even so the medicine takes on an orange color, he must, Dona Soraia in necktie and vest con-senting to an engagement, consenting to getting married

—It wasn't anything mother

the kangaroo, the other frame, a plastic doll with sketched-on features

the rosy right cheek was missing

on top of the wardrobe, it's telling the old folks, it's telling us that your son was working at night in a women's clothing store, he'd come home smelling of perfume, he didn't go back to making love out of respect for the dead woman in spite of your insisting

didn't you insist, old girl?

—Be quiet father, if you're not quiet I'll

when you came out, there was a colleague with him, he would bring you little items that warmed your heart, painted owls, little rings, sugar bunnies and you were glowing all over, old girl, the bunny was so pretty with this ribbon Silvestre, it's a shame to eat it, one, two, three, eight, eleven bunnies as escorts for the kangaroo, when the paper was taken off there were fungus marks on the sugar or maybe, with the heat, a drop slipped down over its ear, the afternoon when your son's fiancée wanted to talk to you on the edge of the sofa where we are now

Alcides pointing at my mother, the package with the sandwich, the apple, the grapes

—Do you know that peasant-looking woman, Soraia?

when your son's fiancée wanted to talk to you and your husband was in the hospital there wasn't much time to remember, you kept twisting the catch on your purse

is it true?

the words that wouldn't come out, the commiseration, your pity, the straw hat in the place where Marlene, a cup of linden tea to help the conversation and your old lady, whom you were born to serve

—Father is a no-good a no-good

was warming up the teapot, leave it alone don't bother about the gas jet I have to unplug, snapping the match, I had to light it by blowing on it, scrape the tea leaves from the tin with the scratched picture you inherited you don't remember who from, *Souvenir de Toulouse,* your son's fiancée saying it's late, I'll be back Dona Isidora, we'll talk later, the steam from the tea spreading through the room, Marlene wiping the dressing-room mirror with a quick brush, the manager angry, telling them to start the music sometime today

—Will it be sometime today, Marlene?

and later on your son's fiancée sick, little paper lips listless, unable to drink tea, visiting you, chatting with you, well-being that might not be well-being, the little flame on oil lamps when the oil is giving out, rising up for a minute and disappearing for good, the useless straw hat forgotten on the floor, the impression

and I can't believe it, and I was fooling myself

that your son relieved, taking her by the fingers that weren't fingers anymore, and you can't believe it, you were fooling yourself, he doesn't want

—Don't torment her, father

her to get better, be cured, close her eyes quickly, tie a handkerchief around her chin and he didn't speak, didn't speak

—Don't believe my father, he was fooling, it's a lie ma'am

of course it's a lie, the proof is in the fact that my son has taken charge of the funeral and the dinner, consoling everybody, a piece of cake, a drink, the dead woman's virtues, he swore to me that he'd skip work that night and not reek of perfume, I'm so upset that I won't get married, mother, after a year, after two years if I insisted to him, do you remember what I swore to you, do you want me to break a pledge, do you want me to suffer in hell, I've kept the straw hat in the trunk because it'll always be a remembrance, girls, the girls don't think so, and the medal and the uniform, the brim has been frayed by time but the top is perfect, it protected her from the sun because she was always frail, a child almost, and the child was coming to me through the door, picking up the kangaroo, deciding

—I want to talk to you

the skin was so delicate, so white, she didn't need any whitening in the coffin, not just the lips, two bits of tissue paper, girls, the eyelids, the forehead, the little bracelet that my son gave her and she took along to the cemetery with her, one afternoon I asked her about the bracelet and her face suddenly grew hard, the only time it wasn't paper, it was stone

—About the bracelet

she lowered her head, twirled it around her arm, fell silent and I asked

—So, what about the bracelet?

and there was a strange expression, a movement that wasn't getting rid of me, was getting rid of something or other in her, a suspicion, a sureness almost, a sureness and at that point I got the feeling of a lashing of leaves on her face, the leaves that the wind suddenly picks up and hurls at me as she got rid of them with her handkerchief

—It was nothing

and for a second there were remains of moss in her hair, the bits from trees that blind us sometimes, my husband opening the umbrella in spite of the sun

—Be careful of the wind, Isidora

you were digging through garbage, old girl, digging through dust and perfect loves and veils against dampness, if you give me a moment there must be a picture where she looks better and in the picture it's not the deceased, Judite with the mantilla that a fellow worker had lent her, clutching a small package where maybe there was a sandwich, a slice of apple, a bunch of grapes she didn't know where to put, in the picture I was coming out with Alcides, running into that scarecrow

—*It's the last time I'm warning you, father*

—*Aren't you coming home Carlos?*

almost like an urchin in the village inventing the

—Can't you smell the mimosas, tell me you smell the mimosas

and I said to my wife

—The mimosas are finished Judite

I said to Alcides who was asking do you know that scarecrow, Soraia

—Some nut, I guess

a nut who hid the bottles in the washtub, taught in Almada

unless I'm mistaking her for a person I think taught in Almada

I met her in the coffee shop, we strolled along the wall by the Tagus, she's living with somebody or other in a Gypsy settlement or a place with retirees or something like that, Alto do Galo, São João, Trafaria, they tell me she has a son

—*You can't be my father, why?*

who doesn't know his father, gossip says the owner of the café, the electrician, a pack of pups among the leftovers on the beach who gave her money, there's nothing to guarantee for me that it wasn't one of the Gypsies camping in the woods, the government took the son away from her because of the wine and turned him over

they told me

to a couple in Anjos who'd lost a girl and were interested in him,
I gave Alcides my arm and Judite was silent, if she said anything to
me, whatever it was, I didn't hear, it was the sea I was hearing

—Don't take it to heart but I can't hear you, all mixed up with
the waves

not really the sea, the Tagus estuary, the sea was farther out, the
lonely lighthouse that ran on diesel fuel moaning in the rain, the
old woman settling Judite on the trunk

—She was a countess wasn't she?

a countess begging for pints, accepting money, you fool me old
girl, I was rumpling and smoothing the bedspread, she asked the
wardrobe mirror

—Where have you been, Carlos?

and he was fooling me old girl, Micaela said to me

—Soraia

not

—Dona Soraia

Dona Soraia, like the dead woman, the old woman saying to
Micaela, trying to figure it out

—Dona Soraia, miss?

and you didn't catch on, old girl, it was impossible for you to
catch on, for you to dream that your paratrooper who worked at
night, not my Silvestre no

—Are you sure her name is Dona Soraia, miss?

or catching on and warming up the teapot in order to stop
thinking, her husband's crutch that had propped him up was propping me up, when I was in pain after doing the tests and it was hard
for me to walk because of this thing in my bones, the doctor was
sympathetic, accepting misfortunes that weren't yours, suggesting
to Rui

—A crutch would help

advising me to take some shots, pills, the steam from the teapot
that stopped me from seeing, repeating not my Silvestre

—Not my Silvestre

and, still and all, I'm sure that her voice was hesitant looking for
support, offering her the crutch

—Take the crutch, old girl

get your glasses, which must be on the tray with the kangaroo on top of the missal because you go to mass, Our Lady of the Ascension helped you with your erysipelas, after a novena she'll look after you, have pity, Dona Amélia scolding me with little imbecilic signs that meant

—Shut up

in spite of Marlene

—Shut up

I have to hurt you, all I can do is hurt you

—Her name was Dona Soraia, ma'am

while Judite with her stupid little package and Alcides

—How awful

I said through the steam coming from the teakettle

—Her name's Dona Soraia, ma'am

what's become of the mimosas, Judite, you've lost the mimosas

—*Have a good day, father, go to hell*

you haven't lost, in just a bit there'll be Bico da Areia, the help of some wine and peace or indifference again, you have a bottle in the wardrobe, I'll help you, have a drink, don't pay any attention to the pine cones on the window, it's the pups, money, accept it

—Come in

so disheveled, so afraid of you, show them, Marlene covering my face with the fan

—Stop that, Soraia

and I couldn't stop, don't let them order me to stop, I'm not me, it's something that's not mine inside of me, remorse or not remorse, uneasiness, hate, so what, I'm not interested, what I don't know or whatever it is and it makes me go on right up to the end, Marlene, the old woman moving the teakettle aside and staring at me with a feeling of panic, her mouth

—Miss

not her mouth, the space between her gums where one tooth, two teeth

—Miss

three teeth, who cares, I'll give you three teeth, old woman, the girl in the picture scolding me, the plastic doll angry with me, maybe the dwarf from Snow White hating me over on the other bank of the river, the dwarf bothers me, don't cover my face, Marlene, don't stop me from talking, just a little while from now we'll be on stage pretending to be singing, the music that's slow to pick up, the padding that gives me what I don't have, that gave your son what he didn't have, old woman, Rui like when he was asleep

you're asleep Rui, don't be surprised that you're asleep

—Is my wife going to be all right, doctor?

and when you wake up it won't have been anything, I promise you it won't have been anything, you're not going to remember anything, at most this night seems to me to be a dream that you were sick Soraia, a doctor who I don't remember was saying terrible things and I was stroking your head, they're dreams of health, don't upset yourself, my darling boy, dreams of a long life, my love, next year we'll change the sofas in the living room and put the place in shape, a proper bathtub, faucets that work, pay the plasterer to fix the ceiling, a long life, such a long life, I'm going to be left without any hair but with a very long life, grabbing the plastic doll and turning it around, don't bother me, stop looking at me, but it was the doll, it was the manager of the club

—We have got to accept the fact that we get old, Soraia, I've grown old too but I'm not a dancer

it was my son

—Paulo

hard to make out in the steam from the teakettle, the autumn haze at Bico da Areia where Judite goes back with the little package in her hand, I must confess there are moments when I get longings

not really longing longings, just missing you

I mean missing the horses, the bridge, your setting the table, the way you'd shake the hair back from your forehead and when you shook it you were so young, the feeling that a door

none of the doors we had

was going to open and I was changing, my uncle's wife was giving me a bath in the tub

—Let's get out of the water Carlos

but it's impossible to separate the steam of the bath from the steam of the teakettle, the old woman leaving the stove

get yourself a new apron, old girl, a pair of proper slippers, don't pretend to be poor, don't ask me for things as though you were my servant, pouring tea into the cups, almost indignant, humble

—Don't say bad things about my son, miss

your coward of a son who hid what he was from you, I'm working in a store at night, mama

mama?

two locked drawers, those manias men have, where he wouldn't allow you to snoop

—They're things from the shop, don't peek

a way of walking that intrigues me, a wave with two fingers, her colleagues from school, secrets, whispering, Judite's surprise on the step to the yard

—Carlos

or maybe her colleagues defending themselves, old girl, defending me, the shock, the outrage, the marks on your neck when you get upset, it can't be, I don't believe it, it makes no sense that my husband, my uncle's wife laying me down on the bed wrapped in the towel, she was unbuttoning her dress, I'm going to show you what this is, you scamp, you scamp, gentian branches darkening the window as though people were watching us, the sound of footsteps in the branches, take it easy, it's not your parents, it's a gentian silly, whenever I touched the gentian at Bico da Areia, I'm going to show you what this is, you scamp, you scamp, my uncle's joviality melting away, chin muscles stiffening and she, I can't believe you're jealous of a kid, Fernando, if Judite took my arm in Almada I felt that they were hugging me, my uncle's wife with a pitcher and soap

—Time for your bath, Carlos

and now this steam from the tub is in the teakettle, the plastic doll, you scamp, you scamp, Rui in his dream

because it was a dream, one of those dreams that predict long, happy lives

—I think I dreamt you were sick, palpitations

Soraia's going to lose her hair, doctor, and the physician availing himself of the test, because there are miracles and numbers do change

but there aren't any miracles and numbers don't change

studying the ceiling without studying the ceiling, studying us, a man on a stepladder was whitewashing the laboratory and while I was looking at the man, death was so far away, everyday movements that hold back death throes, misfortunes, and yet the doctor, who didn't notice the man on the stepladder, in my opinion we should begin the treatment on Thursday, but what treatment's that, because it was a dream of Rui's, doctor, I may be a little listless, a little pale, I haven't had much rest lately, that's all, I can't stop work, I'm behind in my bills, the two-month loan on the dishwasher, the problem of the rent, the debts of my husband and to some friends in Chelas, maybe Judite could ask for some help from the café owner, the electrician, the pups, they might give you a handout

I'm not interested in the reasons why they should give you the handout

and then I'll pay as soon as I get better, Judite, as soon as I go back

I'm going to go back

to work at night in a dress shop where I'm filling in for a fellow worker named Soraia and out of habit or as a joke the other clerks call me Soraia too, not making fun, out of respect, to keep the deceased woman alive the way you keep yourself alive in me, one of these days when you least expect it, I'll be back in Bico da Areia, you'll hear a knock on the door and it'll be me

it'll be me

you'll hear someone by the gentian and it'll be me in the yard reviving the marigolds, decorating the flower beds with colored stones, pieces of tile, pebbles, opening my wallet

a man's wallet

and giving you back the money, Judite, I'll bring a chair up to the gate and sit looking at the waves in the afternoon until the lights in Lisbon and the herons on the bridge and then I'll sit down at the table with you, if you look for me at work again and see me with Alcides, a partner of the boss's, a chum

—Let me introduce you to my wife, Alcides

the cashiers at the store, Marlene, Micaela, Dona Amélia, Sissi
the hateful Vânia

happy to know you, with no intention of disappearing

—Is that your wife, Soraia?

you're surprised and they correct themselves right away, man-
nerly, pleasant

—We're just fooling around, don't pay any attention, are you
Carlos's wife?

but consider those bills a loan, Judite, until the doctor, a couple
of months from now, lets me go back to the shop that looks like a
club because of its neon signs and the posters but it's not a club, it's
a store, the doctor and an ever so normal test

—The worst is over, Dona Soraia

I made a mistake, out of habit

—The worst is over, Mr. Carlos

I had good color, I was stronger, you think you're sick and you're
not really sick, we invent ailments in our heads, the secret is not to
let ourselves be beaten down, Judite, and I'm not going to let myself
get beaten down, a passing annoyance, he said, these autumn
viruses of no importance, he said, we get too upset, we're afraid and
you'll see, we're fine, I'm fine, if they told you I was let go, that the
manager called me to his office and said

—You've grown old

don't you believe it, just talk, the proof is that pretty soon they'll
be naming me supervisor, I'm going to be in charge, if they tell you
I'm living with a guy on Príncipe Real, don't believe them, just talk,
every so often some guy or other sleeps over for a few nights, they're
there because they're doing work at their place and right away people's evil tongues will wag, twisting things and

you can't hear the albatrosses, albatrosses I'll bet, it's been so
long since I've heard the albatrosses

and they foul everything up, I've been by myself ever since I left
you, why shouldn't I be by myself, because it was you that I left

and being by myself I accept your help, I open the door to the
café owner myself, to the electrician, to the pups, I'll go out to the

backyard wall and work on it, no farther, this side of the spigot, ready to come if you call me, if you need a beer, a clean towel, the saucer that serves as an ashtray, without looking at me and point-ing with your mouth you say

—Take the money on the table

which someone, and I don't ask who

my usual discretion Judite, somebody's footsteps on the street

left sticking out separate from the pitcher, a few sweaty bills, a few dull coins, I stuff them into my pocket without looking at you either, picking up a little leaf that had fallen onto the tablecloth

and that makes me feel guilty, I don't know why

the leaf I kept in my hand like some small living thing, promis-ing you that tomorrow at nine o'clock, the day after at most, Tues-day without fail I'll come by to finish the wall, I'll take over my half of the clothes closet, I'll live with you

where would I live if it wasn't with you, Judite?

just the time I need to clear up two or three matters, to get rid of a few bothersome things I'm not going to bore you about, to resolve a few small, unimportant matters and still I was hanging around aimlessly, holding my hand out to you, saying good-bye, trying to kiss you, succeeding in kissing you on your cheek, which feels like it doesn't believe, inert, sure that your lips are trembling, a wet thread is coming down to your chin

I'm exaggerating obviously, there's no wet thread

I go on to the bus stop with the little leaf in my hand, I forget about the little leaf and back at Príncipe Real I find it in my fingers again, insignificant, yellow, sticking to my skin, asking myself

—What's this?

remembering, shrugging my shoulders, throwing it into the washbasin, dragging the sideboard over to the other corner of the living room, testing the print for the place where the afternoon light as it passes through the curtains transforms the trees into the movement of water that's flowing endlessly across the wall, I open the shoebox with the two of us inside, or, I mean, the little figures from the wedding cake intact, intact except for the man's foot, which is missing an ankle and the woman is missing a corner of her veil, standing them up on the dresser, remembering so many things, forgetting them, and going back to realizing that they exist when my elbow

I think it's my elbow

happens to knock them over and I notice, without any sorrow, that they've broken into pieces on the floor.

CHAPTER

IT'S NOT A MATTER of wanting to write, I have enough already with what I'm obliged to write at work to have the patience to waste my evenings and break my head with a pen and a notebook, but it's the only way I have of trying to find you, even though I carry my plate and glass into the kitchen to wash on Sunday

I say wash them on Sunday out of habit because I hope that someone will wash them for me

where can you be, Gabriela?

for example, a woman I run into in the café where because I'm timid I don't get to meet, it doesn't matter who it is, the girl in accounting at work who, as soon as she smiles, regrets having smiled at me and right away she huddles down into the thorny virtue of ugly women, the switchboard operator who has looked right through me ever since the lawyer started giving her goodies, I carry my plate and glass into the kitchen, I fold up the tablecloth

the same one from six months ago, which is going to last another six months

in that way I can free a corner of the table and turn loose the hounds of words with hopes that one of them, wagging its merry consonant tail, will discover all of you alive

as though you could be alive

under the rubble of years and years and all the debris of recrimination, anger, gentians, with hopes that something there will gather together the plaster shards of the past which I'd imagined to be at rest forever and right then and there, more words come together, agitated, happy, breaking away from the leash of the pen as I bring my nose closer to the paper and look for all of you, submerged in the lines is a faint little voice saying

—Paulo

that I think I recognize in spite of the tricks of memory that distort things and snuff them out, or the deafness that's been bothering me for months now and your audiogram has gotten worse, friend, you'd better get used to the idea of a little device so the world doesn't turn into a fishbowl with no fish and the isolation of plastic grass among the pebbles at the bottom of it, the little voice repeating

—Paulo

that's sniffed out by the frenzy of the words that make me run after them as they tug at my arm, on the track of hurried phrases through the notebook, I'm off balance and running along unwillingly so they won't get away for good, dozens of diphthong snouts and vowel eyes pointing out to me what I think I want and it scares me now, the little voice gets closer

—Paulo

along with the little voice is something that takes on the look of a face I can see better on the next page, if I manage to catch up with the pen that's running away from me and barking out adjectives at a shadow, a silhouette, a man who enters a house

what house is that?

on a street that's becoming clearer paragraph by paragraph, or looking like a corner with tileworks, the newsstand where my father

I'm so curious and the words are getting ahead of the pen, presuming, inventing, pushing hazy months to the side and in the end it's not a newsstand, it's a phone booth

the corner with tilework, the phone booth is a type no longer used, the little voice takes on body and becomes part of Sissi, who's waving to me with her umbrella during the time when after the maid from the dining room I was living with her in Campolide, in companionate marriage, in what Sissi called home

a man who's coming home, the pen announced just now, and I

was surprised, staring at a first floor that could be a club because of the lack of light and the oak trees on a slope, much too high over our heads, like the olive trees in Chelas when I used to fly at ground level, mixing in with the clouds

it's not a matter of wanting to write, tired from whistling, shouting their names at them and slapping my thigh, the syllables won't obey me and bring up episodes and people that they bury again, making mistakes and giving me memories that aren't mine, other people's days, relatives I didn't have, I ask Sissi as though Sissi was still with me

—Do they belong to you?

Sissi interrupts her landscaping an eyelid

—Who in hell knows who they are

so I ask them, all tangled up in excuses

—Go back to where you were, ladies and gentlemen

offended, they return to oblivion, lingering on the pretext of examining Sissi's piggy bank in whose gullet unfortunately there were no coins

—Are you sure you don't want us to stay?

annoyed at living in the eternity of photograph albums and the memory of grandchildren whose names are all mixed up, so presentable, so worthy, so ennobled by their distant mustaches, the Sunday clothes, pleated cheviots, perfectly combed hair, made just right by the photographer

—Lean forward and rest your chin in your hand, madame

whose authoritarian finger could be seen freezing the poses, the finger pointing at me

Estúdio Nadal, Estúdio Águia D'Ouro, Estúdio Endústria

—Let them stay, boy

the way Sissi was letting me stay

out of respect for your father who was a real lady, Paulo

on her planet of double-chinned piglets, Dona Amélia

—You're like two of my children to me

was tripping over the mistaken coins the words were giving me, hanging onto the teeth of accent marks and her cordial

—People you know, Paulo?

looking at bangs, boys in sailor suits, a gentleman in plus fours with a picnic basket on his arm suggesting in a whisper

—Not even a minute or two together at least?

more interested in Sissi than in me, the pen picking up on her relatives and forgetting mine, the words bringing out of the past a woman playing the piano, a fireman, a man with a sick throat who was interrupting the swabbing of it by raising his muffler

—It looks like Esmeralda's niece, doesn't it?

creatures that I buried in the notebook, going right back to the page

—You're not the ones I want

the sound of the piano was prolonged just a bit in spite of my covering it with paragraphs, notes that were fainter, more spaced, the sick-throated man hacking far off in a sanatorium up north and drinking spoonfuls of quinine every half hour, I killed him by rubbing him out with the tip of the pen

—He's all through

or dissolving him in an erasure, good-bye, the gentleman in plus fours trying to distract me with the picnic basket

—Would you like something?

lines of hurried writing, not looking like my hand, where deciphered under a checked napkin there were a chicken wing, hard-boiled eggs, lemonade, the notebook covered by the tablecloth and the gentleman offended maybe, but certainly silent, squatting by the side of a road with the boys in sailor suits, while quail sobbed in a thicket at the start of the century and a chalet appeared that hasn't existed for a long time in Lisbon, at least Sissi fascinated

—If I were you, I'd let the chalet stay

in spite of her not living with me

I'm living alone in this fifth floor left because the girl in accounting hasn't stopped sticking out her virtuous thorns, even though I'm living alone I think I hear Sissi

—If I were you, I'd let the chalet stay

inside which she stubbornly lived, in spite of the customers at

table nine, a boy with bangs, from time to time she'd talk about getting married

—There are women who interest me, did you know that?

and according to what they told me

or I invent their telling me

or I confirm to myself

or I say with the tip of the pen without dwelling on what I'm
saying

she left the country for a club in Marseille, a little Christmas card
and a little postcard in the summer, insinuations that we could
have been happy if I, after a note in which she recalled to me a photograph from the last show, that she was thinking about getting a
sex change in a Brazilian clinic, and the evil omen of a silence that's
lasted until today, and the piano I ruined giving out a mournful *re*,
swallowed up as the piggy bank filled its gullet, the lack of coins,
remembrances from strangers, which resulted in the idea to heal up
one wound by opening up another right next to it, I don't know
whether it's a bother or not, as I guide the words along toward
Anjos or Bico da Areia, going up the Avenida Almirante Reis with
all those eating places and all those furniture stores or crossing the
Tagus on a warship that's fastened to the water by its cannons,
going by Príncipe Real where there's another building instead of
ours, hearing Rui

—Paulo

hoping to help him discover, in the midst of so many balconies,
the one that didn't exist, going back to the beginning of the notebook, showing him

—This is the one

climbing the stairs with him, inviting him in, redoing the chandelier, the sofa, the window that looks out on the cedar, reassuring
him

—You can see, can't you, don't you see?

the bit about looking for the mastiff with a bow, writing it down
secretly while he's thoughtful

—Didn't they find me years ago in Fonte da Telha?

pretending not to hear him, completing one of his legs so I can stop him from limping, Rui noticing the dust on the furniture, the clothes to be ironed, the closets with no dresses, only male things, a drawer on the floor

—Soraia?

Soraia, the one the words were looking for and couldn't find, skipping lines, changing pronouns, piling it all up

what for?

at the top of the page in a tiny hand, I catch sight of my uncle, Dona Helena, Mr. Vivaldo with the redheaded maid, nothing of my father, I ask the tip of the pen to bring him to me and the tip goes off course, reappearing with Noémia, wearing bangs, pedaling the tricycle

—It wasn't Noémia who was pedaling the tricycle, it was Dália

and Dália is in the room in Anjos with flowers in a vase, the sentences are so stupid, such jackass stuff, I get mad at them, correct them, put Noémia and Dália where they're supposed to be, take a good look, this is the way it is, the tricycle belongs to the second one, the flowers to the first, apologizing

—I'm sorry

especially in regard to Noémia, who's envious of the tricycle, spending almost an entire paragraph consoling her by pumping up the tires on the bicycle in the laundry room, raising the seat for her because she'd grown in the meantime, and repairing the light

—You've got a bicycle all for yourself and Dália hasn't any, so let's not be jealous, Noémia

Rui is suspicious that I was hiding my father from him

—Who are you talking to?

from Fonte da Telha, persisting in the idea, a syringe, cliffs

—I could almost have sworn there were cliffs

insisting that he'd lain down on the beach, I'd left him twenty feet from the waves

—Not right there, farther back, put a dune in the notebook

a dune to please him, one he hadn't even seen, as he insisted

—I think I died, I couldn't have

cabins, the little train carrying people every fifteen minutes through dunes and reeds and where he and my father so many times

with the bored silence of married couples?

in search of a moment without any neighbors or scandal, I went on at length

—Look

in descriptions of August afternoons when Micaela or Marlene was with them

never the two together, Micaela some afternoons and Marlene others, cold at that time, because of the major on Tuesdays, because I don't know who stole from whom, with rumors of hair loss that could have been syphilis, I polished my prose, made it a perfect summer, free of clouds and accusatives

I made good use of the moment when Rui

—Soraia?

making demands of the words, busy in bringing back the maid from the dining room and the accordion without keys, how about a little tune Gabriela

—Give me my father right now

mad at the pen for foisting on me what I didn't want, Dona Aurorinha, for example, resting her shopping bag on a step in the dark before evaporating, grateful

—Thanks for remembering me, Paulinho

the nephritic man swaying on the stretcher on the way to the hospital, sighing when he brushed against me, out of the corner of his mouth

—This has been going on for a long time, young fellow, it started I don't know when

Vânia, for example, who was run over and died and I was quick to send her away before a bandage was unwound from her forehead and the leg the truck had left all twisted and strange

—We haven't got anything of interest for you, and besides, you're dead now, so get lost

Vânia hiding the bandage in a tulle head-covering and hiding the leg with her small bag

—You're mistaken Paulo, I'm alive

reprimanding the words for giving me ghosts, locking them up in parentheses, explaining to Rui, who was wandering about in the hallway as if in the dream of a dream

—Didn't they find me years ago in Fonte da Telha?

because my father must be on his way, he was delayed by a rehearsal and his body was lying there, the lights from the police car making it all the more naked, an almost adolescent body, where I got the impression that flies

and as soon as I write

flies

the flies are there, if only I could stop writing, wash the dishes, forget

the police, who put up some sticks and yellow tape as they kept the sea away

—Keep away from the body, keep moving keep moving

and the sea, poor thing, in an ebb tide that didn't dare come back in, tiny little waves, that sound of pennies as the water obeys, a man picking up the syringe, showing something, preventing Rui from seeing the writing about a blonde wig there in the garden

—Do you see a blonde wig there in the garden?

summoning my father and still Rui was examining the body, keep moving keep moving

—Doesn't it look like me?

cursing the pen's deceits, changing pronouns, multiplying ellipses, it doesn't look like you, it's not you, that's silly, a tramp, some poor devil, one of those unfortunates who was looking for mussels on the cliffs and, all of a sudden, a slip, a weak heart, a drunken argument, and someone with a club, you're younger, better put together, we missed you, didn't you know, see how happy my father is to see you, thank God for the words that sketch out my father and the street door, heels on the stairs, the lock that groaned before its final turn

I haven't forgotten the lock that groaned before its final turn

so I can relax for a bit, think about the switchboard operator who pierced me with the eyes that didn't stop on me, extension one twenty-six, it was really a kind of cocoon with an old array of wires and plugs

—Extension one twenty-six, good morning

that I didn't dare connect with, displeased with my uncomfortable bachelor's furniture, the flotsam from the shipwreck of a relationship after Gabriela that I won't go into because it will invade my prose with a lot of bitter arguments, jealousies back and forth, and end up with a hefty brother-in-law taking her out to the elevator and calling me a bum and coming back with a van that carried off all the household appliances and left me with this trash, the last word

—Bum

falling thunderously from six feet of flannel and disdain and all of which the neighbors heard, thinking about the girl from accounting in the same way, washing away what had been washed away already or picking up her mother's wedding ring and wondering how it would look on her ringless finger, wondering about someone like me in the café at that time, available, sincere, proper, a matter of great seriousness, please abstain in case you are unable to fulfill the required conditions, please reply to this newspaper at Box 472, remembering the maid from the dining room, remembering you, picking up my pen again

because there are things that weigh heavily on me

where the ink dries up, drawing some spirals

bringing the tip back to life

clearer and clearer, the scribbling as the metal gets rid of a piece of dirt or something and the piece of dirt is imprisoned in a blue stain, another way of writing, telling a story

what story?

mine too maybe mine or the reverse of mine which I'll never read, and no sooner does the thing start a capital letter in its meanderings to get working again than my father

the words were calling for Vânia but I held them back in time

my father

I looked and my father was still there, still

on the ground floor that didn't go away so long ago, sitting on the sofa, taking off his wig checking whether some pigeon because the pigeons used to, not like today when there are almost no birds in Príncipe Real because there's almost no old man with leftover bread in his pockets, you'd wake up in the morning and all those wings in the treetops, when Dona Aurorinha with her little jacket that was missing buttons and missing color, sentimental, emotional, and nothing but bones now

—Thanks for remembering me, Paulinho

Rui staring at my father paying no attention to him, holding his stomach where a pain, an indisposition

—I swear by my mother I'm not on drugs, Soraia

the trembling of his hands, not counting the money my father was giving him on the first week of the month and the rest of the time he stole things, that rigamarole about a friend with a radio in hock, medicine for a classmate in school and you can be sure that tomorrow, without fail, if only the letters could help my father rumple and smooth a quilt, if I could only let him know through the notebook with the same clarity as when I jot down his little items of glass jewelry, if it could only explain why, could show me how to help him and because I didn't know how to help him, this remorse that I disguise as indifference, distance, during the times I ask myself what I feel for him, the pen is busy sniffing out Dona Helena in the rubble or the Cape Verdeans in Chelas, sinking me into a page where a Mulatto in dark glasses is opening and closing a jackknife on the riverbank, if I try to make him out, behind him it's not the heroin district, not the wall, not the jackdaw, it's the Tagus, somewhere in the Tagus is what I've been looking for all these years, half a gate, a plaster dwarf on the refrigerator, peace, a difficult peace now that Rui

—Soraia

now that my father notices him and slips a bill into his open neck, getting to the

—Would you mind waiting outside a bit, Paulo?

and me

today nobody is there for me

—Would you mind waiting outside a bit, Paulo?

back to the cedar and its nightlike shadow on a March afternoon, trying to find out without Mr. Couceiro everything is all mixed up without Mr. Couceiro

how do you say cedar in Latin, adding up the number of white cars, betting that before twenty

twenty-five at most

a fold in the curtain and my father calling me, not dressed, in a bathrobe and with his wig at an angle, thanking Rui, annoyed with me

—What are you looking at?

and on his face not me, my mother protesting in silence or picking off a drop of disappointment from inside her eyelid with her pinky

—Carlos

the words trotting along among us with the exaltation of discovery

we've brought them together, we've brought them together

pulling him, pulling me, bringing us closer together, bringing me closer to him, that is

and I with no desire at all

clutching my sleeve with exclamation points, the molars of ellipses, the tittles in the shape of lips, my father working on his makeup, the stockings that my sloppy son

I never saw anything like it

is sure to tear on me

—I hate for you to grab me

you never liked me to hug you, isn't that right, father, if I sit on your lap you stiffen up, not moving, your head turning away from me complaining about the wrinkle in your pants, my mother always taking your part, don't annoy your father Paulo, at most a pat on the head, excuses, lies

—I've got a cold and I'll give it to you

the mole on his ear that intrigued me and I had the urge to touch it, I'd reach out my finger and he'd say not now you're dirty, careful with my shirt, dummy, running to the mirror on the wardrobe, what a pest this kid is, checking the damage, bawling me out because of a stain and in the end a defect in the mirror that he would check with his fingernail, and then he'd move a bit and his

nose was now fat now thin, a big gap between chin and mouth and
right after that no gap at all, my father annoyed with the house and
the marigolds that were withering

—Not even the mirror's any good

two men came from Costa da Caparica with a new mirror all
wrapped in newspapers, the one who seemed to be in charge, take a
look and see if you like it, ma'am, as his partner studied the dwarf,
my mother's reflection and the one of the man who seemed to be in
charge with the window behind him, the café to the left instead of
to the right, the herons that were arriving in the reflection and
going away outside, the bed with the pillows was changed, my
mother's was on top with my father's underneath, the man from
Costa da Caparica, so young and already married, ma'am, is the kid
yours, I got the idea of somebody touching somebody and they
weren't touching me and just the three of us in the room, the one
studying the dwarf, come here boy, the one who seemed to be in
charge, such a young woman, such a young woman, Rui told me
that in his aunt and uncle's house the maid would hold her daughter up against the desk by the ankles as she protested and struggled

—Don't get the doctor mad, Matilde

so the uncle could touch her, she'd lead her into the study the
way you lead a lamb, unbutton her blouse here she is, mister architect, she'd pinch her belly telling the

—A thirteen-year-old skin, mister architect, nice and firm

a slap for the first refusal

—Show some respect for your boss, Matilde

Rui told me that the girl would stop resisting, crying, she'd look
at me all the time and not ask for anything, she helped out in the
kitchen, served us at table, if she happened to get the plates mixed
up my aunt, right away, would say clumsy, the one who seemed to
be in charge to my mother

—I can give you a little discount on the mirror

as soon as they'd left the café owner said

—You don't look all that ashamed

Rui, proud of his family, said the old man wasn't up to it, admi-
ration, envy, the pen all aroused too

—The old man wasn't up to it?

asking Rui to hold the legs of the girl from accounting, lifting up her clothes struggling with the cheap fabric

—They don't pay you very much do they, how long has it been since you've bought a blouse?

in an apartment I suppose was like mine, little pieces of store-bought furniture, framed prints of kittens and flowers, a mouse masquerading as a peasant girl flirting with a mouse masquerading as a soldier leaning on his rifle like a dandy on his cane, I want to be your mouse, I want to be your soldier, be quiet, don't cry, you'll be sorry if you hurt me, Rui was furious with teeth marks on his hand, you almost drew blood you idiot, look at this, look, pulling the picture off the wall

—Show some respect

and smashing it on the floor, his shoe broke the glass, he turned on the faucet in the bathroom to wash off the wound, searching in the closet for some iodine, a tube of lipstick and there wasn't any lipstick, if you could only smile at me, really say hello

—How are you Mr. Paulo?

have lunch with me in a restaurant with tiled walls that smelled of cooking, the menu on the blackboard halfway erased from the previous day, yesterday lamb stew, swordfish, vermicelli, the black waitress, the busboy with a pimple on his chin

—I'll bet you hurt him too

the girl was skinny, withdrawn, demanding that we split the check, fishing through the patent-leather change purse where there were subway tickets, pieces of paper, the photograph of a man

—Your boyfriend

her finger covered the picture of the man, she wasn't offended or upset, I haven't got time for any love affairs

—My brother, Mr. Paulo

asking me to leave first not for her sake, for mine, I don't want to get you hung up, Mr. Paulo, there are a lot of pretty girls in the office, Belmira, Susana, have you talked to Susana yet

I wonder which one is Susana?

I'm not worth a cent, quick legs on the stairs, bumping into the busboy and I'm sorry, the second shoulder of my coat that's hard to get into and then the whole afternoon over the books, my shoelaces get undone without my realizing it, the ballpoint gets tangled in hair, wanting

who can explain it for me?

to torment her, upset her, make fun of her brother

—Your brother's really ugly

off in the provinces somewhere, Venezuela, Paris, and revulsion with myself inside, a surge of guilt

—My brother's dead, Mr. Paulo

not sad, her normal tone of voice, just information

—My brother's dead, Mr. Paulo

a fork slashing in my insides, slicing and before I'm obliged to continue, a coffin in a hearse with a mother or a godmother all upset and rosaries and her, twisting her hair on Castelo Branco or Lagos, buying her a print with

why not?

a pair of puppies looking at each other with liquid tenderness, aren't they cute, my father to Rui, which the pen wrote down, stronger, in a checked vest

—There's something different about you, I don't know what

my father is a puppy with liquid tenderness and inside the liquid tenderness mistrust, suspicions, a sneaky glance at the notebook that he couldn't see because he's at Príncipe Real, not here

—What have you done with him, Paulo?

hiding the girl from accounting, the prints, the brother, discreet with an expression that was asking forgiveness for having lived thirty years, he would have liked the mice, the needlepoint pillow on the leather easy chair, the girl straightening out her skirt, a reproach that wasn't a reproach

Mr. Paulo

and was making me hate her

—I hate myself

I was surprised with the mistake she didn't hear, desolated by the mouse masquerading as a soldier in a useless little rag, the teeth marks on her hand, did you see this, silly, did you see this

—I hate you

and yes, I spoke the truth

—I hate you

I don't hate myself what an idea, why should I hate myself, if you lived with me you'd wash the dishes on Sunday, you'd put up a little picture in the living room, another one in the bedroom, you'd pretty up the house for me, maybe we could talk every so often, me who doesn't talk much but even without talking I'd feel you close by and calm down, do you understand, with a bit of luck I'd forget my father, Príncipe Real, this notebook where the past becomes the present and comes after me, smothers me, my father, pointing to Rui's place on the sofa

—What have you done with him, Paulo?

the café that's probably finished lighting up outside, Marlene and Micaela who've also finished or gotten so old then, my God, calling from the street

—It's us, Soraia

music from a loudspeaker hidden, certainly, but where, in what place, I search behind the curtain, in the shadow of the end table, in a vase that was supposed to be Egyptian

—It's Egyptian, Paulo

Egyptian my foot, it was missing its top and had been bought in a flea market, an orange spot crossed by a grayish spot, Dona Amélia crossed the room with her perfume tray

—Aren't you ready, girls?

I found it last week or two weeks ago

it's just a matter of looking in my datebook

leaving a church near the dentist's, she was too busy with the trouble in her ankles to pay attention to me and I'd lost the left half of my mouth because of the anesthesia, up to the neck a complete person, from the neck up a fragment of a face with no cheek or tongue, tongue and cheek were missing

—Dona Amélia

according to the photograph, of course

—Paulo

not getting to hear them, the dead brother's, I suspect

—Mr. Paulo

interceding for the girl, a

—Mr. Paulo

useless in the patent-leather purse while Dona Amélia's leg was searching through the emptiness of the steps, a small jacket that looked like mourning wear

the husband?

some colorless shreds of hair, remains of old makeup whitening her cheeks, she limped slowly into the room with the tray from which perfumes were sliding off

—Aren't you ready, girls?

the words were mocking me, they dispersed and went back with Mr. Couceiro and while Mr. Couceiro said

—Son

before I could say

—Don't call me son

I'm your son, I'm your son

they left him in the laundry room with the lack of interest of someone throwing away an empty overcoat, they were changing him into my grandmother, smothered in mimosas or God ruling the world up on the roof of a boardinghouse, the orange spotlight

or the gray one?

lingered on him and left him, went on to a girl playing hop-scotch in the living room

—Mother

the girl standing and the words placing a grave close by and waving laurel branches

—It's the wind, pay no attention

and I guess that it was the wind because the clouds on the mountains were growing longer, the curtains at Príncipe Real were wrapping up my father, dragging him far away, Micaela, Sissi, Marlene with a tone of censure

—We could have been friends, Paulo

not seeing the cedar or me on the bench waiting, my father got up from the sofa to lock the window

—It's all over, Paulinho

Paulinho finally, not Paulo

—It's all over, Paulinho

hiding his face on his chest, the falsies don't upset me, the spangles don't upset me, you're my father aren't you, tell me that you're my father, play piggyback with me

do you remember playing piggyback with me?

toward the bridge, show me the gull eggs, Alto do Galo, remember that time on the carousel at the fair, the animals shaking as they went around, gallop faster, don't let me fall, don't worry about the pups, their laughing, the pine cones that don't bother us, see there, written in the notebook, how they don't bother us, you don't have to disguise yourself as a clown, lip-synch the singers, accept table nine

—Did they want to talk to me?

sit down on a beam, relax, I closed the notebook didn't you see, the customers are all finished, we're going home, going by the reeds, the Gypsies

—Mr. Carlos

admiring you, high regard for you, people have a high regard for you, father, they don't belittle you, all you have to do is not make yourself up with those ridiculous things, there should be a place for us next Sunday

—No problem, friends, stay here on the terrace

in the restaurant at Cova do Vapor, mother seasoning your salad, me running on the float, in September we'll take the train to the village, we'll get up in the morning when the wasps are swarming, remember mother sleeping with her arm over her head in the position of a dancer, with the look of a little girl, if we tickled her

—What is it what is it?

not recognizing us, recognizing us, sitting up in bed, not recognizing the room, recognizing it, asking what time it was

—Nine o'clock, really?

the words are so quiet in the notebook

I'll never again let them out, I promise

the window is opened and the chestnut trees, the vine

no sentence contradicting me, getting away

the backyard really here

no sentence contradicting me except for an instant, a tiny instant, don't be frightened, Marlene from the street, her plumes, her tiara

—Where have you been, Soraia?

that my mother didn't notice, I pretended not to notice, don't be afraid, father, Marlene in the notebook forever, it's all over, look, mother

—Nine o'clock, really?

Looking for her sweater

—Turn your back, Paulo

fixing her hair, tightening it into a braid like in the days when she played hopscotch on the gravestones, all you had to do was draw the squares, toss the pebble, leap on one foot up to the last one you'd drawn, pick up the stone, go back to where we are, aim at the next square and leap again and, meanwhile, the smell of mountains that she

—The mimosas

and in the meantime the two of us on our way to the sluiceway because sometimes a little fish or a frog or a bird, whoever catches the little fish or a frog or a bird wins, and the last one to get there

it's well known

is a faggot.

CHAPTER

IF ONLY WE COULD TALK, it doesn't matter where
   the beach house, Anjos, Príncipe Real, the club
   a place where we wouldn't be the ghosts of now but the people from before, the ghosts are you, people that I've lost and a ghost is me, looking for you in the shadows, talking to you the way dead people talk and with my own words answering, not yours, what do I expect you to say, knowing that you wouldn't be talking like this, if you could only tell me what I don't know or maybe what I'd rather not know, what happened before I was born or when I was too small to understand what was going on and all I can do is invent, the way old letters invent the past
   they don't explain anything about him to me, they invent
   the way the lemon tree in the yard invents maybe
   —Paulinho
   or I invent for it because whenever I was in the village, the lemon tree was silent, watching along with me the druggist in the cemetery as he held out a bowl over his daughter's crucifix
   —I've made you a little soup, Luísa
   lifting the lid off the bowl, filling a spoon, blowing on it as he offers her the spoon
   —A little bean soup the way you like it, Luísa
   and staying there with his arm out in the shadows from the sun
   —Bean soup, Luísa
   ending up by putting the bowl down into the grass that was smothering the chrysanthemums

—Have it when you feel like it, there it is

and she must have had it when she felt like it, at a time when there was no one there except a lamb munching thistles in the distance, because when I went over, there was no soup in it, talking to you two from this fifth floor where I'm living and I call you, seeing you coming from the balcony, not at the age you'd be today, at the age I remember you both, the branch of a mulberry tree making your smiles bigger

—Son

seeing the three of us in the wardrobe mirror which I suppose was sold when you sold the house, mother, and when I asked the ones who'd bought it, they didn't know anything about you, I was next to the small entrance where there was a new porch

I mean, just a porch, we never had a porch, an attic we didn't have either and a child who wasn't me, with a locomotive, looking like me

or a car with wooden wheels?

hugging it to his chest, staring at me

not just the child staring at me, the whole house staring at me

—Is there something you want here?

not our house, how strange, a different house, the refrigerator without the dwarf from Snow White on top, the supports that held up the gentian showing, but with an unfamiliar vine growing that had little blue flowers and that my father hadn't watered, no gulls or pups, the remains of the bridge, a woman not like you, fatter, protecting the child

—Is there something you want here, mister?

she probly idn't ask me that, she answered

if you could have been here, mother, you wouldn't have told the man to send me away, don't play with your cameo, answer me

—Send the faggot's son away

my father without any quilt to rumple and smooth, rumpling and smoothing his skirt, moistening his fingers with perfume and touching his neck with them, taking off the right earring that was hurting his earlobe

—I don't believe it, Judite

with the shrug of his shoulders accepting the applause, the invitation from table nine that Dona Amélia

—Table nine, Soraia

his uncle's wife taking off his pants, shirt

—Bath time, Carlos

if we could only talk, it doesn't matter where

his uncle's wife, he searched for her to get his revenge many years later

To get my revenge on her, can't you see, my reluctance to ask her to

—Pet me

unable to stand her petting me and asking her

—Pet me

and when I asked

—Pet me

as the towel came off my body and her hands were on my belly, the twisting of her mouth which I'll never forget, her breast weighing down on me

I don't know if it was weighing down on me

weighing down on my knee

—*Such nice skin such nice skin*

his uncle's wife, he searched for her many years later to get his revenge on her, asking her to

—Pet me

or confessing to her

—You're the only woman I let pet me and I can't stand you because of it

the aunt was an old creature peeking through the little crack in the door without releasing the chain, looking for her glasses to see things better, deciding that a beggar, a thief, a door-to-door salesman

—I don't need anything

pushing on the doorknob to get rid of you and you, father

do you remember?

father was so comical on the landing, with no makeup on, no earrings, the polish off his nails and his nails trimmed

don't keep insisting that it wasn't like that, it was like that

the old creature through the crack in the door

—I don't need anything

going back twenty years all of a sudden

twenty-five, twenty-seven years

her mouth twisted like before, shucking off her old age

hovering over me

hovering over my father, all red, enormous, her arms wet with soap and water

one afternoon, kissing my uncle in the yard, the same twisting of her mouth, the same arms, pruning shears in her hand, the tip of the shears against my uncle's back, she stood on tiptoes to reach his throat

and yet, so big

I found myself telling her

—Kill him

her arms were wet with soap and water and instead of

—Such nice skin such nice skin

the short robe, a button instead of a pin, a soft stomach that was quivering

—I don't need anything

suspicious of the beggar or the thief or the door-to-door sales-man, unable to make out his features and if she did, not asking

—Do I know you?

my father looking for the pruning shears that weren't there, aware of his voice

—I'm going to kill you

and unable to get angry, tiny, naked, lying on a towel

if only we could talk, it doesn't matter where

in the same tone of voice as hating her, asking her to

—Pet me

my uncle was hunting wild doves in the bedroom, in pajamas, resting on the pillow with the shotgun, he would fire as soon as there was a flock in the window, he would lay down the shotgun, linger for an eternity flicking his cigarette lighter, another eternity putting it out with the first puff of smoke and it went out with the first puff of smoke not him, the little beacon light on the cigarette

—Go get the doves, Carlos

and my father

if only we could

picking up the handkerchiefs with dirty wings

talk, it doesn't matter where

in the brambles, by the walnut trees, at the godmother's feet as she came back from the well with her buckets, my father to the aged creature, convinced he'd been aiming at her with the shotgun which they later sold to the sacristan because of thieves in the church, the sacristan, we'll show them

—I'm Carlos

the creature's expression was stagnant

her arms were wet with soap and water and taking away the towel, give me your arms, aunt, she'd pick me up, lift me out of the tub do you remember

—Bath's over

carry me into the next room and I'd smooth and rumple the quilt, waiting for her, smoothing and rumpling the quilt until my wife

—Why Carlos?

until you, ma'am

—Such nice skin such nice skin

the creature wasn't looking at me

her mouth was twisted, a muscle stretching out, the head of thin hair that leaped up into my nose

—Carlos?

Carlos, the faggot, the clown dancing in a club, taking care of customers in the boardinghouse in Beato, the one who's living with a boy his son's age and Dona Aurorinha

—God forgive her, poor thing

remember undressing me at night, turning out the light for me, I'm sure of you, ma'am, looking at me from the door

—Sleep well

going away having forgotten me

why have you forgotten me?

toward the conversations and coughs of the grownups

the crazy man who lived in the station robbed me and tomorrow my corpse the little that's left of me in a bag, still asking for help

the voice of my uncle's wife knowing that they were going to kill and yet diluted by the voices of the godmother, the druggist, the cousins, hastier, quicker, telling them

it was obvious

—The crazy man at the station is going to take Carlos out of the bedroom

he comes in through the window in spite of the fact that nobody at all could fit in the window and Carlos, unable to scream, see how he's carrying him on his shoulder, the way he trots with him through the lettuce patch, the way the leaves can be heard telling us

—They've taken Carlos away

and us with our little hands over our ears

—What?

my uncle's wife not in the living room, through a crack in the door

if only we could talk, it doesn't matter where

the beach house, Anjos, Príncipe Real, the club

a place where we wouldn't be the ghosts of today but the people from before, we wouldn't be ghosts, people

looking at the oversize jacket, the too-long pants, the almost-empty vest

—I'm Carlos

a child lost in adult clothes, not wanting to be sent away, not wanting to be scorned, moving closer on the doormat

do you want me to take care of you, father, do you want me to stay with you?

—I'm Carlos

forgetting about the pruning shears, the shotgun for doves that he brought to his uncle and his uncle with his eyes closed on the bed

—I'm not interested in birds today, beat it

my father giving in, going down the steps, thinking

—Carlos?

but maybe not the old woman, his hope that the old woman

—Carlos?

would undo the bolt and invite him in

—Come in

a tub in the kitchen, Vânia helping his uncle's wife

—Let me take your shoes off, Soraia

the manager to the ceiling where the light man

—The green spot now

a second spotlight on the audience, Mr. Couceiro, Gabriela, my mother, the father of the maid from the dining room holding out the accordion at arm's length

—How about a little tune, young fellow?

the pups throwing pine cones on the beach

and the pine cones they were throwing on top of you, add the pine cones they were throwing on top of you

the Gypsies' horses that Dona Amélia was ordering to gallop on stage, his uncle's wife repeating to herself

—Carlos?

and it was at that moment that you died, father, not later, not when the doctor was feeling sorry for you because, after all, nobody wants them, a hard life, poor things

—We'll start the treatment tomorrow

it was knowing that you were dead in her, you'd always been dead in her, you never touched my mother or any other woman because of her

convinced that one day in Bico da Areia, Príncipe Real, in the lodging houses where they still accepted you, the old woman leaning over you, taking you by the wrists

—Bath time, Carlos

—Sleep time, Carlos

—Petting-me time, Carlos

if only we could talk, it doesn't matter where

or I preferred thinking that maybe I was telling him that because by telling him that my father isn't a faggot, a clown, he's an urchin looking for wounded doves in the brambles and his uncle in pajamas turning the shotgun toward him, firing and instead of the sound that he expected, silence, the pain that would certainly be coming, nothing, the music interrupted, the lights out, the Gypsies' horses in the middle of their trot, the same wave curved eternally over the beach of days gone by and the same bridge where I piggyback on your shoulders, slipping down, the tables in the club deserted, Dona Amélia's tray abandoned on the bar, the first light coming down through the small window hidden by a piece of calico and if I say coming down I mean lighting up the platform they called a stage or an oval of boards with drapes around, the workers' jackets on the cane stand for the customers, no one except you

father

rehearsing a step, another step, disappearing into your fan and emerging out of the fan, mimicking a song that's not playing, look, the posters announcing

Soraia

announcing Soraia, Micaela's nervousness

—Don't hurt him, Paulo

and as I turned toward Micaela a trace of cologne or not a trace, an absence, it was the absence who said

—Don't hurt him, Paulo

a faggot sorry for another faggot, isn't that funny, father, a clown sorry for another clown, isn't that amusing, father, if we went to the circus they'd enlarge your face, paint it with lipstick into an endless howl, and I believed in them the way I believed in you, the way my mother believed in you, in your night job, in your excuses, in your silence

—Carlos

asking herself, facing the wardrobe, what's wrong with me, what have I done, buying new blouses, new sandals, the necklace she bought on time behind my father's back and the jeweler saying

—There are other ways of paying, miss

with me sitting on the floor and my mother to me in front of the jeweler

if only we could talk, if only we could talk at least, if I could talk to Dona Helena she'd listen to me

—Nuisance

the jeweler behind a cheap cigar which was his whole face except for the invitation under the cigar

—There are other ways of paying, miss

reaching out his hand and patting me on the head to please her
there was a raffia mat in the kitchen, remember?

—I have a nuisance, too, forget about him

his hand was moving toward her with the pretext of straightening her necklace and my mother's throat, not alive, inert, like when
the owner of the café, the pups, like when I'd go to her and her body
would immediately draw back, disgusted with me

—The way he clings to people

judging that my father hated me because she'd had me by some
man he probably didn't know, men she slept with in order to sleep
with you, father, closing her eyes and being sure it was you, calling
them by your name, imagining you with her, hearing your footsteps in the yard, your fingers on the marigolds, your hand
stroking her and sliding along her thighs, the gentian branches
that folded over her and folded up her bones, bending her, putting
her to sleep, waking her up and when she woke up my mother
saying

—Carlos

and

—Carlos

and

—Carlos

because no other name made sense, it was you, understand, you
were that heavy breathing, you were those kisses, those aimless
words and as a result you, father, not the owner of the café, the electrician, one of the Gypsies, if it happened that a mare was lingering
in the yard, and being my father frightened you because you had no
right to be a father, your uncle's wife

an old woman through a crack in the door

looking at him with a kind of happiness or surprise

—I never dreamed that you

that's the way it was, wasn't it, father, agree that it was that way,
your uncle's wife who didn't order you

—Bath time, Carlos

she didn't even touch you

and the pump from the well that breathed like a man, not really
breathing like a man, that agony before relaxing, the sadness

the maid from the dining room to me

—*Who are you talking to, Paulo?*

and I on my back

you mustn't see my face

as calm as I could manage

—*Nobody, go to sleep, it was a car from down below that woke you up,*
I'm not talking to anybody

and, as a matter of fact, I wasn't talking to anybody except ghosts I've lost
and I was a ghost too, looking for them in the shadows, go to sleep, my blind
grandmother going over the contours of bones, suspecting, getting up, going
off in silence

a car from down below that woke you up, go to sleep

my grandmother heading toward the stove, disappearing into the wood-
pile where the invisible clock was striking

and I on my back

—*Go to sleep*

the peaceful heart of a fat man

your uncle's wife looking at you with a kind of happiness or surprise as if you

—I never dreamed that you

the way you look at an adult, without ordering you

—Bath time, Carlos

without even touching you, putting her hand on her own belly
and looking at you while the shotgun was fading in the smoke

—Go get the doves, Carlos

handkerchiefs with dirty wings in the brambles, at the base of
the walnut trees, at the feet of my godmother coming back with the
buckets from the well, in the calf pen as they trembled with fright
and you were looking at her in turn, almost demanding

—Pet me

not begging, an urgency that surprised her

—Pet me

the flocks of geese and the toads from the ditch suddenly there,
the engine on the seven o'clock train crushing through trunks,

breaking through the house, someone you didn't see

—Carlos

your uncle's wife running off toward the threshing floor as though with a spasm or a vomiting attack or an upset or something like that, you were getting undressed without any help, going to bed without any help, avoiding my mother

—I'm sorry

no, only years later, avoiding my mother

—I'm sorry

going to bed without any help in the room sunk in a vastness of chestnut trees and drains, the way, later on, by the sea

not really by the sea yet, by the Tagus

the way later on at the point where the Tagus becomes the sea, at Bico da Areia, with my mother beside you and the flowers that follow you nonstop reminding you

—Your uncle's wife, do you remember your uncle's wife?

the flowers or the pine grove or the thicket or the clouds from Trafaria where autumn begins or my mother's elbow that faded into yours

the maid from the dining room to me

—Who are you talking to, Paulo?

Marina & Diogo, Marina & Diogo, maybe if you write our names

I'm not going to rot away in this dump with you

I'll kill you

I left you like a chicken thief and today I think that

you, who couldn't catch on at that time, stayed waiting for the arms wet with soap and water, that your uncle's wife held

—Go pick up the doves, Carlos

floating over you, one of the doves had no head, another dove was a muddy little pile of feathers, another dove was pieces of cartilage that fell apart in your fingers, your uncle's wife in the Lamego hospital

you didn't find her at dinner and they told you in the Lamego hospital, which is a big building with aluminum sounds and some character ordering

—Silence

in spite of the silence a fan, faucets, a woman to an unseen person

—I never dreamed that he

drafts, echoes, the uncle without his shotgun, elbows on his knees, attempting a smile that wouldn't detach itself from his face

—Next week without fail I'm going to give you more doves, Carlos

and the smile wavering, letting the godmother accompany him into the courtyard where the lady doctor

—With this miscarriage and the operation on her uterus she'll be spared the trouble of any more children won't she?

a stone fountain, an East Indian in a wheelchair predicting my knee never fools me, there's going to be rain tomorrow

when they die they wash the intestines so they can go into the ground clean, your uncle's wife almost a month without talking to anyone, looking out at the countryside through the window of the nursing home, a few buildings, that is, the town hall and its flag-pole without a flag, a row of elms, when they lifted her up for a visit she didn't notice you

and it was then that you began not to exist, father, it was then

not later, but only after many years you'd come to realize

that you'd begun to die, when they went to get her, the son of the Indian in the wheelchair was cleaning his father's intestines, through the window there was more countryside, the mill where a girl, naked from the waist down

—Such nice skin such nice skin

was swaying with the bumps just like mechanical toys, the doves that your uncle hadn't had time to kill, busy adjusting the pillow on the bed, your uncle's wife looking out over the yard, the henhouse, the furniture, at least with this miscarriage and the operation on her uterus, she'll be spared the trouble of more children, isn't that so, and your father

—Any more children?

who as soon as you knew that I was going to be born understood

a child again, a child again

your uncle's wife went with the in-laws, bouncing along just like a mechanical toy, she plucked the poultry, ironed, sewed, because of you they cleaned out her intestines with no need of any help until hollow, empty

—Carlos

Carlos, the faggot, the clown, dancing in a club, taking care of customers in boardinghouses in Beato, who lives with a boy the age of his son and Dona Aurorinha

—God forgive her, poor thing

if they mentioned your name, your uncle's wife would interrupt her sweeping, not looking at you but at the handkerchiefs of dirty wings they told you to pick up

—Go get the doves, Carlos

from the base of the walnut trees, their breasts crushed, their heads hanging by the thread of a tendon and your uncle's wife

—Carlos

because it did happen that way, didn't it, father, a child with her, a child, your uncle's wife

—Carlos

and yet if only we could talk, it doesn't matter where

the beach house, Anjos, Príncipe Real, the club

you agreed with me

and yet

—Not now Judite

yet

—On the Saturday I'm off work, Judite

until admitting, accepting, you said in a small, soft childlike voice that frightened you and where it was

—Pet me

you surprised with the

—Pet me

thinking it's not true, I don't believe what's true is true, you were smoothing and rumpling the quilt

or a towel

the quilt

—I can't, Judite

my grandmother, not blind yet, brought her husband from the tavern in a wheelbarrow

—Wretch

you were taking down the suitcase from the top of the wardrobe

—I can't, Judite

and as you opened it on the bed where there was no towel, no woman with arms wet from soap and water, no twisted mouth, my mother was placing herself between you and the suitcase and you were picking up your topcoat, getting to the door, pushing me aside with your foot as though I too, avoiding the gentian as though the gentian too, you said to the gentian or to me

to the gentian that was trying to stop you from getting to the gate, you broke off a branch and a clump was spinning and spinning in your memory

—I can't, Judite

in the same way that the horses and the gulls and the pups and the waves were spinning around you, I'm going to clean your intestines, father, so you can go clean into the ground now that we can talk, I'm able to talk, the sea is calm, notice, the bridge is peaceful, the pine grove is at rest, now that I'm before you all at Cova do Vapor or on the carousel or in the village, I'm talking to you who haven't died yet or haven't gone away, the proof is fingers on my cheeks, ears, mouth

—You're Paulo, aren't you?

your smells, your footsteps, your voices, the tub you bathed me in, which my father changed into a flower bed for begonias, I happened to surprise him taking care of them, imagining my mother and me at the café or at the butcher's or admiring Dália, who was going to marry a doctor, pedaling in the yard, taking care of the begonias the way he would a little boy we couldn't see, announcing to him

—Bath time, Carlos

washing his body, lifting him up out of the tub, laying him down on the flower bed bordered with pieces of colored glass, the one where the marigolds follow the light in a lazy rotation before lowering their more white than yellow eyelids

—Such nice skin such nice skin

on the stomach of the earth and once laid down, wrapping him in an invisible towel, not like your uncle's wife

—I never dreamed that you

the navel that is getting larger and something that

not like your uncle's wife

—Sleep time, Carlos

helping you climb up onto the bed, stopping for a prayer because there was an owl in the acacia and therefore a soul was pleading for repose, ending the prayer, checking to see if the owl was silent and therefore the soul

—Thank you, ma'am

picking out a blanket, two blankets, putting out the light and the window was there, nothing existed

not the bed not the room

beyond the window, the frames where a branch was leaning in a curtsy

—Hello, Carlos, good evening

along with the branch more branches, oranges, the druggist holding out his bowl to his daughter's crucifix

—I've made you a little soup, Luísa

the doctor's widow

Dona Susete

smoking in the movies without the theater owner's daring to say with a flashlight between the rows

—Please wait, madame

the window where a wheelbarrow was approaching, a ghost carrying another ghost

ghosts of you who'd died or I'd lost and I was a ghost looking for you in the shadows, telling you, stating to you

swears to you a wheelbarrow's approaching, my father pushes himself right up to the henhouse, looking for the latch on the door in the wire fence with the light shining on round onion tears, driving the hens off their roost, dumping himself into the rubble

—There you are, wretch

condemning himself to wake up, all caught up in the rain with cans of corn and pieces of bread, calling to my mother

—Judite

calling to me

—Son

and as he calls to me

—Son

drawing me out of the begonias in the tub, all wet with water, soap, membranes, fat, blood, realizing that I was there, all shriveled and slippery, defenseless, at the brink of a wail and incapable of a wail, beginning to be born.

CHAPTER

MY SON PAULO lets himself make up whatever he feels like

and you believe him and write or pretend you believe him and you write or you don't even believe him but you write

about the smell of the gentian in Bico da Areia which for my part I never caught at all: that bit about the ebb tide, yes, down below there, when the beach got wider and you got the impression

or the certainty

that you could cross the river on foot and get to Lisbon, that bit about the ebb tide reaching me in the living room the same as the wind from the woods while I waited for my husband, fixing my hair

because I fixed my hair for him in those days

or waking up when I was sleeping alone in my half of the bed because when I reached out my arm nobody there, when I'd open my eyes nobody there, when I'd call out

—Carlos

nobody there, the bedroom was huge or maybe it wasn't so huge, it was made bigger by my being upset because he wasn't there, that always happens when there's no answer and my husband's at the window all alone too, his legs are in the room, but his body is in the dark and I can swear there's no smell of gentian over us

Paulo can make things up but your writing down lies for him has to have an effect on me

the woods maybe, the pine grove if you want, and after my husband left, not the pine grove, not the woods, the wine stains that turn the sheets sour, a stranger or someone that sleep turned into a stranger or who'd always been a stranger

asking

—Did you have a nightmare, Judite?

leaving before morning because of family or work or afraid that the neighbors would run into him leaving this house, a motor scooter down the drive, fast like a thief, Paulo inventing

—The gentian

but what gentian, dammit, the one that grew in Lisbon or, at least, they guaranteed me it would grow in Lisbon, that place which you can reach on foot, every six hours, at the time when the Tagus steals the trawlers away from me, not even any reflection of my weariness, the mirror on the wardrobe isn't nice to me and it sneers and gives me

—There it is

this hair that's turning gray and makes me wonder, strikes me, what does he know about the gentian and Bico da Areia, my son, who never wanted to come back, brought up by some rich people

they told me

who made him forget me, maybe today if we crossed paths and I said

—Paulo

no matter how much time has changed them, there are things that stay the same in people, little pieces, fragments, a movement that begins at the shoulder and holds back until it reaches the fingers, just where it held back before, maybe if

there's an example

we crossed paths on the street and I said

—Paulo

things like that, you see, there are times when a raised eyebrow is enough for me, you hang onto an eyebrow and the rest

right away, immediately, would be saying without any fault on my part, building, building up by itself, I said

—Paulo

and the fibber comes up with the gentian, well dressed, of course some rich people moves his head back and forth, notices me, wonders

—Some maid out of the past?

strokes his tie with his finger and the finger grows all over him

—Me?

on his face

it's obvious

who can it be, who can it be, some dame telling me about her sickness, pulling some trick on me, asking me for money, the seamstress we had once, the day maid, the first visitor to a room where they were waiting for him

Otília Margarida Berta

and where he could only notice a wicker chair and the brand name on the mattress

Medicinal Somnium

or Ortopédico Somnium?

instead of the person with no contours or face, the fibber kept repeating Medicinal Somnium until an elbow pulled an item of clothing out from under the sheet and he waved it for a moment before letting it drop onto the floor

—Let's get this over with fast, I've got my niece waiting

the fibber with a taste of defeat in his mind getting alarmed facing me

—Otília?

or maybe the seamstress who'd brought in lunch on a wooden tray, holding out the fork with the modesty poor people have, that offering of chicken and potatoes

—Won't you have some?

Margarida

unable, that's obvious, to explain who I am, much less the gentian, which was there

agreed

a vine or a weed that had taken on strength and tendrils, but a gentian, no way, one of those bushes that grows in damp places, that almost lifts up the soil and goes along gobbling up walls, just like some sunflowers that had been there

not marigolds

that my husband watered and that didn't last six months, skinny little blossoms in flower beds

that's the real truth and it's hard to believe that any truths could have come from my son's mouth

bothered by the bricks that Carlos was sticking into the ground that stray cats destroyed in the fall or that I destroyed

the stray cats didn't ruin anything, there aren't any stray cats by the sea, I ruined them with a hammer on the day my husband was putting his junk in a suitcase, I mean what were his mistress's clothes

not his, how can you ask that, how could they have been his?

—I'm leaving, Judite

and I kept on destroying them with the hammer right to today, destroying Carlos too, kneeling in the yard with Paulo, whimpering that he knew what he was doing, luckily a friend of mine who ran the nearby café called on me to do some work that helped us stay alive, some quick quarter-hours with no useless words and with closed curtains as at the same time there was barking in the street and pine cones on the roof, episodes my son doesn't know about because I let him play by the gate, charmed, a half-dozen shacks farther on, by a girl on a tricycle who married a doctor and all that

look what we've come to

as for the gentians, who cares, the only one I can remember was when I went to Almada, on the corner below the school

no, before Almada, studying in Setúbal, in a chalet with a slate roof where nobody lived, even though it was deserted an aimless light wandering through the rooms warned me

—You're going to die, Judite

and I, who was always dumb, listening to my heart, afraid that it would stop and it was stopping

and, having died, weeping, all sorry for myself on the pillow, wondering, maybe it was a gentian here in Bico da Areia and right off I remembered death, my mother who even though she was blind and, no matter how many coins were laid on her eyes, scolding me from her coffin

—I always told you

and Paulo would immediately think, for no reason at all, that it was because of his father, that mania about his father, that a clown, a faggot, and songs, and dances, when in fact he was a clerk in a jewelry store on the courthouse square, thousands of different hours behind thousands of different counters, chimes, pendulums, cuckoos bowing and not bowing which, adding them all up, with a line underneath, gave the age of the world and the age of the world must have got him all mixed up because he got the days mixed up and he'd miss meetings with me, he went with me on the train to my mother's, the windowpane was clear but it was little more than a shape on the seat beside me, grade crossings, a cow running away in a whirl by a curve, head, flank, tail, if I held out a piece of fruit from the basket from the reflection came

—I don't feel like any, Judite

I could make out, against a clump of willows, my colleagues who were spiteful with envy

—We always said that he

intrigued with that fiancé who was impossible to touch, whose lips didn't give off words even though they fogged up the landscape

he'd draw my name with his finger for what he was telling me

my mother would run over his features and model an absence in the air

—What is it about your husband, Judite?

I would point to the window when the shadow of the medlar tree cast its shadow over the veranda

—Try the medlar tree, mother

not a gentian

Carlos, in the reverse of things, except on the wardrobe mirror where the present was authentic,

—Carlos

at first just the dresser with more objects than there was room for, including the little copper fish I thought was lost and it is back there

looking at it without any fish being in the mirror anymore

the usual curtains in reverse, a corner of the wall left-handed, I spoke to the wardrobe, happy about the fish with its tail up

—Carlos

and sad at losing it when I got out of bed

maybe if I went back quickly and didn't give the dresser time to hide it, I could still find it

—I want my fish, Carlos

even though Carlos hadn't reached the wardrobe mirror, waiting on Carlos a bit, and Carlos asked

—What fish?

the curtains, yes, the corner of the wall, yes, for a minute the gravestone where I played hopscotch and when I took a better look the terrace café, the owner coming for me through the alley and on into the yard

—I know quite well that you're alone, open the door, Judite

because my husband, because before there was my husband and my husband would take his jacket off the hook and with the dish-cloth hanging around his neck

—I'm going into the woods for a bit

with the pups behind him in a flurry of pine cones and clumps of turf, old cuckold, old cuckold, strange as it may seem it still happens to me, almost without my noticing it, settling onto the bed, facing the wardrobe where there's another dresser, the drapes I replaced ten months ago in July and instead of the café and the bridge there's a hairdresser, a movie, a firehouse, no café owner, no trace of Gypsies, I look at the wardrobe where there are flowerpots, balconies, the twins in the pink building braiding each other's hair, I say

—Carlos

realizing that I'm saying

—Carlos

after calling him

not true, knowing that I'm calling you

—Carlos

in the hope that they can't hear me in there when

—Carlos

I can't see you appear in the mirror, suspicious of me, a touch of leftover makeup on the corner of your mouth, this furniture that repeats you and I'm annoyed with you

—What's this all about?

or maybe I'm annoyed with you because you say

—I'm not capable, Judite

only in the mirror, not in the room, in the mirror, with the little fish with its tail up in your hand

—I'm not capable, Judite

or the hoe for working on the gentian as though there was a gentian, agreeing that a gentian did exist, ever since you stayed there in the mirror for a second, ever since I imagined Paulo coming for me in Bico da Areia, worried about me

can you assure me that he's worried about me, sir?

and Bico da Areia, Alto do Galo, Trafaria, so different now, no more horses, or maybe they're still in the reflection of a reflection that I just happened upon in a patch of rain with my nose above it, sniffing out the past, somebody hard to recognize drawing squares in chalk on a stone surrounded by laurels where letters and dates, the letters gave me the idea that it's my name, the dates are worn off, the caretaker of the cemetery, who used to say Juditinha

—When will it be your turn, Judite?

and, most of all, my husband who doesn't want to cross through the mirror and touch me, if only his hand

Stop your kidding

was getting close to mine a voice that was a funny little laugh

—Bath time, Carlos

that stole him away from me and my husband, I don't know where, I think someplace with wild doves and a man fixing his pillow while he picked up his shotgun, said

—It's not my fault, Judite

and since it wasn't his fault, a blonde wig like the one on the woman who was wrapping him up in a towel, who held him in her arms and passed by me without seeing us on her way to the bedroom, my son would disappear from underfoot whenever someone, the owner of the café, the electrician, the school principal called

—Judite

Carlos hiding in the palm trees while the gentian

let's admit it

was breaking up in the wind, with every crack dirty wings in the brambles, a bird quieting down and stretching out a claw

—Go get the doves, boy

the vine kept on waving in the wind even though there's no wall, I've sold the house, I live far away from the pine grove, the waves, the flower beds, lilac petals fall into my eyes so I can't see you running from the beach to the house or me on the steps waiting, you don't have to believe me, but there were never any other men, Carlos, it was always you, you were the one who gave me wine and lowered your voice, you said you were there but you didn't dare come in, you weren't like a child, you were a child, I've brought some money Dona Judite, I'll pay, a child, and I unbutton my blouse, in no hurry, stockings, panties

—Sleepy time, Carlos

putting out the light, hesitating for a minute, thinking there are footsteps and no footsteps, they were the trees in the orchard, I was wrong, his breath, his smell, the surprise that scares me at first and charms me afterward

—I never dreamed that you

what I mean is, that even though I waited for you to I didn't dream that the café owner

what do I care about the café owner, I didn't dream that you, say Judite, please say Judite, don't go to sleep now

—Sleep time, Carlos

make me feel that I, believe that I, my colleagues spotting my new lipstick, my lighter hair, almost blonde

blonde

their curiosity you've got to tell us, Judite

—We never dreamed that he

the mulberry trees in Almada playing checkers with the shadows, going down to the river, here there was a wall, here in olden days the kings, here was an old arch, the ground-floor flat of the police informer they'd pull along by a leash and the poor devil, sobbing with fright, up to the station house, you were looking at me as though you didn't see me and you knew I was looking at you, my braid got undone and rubbed against your nose, for the first time I in the wardrobe mirror with the little copper fish, the corner of the wall, left-handed, and you're here, you're here, we can cross the river on foot and get to Lisbon, hold out an arm wet with soap and water and find your shoulder because I'm not sleeping alone, the surprise of a body

because I'm not dreaming of you, I don't tell my colleagues, and they say you've got to tell us, Judite, what's it feel like afterward, what do you say, did you feel

we imagine

like singing, sure that everybody on the street understands, is looking at us and noticing how horrible and then at home my father, aren't you ashamed, Dolores, I don't know if I can take it, all those heads together in the coffee shop

—We never dreamed that he imagined he

asking the waiter for another coffee, blushing, satisfied, another coffee hurry up, the rice cake between plate and mouth, my father leaving, from this moment on, you're no longer my daughter Dolores, my mother behind my father telling the dog to be quiet and the dog wasn't quiet, don't do that, Joaquim, I'm lucky I haven't got a father Dolores, my mother in the village running her hand over my face, believing me, too much sugar in the coffee because I was distracted by the talk, his chest is bony, his beard prickled at first, it left a little mark and later on it didn't prickle, if Carlos had a mustache maybe tickling on the lip, I would laugh at the tickling and out of nervousness too

just out of nervousness I think, the mustache would be fine, he'd get mad

—Do you think I'd be enough of a boob to have a mustache, Judite?

and that was the end of the tickling, and, pleasantly, this coffee is mush with all the sugar in it, little secrets, whispering, the waiter in the coffee shop flirting under the pretext of drying the table for us

—It's all wet, sweeties

Dolores, going along, batting her eyelids like she was with Carlos, maybe lover's got a friend, you've got to ask him, casually like, if maybe he's got a friend, a little innocent question, see, in the middle of a conversation, the waiter with his wiping and Dolores, with lots of blinking, Dolores to a man who was already old and was wearing a wedding ring

didn't you notice the wedding ring?

plenty of white hairs, a pencil behind his ear, his way of talking

—It's all wet, sweeties

thirty years old at least, he was missing a tooth on one side

—It's all wet, sweeties

the mulberry trees in Almada playing checkers with the shadows, we'd go down to the river and there was a wall here, probably there were kings here in other times

Dom Pedro would arrive with his ships

there's a very old archway here, the police informer accepted the leash, walked on his knees, there was something about Carlos's expression, his fright, a woman was beating him with the wicker mat, the garbage can they'd turned upside down, the herons coming back were pecking at the oil on the river where Dom Pedro kept his ships

—I'm not capable, Judite

meaning

—I'm not a fascist, comrades

don't rumple the quilt, blood on his lips, hands begging

—I'm not a fascist, comrades

Lisbon was waiting for the king with torches

Great friende he wast of merrymente

and Dom Pedro's ships in the mud were all decorated, his tomb is in Alcobaça isn't it, the stone beard that never prickled anybody, tell us what it was like, what do you say to them, what do you feel afterward

you feel a wish to die, feel that sin is suffocating us, that the sea is covering this house, that the decorated vessels, canoes, trawlers, those ships that have oars as the hooks and blades of the oars crossed back and forth across the benches

the fishermen on the shore

—Come with us, Judite

my husband was in the window, his legs were in the room, his body was in the darkness, disappearing in the pine grove among the mares and the owls, taking him in my arms, announcing

you've got to tell us, Judite, what was it like, what's it like, chubby Dolores, from this moment on you're no longer my daughter

—Bath time, Carlos

you don't feel like dying, you feel that we've changed, you don't understand in what direction but we've changed, a thickness in the bones we didn't have before, a quiet fire in the blood, a door that's being opened to the inside of things, people are considerate

—Dona Judite

from one moment to the next

—Dona Judite

I'm solemn with myself

—Dona Judite

my mother was asking my opinion, should I do it this way or do it that way and she did it

—You're right

Dom Pedro's ships were slowly leaving, the stone beard

—Milady

friendly, well mannered, not the least bit shrouded in his tomb, reaching out his arm to me

—Do me the honor, Dona Judite

you feel such great peace, if they would only let me

word of honor

I would stay like this for the rest of my life and the king, approving me

not like your father, approving me

—I am in agreement, milady

not loving his squire more than should be mentioned in these pages, loving me

picking you up and laying you on the bed, nothing to prickle or hurt, the smooth skin

—Carlos

the fingers reaching over this clamp, this mole, your not seeing me and looking at me at the same time that you didn't see me and you knew that I was looking at you for the first time, with me in the mirror with the little copper fish *you feel the way a little copper fish feels when it's come back out of the dresser drawer from among bottles, pictures, the empty matchbox that was there by mistake*

and you're here, you're here, don't let my colleagues

—We never dreamed that he

mimic your gestures, make fun of me, forbid me, at a different table, to give in, swaying

—Such long lashes, Judite

the waiter with the wedding ring on the pretext of wiping the table

—It's all wet, sweetie

spare me the railroad station where there's no ship of Dom Pedro's, a parking lot on one side, a marketplace with no market on the other, a few tumbledown stands that is, and a poster that's peeling off a tree

a faggot, a clown, he puts on makeup, a wig, make the people laugh, Carlos

a rabbit in a cage to keep him company, without his workcoat on, the waiter is older, thirty-six, thirty-seven, those smells of age, pointing to the animal that was pushing up against the cage

—He knows me, sweetie

that was pushing up against the cage all the while, he opened up the little door and gave a whack on the back of its neck, the kind my mother knew how to give and I didn't, no more

—Dona Judite

Judite once more, she doesn't ask my opinions, whether I should do it this way or that way, covering my words with her hand

—Be quiet

handing him the hanging thing that had stopped snuffling

—Take your silly animal

and the waiter, who might not have been telling me

—The poor little critter hasn't done you any harm, sweetie

because with the maneuvering of the locomotive no sounds could be heard, the train was quiet and as soon as the train was quiet, there was a soft little voice that made me hate him all the more, you won't protest, you won't get excited, you'll take it, I'll bet that there've been a lot of orphanages in your life, a lot of buried dogs, a lot of women, take care, so long

—Come on out of here, sweetie

in the empty cage there was some lettuce or something like it, the waiter was nudging the rabbit in hopes it would give a little leap

—Give it up, he's not jumping

I even peeked into the flat but it couldn't be seen from the street, the locomotive could be seen, filling everything with smoke, a guy with a lever was directing the operation, on the circus poster my husband was dancing

—Dance, Carlos

tents with little curtains left over, a cot in one of them

or so it seemed to me

where a pregnant cat got mad at me, the hair on the mustache gives the impression that it prickles and it doesn't prickle, little secrets, sighs, grade crossings under the herons by the Tagus where there are faded houses and sickly olive trees, deserted tennis courts with an echo of balls

Paulo, who makes things up as he sees fit and you believe him and writing

the waiter from the coffee shop put the rabbit back into its cage with the intention that the animal

—Your stupid animal

if only he'd nudge him again and he doesn't nudge him, I guarantee, a lot of orphanages, a lot of buried dogs, a lot of women like him

on in years and in pencil

having fun with the rabbit because poor devils like us and while the rabbit stopped answering take care, so long, if I asked

—What about your wife?

the hopeful little look

—One of these days she'll come back, sweetie

so there was a rose in the napkin as he served it with the soup bowl, held on by a piece of tape

—I kept the chicken soup for you

the next day when he served me my coffee he sent over the tray with the flair of a magician

—Good afternoon, sweetie

Dolores's teasing

—He's crazy about you

curious heads, alert

—What do you feel afterward?

you feel that you're a little copper fish calling for help, that the marigolds have forgotten about me, that the sea has disappeared, that the bridge doesn't exist, that you're facing the mirror that's a darker piece of sky

—What about the sky?

asking the waiter if he'd lend me the rabbit, my wife didn't understand but the rabbit did, the waiter said the animal didn't hurt her

—Go away, sweetie

it didn't bother her, it didn't hate her, but how do you say

what do you say

you people teach me

to a waiter in a coffee shop that it had nothing to do with his annoying me or getting me mad or hurting me, it's not that

how do you tell a waiter in a coffee shop over a railroad station that the rabbit doesn't matter to me

how could a rabbit bother me?

that I haven't found any other way of protesting against

I haven't found any other way of protesting against myself, against the café owner

—Don't lock the door on me because I'll knock it down, Judite

against the pine cones on the wall and me all alone inside here, being dragged naked to the station house, if I went to the butcher in São João they'd dance around me, your husband's a faggot, how do you tell a waiter in a coffee shop who's buried so much poverty behind him, so many women, so many pups and the locomotive whistle stops me from hearing

—Be patient and bury me

and he kept the soup bowl in the cupboard because my wife will be coming back, she's going to come back, maybe a schoolteacher when I wipe the table for them.

—It's all wet, be careful

will come up with me on my Tuesdays off, I'll serve them the wedding glasses of which I've got four left, the locomotive with one last jerk, just like the rabbit before the rabbit went on my fingers, it wasn't the rabbit, what do I mean the rabbit, it was me, leaning over the wardrobe

—Carlos?

and in the wardrobe mirror, ships in which Dom Pedro was coming from Almada to Lisbon, what's it like, what was it like, what do you feel afterward, you have to tell us Judite, expressions of envy or of doubt, and I said

—I'm not exaggerating, word of honor, you feel a joy that's so gre . . .

if only my mother could stick her hand into the cage that's the house, grab me by the behind, pull me out

—Come here

my nose was always twitching, lady, lady

hold me up by her arm, wet with soap and water

—*Bath time, Carlos*

what can I look for you with, a knee that bumps up against your absence, the head that slips off my pillow over to yours and there's nobody on the pillow, even though there's nobody on the pillow

I'm not exaggerating, word of honor, happiness so big

I give in completely, make such eyes at a faggot that it's too much, my mother says

—Your making all those eyes at a faggot is too much

grabbing me by the ears, finding the spot between my vertebrae, giving me a lesson and I'm all stiff, whimpering

not so stiff, maybe my tail a little

I'm stiff, whimpering, the slap, the mimosas, at least you can hope it's the mimosas, me as a bride coming out of the church

—This is where it hits you, watch out

the photographer hidden in his camera

—Closer together, closer together

Paulo, who makes up whatever he feels like, and you believe him and

write or pretend to be writing that you believe him and you write, not even
believing him but you write

if you believe me, write about my husband giving me the little
copper fish

—Judite

in Bico da Areia or here

—I've come to get you, Judite

write about the smell of the gentian, which for my part I never
caught, the smell of the ebb tide, yes, just as soon as the beach grew
wider, and you got the impression

sure

that you could cross the river on foot and get to Lisbon, the ebb
tide getting into me in the living room all mixed in with the river
while I was combing my hair

because I'd comb my hair for him in those days, write about
flower beds bordered by pieces of tile that my husband was sticking
into the ground and that I smashed with the hammer on the day
when he

I didn't do it with the hammer, write that the flower beds are
intact, the vine's alive, the waiter at the coffee shop

—Your coffee, sweetie

you can write that I'm fine, tell Paulo I'm fine, I haven't changed
all that much, I think about him sometimes, every now and then

you need time, better clothes, dyed hair

I give him permission to visit me, I promise, he can poke his
hand into the cage that's the house, find me in some corner drawing back and wanting, he grabs me by the behind, pulls me out

—Come here, mother

I'm not exaggerating, word of honor, such happiness

finds the spot between my vertebrae, the blade of his hand while
I'm stiff, whimpering

not stiff, my tail just a little, I propose to him

—Now

now that the king is arriving in his ships from Almada, write
down a railroad station with a locomotive that's maneuvering and
yet there's no danger of my being heard, the marketplace without a

market, a poster hanging from a tree trunk and showing a clown dancing, write that my son is putting me back into the cage, closing the little wire door, checking in the wardrobe mirror to see if his father is with me

and since his father's with me, he waits in the yard at Bico da Areia until we call him

—Paulo

waiting by the cedar tree at Príncipe Real until one of us

one of the rabbits that are pushing, silent, furtive

—He knows me, sweetie

raises the shade, lifts the curtain and Paulo at the entrance to the living room is holding a car with wooden wheels and looking at us in the mirror where lips move without giving off any words, we go dim, little by little, as the light grows dim

believe me and write or pretend that you believe me and write or don't believe me, but write that we're growing dim with the dimming of the light and only the Gypsies' horses coming back from the beach and thirty or forty feet away is the ragamuffin who was to marry a doctor and nobody can say whether or not she got married, paying no attention to Paulo until the ragamuffin grows dim too and the mirror is finally dark, the bedroom is dark, the living room is dark and anything else that can't be seen, of course, but I could make out the little copper fish I thought was lost and now that it was impossible to touch it, I realized that it had never gone away from there.

CHAPTER

WHEN I THINK ABOUT those performers dressed like Chinese who set up a table in the center of the stage, some bamboo poles standing up on the table and on the top of each pole there's a plate spinning around, eight or nine of them, that is

—The customer at table nine, Soraia

eight or nine plates spinning around, horizontal and fast at first and then slower and slower and more and more wobbly, about to fall off and stopped from falling by the little man who keeps running back and forth and giving them another spin by twirling the bamboo pole, one or two plates always off balance, one or two plates slipping, one or two plates that you can picture in pieces on the floor and yet they start moving again, saved by just a few seconds, tilting and hesitating and still dancing, when I think about myself I think about the little man trotting beside the table in his fake Oriental costume and his mandarin mustache that is ready to fall off, stuck under his nose with some glue, as he rushes from right to left and works hard to keep all those tears dancing, each plate's a tear that has to be kept from falling and so he gives a pole a spin, another pole, the one on the end that no smile could ever hold back, yesterday I thought I saw my father, knowing that it couldn't be my father, my father's dead, with Sissi who couldn't have been Sissi, Sissi's in Spain or maybe back to being a man

and again trouble with the plates on the bamboo poles, I go left and right running to help hold the tears, the mandarin mustache blows off and gets into my mouth, I keep them from falling onto the floor

—Don't do that on me, don't break

or maybe

—Sissi

or maybe

—Father

he's disappearing down a side street with garages where I got the idea that Rui, and Rui's in the cemetery too or with a syringe in Chelas, seeing me without seeing me

—Not now, Paulo

and that plate, the last one, careful with the last one, spinning the pole until the pieces come back into place, fragments, disconnected episodes that memory was bringing together and forming an afternoon on the beach with Vânia for example

—Come here, Rui, quick

and to me, if I got there with him, stiffening in her blouse

—I don't want any gab with you

the plane tree at the hospital where Mr. Vivaldo wasn't touching the ground, the maid from the dining room in the silence of the bedroom

—Aren't you sleepy, Paulo?

Dona Helena facing the bicycle in the laundry room not a person, just a kerchief, everything swirling about side by side on the table, yesterday my father with Sissi and their not recognizing me but how could they have recognized me since I've changed over the years, I had hopes that my uncle

—Your father's coming to work with me, did you know that?

convinced that the plates should be moving in the opposite direction

if only I could make them move in the opposite direction

a different life I've invented, such foolishness, looking at what's happened to us afterward, I thought I was living with an old couple

who couldn't even take care of themselves

who took care of me and my wife from the kitchen

I must have had a wife

—Word of honor?

nothing but voice and astonishment, a pause in the chinaware and in that pause the bamboos were spinning faster, a screech of clowns or the cackle of a lipstick kiss looking for me in the living room

—What are you looking for?

no stage, no mandarin worried about a dozen

eight or nine

—*The customer at table nine, Soraia*

plates, visiting my father without understanding why in spite of Dona Helena and Mr. Couceiro, who scolded me by not scolding, the sketching with the cane meant

—I forbid you

or not even I forbid you, asking

—Don't go

my father was opening the door grudgingly and looking over his shoulder at someone or other who was disappearing into the bedroom, hiding I don't know what he'd picked up from the rug, a pearl, a brooch

that showed what he was

in his pocket

—Come in

my wish spotted right away, my not accusing him

I wasn't accusing him

reproaching him

I wasn't reproaching him

my son or the one who thinks he's my son

if I could only get to tell him at least

—*You're not my son*

and his not believing

believing

his not believing

—*Father*

I, *who can't do it, I'd love to do it but I can't do it, the woman before Judite, squeezing her hand against her breast, says*

—*Don't be upset, Carlos*

or maybe

—Bath time, Carlos

or maybe I say

—Pet me

and my uncle taking aim at the wild doves, a rag pile of wings in the brambles, little hearts beating with the blood all run out, the woman separating my fingers one by one and my fingers

—No

feeling the sticky warmth of the blood, I was thinking don't make me, I don't want to and she said

—Feel me, Carlos

as though nothing existed anymore except the wild doves, the bath, the woman, my uncle's wife, that is, grieving under the blanket, you're going to kill me boy, you're killing me boy

—Feel me, Carlos

my son accusing me, reproaching me, my uncle's dog

—Go get the doves, Carlos

calling me one Sunday while he tied up the setter by the collar at the end of the judge's vineyard

—Look what I do to dogs that don't obey, Carlos

and the judge, in shirtsleeves, watching him

—Look what I do to dogs that don't obey, Carlos

a two-year-old male that had run off with a dove, my uncle slipped in a cartridge without letting go of the leash, ordering me

—Take hold of the stock, Carlos

and the police informer, unfolding the dirty feathers that were his arms, waved his little wings

—I'm not a fascist, I'm your friend, comrades

a boy with a hammer, and one with a pistol

—Take hold of the stock, Carlos

the cartridge disappearing with a click, the judge on a stepladder with the basket of oranges, the setter rubbing up against us, licking us, whimpering with pleasure, my uncle tugged on the leash and a kind of whine of surprise, his jaw dropped, looking for us, the judge was peeling an orange, his mouth almost saying

—Alberto

*but only the orange getting crushed in his hand, a small thread of piss on
my uncle's shoe and my uncle tightening the leash*
—You son of a bitch
ordering me
—Put the butt to your shoulder, Carlos
*pressing the butt against my shoulder then, placing the barrel at the ear of
the dog, who was beginning to understand, who understood*
I remember the orchard, I remember the orchard so well
the police informer's face, all eyebrows, all gums when the pistol
—Comrades
crumpling onto the ground and pushing stones along with his
nose, breaking them up with his fingernails
—Comrades
his neck was bent over and the pistol was at the back, the hammer was waiting
—So?
*my uncle aimed at the setter's ear and the branches on the trees were so
thick that no one could hear the shot, no one heard the shot so that no one, not
even me almost, heard*
—The trigger
*it's a little tongue that's not hard to move, you tighten up, that is, you bend
your finger, you look beyond the judge who was shaded by the treetops, not by
the shot, you don't notice the shot, you notice your shoulder jumped, my uncle
let go of the leash and the setter was inert, brown and white marks*
not a single red mark
*brown and white marks, the remains of some piss, a tooth in the space
between his lips, the judge took off his cap, my uncle's wife was separating my
fingers one by one, and my fingers said I don't want to*
—Feel me, Carlos
—Don't worry, Carlos
—Feel me, Carlos
*my uncle leaned over the setter the way the boy with the pistol did over the
police informer, who kept on squeezing the orange*
a stone
in his hand, not a single red mark
—I'm not a fascist, I'm a friend, comrades

a sandal in a strange position, the boy with the hammer took off the man's wristwatch or the little heart of the doves, it's a mistake, comrades, ask the authorities if it isn't a mistake, a square watch, lines instead of numbers, the boy with the hammer said to the boy with the pistol

no, to everybody

no, to himself

—It won't be any use to him anymore, will it?

my uncle said to the judge who, because of a problem of water rights had sent my grandfather off to Africa, was wiping the lining of his cap with a cloth

—You bury him

if my mother was talking to her sister-in-law by the threshing floor we could catch her words over here, people's conversations carry farther than the wind, the shotgun blast got to the judge who'd sent my grandfather to Africa

—Get a shovel and bury him, not in my vineyard, in yours

he went through the fence, knocking down one of the posts, scattering the oranges with his shoe, my grandfather had come back from Angola with fevers, the police informer's watch kept going, Judite said that the king, great friende he wast of merrymente, was leaving Almada aboard his ships or maybe on the trawlers that were all decorated along the river, the shotgun followed the judge as the shovel dug, you just saw what I do to dogs that don't obey me, doctor, the judge was cleaning his cap, my uncle was sitting with me on a rock

—Rest here, Carlos

filled with the emotion of the orchard, the blackcaps imitating commas as they mussed up the grass, does this thing work or doesn't it, neighbor, give me an orange to taste, he tasted it, threw it away, not even the fruit's any good, doctor, the orange hit the judge's legs and went off, feel me, Carlos, not there, on this side where I'm more me, don't be afraid, feel me, little dove bones, the sticky warmth of blood, don't make me, I don't want to

the judge finished covering the setter with dirt

—Do I have your permission to leave, Alberto?

the cap that he didn't dare put back on his head and that the cloth had kept cleaning, the gleam of the oranges in an acid light, my grandfather recovered from the fevers from Africa

—Alberto

I remember a couple of men

my grandfather and someone else?

playing checkers under the trellis but how could it be my grandfather since my grandfather's sick

—*Alberto*

I remember an oil wick in the shadows, our cooling his forehead, my uncle's wife pouring water into the tub, bath time Carlos, table nine Soraia, and I was turning down vermouth, as though the manager was my servant, and the manager was obsequious, ordering a bottle of French champagne, please, arms that unwrapped me from the towel

—*I never dreamed that you*

my son straightening out the plates that were tears

—*Sissi*

my son

—*Father*

the judge

—*Do I have your permission to leave, Alberto?*

my uncle's shotgun rose up from his belly to his head and went back to his belly

the gleam of the oranges in an acid light while my grandfather's coffin, decorated like the king's ships, was on the mule cart, my uncle got up from the rock, calling me

—*Carlos*

he crossed over the wire fence beside me, knocking down another post, without even a side glance at the cap that lived all alone in the big house

—*You can go to shitty hell, judge*

and as we walked back home, accompanied by the creaking of the trees, I realized that I was ceasing to exist for him, my mother was looking at me, my younger brother, held by the hoe

—*You hurt me*

so I stopped to watch the ants in a crack in the tile

my father was opening the door grudgingly and looking over his shoulder at someone or other who was disappearing into the bedroom, he received me while hiding I don't know what he'd picked up from the rug

a pearl, a brooch

that showed what he was, in his pocket

—Come in

my wish, spotted right away, of not being there accusing him
reproaching him

I wasn't reproaching him

I'm not reproaching you father, you've got your bamboo poles
too, your plates that spin horizontally and fast at first and
afterward

right afterward spin slowly and wobbly, about to fall and you
spin them again, there are always one or two slipping now and you
picture them in pieces on the floor and in spite of that, all of them
saved in a matter of seconds

—Who's in the bedroom, father?

the bamboo poles go faster faster

—Nobody

in the same way that nobody's dead in Almada, a pickup truck
took him away just as the police lieutenant

—You made a mistake, lieutenant, there's no informer here

—Who's in the bedroom, father?

my father rumpling and smoothing the pillow on the sofa for
lack of a cap he could clean

—What do you mean bedroom?

keeping all those tears spinning

what my son calls all those tears

the one from the maid from the dining room for example

—Are you really leaving, Paulo?

not stopping me, not getting mad, the covered window uncovered and in the window was a small hill with a crown of cabbages,
and beyond the crown of cabbages the Jewish cemetery, marble
tombs without names or flowers, a six-pointed star on the gate
keeping watch over the deceased, the blouse with anchors helped
me fold the clothes in two parallel lines

two plates had fallen off the poles

onto her cheeks, onto her chin, onto the overcoat where she hadn't
sewn the hem

—Are you really leaving, Paulo?

yesterday I thought I saw my father just the way I seem to run into Gabriela sometimes, that is, Gabriela I'm sure in the distance, her way of walking, of tilting her head, maybe Gabriela when she's gotten a few steps closer, she's gotten a bit fat, she's dyed her hair darker and, a few seconds later, the skirt is maroon instead of scarlet, the nose is changing, it's pointed, long, not Gabriela, a stranger startled by my extended hand, visiting you in the hospital dining room, seeing you without your seeing me

God damn it, pretending you don't see me

with the cart of pots and pans, getting you mixed up with the redhead who works with you or wanting you to be the redhead and seeing that it is you, the way you push the cart, wave to a patient

—Are you really leaving, Paulo?

no quivering lip showing as it covered her lower teeth, holding back the tip of her tongue and her upset in the same way that she would hold the knife cutting bread, the blade on the board and the tongue on alert, giving orders, you're back in the dining room and you notice me

you don't notice me

the

—Hi Paulo

no suffering or parallel tears or even surprise

you're faking, I don't believe it, you've got to be faking

a jolly camaraderie, the naturalness that crushes me

—Hi Paulo

and you're not faking, you're sincere, I'm dead in you, how unjust, please explain to me how a person can forget so fast, that camaraderie, that naturalness, that I didn't treat you all that bad did I?

—Hi Paulo

when just a few months ago

six, seven, fewer than seven?

stopping me from looking into your face, the pillowcase whispering don't say anything, I'm fine, relax, I'd never noticed your mole or that gleam in your hair, the mole maybe, at first, because people do lose those things, but the gleam in your hair, and now the gleam in your hair, your scorning me, the casual way with which the rich dribble out their alms while

I don't know who to

—Just a minute, I'll be right back

your alms

—Hi Paulo

staring at me in a hurry, with no pillowcase, lighting up for a patient

—Carmindo

the little folds of your eyes aren't for me, they're for him, you, filling out your smock, emptying out for me

—It's been a long time hasn't it?

your taking a step, two steps, to hide this thing here in the throat, attempting a happy expression that doesn't come, calling to you before you stop hearing me, insisting that I, guaranteeing that I, that both of us, that the mole, that the gleam in your hair, four steps, five steps, the tree trunk where Mr. Vivaldo swung all night, it's funny the way he was empty and wasn't, seven steps, I mustn't forget

eight steps and right away it's impossible, the hole in Mr. Vivaldo's sole and through the hole his sock, I'll tell you about the hole

not about the hole

I'll tell you anything at all, eleven steps, twelve steps, which will make you leave the patient and you stay there, it could have been that you're still in the bedroom, my suitcase is still in the closet, beside the mailbox and on the wall of the stairway Marina & Diogo, replace the Marina & Diogo with Gabriela & Paulo, don't you like Gabriela & Paulo, don't you think it's better than Gabriela & Carmindo, Gabriela & Carmindo sounds funny, there's no ring to it, it's off, it doesn't fit, the cart twenty steps away and good-bye going into the dining room with a clatter of aluminum, who's in the bedroom father, and my father smoothing and rumpling the sofa for lack of a cap he could clean, for lack of a quilt

—What do you mean bedroom?

the redhead waiting for you to help with the dishes, crates could be seen, heads of hair, the glow of a stove, quite clearly you could see the chalk, the charcoal, the pencil, I was going to swear that with my blood too, how stupid since I was the one who was through, not she, I got tired of you, on every plane tree, even on Mr. Vivaldo's, you noticed Gabriela & Carmindo and I'll almost bet Gabriela & Carmindo while the two of us together, women's lies, women's little betrayals, I'm fine, relax, such a rigmarole, don't say anything what an act, so credulous, so dumb, Gabriela at the door to the dining room

too many steps, it was over

—It was nice seeing you, Paulo

just like that, from a distance, not Gabriela, somebody else, I really don't know who, but somebody else, some stranger because only a stranger

—It was nice seeing you, Paulo

not Gabriela, Gabriela's waiting for me

of course

and I'm emptying the suitcase, giving in to weakness, to pity, not to weakness, to pity

settling into the chair facing the window where there's the small hill with a crown of cabbages, the marble tombs of the Jewish cemetery, listening to you bustling about the room with a basin or a scrub brush, setting up the ironing board on its lame legs and Gabriela & Paulo, an indulgence on my part, Gabriela & Paulo, the oil lamp spitting out bits of anger that could have been mine

—Who's in the bedroom, father?

I mean

—Who's in the bedroom, Gabriela?

Gabriela surprised at me, the bamboo poles

faster, faster

pretending

—Nobody

like my father

—Nobody

his eyes were so easy to understand

—Have pity on me, Paulo

just like the eyes on the judge burying the setter in the gleam of the oranges, he diverted my great-grandfather's water to his orchard, his cornfield, my great-grandfather set fire to his barn, he was having dinner when they came for him

I wonder if the orchard still exists

my father's uncle, little at that time, silent in a corner and twelve years in Zemza do Itombe from where an ivory doll yellow with age was left, a black woman with a little black boy on her back, unwrapping it, my father's uncle was almost a man by then, silent in a corner, the doctor with the return of the fevers

the orchard existed then

increasing the injections, an oil wick in the shadows, cousins who were playing checkers under the trellis waiting, in their Sunday suits which served as mourning clothes

—Is he dead?

the judge, without taking off his cap, following the funeral from his balcony

Gabriela & Carmindo, Carmindo's suitcase instead of mine, a bronze mermaid decorating the radio

the next morning my father's uncle

—Go get the doves, Carlos

I say to my father, pointing to the door of the bedroom that didn't open on Príncipe Real, it opened on the Travessa do Abarracamento in Peniche, an office building where there were desks, file cabinets, telephones

—Go get the dove, father

every time the dove moved, even muffling its cough, even on tiptoes, a floorboard telling me

—It's there

if only I'd waited for Gabriela and followed her and even if I hadn't waited for Gabriela, hadn't followed her, I spent the night on the street, I saw Marina's window lighted and ours was out, climbing up the little hill with cabbages nothing but an old man heating a coffeepot on the third floor left and every time the floorboard creaked my father's eyes

—Have pity on me, Paulo

as if I could have pity that I didn't have on him, I was holding a setter by the leash, lick my pant legs, go ahead, weep with pleasure, go ahead, see what I do to dogs that don't obey, doctor, my father's eyes

—I make so little at the club

and why should it bother me that he makes so little at the club, tell me, don't draw back, stop pissing, stop wetting my legs

cut out that pissing on my legs

putting the butt against my shoulder, turning the barrel toward you as you were starting to understand, understood, trying to get away with a whisper

—Paulo

I didn't wait for Gabriela, didn't follow her, I went back to the hospital a month later

no, a week later

no, three days later

the psychiatric section, the emergency room, a butt friend, a coin for a cup of coffee friend, the plane trees where Carmindo wouldn't hang himself, why not, if Mr. Vivaldo, who was more important, hung himself, the cart with pots and pans, bowls, let me help you, let me take it, and instead of

—Hi Paulo

a gesture of annoyance, a patient sleeping in a flower bed with pieces of paper sticking out of his pockets, the redhead taking your part

—What do you want nosing around here, you dope, beat it

I was swinging on that plane tree with the hole in the sole of my empty shoe

my father at Príncipe Real just like on the rock with his uncle while the judge was burying the setter, not a doctor of laws with his authority and his black robes, a peasant in a cap afraid of people, which was obvious from the way his jaw was muttering fear, the stones in the dirt on which the shovel was sliding

—How'd you like an ivory black woman, judge?

his foreman, farther on, forgetting about his repairs on the tractor, watching them

—Because you need a black woman, judge, an ivory statue to fix your lunch

my father with no blonde wig but with false eyelashes

no, my father in shorts with a bandage on a healthy knee because he liked bandages, when I think about myself I think about those performers who set up a table in the center of the stage

—What happened to the bandage, father?

and the false lashes blinked in surprise, as he opened the powder box and used his little fingers to fix the corner of his eyelid, you can rest easy, father, they're not falling off

—The bandage?

the small living room was intact in my memory, traces of ashes on the yellow sofa, the answering machine where there were never any messages, the start of some breathing and the sound of hanging up, the customer apologizing to reporters, recognize the voices Soraia and just imagine the little present they'd get for free, it's not that I don't trust you but put yourself in my place, don't get all worked up

the posters, the bottles, almost always near empty

one of them without a stopper

the pot where they left the money, bills slowly extracted from a wallet, spit on the finger and I thought there were two and in the end just one, it's the same price, isn't it, ridiculous little gifts, key rings, datebooks, Peruvian earrings that weren't worth a cent

—Take a look at the silverwork, all hand done with a chisel, it's some Inca god from down there

the drapes held by tasseled cords and gilded hooks, the cigarette burn that a fold meant to hide it only made larger, the Persian rug that high heels and the mastiff with a bow were making fray on the edges

—Who's in the bedroom, father?

in spite of the cough and the creaking floorboard, my father was blocking the hallway on me

—Don't go in there, you'll only get him all excited, it's the mastiff

clean yourself with a cloth like the judge, father, don't be a coward, the small living room is intact in my memory, every crack, every cranny, every smell of leftover smoke, the pond in the square was filling up with shadows, just like the Tagus at Bico da Areia, my mother at the age when she played hopscotch, holding back, looking at it, a pebble in her hand, almost forgetting about the chalk scratchings, picking me up in her arms, tightening her fingers, and the shadow of her fingers

—Look, Paulo

(the plate in my idea of her that's spinning horizontally, it doesn't slow down, it doesn't fall)

taking me by the hand and by the shadow of my hand at the same time, I drew it back and the white hand was alive, my mother said

—A great faggot, gentlemen

and catching the

—A great faggot

and suddenly falling silent

no, not falling silent, hugging me against her, running away from the gentian

—I'm sorry

as though the gentian

(her plate, a tear)

was some illness, a poison, the medicines that are kept on upper shelves, the bottle of lye, the roach poison with the skull on its label, my mother going out into the yard with the fish shears and cutting off its branches, leaves, pulling it up by the roots, insulting it

—Faggot

the clusters clinging together in the air, rising and falling, a flurry of petals that landed on her shoulders, my mother shaking them off

—Faggot

noticing me on the steps, tossing away the shears, hugging me again

(her plate must have fallen off the bamboo pole because my cheek was wet)

the waves of the incoming tide got stronger in the afternoon, reaching the refrigerator, the dwarf, the liquid with the skull, my mother looked at the liquid with the skull, she left me on the walk and brought up a stool, stopped, trotted over to the bed where the pillow was over her head hiding her, my mother with no head and even with no head

—Faggot, faggot

my mother, two ankles on the mattress, shoes coming off by themselves

—Faggot

still pounding, asking her about the mimosas, lifting the pillow

—Do you want the mimosas, mother?

but at Bico da Areia there were only woods, the pine trees, reeds down by the bridge, I'll go get some reeds for you

—Would you like some reeds, mother?

the shadows on the Tagus were calming down with night, my father was at work, the two of us were all alone, talking about reeds, about my drawing the hopscotch, five squares in front, a pair of horizontal squares after that, a half circle over the horizontal squares

—What's that?

not understanding at first, understanding afterward, and two eyes, the face, all of her in the wardrobe mirror, smoothing her dress, disappearing from the wardrobe mirror and I was in her arms, what seemed to be a smile

what was a smile

(her plate, like a tear, intact on the pole, horizontal, secure, spinning happily)

what was a smile

—It's all right, Paulo

and even though it was almost night and it was hard for us to see each other, even though the Gypsies, the mares, the threats of dusk were outlining the cistern in the back of the yard, she was drawing the lines of the hopscotch with the fish shears in spite of the stump of the peach tree that we'd cut down years before, that ditch with wasps that held out all through summer, five squares in front, a pair of horizontal squares, the half circle over the horizontal squares, where we turned back after a leap, tossing the piece of tile to the farthest square in order to pick who'd start, I hope I miss and she hits, I hope she starts, my tile is off, hers is next to the cistern

—You start, Paulo

putting your feet together at the starting line

—It has to be with your feet together

so I put my feet together, I think I made a mistake with the marks but I certainly didn't make a mistake

didn't I make a mistake?

because my mother clapped, I turned around with a perfect jump, I picked up the piece of tile without touching the ground with my fingers, I'd beaten her, an owl flew up from where the Gypsies were over our roof and disappeared into the café, you couldn't hear the river, you couldn't hear the mares, one of the pups might be calling its buddies from the bridge or maybe it wasn't one of the pups maybe it was the mimosas

the reeds

I didn't say reeds, I said maybe it was the mimosas

I'm sure the mimosas were coming down out of the mountains, greeting

—Judite

and my mother's plate was secure, the only plate that was spinning, not my father's, not Mr. Couceiro's, not Dona Helena's, not the maid's from the dining room

most especially not the maid's from the dining room

Gabriela

my mother's plate all alone in the center of the stage, gleaming, calm, with no need for bamboo and the whole world around, has now fallen, was in the darkness.

CHAPTER

I LIKE THIS PLACE because this was where my mother stirred the soup. In those days night would come on earlier, there wasn't any laundry room or any fluorescent light on the ceiling, we had the balcony facing the Anjos church and a weak bulb, darkness would come fast into the kitchen, my mother would be seen standing by the stove tasting what was in the pot and going back to stirring, while I got the impression that the floor tiles were gleaming here and there, with the reflections from that weak bulb, but the jaws of alligators were in wait, my mother said

—Helena

the alligators went off annoyed, dragging themselves along, disappearing into the mud in the floor below, the eyes of the pots and pans, spying on me from their hooks, stopped threatening me, the sounds of the firewood in the stove stopped turning into the sounds of the sea on some invisible beach, a cove of echoes where the cliffs of the furniture were quivering, the furniture too said

—Helena

my mother was indifferent to the alligators and the cliffs, adding a touch of oil, and the jaws were coming back, spreading over the floor, my father turned on the light in the living room and the apartment

quivered

hiding the cove and the sea in the silverware drawer, if I opened the drawer there was nothing but forks and knives, when my daughter was alive or Paulo was little, they'd go up to the cupboard but I held back from warning them, worried about them

—Careful of the waves

even though an aneurysm has taken my mother away now, the fluorescent light has stopped the animals from coming and the laundry room has given the apartment the look of a place where people live, a sideboard, the newspaper

—Put on your glasses and thumb through me

Noémia's picture with the vase beside it

—I'm still here, didn't you know?

so difficult to make out behind the glass sometimes, at other times so easy, especially on Sunday mornings, when we get back from visiting the cemetery, my husband is sitting on the fence around the grave and I wipe her name clean, not sad, not talking, because the years have turned our marriage into a hope for that vague, unimportant time when the clock in the living room would stop. Or maybe it did stop in April when Paulo left us with no explanation

when I went into his room I didn't find his things, I told my husband and my husband raised his cane a little and that was that

from then on, it showed a perpetual twenty-after-five, the way it remained for months and at twelve-after-seven at the time when the doctor looked up at us over Noémia's bed

we hadn't bought the cane yet, so my husband raised his eyebrows and I just understood

and both times I was pleased that my mother was in the kitchen stirring the soup, tasting it from the big spoon with the tip of her tongue. Although she wasn't with us anymore, we did what we had to do in a way she would have approved of; in Noémia's case, my husband took care of the church, the priest, and the funeral with a calmness and without any useless exaggerations, I told my old friend who was coming down the street for a discreet visit, and the three of us went along with her on little paths that were freckled with sunlight where widows sat on little canvas stools and stretched out their legs in the August heat after they'd polished the medallions on the stones. It's possible that the other tenants had noticed that the bicycle was missing from the yard, the silence of our radio might have told them. For weeks I had the notion that the alligators were dragging themselves along on the tiles again, the invisible beach and the cove with its echoes, but I'd turn on the fluorescent light, and night would disappear immediately, the knives and forks would move about in the drawer, gathering together to calm us down

—There aren't any waves here

the overhang defended us from the church sparrows, my husband, in the easy chair where my father used to work on his stamps, was obeying the newspaper and slowly thumbing through it

—I'm reading, can't you see?

while he peeked over the pages, not at the buildings across the way but at a piece of sky that remained between rooftops, reminding us of the pieces of cloth left over after the curtains had stopped growing old in the chest in hopes that they could be used in some future that will never come. A piece of sky that my husband was living and reliving as he thought

—What's the use of my wanting that?

until he ended up letting it fade away, picking up dust and charcoal from chimneys, the evening breeze brushed his fingers and forgot, just the way the apartment was forgetting Noémia, because it kept running into fewer toys in corners, fewer dresses on clothes racks, fewer multiplication tables that the sea by the invisible beach was taking away with itself, I mentioned that to my husband who'd bought his cane by then, my husband lifted the cane a bit and, immediately, the jaws of the alligators swallowed up memory and nostalgia, the evening breeze touched us both and forgot about us, maybe in the neighborhood they thought we were dead, and I think we would have died if it hadn't been for the memory of my mother stirring the soup in the kitchen and adding a touch of oil

—Pass me the cruet, Helena

worried about my father's diabetes while he was anchored in his easy chair and changing stamps in his album, I remember one from the Belgian Congo with a rhinoceros and one from Mexico with a snake not as terrifying as the eyes of the pots and pans that were spying on me from their hooks

—God help you if we ever get our hands on you, Helena

coming from the chicken broth in the teacup and the pale fingernails, from the kisses that smelled of sweet violets

—See you tomorrow, Leninha

whose perfume had turned their purple into a condensation of fruit preserves, Noémia laid her bicycle against the laundry tub, I happened to touch the bell by mistake and there was a rusty tinkle, a protest

—What's that?

rudeness from my daughter who was always obedient, docile, doing her homework from school on the dining-room table, nothing but erasers, elbows, and her nose in a book, Paulo, him, yes

—What's that?

and my husband's cane rose up and went back down onto the floor

Paulo, who refused to go into the kitchen, pointing at the tiles

—I'm afraid of the alligators, I don't want to

and, as a matter of fact, there were waiting jaws, a cove with echoes, muddy, dark waves just like the ones at Bico da Areia where we'd gone to pick him up, you passed through a pine grove and there were some ramshackle houses, herons, boys with their pockets bulging with pine cones, horses whinnying deep in the woods and, most of all, the water

—Run away from us, Helena

and in the water were great scaly jaws dragging along, waiting for me, my husband waited for us by the gate looking for a piece of sky over the rooftops of Lisbon, a kitchen where my mother wasn't stirring the soup

—Mother

a wardrobe where the edge of a blonde wig could be seen, a woman with a bottle in her hand was pointing to the wig

—Carlos

the wig disappeared from the mirror

—I'm terribly sorry for not receiving you properly

a vine asked me, showing its leaves

—I'm a gentian, isn't that right?

Noémia's room with the photograph and the vase, the crucifix that gave the impression that it was suffering along with her, the same thin body, the bones showing, the same surprised features that were being eaten away by verdigris, Paulo was in the other bedroom, the one in the rear that had been my parents' and where the smell of violets persisted and was still turning things purple, night from long ago before there was fluorescent lighting, and inside the sideboard were the beach, the cove, the furniture, my fear, the alligators chewing on a piece of me

—Stir the soup, mommy

Paulo, when we'd take him to Príncipe Real on Saturdays, a long silence, slippers that were annoyed and calling out in the silence

—Soraia

more silence, more slippers, coming out of the well of sleep

—What time is it?

a drape that finally opened, a single hazy eye in a disorder of lashes

—The old couple with the kid, what a bother

objects were quickly hidden, a man's pants and a woman's blouse, yawning behind the pants and the blouse was a guy with a mustache who was hitching up his pajamas, my husband was near a pond where there weren't any alligators dragging along, just some dirty ducks squatting

not moving

on the muddy surface, I had an urge to move that one duck so there'd be three on each side of the fountain, if it had been up to me and I knew people were coming, I'd have shown the courtesy of arranging the ducks, just the same as I'd close the kitchen door so they wouldn't come up to my mother stirring the soup on the stove or so that the jaws on the tiles wouldn't gobble them up, the yawn dissolved into a blonde wig that spoke to Paulo

—Come in

and the cane

what did you expect?

rising up a bit, while maybe on an invisible beach, a cove full of echoes, before diabetes reduced him to his stamp collection, I'd go with my father to the home of some single lady cousins who looked to me like a pair of antique dolls masquerading as old women, porcelain faces that mold, not time, had left all wrinkled, the cousins would take the protective felt cover off the piano and then, yes, the waves, notes that came and went without anyone touching the keys, the cousins clapped their hands, gushed over me

—So proper, so grown up

little powder boxes that were transparent swans that sailed along the varnished wood to the rhythm of the music, barking could be heard on the imitation marble stairway that drowned out the little lily voices of the dolls as they asked me my age with ecstatic wonder

—Are you serious?

when the sun went down they probably sat down on the bed, mantillas over their shoulders, and slept with their arms held out, all stiff on the bedcovers, piercing the darkness with their little ceramic eyes, my aged father was suddenly so young, how strange that people existed who were born before you were, father, mentioning deceased people by name and the deceased people were happy

—We're right here, girls

as the waves grew stronger and cats jumped off the consoles, my daughter died all over again when Paulo left here, for a moment I got the impression that Noémia was doing her schoolwork on the dining-room table, her nose in the book, I said

—Noémia

and nothing but the shadow of the church or the outline of the sideboard, which at certain times

at the end of the day, in January, for example,

looks like a face, my mother asked the soup

—A face?

I couldn't find his jacket or his clothes, I found a piece of newspaper with some brown stuff I didn't dare pick up, maybe Paulo

—What's going on?

if I were to tell the dolls, the lilies of their little voices, alarmed, would say

—Good heavens!

at Príncipe Real there was a lady in a fur stole with crusts of bread for the pigeons

—Nobody lives here, madame, they passed away

that's not true, a blonde wig lives here and a fellow with a mustache, Paulo introduced the wig while the ducks arranged themselves as they should be, and one of the swans on the piano

—My father, Dona Helena

I was saying that one of the swans on the piano was changing from transparent to opaque, my father, Dona Helena, and dozens of alligator jaws dragging along the floor

not dragging, coming this way

crossing the hallway, walking over to meet me on their slow legs, run away, run, leave the cousins' little place with boxes of citron and thyme, I was sure that when we weren't there, the dolls in a corner on the floor wanted us to come back in July, tender, happy

—So proper, so grown up

not hearing

—My father, Dona Helena

not shaking his hand, the man's pants, the woman's blouse, something he was holding back, excusing himself, and my husband's cane sinking into the ground

—I didn't have time to change, please excuse me

clearing papers off the sofa, a plate with some food on it

your soup, mother

a fan plucked clean of feathers between the end table and the wall

—Please, please

the guy with the mustache

—A friend

taking money out of a woman's purse

—I'll pay you later, Soraia

Paulo's father getting angry, aware of me, excusing himself

—A friend

turning the dwarf on the refrigerator around, introducing a man in an apron, stopping to reassure myself in front of the mirror his wife at Bico da Areia didn't hear us

Dona Judite, I believe

—I used to be pretty, you know

and the vine on the wall didn't believe her, clouds where if it rained it wasn't really raining, making things damp with fever, Noémia was staring at us from the sheets

not allowing her to die

—Would you like your bicycle, Noémia?

and the eyes that weren't hers, much larger than hers, my father's, for example, checking his stamps, the rhinoceros from the Belgian Congo, the Mexican snake, shaking Noémia until my husband stops me, wagging my finger at her, scolding her

—Where did you get those eyes?

the first time my husband and I did it, his eyes were like that, words weren't coming out of my mouth, were coming from the hand on my throat and I was getting to see that I had cartilages and muscles, just like the chart at the Health Center with a person displaying his insides with numbers, I've got numbered insides, how awful, twenty-seven biliary vesicle, thirty-two spleen, forty-one ovaries, my husband was hurting my number seven, pharynx, where did you get those eyes

—How many men, Helena, tell me how many men, hurry up

there was no laundry room or fluorescent light, we had the balcony that faced the Anjos church and a weak bulb, night came so fast into the bedroom, Paulo's father, his face covered with the cousins' powder, and a voice like theirs

—I'm a performer, ma'am, it's my theater costume

the piano was open, notes coming and going with no keys touched, pictures of Paulo's father and others from the show, I said to my husband, not understanding

—How many men?

at that time night came so quickly into the kitchen, my mother was standing by the stove, tasting what was in the pot and stirring again, paying no attention to Paulo's father

—I'm a performer, ma'am

begging me to come in, not take his son away, it's all right, you're a performer, Mr. Carlos, we've brought you your son

—We've brought you your son

Paulo was on the bench in the laundry room while I starched or ironed shirts

—My father works as a clown, Dona Helena

a jaw was getting bigger, snapping shut over him and over me

—Paulo

taking him in my arms

—What's that?

a door slammed in the hallway, not in my room, not in Noémia's room, in some other room, but what room was it and where, the invisible beach, coves, bays, small compartments I don't know about, where maybe there's a stamp album, my parents, my daughter doing her homework, not under the laurels, right here, my daughter thirty years old

thirty-two in September

holding out a bit of oil to me, pleased to see me

—Don't you stir the soup like grandmother, mother?

she works in a law firm, maybe she'll get married, she worries about us

—Aren't you stronger than grandfather, father?

walking with her over to the cousins', the porcelain dolls in a frenzy of joy

—So proper, so grown up

they had a little machine that could tell you what the weather was if you were too impatient to look out the window, a small house with two people taking turns, one in a raincoat and hat, the other with a basket of flowers, if it was raining, the one in the coat would come jerking out, if the sun was shining, the one with the basket would struggle out, if the weather was in between, both at the doorsill, you first then me, maybe two lady cousins worried about the clouds, today I don't even know which room Paulo had been living in when he went away, maybe if I ask him

—Paulo

a sound of people and, please tell me where, he didn't leave, he'd never leave, who'll put another blanket on him in winter, who'll wait up for him at night

—Who's there?

who'll make cookies for him to nibble on while I pretend going to bed, my husband, from under the sheets, says

—Is it the boy?

and I say

—Be quiet

because I'm not going to let him die the way Noémia did, you're not going to die, Paulo, no laurel tree on the hillside in Chelas with a piece of netting over you, no drawer, I won't allow it, I followed him up there

no, a wall on a hillside and the magical jumping-about of a jack-daw all around, something like what was left of a trunk in the weeds, it was my grandmother's that my mother had tripped over as she left the soup for a minute

—Don't leave the soup, mother, keep on stirring, I'm still here

clamps, needles, spiders

—What do I want with all that?

with its gold catches and leather all faded, the cover was off and I searched for it in the weeds and a gleam of jaws was snapping at me

—Hurry back to the stove, Helena

the corpses of cars, alligators lying in wait and among the alliga-tors were people tying their arms up with pieces of cord, I followed him to the hill in Chelas where a Mulatto with a jackknife helped me up the embankment that led to some shacks, more people with their sleeves rolled up, a black woman piercing eggs with a tooth-pick, sucking out the insides, and tossing away the shells, my grandmother used to darn socks by putting a wooden egg inside, looking for the egg the way I was looking for the trunk lid, and my grandmother saying

—I got you

I don't remember her, I remember her voice

—I got you

and if I don't remember, nobody else will anymore, time
an alligator that's different from these
has gobbled her up, it's all over, quit your
—I got you
because you're not giving me orders anymore, you don't even
have a name you can see, you're giving orders to anyone who's
around now, the Mulatto with the jackknife said
—Go ahead, auntie
I was all stuck-up with my copper brooch and its arabesques
—*You're all stuck-up, Dona Helena, what's this all about?*
—The faggot's son, it's the old dame who's paying
giving them the brooch that they took to be bronze, Paulo,
pointing to a girl who was wearing a man's coat and studying her
hands beside a broken-down wall
—Don't you think Dália does well on her tricycle?
the way Paulo used to study his hands, not in Chelas, not with
us in Anjos, at Príncipe Real, at Bico da Areia piggyback on his
father
in a restaurant at Cova do Vapor
in a restaurant at Cova do Vapor, chasing after the herons that
went hopping off
watching Dália pedal
watching the girl in
a small white skirt
a man's coat studying her hands from out of my grandmother's
trunk that she'd found in the weeds, just the way she'd found a
brooch, a box of pills, pebbles
wearing a ring, did you know that?
and convinced that her hands could save her from I don't know
what, I don't know how, studying them, all caught up in them,
saying
—Dália
saying it louder
—Dália
and Dália nothing but slippers and caked with mud or scabs,
Paulo said to me

—She's going to marry a doctor

the Mulatto with the jackknife taking me back to Olaias, worried about me

—Be careful you don't get robbed, old girl

the doctor's bride was going down the hill ahead of us, dragging what once had been a scarf and that made her steps look longer, we were invisible

I was always invisible for Dália, Dona Helena, never a hello

the spiders, the packages of pills, and the trunk all far away, the Mulatto with the jackknife summoning up all his good manners

—Did anyone do anything to offend you, old girl?

my husband offended me

—How many men, Helena?

back in the days when there was no laundry room or fluorescent light, the balcony looking out on Anjos church, a weak bulb and here and there on the floor tiles there were jaws lying in wait, Paulo's father, introducing us to Rui

—A cousin of mine, ma'am

a cousin, a nephew, a younger brother, a godson, ma'am, say hello to my little boy's godmother, a brandy glass lost in his fingers, Noémia thirty years old

thirty-two

—Are they your friends, mother?

my husband who even today without speaking asks

—How many men, Helena?

Noémia works in a law office, she'll be here any minute now, where did you get those eyes

—How many men, Noémia?

Paulo's father passing out little glasses of anisette, his wife in Bico da Areia wasn't talking to us, talking to the mirror and the mirror, yes

—Paulo has no father, he only belongs to me

up on the bicycle in the laundry room while I iron, while I sew, my husband lifts his cane a bit

—I wasn't the first, Helena, confess that I wasn't the first

because Paulo has no father, he only belongs to her, a poor

woman looking for bottles on the floor, dragging herself along, puffing her cheeks out at no one

—I was pretty once, you know

if Paulo doesn't have a father, who's Noémia's father, features without an echo of mine, the one we'd visit on Saturdays, the one on whose grave there's

the one who won't be here in just a minute now

that carved name, those flowers, the one who's fading away in the picture frame, disappearing, we never got to talk, we didn't have an opportunity to talk, maybe I only thought you were going to talk, even after so many years, even today, Paulo's father in the middle of all his posters and paper stars, worried that maybe we wouldn't let him see his son

—Wouldn't you like a little drink?

and he bustled about, a theatrical gesture, maybe I'm growing old waiting for an answer, I go on ahead and I don't find the kitchen

—It needs a touch of oil

and my husband tells me to wait, tells me to be quiet, puts his finger to his lips

—Just a minute

I say to my husband

—Be patient, just a minute

and there's a light on a stage, there's some music starting up, the manager says

—Soraia

Paulo's father's in the small living room with posters and paper stars at Príncipe Real where a mastiff with a bow was rubbing against our knees

—I've been dancing for thirty years now and I'm tired, you see

and I brought him his son from Chelas, I was so stuck-up, the copper brooch with arabesques, my husband said

—Who gave you the brooch, Helena?

Paulo was quiet for a moment, he wasn't hollering at his father

—Clown

getting indignant

—Why did you abandon us, clown?

meaning himself and the woman in the wardrobe mirror

—I was pretty once, you know

wasn't listening to us the way he never listened to anyone, busy looking out the window, not at the café, not at the beach, not at Lisbon, at something that was floating in time, I could have sworn it was a wedding picture, a wedding cake with two figures on top, a village set into cliffs, a blind peasant woman

—Judite

I could have sworn she was in Almada and there were the king's ships, I could almost have sworn about my age, just the way I could almost have sworn that Dália and the people in the weeds in Chelas were my age too, a horror of skin and bones draped in threadbare clothes, shapeless vests, shirts, frock coats, great laughing gums, scarred cheeks, imagining a yard for them, telling them

—Pedal, pedal, keep on pedaling, pedal

and they go along spinning in front of me with their bony shoulders, their skinny little necks, their swollen ankles that make it hard for them to move

—Pedal

Paulo says

—Why did you abandon us, clown?

pedaling along with them, the same dark teeth, the same aimless movements, the same obedience, not humble, indifferent, sleeping on market benches with open eyes, on overhangs by the Tagus, in empty containers up against a fruit crate or a garden fence that hadn't been knocked down yet, not just Paulo, Paulo's mother, Paulo's father with his red lipstick

—I've been dancing for twenty years, I'm tired

in a ground-floor apartment where some floorboards are missing, underneath the boards is the center of the earth, the same as my grandmother's trunk, which would turn up in the Mulattoes' garbage heap any day now, feathers, fake fox furs, makeup cases and skinny necks poking in the trash, spotting a necklace or a tulle rose and dropping them while a palm tree stood there in the wind, while the storks of April, while my mother said

—Pass me the oil, Helena

the ground-floor flat was all topsy-turvy in its abandonment, its silence, all that was left were the cedar tree and the ducks in the pond that would have to be lined up, three on the right and three on the left, they aren't moving now, Paulo, who wasn't with us when I, my husband looked at me saying

—How many men, Helena?

and I was helping the orderly

—Be patient, just a moment

propping him up in bed so he could see the mountains of Timor, hazy rice paddies where buffaloes were sinking in, my mother was stirring the soup in the kitchen, the cane I'd given my husband so he could rise up an inch

—Helena

and it slid onto the floor, his face was fading away

feature by feature

leaving his face with no eyebrows, wrinkles and other things, the orderly took out his false teeth and the wrinkles were bigger, he was looking for me in the room at places where I wasn't until I got to understand that he wasn't looking for me because he'd forgotten me, I was lost in the midst of waves, bays

—Noémia

dark waters were coming and going, the cousins were charmed, happy

—So proper, so grown up

stiff and straight on the coverlet, porcelain faces that mold not time

had frozen, asking my age with a drawn-out surprise

—Good heavens

my husband's face asking

—How many men?

one of the alligators drew back chewing, and the orderly

—It's over

the wrinkles I was leaving behind and Paulo wasn't

—Dona Helena

leading me, my son Paulo, my son because he's not my son and I had

—It's the old lady who's paying

brought him from Príncipe Real, from Bico da Areia, from Chelas, and he was laughing, he was returning from the cemetery laughing, I shook his arm and Paulo said

—What's that for?

and he was laughing at me, thinking I hope I can keep on laughing, I hope I never stop laughing, I hope I can laugh until I'm left all alone with my mother, my father, Rui at Fonte da Telha encircled by police headlights, Paulo said

—Dona Helena

and before I

before I could lay down the iron on the board

—Don't call me son

and he was laughing, Paulo was saying to me, you can't know, you don't know, but when I'm laughing and hating I'm capable, you don't understand

don't understand

how much I hate my laughing and what comes after my laughing, your husband, my father, my mother, you, it makes me so damned uncomfortable having you love me, Paulo was at the window looking out on the Anjos church and the sparrows and the trees

—Clown

Paulo said to the afternoon on Avenida Almirante Reis, to the shops, to the newsstands, to the furniture stores

—Faggot

turning back inside and laughing again, Paulo said to the bicycle or to the basket of clothes

—A clown, a faggot

grabbing my arm, no I was grabbing his arm, he was grabbing my arm

—Do you remember my mother, Dona Helena, do you remember coming to get me?

he backed off, up to the washbasin, laughing

—How long ago was it that you came to get me, Dona Helena?

they were the movements a body makes when somebody's laughing, the eyes that aren't his, where did you get those eyes

—Was I happy, Dona Helena?

with the voice of the dolls masquerading as old women who asked me my age with great surprise

—So proper, so grown up

porcelain faces that mold, not time, had hardened, opening the piano that was protected by a felt mat and then, yes, the waves, not Paulo, the waves

—Was I happy, Dona Helena?

you could tell they were coming and going and not touching the keys, transparent swans in time to the music on the varnished wood, when the sun went down they probably sat on the bed together and summoned up the dead, name by name, and the dead, with their celluloid collars saying

—Here we are, girls

while the waves got bigger and cats escaped out of sideboards, my father, so aged and suddenly so young, how strange that people born before you can exist, father, Paulo's voice was a candle about to go out, along with his laughing, and there were just the two of us at home

nothing but the coves, the beach, the jaws dragging along the floor, alligator jaws lying in wait

—Tell me if I was happy, Dona Helena

not

—Tell me if I was happy, Dona Helena

a more urgent request, his body wasn't moving, waiting

—Please tell me if I was happy, Dona Helena

of course you were happy, how could you not be happy, your parents, the gentian

—Am I a gentian maybe?

the car with wooden wheels, all those things, lunches at Cova do Vapor, for example, the ships of the king, a great friende of merrymente wast he, when you'd get close to the bridge

—Gallop, gallop

all those things, how could you not be happy with all those things, Paulo, the rooftops along Avenida Almirante Reis were almost pink now as the sun sank lower over the Tagus, the church was getting bigger with sparrows, at any moment now the chimes would ring

—Seven o'clock

just as stone still as when my daughter

I told you, I already said to you, I told you

and there was a piece of leftover sky between the buildings, a fragment of cloth after the curtains have gone with the hope that we can use it in some future that won't be happening

—You were happy, Paulo

they finally fade away, picking up dust and chimney ash, dusk is painful on your fingers and I forget him in just the same way that the apartment has forgotten us

—Who are these people?

you were happy, you are happy, I'm happy, don't move, don't turn on the light, don't see me now, it would be hard on me if you saw me now, I couldn't stand it if my husband or my daughter saw me now

—What happened, Helena?

take me by the elbow and turn me toward where my mother is stirring the soup and pass me the oil, boy, instead of words, pass me the oil, boy, if you liked this home

I don't like this home

if we'd liked this home

—It's not home, ma'am, it's a different home here

if we'd liked this home maybe we could have come around to staying, living in it, sitting in the little living room while my husband lifts his cane and Noémia, with her nose in the book doing her homework from school, the place where my mother stirred the soup

stirs the soup, look at her by the stove tasting, stirring again, in those days night came on earlier

there was the balcony, a weak bulb, I seem to see the alligator jaws in wait on the tiles, my mother

—Helena

like me

—Paulo

like me to you

—Paulo

I'm happy because you're happy and yet

—Paulo

an invisible beach, a cove of echoes where the furniture was
quivering

was quivering

where the furniture was quivering and the furniture also said

—Paulo

the furniture said

—Paulo

just the way I say to you

—Paulo

the two of us at home, sitting in the dark across from each other
without seeing each other because we won't be seeing each other
anymore, it's impossible for us to see each other, you went away for
good, a room with no window and a maid from the hospital, they
told me, and I died, it was all over, the way it was all over on Príncipe
Real, at Bico da Areia with no terrace café, no Gypsies, no horses,
where you don't recognize

I don't recognize

whoever it was or whoever it is doesn't recognize you, not the
electrician, not the pups, not Dália

—Pedal, Dália

you hesitate

—Which street did we live on?

—Aren't there any marigolds?

—Which was our wall?

and no street, no marigolds, no wall, the pine grove, if even that,
the woods if even that or no pine grove or woods, nothing, you
think the outline of a medlar tree is a mare, a flight of pelicans is a
whinny, the bridge is in ruins, you think you catch sight of him

coming home with a suitcase and a smile and it's only some suspicious woman hanging wash on a line

—*Paulo has no father, he only belongs to me*

it's all over, Paulo, it's all over, don't ask me if you were happy because I can't tell you, I can only hope along with you that dawn will be coming

but it doesn't dawn anymore, the clock stopped at seven o'clock today, next week, a month from now, what does my age matter to you since someday when you're my age, Paulo, you'll

—So proper, so grown up

remember this in some room I can't imagine where, writing your copywork with your nose in the notebook, erasing what you wrote, getting desperate because it wasn't that way, there are missing sentences or I put in too many sentences or I was wrong or I'm not capable or Dona Helena so different dammit, it wasn't that way

not that way

and in the end it was so simple Paulo, so much simpler than you think, just your asking me

—Was I happy, Dona Helena?

—Tell me, was I happy, Dona Helena?

—Please tell me, was I happy, Dona Helena?

and you were surprised because night comes on earlier

there's no laundry room or fluorescent lighting on the ceiling

there's the balcony looking out on the Anjos church and a weak bulb and my mother stirring the soup

I like this place because it was where my mother stirred the soup

she would stand beside the stove, tasting it from the window, and she was still stirring while here and there on the tiles there were no reflections of that weak bulb

write that, no reflections of that weak bulb

write no reflections of that weak bulb but alligator jaws that stopped lying in wait for you and went off, annoyed, dragging along, disappearing into the mud on the floor below, the wood in the stove stopped turning and there was the sound of the sea on an invisible beach and I said

—Of course you were happy, Paulo

I was sincere

—Of course you were happy, Paulo

and we dissolved into the frame together along with Noémia, two shapes with no features beside an empty vase.

CHAPTER

THERE ARE TIMES when I think yes, I can think whatever I want to and what I think is true, that everything keeps on just the same, for example, that nothing's happened, we're fine, my father is still living with Rui and pretending he's singing in spite of his age, I visit my mother at Bico da Areia, I'm living with Dona Helena and Mr. Couceiro in Anjos or, at least, I do drop in on them from time to time

I drop in on them from time to time

but, naturally, all these things are nothing but ideas of mine, pure fantasy, with me ringing the old folks' bell and a smile on my face while I wrap up a present, tying it tighter with my teeth, Dona Helena wiping her hands on her skirt, signaling to her husband

—It's Paulo

our son, as she liked to say, all they had left if they'd ever had anything, still wiping her hand on her skirt after the door's been opened, taking the package with her fingertips, undoing the string with a smile, a painted mug that she held out, turning around to show it to the living room

—Look what our boy's brought me

where Mr. Couceiro was starting his operation of getting up

old when he was sitting down, old as he hesitated over his armchair, old when he was almost on his feet, old, thank God, when he was standing and putting his hand to his ear asking

—What did you say?

Dona Helena placed the mug on the center of the sideboard and pushed aside the mugs from previous Saturdays, letting me know by signs that Mr. Couceiro was hard of hearing, repeating in a louder voice, shouting, syllable by syllable, in the vocal tone we reserve for the deaf

—Look what Paulo's brought us

Mr. Couceiro staggered around his armchair with every part of him going its own way as he fell into long, aimless steps, one ear keeping in touch with the world

—What?

not understanding about the present

stumbling and unaware that he was stumbling, examining the mug that Dona Helena was holding tight by the handle, afraid she might drop it too

—He's gotten so clumsy, you know

Mr. Couceiro arriving at my jacket, my shirt, as I was being gathered together into a person, my features possibly, my legs maybe, the shape of my arms, my nose

almost a nose

opposite mine, the space under the nose

was it a mouth?

where a vague look of surprise was swimming about

—Paulo

and I was doubtful

—Can it be me?

Dona Helena was all a-flutter, praising the mug to the sky as she apologized to me with a shrug of her shoulders that was asking me to be patient

—He gave us this, Jaime

Mr. Couceiro was baffled by the combination of me and the mug all mixed up in his mind and bewildering him, aware that it was bewildering him and scratching the space under his nose, covering up

—Of course

while some part of him was moving away from us, we could make out a woman

his mother?

waving from the window of a railroad car and Mr. Couceiro, eight years old, was waving too, Dona Helena brought him back, annoyed at her mother-in-law

—Aren't you going to say hello to Paulo?

the space under his nose said

—Mother

angry with Dona Helena, who was taking her away from him, the train went around a bend and the car was lost, what was left was the mug that had no meaning at all, what was the mug to him

what mug?

a man he knew and didn't know or maybe there were still moments when he knew who it was

the friend of his parents who'd take him for a walk in Abrantes, a comrade from Timor?

maybe it was Paulo, but what does Paulo mean, a connection inside him was breaking off, his gums were going on all by themselves

—Paulo

the woman who was talking to him, his wife

—What's your wife's name, Mr. Couceiro?

the question aroused dusty echoes, his daughter was calling him, a blonde wig that passed by in a dance, Dona Helena answering for him, eager for a place in that opaque desert

—Her name is Helena

Mr. Couceiro, satisfied, made use of the information

—Her name is Helena

even though it was meaningless information, what does Helena do, what's Helena made of, there was his mother waving to him, he caught sight of the railroad car, caught the smell of coal and as soon as he began to wave back, the car disappeared, a sudden gap, his nose was close to mine, his eyes were finally clear, his hand was on my shoulder with its former strength, his face was the one from before

—Paulo

capable of reciting the names of trees in Latin without a single

mistake, my wife is Dona Helena, my daughter is Noémia, my godson is Paulo, the cane, explaining

—There are moments when my memory

our boy, Paulo, Paulo, of course, how foolish of me, Dona
Helena's voice rising

—He brought us a present, look

Mr. Couceiro moved his cane from one hand to the other in
order to take the present, some of his fingers were dead but one or
two were in working order, not connected to the defunct knuckles,
we don't need you for anything

—Yes, gentlemen, yes, gentlemen

his mouth was like ours for an instant, it had lips, a tongue

—Yes, gentlemen, yes, gentlemen

and, right away, good-bye mouth, fragments that were breaking
apart, hair, forehead, cheeks all running about the living room, his
mother was waving, I think, the sound of a locomotive moving the
rug out of place, the space under his nose showed no surprise

—Did I say, yes, gentlemen

my mother waving to those strangers I know

don't know

who assure me that I do know them and I don't know who they are, she
brings in a bowl and a napkin at night, puts a spoon into the bowl and comes
toward me, dribbling porcelain drops and asking me to swallow them

—It loses its taste if it gets cold

not soup, not vegetables, not rice, it's the design on the plate that she's ask-
ing me to swallow after she blows on it because there's steam in the design

—It loses its taste if it gets cold

my mother, not this one, the one who's dribbling drops of skin

—Now you've made me cry

she didn't treat me like this, she waved to me from the railroad car with
her furled umbrella, a man in a derby

my stepfather

—All mushy and sentimental, Isabel

Isabel went away, that is the light on the end of the train faded over a
bridge and I to Isabel

—I'll see you later, mother

but going over things slowly because I won't get lost if I go slowly, Isabel did exist, my stepfather, the station, the bowl, they all existed and the napkin and the strange woman asking me to eat

—It loses its taste if it gets cold

the one they swear to me is Paulo is staring at me with a sorrowful look and why is he sorrowful because I

but why is he sorrowful because I'm fine, the train that's going off, they'll take care of me, my brother-in-law took care of me

—You're going to work in the store

why is he sorrowful then, the strange woman talking to Paulo is shedding pieces of skin

I know Paulo, he lived with me, I know him

—He was so smart that it made you feel sorry, didn't it?

I also know the strange woman, my wife,

Helena, obviously Helena, going back over it slowly

I was sure, I was smart, wasn't I?

things fall together, they fall into shape, perfect or orderly, the apartment in Anjos, Helena, Paulo, I had a daughter, Noémia

I have a daughter

slow down, I said, say I had a daughter

I had a daughter Noémia, the impression that at some time I'd shed drops of skin for her just like

I suppose

I shed pieces of skin for that one here, my brother-in-law in the store was piling up boxes one on top of the other, furious with the boxes as though every box was my mother

—Quit that bawling, dummy

Paulo was leading me to the sofa, handing me my cane, calming me down, picking up the mug and handing it to

—I'm your wife, Helena

Helena?

—Don't worry about the present, Mr. Couceiro

my mother's name was Isabel Lopes Martins, my mother's father was Abel Lopes Martins, my mother's mother was Maria da Soledade, the glove

that stroked me as she got into the railroad car had trimming at the wrist,
Paulo said to Dona Helena, covering my knees with a blanket
  she wasn't Helena to him, she was Dona Helena
  —*It's sad, isn't it?*
  and I laughed
  —*Sad?*
I laughed and my brother-in-law, box on top of box, with every box he
was crushing my mother
  —*Quit that bawling, dummy*
shoeboxes with my mother inside waving, still waving today, and Paulo
taking my arm
  —*I'm not leaving, Mr. Couceiro, don't say good-bye to me*
  I think it made me sad that my mother
I'm their son, as she likes to say, all they have left, I say, if they
ever had anything, boosting Dona Helena's spirits
  —On my next visit I'll bring him a bigger mug
if they ever had anything except the trees in Latin and the grave
in the cemetery where they always took in a deep breath of air from
the laurels as they faced it
  if I could only crush all the shoeboxes, crushing you mother, crushing you
and they'd forget about Avenida Almirante Reis where everything grows old along with them, even the sparrows on the church
limping between the clock and the balcony, not even sparrows
almost, dry leaves maybe, little twigs for legs, cedilla marks for
wings just like me maybe
  no, not me yet
and yet there are moments when I think, yes, I can think whatever I want and what I think is true, for example, everything is going
along just the same, nothing's happened, we're fine, but these are
ideas of mine, pure fantasy of course, Príncipe Real without these
buildings where there are American companies and insurance
firms, buildings that were put up later, there's a fellow who helps
park cars wearing a military cap he found in the morning trash
  God, if I could only talk someday about the night's garbage that piles up
on sidewalks, boots, pots and pans, statues of saints, encyclopedias even,

washing machines even, even psyches, whole lives there and yet no people to bring them to life, only their absence like a fold in things or voices that stay on through fingerprints, a footprint on a pillowcase, a key that opens doors in the emptiness if it's turned and after the doors, I'll bet, me, the time when night spits us out, sends us away, deposits us into the street

the beggar in the military cap salutes

—I was a lieutenant

showing the leg he called wounded but there's no scar, only the swellings from wine, the marbling of varicose veins showing over his sock

—A stray bullet, friend

and since I can think whatever I want to and what I think is true, there you have Dona Aurorinha with her plastic shopping bag, fussing through shoes, pots and pans, statues of saints

—You never know, Paulo

you never know what?

—You never know what, Dona Aurorinha?

and she was fishing through the trash where tin cans clinked, cans that at one time had meant tea, cereal, almonds, had been pots of clover for rabbits on the doorsill of the laundry room, Dona Aurorinha was telling the whole universe about it or about the X-ray of her spinal column, which the doctor hadn't shown her yet, that had splotches swirling about in a great big envelope

—You never know, Paulo

the beggar lieutenant, Dona Aurorinha, who leaves the trash and heads for home, the lady in the Persian lamb coat on her bench

it's been months since I've thought about her

throwing crumbs to the pigeons and if I take to following Dona Aurorinha, my father in the ground-floor flat, because I'm grown up now and I'm quite capable of rapping on the window

I can think whatever I want to and what I think is true, so number twelve is here

the printing that's faded from the wood on the crates where the dough is oozing out

rapping on the window and through the window was a chandelier that was missing its hooks, the open wound was suppurating plaster

from the previous chandelier, ideas of mine, things you invent and still, what can my father be like after fifteen years

fifteen is just a fantasy, sixteen, seventeen

fifteen years gone by, the cedar tree is just the same, the pond where a worker was cleaning out the slime, first pouring the fish into a bucket

when the water went down, they'd been left thrashing on the cement, a tiny motor made up of gills, while in the bucket only peaceful knives, every so often the wiggle of a blade

rapping on the window and

like before

silence, distance, the wound from the previous chandelier with a nail twisted into a hook, the back of the sofa protected by a cloth and on the cloth an eyeglass case that was missing its top and a teacup that was spilling barley broth, Dona Aurorinha

in the cypresses ages ago

struggling with the brass doorknob that was missing some screws

—Aren't you coming in, child?

the keys from the night's garbage, on the contrary, turn so easily in the air

her little head, what must have been a body, the satin slippers from a youth with town bands as saxophones and drums began their concert

—I had lots of boys after me

and characters in velvet collars, not lots of them, three or four, with me there looking at her

the light from the bulb in my father's apartment making the doormat curl up

—It's me, father

and breathe

ideas of mine, just fantasies

no angry exclamations, no footsteps, a tiny motor made of gills or a knife in a bucket

you've turned into a fish, father

checking the wig, the dressing gown or no dressing gown or wig, those pajamas for lounging and dozing in chairs on Sundays and the pajamas, ashamed of having been found in last night's garbage, maybe one of the spotlights from the stage, maybe Dona Amélia with her tray of candy and cigarettes half hidden in a sideboard

I don't want my son to see me in last night's garbage

the breathing said to me

—I've got no openings, beat it

he couldn't have been dancing anymore, his fat, his age, he'd walk through the club during breaks in the songs also carrying a tray, he'd call to Vânia or Sissi, waving the invitation from a customer, and the manager said you've got to accept it because it's an important job, champagne, friends who get the police to close their eyes

—Table nine, girls

Rui far away, years ago

ideas of mine, the things people invent

the mastiff with a bow inside a bag on the sidewalk, he couldn't see anymore, poor thing, he'd bump into furniture, we'd stick his food under his nose, from time to time my father with

(with his breath chasing me away

—I have no openings, beat it)

an old customer to talk to about gout and glory, so you remember that Argentine number, Mr. João, me as a tango dancer, and Mr. João

—As a tango dancer, I haven't the least notion, Soraia

actually more than a customer, company, they'd go over names, Alcides, Micaela, Marlene, that other one

—What was the name of the one who lost her leg in an accident?

and the two of them searched, beaming as they came up with it

—Samanta

they shared the remains of some egg brandy in a cocktail glass that was a water glass, because as far as cocktail glasses were concerned

—How do you like your drink, Mr. João?

I never saw anything more delicate, a kiss on the cheek, a bill in the ashtray

—Give it to the parish priest and have him say a little mass for me

a farewell with recommendations back and forth to keep warm and take some calcium for the bones, as soon as he was alone my father took another drink that would serve him as dinner since the toaster oven wasn't working

—*As far as toaster ovens are concerned, I've never seen anything so fragile*

maybe when I left I'd catch sight of him from the cedar with him catching sight of me from the curtain, not the blonde wig, a bald head on which the chandelier was being reflected in little gold spots

(he thinks you invent things or maybe that you don't invent things)

and I said from the cedar

—Good-bye, father

things I invent or maybe don't invent, if he hadn't died it would have been just like that, more or less, Rui with Vânia, my father a bit of afternoon in the park, it's not hard for me to imagine that furtive little pat at the employees' exit, it's not hard for me to imagine the telephone operators

—How about that?

(you were always a clown and you'd end up a clown wouldn't you?)

so it's not hard for me to imagine your hanging around the club at night, with the rags you had left fluttering around you and a few daubs of makeup put on haphazardly

(a genuine clown)

under the eyes of the doorman as he called over his chums

—Do you still know how to dance?

and my father

(—Be careful, I'm not interested in seeing you, thanks)

convinced that the chandeliers were turning red, yellow, purple, were searching for him on the asphalt pavement, convinced that they were turning on the music

the crackling of the speakers before the needle took hold

a ballad, a *pasodoble*, a fado, the doorman signaled to his friends

—Well, Soraia?

(—I said I wasn't interested in seeing you, didn't I)

and my father was stomping out *alegrías*, bouncing, stopping, doing a spin

for moments he was almost a woman, almost young, the rags were a real dress, the daubs of makeup a perfect base

and I said for moments because my father was waiting for applause, the doorman called the manager

—Soraia's back

the dress rags, the daubs of makeup, the manager, who wasn't coming, the doorman calling a cab

—Good night, engineer, sir

whispering to my father

—Now that you've shown us what you can do, beat it

posters of that imbecile Vânia, of a ludicrous Mulatto, of others who'd been nothing in my time, one of them, I think he was the messenger boy whose mother would bring him and pick him up before Alcides, artistic, taking care of things, his mother, thankful, was shaking both of Alcides's hands, Alcides quite a bit older, but with his generosity intact

—We've got to take care of each other, ma'am, I was made to help young people

the same kerchief around the neck, the ring on the pinky with the setting of a Libra held by three silver clamps, the messenger boy photographed from an angle

beautiful Cristiana

bare-shouldered, smiling

—The engineer at table nine, Cristiana

if they'd only let me sit in the audience for a bit, if they'd only let me watch, I won't interrupt, I won't misbehave, if only my son

—A clown

I pretend I don't hear, I don't answer, I remain quiet

—I don't have any openings, beat it

and he was by the cedar observing me while I was at the curtain watching him

I haven't got the strength to carry him piggyback from the yard to the bridge, with him digging his heels into my ribs, forgetting about the

—Now that you've shown us what you can do, beat it

pointing out the gulls and the pups throwing pine cones at us, he was demanding

—Giddyup

when I could barely hear myself, my heart, my lungs, the sand was throwing me off balance, going forward, still running

if that could be called running

with all my strength gone

—I can't

the way I can't dance if they ask me to, my body not used to it, no rhythm, certain that my mouth is out of sync with the lyrics, mouthing the words when the words are finished and there are only saxophones, violins, certain that the manager's in the wings making furious signals to me, the light man turning the spot off me, Vânia with plumes I'd bought for her, they were mine

—Didn't I tell you, didn't I tell you?

or maybe it was my wife who said

—Didn't I tell you, didn't I tell you?

the day she was waiting for me at the entrance to the club, prettier than in my memory of her, taller, and along with my wife the gentians in front, the screeching of herons, the wind from the pine grove bringing along the hoof-beats of the mares, wanting to ask about Paulo, and instead of asking

—How's Paulo?

growing impatient

—I haven't got any openings, beat it

while the moving van was outside and a hunchback was carrying out my junk

—Eight months and no rent, you've used up all your credit, girl

the ducks on the pond, the cedar, the woman in the fur jacket moved over on the bench to make room for me next to her, and the two of us were there all afternoon, with no need for conversation, watching the pigeons

even though you can think whatever you want to and what you think is true, that everything is still the same, for example, that nothing's happened, we're fine

(ideas of mine, nothing but fantasies)

it wasn't my father on the other side of the door hinges, quickly checking his wig, his robe, my father was probably in the night's garbage piled up on the sidewalk, boots, pots and pans, statues of saints, even encyclopedias, even washing machines, psyches even, a key that turns to open doors to emptiness and behind the doors him, not in the hospital, not in the cemetery, what place, where

—Papa

with Micaela, Marlene, in the kitchen, where his uncle's wife was unbuttoning his clothes

—Bath time, Carlos

my father in the newspapers from long-ago days where the pictures are losing their clarity and turning black in the drawer, you can make out a top hat, a walking stick, a knee, Marlene in profile

with a wire mustache and rabbit ears

throwing a kiss to the readers, pages that leave me with Soraia in the form of carbon on my fingertips and some of her that still hasn't changed into carbon

maybe there's still some part of her that hasn't changed into carbon after so many years under a gravestone

I think

(I can think whatever I want to and what I think is true)

that somewhere Micaela, too, on the other side of the river, São João da Caparica, Trafaria, Alto do Galo, is coming slowly toward me, not seeing me

not seeing me?

from Bico da Areia or from a little provincial village where the mimosa scent wafted down from the mountains

no, just from Bico da Areia, the small yard, the wall, my father and Micaela in the house my mother left

(the things you invent, nothing but fantasies)

two clowns caught by the waves and I understood that in Bico da Areia it wasn't them, it was me, duplicated in the wardrobe mirror almost beside the bed

beside the bed

asking me

—Why?

and worried that I'd answer myself, the suspicion that it was the maid from the dining room, maybe

—Why, Gabriela?

nervous because of Carmindo's jealousy

—I'll only take a minute of your time, I'm sorry

the protection of a plane tree so that nobody would notice I was upset

not really upset, curious

—Why?

Gabriela fixing her hair, because there are times when if you fix your hair, your brain will become clean, asking me

—Hold the tray

so she could fix a hairpin, taking back the tray, making up her mind and leaving me

—I haven't the slightest idea

while I was swaying up against a tree trunk like Mr. Vivaldo, a gray cat, all eyes, was slipping away, all liquid and solid

solid at rest and liquid going away

behind the bushes, the redhead with her freckles glowing, saying to Gabriela

—This isn't the . . .

scratching a knee, forgetting me, the feeling that not even my shadow was left, searching for names and people without any shadow, too

names or a recollection of names, people all dissolved into a fold in time

the name of a clown, or a woman looking for bottles in the kitchen, the stray dog of my love for them who follows me at a distance, if I get close to him he'll run away, leaping off, if I forget him, he'll come back, repeating

—Your father, your father

until he lingers beside the trunk of a tree or a tire, noticing that the dog is missing, I go back and I've lost him, the performers with silver garlands, in just a little while Dona Amélia

the one who replaced Dona Amélia

the manager

they didn't replace the manager

if I wait long enough in this café I'll be sure to see him, picking out a table from where you can see the street and as soon as he comes down the street I'll spot him, a quarter after six on the wall clock that's shaped like the rudder of a fishing boat, guessing the number of milk cartons on the counter, how long it took the guy on the left to smoke his cigarette

he put it out too soon, mumbling three minutes

a kid was hopping on one leg by the door and with every five hops he'd look at us with pride and switch legs, the waitress annoyed with his hopping

—Leandro

Leandro with a bracelet of glass beads and traces of gouache on his forehead started hopping again, hands on his hips, with the obstinacy of an Indian chief

—I'm stronger than you are

from my place the number of cartons was twenty-five, getting up to check, thirty-one, I was wrong, the guy with the cigarette was watching me counting them as I held out my finger, Leandro asked me, interrupting his Redskin challenges

—What's your name?

when I sat down his interest in me vanished, he was busy taking a turn about the room, avoiding stepping on the cracks between the floor tiles, when he finished his turn he picked up the wastebasket, where there were napkins and fruit rinds, threatened to throw it at the girl, the girl threatened to use the meat cleaver

—How'd you like me to slice you up, Leandro?

bungling a cut, almost slicing off her little finger, sucking the finger with eyes full of tears

—When I get home I'm going to tell mother, Leandro

identical noses, the shape of the mouths, the dimples on the chins, the girl was fifteen, sixteen years old, seventeen at most, still almost a child and yet, sandwiches, beer, change, her father at the end of the day wrote down figures on a piece of paper

—There's some money missing here, Matilde

six-forty, six-forty-one, the second hand was about to stop and the mechanism was annoyed

—I won't stand for any loafing

Leandro, who didn't care about little fingers

—Come off it

sneaking a sugar cube and rolling it around in his mouth, some of the crystals rolled down his shirt front, shining, he squeezed the cube into a ball, threw it at me, missing

—How old are you?

the second hand pretended to move and it wasn't moving because it was six-forty-one some time back, taking the clock down from its hook in case some cog had decided not to work, the cog reacted and it was immediately six-forty-two, one of the sugar cubes fell onto the table next to me, I picked it up with my thumb and it didn't taste like anything

—Do you also suck like my sister?

with the sun gone and night coming on

not night, the clouds that announce it

the squares of the tiles were turning gray, one by one, Dona Helena and I were in the laundry room with the clouds all gilded and brown on the church side, if they got any closer, Dona Helena could have picked up her crochet needle and turned them into the fringes of a sheet or sofa coverings, so they disappeared into the neighborhood, outlining chimneys, attics, Mr. Couceiro, who hadn't paid any attention to the clouds, was pounding his cane on the floor and asking for his medicines, Dona Helena

six-fifty

was releasing the clouds, unwillingly

—Have you seen his syrup, Paulo?

a medicine that must be related to Leandro, always changing places, we were sure it was on top of the fruit bowl and there it was among the aluminum pots in the kitchen, Dona Helena said

—Are you alive or something?

to the sticky label, the spoon that's hard to pull off the instructions as the print stuck to the handle, the clouds out of reach of her needles were slipping along over the rooftops, heading far away from us, the sugar crystal of a star was halfway between the church and a slanted building

—Can't you get it, Dona Helena?

521

you wet your thumb, lift it to your mouth and there you have it
the hands on the clock

how about that?

seven-fourteen, Leandro was calm all of a sudden with the arrival
of his mother, he did attempt one more turn around the café without stepping on the cracks between the tiles and hopping over
three, lifting his shoe almost to face level, his mother said

—Leandro

and the Indian chief, humiliated by the tyranny of the white
men, took himself off muttering resentments, to the rear where he
hid, surly, turning a flashlight on and off

the flashlight in his hand was now pink, now white, his mother
opened the cash register, calculated the profits and closed it again,
a sharp piercing glance at

seven-thirty-nine

the daughter

—Have you got it all together here, Matilde?

folds of disbelief on the corners of her mouth and my father
wasn't coming, he used to get so worried about being late

—Close the snap for me, hurry up

Sissi with her hair in a net, Samanta escorted and protected by
Alcides who was clumsy but a gentleman, no cloud was showing,
some sugar crystals but they were lost on other tables where my
thumb couldn't reach, my hand couldn't grasp anything except the
oh-so-slow hands on the clock that were mocking me, thirty-one
milk cartons

no, thirty, the girl was emptying one of them into a glass, thirty
milk cartons, twenty-six bottles on the shelf, with nineteen turned
frontward and the rest to the side, seven-fifty on the dot, another
tick, almost seven-fifty-one

seven-fifty-one

a pair of unknown clowns, in costume already, the doorman was
kissing them and gushing, one of them took off a shoe to have a
look at the heel and she straightened it out on the step, Dona
Helena with the spoonful of syrup in the laundry room

—What's that about the clouds, Paulo?

I would have liked so much to have given you a cloud, Dona Helena

—Take it

and yet

are you watching?

I haven't got any, a round, pretty one to decorate the sideboard, if the roof tiles scratched it, you can give it a stitch, she'd made hundreds of stitches in my mufflers, my sweaters

—Be careful with the hooks, don't tear it again

don't worry, I'll be careful, Dona Helena, I'll keep away from hooks, I won't tear it again, and I won't let my father run away on me, the clown was testing the heel with a prudent step and smiling at the doorman, coming home with a cloud for her birthday and Dona Helena showing it to Mr. Couceiro, holding it carefully so it wouldn't rain

—See what our boy's brought, a cloud

hesitating between the back of the armchair and Noémia's room

—Don't you think it would go well with

the bridge at Bico da Areia, where the herons sleep, invisible in the dark, Leandro's mother closing the shutters

—Let's close up

Leandro was lying on the chair opposite me, softened by sleep, his sister was washing the beer glasses, sweeping the floor, appearing with a mop, asking me to lift my feet

—Please

and the floor under me was gleaming with reflections, the clock on the floor said nine-thirty-eight and I leaned over to look at it

while Leandro's mother closed the glass door to the water meter

my shoulders, my neck, my face were lowered, these ears, this mouth

nine-forty

ten o'clock

the bucket on top?

Mr. Couceiro checked it, bringing it closer, and Dona Helena said

—Careful

careful with the mufflers, careful with the clouds because there are so many treacherous hooks, good heavens, the club sign was lighted

pink

the light was growing stronger in the neon tubes, the square of bulbs was out of balance, with one burned out, stumbling on and continuing its spin

—With so many bulbs burned out, there won't be enough lights in this place someday

the laundry room was lighted up, the kitchen was lighted up, ten-twenty

those eyes, that hand touching the chin

no, the cheek

no, the earlobe

no, past the earlobe, that hand adjusting a blonde wig and staying up in the air, opening and closing, greeting, hi Paulo.

CHAPTER

SOMETHING'S GOT TO HAPPEN before tomorrow morning, I can't believe that everything

these people, these years, my life

is ending like this, it's not even an ending, just a halt, a pause, an absurd misunderstanding with me looking for myself in the place where I ought to be

—Paulo

and there's nothing, the house, the other houses, the small café, the mother and her two children have left now, after setting padlocks and the little lights that alternate

one white, one red

on the alarm which the police paid no attention to because the wind would set it howling away, the mother is in front, putting the keys in her pocket, the girl holds Leandro asleep in her arms as she complains about his weight, the Indian chief is hugging her around the neck, I imagine that they can't live too far away because they're walking in the opposite direction from the bus stop, the mother is fatter, smaller now, but with the same nose, the same mole, turning around

—Matilde

maybe they live near Príncipe Real without my ever having run into them

Leandro hopping around the pond

maybe they ran into my father and the girl would have been jealous of his wig, his dresses, scandalizing her mother

—What do you think you're looking at?

Leandro shooting imaginary arrows at the mastiff with a bow

—I got him in the heart

the same nose, the same mole, the same chin, I don't look like my parents, when they'd ask about them saying

—Who does he look like?

my mother would make a motion like closing a curtain to hide a corner in the past that they were ashamed of

—He takes after his father's family

behind the curtain was a voice that was bent over in defeat, not even a voice, some inert creature

—I can't do it, Judite

and she pulled the curtain a little tighter so the creature wouldn't be visible and they wouldn't hear the voice, muffling both by repeating loudly

—He takes after his father's family

and the bedsprings can't be heard, it could be the sea rattling the pebbles on the beach, but what do I care about pebbles because they don't give me away, they stay where they are, moving around aimlessly, who's going to believe the sea

—Don't believe the sea

when a teacher friend from school pointed toward the waves and asked me

—What did he say, Judite?

the usual falsehoods, lies, forget about it, what interest can there be in the gossip of castaways, the ebb tide goes out, you forget about them, and that's that, they have to talk about something, don't they, my friend didn't believe me, looking at the bridge or at a flock of herons

in August there were swallows, toucans

amused by the gentian's nodding, yes

—Since when have you put any trust in gentians, Dolores?

the girl, putting down Leandro

—I haven't got the strength, ma'am

and Leandro was crying, if their mother would only let me help him and she won't, she's suspicious of me, a customer who counts milk cartons in a café

a nut, a thief?

something's got to happen before tomorrow morning, in order to clear things up, to explain to me, the river

—Explain what to you?

was all ready, if I could only believe the river, falsehoods, lies, the gossip of castaways, forget about it, tomorrow morning

no, before tomorrow morning, tonight, the mother and her children had disappeared into a small doorway on the Rua do Século and the lights went on in a second-floor apartment, Matilde or the friend from school while the pebbles were unsuccessfully trying to whisper the truth to her

—What are they saying to you, Judite?

my father appeared on the balcony and he must have spotted me because he pulled the shade down just the way Carmindo would if he spotted me from your place and he'd pull the shade down, Gabriela, the diamond of light that would draw me out of the darkness disappeared and I don't exist anymore, I'm a piece of masonry, the branch of a tree, my mother's friend, interested in me, must have asked

—What did he say, Judite?

getting me all confused with the pebbles and the bridge beams, my mother would check the curtain so it wouldn't let the past be seen, he takes after his father's family

—Don't believe that, Dolores

but who was my father, outside the bar on the next block were the municipal workers with hoses over their shoulders, women waiting, a tank with spider crabs on a base of sand, my mother was contradicting the waves

—He takes after his father's family

and my father was agreeing, pretending with pride, Rui with an ant in his ear at Fonte da Telha, the scratchy pebbles all piled up, the municipal workers hosing down the sidewalk, one of the women waiting called me and I used the pretext of the sea, saying

—The sea, you know

saying

—I'm sorry, I didn't hear, I'm sorry

saying

—What's that?

and the sea really was stopping me, my mother was at the window facing the wet wind that was mussing her hair

—Sleep is impossible

telling the woman that my mother, at night, while the unseen waiter in the beer parlor next to the treetops in the woods said

—You're paying the lady's bill, aren't you?

my mother, acting as though she didn't see me, was looking at the wardrobe mirror

—Aren't you going to bed, Judite?

one afternoon we found the electrician dead, one of the Gypsies had spotted him because the mares were running away from the house and the door was open, he'd slipped off his bed, the woman came up to me because Dona Amélia was giving her candy and whispering messages

—The customer at table nine is waiting, Micaela, the customer at table nine is waiting, Sissi

and an orchid as a remembrance of this meeting, an order of champagne to help conversation, which is a bit flighty, as is well known, champagne loosens it up

—Here's your present, Mr. Paulo, take good care of it, take a look at it

less timid, a knee shaking off bashfulness as it touched my knee and applause for the old man who's adjusting the microphone on stage, getting ready for a bolero, the manager plucking a hair off my neck

no, a grain of sand

no, nothing and crumbling at the nothing in his fingers

—You've picked the best of my dolls, congratulations, you have a good eye

and Dona Amélia agreed, familiar with my fine qualities

(the doctor, without looking at the electrician

—His heart, obviously)

another orchid, cigarettes, my mother at the burial, maybe a hopscotch on some gravestones, and yet no trace of chalk for my mother, her nostrils got big, not because of the mimosas, there weren't any mimosas or any mountains from where the mimosa scent could come, there were half a dozen crosses, a few words into her handkerchief in the tone you use when you talk in your sleep or when you're out of touch with everything

—Poor devil

she'd lent him one of my father's suits, a necktie, a sweater, if only she could have taken one of Dona Amélia's orchids and given it to the dead man

—It's for you, take it

after the burial

from remembering the mimosas, I think

a pint of wine under the archway of a tomb, my grandmother appeared with her look

—Grandmother

and as soon as I said

—Grandmother

she went away without a word, my mother saying to me

—I'll tell you someday, Paulo

you'll tell me what, someday, what is it you want to tell me, there's nothing to tell, is there, in the electrician's house there was broken-down furniture, a toolbox that the pups carried off, a bundle of letters that he never got to send, they began with Judite and my mother burned them

—I'll tell you someday, Paulo

as soon as she guessed what the bundle was and yet while my mother was undoing it, there were letters, a picture

—Of you, mother?

a small lead heart painted once and faded now, she folded her handkerchief with the word inside

—Poor devil

looking into the handkerchief and the word wasn't there anymore

—What happened to the word, mother?

something has to happen before tomorrow morning, I can't believe that it's all going to end like this, not even an ending, just a halt, a pause, an absurd misunderstanding with me searching for myself in the places where I ought to be, the woman in the beer parlor

or Marlene or Sissi

—Is it today or what?

my father in the hospital, asking for his glasses, feeling around for the night table, the nurse was changing his serum, the manager was giving him his glasses

—My best doll, Mr. Paulo

and my father was unable to get hold of the frame

—I want to see myself, leave

a match and the picture that belonged to the electrician had been transformed into a gray square

I never got to decipher it

that fluttered for a few seconds, turned black, disappeared, before it had become a gray square it looked to me like a girl or something, but maybe I was presuming things, I'll tell you some-day, Paulo

—Was it you, mother?

where could Sissi or Marlene be living, on what block, how old, the customer at table nine, girls, Mr. Paulo, a friend, two bottles of champagne, a bit of French perfume, whose picture was that mother, the woman who was calling to me, standing

—Your time has begun its countdown

my countdown began ages ago and there's not much time left to the end of my story, say, for example, that the woman

—Dina

the usual lie, they always lie about their names and I never catch the reason why, they hide them the way they hide their lives, their childhood, their age

—I'm whatever age you want, don't let it worry you

they make us stop the car a long way from where they live, they point out the wrong building, any old apartment house

—Let me out here, you go on

and as soon as they think we can't see, they open up their umbrella, start running and it's a different building on a different street, if we kept their purse we feel something hard, a sap, a knife, their body is always on guard, the eyes of someone looking out for them

only eyes and the tip of a polished shoe

two lamp posts farther on, Rui is in the park watching the blinds for a signal light, before Rui it was Eurico, Fernando, the electrician is standing staring at me, the car with wooden wheels, not bought in a store, carved by a jackknife with passengers drawn on the windows, an electrician had been drawn, a child

me?

a woman beside the electrician, my mother was blocking my view of him

—He's the one who sent it

and he had a bag for mussels on the bridge, leaving us, he never came to call

never came to call?

I never saw them talking, I don't believe him

women always lie

they would pass each other without saying anything, the owner of the café made him get out from under the awning

—I'll tell you someday, Paulo

he told him not to come there

—You stink

tell me what, mother, there's nothing to tell, whatever it might be, a mania, when at night you say

—Sleep is impossible

he was squatting on the beach warming himself over a small fire of pine cones, for the last few months something had been wrong with his back, he had a crutch to help him walk, I was on the steps with the car, ready to throw a stone at him if he tried to steal it from me, and he was next to me, not saying anything, he looked as if he was going to say something and no words came out, the impression

it must have been an impression

that my father was avoiding him, he'd disappear into the flower
beds or gallop off with me on his back to get away from him, his
neck was bent over as though
—What's wrong, father?
as though nothing
—It wasn't anything
the usual lies, I lie all the time too, don't stumble, don't slow
down, keep on straight ahead, straighten up, the electrician was
beside me with a crutch, in the house along with the cheap furniture and the mattress, a car with wooden wheels with no passengers
drawn on it, I mean, he'd drawn the woman, the child and the man
were missing, the woman with her nose in the air
—Do you smell the mimosas, Paulo?
I'm sorry, the woman was dripping a few words onto her
handkerchief
—Poor devil
putting the handkerchief away before I could say
—Let me see
and a small lead heart, it looked to me like the mares and yet the
mare on the beach was a different horse from the one I told
—Faster
Sissi or Marlene or the woman with me, orchids, bashful, I'm not
what I seem to be, Mr. Paulo, next month I'm going to be in the theater in Morocco, the manager, dusting off my lapel, the best chick
of all, congratulations, just right, respectful, my father
Soraia
ordering more champagne, so many rings and so coarse, father,
seriously, did you need all that jewelry?
—Very interesting, Mr. Paulo
bolero after bolero, Dona Amélia worried
—That lover there?
and how about a little perfume, a gardenia, Alcides's finger
telling her to hurry up and yet I said to the woman who went with
the finger
—Where to?

without touching the champagne, because the champagne was beer, the lipstick smeared around her mouth

—I'm not Soraia, I'm Dina

you're not Soraia, you're Dina, and yet there's a wig, falsies, the woman was offended, holding out strands of her hair to me in a boardinghouse in São Bento

—A wig?

the three poorly lighted floors that I expected, certain that I was being watched without seeing anybody, I was careful to see that Dona Aurorinha gave her lungs a rest along with her shopping bag

—I know it's you, Dona Aurorinha, answer me, ma'am

and, finally, a faucet breaking up the wall and dripping down to the floor, every drop

—Poor devil

hide them in your handkerchief, mother, don't let me hear, doors to the right and to the left, the washbasin in the rear where a Mulatto woman says to Dina

—Hello Teresa

not really Mulatto, Pakistani, Timorese, drying her hands farther down the hallway without realizing that she was getting us wet, she opened a door to where a fellow was sitting on the bed and tying his shoes, for a moment his eyes

no, the eyes of the manager, always careful with me, pointing out the second room, the balcony over a warehouse, the aluminum sunshade

—Is it all right, Mr. Paulo?

or Sissi feeling for the catches on the dress she'd inherited from my father and tightening it on her hips where the stitches were giving way

—Is it all right, Paulinho?

something's got to happen before tomorrow morning, I can't believe it's all going to end this way, I mean this woman, the shade, the warehouse, my hesitation about getting undressed, I don't get undressed, what else can I do, getting undressed, on the edge of the bed with my mouth on the pillow, avoiding her or unable to avoid her, the bedsprings warning me, I won't let them see my face and in my face the doves, the bath, this scorn for

not for you, not for you

—*I'm not capable, Judite*

the fear that you'll stroke me and wanting you to stroke me and if I want you to stroke me, the gentian

not my uncle, the gentian

—*Carlos*

not the gentian, my mother stealing me away from my uncle's wife

—*Carlos*

and then the pulley on the well, the bucket touching bottom in the darkness and bringing me up, the afternoon by the chestnut tree outside the kitchen or at Bico da Areia or on the sheets on which my son is getting undressed now, every button on his shirt a great effort, the belt on his pants, which refuses to loosen, Dina

or Teresa

impatient, fed up

—*You've got twenty minutes left*

or not even twenty minutes, your time's run out, you understand, your time's run out, you don't have any left, I knew from when I was a child, I lost it when I was a boy, I don't know it as a man, the orderly referring to him or to me

to him because I'm fine, I'm alive

—*He doesn't have anything left anymore*

with Paulo thinking not even an ending, just a postponement, a pause, an absurd misunderstanding, my son Paulo thinking an absurd misunderstanding and no misunderstanding, if I could only make him listen to me, tell him that even though there were steps in the hallway and loud laughing and orders

and along with the footsteps, the laughter, the orders to the Mulatto woman, or Pakistani or Timorese

—Good-bye, Teresa

outside, the woman asks

Sissi?

helping me with the belt, fooling with my socks and leaving the socks alone, asking me, listlessly

—What's your name?

without bothering about an answer, from the balcony the
herons, the bridge, the waves are stopping me from falling asleep,
Gabriela giving her arm to Carmindo

—What did you expect, Paulo, you went away, didn't you?

and the woman, in the tone of someone recalling an episode that
fades away and has no connection to me

—Paulo?

not me, a lover, a cousin, one of those relatives who come back
sometimes because of, how should I know, what goes on in a dream
and follows us, annoyed with us

—What are you doing here?

looking for objects whose places we've changed, always farther
back on the shelves, a baptismal ladle, rosaries, tin ashtrays, my
father to my mother, picking me up

—I'd rather have had a daughter, Judite

*a daughter wouldn't have to go through what I've gone through, women
are capable of what I'm not, they adjust themselves to what's happened, they
live in it, they breathe in it, they can tell from the direction of the wind the
tombs they'll inhabit, a daughter wouldn't feel what I feel, those hands that
pull me, tug at me, grab me, women drink in their suffering like plants or
mares or the ground or the trees, women are mares and they keep up a secret
dialogue with death, they know the dark places of their bodies where I wan-
der blindly and where peace is to be found, a daughter could have done what
I can't*

could have decided what I can't

a daughter nev . . .

so that Sissi or Marlene

Sissi

Dina, Teresa in the tone of someone who remembers a fading
episode that has no connection to me

—Paulo?

only the letters of my name, I'm all alone, the doctor, not looking at me

—His heart, obviously

while I slid across the mattress, I said to the Mulatto girl

not Mulatto, Oriental, Pakistani, Timorese
—*I can't do it, Judite*
escaping from out of the wardrobe mirror, taking refuge in the gentian
and it wasn't the gentian, wasn't the waves, Rui, holding me by the shoulders
—*Soraia*
I mean, not Rui, father, leave me, the woman
—Your hour is up
slippers or shoes in the hallway, a door that hits a corner of the
sideboard or the back of a bed, windowpanes shaking, a plea
—No
louder, closer
—No
farther away
—No
somebody falling or I think had fallen, a voice outside
—Joana
again
—Open up, Joana
and again
(a second voice)
—What's going on, Joana?
the second voice pushing on something because there was the
sound of something on wood, telling the rooms
—The party's over, ladies and gentlemen
taking out a knife
or what looked like a knife
to a man who was looking at us, astonished, the legs of another
man on the floor, the Mulatto girl
the Oriental girl, the Pakistani girl, the Timorese girl drying her
hands by waving them
and it wasn't water, not water
wetting my chest, not noticing that she was wetting me
not water
as if she didn't realize she was waving them until the first voice
pushed her toward the room
—Joana

I mean, he wasn't pushing the Mulatto girl
or Pakistani or Timorese, what difference does it make
he was moving a cardboard figure, a silhouette, a doll, he closed
the door, turned the key
—The party's over, ladies and gentlemen
suggesting
not ordering
suggesting to the man who was looking at us astonished
—Beat it, Marçal
*and in April I sensed something strange for the first time, she didn't tell me
and it was the child, I found her hugging her knees and I didn't understand,
I thought she wasn't feeling well, an upset, one of those letters her mother dictated to the woman in the post office asking for the sky*
—*Did you put in everything I said?*
while her fingers sketched figures in the air
instead of leaving, the man was quieter, empty rooms, bedcovers
thrown back, balconies just like mine and on the balconies there
was silence
not even night, night hadn't been noticed, what had been
noticed was the breathing silence as a substitute for night and I said
to myself something has to happen by tomorrow morning, I can't
believe that all this
these people, these years, my life
is ending this way, a postponement, a pause, an absurd misunderstanding, Joana was in the locked room, the second voice was
sending the man away, first with the hilt of his knife, then waving
his arm
—Beat it, Marçal
making him go down onto the street as he picked up speed landing by landing, almost running now and no longer looking at us, he
emerged into the light of the street lamp and was lost, I was sure
Joana was shaking off what wasn't water from her hands, that they
brought up a van and there was a long shape in it that they tossed
into the river with the help of a rock or some bricks and that was
that, the rock or the bricks released near Vila Franca along with factory waste or the keel of some ship, nothing but a bundle of clothes,

a spongy piece of something that the fish rejected and that fell apart into rags on its way to the sea, a month or two later the Mulatto woman

or the Oriental woman or etc.

was drying her hands by shaking them and there was water again, the man was waiting for her below, not worried, why should he be worried about us

my wife wasn't getting annoyed with me, she'd look herself over, take stock of herself, go back to looking herself over, lunch was untouched on the table, dinner was still to be made, the year the marigolds bloomed twice, in April and in July, the woman at the post office read the letter to the blind woman, your daughter says the marigolds bloomed twice this year, and the blind woman, looking at the ceiling, it's a mistake, it can't be, it's a mistake, and then becoming alarmed she said

—Repeat that

not loud, in a low voice and

—Wait a minute

and in an even lower voice

—Maybe

gathering up her skirts, looking beyond the scale, the messages no one else noticed, this is my son, the car with wooden wheels, the electrician leaning on a crutch, turning his head, the doctor, without coming in

—His heart, obviously

Judite's mother

—Maybe

finding the sidewalk that led to the square without any help, guided by the drowsiness of the goats, during the time I knew her she was still working in the garden, she could sense the gleam of the onions but was beginning to get confused in the darkness just like us, but at midday, if we lighted a lamp she wouldn't blink or squint, there was a cloud over her eyes, a touch of winter, making a mistake this time because

—Judite

and Judite and Paulo at the cemetery or in the market, I was the one going around the sideboard, avoiding the loose tile because if I stepped on it she'd catch on

my steps were wider, my weight

setting myself down on the stool noiselessly, almost without breathing, when the blind woman said

—Judite

reaching out and missing me, every finger was an antenna or those claws lobsters have that people tie up, her arm knowing, stopping, returning to her lap

—You're Carlos

the disappointment with my name

—You're Carlos

her blank eyes toward me

—You're Carlos

not angry with me, scorning me, if I was sitting in Judite's place and passed the dinner plate to her, she wouldn't accept it, if Judite was in my place

—Thank you

her arm knew, stopped, went back to her lap

—You're not the father of my grandchild

and I said in a whisper so we wouldn't be heard

—I'm nobody's father

taking her by the wrist, whispering into her ear, while the electrician was approaching from the bridge, scattering the gulls, the horses of the Gypsies, and the horses on the carousel were spinning around in my head and colored lights and music and customers and Paulo waving to us

—He takes after his father's family

I whispered into her ear

—I'm nobody's father, you can be satisfied with the fact that I'm nobody's father

the two wrists, the neck, the throat of the old woman so easy to squeeze until a muscle, a bone, a cartilage

so easy

That it gave way, broke, withered in the palms of my hands

So easy

—I'm nobody's father

the man from the boardinghouse appeared for a moment under a streetlight where municipal workers were hosing down the sidewalk, I tried to pick him out and I couldn't, a beam from some scaffolding, I thought it was Joana on the balcony and it wasn't, a gutter, the quivering of some blinds, I can't believe it's all going to end like this, not even an ending, a pause, a rumble from the direction of the docks, derricks, a corvette, the breeze is slower now because something's about to happen, is happening, happens, Bico da Areia slowly emerging, moments from now the owner of the terrace will unfurl his awning, a heron

six herons

their bills asking me

—Was this what you expected, Paulo?

not a postponement, a pause, an absurd misunderstanding, the maid from the dining room

Marina & Diogo

looking for her clothes on a chair, dropping them, clenching her fist and starting to dress, Carmindo asked

—Gabriela

not Marina & Diogo, Gabriela & Carmindo, on every floor Gabriela & Carmindo, on the mailbox Gabriela & Carmindo, never Gabriela & Paulo, Gabriela & Carmindo, Carmindo asked

—Whatever happened to Paulo?

and a forehead showing surprise

—What Paulo?

a forehead remembering

—Why should I know anything about that Paulo

luckily Sissi

—Good morning, Sissi

reaching the place on Penha de França, in Sapadores, in Estefânia, a neighborhood as bright as day, taking off necklaces, putting them into the little basket where

on a blue mat

other necklaces, bracelets, taking off makeup

—Tired, Sissi?

with the dish towel, warming up the tisane, dipping a little bag into the water, watching

not watching, Sissi unhooking her bra

the teapot taking on color, losing the thread on the little bag, fishing it out with a fork and throwing it into the garbage

—Tired, Sissi?

tired tired I'm so tired, Paulo

looking for something

—Where's the fucking teacup?

a teacup for me, finding an empty bean can, holding the can out to me, in the bread bag a crust, crumbs

Gabriela & Carmindo on every landing, on every turn in the railing Gabriela & Carmindo, Sissi excusing herself

—I didn't expect you, you know

annoyed with a run in her stocking, covering the run with saliva

—Can you notice it now, Paulo?

and even though I noticed it, I stroked her shoulder, assuring her

—It doesn't show, don't worry

Sissi was my age, the same color hair and that beard stubble on her cheeks, her chin

—I could be you

Sissi or me, I think me, I think one of us

—I could be you

not one of us, me

—I could be you

if I got dressed as a woman, if I painted my face

I don't get dressed as a woman, I don't paint my face, I'm a man who doesn't get dressed like a woman, doesn't paint his face, doesn't take care of the customers at table nine after the show

—The customer at table nine, Paulo

candy, cigarettes, the manager demanding

(—It'll be too bad for you if the customer doesn't buy some drinks, Paulo)

picking hairs off his lapel, a speck of dust, nothing, flicking the dust away with his fingers

—You've picked the best chick, congratulations, you've got a good eye

Sissi and I on checked sofa, I was going to say found in the night's garbage

something has to happen before tomorrow morning

where the telephone book was standing in for a leg, Sissi and I weren't talking, not even

—I could be you

while my mother hid us, ashamed by a slight movement of the curtain and behind the curtain the two of us, maybe the sea in the distance was whispering through its pebbles

—Don't believe anything the sea says

and a marigold that bloomed in order to protect us from the day.

CHAPTER

WHEN YOU COME right down to it, it's just a matter of being sure that people no longer exist, that they pass by without noticing me, their faces indifferent, their minds somewhere else, no voice, no presence, nothing, with me just as far away, I see myself leaving home, returning home and I don't ask

—How's it all going, Paulo?

—What's with your life, Paulo?

—What about tomorrow, Paulo?

I stand there observing myself from the door, I take a little time, I leave and the apartment is deserted, the furniture gets bigger as it always does because nobody exists

we get home and can tell that the place where we live hates us, it pushes us back out onto the doormat, it wants to get rid of us

the doorknobs are huge, the defects in the wood enormous. the window is strangled by hinges and blinds

and I'm so tiny in the middle of it all until the glass cupboard or the chest hides me completely and when they hide me, they also hide these clowns, these old men, this idea of waves, not real waves, the ones I make up for myself when the glass cupboard and the chest will let me, as they combine the reflection of the sun in a bot-tle with the rippling of the curtain or the river, that is, and what's missing

the bridge etc., the Gypsies etc

unfolds at my feet, the sun leaps out of the neck of the bottle, reaches the ceiling, falls back and immediately says

naturally
—It's the changing of the tides
the curtain draws back
let's suppose
and you notice right away
how could you think otherwise?
a change of wind in the pine trees, a wind with little printed flowers and the tear made by the screw on the door through which the switchboard operator at work hands me the phone
—For you, Mr. Paulo
a childhood scar on the edge of her lip that prevents me from noticing the receiver, hearing
—For you, Mr. Paulo
because a little girl inside her had fallen down in the schoolyard and was starting to cry, holding her hands over the cut on her mouth, I picked her up in my arms and assured her
—It was nothing
holding her tight
—It's all over now
the little girl gave way to a woman waving the plastic object back and forth
—I haven't got all day, it's for you
the string around her neck with the small medallion of her zodiac sign
Pisces
two robalos or some fish like that and before I could say
—I love you
the robalos disconnected the call
—If you don't want to answer, that's your business
and it wasn't the sign, the scar on her lip, the back of her indifferent neck, her indifferent back dialing a number with a pencil
—Personnel Department?
there's a pimple that hurts her looks
hurts her looks?
it doesn't hurt her looks, it makes her vulnerable, human

she's the child again for a second, I grab the phone and the pimple, not the child, pushes me away with the pencil

—It's too late now, forget it

a bare ankle bends and stretches out, she removes a clip-on earring to make it easier to talk on the phone, examining it in her
hand, a coral pomegranate

how many years ago was she secretly prancing about in her room
wearing her mother's earrings and shoes?

I take the phone all the same because maybe the little girl is on
my side, I can see her quite clearly through the small openings in
the plastic

—Mr. Paulo

and here's the schoolyard with its tree in the center, three rows
of desks in the ground-floor room, the crucifix over the blackboard
where there are the remains of lessons in addition, archipelagos,
verbs, a lot of numbers, a lot of islands, and a lot of past perfects
that pour down onto a bare ankle that's bending and stretching
and onto the little plugs that connect the Personnel Department to
Accounting or to Human Resources, if I could only say to her

Júlia

say

—I'm talking about you, Júlia

—or is it Dona Júlia?

—I'm talking about you, Dona Júlia?

no

—I'm talking about you, Júlia

could only tell her that people had stopped existing around me,
that I have nothing left except the waves on the curtain and you in
the tear in the curtain, my life reminds me of those games in the

Children's Section

on the next to the last page in the newspaper, underneath the
columns on bridge and on chess, a square with connecting threads
and each thread's a path, on each side of the square are five threads
starting, at the start of each path is a different color Prince, on the
opposite side is the Princess that one of the threads reaches, find

out which Prince will marry the Princess, the answer is upside down in tiny letters

The Blue Prince

I twist my head so I can decipher the answer, I follow the Blue Prince's thread with my finger as it comes to an end without reaching the Princess, I try the Green Prince, the Yellow Prince, the Brown Prince, the Red Prince and the Princess is still unmarried, I go back over the path starting from the Princess with endless spirals, not noticing that my finger's over the page where there's no Prince, there's a photo of a gentleman giving grammar lessons to readers who are meticulously reduced to initials, a comma, and city, C. F., Coimbra, J. H., Santarém, P. M., Gaia

Consultant in the Portuguese Language

or after that, in order to protect secrets, Properly Identified Reader, Évora, creatures tormented by plurals and the predicate nominative of the subject, the one the Princess marries is no Prince at all, it's Professor Maia Onofre, promise me that it will be for always, for ten years, for one year, for a month, for a day, for a few hours, whatever

erase anything of no interest

Professor Maia Onofre, send me a letter, ask me something, if you're worried or have any doubts that I'll respect your anonymity, I'll reduce you to initials, check with philologists, opinions, dictionaries, bring up phrases in Latin, print them in italics, treat you as an esteemed friend, furnish examples, oddities, variants, explain it all through an encyclopedia

encyclopedias are pleasant and light things when I thumb through them

I'll stop you from falling down at recess, from crying, I'll erase the verbs on the blackboard and in place of the verbs, in huge capital letters,

I love you, Júlia

you can't imagine how much fun I can be, I know how to play cards, how to set a nail with my left hand, pull coins out of my nose, dance, I learned that from my father, a clown, he lived in Bico da Areia, then on a square, then in the hospital, then off the square, then, a very short time later, in the hospital, and then he died, from the distance now you can imagine that he lived his life

just like I do

later on, entangled threads that broke off in the air or poured over Professor Maia Onofre at table nine with his flower and his little cup of chocolate raised in a toast, pleasant, all fingers, adjusting his voice and the knot in his tie

—Would you care for something, dear lady?

my father is a Properly Identified Lady Reader, Júlia, Dona Amélia was handing him a slip of paper from the manager reminding him of his duties, the norms of conduct and the percentages, my father was holding the note out in front of him, moving his eyes closer to it and back in order to put it into focus, he was learning that Professor Maia Onofre, table nine, eleven percent, he put away the information, folded, in his false décolleté and the next day I came upon Professor Maia Onofre saying good-bye, less chubby than on the night before and smelling of orchids, on the bottom landing, Dona Aurorinha, who was coming down to go shopping and leaning on the rail asked

—A relative of yours, Carlos?

Rui

another relative

delivering the note in the club, collecting the eleven percent and inviting me to go with him to the broken-down wall in Chelas near an invisible jackdaw, me, who at the time was living with some older people, dead years ago and whose names aren't worth mentioning

the family keeps getting bigger, Júlia

on the sidewalk in front of the Anjos church and just because I wasn't dreaming of you at the switchboard at work, I didn't bring the bicycle we had there down to the street, even with its flat tires and its flopping light, I'd pedal up to you, to the robalos, to the scar on your lip, to the scorn with which you handed me the phone, paying no attention to me or annoyed with me

—For you, Mr. Paulo

to the girl crying with her hands over her mouth that I said

—It's all over now

and both of us, Júlia, sure that it wasn't all over, that it hasn't gone away, the tree in the schoolyard with no leaves thirty years ago, in an ancient October with puddles left over from the rain and the bricks turning red with something looking like blood, your blood, my blood, our blood, because we drew a line with the jackknife across our skins and rubbed them against each other

me, the Blue Prince, you, the Princess

and we solemnly rubbed against each other

we're so young, aren't we?

one into the other, a pact that seals our love, swapping palindromes, sticks of gum, my blood when the syringe drew it up in Chelas, and the color on the glass got dark with the heroin, it was her blood because even though she's lying down, it keeps on dripping every night, before going to sleep, in a room where it's easy to imagine the white lacquered dressing table with its copper trim, small cookie tins, a nickel-plated dolphin balancing the globe on its nose, a box with tissues folded into each other from which you manage to pull out just one and I get an endless accordion of pink rectangles that I shove back into the box

and get all wrinkled

in hopes that you won't see, your smile in a bathrobe by the doorway

—You're so clumsy, Paulo

slippers with Hotel Sevilla printed on them, revealing a charge of kleptomania that her fellow workers aren't aware of, that travel agents deplore, and that I find charming, a picture in a bathing suit, probably by the pool of the aforesaid Hotel Sevilla

(in the vacation schedule: third day, Hotel Sevilla in Seville, unforgettable city, mosques, afternoon free)

in a bamboo frame, the lamps on the night tables have chimney sweeps holding up their brooms and on the sweeping end are the bulbs with satin shades of starry skies, your name embroidered with cherries around it that you had on the wall in a frame and in spite of the name that your mother or your sister or you were writing out while you were getting over a bad case of flu, in spite of the wardrobe, which was also lacquered, matching the dresser, in spite of the light filtering through the window blinds and spreading out long-lost ecstatic memories in the room, first communions, birthday cakes, the garden at Caldas da Rainha was still waiting for you, you keep on falling down, Julia, you keep on falling backward, in childhood, you stumble on the second jump over the rope that two schoolmates are swinging

—Your turn, Júlia

leaping in quickly with your book bag on your back, saying one two three, jumping in rhythm and yet, somebody

or it seemed to you that somebody

called your name

or a muscle was too slow, or it was a trick of your schoolmates

oh, Júlia

and the surprise, the stumble, a cry, me running over to you

—It was nothing

and you're sitting up in bed and holding your hand to your mouth, finding the blood, hiding on my shoulder

—What a nightmare, Paulo

the bare ankle that bends and stretches out, the pomegranate earring in her hand and instead of

—I haven't got all day for you

your hair, which I slowly stroke, the shoulder that's free of a strap grows small in my hand, a voice that's unrecognizable because it's so long ago and yet it's yours, in a kind of childlike abandon

—What a nightmare, Paulo

the relaxation was helped by covering the chimney sweep with a pajama top because the shadow helps, turning me into Professor Maia Onofre discoursing on gerunds, the Blue Prince holds out his finger following the twists and turns of a thread on his skin, the robalos of the zodiac sign, the beginning of your arm, the little pillow of flesh protecting your armpit, and no blood on your hand, look, see how there's no blood on your hand, your hand's clean

at other times, after the heroin, she'd dry it on her blouse

your clean hand on a phone that I lift to my ear and you drive me off with your pencil

—It's too late now, forget it

at other times, after the heroin, she'd dry it on her blouse, bend over me sitting on a rock and the colic was gone, my sweats were gone, my kidneys weren't on fire, the jackdaw

probably

but the jackdaw amused me, completely unimportant, you know, and I was in the garbage and the weeds, forgetting about the scar and taking you in my arms, hanging over you, it was during those days

I'm sorry

that I remembered my father, the clown, and his belief in some kind of miracle, he'd close up his fan and stare at me, I would get annoyed while he hesitated

—Don't be mad at me, father

just the way other people stared at me, you, for example, I would have been annoyed too, you and the Mulatto with the jackknife flicking out the blade, making me get up, leave

—You piece of garbage

stumbling down over the uneven ground, coming upon a dead cat, the maid from the dining room with her sleeve rolled up, examining the syringe

—Promise me it won't hurt, Paulo

how in hell can it hurt, it's great, it won't hurt, I'm here I'm not here, I talk to you I don't talk, it won't hurt at all

you'll feel better, I'm not even worried about my father, Gabriela Judite & Carlos

and the maid from the dining room

—Your father?

she didn't know about my father, she knew about the singer at the hospital, Mr. Vivaldo coming over and flirting

—Can I help you, sweetie?

my father opening his fan, his eyelashes were also two fans, three fans fluttering at Mr. Vivaldo, a quick question that grew long, taking possession of him, tying him up and taking him from table nine to the ground floor at Príncipe Real, posters, decorations, petunias in the vase

—I beg your pardon, sir?

things that come into my head, crazy things that I think about, a lacquered dressing table at your place, your name surrounded by poppies on the wall

cherries

Julinha

the way we sink into ourselves even at night, first communions, birthday cakes

ten candles, eleven candles

Caldas da Rainha waiting and then Caldas da Rainha hazy, the candles going out, we're about to doze off and boom, the raindrops

speaking of rain, did you notice all that blood?

the tree, the schoolyard, we try to go back, we try to run away, and yet always the schoolmates

—Don't stop

knowing that we can't jump, we're not going to jump, the rope beneath us and above us, coming back, going away

—Don't stop

take care of the switchboard, don't listen to them, transfer a call, change the order of the plugs, ask the little holes

—Personnel Department?

or Accounting or Main Office or Human Resources, not school-mates, clerks who don't jump rope, stop the raindrops from spread-ing over the bricks, where there are candy wrappers, rotting leaves, maybe we're reflected in the raindrops just like we are now, just like you are now with a chain around your neck and a blouse with polka dots and yet

—I don't feel myself, how strange

wrinkles that I don't have, freckles all over my skin like old peo-ple have I swear, my hair's ridiculous, the scar on my lip

—I don't feel myself, how strange

and yet

—It was nothing

and yet

—It's all over now

and it's not really all over, it goes on, even with my father dead I happen to detour over to the club and for a few minutes I stare at I don't know what by the entrance where my mother would wait for him, I just happen to go back to the church in Anjos to take a look at the building that no longer exists under scaffolding, canvas, I watch the workmen dismantling laundry rooms with hopes of seeing a little woman ironing beside the sink and saying from a distance, not waving her arms, not shouting, discreetly

I was always discreet, Júlia

—It's me

as the clock goes along blowing away the five o'clock sparrows with a ringing of wings I seem to see a little old man with a cane walking toward me

and it's not a little old man, I was wrong, it's a beggar who can't even see me as he waves his lottery tickets or his bad arm

I stopped seeing him too

so every night, it's not true, we fall, I mean I fall and you're not handing me the phone

once in your life you're not handing me the phone

you're scared by me, letting me lean my head on the robalos

—It was nothing, Mr. Paulo

let's suppose that in spite of the telephones to the right and to the left

—An outside call for you

what a word, outside, as though there was an outside, from nine till six there are confirmations of expenditures, duplications, bills, and, as for outside, the violin of a beggar putting my guts out of tune, just let me imagine that you're about to embrace me, about to hug me

—It's all over now

just imagine that your embroidered name in its frame is giving me some help, through the blinds, instead of morning on the street it's the park in Caldas da Rainha with statues in the flower beds, the museum, the palace, your home close by, I think, over a restaurant or a furniture store, the small balcony, the window, and inside, your family, you, a fireman's hat

your father's, your brother's?

because you must have brothers, Júlia, you don't have anything to do with them but they exist, one's off in Luxembourg and the other one, older, is an elementary school teacher in Coimbra, your father, who worked in a pharmacy, your mother taking in sewing to make ends meet when the month was over, you, after grammar and high school, your boyfriend, the son of the owner of a candy factory and a fireman, too, turning on the siren of his fire engine when he'd see you on the street and your mother would frown, they closed the park at seven o'clock, and still

was I right?

some steps, the palace all lighted up, the watchman far off, a flower bed right there, not damp in May, a lot of bats in the treetops and with your fear of bats and his body close by, words that didn't mean anything, fingers that hesitated a little, made it finally with the help of something

a rat?

that appeared, disappeared and couldn't be seen clearly, dry branches, a moan, noises, the fireman stamping on the ground, pretending there was panic, it was nothing, it's all over now, don't be scared, the next day your mother showing you the skirt where you didn't know what it was, a stain or something like that

but from what?

—You can't tell me, Júlia

so it was Lisbon and the room of a cousin who forgave sins, the first job as a cashier, the second job in a laundry, the boardinghouse because my cousin only had a narrow little couch, my brother from Luxembourg boiling over with threats, my brother from Coimbra deaf to my cousin's attempts, she shouldn't write me, she's dead, luckily the third job at this switchboard because of a customer at the dry-cleaning place who wanted me to have some comfort and peace, thank God, the copper decorations, the lacquered furniture that he let me pick out, I brought the little frame with my name embroidered on it so long ago, my grandmother taught me

—I'll teach you, child

not on my mother's side, on my father's, she lived in Foz do Arelho, my grandfather had a seaside restaurant and after he died the gulls so they told me

ate him, hundreds of gulls tugging at the reed roof and the shellfish left over in their tub and no customer to buy them, in the morning there was mist on the estuary and my grandmother, invisible, said

—Julita

not Júlia or Julinha, Julita

I don't like my name

coming out of the gold-colored mist, taking me by the shoulder and I gave a start

—You scared me

the restaurant that had belonged to the dead man was nothing but dried shrimp, a few scattered reeds, the hat that she dug up, not the whole hat, just the crown and a piece of brim

—We worked there

I wondered if maybe the gulls had eaten my grandmother too, what time had left of her, that is, the years had gotten inside her and they were gnawing away, gnawing away

—Your muscles were all finished, your flesh was all finished

my grandmother was nothing but the scarf around her head, her mourning dress and her hand on my shoulder as it came out of the empty shawl

—Julita

the two wedding rings stuck together, the dead man's and hers, in the afternoon we'd bring our stools together, a pair of eyeglasses under the shawl and behind the glasses were boats, the diamond-shaped cloth over the knees she didn't have, the needle was turning out cherry after cherry around the letters until the gulls decided to gobble up the dress and the kerchief, I grabbed the embroidery before the sea carried it off and the waves were swirling about madly, splattering me

the sea has a speech defect

—If we could only grab you, Júlia

what I remember is light, the clear sky, a window blind wandering among the cliffs, if my brother in Coimbra would only answer my letters I'd ask him

—Do we still own the house the old girl had in Foz do Arelho, Clemente?

the day before yesterday, without knowing why, I almost asked Mr. Paulo at the office, a skinny fellow, always checking up on his baldness where there's a reflecting surface, the metal plaque on the door, for instance, he'll plant himself in front of it, push back his hair, turn his nose to one side and roll his eyes, if he's wanted on the phone

he's almost never wanted on the phone, who's going to call him

and I hand him the receiver, he lingers at the window looking at me and mumbling silly things that don't mean anything

—It was nothing

like

—It's all over now

folding his arms in a rocking motion, and me with a million extensions and lights going on, a hundred eighteen, a hundred nineteen, two hundred forty-seven

—I haven't got all day for you

his arms are hugging a non-existent little girl to his chest, I was being driven by the light from the main office

all by itself at the top of the board

asking for a ministry, a bank, the secretary's daughter's nursery school

—If you don't want to answer, that's your business

and his mouth isn't where it should be but is roaming around his face, by his nose now, on his forehead now, coming to roost on his collar, declaring now

—I love you

following me to the photocopier, when the top is closed it starts to rumble and gives us paper in a small grated tray, coming back from there, he's nothing but a mouth wandering around without a stop

—I love you

to the coffee machine, which pours coffee into cardboard cups that will burn you, a cup comes out and right away the chrome spout dribbles out steam in tired gurgles, I'm in a great hurry bumping against the machine and Mr. Paulo says to the coin slot

—I love you

going into some strange lecture about schoolyards, raindrops, and girls jumping rope, two turning it and the third jumping, I go to get my jacket in the closet and he's consoling the closet

—Don't cry

going on with silly talk about torn curtains and pine trees and a wind of little printed flowers that leads to a ladder by a wall, I can't remember any ladder at Caldas da Rainha, I remember the statues on the lawn, the bats in the garden, looking for places during the day where we were at sunset, near the boats on the pond, and a man was trimming a hedge and not paying any attention to us, a man or a Mr. Paulo

—Dona Júlia

greeting me from the museum, I look at the museum and Mr. Paulo has disappeared, I stop looking and Mr. Paulo returns, I can't get a good look at him, but I'd swear it's him, suddenly I'm back by the pond and no one's paying any attention to me

I think

and Mr. Paulo is turning into the trunk of an ash tree or into the bust of a painter

—Pardon me

examining my zodiac sign reverently

—Please let me talk to you about us

the robalos are all teeth and Mr. Paulo is drawing back

—Pardon me

in the apartment there is no lacquered furniture, no bronze decorations, a few pathetic items

—*They belonged to my father*

that belonged to his father

—*My father's dead*

a lot of little ribbons, cretonne stars, and gaudy fripperies, a wardrobe mirror where I'm sure there's a woman with a fork in her hand and a man in an apron smiling at me, or not smiling, just looking me over, the man in the apron saying in a kind of mocking voice

—Maybe your son won't turn out to be a faggot, Judite

comparing Mr. Paulo to the character who was rumpling and smoothing a portion of a spread, thinking, I'm sure

—I must be crazy, it's a lie

of some lame mares trotting, animals that the Gypsies haul from fair to fair, prodding them along with insults and pleas

—I must be crazy, it's a lie

Mr. Paulo brings up some chairs

—Please sit down, girl

girl, how idiotic, I stopped being a girl twenty-one years ago in the garden at Caldas da Rainha when the rat ran over us in the flower bed where there was no May dampness

yellow carnations, zinnias, my mother showing me the skirt

—You're not going to tell me, Júlia

my not understanding

—What's wrong with a stain?

she drove me into the bedroom making mysterious gestures, my father

—Mercês

and she gave a signal

—Not now

a signal

—Wait

she closed the door, unfolded the skirt in front of me, and there was a small clear stain

—You're not going to tell me, Júlia

my not understanding

—Not tell you what?

concentrating on the little stain, understanding suddenly, zinnias, zinnias, the lights were on in the palace, afraid of the bats, the other body got closer, some schoolmates and I took a hammer and knocked down the boards of a closed-up house and went in, hidden rooms, a flowerpot with some narcissus on the terrace, my boyfriend, or let's say the fingers that ruined me, Julinha Julinha, he grabbed the narcissus pot and broke it

—Not tell you what?

I heard my schoolmates laughing, or it was the shards of the pot that seemed to be bleeding, pink and red pieces of pottery, you're not going to tell me, Júlia, not going to tell you what, what is there to tell, what do you want me to tell, the green narcissus, oozing green, murmuring green, almost shouting

—I don't shout

green, lots of narcissus, lots of pieces of pottery, pink, red, and green all blended in my eyes, my father got up from his chair

—Mercês

wearing an undershirt and suspenders that weren't pink or red or green on top of it

brown?

his suspenders were so vivid, I'd never seen them so vivid, when he shaved in that piece of mirror they were drooped down to his hips and now they

my mother

—Not now

—Wait

now they were so clear, my brother, the elementary-school teacher in Coimbra, don't let her write me, she's dead

—You're not going to tell me, Júlia

in front of me in the bedroom, unfolding the skirt, a light stain and I said

—It's so light

bats and rats, the flower bed I thought was dry, I took a look and I was wrong, it was wet, my schoolmates and I went back to pounding on the boards and the boards weren't secure, they fell down, the twisted nails scraping the wood

they fell down

Ernestina, Rute, Sofia, who was big, Sofia died of septicemia, the first dead person I ever saw in a coffin, a piece of pottery not pink or red

dim, translucent

that I saw in her coffin, she could run faster, she was stronger than I, the small light stain, you're not going to tell me Júlia, my father with a third of his face shaved, turning the knob

—Mercês

use the hammer, father, use your fingers, hold your fingers like this in the dark next to me, near the palace you can barely see the museum, use your fingers, dry branches, sounds that don't mean anything, words that don't mean anything, my love, I adore you
—I don't believe you
—I adore you
— How much do you adore me?
—I adore you because I'll only be adoring you for a little while
Mr. Paulo
—Excuse me?
taking my zodiac medallion, turning it over
his happiness
his mouth
—Excuse me
and because I knew the rest, his knee between my knees
—Open them up
the other knee asking
—Let me be just like this
the other knee, both knees, four knees counting mine, my knees up, not his
—Open them up
the hammer we used to knock down the boards and after the boards the thick, stagnant air, a few sofas and after the sofas the flowerpot on a clay base, the way I knew the I adore you, the be patient, the just a little while longer, I adore you, I allowed Paulo to hold my little zodiac medallion, to say
—I love you
at the same time that he said
—I thought they were robalos, they're porgies
I asked
—What?
I asked
—I beg your pardon?
and he said, pointing to the cord
—What I thought were robalos were porgies
the porgies were joined to his love for me, the wardrobe mirror

where a woman with a bottle in her hand and a man in an apron were smiling at me, the Gypsies' mares, some boys on the beach

could it have been a beach?

who were throwing pine cones at the herons, Paulo going to the curtain and asking me

—Look

insisting, afraid I might say no

—Can you see the clown, Júlia?

Dona Júlia?

Dona Júlia's no good, Júlia

—*Can you see the clown, Júlia?*

—Can you see the clown, Júlia?

and I said, in order to calm him down, yes

—I see the clown, Mr. Paulo

when what I was really seeing was the sun leaping out of the neck of a bottle, reaching the ceiling, and he saying right away

naturally

and he saying right away, naturally

—It's the changing of the tide

and it might just be happening

it really happened

because along with the tide, the curtain was furling up and the wind in the pine trees, a wind with little printed flowers and a torn spot because of the screw on the door latch through which the switchboard operator at her job

me?

holding the phone out to him

—For you, Mr. Paulo

and Paulo stroking my skin with his finger, slowly following the thread of the Blue Prince on his way to me.

CHAPTER

WHEN WE WERE ALL living together, they'd put me to bed on the mattress they kept under the bed, they'd unroll it in the kitchen, explaining

—It's nighttime, Paulo

and I'd stay there in the dark listening to what we called the sea down there, and it was nothing but the river, the mouth of the river, the place near the bridge where the Tagus, tired of bumping into mountains, dams, castles, mills, desolate

I imagined

plains, finally reaches the ocean and dissolves into it with a kind of sigh or something like that, when we were all living together and I stayed in the dark looking at the door to the backyard that rose up like a halo on the wall, I always thought that the tears, the arguments and the questions were finished, my parents

you

went to bed too, at peace with each other in that ember of harmony that old people have in spite of the fact that you hadn't reached the age of thirty at the time, and how peaceful you were, I was peaceful too, moving about on the mattress in search of sleep, a bit of straw or a rag or a piece of basket that the waves pick up and drop and leave on the last beach where a tricycle and a car with wooden wheels lay sunken, and then, in the silence, seeing myself in the kitchen under a striped blanket, it seemed to me that

it didn't seem to me, I was sure you two were fine, it was all right for me to be away from you because we were

I mean it
a family, nobody
not even me
asking
—Take care of us
and yet I said good-bye to us, I went along through the daytime, treetops with no feeling of remorse, it was ending just the way I'm ending my story, father, and afterward we never existed, the way none of us existed when I was asleep, the beach, we can agree on that, the car with wooden wheels, we can agree on that, the tricycle, we can agree on that, that child on the mattress

what child?

whose name I don't know anymore and whom we don't see, all that's left to be said is that it's February, Friday, February twenty-third, that it's raining, I don't remember its raining during those days except on one or two occasions, tears on the window and the smell of the woods closer by

February too?

clouds from Trafaria making the gulls nervous, the marigolds complaining from hunger

—Feed them, father

you had the package of fertilizer, your mouth was twitching with annoyance, the act

—Don't put on an act with me, sir

and a side glance, not angry, offended, my mother yes, angry

—Paulo

I was big and small at the same time, how strange, where did I go looking for those marigolds, please tell me, I never think about them, I never saw them again, the stems as tall as I was at the time

enormous

—*Do you like marigolds, Paulo?*

wasps on the petals and my father says

—*A wasp, keep away, watch out*

the bricks beneath the cement of the wall, the cracks between the bricks is where the wasps

saying it's February, Friday, the twenty- . . .

make their nests like paper roses and they hide, quivering in the petals

third of February, it's raining, since I didn't take the clothes off the line there's a shirt fluttering on the clothespins, if my father were here, the collar would be left and right, the shirttail would be flapping, the arms would be dancing aimlessly, I open the window to stop it from falling into the street and the people around are looking at the ground, looking at my fifth floor

—A clown

are going to think I pushed him

I hug the wet cloth and when I notice I'm hugging it against me, I let go of it, angry

—Don't grab me, father

stop getting me upset, get lost, one afternoon you rang the bell at Anjos, Dona Helena was on tiptoes peeking through the peephole, staring at me, wiping her hands on the hem of her skirt, shouting

—Just a minute

staring at me again, fixing her hair, straightening the topcoat on the coatrack

it was the same thing

huge wasps on the stamens that weren't black anymore, scorched, their buzzing would get louder by the tank during the summer, taking my shoes off and smashing the paper roses with my shoe, someone pulling me away

—*Leave them alone, be careful*

at first the landing was dark, the skylight was visible but what's the use of a skylight that's all dirty from pigeons and leaves and trash, Dona Helena opened the door, annoyed by the coatrack where the topcoat

after the doorbell rang

was getting all wrinkled and my father, without a wig, without a dress, modest, a rose of wasps, timidly excusing himself

—If it's all right with you, ma'am, I'd like to see my son

I said to myself, hiding on the sofa

—Leave them alone, be careful

no paper petals in December, only moss, the cement was crumbling to dust and the bricks on the wall were too, a bridge beam that had become detached from the planks, it spun around in a wave and went off slowly, my mother blowing her red nose

—I don't like this, Carlos, didn't you say you were going to get us a place in Lisbon?

there was no Lisbon, there was the fog that came up from the water, the herons were numbed, the owner of the café chewing on his cigar

I've come to the end of my story, father

you're just like other fathers, without any makeup or fans, if only I could have seen my mother looking proud, pointing you out to her friends

—Carlos

after my father went away, I found her in the kitchen holding her wedding ring, aware that I was there, she threw it into the silverware drawer and closed it with her hip, the next day I couldn't find it in the drawer or on her finger, I looked among the forks, the tea-spoons, alongside the fish-scaling knife still pink with blood, I came across some old pennies, the cover to a pen, no wedding ring, and I began to cry

clouds from Trafaria, clouds from Alto do Galo, I didn't see any roofs or walls, I saw the curtain of my eyelids, I caught the tears with my tongue and they tasted like raw eel, rust

—Where's your wedding ring, mother?

while my father was on the landing at Anjos, I caught sight of the wedding ring before I caught sight of him, my mother showing it off to her friends

—Didn't I tell you that you were wrong?

—*Promise me you two won't start arguing, mother*

the friends who could see and Dona Helena couldn't, look at my mother's friends, Dona Helena, the schoolteachers agreeing, in smocks, interrupting the dictation

—It's true, Judite

my father, who was going to take me to Bico da Areia, and the three of us were going to live with no arguments or questions, going to bed at night on the mattress, listening to what we called the sea down there, and it was nothing but the river, the mouth of the river, the place where the Tagus, tired of bumping into mountains, dams, castles, mills, desolate

I imagined

plains, finally reaches the ocean and dissolves into it with a kind of sigh or something like that, a shrug of its shoulders, a shaking of its long foamy hair, I was in the dark looking at the door to the backyard that rose up like a halo on the wall, a gleam of aluminum, a rusty edge, the windowpane where there were black tree trunks in the woods, help me put my clothes into a bag

Dona Helena helps

takes my jacket off the hook because I can't reach that high, that one with the velvet collar hasn't fit me for more than a year, the other one, the blue one, because we're losing time here while Dona Helena worried about me because why in the world, my father sure I don't see him, making all kinds of signals, what are those signals for, there must be a bus straight home, mustn't there, you catch it on the Avenida Almirante Reis, good-bye Dona Helena, cross the Tagus, to Costa da Caparica and right after that, boom, a second bus, almost always empty, makes a right turn by the campground near the pharmacy

at night only the store windows are lighted, no building fronts or trees

my mother waiting for us, my mattress in the kitchen, Dália's aunt raising her eyebrows

—Have you come back?

we only talk to a few people, indifferent to the rest, when my mother got annoyed with my father, only half her face would argue, her hands kept on cooking the rice and her eyes kept watch over her hands, from time to time her eyes would join her mouth and get angry too, her shoulders, indifferent until then, would go into furious agitation, I knew the schoolteacher was scolding somebody because her hip was leaping about under her skirt, her absent-minded fingers were gripping the piece of chalk, the shoes weren't concerned with us, Dona Helena was concerned about me, asking my father are you going to work in Spain

—I can't go to Bico da Areia, Paulo

running into the laundry room, refusing to eat, lying down on my back until the next day, Dona Helena mumbling in the dark

—Don't be upset, Paulo

trying to console me but she wasn't doing it, if she happened to straighten out my sheets

—Go take care of your daughter, leave me alone

there's Mr. Couceiro, just the way I said, nothing but the cane, staying awake, grabbing my clothes

—Are you going to work in Spain?

and running away, the church not looking at all like a church through the curtains, something else that was waiting for me, threatening me

—Don't go down the stairs, Paulo

since when have churches talked to me?

streetlights that grew smaller all the way to Martim Moniz, in just a few hours the garbage truck, if they caught me on the street, the men who emptied garbage cans into it would gag me and good-bye, Mr. Couceiro's footsteps in the hall and Dona Helena farther off, intent on her crocheting because her syllables were correcting a stitch

—Don't bother him now

leaving the sentence half done, finishing it right afterward, laying the needle and the ball of thread in her lap, the sentence, free of the crocheting

—Don't bother him now

—*Where's Spain?*

not the same as the daytime Dona Helena because darkness changes people, makes them more important, more serious, even the sea, for example, even the creaking of furniture in the pine grove, lots and lots of chairs, couches, tables, the picture of Noémia

or my father

—I can't go to Bico da Areia, Paulo

and the world in pieces, pieces of horses galloping in the woods, my mother with the owner of the café, with the electrician, with the pups

—I'd really like to go back with the two of you

turning to them, smiling at them, ordering me to go play in the yard

—Until I call you, Paulo

or just let me stay and wait, I've spent most of my life plunked down like a boob on a step or on the bench by the cedar waiting for you people, I'm fed up, my father looking around for some help

—Loosen your tie, father

you understand, don't you, Dona Helena, and Dona Helena straightening out the topcoat, a month in Mérida in the theater, at least I'll be able to put a little money together, there'll be no more of my being behind on my rent, I'll pay you for my son's upkeep, Dona Helena lying, busy with the topcoat, we don't need anything, Mr. Carlos, they hid money in a can, they kept accounts in pencil, Mr. Couceiro asked for more time to pay the electric bills

—Not for too long

they put a candle in a saucer and the living room began to tremble, our bodies went from fat to thin, in the morning a halo of soot on the ceiling, Mr. Couceiro would wrap up some enameled objects in a newspaper, leave with them, and after a few hours the light switches were working, my father was also lying

—I'll pay for my son's upkeep

if they'd only given him a mattress to rumple and smooth at least, Alcides was in the car waiting with bundles and suitcases, a month is only a minute, Paulo, everything's so quick, isn't that so, Dona Helena, just a minute ago summer was just beginning and now we're already well into it

I was in the laundry room looking at the orange-colored top of the building

before you know it, I'll be back with you again

two parakeets at first, they ate seeds from a package, they didn't fly, they didn't sing, they didn't pay attention to anything at all, the one who must have been the female died

Friday, February twenty-third, and it's raining, I don't remember its raining at that time, I remember my mother saying to a man who wasn't the electrician or the owner of the café

—Not in front of the child

there was a pair of white pants with a trace of oil on the crease, a tinkle of keys

or a laugh

and the tinkle of keys walking over to my mother, her blouse, her neck

—He won't notice

my mother rubbing her neck, checking her blouse, taking the bottle out of the oven, drying two glasses and

—Just a minute ago summer was just beginning and now we're already well into

placing them

it

on the tablecloth, if I could only have dipped my finger in and tasted it, the tinkling keys drinking the wine

—What shall we do with him, kill him, throw him into the river?

white pants up against my mother's legs and my mother leaning against the sink, breathing hard

—Wait

looking for some coins in her purse and there weren't any coins, an expired bus ticket, in the sink were pots, ants, my mother letting go of the neck of the bottle

—Haven't you got some change at least?

white pants poking around annoyed

—If I'd known about the kid I wouldn't have come

the river, the mouth of the river, the place near the bridge where the Tagus is tired of bumping into mountains, castles, dams, mills, desolate

I imagined

plains, finally reaches the ocean and dissolves into it among herons' calls, with a kind of sigh or something like that

he gave my mother a coin and she gave it to me

—For his upkeep

she picked me up from the floor, sat me down by the cistern, gave me a saucepan and a wooden spoon, signaled to me from the window, showing how I should pound on the saucepan with the spoon

—You can pound on it as long as you want to

to please her, I tried a whack and I didn't feel like it, I felt like taking a pee, I felt like eating and I was afraid of the herons, of the bridge that was changing color, of an animal that was sighing and talking and devouring itself in the kitchen, it wasn't my mother or white pants, it was a shape with two backs and no chest, two backs of necks and no face from which arms came out and went back in again, teeth and feet, the electrician was wandering about picking up things that the waves had left, I imagined that he hated me and yet if the pups threw pine cones at me, I'd thought he'd be silent but he'd curse the pups, he'd leave us shells on the wall, the café owner's wife was going about wiping the tables and I imagined that her husband, hands on his hips, was saying nasty things about my mother or me

about my mother

the Gypsy women were coming back from the beach with buckets and in the buckets were crabs, mussels, if a dolphin was beached on the sand they'd call to each other in Galician, white pants left, along with the animal, on a scooter that sounded like popping corn, my mother was softly scraping the spoon over the saucepan

—The coin

scraping the spoon harder over the saucepan

—The coin, Paulo

furious with me

with me I think

with me

furious with me

—The coin

the coin in my hand, a little one that was good for buying almost nothing, five or six pieces of candy, a stick of bubble gum, not even a cheap piece of chocolate, my mother not believing me

—Is this what the bastard gave you?

all that's left to say is that it's February, Friday the twenty-third of February, that it's raining, through the opening in the curtain the building is massive, opaque, writing a letter to the maid from the dining room and in the letter Paulo & Gabriela saying that when you smile your mouth

she dropped the coin into the pan and went back to the kitchen, then the spoon on the saucepan, the spoon on the neck of the bottle, the spoon on the neck of the bottle again, a crash, two crashes, as she smashed the bottle against the stove first and then hit it with the door beam, I wanted to ask

—Mother

and my voice refused to call her, one of the shards from the bottle had caught her on the chin, my mother showed me the saucepan

—One coin, the cheapskate

taking me by the hair and pulling me up against the stove, which was unpolished and had one burner out of shape

—One coin for half an hour, do you think I'm only worth one coin for half an hour, Paulo?

saying it hadn't rained during that time except on one or two occasions, sunset at three o'clock in the afternoon and the Gypsies' horses sobbing with fear, the café owner's wife was picking up plates with one of her husband's berets on her head, raindrops were bouncing in the yard

tears were coming down onto the window

the smell of the woods was closer, the vine was growing cold

—The vine, father

before moving to Lisbon he would protect it with reeds and string, he'd form a mantle that he draped over it, he'd come back into the house and my mother would say

—What about me, Carlos?

tears there, too

—You're not a window, so don't let it start raining

and she, not hearing me

—What about me, Carlos?

you're not my mother, I never saw her, who are you, lying on your back on the bed, she would disappear into the pillow repeating

—What about me, Carlos?

my father's hand didn't reach her, it stayed up in the air, stopped, my father was my father, she wasn't

my father finally opened the door and walked out into the rain

the coin

—Do you think I'm only worth one coin for half an hour, Paulo?

it fell onto the saucepan and rolled along the floor, not in a straight line, in a hesitating arch, taking its time, bumping into the refrigerator, it was silent, the dwarf from Snow White said to me in a stern voice, we used to spend many afternoons together with nobody else at home

—Looking out for each other

if I grabbed the shears, the dwarf immediately said

—Watch out

he'd stop me from cutting up dresses, tasting the pills, turning the bathtub into a lake

—Forget it

if I'd followed his advice I wouldn't have left Gabriela, I can see him with us scolding me

—You're such a jackass, Paulo

the maid from the dining room, surprised, looking at the boards over the windows, asking

—Who were you talking to?

my father was back from Spain less bouncy, thinner

—They tricked me

the church was tolling hours that were impossible to count, fifteen, seventeen, six hundred, and Mr. Couceiro was growing older with each one of them, no packages or suitcases in Alcides's car, a bowl of apples on top of the blonde wig, Noémia's picture of interest for a moment and then gone, the frame was still there, that is, and the vase, not Noémia

—Not even a theater, Dona Helena, they wanted me to

not even a theater, a dump on the outskirts of Mérida and we were held there inside, Alcides ate with them, played cards with them, he lost my money, we performers had a different table, four Spanish girls, a short little Romanian and me, the customers would make their choice in the main room where we painted our nails and listened to music, if I said

—*Alcides*

Alcides would get angry with his cards, checking his hand for trump cards

—*If you haven't got any toys to play with, how'd you like me to break one of your arms?*

the little Romanian tried to run away, they caught her in the mail truck, they called us in while they held her head and broke one of her molars, a long scream, a faint, get up, you fag

—Watch out for your teeth, ladies

and I was thinking about swings, I'd help it along with my body, push out with my feet, and they couldn't catch me because I was going up into the sky

the café owner's wife was taking down the awning and a heron or two were on the bridge wall, her husband, grabbing my mother

—What's all this about?

who was pounding on the stove with the door beam, she stopped pounding looking for the bench in the kitchen, where she flopped down in silence, not my mother, just a slipper, some lips that were whispering something you couldn't understand, I went over to her and said

—I'm sorry

fingers that squeezed my shoulder, her lips against my ear

—I'm sorry

the electrician could be seen through the window taking something or other out of his pocket

a conch shell

and laying the shell down on the wall, when I got to the marigolds, the crutch was on the beach, I think he was waving it, but maybe I was wrong, all that's needed is for the light to change or a change in the pine trees for us to think there are people, a pine cone rolled down the roof and the owner of the café

—Bastards

my father at Príncipe Real, in a blonde wig, was burying jewelry in a bag of flour

chokers, tiaras, my mother's medallion, a tortoise shell encrusted with silver

unicorns, dragons

in heels he grew a couple of inches taller and it took me a little while to recognize him under the eyelashes, when we got to the street, Dona Aurorinha said

—My, you're looking pretty

he kept the sunlight off with a paper parasol that the trees

praised in Latin, my mother said to the owner of the café, I'm sorry,
the dwarf from Snow White was lording it over everybody

—I've got a headache

was carrying a pick and a lantern that didn't throw any light on
anyone, but if I were to pick up the shears, he'd get scared,
whispering

—Watch out

time was wearing him down the way it does walls, my mother
had grabbed him more than once to toss him into the garbage

—We've got to buy another doll, Paulo

she'd lift up the lid of the trash can, moments from so long ago
would pass through her memory, she'd repent, explain to the dwarf

—You're safe for now

she pretended to kiss him

—*What about me, Carlos?*

tears there, too

—*You're not a window, so don't let it start raining*
and she wasn't hearing me, so tiny in a corner

—*What about me, Carlos?*

she'd look at me, put him back on the refrigerator

my father's hand didn't reach her, it stayed up in the air, stopped, he
finally opened the door and walked out into the rain

she was getting lunch ready, making too many movements and
too much noise, annoyed with me on the floor with the saucepan
and the spoon

—You good-for-nothing

I wasn't at Bico da Areia, I was with my father in the store, you
came off Príncipe Real and after three blocks there was an antiques
shop and a lunchroom, in the antiques shop a woman was thumbing through an album, in the lunchroom a waiter was whistling in
the middle of the flies, in the shop window

porcelain figures, clocks, small ivory animals, candlesticks

—*No theater at all, Dona Helena, they wanted me to*

a creature was eating out of a bowl, the only thing she was looking at was the paper parasol, the creature was chewing

I don't remember its raining at that time

—What have you got for me today, Soraia?

the marigolds were crackling with hunger, disappointing the gulls, you had on my mother's apron and were carrying the fertilizer, your wiggly stage walk, your little head was worried, stop putting on an act for me, father

my father emptied the flour bag onto the counter and a sharp gleam of stones, the creature with the bowl came limpng over, one of his legs just like mine, the other flopping, slow, one of those rolls on a window shade worn by use

I picked up the electrician's conch shell and from the shell the sea said
—Hello, Paulo

and while my mother explained to the dwarf
—You're safe for now

the creature was separating diadems, medallions, and buckles, putting her knife down, she held a pin up to the light, pushed everything toward the bag of flour, her look going from my father to the bowl
—Do you like playing games, Soraia?

playing games in a one-story place on the outskirts of Mérida, oak trees, poplars, they held her by her head, Alcides held open her jaw with a piece of metal
—Oh, such a pretty little mouth

when they hit the nerve it wasn't pain, it was the jab of a light-ning bolt, all her bones were on fire, turning into mushy lard and then on fire again, maybe a scream, I don't know, father, how can somebody scream and not know she's screaming?

think about swings, stretch out the tips of your toes, go up into the sky, you remember hogs being butchered, their guts torn out, the buckets of blood, your blood, stretch out the tips of your toes, why don't you scream, you don't exist, the hope of dying exists, scarlet flowers, your uncle's wife undressing you, a single scarlet flower that sobs, the moans you turned into, Alcides doesn't exist, the drill doesn't exist, you don't exist, the pain exists, understand, the pain exists
—The boob fainted, give him some water

the pain exists, I didn't faint
—Give him some water

the pain exists, a jab of fire you don't understand, your wife on the pillow, repeating

—What about me, Carlos?

the pain exists and in the middle of the pain, the creature was pushing the bowl up against his chest

—Do you like playing games, Soraia?

in the bowl were olives, chicken, vegetables, the pain exists, how can I show the creature, how can I make her see

—I'm flat broke, Dona Odete, there must be an emerald there that's worth something

the bowl and the knife mocking him

—Emeralds?

the bowl and the knife noticing me

—Is that your son?

how to make him see that the pain exists, they'd taken his fox fur piece, his gold earrings

—They took my fox fur piece and my gold earrings, there must be an emerald there that's worth something

how to make him see that the pain exists and there's no swing on which to escape the pain, it's impossible to touch the sky with the tips of his toes, to find a mail truck to take us away, an electrician who leaves a shell on the wall, oak trees, poplars, Alcides was checking out the room, feeling the pillow, you and the mattress were huddled against the wall, father, you, a clown, you, a scarlet flower, sobbing

—There's money missing here, Soraia

not remembering my mother or me, he was remembering the rent to be paid, the music that was turned up just when the drill

—Don't move

I was pounding the spoon on the saucepan when they held open his mouth with the piece of metal

pain exists

Friday, February twenty-third, so as not to hear his piglet squeals, not to hear his guts being torn out, the buckets of blood, his hope that there might be an emerald that's worth something, and the bowl

—Emeralds?

the bowl of chicken and vegetables or the limping leg

—Take that junk away, Soraia

pounding on the saucepan, keeping up my pounding on the saucepan, I found the coin under the refrigerator, I gave it to my mother and my mother to white pants, to the owner of the café, to me

—Do you really think all I'm worth is one coin?

not a grown woman, a child talking in her sleep, in my grandmother's house I came across a picture of her in a drawer and cramped writing, where you could imagine erasures and a nose over her shoulder

—Just look at that handwriting

lines in pencil so there'll be no mistakes an eraser couldn't remove, the tip of the pencil catching on the paper, the nose threatening her

—Oh, my

To my aunt and uncle from Judite, and a date written out

—Don't you know how to write numbers, Judite?

don't ask me if all you're worth is one coin, don't make me talk, I read

To my aunt and uncle from Judite, once, twice, eight times and it wasn't you, a girl younger than I, dark, skinny, To my aunt and uncle from Judite, you were never that one, mother, you didn't have any aunt and uncle, you were a schoolteacher, you married my father and that was that, you were looking at the stove noticing the broken burner and the enamel you'd pulled off, buttoning up your dress without getting it right

—I'm sorry

bumping into yourself in the wardrobe mirror, a child amazed at the conch shell on the wall, amazed at us, a clump of gentian detached from the branch, scarlet flowers, the only scarlet flowers that scream, my grandmother running her finger over the picture

—Your mother

a dark child, skinny, crouching timidly

—I'm sorry

tears on the window and the smell of the woods closer by, wild fig trees, acacias, firs, the ebb-tide waves that the horses were licking, the place where the Tagus, tired of bumping into mountains, castles, dams, mills, desolate

I thought

plains, finally reaches the ocean and dissolves in it with a kind of sigh or something like that, I'm finishing my story and there's not much left to say, just say my father at Príncipe Real with the bag of flour and with me, lay off the theatrics, father, Alcides waiting for us in the armchair in the living room in the midst of open trunks, showing the wallet and there were no coins

—There's money missing here, Soraia

not just Alcides, a buddy in white pants with him, I didn't look at the buddy, I only looked at the pants, the trace of an oil stain on the crease, the tinkling of keys and the tinkling of keys saying

—Shall we kill him and throw him in the river, shall we lock him up in the closet?

Alcides checking the lock on the bedroom door, the bathroom, the pantry, looking at me, at my father, locking me in the pantry

—We're going to play hide-and-seek, so you hide here

my father

—Paulo

I wanted my father to say

—Paulo

Mr. Couceiro to say

—Paulo

Dona Helena to say

—Paulo

I wanted my mother to say to Alcides

—Just a minute

my mother to say to white pants

—Wait

putting me down beside the cistern, giving me a saucepan and a wooden spoon, the Gypsy women were coming back from the beach with buckets and in the buckets were crabs, mussels, if a dolphin was beached on the sand they'd call to each other in Galician, when my father reaches the beach, counting the oaks and poplars of Mérida, the short little Romanian will climb up onto the first-floor balcony and

a flowerpot

falling down along with her, the railroad station that called us at night, farther away than I'd imagined by the sound of the trains

the sound was quite close by

everything was close by in the darkness, the pups, the moon, or the clock on the roof of the station, slipping through underbrush, staggering, running, this shoe, that shoe, I thought I heard voices looking for him and now barefoot, running, maybe not even voices, oaks, poplars, lungs, the ramp where he hurts himself, running, stopping, but nobody there, the spoon on the saucepan and the coin

—Paulo

running, the silence of the pantry, the silence of the house, the silence of Príncipe Real, Dona Aurorinha on the landing, and running, reaching the station through some warehouses on a slope, my grandmother sketching the picture with her finger

—Your mother

and running, a dark, skinny girl. To my aunt and uncle from Judite, the tip of the pencil catching, the nose over her shoulder, just look at that handwriting

running

they brought the pig in on a plank, its feet were tied, a piece of swill was still in its throat, faded eyelids, not eyelids with makeup, skin in need of a shave, little eyes that didn't see

running

Alcides and white pants hung him from the hook, do you want my conch shell, father, and running, the glass bowls, my uncle's wife undressing him, bath time, Carlos, the water pump back and forth, the wasps' paper roses, no more arguments, no questions, the twenty-third of February, Friday, not bothered by the rain

running

Dona Helena was straightening out the topcoat by the landing in Anjos, trying to help us, why is my father signaling, thinking I don't see, the campground, the pharmacy, my mother waiting for us, the mattress in the kitchen, Dália's aunt

—Have you come back?

so they brought me back from the station and I was obedient, silent, they held me by the head and I let them hold me by the head, they ordered me not to move and I didn't move, they ordered me to open my mouth and I opened my mouth, they kept it open with a piece of metal, they tied my ankles to the back of the chair, they folded my arms, they placed a second piece of metal on my back, they brought up a lamp and I didn't turn away from the lamp, I accepted it because it wasn't the drill, it was wasps, my father saying, don't touch, be careful, and suddenly, thank God, near the bridge, I reached the ocean and dissolved in it with a kind of sigh or something like that, I was all alone in the dark facing the wall, looking at the refrigerator, the stove

—Judite

the steps in the yard came up inch by inch, my wife

—What about me, Carlos?

and even though my wife didn't reach it

she stood there hesitating, stopped

I'm sure she recognized me, saw me, moved to one side, because of the wardrobe mirror the two of us, my son walking toward us, sitting on the ground with a saucepan and a wooden spoon, scraping the spoon softly over the saucepan, and I must have dozed off

not fainted, dozed off

I must have dozed off because Alcides wasn't there, or the diadems, the medallions, the buckles either, there was the cedar at Príncipe Real chatting with me in Latin, a lot of herons on the bridge beams, and Judite handing me a coin in her cupped hand.

CHAPTER

YOU KNOW WHO you can rely on and I've learned in this life of ours never to rely on anyone but myself. Maybe that's why I've done everything by myself: the club, the restaurant in Campolide, the house on the Sintra road

(not really Sintra, Mem Martins, near the railroad station, I like the trains at night, my late mother pausing to listen

—The eleven o'clock mail train

and it was just as though we were still together)

purchased quite cheaply

what I mean to say is at a good price because I hate bragging

from the English people who were going back home and were complaining about the climate, the dampness, their bones taking on water and I, yes indeed, yessir, I agree completely, Mister, sir, rheumatism all over their bodies, pains in their joints, it's time to go, go back to sunny London, here's your check

I enlarged the pool, put in a statue and some lights, built a new gate with elephants on the posts, kept their sofas, my wife had wanted something in cretonne

—Keep those sofas?

but I was up on civilized matters and in agreement with the fact that Europeans and monarchies are way ahead of us

—If the English people can relax on them, it means they're good

holding back no secrets, without any talk, I limited myself to opening my eyes wide and speaking more softly

—If the English people can relax on them, it means they're good

580

she was submissive, shrugging her shoulders, shrug your shoulders all you want because I don't even notice it, girl, if my mother were living with us

—Be quiet

smiling, looking toward the window

—The eleven o'clock mail train

it says in the Bible that woman has to obey man and no matter how intelligent my wife may be, and that's not really the case, who's going to argue with the Bible, even though nothing is there

I think

about forbidding you to shrug your shoulders, I pretended it wasn't important, what's the point in wasting gunpowder on sparrows, if she grumbled, that was something else, but that's only her way of doing her gymnastics to avoid getting all hunched over, it was logical for the sofas to be in the living room, big, ugly, solid, leather, not all that comfortable, hogging all the space, my wife, pointing to those monstrosities, asked

—What is it about all this stuff?

and even though I agree with her and I know there's no reason whatever for any of it, if I give in to her, good-bye authority, so I light a cigarette or play with the dog or whistle, all cuddled up on the sofa so she'll think I'm fine, and I was thinking it'll be too bad if you think I look uncomfortable

when I remember my mother, I remember her cupping her hand to her ear

—*The eleven o'clock mail train*

my wife seems to understand me then, with those female antennae of hers, and she goes back to the peace of her crocheting, uncomfortable too, while I wonder and ask myself

my mother

—*Who's she?*

—Whatever got into my skull to get myself hooked up with you? getting on in age the way you are

two years older than I

my mother rolling her eyes

—*Two years older than you?*

with the bulb in her heart blinking, plugged in poorly or maybe a loose connection, the doctor

—Rest and cut down on salt

lunch was tasteless, broiled fish and broiled meat that didn't taste like anything anymore, and then broccoli and carrots instead of rice, sauce, potatoes, I explained to the doctor, the doctor lowered his glasses looking down at my belly

—You could lose some weight too, my friend

forget about the trains and confess to me that I've gotten fat, mother

and since he's an expensive doctor and a professor of medicine at the hospital, before he gets to my spleen, he asks me if I drink and I lie to him, swearing

—Never touch it

unfortunately I have to drink, not because of any urge or addiction but because of my job of sitting down with the customers, except that most of the time I drink the same little cup of tea as the girls while the men have their bubbly, I go from table to table with a little glass in my hand, avoiding any invitations with a word, a hello, praise

—Always in the best of health, mister engineer

taking care of their requests

—If you don't mind, could you introduce me to the lady who closes the show?

I tell Dona Amélia, discreetly because customers demand good manners, respect

—Send Marlene to number nine

and if Marlene or Micaela or Vanda or Sissi, having forgotten the rules and the fact that I make sacrifices for my people, say

—I'm tired

I trot right over and set them straight and point to the street door

—There's the way out

because as soon as they feel secure, they start to act up and take advantage, I've been in the racket for thirty years, fighting with transvestites

thirty-one on the eighth of January

and I give what advice I can to beginners, although I wouldn't recommend this miserable existence to anybody, it's

—Don't let them act up with you, don't let them take advantage

what happened to the eleven o'clock mail train?

or hit them with a fine against their percentage from time to time so the fine ladies will get it into their heads who's in charge

God wrote it in the Bible

and other than that, I treat them according to what they think they are and leave them alone, as far as I'm concerned as long as they do their job they can even kill themselves, far away from the disco, it's no business of mine, they come into my office all the time asking for work, they line up in the hallway, shaking their falsies

—I'm a girl, didn't you know?

they swear that nature made a mistake, as if nature's mistakes would soften me up: they only help me make a living. Thank God that nature spends its time making mistakes because that's why they show up in my office, half-bashful and half-aggressive, with shaved chins and a transparent little blouse

—I'm a girl, didn't you know?

ready for Dona Amélia to teach them how to dance and pretend that they're singing

—Move this way, move that way, look sad here and laugh here

escorted by characters who look at me out of the corners of their eyes and, after coming up against the bartender, settle right down

—I'm only here because I'm a friend, I swear

they simmer down, scratching an ear

—I don't want any trouble, I don't want any trouble

all of a sudden polite, humble, good boys basically, agreeing that we're helping them out with a little lesson in life, wiping their mouths with a handkerchief, checking the handkerchief, wiping again, the bartender, like a buddy, giving them his

—I was only thinking about your future, you'll thank me for it later on

and most of the time they really do thank him

—I'll never forget that friendly little whack

a few who seem intelligent to me do odd jobs for me, I've got Fausto, Romeu, Alcides looking over the market according to my rules, if they piss outside the pot the bartender says

—You'd better take good care of your lip

too bad for the eleven o'clock mail train in Pinhel, too bad for me

there are still two days

it's an example

Alcides is tapping me on the shoulder, he only taps me on the shoulder when it's something important

—Thursday at six o'clock I'm bringing in a little something that will be of interest to you, boss

and that afternoon he did introduce me to a boy who reminded me of somebody, I don't know who, I heard him speak and said to myself

—I know you

without catching on to where I knew him from, I swear, I said to myself

—I've seen that face before

that face, that way of walking, that voice, just the same as I'd seen the suitcase he was carrying, not a new suitcase, the catch was repaired with adhesive tape and wire

and underneath the plumes I was also sure I'd seen, a blonde wig I'll bet

not a redhead, not platinum, blonde

purple nail polish, strapped shoes, I told him to go fix himself up to be examined in the dressing room that used to be a pantry during the time when the club had been an apartment

it still smelled of rats and peach preserves

Alcides was nervous

—Anything wrong, boss?

while I was wringing out the rags of memory that weren't dribbling anything out except mothers and trains

—I know you, I know you

Alcides, careful

—What's that?

uncorking the mineral water that the doctor had recommended to me for cleaning out my bladder, I said

—I know you

becoming aware of the

—I know you

getting irritated, correcting

—That's enough

Alcides was offended but nice and quiet, just like my wife, with the only difference that we weren't living together, if he ever came across the English people's sofas, I can guarantee what his reaction would be

—Those sofas?

shrugging his shoulders in silence, all cramped up there without my noticing and I was saying to myself

—I know you

not hitting on what place, you remind me of someone but what someone, I could swear we've met somewhere, spent some years together, we spoke, Alcides was acting like an orderly

—Mr. Sales

I must have scared him, because he sank into the chair waving his little hands, repeating

—All set, all set

when the other one came back, I didn't need a diagram, here it was at last, it certainly looked to me that this was it, the spangled waistband, the silken eyebrows, the beauty spot on the cheek, Alcides, with the gesture of an impresario, saying

—I give you Paulo

and then what I was expecting happened, everything came together, everything was finally clear

why hadn't I known right away, why hadn't I realized?

I knew the rings, I knew the earrings, the merry little pirouette that brought back memories, the bracelets that went up to Alcides's chin with a tender little pinch, the red lipstick completing the effect, and then

how was it I hadn't realized, I'm so dumb, you were right, mama, and then

what did you expect?

—My name is Soraia

she said.

ABOUT THE TRANSLATOR

Born in Yonkers in 1922, Gregory Rabassa attended Dartmouth College and served in the OSS during the Second World War. After receiving his PhD in Spanish and Portuguese literature from Columbia University in the early 1960s, he began translating the work of Julio Cortázar. Regarded as one of the leading translators of Spanish and Portuguese literature in the world, Rabassa has translated over thirty books and has won numerous prizes, including several PEN awards, for his translations of the work of Gabriel García Márquez, Jorge Amado, and Machado de Assis. His translation of Cortázar's *Hopscotch* received the National Book Award for Translation, and he is the recipient of the National Medal of the Arts, as well as a member of the Order of the Rio Branco, one of Brazil's highest honors. He is the author of a memoir, *If This Be Treason: Translation and Its Dyscontents,* and a distinguished professor emeritus at Queens College. He lives with his wife in New York City.

ABOUT THE AUTHOR

Born in Lisbon on September 1, 1942, António Lobo Antunes grew up during the repressive years of the Salazar dictatorship. He was thirty-one when the Carnation Revolution transformed Portugal from a virtual police state into a liberal democracy, but it was the political repression that he experienced during his youth that highly influenced his adult consciousness and would inform much of his fiction.

At the urging of his father, Lobo Antunes opted as a young man to go to medical school and specialized in psychiatry. Required to serve in the army, he became a military doctor in Portugal's doomed colonial war in Angola, and it was this experience that influenced many of his novels. After his return to Lisbon in 1973, he began working as a clinical psychiatrist before devoting himself primarily to literature.

Lobo Antunes has written eighteen novels, which have been translated into more than twenty languages. His first novel, *Memory of an Elephant*, was published in 1979. In the same year, his second novel, *South of Nowhere*, a frantic monologue by a former soldier in Angola delivered to a lonely woman he meets in a bar, was published to international acclaim. His more recent novels, *The Inquisitors' Manual*, about life during the Salazar dictatorship, and *The Return of the Caravels*, about the breakup of Portugal's colonial dominion in the 1970s, have both been named *New York Times* Notable Books of the Year.

Lobo Antunes is considered by many to be the greatest novelist on the Iberian peninsula. For George Steiner he is the "heir to Conrad and Faulkner." In fact, the *Los Angeles Times Book Review* commented that Antunes writes "with the insight of Faulkner, of a man who knows the scent and taste of the dust from which his characters are begotten."

António Lobo Antunes has received numerous literary awards, such as the Jerusalem Prize for the Freedom of the Individual in Society (2005) and the Camões Prize, the most important literary prize for the Portuguese language (2007). He lives in Lisbon.